Books by

D. M. ALMOND

Chronicles of Acadia

Book One: *Secrets of the Elders*

Book Two: *Land of the Giants*

Book Three: *Necromancer's Curse - coming Summer 2015*

A Dark Rising – *coming Fall 2015*

LAND of the GIANTS

Chronicles of Acadia
Book II

D. M. ALMOND

To Jaime

D. M. *(signature)*

The characters and events portrayed in this book are fictitious. Any similarity to real persons, living or dead, is coincidental and completely a byproduct of the reader's overactive imagination. So you have come back for more, silly little reader. Do not draw comparisons between this world and your own, lest you lose yourself in dreams of fantasy.

Cover illustration by Victor A. Minguez

Edited by Jessica Barnes

ISBN 978-1508943273

To my crazy doppelganger, Don.

The best brother an Acadian could want.

Table of Contents

Prologue

Logan Walker hated the infernal surface of Acadia. Thick, rank mud sucked at his boots as he willed his stiff legs to keep trudging through the marshlands. He was in a bad mood, most likely due to the overpowering light of Themis, the daystar, beating down on his brow, the weight of it like ten sacks of silt piled across his back. Logan's skin was covered with a thick sheen of sweat, and he grunted with each aching step forward through the heat.

Or perhaps his current disposition was more likely a byproduct of the incessant prodding by the lizardman behind him, who seemed to deem it necessary to periodically jab him in the spine with the butt of a primitive wooden spear, despite the fact that he was willingly complying with their commands and marching through the dense jungle wetlands like a good little prisoner.

The next time he does that I'm going to stick my fist straight down his scaly throat, Logan thought, gritting his teeth and wincing at the most recent blow.

Another Agmawor gave Bipp an identical hit, knocking the three-foot gnome onto his hands and knees. The diminutive gnome was barely able to hold himself up in the deep mud with his bound wrists.

Logan's small friend was having a rough time trekking through the dense mud, his stubby legs working hard to maneuver through the marshland at the same pace as the lizardmen, who were brutally pushing them to maintain their swift trek. Mud caked Bipp's leather bracers and stained his silver hair, rivulets of it clinging to his bushy mutton chops and large, bulbous nose. The normally jovial engineer was looking rough.

Logan sludged over to help him out of the muck before he fell over completely and drowned in the foul-smelling mud.

As Logan helped the gnome to his feet, a sharp blow cracked against his neck. An explosion of stars washed across his vision, knocking him a couple steps forward. As he regained his footing, growling like a feral beast, Bipp caught his forearm, throwing Logan a knowing look and stopping him before he could do anything rash. Logan squared his shoulders and glared hatefully at the lizardman who stood gloating before him.

He knew there was not much special about his appearance, as he looked just like most other twenty-two-year-olds hailing from his village, Riverbell, in the underground kingdom of New Fal. He stood five-foot-eleven, with dark, walnut hair that he kept cropped short and wild, looking as if he had just rolled out of bed. His normally pale skin was a deep shade of raw pink, unused to the scorching heat of Themis, the daystar, which beat down on the surface world. Themis' light was so bright that his crystal clear emerald-colored eyes stung even under the magical dweomer placed over them.

All in all he was pretty typical for your everyday, run-of-the-mill villager, with one exception, which was his mechanical fist. It was crafted from adamantine and gifted to him by the Council of Twelve to replace the hand he had lost defending the capitol from an invading horde of skex. That was before he was setup for murder and had to flee his homeland.

Logan thought for a fleeting moment about ramming that fist straight through the lizardman's filthy muzzle. But his friend Nero, the only other member of his party to be caught by the lizardmen, shook his head slightly, silently reminding Logan that they were far outnumbered and grossly under-equipped for such a daring move.

He knew his companion was correct, that even as fast as he was, there was no way he could take out enough of the creatures before they gutted him like a pig, or even worse, harmed his friends. Wading through the mire, with poison-tipped spears aimed their way, his companions were in no position to mount an offense.

The Agmawor commanded him in its sickly, guttural voice, motioning for the soft-skin to keep moving. Logan looked deep into the stinking lizard's yellow-slit eyes and curled his lips, but turned to comply anyhow, earning what he assumed was a laugh from their captors, rows of needle sharp teeth clicking together and tongues slithering from between quivering, scaly lips.

From the corner of his eye, Logan looked for Tiko, his Agma companion, who he assumed was following them from high up in the trees. The Agma was nowhere to be seen, which Logan knew was a good thing. He could only hope that his brother Corbin was having better luck with Kyra and Stur. Picturing them in his mind's eye, Logan wondered where they were at that moment and whether they were safe.

Bipp groaned as they resumed their trek through the mud. Logan could not help looking at his companion and wondering how they got themselves into this mess in the first place. Only hours before, everything was working out so well, yet here they were, trudging through the Sunken Marshes of Ithiki on the surface of Acadia, prisoners of the cannibal Agmawor tribe, being led the gods knew where. The deeper he thought on it, the further his mind wandered back, to the beginning of their journey. Back to before they set out for the surface of Acadia.

Chapter 1: The Citadel

The young woman groaned for the third time that day.

"I think she's coming around," Bipp said, his voice strained with excitement.

Logan Walker sat with his back pressed firmly against the wall. His eyes remained transfixed on the adjoining hall, peering through the yawning hole he had blasted through the door when battling the second wave of spiders two days ago. The hall beyond the hole was as wide as two homes put side by side and as long as anything they had ever seen, with row upon row of glass tubes, each larger than a man. Those containers seemed to be filled with some sort of ice and radiated a faint blue glow. Even more unsettling, they seemed to each house a sleeping human.

Logan and Bipp had wanted to explore the mysterious chamber, but they had yet to step foot inside. Corbin had pointed out that they could not leave this woman, whom they had rescued from a pack of spiders the size of small dogs. In her condition, she would be completely defenseless if left on her own. Splitting up was not a good idea either, as there was no telling how many more spiders existed in this structure, and the three of them had had their hands full dealing with the beasts as it was.

This turned out to be a wise choice, as that very evening, when everyone fell asleep, another pack of spiders attacked. Logan did not want to think about what might have happened if they had not been all together for that assault. His body gave an involuntary shudder.

They'd spent two whole days guarding a stranger in a strange room. The walls were made of some sort of metal Bipp did not recognize, and for a gnome engineer to be unable to place a metal was saying something. They had used some flint to create a makeshift torch and clear large areas of the floor and walls, burning away the thick strands of spider webbing. And then they had sat. And waited.

If Logan had to spend another day inside the cramped space, with the constant threat of arachnids attacking, he might lose his mind.

"I think our friend is right," Corbin said, bumping Logan's shoulder and pointing at the unconscious woman. "It appears she is waking up."

Logan's head perked up and he scrambled to his knees on the other side of her. They had propped the woman's head on his pack and covered her in some extra tunics. Corbin said it was to keep her warm, but Logan thought she must be fine, since she had been sweating like a fevered pig since last night.

The woman's eyes fluttered open, shifting this way and that, clearly trying to take in her surroundings. She tried to push herself up to a sitting position but found her muscles weaker than her feverish intent. Bipp caught the back of her head before it hit the floor and gently guided it onto the pack again. Her lips began trembling open and closed. It looked like she had a fish swimming around inside her mouth and was trying to blow out.

"Is she having a seizure?" Logan asked.

"I think she's trying to speak," Corbin said.

Bipp brought their flask to her mouth and let the water dribble over her cracked lips.

"What are you doing?" Logan said. "That's all the water we have left."

They had spent two days, at least, sitting in this cramped room, and before that, they had traveled for days through desolate tunnels before they stumbled upon the shaft that led them here. In that time, they had completely run out of food, and clean water was a scarce commodity they were carefully rationing. There was no way to find provisions without leaving the unconscious woman or splitting up.

Bipp ignored his protests and helped the woman to another drink of water. She began to cough, turning her head and spraying flecks of spittle on Logan's knees. Logan gritted his teeth and fought the urge to complain.

"W-when did we a-arrive?" she asked.

"Arrive?" Bipp asked. "We only stumbled across you two evenings ago, lass."

She shook her head, trying to clear her thoughts, and squinted at him. Her eyes went wide then pinched tight again, and she craned her neck away.

Bipp patted her shoulder. "You've been through a lot. Best you rest for a spell and regain your strength."

She gaped at him. "What *are* you?"

Corbin looked concerned. "Do you think she's lost her...you know...do you think she's still *normal*?"

Logan rotated his finger near his ear in response.

The woman scowled at them in a way that immediately cowed his teasing. "I am not crazy. There's a little...I don't know...*man* standing beside me, isn't there?"

Bipp proudly put his hands on his hips and puffed out his chest. "Damn straight, I'm a man. Older than both of these pups combined. Well, not really, but I *am* the oldest of the group."

She tried to sit up again. Logan moved to help, but she shook him away. "But you're so...*small*." She thought for a moment, and her eyes widened. "Oh no! Is this a side effect of our trip?"

The three of them exchanged looks, and Corbin shrugged. "We don't know what you're referring to. My guess is you're still a little off from the spider's venom."

Her lips curled back and nostrils flared as if she smelled spoiled milk. "Yuck, I hate spiders. Wait, what are you wearing?" She looked them up and down as if she had never seen clothing before.

Logan looked down at his torn tunic and worn pants and could only guess how disheveled they must seem. Bipp whistled and did his own rendition of the waggling-finger–by-the-ear gesture, though it came out funnier than when Logan did it.

The woman did not miss a beat and threw a dark look at him. "I am not crazy." She slowly pronounced each word so they knew she meant business. Obviously it did not have the desired effect, because Bipp and Logan began to chuckle.

"C'mon guys," Corbin butted in, ever the ambassador, "the lady is obviously disoriented and confused." He turned his attention to her. "Can you remember your name?"

Her eyes squinted again. "Do you not know me?"

Corbin shook his head.

"I am Kyra Tarvano," she said. "*Kyra. Kyra Tarvano?*"

Logan nodded and turned to his younger brother. "Well, she remembers her name, at least."

She tried to rise, but her legs were too weak. Her face was a mask of puzzlement, and she suddenly reminded Logan very much of a scared puppy. "Who are you people? Where am I? Why am I here? I have to go!"

Logan dropped his mirth and grabbed her, steadying her and helping her sit back down while speaking soothingly. "Whoa there, lady, calm down, everything is alright. We are not here to hurt you. We only want to help, honest." He seemed to be getting through to her, as she dropped her flailing arms and slowly grew rigid. "Now why don't you just settle down before you hurt yourself?"

Her eyes cleared and she shook her head, sitting back on the floor. Without speaking, she began to take in the room, studying the walls, the open door of the shaft, the three strange men kneeling around her. Her dark eyes rested on the shattered portal to the next room and tightened. "What happened there?"

"Where?" Logan looked over his shoulder. "Oh that? I guess I got a teensie bit *overzealous* taking out one of those creepy crawlers."

"Is the rest of the crew safe? How are the citizens?"

"You'll pardon me," Corbin said in a gentle voice, "but we have no idea what you mean. Perhaps you could explain how you got here so we can understand?"

She scrunched up her face.

"Listen, lady, what my brother means is that we don't have a clue what you're prattling on about. Why don't you start with how the spiders got you and your friend there?"

Corbin shot his brother a look, silently pleading with him to be more tactful.

Kyra's eyes followed his pointing finger and locked onto the mummified remains of the man who rested inside the half-opened spider sac on the far side of the room. Her lips recoiled in disgust. She studied the remains and shifted her attention back to them. There was a visible change in her attitude. She seemed to gather her composure, becoming stolid, shoulder firmed and jaw clenched tight. Her face fell grim and her eyes tightened.

"Tell me who *you* are." She said it as a demand, and not one from someone who trusted them.

"My name is Corbin Walker. This is my brother, Logan, and our friend here is the goodly gnome Brillfilbipp Bobblefuzz."

"That's Bipp to my friends," Bipp interjected, waggling his bushy silver eyebrows at her.

"We are on a journey." Corbin stopped to find the right words. "You see, a swarm of Skex attacked our village—"

"Skex?"

"Yes, a whole swarm of them, and we had to get to Fal so we could warn the people—"

"Fahl? The robotics company?"

"No, not *Fahl*. Fal, our capitol. Anyhow, Logan murdered Mr. Beauford and then—"

She recoiled from Logan and eyed him warily. "You murdered someone?"

"No. That's not right, what I meant was..." Corbin fumbled over his words.

If Logan had not been laughing so hard, he might have been annoyed. But both the sight of his brother squirming and Bipp biting his fist to keep from bursting into tears of laughter stayed his anger. "Wow, you really suck at this, huh?"

Bipp slapped his knee and chortled at a red-faced Corbin.

"Let's start over?" Logan offered to the woman.

She nodded and he told their story. He told her about the insect attack that brutalized their village, and about their race to warn the capitol. He told her how he was *falsely* accused of murder and had to go into exile in the wastelands, and how he met Bipp on his journey. He told her he had followed his dying friend's cryptic demand that he *seek the truth*, and how that led to the ruins of Ul'Kor, where they discovered the horrible secret about their kingdom.

"You mean the entire place was built by *gnomes*?" she interrupted.

"That's right." Bipp grinned. "Finest builders in all of Vanidriell, after all."

She blinked a couple times and sat back against the wall. Logan was happy to see she was regaining her strength. "I'm sorry. This is all a bit much to take in."

Logan shrugged and shook his head. "All good adventures are, eh?"

"I'm not sure I would call that an adventure. Sounds more like a nightmare to me. So what was this secret you uncovered?"

"Our god is not real," Corbin said grimly. As much as it used to annoy Logan that his brother was so devout, it pained him to see the look of emptiness in Corbin's eyes. "The Great Crystal, that which provides life for all of New Fal, Baetylus, is a false god. Our people worship a false idol, and in turn, this insidious creature feeds off of my people, absorbing their souls and sucking away their life force. On top of that, he holds mastery over them and sways their thoughts with his loathsome power."

Kyra groaned. "So we really are still on Acadia?"

Logan cocked his head to one side, trying to make sense of that statement. "The surface? What do you mean?"

"Only on Acadia could such nightmares be true."

"No, not that. What do you mean by *Acadia*?" he corrected.

"This is Acadia, isn't it?" Her eyes narrowed and she fell into a state of self-reflection, shaking her head in sorrow. "We never left, did we?"

"Acadia is the surface world, lady. Nobody has been up there in centuries." Logan frowned at her. "Geez, Bipp, I think Corbin was right about that venom addling her brain."

"I don't think so," Corbin said evenly, tapping a finger on his chin and studying Kyra. "Why don't you tell us *your* story?"

Kyra helplessly looked around as if searching for a way out. She clearly did not want to share her secrets but saw no better option, and if their story was true, these men had saved her life. She took a deep breath and tried to think where to begin.

"My name is Kyra Tarvano. I am the High Marshal to the Kingdom of Agarta, charged with protecting my people and leading our military. I see by your reaction you are surprised to hear this. Make no amends, I am not offended. I find your tale quite amazing, almost fantastical. You see, there are no such things as gnomes. They are the stuff of bedtime stories told by old handmaidens. Tales whispered of a race long lost to Acadia, who ages past left man to his plight and crept into the bowels of our planet to live in peace. To see you here in flesh and blood, with your diminutive size and silver hair, I now know that those stories had a truth to them."

Bipp grinned sheepishly at her.

"I know nothing of any kingdom of man that dwells alongside the gnomes, or of any forgotten lands called Vanidriell. However, your tale speaks of truth. For Acadia has certainly been invaded, conquered, most likely. The jotnar, a brutal legion of ice giants, descended upon our lands with a fury and darkness we have never known. The brutal blue-skinned devils were wiping every human from the planet like a tidal wave of death and destruction. There is...was...nothing we could do to stop them. With our future bleak and extinction near at hand, it was decided that we would construct the Citadel before all was lost."

"Is that what this building is called, the Citadel?" Logan asked.

Kyra opened her arms wide, gesturing all about them. "This is the Citadel, our salvation. She is not a building but a ship, an ark, a *vessel* to wade through the sea of stars and bring us to a new home."

"Where is this sea of stars?" Corbin asked. "We have not seen any signs of water in some time now."

Kyra smiled. "I don't mean a *sea*. It's to the heavens I refer. The Citadel was created to take us deep into the heavens and bring us to a new land, one safe from the jotnar."

Corbin gulped. He had read of the heavens in Elder Morgana's books. They spoke of an infinite night sky. The idea of it had always left him unsettled. He wondered how his ancestors had been able to live without fear of falling into the limitless void over their heads. Judging by Logan's face, he was thinking much the same.

"Then why are you still here?" Bipp gave voice to the question in all their minds.

Kyra pulled herself upright, steadying her weak legs by leaning against the wall. Logan wanted to help her, but she looked like she might attack him if he offered. Her eyes were locked on the adjoining chamber and its rows of frozen glass tubes.

"That, gentlemen, is exactly what I intend to find out."

Kyra recovered in no time, having the stamina of a healthy young woman with concerns far too important to waste time lying about being sick and feeling sorry for herself.

As the poison worked its way out of her system, Logan could see color returning to her bronze skin, which was a good deal darker than the underworld dwellers of Vanidriell. Though he knew it must be true, the whole idea of her being from Acadia seemed absurd to him. The Elders had always taught that the surface world was destroyed in the Jotnar Invasion, scorched under the melting devastation of doomsday devices. Yet there she was, defying the old stories.

Kyra may have been smaller than Logan and Corbin, but she was taller than most women Logan knew and commanded a presence that conveyed to all she met that she was, without a doubt, in charge. She led them into the adjoining room, the "Sleeping Chamber," and searched for some sign of what had happened.

They entered with weapons drawn, ready to fight at the first hint of a spider attack. Iridescent blue light washed over them as they entered. Logan immediately realized that he had misjudged the size of this chamber. It was easily twice as large as he originally thought.

As they came to the first row of "sleeping chambers," he paused to look up. The glass capsule was capped on both ends with metalwork that was attached to all manner of tubes and rested a good three feet off the floor. Its glass was frosted over so that he could only dimly make out the humanoid shape locked inside the ice.

Logan took a step back. His arms fell to his sides and he stared up the rows in awe. How had his life become so complex? When did he go from the village laze-about to crazed adventurer? He wondered if the two were even exclusive concepts. He certainly felt like the same old Logan. Yet here he was, in a room filled with his frozen ancestors from a time they knew of only from fairy tales. He could only hope that he was ready for what might lie ahead.

They followed Kyra farther into the great hall until they found several broken glass chambers. Sheets of webbing covered the area.

Kyra judged that the arachnids had worked for a long time to weaken the integrity of each stasis chamber until they were finally able to get inside.

"They're so big," Corbin whispered, taking in the height of the frozen men.

Kyra explained that the two of them were smaller than most Acadian men. She assumed it had something to do with the effects of gravity, having lived so deep inside the planet of Acadia. She noticed Bipp's disapproving frown and quickly added that he seemed the perfect height for a gnome. He gave her an appreciative smile at this.

"Follow me," she ordered, heading into an adjoining corridor.

Kyra's clothing was torn and sticky from the webbing, and she was, for lack of a better word, a mess. After they passed through the Sleeping Chamber, she wasted no time finding the Waking Room and changed into her military gear. Donning tight, black leather pants with grey padding on the side of either thigh and a matching leather jacket with protective padding on the sleeves, she felt slightly better. She wore the jacket over a form fitting black shirt with a modest square collar.

Seeing her dressed for combat, Logan began to get a better picture of her as a military leader. Her long, raven-black hair was pulled into a more practical pony tail, and the tight jacket collar accentuated her high cheekbones. When Kyra looked at Logan with her chocolate-colored almond eyes, he felt like a scrutinized ant.

Wasting no time, she led them down another hall into a larger tiered area. Various mechanical devices jutted up out of the floor, each with glass cubes resting in their centers and rows of buttons with symbols on them underneath. Kyra moved to the closest terminal and tried punching keys, but nothing happened.

"We need to get one of these back up," she said, opening a panel and fidgeting with the innards.

"Shouldn't we try to find some sort of record of what happened here first?" Logan wondered, mulling over the dilemma. He was not comfortable being so exposed. Though Kyra seemed to be quite comfortable with her surroundings, they had no idea what to expect or what might be around each corner.

"That's exactly what this unit can tell us...*if* we can get it operational again." She frowned at the broken terminal. "I'm going to try to repair this. Keep an eye out in case some of those creepy spiders try sneaking up on us."

She did not wait for him to answer, crouching down and falling to work messing with the guts of the terminal. She worked for some time until, finally, she gave up and blew some loose strands of hair out of her face. "It's no use," she huffed, biting her lip and stepping back to scowl at the broken machinery. "We're just going to have to wake some of the others."

"Wait, you mean you can actually dispel the ice surrounding them?" Corbin asked excitedly.

"Of course. That *is* what we built the Sleeping Chambers for."

"B-but that's..." Corbin's voice trailed off and a wild look bloomed behind his eyes.

"Science?" Kyra offered.

Corbin snapped his attention back to them, and for a split second Logan thought his brother might try and hug her. "No! That's incredible!" He grinned like a madman, and Kyra took a step back. "I'm sorry, I should explain myself. Lady Cassandra said we needed to travel long and far and find the surface dweller Isaac. And now here we are, talking with an actual Acadian and about to wake up more!"

Kyra shook her head. "I've never heard of anyone named Isaac." Logan could see she did not want Corbin to get his hopes up.

"But there have to be hundreds of men and women in that room," Corbin said.

"Thousands, actually."

"So it stands to reason one of them is named Isaac?"

"I guess, sure."

Corbin beamed. "Then we will help you wake your people, and you will lead us to this man Isaac."

Kyra twirled on her heel and headed back to the Sleeping Chamber. "C'mon, men, follow me."

Over the next day and half, they helped her wake one after another of the frozen humans. Each required the same care and thoughtful consideration as they broke the news that they were not only still on Acadia, but that several centuries had passed. Some took it well, but others broke down in tears, raging over the injustice of it all.

It was amazing, however, the speed with which they became clear-headed and functional again. Bipp said they recovered so easy because there was no spider venom in their systems.

As they woke more of Kyra's crew, things sped up exponentially with more hands able to help in the awakenings. It did not take long before Logan, Corbin, and Bipp were not needed and told to wait patiently until the work was completed. The Citadel residents reminded Logan of worker ants busy taking care of the nest. An entire brigade of men and women filled the area, working diligently to bring the exotic equipment around them back to life.

These were the ancestors of his people. He had heard stories and read snippets of lore on how the Acadians relied on technology, but never in a million years did Logan expect to witness it firsthand. Glass screens became like living things, with floating words and images he did not understand. Heating systems turned on, warming the rooms, and all manner of oddities he could not explain were happening all around him.

At first he and his companions were thankful for the respite, and even for the dried, paper-like food they were offered. It tasted like licking dirt but satisfied their hunger and gave them strength again. But then, as more time passed, he began to grow impatient.

"This is getting ridiculous," Logan said. "She's treating us like second class citizens." He paced back and forth while complaining loudly to Bipp, who just shrugged in silence from his perch on the countertop.

"Logan, keep your voice down," Corbin cautioned, looking around to see if any of the nearby workers had paid them any notice.

"What in the blazes do I care if these Acadians hear me?" Logan glowered, raising his voice even louder, as if daring some of the workers to pay attention.

"I'm sure the marshal has her reasons for being away," Corbin said, gesturing to all the men and women bringing the Citadel back to life. "It has only been a couple days, and there seems to be a lot going on that requires her attention."

"Even so, there has to be something we can do other than sit here twiddling our thumbs," Logan said, making the gnome chuckle.

Corbin cocked his head to the side and tapped his lips thoughtfully. "Hmm, as far back as I can recall, not once do I ever remember my older brother actually looking for something productive to do," he teased, sharing a smirk with Bipp. "In fact, Bipp, did Logan ever tell you exactly how productive he used to be back home? Oh yes, he was always getting to the fields at harvest…just in time to sneak off for a nap, that is. One time he slept for five hours straight, and old man Harper almost shaved the nose clean off his face working a scythe through the crops!"

Bipp giggled at the mental imagery, and Logan folded his arms over his chest. Maybe it was true that in the past he had spent more time lying about than doing meaningful work, but that was then, and things had changed. Now life was filled with adventure, and he wanted to run after it with both arms.

"How can you just sit idly by while Elise is down there fighting for her life?" Logan snapped at his brother.

The instant he said it, he regretted his choice of words. Corbin's face dropped, and he glared shamefully at the floor, his thoughts drifting inward to his fiancée, who was on the run with their entire village, trying to escape the tyranny of Magistrate Fafnir.

"I-I'm sorry, Corbin. I didn't mean that."

Corbin nodded slowly, brushing away the notion with a wave of his hand. He knew better than to take his brother's words to heart. Logan could be gruff and brash at times, but Corbin had to believe his heart was always in the right place. And anyhow, his words did ring with a little truth. Though it was all Corbin could do not to dwell on thoughts of the woman he loved fleeing execution from the capitol, he had given his word that he would find the man named Isaac. According to Cassandra, he was the key to freeing them from Baetylus.

"I know you didn't. Elise is always on my mind," Corbin said. "I just think it's better if we stay on good terms with these people. The last thing we need is the marshal becoming angry with us and turning her back on locating this Isaac fellow in her ranks."

"Are you kidding? We haven't seen her for days. That woman has abandoned us. The least she could do is come back around so I could check out that nice little backside of hers, though, eh?" Logan joked, elbowing his gnome friend, who laughed harder than he thought warranted and almost fell off the counter.

"Um..." Corbin stared at something over Logan's shoulder, his mouth open in surprise.

Logan felt a flush of warmth creep up his neck at the realization that someone was standing behind him. When Kyra cleared her throat, he felt twelve inches tall. He turned to face her, wearing a sheepish grin on his reddening face. For all his bravado, there was something disarming about Kyra that he could not put into words.

"The technicians said you've been creating quite a commotion, demanding my presence?" Kyra spoke it as a question, but it felt more like an accusation. She held her arms crossed and her hip cocked to the side.

"Um...oh...well...." Logan scrambled to gather his thoughts under her withering stare.

"What my brother means to say, Marshal Tarvano, is that we feel our group could be useful to you and would like to be included in some of your plans." Corbin extended the olive branch, hoping to diffuse the situation.

"Oh, I see. So tell me, which of you would like to get to work on the quantum drives, and which has a degree in micro-holobionetic design?" Kyra asked without the slightest trace of sarcasm in her voice.

Logan looked at his friends in defeat, hoping they would have a witty comeback. Bipp just shrugged again, which made Logan's blood boil.

"Exactly. Leave my people alone and stop causing a ruckus. They are trying to do their job and get the Citadel functional again," Kyra said, gesturing around the control room.

Logan wasn't sure if it was something in her body language, an overreaction to his embarrassment, or if it was the ape of a man standing at her side glowering down at him, but something inside him snapped at her words, and he could not contain himself.

"Listen, *sweetie*, I dig that we don't fit in around here, and we probably seem a little backwards to you—you know, 'cause us Falians didn't grow up with all these fancy doohickeys. But who the hell saved your sorry behind when it was being sucked dry, wrapped nice and tight with a tiny spider's bow?" Logan asked, moving in nice and close to the brute for good measure.

Bipp stood on the countertop, his jaw hanging low, and Corbin rubbed his forehead in frustration. Kyra just stared at Logan in expressionless silence. The longer she glared, the more his resolve broke, and he could see the silliness of the whole situation.

"It would appear you are correct," Kyra said. The last words he expected to hear.

"I am?" Logan asked.

"Make no mistake about the value I place on what you did for us. We've found hundreds of stasis tubes destroyed by those spiders. They must have been feasting on our people for generations now. Had you not come along, I would not be alive today, and for that, I am forever grateful," Kyra said with little to no emotion while the large man beside her smiled warmly at them.

Logan was at a loss for words, all this time he had been letting himself get worked up over her seeming dismissal of them once her own people were awake. Now he felt like a petty child for seeing it as a slight.

"The lad is exactly as you have described, my lady," the large man said in a deep, brassy voice that came from somewhere beneath the thick yet carefully trimmed brown beard which covered his upper lip and chin. Logan caught himself staring at the man's facial scar, which ran across his cheek and over his upper lip, disappearing into the mass of hair.

"Gentleman, this is my weapon master, Stur Skorsgard, head of the Silver Lions, leader of the Agarta Footmen, and Arch-Guardian to the kingdom," Kyra introduced the brute, who towered over the men with broad, rounded shoulders and arms the size of tree trunks. He was fully geared for battle, wearing a brigandine with elaborate golden lace patterns woven into the black fabric. A padded leather jacket hung down to his knees and split at the waist so he could move quickly. The entire suit of armor was made of a flexible network of interlocking plates stitched inside the fabric. Across his chest and arms, the padding was dyed blue with an indigo roaring lion standard on both shoulders. He wore black steel gauntlets that covered his forearms and had a man-sized broadsword strapped across his back. The blade was so large, Logan wondered how he could even wield it fast enough to actually fight. Then again, judging by the size of the behemoth, he guessed the warrior could handle himself even without the weapon.

"Goodly met, lads." Stur placed his fist in an open palm and bowed slightly, and Corbin and Bipp awkwardly returned the salute. "You have my undying gratitude for keeping the Lady Tarvano safe when I could not."

"We were just in the right place at the right time, Weapon Master," Corbin sincerely replied. "We only did what anyone would in the same situation."

Stur shared a look with the marshal that was difficult to gauge under his bushy eyebrows. "I see much has changed during our long slumber. Please, call me Stur. Weapon Master just feels so stiff."

"Yes, and the lot of you better stop calling me *Lady* or Marshal. Kyra will do just fine," Kyra commanded, adding, "And that includes you too, Stur." She left no room for any objection, not that Logan minded. He had no inclination to grovel before the Acadian like his dutiful brother.

"Looks like the two of you are ready for a fight. Where are you headed?" Logan asked, having noticed Kyra also wore a bronze xiphos, a style of short sword with a blade that was shaped almost like a teardrop, strapped to her slender waist.

"We were coming to find you," she stated flatly, making him feel even more foolish for getting worked up earlier.

"Now we're talking!" Bipp exclaimed. "We have been bored out of our brains waiting in here!" He hopped off the counter, rubbing his palms together eagerly.

"How can we be of service, Marsha—err, Kyra?" Corbin asked. Logan rolled his eyes, which did not go unnoticed by the massive weapon master.

"The main transport has been repaired, but it seems to be stuck on something up on level five. It's only a short walk to get there, but we deemed it wise to have you accompany us," Kyra explained.

"All these people awake, and you need us to help get an elevator moving?" Logan questioned.

"These men and women are scientists, and they have enough work to do as it is. Stur is one of the only warriors we have awakened, and I have his men busy clearing the lower level exits of those monstrous spiders. We've decided not to wake any more of the soldiers until we better understand our situation," Kyra explained with an edge of acid in her voice at being questioned.

Logan smirked, holding his palms forward. "Whoa, whoa, relax, there *Lady Tarvano*. I'm only messing around with you. We are *more* than happy to get out of this room and have something to do."

Kyra turned and headed for the corridor. "Alright then, fall out, men," she commanded over her shoulder, twirling her finger in the air. "But Logan, perhaps you should stay close by my side." Logan moved right up next to the marshal, wearing a cocky grin. "This way I don't have to worry about you staring at my 'nice little backside'," she added, wiping the foolish grin from his face and causing Stur and Bipp to chuckle in unison.

True to Kyra's word, it was a quick hike through the network of dusty rooms before they arrived at their destination. Logan had grown up in a log cabin in Riverbell. Since leaving the small village, he had come across many strange and fascinating structures in his travels. However, none of them could have prepared him for the oddly comforting rooms and corridors in the Citadel. The place was both sterile and familiar. Most rooms remained unlit, but a good portion of this floor was lined with artificial lighting that ran parallel to the floor in lines that clung to the metal walls.

They took a hard right out of the corridor into a rounded out lobby that connected to other hallways in the complex. An androgynous looking fellow waited for them at the elevator shaft in the center of the room, holding a kopis and kite shield as if they were a bundle of laundry. As they approached, he became oddly animated, springing forward to meet the party.

"Greetings, Marshal Kyra Tarvano. This one has procured the requested equipment." He spoke oddly, rhythmically enunciating each syllable.

Bipp walked right up to him, gazing at his side and looking around at his back as if he were a museum piece.

"Excellent work, Nero. Please give those to Logan Walker here." She gestured to Logan.

Logan looked down at the offered bundle, puzzled. "What's this, then? Is it my birthday so soon?" He took the kopis, feeling the weight of the curved sword. The pommel felt secure in his fist, and he admired the sharp studs on the curved bar that protected his knuckles. "Me likey. But hey, how about a revolver instead, eh?"

"My sincere apologies for your disappointment, Master Logan Walker, but the armory did not fare well through the strains of time," Nero offered.

"That's a shame. I was hoping to get my hands on another of them laser rifles," he jested, keeping the sword and waving away the other equipment Nero offered.

"It is somewhat of a surprise to hear your people are still using such advanced weaponry, after hearing from Lady Kyra about your humble roots," Stur observed, truly interested to hear more about the Falian people.

"Ah, we don't really have too many of those," Logan lamented. "I mean, I used to own one, but that's a long story." He had grown very fond of the laser rifle Elder Morgana bequeathed him on her deathbed and missed it ever since it was destroyed at the ruins of Ul'kor.

"Logan Walker, are you positive you would not like this shield? Statistics show that warriors who wield a shield in combat are thirty-three percent less likely to experience fatality." Nero offered the kite shield again.

"What's with this guy?" Logan arched his eyebrow at the strange man. The Acadians had no idea his right hand was mechanical since he had been wearing leather gloves he found in the Citadel, nor the devastating capabilities it possessed, and he was not going to reveal his ace card at the moment. "Nah, I'm good pal, thanks for the sword, though."

"He's not real," Bipp explained, flicking the man's leg as if he were testing a theory.

"Ow." Nero backed away from the prodding gnome, who was surprised to be incorrect.

"That is quite enough," Kyra reprimanded before dismissing Nero, who walked in the oddest manner quickly down the corridor, leaving them alone in front of the open elevator shaft. Once he was out of earshot, Kyra directed her gaze to Bipp. "You are wise to see the truth of Nero, yet not completely correct. He is what we call an android, an artificial life form created to serve the Empire in times of war," she explained.

"What is that supposed to mean? So the guy's, what...like a machine or something?" Logan asked doubtfully, looking down the hall the man had disappeared into.

"Yes and no," Kyra said. "Originally the androids were created just as machines to serve us in the same way as any other tool would. Yet over time we saw these creations had a spirit, not unlike a soul." She hopped across the expanse of the open portal into the shaft, grabbing a ladder rung and beckoning for the party to follow suit.

"Interesting construct. I would love to pick your brain more on the subject another time, if you don't mind?" Bipp asked, enthusiastically pondering the useful applications such beings could pose to gnome civilization.

"Sounds like more witchcraft to me," Logan grumbled, wary of anything new after his recent turn of luck. "How many of those people you woke up are these android things?"

"They do not like being called things. They prefer the names they are given at creation, much like us," Stur corrected, taking the rear as he entered the unlit shaft.

The air inside was thick and dusty. It tickled Logan's throat and he had to cough to clear it. Corbin looked uneasy at far down the shaft went and seemed determined to keep his eyes upward.

"And Nero is the only android we have awoken. Hang on, we are almost there," Kyra called down. She had outpaced them fairly quickly, moving lithely up the shaft on iron rungs.

Reaching the half-opened door above, Kyra slipped through the narrow gap where the elevator cabin was stuck between two floors. Logan was not sure the giant weapon master could fit through the small opening, but Stur forced his way past, rocking the suspended room above. Logan gulped a knot that swelled in his throat, looking at the shaky outline of the cabin above. He was happy to climb out through the gap.

After they were all in the dark hallway, Kyra motioned for them to help her back inside the shaft, this time entering the stuck cabin through a wide opening where the doors were stuck ajar.

Before they entered, Kyra stopped to whisper, "We have been clearing out spiders for days now. But nobody has had a chance to take care of the upper levels yet, so keep your eyes peeled."

"Bossy lady, eh?" Logan jested, nudging the large man, who glowered down at Logan's open show of disrespect in the middle of a serious situation. Logan took note of this and sobered up, brandishing his new weapon in his left hand and eyeing Stur's massive sword.

"Corbin, give me a boost," Kyra said.

She jumped off his cupped hands into the elevator then pulled him inside after her. Stur lifted Bipp like he was no heavier than a babe and gently set him inside the compartment before joining them. While

Logan was still pulling himself into the cabin, the small room jolted downward an inch, letting out a sharp screech of grinding metal that echoed up and down the elevator shaft.

Kyra shot him a dirty look from where she stood perched on Corbin's shoulders, opening the overhead emergency hatch.

Logan scowled back. "What? Like I'm any heavier than the ox over there?" He pointed at Stur.

Kyra was halfway through the ceiling hatch when Corbin asked what she saw blocking the way. She deftly slipped off his shoulders onto the elevator's roof and motioned for them to be quiet and join her. Stur was far too large to make it through the opening, so he helped both brothers up in turn. As the weapon master lifted him, Logan could not help thinking how the man's hands were as big as his head.

It took his eyes a couple moments to adjust to the darkness after spending all that time in the artificial light of Kyra's base. Once they did, his heart jumped and his skin crawled. All around them were the familiar thick strands of spider webbing, exactly like those they had encountered when they first made it into the Citadel and found Kyra hanging in a feeding sac.

Unfortunately, it was not just webbing that surrounded them. There were also spiders the size of dogs, their long legs curled around fat hairy abdomens that moved ever so slightly, as if in slumber. There had to be six or seven of the black arachnids huddled together along the walls.

"Guess we found what's been blocking your machine." Logan's whisper bounced off the walls, echoing up the shaft. The group tensed up. Wincing, Logan started to apologize but Kyra covered his mouth with her palm and put a finger to her lips before directing Corbin to take the left flank with surprisingly straightforward hand gestures. She popped her head and arm through the elevator porthole and signaled Stur to be ready then slid over to put her back against Corbin's. Signaling with her fingers, she counted down—three...two...one—and then made a fist.

As her last finger went down, the party exploded into action. Corbin vaulted into the air, slicing down two of the oversized monsters. Kyra jumped against the wall to throw herself up high, cutting down another, and even Bipp let his small hammer fly, knocking one of the creatures loose from the wall onto its back.

Logan ran in before the dangerous fanged predator could flip over and traced a line across its exposed hairy abdomen with his sword. As he moved out, the creature wildly thrashed its eight legs and mewled like a wounded feline, trying to escape the stinging feeling of death.

It all flew by in the blink of an eye. Yet no sooner had they dispatched the first four beasts than the three others woke from their slumber to unfurl long, hairy legs and drop from the wall, ready to turn the tables on their attackers, while a fourth scurried faster than they could hope to catch up the shaft away from them.

Logan tried to warn Bipp away from the spider that had landed behind him, but having eight legs made the wretched thing swifter than he anticipated. Bipp let out a cry as the large, fat fangs clamped into his back, lifting him into the air and tossing his already paralyzing body aside like a ragdoll.

Logan lunged in, howling for his friend, and stabbed his blade deep into the creature's fanged maw. Desperate yellow eyes flickered up to him as the spider tried to backpedal and escape the blade lodged in its face. As it moved away, Logan's sword went with it. Before the monster could escape, though, Logan clamped onto one of the two-foot-long legs with his metal fist. He squeezed hard enough to snap the leg in half and gave himself enough leverage to pull the beast back toward him. Another thrashing leg almost bowled him over as the terrified predator turned prey desperately thrashed about, trying to escape. Logan rolled with the blow, throwing himself sideways to the floor and feigning unconsciousness.

Kyra saw him and moved to help, but Corbin blocked her path, shaking his head. He knew his older brother well enough to know a ruse when he saw one.

The spider moved in to claim its new prize, and Logan spun from the floor to grasp his sword with both hands and wrench it through the bottom of the monster's face. Sickly yellow ooze poured out of the spider's ruined head.

Kyra was already focused back on the two dangerous arachnids facing her. Corbin danced in toward one that was circling them. The creatures ran around the wall to their left, and Corbin jumped back, rhythmically avoiding a hissing stream of poison shot at his feet.

Another spider violently charged in, planning to overwhelm Kyra's small form. The experienced and battle-hardened woman deftly rolled out of the way, letting the spider barrel past her. In the blink of an eye, she was up on one knee and released a cord on her gauntlet. Rows of platemail spun open clockwise, locking in place across her forearm to form a shield, which she used to ram the surprised beast from the side, knocking it down the exposed opening into the elevator below. Before the surprised monster even had time to react to her ruse, Stur had sliced it into three separate, twitching pieces.

Corbin ran to the right, danced out of the way of another stream of poison, then spun to the left. Coming in hard, his feet clambered right up the wall with such speed it seemed as if he were walking sideways up the shaft. Hopping off the wall to land behind the cornered spider, he rolled into a ball, spinning sideways with the blade of his voulge sticking out like a top. By the time he stopped, the headless spider was already falling to the roof of the elevator, dead on arrival.

Logan pulled his friend's body off the floor, slapping his sickly grey cheeks. "Bipp! Bipp, wake up, buddy!"

Kyra ran over to give him a hand, propping the gnome on Logan's lap and lifting one of Bipp's eyelids to reveal an undilated, yellow, bloodshot eye. "He will live, but the poison is paralyzing, as I know only too well. Bipp can understand us, he just can't move. Help me lower him back into the cab."

Logan was relieved to hear the good news. His mind had gone into shock from the moment he saw his friend get bitten. Together, he and Kyra carefully lowered Bipp's limp body into Stur's waiting hands below, while Corbin worked with his voulge to clear the thick clumps of sticky webbing built up around the elevators wheels preventing them from rolling up the tracks set in the four corners of the shaft. Once enough was cleared away from the mechanism, which had been pushing against the webbing all this time, the entire cabin suddenly heaved upward, grinding past the remaining filament and tossing everyone about as it settled to a stop.

Kyra called for them to get inside the cab, and they rode it back down to the third level, where she had some attendants take Bipp to the Waking Chamber for medical attention. Logan felt guilty for not sticking by his friend's side, but Kyra assured him the gnome would be fine and insisted he accompany them to the top level, where she reasoned they would most likely need his skills.

The party stood huddled together, silently brooding over their sloppy victory as the elevator headed for the surface. Despite Bipp's injuries, Logan could not help feeling a trickle of excitement grow inside him, eager to see what was above. Growing up in the underworld lands of Vanidriell, deep inside Acadia's core, the young man had often found himself daydreaming of adventures and was the first to gather around when the traveling bard, Claudio, came to town with stories of epic battles from the days when humanity stilled dwelled on the surface world. The companions had travelled long and far to get to this point, and he could barely contain his excitement.

As the elevator whirred up the shaft, the car jarred, hitting something heavy overhead, which slowed it for only a second. Logan looked to Kyra for an explanation, but it was Stur who spoke.

"Another of the arachnids, no doubt. Unless it knows how to open emergency hatches, I'd say the abomination is about to become spider pâté," the weapon master said confidently, pointing at the ceiling hatch.

Logan was about to ask what pâté was when the car suddenly slowed to a jerking halt, reaching its destination. The trapped spider above screeched as it was crushed to death between the cab and the top of the shaft.

"Top floor, men. Get ready and stay on your guard," Kyra ordered, flicking open her folding shield and assuming a battle stance.

Logan was too excited to see what lay beyond the elevator doors to be annoyed with being ordered around. He did not typically go in for filling the role of an obedient follower, and last time he made an exception, a man was murdered.

The cab gave a low ding and the metal doors slid open, flooding the small compartment with blinding light from the room beyond. It was as if someone had thrown stinging water in Logan's eyes. He clamped them shut immediately as the bright light flooded the cabin. Blocking the light with his hands, he could barely make out that his brother was encountering the same problem, but their Acadian companions were not. Kyra and Stur exchanged questioning looks at the men's reaction.

"I was afraid of this," Kyra said. "Your people have lived in the underworld so long your eyes cannot take the light of the surface." She moved her body to shield some of the light from his face. Stur had moved out of the cab, surveying the room beyond for more enemies.

"Maybe that was something you could have mentioned to us *before* the doors opened, lady. I think I'm blind," Logan grumbled, his eyes squinted so tight the marshal became no more than a blurred dark shape against a backdrop of blinding white light. He could hear cloth tearing and saw a blotchy form moving toward him. Logan lifted his sword to defend himself.

"Would you put that down before you hurt yourself?" Kyra scolded as Corbin pressed a strip of cloth to his brother's face, dulling the light to something more manageable for his sensitive Falian eyes.

Logan tied the piece of beige fabric across his eyes, complimenting his little brother on the idea. He had to press the fabric against his eyelids to dab away the tears welling up, but he could see much better through it than he had by squinting. Making out some fuzzy details of the room, he found himself working his gaze up Kyra's thighs to take in her perfectly rounded bottom. His smirk told her he could see again, and she rolled her eyes. It was not as good as regular vision, but it would do for the time being.

"Lady Tarvano, you have to come see this," Stur motioned for her to join him. "I-I do not know what to make of it."

"Stur, you must stop calling me *Lady*," Kyra replied, making her way into the room while leading Corbin by the arm and beckoning for Logan to follow.

He entered the large domed room. Its glass walls curved from the outer edge all the way to the ceiling, supported by intervals of arched steel beams. Logan guessed this was some sort of viewing area. From this vantage point, you would probably be able to see all around the ship's exterior. However, all he could see of the outside world was a solid wall of shifting gray, white, and black sands, like ants dancing across the glass.

"What is that stuff?" he asked, trying to figure out if the spectacle actually looked as odd as he thought, or if this was some byproduct of seeing it through torn cloth.

"It looks like some sort of static layer is covering the Citadel," Kyra announced, her broken voice hinting of similar puzzlement.

Stur moved up beside them and pointed toward the edges of the room to the left and right. At either spot stood a dark shape Logan could not comprehend with his limited view. The sound of Kyra's gasp told him they were significant in some way.

"What is it?" Corbin asked readying his weapon and shifting to a defensive stance. Stur placed a comforting hand to his shoulder.

"They are our arch mages," Kyra said. "The finest Agarta has to offer. Both of them possess absolute mastery over the elemental arts."

Logan could hear the pain in the marshal's voice. He knew there was something he was missing and moved closer to the dark shapes, trying to get a better view. One of the men stood with a grey hood over his head, arms held out wide and white-bearded mouth agape. Crackling rivers of static energy flowed from floating orbs encompassing both hands, streaming in and out through his mouth and empty eye sockets. The sight was both impressive and gruesome.

"They sacrificed themselves to protect us," Kyra murmured. He could hear her reverence for the magic users.

"This magical shield answers some of our questions," Stur called from across the room, where he was examining the other mage.

"Now we know how the jotnar were unable to detect us for over two centuries. This is powerful magic, as potent as it comes. It seems to be acting as a cloak, hiding the Citadel from the outside world. Even the ever devious jotnar would have been blind to the base under this spell."

Kyra agreed, nodding at the sound reasoning. Stur had far more experience with magic users than she, but even a layperson could see the logic in it plain as day. "That still leaves the mystery of why they had to do it in the first place, and why the Citadel never launched."

"Well, you are forgetting one other important question," Corbin said, catching their attention. "What really happened to the surface of Acadia two centuries ago?"

Stur grimly rubbed his beard. They really had no idea what the surface looked like or whether the jotnar invaders even existed anymore. After all, it had been over two centuries since the invasion. For all they knew, the planet was a desolate wasteland just as the New Fal historians taught. At the same time, it was just as likely that a city filled with the giants existed just outside of the base, making a launch into space absolute suicide.

"Why don't we just wake these guys up from their trance and ask them?" Logan asked, trying to brainstorm a solution.

"I'm afraid that would be a dangerous mistake," Stur said. "As you have pointed out, we have no idea what lies beyond this barrier. And the arch mages are not simply in some deep slumber. Magic like this would only be possible if their souls were stuck between two shifting planes of existence. Long past, these noble men forfeited their lives to protect our people, knowing the only way to take down this barrier would be to kill them. Even if we could wake them, the sands of time would catch up all at once, aging the mages to dust." Stur's words hung in the dry air as they all somberly looked at the two mages who had given their lives to defend the last remnants of their society.

"And once the barrier is down, we would be like sitting ducks for the outside world," Kyra finished his reasoning. She gathered the men back into the waiting elevator and pushed a small lever down to the third level they had come from.

"So what's next for you guys?" Logan asked, unsure he wanted to hear the answer.

Kyra silently gave Stur a questioning look, receiving an acknowledgment to some private conversation they must have engaged in prior to meeting with the men. Corbin did not like the implications of their exchange, and he rubbed his stinging eyes as they adjusted to the 'normal' lighting.

Alarm bells went off in Logan's head. He had a hunch about the Acadians' next actions. "You guys can't be serious."

"It is the only logical course of action," Kyra replied, confirming his suspicions.

"What are the two of you talking about?" Corbin cautiously asked.

"Isn't it obvious? They're going to travel to the surface," Logan answered for the silent pair.

"But that's crazy," Corbin said in disbelief. "What you're thinking would be suicide."

When the elevator came to a stop, he moved out of the way, allowing Kyra to exit first. As he untied the cloth from his eyes, he saw Nero was already there, dutifully waiting for their return like a faithful watchdog.

"Access is clear," Kyra said. "Take a novice and study the magical barrier protecting the citadel." As the android gave a slight bow, she added, "Report back to me as soon as you have the appropriate data in hand."

"It will be done on the hour. Word has come back from delta squad," Nero replied in his odd manner, speaking with a slight rhythmic pause between each word.

The pair stepped aside to discuss something in private. Logan heard the marshal snort. "I will find Oram and discuss this with him personally. In the meantime, get started on the analysis," she ordered, catching the android before he could walk away and adding, "Oh, and Nero...do *not* allow anyone to touch the arch mages until I give the word."

"As you wish, Marshal Tarvano." Nero bowed before hurrying to his next objective, leaving them standing alone outside the elevator doors.

Kyra turned her attention back to Logan. "We will leave for the surface first thing in the morning. Make sure you are both well rested and re-supplied."

Corbin started to reply, but Logan did not give him the chance. "Listen, lady, we don't take orders from you. Maybe around here you're some hotshot everyone fights to grovel in front of, but we are not your disciples. The sooner you get that straight in that pretty head of yours, the better off we will all be." Logan folded his arms over his chest, slowly feeling his bravado wavering under the woman's brooding glare.

"Are you quite finished?" she asked, not waiting for an answer before continuing. "Like it or not, we *do* need you right now. However, I will not force this task upon you. You are free to do as you must. But I will be leaving for the surface with a scouting party regardless of your next actions and would think your honor would guide you to accompany us."

Logan did not know why he found her personality so scathing. Who was this lady to talk to him about honor? They owed her nothing, as far as he could see.

Corbin held up his hand, begging Logan not to say another word just yet. "Listen, I agree with my brother," Corbin said. "Maybe not in the way he conveyed the sentiment, but still, Logan's correct all the same. By all accounts, the surface in uninhabitable, and we cannot afford to frivolously risk our lives there when our people are in grave peril. We have a responsibility, first and foremost, to wake the man called Isaac and find out what answers he may hold to freeing Fal from the sentient crystal, Baetylus."

Kyra mulled over his words for a moment, weighing the possible courses of action presented to her. "Be that as it may, if you do not accompany us to the surface for this expedition, there is little I can do for you until my return." She spoke quickly, trying to leave no room for argument. "I hear your point of view, but you are in no position to barter for information, and none will be provided if you do not accompany us. Like you, my responsibilities lie solely on the survival and wellbeing of my people."

Corbin was stunned by the veiled threat, stepping back as if slapped in the face. He could not comprehend how this woman, whom they had saved from certain death, could be so callous and cold to their own cause. Even the weapon master looked surprised by her sudden ultimatum.

"You hag!" Logan hissed, twisting his face in disgust. Kyra belied no emotion at his stinging words, not even batting an eyelash as she continued to stare impassively at Corbin.

Stur moved between them, holding his massive arms out with palms raised. "Whoa now, everyone calm down for a moment. We all need to think about this a bit more rationally. The Citadel's systems are not even back up and running yet, and it'll most likely be a good week before they are. Think on it. In that time, what else would you three be doing but sitting in the control room, brooding over your boredom, just as you did this very day?"

Logan could see the wisdom and discipline Stur possessed. The experienced weapon master could no doubt easily cut him down for his disrespectful words, which he could see bothered Stur more than they did Kyra. Yet Stur played diplomat to the potentially explosive situation instead, acting as if there were some false compromise to be had between them. Both brothers understood the veiled threat Kyra had laid down. Either they helped in this task, or she had no intention of searching the cryo chambers for the man named Isaac.

"You can sugarcoat it all you want, but a threat is a threat," Logan said to Stur.

Corbin stepped forward. "If we help you scout the surface, will you give us your word to bring me to this man Isaac?"

"You have my word," Kyra agreed, finally blinking.

"As if *your* word means anything to us," Logan snapped, testing the mighty guardian's patience. Kyra placed the back of her hand on Stur's stomach, halting his grumbling response at her honor being called into question yet again.

"Ah, but up until now, I've never given you my word, Logan Walker," she coolly pointed out.

Logan ran over the conversations they had had over the last week and realized the devious marshal was correct. Kyra had never actually promised to help them, only vaguely alluded to the possibility. Despite his annoyance over being backed into a corner, he could not help smirking at her cleverness.

Corbin spoke in his mind. *"We have no choice for now. We must do as the Acadian says."* Through their telepathic connection, Logan could feel his brother's ire but also his acquiescence.

"Well, men, what is your decision?" Kyra impatiently prodded, unaware of the mental exchange.

Logan nodded silently at his brother.

Chapter 2: Homecoming

They had only been inside the manmade Citadel for a week, but it felt like forever since Corbin had seen underground tunnels. Their familiar winding tightness and the smell of rocks mingled with dirt gave him a feeling of calm. He had not realized what homesick could be until Kyra led the party out one of the Citadel's emergency exits, which led to a network of underground tunnels shooting miles away from the Citadel. From the moment he stepped back onto the firm bedrock, Corbin was at peace once more.

He noticed Bipp was making good progress. He even had a little extra pep in his step, no doubt from the medicine the healers had given him. The gnome was in such high spirits, he was even trading barbs with Logan again, the two of them chuckling and trailing leisurely behind the rest of the group. Despite Logan's reluctance to be subject to Kyra's command, he was falling in line so they could get through this little scouting expedition and get on to their real task as soon as possible.

Nero carried some extra supplies they would need. Though he was lean and not very muscular, even a bit soft-looking, with skin like a young boy, the android was stronger than he looked. Nero also carried a longbow and a quiver of arrows, and Stur claimed he was a proficient archer. Kyra brought along four Agartan soldiers, Oram, Rod, Lars, and Erol. Corbin half-expected them to be brandishing military grade muskets or even pistols, but instead they carried the same standard-issue sword given to his brother, the kopis blade, which Corbin considered nothing more than a slightly curved, oversized machete. A good deal of the Acadians' weapon stockpile had not survived the ages nor the corrosive effects of the rabid spiders' webbing.

Corbin caught another dirty look from Oram as the soldier brusquely shouldered past him to catch up with Kyra and the weapon master. No doubt it was to once again express his deep displeasure with having the *untrustworthy* Falians along for the ride. Corbin did not know what Oram's problem was. Maybe his thick, matted hair was wound too tight? Corbin did not generally find himself an unreasonable man, but something about Oram's beady eyes, dark greasy hair, and cocky strut made him want to punch the guy in the throat.

No sooner did the idea bloom than Corbin instantly felt guilty for the sentiment, dismissing it as a byproduct of stress from being so long out of touch with the woman he loved, Elise Ivarone. He had not spoken to her for over a week now, and every day that passed when they were not in contact filled his imagination with the darkest possible scenarios. Sometimes he would get so worked up over the thought of her down there all alone, trying to get the people of Riverbell to safety, that it felt as if his skin would explode.

Just after they arrived in the Citadel, he had chanced to speak with Elise. During a dream the very night they rescued Kyra, he had drifted across the vast distance to the realms of Vanidriell, like a psychic fog creeping over the rocky terrain, whispering her name until, at last, he found her sleeping in a cave in the hills around Mount Monkton. She was a good three leagues from their hometown, Riverbell.

Elise lay against the cool rock of the underground mountain, dreaming of the past. He entered her mind and found Elder Morgana, the woman who had raised Corbin and his brother when their parents died, laughing beside a fire and telling tales of the great surface kings and queens to a huddled gathering of children. Becoming part of the dream, Corbin found himself sitting beside a six-year-old version of Elise, the two of them intently gobbling up every word Elder Morgana had to say. His seven-year-old self giggled, looking at her with a warm smile.

Corbin looked around the fire at the familiar faces of his friends, people he had known all his life, who were no doubt this very minute sleeping in the caves around Elise, on the run from the corrupt Magistrate Fafnir's lawmen. Though he knew this was a dream, it felt and looked real. Corbin's heart ached to see Morgana's face, wrinkled and smiling with that gleam of love in her eyes as she told the children the tale of Jogah, the nature spirit. It was a story he had heard too many times growing up. And yet it never got old.

Morgana finished the story, laughing at a comment young Tolly made. "Okay, children, it's time for bed now." She beamed. Corbin found himself joining in with the other children's protests. "Okay, you eager little mice, maybe one more tale," Morgana teased, throwing him a wink. "Who wants to hear the story of our God Baetylus?"

The children cheered, and the wrinkles around Morgana's lips deepened as she smiled affectionately.

"You knew, didn't you?" Corbin asked her across the fire, knowing the dream Morgana would not hear him. "The whole time we were growing up, you were telling us lies. But why?"

"Corbin?" Elise asked.

Everyone around the fire froze in place, their eyes intent in his direction. Corbin pulled away from the group. When he looked at Elise, she was a wee lass, standing beside him with her head cocked as if trying to place something she could not remember.

"I'm sorry, Elise. This should be a happy dream!" He beamed.

The little girl version of Elise opened her eyes wide, surprised at the boy's words, which shook her out of the illusion. Recognition washed over her face, and the small girl stretched into the young woman Elise now was, standing over him with flowing blond curls and eyes like sapphires that melted his heart, lighting up her round face and fair skin.

"Corbin....is that...are you here?" she asked, now fully aware she was dreaming and certain the boy was out of place.

"Yes, my love, I am here!" he rejoiced, flashing into his adult self as the scene dissipated to be replaced by the cave she was sleeping in.

Elise sighed, crumpling against his dream form to bury her face in his chest. "I was so worried. So much has happened since we last spoke, back in the dungeon. You don't know how sick to my stomach I've been, wondering whether you were able to make it back to your body in time." The emotional release hit her, and she let herself sob lightly, clutching him tighter.

It struck Corbin that he probably should have reached out to Elise earlier and let her know he was safe, but so much had happened after they spoke that he never had time to think about anything but survival.

Guilt filled him, and he tried to console her. "Logan and I are both safe. We made it out of the ruins and found other humans. Here, let me show you." Corbin projected images of all that he had been through, each one slipping into Elise's mind as a sheet of moving memory that conveyed far more than mere words ever could.

"Who are they?" she whispered staring in awe at the rows of glowing blue cylinders, each one home to a different human.

"We are not entirely sure, but the woman we woke, Kyra, claims to be their marshal, a military leader of sorts, and we are going to begin waking up more of them on the morrow," he explained, though she had already seen as much in the images he shared through their telepathic connection. Corbin had not been practiced in the arts of pscionicism long, having had the talent thrust upon him by a well-intentioned Lady Cassandra. He knew that the memory projections conveyed so much more than mere images, but old habits died hard. "I believe they are actually our ancestors."

"But...how can that be?" Elise asked. "All of the survivors from Old Fal came down into the underworld after the surface was scorched in the Jotnar Invasion." Elise clasped her hands together tapping her thumb as she paced the floor of the cave around the sleeping bodies of her fellow villagers, who lay bundled close together to keep warm.

"I do not mean that they are necessarily from Fal. Kyra mentioned her kingdom was named Agarta, but they are Acadians nonetheless. It seems they were fleeing from the invading jotnar...but enough on that for now. Where are you?" He changed the subject, not wanting to open her mind to the probing influence of Baetylus with thoughts of rebellion.

"Lady Cassandra somehow opened a magical rift that brought me back to Riverbell safely. It was the most spectacular thing I have ever seen, like an event out of one of Elder Morgana's fairy tales." Elise's face lit up for a moment as she recalled her escape from the Fal dungeons, but then the current reality bubbled to the surface, and she grew solemn again. "I was able to convince most of the villagers to come with me and flee our home. Magistrate Fafnir has no doubt sent his men to punish us, and I'll be damned if we are just going to sit around like lost sheep waiting for him," she said, lamenting that so many had refused to leave, stubbornly staying behind and unwilling to listen to her words of reason.

"Elise, that's great news! Then Lady Cassandra can just open another of these rifts and transport you all to the safety of Malbec!" Corbin's heart surged to think his people would finally be out of danger.

Elise's sorrowful eyes told him otherwise. "Would that it could be that way," she said. "There are far too many living in the village...or for now in the hills, for her to transport them all. And besides, she used much of her magic saving me. I have come to understand that in living, Cassandra was a mighty sorceress who trained as a master and could tap into the nearly infinite resources of the universe as easily as you or I could pluck an apple from the tree. She was limited only by the human body's capabilities. However, the sliver of her that exists inside the Onyx is no longer alive. Instead, that fractured sliver of her soul is more akin to a pent up store of magical energy holding together her rational mind like a cocoon. With each expenditure of magic, Cassandra withers away." She stopped speaking to ponder their plight. "Besides, I have not spoken to her since shortly after making it back to Riverbell. I know she said she would need to rest and regain her energy, but it worries me to not hear her when I call out to the stone.

No, I fear we are on our own for now, slowly making our way to Malbec by day and searching for shelter before nightfall."

Corbin felt awful thinking about Cassandra's current plight. Only moments before being unjustly hanged, she had slipped an Onyx stone into Elise's innocent hands. Cassandra was executed for unlocking the power in Corbin to harness the magical psionic energy in the universe, an act she only took as the unwitting puppet of the symbiotic, sentient crystal Baetylus, who feared Logan's path would lead to unraveling the web of lies about its existence on the people of New Fal. Now a small piece of Cassandra's soul, which she had mystically fractured off and stored inside a pocket dimension, lived on inside that Onyx.

"So it is to be a long road through the mountains for our people." Corbin said. "I have faith in you, my love. Lead them to the sanctuary of Malbec while I search for Isaac and find the answers we need to free all the people of Fal from Baetlyus." Corbin held his fiancée in great esteem, knowing the inner strength she possessed, though secretly his heart was filled with dread at the prospect of her being on the run from Falian lawmen.

They had spent a while silently wrapped in each other's arms, thinking on the future set out before them and mourning the innocence lost when their naïve perception of the world had been lifted like a veil.

When Corbin had awoken to the sound of his brother humming an old camp tune, he had had to gather his wits, trying to make sense of the vivid dream. He tried to figure out if it was all just a work of his subconscious mind trying to cope with their situation, or if indeed he had actually been with Elise leagues away. Corbin had to believe the experience was real. That was what kept him going each day, the idea that his actions were working toward something larger than himself.

"Halt," Kyra commanded ahead, shaking him from the melancholy memory. The marshal signaled her troops with an upraised hand. Corbin shouldered past Oram to hear what she was discussing with the android.

"Due to the raised elevation, I would say that is a correct estimation," the android finished.

"And you are sure of this?" Kyra held her chin, fidgeting a finger over her soft, thin lips in concentration.

"I can run the probabilities again if you like, Marshal Kyra Tarvano, but it was eighty-eight-point-four percent likely," Nero confirmed.

"What is?" Corbin interrupted.

"Nero has determined that our path has been altered due to changes on the surface of Acadia," Kyra explained.

"Oh, great. Are you saying the machine got us lost?" Logan asked, eyebrows arched and a thumb pointed over his shoulder at Nero.

"I said nothing of the sort," she replied curtly. "Stur scouted ahead and found...well, you'll see soon enough." After her cryptic explanation, Kyra started the troops moving again, with Stur waiting ahead for their arrival.

When they rounded the last bend, Logan's face grew dark. The tunnel ahead tightened considerably and ended in a wall behind Stur's large frame.

"They've led us down a flippin' dead end," Bipp complained quietly to Logan and Corbin. "Should have let the gnome lead. No man born has a keener sense of direction in Vanidriell," he boasted, proudly patting his chest.

Oram threw a sneer at their banter. "This is not a dead end, savages. Watch and learn."

Stur stood tall, awaiting their arrival, his head almost reaching the top of the cave. On Kyra's signal, he nodded and worked a hidden lever in the rocks, which opened a hatch to the side. The cramped tunnel filled with the sounds and smells of fresh running water, and a warm gentle breeze, the likes of which Corbin had never encountered, ran across his skin. Bipp hopped up and down, then ran forward to get a better view, which Corbin also pressed in to see.

The hatch opened eight feet above deep blue water that was so crystal clear Corbin could see every detail of the sandy bottom. The water lapped in gentle, foamy waves, kicking up a salty taste on Corbin's tongue. The light outside was intense, and he was grateful for the shaded goggles Kyra had provided, sliding them off his head and into place. After their experience in the observatory room with surface light, it was deemed the Falians' eyes would need to be protected from the harmful light until, if ever, they grew accustomed.

Kyra gasped. "That's a hell of a lot of erosion."

"Nero figures the Heltic Ocean has risen four meters to cause such a drastic alteration of the Rainbow Cliffs," Stur explained, tossing a rope, which he had tied around his waist, through the hatch.

"I didn't know marble was water soluble," Kyra said.

"Oh yes, Marshal Kyra Tarvano, marble such as is found in the Rainbow Cliffs of Agarta holds a PH balance of five, giving it an aqueous solubility over time. The two hundred and thirty-six years we have been dormant has been more than sufficient time for this level of erosion to occur." Nero sounded like he was speaking a different language to Corbin.

Kyra nodded, completely understanding his scientific explanation. "Nero, you must address me as only Kyra, please. It is not natural for you to say my entire name every time we are in conversation."

"As Only Kyra wishes, this one shall obey," Nero replied, giving Stur a bit of a chuckle at Kyra's exasperation. Interacting with androids took getting used to, but at least she was giving it real effort.

Kyra's men were already shimmying down the rope while Stur supported their descent, holding the rope like some mega-human version of a paperweight. Bipp pulled a small pack from his bag, which unfurled into a paper-thin aluminum raft.

"Oh my, that is an interesting contraption, isn't it, Stur?"

Bipp beamed at Kyra's praise before waggling his fingers at Corbin and hopping out of the hatch, startling the marshal, who instinctively reached out, thinking he had fallen. The soft splash and giggles of the gnome below told her the reaction was unnecessary. Logan laughed at the marshal, who blushed for the first time since Corbin had met her.

"You're next, Logan," Stur said, bracing himself to hold the Falian's weight.

Logan took the rope, seemed to think for a moment, then smirked at Kyra. "Don't try catching me, now. I'm a little bigger than Bipp. Don't want you to hurt those little arms." He winked and jumped feet first out of the hatch with a splash below.

Corbin thought he could actually hear Kyra growling as she stood there stewing over Logan's insolence. She looked up from the hole to Stur, expecting him to share her annoyance.

"Don't look at me," Stur replied, massive arms held up in surrender. "How do you think I'm getting down?"

Kyra shook her head, only slightly less annoyed, and worked her way down the rope with Corbin fast behind her. The water was surprisingly warm. Corbin had never felt anything like it. All of the lakes, rivers, and wells he encountered in Vanidriell were skin-prickling cold, yet this water was as warm as three blankets and very pleasing to the skin.

Following Nero, they swam through caves of curving marble, soft and smooth to the touch with thick striations of rich pinks, vibrant blues, and creamy whites all swirled together. The water became shallow enough to wade through as they worked their way through a myriad of sloping caves with dozens of directions they could take.

The whole walk took not even ten minutes before they came to a wide, yawning opening revealing the surface of Acadia.

It was a land Corbin only knew from children's stories, a place that was supposed to be lost forever to mankind after the great burning. Through the marble arch of the cave entrance, he could see clear water stretching all the way to eternity, as far as the horizon and beyond, reflecting the tiny pinpricks of light from overhead stars. To the southwest, past a dense jungle, a distant white-capped mountain range reached for the heavens. Entranced by the alien landscape he had only dreamed of, Corbin almost bowled over Oram, so lost in Acadia's magnificence he did not even notice the wormy man's scowl.

Corbin looked at his brother to share this moment and saw that both he and Bipp were equally in awe. He followed their gaze upward and felt the world open up around him. It was that feeling of insignificance one experiences the first time they stare into the night sky, not just with a cursory glance but really gazing into the grandeur of space. He felt silly to have thought the ocean went as far as eternity, when here above him the truth of that word could never be more evident. Layer upon layer of blinking stars blanketed the sky between a carpet of purple and pink galactic clouds. Directly above him, a mighty moon, silky blue, floated haloed by wide concentric rings, dwarfing a smaller green moon that peeked out from behind its sister. Logan tugged on Corbin's arm, pointing to the west at yet a third celestial body, this one alive with swirling seas and clouds. The moons lit up a beach of pure white sands and lazily bent coconut trees swaying in the breeze.

Bipp held onto Logan's leg, steadying himself from the dizzy elation of witnessing the cosmic spectacle. He noticed a tear fall from Logan's right eye and knew in his heart they all shared the same feeling.

Looking over to share this discovery with Kyra and the Acadians, Corbin wondered why they all stared at the trio. Arms crossed, Kyra seemed to be trying to make sense of something. It was then that Corbin realized how close he, Bipp, and his brother had become. They crouched, practically straddling each other for support, afraid of the immensity above. Where they had only ever known life under a cavern ceiling, the idea of nothing overhead was both powerfully enlightening and deeply terrifying on some primal level that concerned itself only with survival and cared nothing for such meager concerns as looking smart.

Logan must have realized it too, as he brushed the others off, clearing his throat and aiming his gaze purposefully down at the lapping waves.

"You boys done making out?" Oram taunted, eliciting a wave of friendly laughter at their expense.

Corbin offered no reply. How could he explain the primal urge he was fighting to run screaming back to the safety of underground, where there was a top to the world? Instead, he, Logan, and Bipp moved to join their new comrades, though they remained a lot closer to each other than normal.

As they made their way toward the beach, Corbin could not help his attention being drawn repeatedly overhead, wondering if somehow they could fall off Acadia and drift endlessly through the heavens. Behind them, the Rainbow Cliffs and their sloping caves moved farther away, eliminating his last chance to retreat back inside the bowels of the planet.

"Is the daylight always this bright?" Logan asked Stur even though the light was not bothering his eyes with the silly goggles on. In fact, he was rather pleased with the lighting, which was much more vivid than New Fal.

Stur snorted, his thick beard shaking. "No, lad, it's not always this bright. Those are the three moons of Acadia, Clotho, Decima, and Atropos. You can see what time of month it is because Decima is in full bloom, bouncing the light of Themis, the daystar, across this *night* landscape."

Logan was impressed by the warrior's knowledge of the celestial bodies. He realized this guy was not just some hired muscle, but nonetheless, he was astounded to hear Stur's correction.

"You mean to tell me this is nighttime?" he asked, scratching the back of his neck and tasting the salt from the sprays of water from lapping waves they waded through. "Geez, if it's this bright at night, I'm not sure I want to be out here when Themis comes out."

To Kyra and the Acadians, having lived all their lives on the surface as children of Themis, the landscape was quite dark. She found it curious that the Falian men thought it bright outside and asked Nero to take note in his logs of this scientific observation.

"Yeah, why don't you jot down that we like to drink scrum too," Logan jested, laughing with Bipp, who pulled a small flask out of his pocket and took a swill for good measure.

"Brillfilbipp Bobblefuzz, may I analyze your scrum?" Nero asked as the men made it to shore and shook the water from their clothing, leaving droplets of brown across the pure white sandy beach.

"When he says it like that, sounds kind of perverted, don't it?" Bipp remarked, handing the android his flask.

The tip of Nero's forefinger popped open, unleashing a thin mechanical hose into the mouth of the flask. After withdrawing exactly a quarter of an ounce, the android's finger returned to normal, and a screen of glowing red calculations popped up, floating in the air before his face. Bipp hopped back a step, startled by the screen's sudden appearance. Numbers flowed by in patterns none of the Falians understood, then just as abruptly, it was over.

"Nero understands. Water, malt extract, sugar, and yeast. What you call scrum is actually an ale of sorts," Nero declared, satisfied at understanding a piece of their language.

"Ain't no *beer*. It's scrum." Bipp scowled, snatching back his flask and wiping the mouthpiece off with his sleeve.

"Stur, look up the side of the mountain." Kyra pointed back the way they had come, high up the face of the Rainbow Cliffs.

Stur nodded thoughtfully, folding his arms over his chest. "I see it, my lady."

Logan looked so confused that Corbin felt compelled to explain. "The Citadel should be right about there, on the face of the cliffs."

"So that barrier those mages put up is camouflaging the whole place, huh?" Logan was impressed that not even the faintest hint of the Citadel could be seen from this vantage point.

"This makes a little more sense," Kyra said, appreciating the weight of the mages' ruse. "If the jotnar could not see the Citadel, they would naturally think we were gone. Brilliant move from the archmages. Without them we would all be dead long ago."

Stur, on the other hand, looked troubled, pointing to the ocean, where a largely populated port city had thrived in their time. There was no trace of the grand city as far as the eye could see. "That does not explain what happened to Wynd."

Kyra had not even thought of Wynd. The landscape was so alien from what they knew, it might as well have been another land altogether. Looking around, she tried to picture the port city she had grown up in. To the Acadians, it had only been weeks ago when they went into cryo-sleep, hoping to arise in a new home. Instead, they woke from their slumber to find their own world had become an alien landscape, Acadian civilization lost to the ages.

Nero began a lengthy discourse. "Kyra, calculating the newly formed elevations from north to south, and factoring in the distance the beach has travelled, while triangulating—"

"Spit it out, droid," Oram snapped, earning a glower from Kyra deadly enough to shrivel his testicles. The grimy soldier ducked behind some of her other men.

"There was an explosion of immense magnitude here, Kyra. It was most likely over two hundred years ago, which would explain how the ocean has moved so far inland and why there is no sign of Port Wynd remaining," Nero explained, his words casting a pall over the Acadians. To know you had outlived the friends and family members you had left behind was one thing. However, to know that those same people had died in a terrible explosion was something else entirely.

The Acadians looked heartbroken, staring out at the lapping waves where their capitol city had been. Corbin could only imagine what memories each of them were reliving, dwelling and aching over the loss of their people. He dared not enter their minds, having vowed to never use his psionicism on allies.

"I am so sorry for your loss," he said, breaking the sobering silence.

Kyra shook her head, shaking off the icy feeling that gripped her throat. She would not cry here in front of her troops, not when there was still so much to be done. "Do you detect any signs of civilization in the area?" she asked Nero.

Again a screen of floating red numbers and words flashed in the air before Nero for an instant. "Kyra, there does appear to be signs of civilization to the west, about eight kilometers from here."

Kyra muttered to Stur that she wished the android would stop saying her name every time it spoke, and he just chuckled.

"Right, then fall out, troops," she ordered.

Corbin caught up with her, walking up the sandy dune toward the jungle. "Marshal, I do not mean to question your judgment, but is it wise for us to enter a jungle none have ever been in before?"

"You *mean* to say, you *do* question my judgment, then?" Kyra said. "You Falians speak oddly. Not that I'll be running my every order past you, but for the sake of your understanding, *if* there is a nearby civilization, we need to investigate it. When the Citadel takes off, it will be seen for leagues, and we cannot risk being vulnerable to a jotnar aerial attack."

Before Corbin could respond, Stur swatted them both like flies, throwing them to the side and roaring as his sword crashed against a pincer claw the size of Corbin's leg that suddenly thrust up at them.

The white sands shifted, rolling down the length of a giant white-shelled crab that was lying in wait. The hulking beast stood to its full height on eight jointed legs, each as thick as Corbin's arm and bred to run through the loose sandy beach, towering over even the weapon master.

The crab flicked its claw, shoving Stur back. The left claw, which was three times the size of the right, clamped down hard on Oram's midsection before the man could even brandish his blade. Blood sprayed across the sand in a red shower as the crab crushed his screaming body in half.

The crab turned in a strange sideways walk to face Logan and the rest of the Acadians, its long eyestalks peering down over its body at them. Logan shouted for the men to get out of the way as he and Bipp raced out of reach. The crab batted another of the men hard with Oram's crushed, mewling body, bowling Rod head over heels down the side of the sand dune and into a shallow pocket. Kyra could only watch on in horror as the pocket filled with a swarm of flesh-eating beetles that tore apart the flesh of his face, greedily burrowing into the howling man's eye sockets.

An arrow swiftly lodged deep into Rod's heart, freeing him from the terror of being eaten alive by insects. Nero was already nocking another in place as the troops fell into a semblance of defensive formation. The crab's element of surprise was over.

It batted at Logan, almost taking him in the side of the head. He howled and threw his blade, which spiraled through the air toward the beast's side. The kopis blade struck its mark but skittered harmlessly down the crustacean to the sand. "Dammit, why does everything I have to fight have armor?" Logan shouted in frustration.

The crab moved in, grasping with the smaller claw and blocking its mouth with Oram's dead body.

Stur swung his mighty blade low, sheering two of the crab's legs off with a crack. The beast did not make any noise but moved with lightning speed sideways away from him, almost trampling Bipp, who rolled between its legs.

Kyra barely had her shield unstrung and up in time to deflect a blow from the deadly pincer. "Corbin, work to distract it! Nero, take out one of those eyes! Lars fall in against the left flank!" she shouted out as she rolled across the ground.

Corbin nodded, dancing inside the beast's claws, which reminded him of the skex he had battled back in New Fal. He viciously pressed the crustacean behemoth with an onslaught of blows from his voulge while dodging the lumbering hulk's attempts to strike him with its claws. An arrow zipped past the defending claw, digging deeply into one of the eyestalks and sending the crab into a violent rage.

Beneath it, Bipp snatched Logan's lost weapon and gave his friend a thumbs up. Logan screamed for him to stop, but the gnome acted too quickly. Grasping the sword pommel with both hands, he smiled triumphantly as he slammed the blade straight up, all the way to the hilt, into the crab's belly.

The beast stopped and stood stock still, trying to understand what had just happened, then toppled hard onto the ground, trying to rub off the weapon.

Logan felt his insides turn to mush as he watched Bipp get crushed under the hulking crab's weight. He let out a cry so blood-curdling even the mighty Stur looked frightened for a moment, and all were shocked out of their wits to see Logan's hand suddenly erupt with blinding light. Energy fueled by his very life force, connected to the universe through a mystical modification his murdered friend Mr. Beauford had installed, burst from the metal fist and melted straight through the crustacean's face, cooking its insides like stew.

Before the light of it even died away, seared across all of their visions in a glowing trail, Logan was already running and calling to the other men to help him. They worked to heave the crab over, hoping beyond all reason to save the gnome. Once Stur joined in, they easily flipped the beast over onto its back.

In the center of the large indent, pushed deep into the sand, Bipp was buried, smiling and rubbing his bulbous nose. "Thank Ferrigan for sand. We should visit the beach more often." The gnome groaned, holding out his stubby hand out for help. When they pulled him to his feet, there was still a perfect indentation where Bipp had been pushed into the sand.

Logan laughed weakly and hugged his friend, while Stur walked up to Corbin, looking curious.

"That is some hand your brother has there. Very interesting." He stroked his beard in consternation.

"He lost his hand in battle. Logan is often a surprise, even to those who know him well," Corbin replied. He noticed that Kyra was deeply disturbed over the loss of her men, as she should be. "Are you alright, Marshal?"

"Two men in less than an hour." She spoke in a low voice, not wanting the other soldiers to hear, while tracing her finger over her face three times, offering a prayer to the Goddess Vaselia. Turning to face the remaining men, she addressed Stur. "This is not the land we once knew. The world of Acadia has grown into a hostile and dangerous land indeed. We must take every precaution from here on out."

Stur nodded, silently agreeing, and ordered the remaining three men to fall into a marching formation, Lars and Erol in the front and Nero taking up the rear. Logan was too weak to walk on his own after expending so much of his life force through his mechanical fist. Corbin and Bipp helped balance Logan's weight and took up position in the center along with Stur and Kyra.

"Fall out, men," he ordered at the marshal's signal, leaving the picked bones of their comrades behind in a dangerous pit of swarming beetles. "Let's find this *civilization* Nero detected and get out of here."

Corbin could not help wondering what kind of people could survive such a dangerous world and dreaded that they would find out soon enough.

Chapter 3: Welcome to the Jungle

For Logan there was stark contrast between the forests of Vanidriell and the jungles of Acadia. If someone had asked him to describe the Muscari Woods, he would use words such as *lush* and *dense*. But now, after travelling through the dank-smelling jungle for half the night, he understood the true meaning of such words. Unlike the forests of Fal, the jungle pressed in all around, with thick vines hanging from fat, tall trees, some with sashes of thick moss blocking his view. It was so hot and humid he could actually see the moisture built up in small pools on the large fronds of ferns, and his clothing clung to him from a sweat the likes of which he had never experienced. The jungle was hotter than anywhere he had ever been. And it was virtually teeming with life, as the sounds of exotic birds, swarming bugs, and the gods only knew what else filled the air.

When they broke for camp, the Falians drifted away from the rest of the group to chat in private. Bipp quickly plopped down in the damp grass and pulled out some flatbread that Kyra had made for their journey. He sniffed at it and wrinkled his nose.

"It's not the bread that smells foul," Logan said, seeing his friend's reaction, "but this infernal bog of a jungle that seems to have been dipped in rot and left to fester." Logan pulled out the kopis blade he had almost lost and began running a sharpening stone over its edge.

Corbin followed suit, crossing his legs in the grass and resting the shaft of his voulge across his lap. He took in the jungle once more. Where Logan found the place to be a constant source of irritation, Corbin could not help but revel in it, marveling at the beauty of the dense woods. "I can't believe the Elders could have been so wrong about the surface. It's amazing up here."

Logan snorted. "Corbin, don't you see?" Corbin shrugged, not following his meaning. "The Elders have been lying to everyone all this time. They lied about the wildlands. They lied about the Crystal. How can we trust in any version of history we have been taught? I can only imagine what else they've misled us about."

Corbin cocked his head, putting the pieces together as his older brother laid them out. His hands rolled across the shaft of his voulge and he drummed his fingers on the bronze spear. Not for the first time in the last month, he felt quite foolish for his naivety. "Yes...of course. What was I thinking?" he said bitterly. "If the Elders have been misleading everyone all this time about everything else that matters, why should I be surprised to find what they told us about the surface is also false?"

"Exactly." Logan rose to pace back and forth, getting more worked up as he thought over the matter. "And another thing—what in the bloody hell was Zacharia doing in a relief carved well over two centuries ago?"

Corbin pictured the carvings they had discovered lining the ceiling of the King's Hall in the cursed ruins of Ul'kor. High Elder Zacharia *had* been pictured there helping the gnomes create the great crystal construct so that they might bring life to previously uninhabitable caverns in Vanidriell. "The curse that fell over Ul'kor was certainly nigh on two centuries ago, there is no mistaking that. And by the accounts Bipp has given, no one has so much as stepped foot in the place since then."

Logan snapped his fingers and pointed at his brother. "Right. So how in the world could Zacharia have been there? You know, they have all these laws against magic use, but how much would you like to bet that damned bastard is a dark wizard?"

"That *would* make sense," Bipp said, eyeballing Logan's portion of bread. "If this Elder fella you're referring to practices the dark arts, he could live a longer lifespan than is typical for your kind."

"How can you know this for certain?" Corbin asked.

"In the Book of Lost Souls, Yuri the Whisperer gives a personal account of how certain necromancers were able to extend their lives long past the moment of death."

Corbin arched his eyebrows and shivered at this revelation. "Oh? How do they do such a ghastly thing?"

"Dunno." Bipp swallowed a hunk of the bread, chasing it down with a hearty gulp of water from his flask. "We only had to read the one excerpt as an assignment in my Arcane Lore Studies. I guess it never occurred to me that the material would ever have any real world application, eh?"

"Well, I'd venture a guess that whatever we find up here is going to be vastly different than what we were taught as children," Logan said.

"I'd say what we've already seen has been enough to make that statement truer than a toad's warts," Bipp agreed.

The three of them fell silent as Stur made his way over to their gathering. "We must go," he said with a sense of urgency. "Erol has found someone traveling through the woods."

"Are they friendly?" Bipp asked.

"We don't know yet," Stur said. "But we're going to break camp post haste and follow them. Perhaps this stranger can lead us back to the civilization Nero detected."

They had been following the woodsman for almost two miles. Stur was like a magician, picking up the trail in this dense foliage. He said it was merely a matter of knowing where to find the information, pointing out the broken or bent plants that were so alien to Logan, he would not be able to tell if they were supposed to look that way or not. He marveled that the muddy ground held no footprints, instead filling back in fairly quickly. When the ground became muddy in New Fal, it was more like clay, holding form to anything pressed in it, while the ground here in the jungle was spongy and resilient.

Kyra held up her hand, halting the party, who were all doing their level best to remain undetected. A few yards in front of her, Stur crouched so low his knuckles touched the ground, trying to hide his hulking form amidst some tall grass.

Logan could not make out what the warrior whispered to Kyra and threw a funny face at Bipp to convey his boredom. The gnome bit his fist to keep from giggling, and Corbin elbowed him with a glower.

"Stur spied a glimpse of our mark through the trees ahead," Nero stated in a voice precisely quiet enough for the situation. The android's superior robotic hearing had picked up the whispers.

Kyra ran through a series of hand gestures, ordering the team into different positions, readying to move forward and corner their target. Once they grabbed the unsuspecting foreigner, they would be able to get information about the area, determining if the Citadel would be in danger.

Logan could see the man's outline through the heavy leaves covering the area. He was only thirty yards ahead, and they crept up on him from the right side.

Something about the man struck Corbin as odd, and he could tell Logan felt it as well. Perhaps it was the way he had stopped in the middle of a clearing, so casually sitting on a rotting log covered with moss and layers of mushroom. Or maybe it was the way he moved, a little more fluidly than seemed normal. Corbin probed for a connection to his brother's mind and shook his head. *Look at his neck. Something's off here,* he said, including Bipp in the telepathic message.

Logan squinted while Kyra and Stur circled around, sliding into position across from them. The man bent over to pick up something from the ground by his feet, and Kyra held her fingers up counting down from five. The stranger's head lifted, and Logan understood his brother's meaning—his neck was longer than it should be.

Bipp grabbed Logan's sleeve, pointing behind them. Something had moved in the trees, rustling leaves as it went. Logan screamed out the warning a second too late as Kyra and the Acadians sprang into action, sprinting from their hiding spots to surround their target with weapons drawn.

Corbin whipped around and held his voulge at full length, the tip of the polearm's blade pressed against the neck of a humanoid that emerged from behind them.

Out of the corner of his eye he could see the *man* they had been tracking standing with his back to Kyra and her men, holding up his hands in mock surrender and flicking a long, thick lizard tail. Logan felt his blood freeze with the realization that *they* were the ones cornered, as all around them the jungle began to move, rustling as shadows emerged from their hiding places.

These humanoids were not the Ul'kor cobolds he had battled before, which were outmatched by his sheer strength and ferocity. No, these were an entirely different threat altogether.

The lizardman in the clearing turned to face Stur, wearing the coy smile of a snake that had lulled its prey into a false sense of security. They were built similar to humans, with lean muscular frames accustomed to survival in these dangerous jungle lands. Their skin was a deep green with smooth scales that glimmered in the fading moonlight peeking through the canopy of trees. They held wooden spears, bows, and makeshift clubs in reptilian clawed hands—three long fingers and a thumb that was smaller than a man's.

Logan counted at least twelve of the lizardmen surrounding them and wondered how long they had been tracking the human explorers before deciding to reveal their ambush. Some of the humanoids had iguana-like protruding faces, with ridges that ran from the top of their smooth heads down their backs, while others had flatter, softer features that were almost human. All were adorned with various bracelets, armbands, and necklaces made of wood and bone, with animal skin loincloths that hung at different lengths around their waist.

The lizardman they had been following appeared to be the leader of the hunting pack. He laughed from the center of the clearing, the sound of it deep like a human, which somehow seemed surreal emanating from this creature's sharp-toothed mouth. His golden eyes sparkled mockingly as he spoke in a language Logan had never heard.

Kyra exchanged confused looks with Stur, who moved slowly and deliberately, motioning for her to put down her weapon. Logan deemed the move wise. Even if they managed to take down a handful of these savages, they would still be hopelessly outnumbered.

Corbin did not share the sentiment, gritting his teeth and growling as he pushed the tip of his weapon harder against the caught lizardman's throat. The leader looked over at them and saw the threat. He called out to his men, ordering three of them to surround Corbin and protect his cornered tribesman.

"Corbin, don't be a fool. Lay down your weapon," Logan coaxed, not wanting the situation to escalate, at least not until they had a better idea of what they were in for.

Corbin's eyes cleared, the cloud of bloodlust washing out of them, and he stepped back slowly, pulling the tip of his blade from the lizardman and laying the bronze spear in the grass, leaving a tiny pinprick of blood on the frightened lizardman's neck.

"Drop your weapons men!" Kyra ordered somewhat reluctantly, cursing herself for not realizing they were walking into an ambush.

The leader said something more in his strange, clicking language, nodding its head in approval of their decision. The freed lizardman behind Corbin slammed the end of a club into the back of his head, knocking him down the hillside into the small moss-covered clearing, where the leader stood. Two others fell on him, repeatedly kicking his prone body while he struggled to block their attacks. The surrounding pack fell into a frenzy, cheering on their mates, and the leader slammed his long spear into the ground, hooting.

Logan lifted one of the lizards by its neck in rage. It weighed as much if not more than he did, but his adrenaline was pumping hard, seeing his brother attacked. Throwing the humanoid into one of his brother's attackers, he grabbed another by the throat, squeezing with the vicelike pressure only his mechanical hand could provide.

"Call off your dogs!" he demanded of the leader, who stood smiling at him amidst his suddenly silent tribe. Logan put more pressure around the lizardman's throat, hard enough to make the humanoid's eyes bulge. "Now!" he snarled for emphasis.

The leader spoke to his men in a series of guttural clicks and grunts.

The lizardmen stepped back from a coughing Corbin, who gasped as he tried to get air back inside his battered chest. The lizardman Corbin had cornered proudly puffed up its chest, demanding to continue reclaiming its honor. This earned it a scathing joke, lighting up the group with a peel of hooting laughter at its expense. The leader waved his proud young warrior off, claiming it had reclaimed more than enough *honor* beating an unarmed soft-skin. Corbin did not understand the words, but the psychic emotions conveyed the meaning all the same.

The leader looked at Logan then held its spear up, pointing at Kyra with the stone tip and speaking more alien words.

"I do not understand you," Logan replied, choking his victim harder in frustration.

"He said let her go or he will kill Kyra," Corbin rasped, pleading with his bleary eyes for Logan to do what only moments before he had done and pull back.

Logan eyed the lizard he was choking with shock, noticing for the first time how flat and feminine her face was and that her breasts were covered with animal skin. Looking around, feeling like a cornered beast, he felt guilt and shame at the realization that he had attacked a woman, and instantly released her into a nearby lizardman's arms.

Other members of the tribe moved in to apply swift justice for his actions, but the leader clicked and clacked, ordering them to halt. They gathered up the party's weapons and separated them into pairs. Kyra and Nero walked in front of Logan and Bipp with lizardmen on either side ready to cut them down if they tried anything. And just like that, the explorers were being led through the jungle as prisoners marching toward an unknown fate.

Kyra edged in close enough to Nero to whisper. "Can you understand their dialect?"

"Kyra, this one processed the reptilian humanoid's language, and it does not come up in any existing linguistic database." The android fell silent, sensing one of the lizardmen moving in closer. It sniffed him curiously, cocking its head and trying to understand what was off about the prisoner, then moving back to its walking companion. "Kyra, their language does have minor qualities of primitive Faluthian," he continued.

"So you *can* process a translation algorithm?" she asked hopefully.

"I can. However, the range will be limited."

Bipp's sensitive gnome ears overheard the conversation. The small scholar knew enough to understand that if these primitive hunters saw the android's holo-screen, they might think it witchcraft and kill him on the spot. The gnome looked up at Logan and winked before pretending to trip on a vine, rolling into one of the lizards from behind and knocking her over.

Kyra saw the charade for what it was and nudged Nero, prompting him to run through the program. In a flash the holo-screen popped up before his face while the lizards were distracted, helping their comrade up.

On her feet again, the lizardwoman prodded Bipp with her foot, not wanting to touch the slimy soft-skin child. One of the humanoids turned, meaning to keep moving, and Logan grabbed its arm, not thinking of a better solution, pulling it back around and away from Nero. The lizardman knocked him backwards with its club, and he held up his hands, gesturing at the gnome, trying to convey he meant only to help his friend. By the time he and the lizard pulled the gnome from the ground, Nero's screen blinked off.

"Stupid soft-skin knows not how to walk straight," one of the lizardmen joked.

"It's just a child, Tiko," the other replied sympathetically.

Logan felt a lump in his throat, alarmed to understand his captors. Nero had set a field of range that encompassed a diameter of forty feet from his location.

"Good work, Nero. Can they understand us?" Kyra whispered, adding the question as a practical afterthought.

"Kyra, I limited the program to our understanding only. If you wish, I can amend the data to include outbound translations," Nero offered.

Kyra quickly grabbed his arm and raised her voice a tad too forcefully. "No, don't do that just yet."

"Shut the female up," one of the lizards said from the front of the line, shoving past Tiko to bat her with his spear.

"Do not damage the merchandise!" the leader ordered from the front of the entourage.

Kyra looked down at the mud, trying to appear as docile as possible.

A flat-faced lizardwoman held a thick vine aside as the retinue made their way over a steep hillock and down into a narrow gorge that broke the jungle on either side.

Logan confirmed that the flat-faced, more human-featured lizards were definitely the females. They wore skins over their firm breasts and brown leather loincloths that looked more like knee-length skirts. He would be lying to himself if he said the lizardwomen were not alluring in their own way. There was something sensual about the curve of their hips and the lusciousness of full, mint-colored lips under golden eyes. He shook off the notion, suddenly nervous that his brother may have overheard his thoughts, though Corbin had promised only to do so if they were in danger.

"Does Tokl mean to sell the soft-skins to Kallix in truth?" the lizardwoman asked her companion, sounding as if she disapproved of the concept.

"Do not be soft, Kalilah. Tokl will do as needs done," Tiko replied stoically.

The lizardwoman hissed, bumping Tiko to the side. "Never has Kalilah been *soft*." She scowled at Tiko, the scales on her body growing rigid. Logan did his best not to show his alarm but moved out of reach just the same. Kalilah's sharp face softened once more, eyeing Bipp with an almost motherly affection. "It is just that the hairy child looks so cute and innocent. What a shame to have to sell it."

Tiko rolled his eyes at her contradiction. Despite their current conundrum, Logan stifled a laugh at his friend's expense, catching the lizardman's attention. His eyes narrowed into shrewd slits, wondering if the soft-skin had just understood his words. Bipp gave the man a doe-eyed response, quelling his curiosity.

"She said I was cute," Bipp whispered, refusing to bite the bait and wiggling his eyebrows at Logan.

"You confuse stupidity with innocence," Tiko corrected the lizardwoman, trying to sound like a wise elder. He could not wrap his head around how his clan mate could think the hairy, big-nosed child was *cute*.

Bipp glowered. "Shows what he knows. Stupidity and innocence are practically the same thing," he grumbled.

"At least now we know why they didn't search you for weapons, eh?" Logan said.

"Either way," Tiko continued, "Kalilah knows we risk Agma safety every moment the soft-skins are in our possession."

Kalilah conceded that fact with a solemn nod, knowing it was dangerous to involve themselves with the soft-skins. They walked the rest of the way in sullen silence.

Logan gathered from other conversations that they were being led to the lizard tribe's camp, to be held there until they could be transported to a slaver named Kallix who would give the primitive lizard people supplies in exchange for wild soft-skins. Logan assumed Kyra caught that detail as well, hinting that there were other humans on the surface potentially living nearby.

Once through the gorge, they came to the lizard camp, which housed hundreds of the humanoids. The leader, Tokl, ordered them to be taken to a clearing between tents and watched over while he went to report their hunt to the tribal leaders.

Only eight of the hunters remained to guard over them, but with the sheer numbers in the camp, they did not dare attempt escape. Many passersby stopped to take in the strange soft-skins with reactions ranging from disgust to exotic curiosity.

"We have to get out of here," Logan urged the group, hoping Stur had a plan.

Kyra looked at Corbin. "Are you wounded?"

He shook his head, silently guarding his bruised ego. When the lizardmen had attacked him, it was all he could do to protect his body from their blows, and now he felt every welt and bruise.

Stur addressed the group of Acadians quietly. "We make no move toward violence until we fully understand our opposition."

"What more is there to understand?" Logan interrupted. "The beasts have us surrounded and plan to hand us over as slaves. Why are we not fighting our way out of this mess yet?"

Stur remained calm and levelheaded. "These lizards were cunning enough to trap us in the first place. So we would do well not to underestimate their potential again."

"If it comes to it, we will fight to the death for Agarta's glory," Lars proclaimed, holding a clenched fist to his chest.

Kyra nodded, gracefully accepting the man's life oath with great care and understanding. "Pray that it does not come to that."

Tokl returned with a pair of muscular lizardmen in tow. These looked different than the hunting party, with horn-beaked snouts and spiny ridges running from their forehead to the back of their neck. The spines were connected by webbed skin covered in orange spots. The strange mane reminded Logan of the feet of a toad. The tribal guard carried heavy cudgels carved from the bone of some enormous creature he hoped to never meet alone.

"Bring the woman and the troublemakers," Tokl ordered. "Nan will see their bones."

Stur hopped to his feet, flexing his corded muscles and towering over the two impressive warriors, who looked up at him in shock. Kyra rose, placing a hand on his chest to calm him. Tokl laughed, goading the man to attack as members of the tribe pressed in all around them with spears at the ready.

The guards looked to Tokl for their next move, and he shrugged, twirling his finger at the entire party. "The brute does not want to leave his slut? Very well. Bring them all."

They were ushered past finely crafted animal-skin huts, giving Logan an idea of the type of people they were dealing with. The place was not littered with refuse, as he had expected, but was instead laid out in an orderly fashion. The more he saw, the more he understood that this was not some primitive band of talking reptiles, unlike the vicious cobolds who lived in filth and squalor. Residing between the boughs of thick tree trunks, the tents were big enough to house a small family, with men and women playing equal roles and smaller lizard children running behind them, trying to get a glimpse of the weird soft-skins.

The group was stopped before a ceramic pot as large as Bipp cooking over a crackling fire, as if the heat of the jungle were not already bad enough for Logan. The smells coming from the strange urn made his belly rumble something fierce, though he thought it was probably prudent to know what was actually in the pot before he let his body have such inclinations.

A large group of the lizard people sat around the area, studying the newcomers with awe. The guards forced them to kneel, shoving them to the dirt with sharp talons digging into their shoulders, while a smaller lizardman began to beat a heavy drum, announcing the arrival of the tribe's shaman and chieftain. Everybody in the area respectfully lowered their heads in reverence. Tokl noticed Logan looking up and rapped the back of his head lightly with the butt of his spear, forcing his eyes down to the ground, though he still peeked through his peripheral vision to see the retinue of lizardmen and women emerging from the large tent in front of them.

A set of four guards, similar to the pair that had escorted them, carried the chieftain on an animal-skin cot. He was an old lizard with wrinkled skin and molting greenish-grey scales. He wore armor from a crustacean over layers of spotted furs and was adorned with brilliantly painted bones and a headdress of bright plumage from some giant bird Logan did not recognize.

Behind the chieftain walked a bent woman, cradling a gnarled wooden cane that looked like the root of some ancient tree. She was also older than any of the lizards around, with grey mottled skin peeling away in thin layers around her crooked hands. Shaman Nan wore skins and furs tied with a leather strap around her waist and over her shoulders. Her face was flat like the other females but was painted with an ashen powder no other wore, and she had a fat, curved bone piercing her septum.

Once the guards lowered their passenger to the warm stone circle, the shaman made her way to stand in front of the prisoners, and the drumming came to a stop.

"Chief Branx, it is Tokl's humble honor to present you this gift of soft-skins," their captor announced as he bowed with a grand flourish of his hands toward the humans.

The tribal leader smacked his rough lips together, snorting at his hunter's offering. "Tokl claims gifts yet only brings danger to our people, bringing these soft-skins to our home," he croaked dryly.

Tokl jolted at his chieftain's flippant dismissal of his trophies. Where he had expected to be honored for his catch, he was being scolded.

"Better that you had brought the Agma food, that we may fill our bellies," Branx goaded the overly proud lizardman further.

"Tokl is sorry, father," Tokl apologized with shallow humility. The tribal leader's words turned the cocky hunter into a simpering, groveling, fool, but Logan could see his ire toward the chieftain for humiliating him.

Chief Branx waved his shaky, curled hand, signaling the warrior to stand and take his leave. "Shaman Nan will see the bones of these soft-skins," the chieftain proclaimed.

Nan had been pacing back and forth, taking measure of the humans. Settling on a position facing Logan and Kyra, she squatted low to the ground, her old bones creaking and cracking with the effort. Up close, Logan could see one of the shaman's eyes was almost closed from either old age or some long forgotten wound, while the other remained open slightly wider than natural, staring through him as if he were only a mirage. Her frail talons unrolled a leather sac filled with oddly carved bones, each with a different rune etched on its face.

"Ah, that kind of bones," Logan mumbled to Kyra, pleased they were not going to be poked and prodded. When he looked up again, Nan wore an amused expression, her one eye staring dead at him.

Clearing her throat, she began chanting loudly enough for all around to hear, rattling the bones in both of her hands like dice. "Oh enchanted spirit of the jungle, protector of the agma, hear my words. Share with this humble soul divine insight, let my ancestor's will flow through me," she intoned, rocking side to side with the chant.

She released the bones sharply across the leather mat, where they rolled into various positions. For a long while she made gibbering noises, studying the bones with dramatic sounds that were more amusing to Logan than serious. Finally, finished with her ruminating, Nan pulled herself shakily up onto her cane and turned to face the chieftain. "To Kallix they are willed," she confirmed, fulfilling her role in the tribe for another year at least.

The lizardmen hooted all around them, excited to find their champion Tokl was correct in bringing the soft-skins to the tribe.

"Bastards think they can sell us off like livestock," Logan snapped, expecting Stur or Kyra to offer an alternative.

Nan froze in place, looking over her shoulder at him inquisitively. Kyra bumped his arm, sensing the woman understood something in his grumbling.

"Mmmm...so you soft-skins understand Nan's people after all?" Nan cackled over the din of jeers, hushing everyone's merriment with the grinning revelation. "No sense playing dumb now, white belly." She prodded Logan with her cane as if she were scolding a pet.

Kyra shot him a look of warning, silently willing him to keep quiet, but since when did he take orders from her? "Yeah, we understand you, old bat," he growled, brushing her cane away.

One of the guards punched him harder than he believed possible in the side of the head for his insolence. None dared touch the Agma tribe's shaman. Somehow, against the laws of nature, Logan managed to stay upright after the blow, angering the guard, who was readying another clenched fist.

"That is enough of that." Nan casually called off her attack dog.

"What transpires amongst us?" the chieftain demanded. "Soft-skins know not the language of the Agma."

Tokl planted himself in front of Stur. "Answer the shaman, white belly. Can you understand us?!"

The weapon master squared his broad shoulders. Even kneeling, he was menacing enough to make the bravest man think twice about yelling at him. Stur looked at his marshal, who blinked and sighed before looking Nan square in the eye and nodding.

A wave of gasps ran through the crowd, though neither the chief nor Nan seemed overly astonished.

"Go ahead, Nero. Get us set up," Kyra ordered.

The android's holo-screen flared to life, frightening the Agma spectators. The guards moved to stand in front of their leader, intending to use their bodies as human shields, while other lizards yelled of witchcraft. Nan held up her hands to silence the gathering, a move which had a significantly less impressive impact than it had earlier. The chief batted his men aside with his staff from where he sat, eyes wide at the technological marvel.

"Kyra, programming is complete," the android said.

"Shaman Nan, we are not your enemies." Kyra spoke firmly and directly, which came out in the reptilian tongue so that all members of the tribe were flabbergasted to hear their language coming out of the soft-skin prisoner's lips.

Awkward silence settled over everyone, broken by the chieftain smacking his lips together. "A soft-skin does chase down an Agma, draws her weapon, and then claims peace?" Branx asked.

Logan could see his point of view. They had stalked and cornered the lizardman, after all.

"We only meant to ask your hunter questions," Kyra began to explain, but she was quickly quieted by his upraised palm.

"Shaman Nan, is there any course of action to take here?" the chieftain asked.

"Erm, well...the bones *have* already spoken. If the soft-skins were going to start speaking, they would been best served doing so before we began," Nan explained with only the faintest hint of nervousness.

"Then it is settled," the chieftain declared, abruptly cut off as an arrow bolted into the top of his headdress. He looked up at the quivering arrow and then, seething with rage, down at the humans, but to his surprise, they held no weapons.

Another arrow zipped into the gathering from the trees, and the camp erupted in chaos.

"It's an Agmawor raid!" Tokl yelled and everyone scattered to gather weapons.

To Logan's astonishment, a tidal wave of lizardmen poured through the trees from the southern side of camp. These raiders looked similar to the Agma but had longer necks and skin that was more of a bluish-green hue, standing out in stark contrast to the Agma's rich green scales. Most wore the skulls or other bones of other lizard people. The invaders mercilessly tore through everyone they saw, skewering defenseless children as readily as the defending warriors.

"Move men, fall in defensive formation!" Kyra called out, gathering her troops in an arrow formation, the tip pointed at the newly arrived raiders.

"Marshal, what are we going to do unarmed?" one of her men shouted in terror.

Stur answered by slamming his fist into an attacker's face and plucking the spear out of his hands like it was a blade of grass. The savage warrior looked down at its empty talons, confused, not even registering the weapon had been taken as it slid through his chest.

Before the creature even hit the ground, Stur lunged forward, pinning another to the ground with the stolen spear.

Logan broke formation to snatch a small child from one of the attackers before it could gnash needle sharp teeth into the babe's face. The blue-scaled lizard hissed at him, opening barbed fans of skin on either side of its jaws. *Where have I seen this nonsense before?* he wondered, jumping back out of the path of the monster's swinging club.

Bipp hopped forward under the swing and crushed the humanoid's knee cap under a blow from his hammer. "I hate cannibals!" the gnome roared, reliving a past nightmare with a degree of hatred. The lizard's leg gave out, bringing his face down low enough that Bipp could crush its skull.

All around them the battle raged, mostly between the two lizard clans. The invaders seemed to decide that the strange soft-skins were too dangerous to approach and easier prey was in abundance elsewhere. Some of the Acadians had pulled the old shaman into the middle of their group, surrounding her in a protective circle, and Logan handed her the child he had rescued for safekeeping.

"Corbin, what do you want to do?" he called to his brother, who was already pondering that very question. Should they help these humanoids who only moments before were ready to sell them to some slaver? Or was this the time to seize the opportunity for flight?

The raiders were a cruel lot, taking a sickening pleasure in the slaughter they committed. The Agma may have taken them captive, but they had not actually done lasting harm to him or his friends. Watching one of the invading lizardmen raping a defenseless Agma woman was more than Corbin could stand. He nodded to Logan, and they broke from Kyra's defensive ranks, running into the fray side by side.

Kyra yelled something to the men about this not being their fight, but she was dumbfounded when Stur suddenly followed their lead. It was the weapon master's honor-bound duty to protect those who could not protect themselves, and he decided that noble calling was not limited to the human race.

Two of the Agmawor broke from their attack, throwing a torch onto one of the supply tents. When one noted Logan rushing in, they turned to face him, eager for the fight.

Logan looked like he tripped on a rock, falling to his knees a couple paces from the reptilians. Corbin ran up his brother's back and did a backflip over the lizardman. The lizards' heads craned back to the tree branches overhead, wondering where Corbin went, as he deftly landed without a sound behind hm.

Despite Logan's surprise at his brother's skillful maneuver, he wasted no time taking the advantage to punch one of the lizardmen square in the jaw with his metal fist. Shards of teeth flew out of the beast's torn face. The other lizard shook off the shock of Corbin's jump and swung a spear at Logan, who leapt back out of the way.

As the lizard thrust his spear again, Corbin smashed a rock into the side of its skull from behind. The Agmawor yelped and gripped its bleeding head while trying to spin and clip him with its swinging cudgel. The lizardman Logan had struck grabbed Corbin from the side, pulling him away from its partner, which staggered backward, blood pouring from its forehead.

Logan jumped forward in a dive, crashing into the raider's midsection and releasing his brother. The two of them tumbled on the ground, blindly lashing out at each other, while Corbin crouched and swept his foot across the dirt to knock the other wounded lizardman onto his back. He snatched up a dropped cudgel and brought it down hard over the raider's face. As he turned, he saw Logan use his mechanical fist to deliver a sharp jab to his own attacker's throat, crushing his windpipe. The lizardman came down hard, smashing the back of its skull on a wooden tent post. It was dead before its body settled on the ground. To their side, Stur was ripping through foes one after the other as if they were nothing more than paper dolls.

On the ground, the lizardman pinned Logan under its considerable weight and decided to savor its victory with a taste of the soft-skin's fingers. Logan blessed his luck, laughing hard at the screaming beast, who cracked more teeth gnashing down on his metal fingertips. Grabbing the monstrous humanoid's face, he dug his thumb right into its eye, wrenching the lizardman off him sideways and groping around on the ground for a large rock, which he slammed repeatedly into the humanoid's face until it barely twitched.

Corbin dodged to the right, avoiding his attacker's spear. The Agmawor had planned the movement, continuing its spin to batter him with its spiked tail. But Corbin had trained half his life to master his reflexes, and he instinctively jumped over the swinging appendage. He came down in a sideways roll, lashing out with the cudgel hard enough to shatter the monster's knee.

Stur held another lizardman above the ground, shaking the hissing beast around like a doll while he choked it. Past him, Corbin could see a heavyset Agmawor towering over the chieftain, the two Agma guards lying dead at the brute's feet. He sent a psychic message to his brother and darted under Stur's arm to the tribal leader's aid. Logan followed his brother, snatching a spear from the ground.

"Queen Nadja sends her regards!" the assassin sneered at the chieftain, as he moved to run the Agma through with a spear carved from solid bone.

Corbin slid low across the ground, batting the assassin's hamstring with his cudgel as Logan hurled another cudgel at the beast's chest. His stolen weapon splintered into shards against the lizardman's bone armor, robbing him of an easy victory.

Even as Logan finished his throw, the assassin had already regained his footing, swinging the bone spear outward like a pendulum. Corbin sprang to his feet, deflecting the attack on his brother with the remaining cudgel. Small specks of bone dust flew off the bone blade, and the force of the blow made Corbin's forearm numb.

Bipp appeared out of nowhere, crushing the lumbering lizard's foot with his hammer and sending the brute stumbling forward under the unbearable pain. Logan met the creature's downward trajectory with a jaw-rattling uppercut from his mechanical fist, hitting so hard he feared the prosthetic hand might dislodge as pain seared through his wrist. When the assassin landed on his back, the last thing he witnessed was the bottom of Stur's boot as he stomped hard onto the lizardman's face.

All around them the tide of battle had shifted, with the raiders fleeing into the night, their mission of death and destruction fulfilled. The camp was filled with cries of mourning as Agma discovered their loved ones slain. Tents were crackling with fire that lit up the forest.

"There is no honor in this." Stur brooded over the scene of carnage, watching the tents burn.

"Seize the soft-skin infidels!" Tokl ordered, surrounding them with warriors.

Logan regretted that he would have to kill these lizardmen, but he had no intention of being anyone's prisoner again.

"Hold your tongue, Tokl," the chieftain commanded from behind them. "You will take this Agmawor scum and tie him up for questioning."

Tokl looked from them to the battered body of the assassin, frowning. "But father...what of the soft-skins? Surely their witchcraft displeased the jungle and cursed our tribe with this attack!" Tokl whined as his men dragged the limp Agmawor away.

"Oh, pish posh. This raid was coming whether the humans were here or not. Stay your hand, Tokl. These creatures just saved Cheiftain Branx's life," Shaman Nan scolded, limping into the fray.

"B-but Shaman Nan," Tokl said, "even the ancestor's spirits spoke ill omen of them through the bones telling."

The chieftain scowled at his son's naivety as Stur helped him to his feet.

Shaman Nan motioned for the righteous hunter to bend down to her level then rapped on his skull, checking if it were hollow. "Honestly, Tokl, they're just bones."

Corbin was not concerned with their bickering, instead moving to help put out the fires, while Kyra ordered the Acadians to help where ever needed.

Logan thanked Bipp for his assistance in the battle.

"Don't mention it. You have done as much for me more times than I could think. Guess we are out of the woods on becoming slaves, eh?"

Logan was not too sure about that. He was pretty confident Bipp was ahead in the '*I bailed you out*' category. But he did not feel much like adding levity to the moment. He could not take his eyes off a woman screaming for her baby to wake up, cradling the bloody boy's limp body to her chest.

"True, my friend. I only wish that freedom had been under better circumstances."

Chapter 4: On the Run

Deep down in the bowels of Acadia, a trio of Falians made their way through the winding Monkton Hills under the dim light of Baetylus, who floated leagues away by the massive cavern's ceiling.

"I think it's just a bit farther," Rygor said, nervously darting his gaze around the woodsy hills for signs of predators.

Rimball shot Elise and Rygor a dark look over his shoulder from ahead. The seasoned hunter did not like all the noise he said they were making. Elise could not blame the older man for his cautious nature and trusted in his expertise. Whereas Rimball had spent a lifetime honing his skills as a hunter, she had next to no experience.

"I think we should keep quiet," she whispered to Rygor, directing his attention to Rimball's back.

The wiry man took in Rimball's crouching form and gulped, nodding. Elise knew he did not mean any harm. It was just that Rygor was very nervous out here, feeling exposed in the rolling hills. They had left the rest of the villagers back in the caves that dotted the Monkton Hillsides southeast of Riverbell so they could scout out the situation. Too many of the villagers had refused to join them in their flight from the village, and she was determined not to leave them behind.

When Elise had first returned to Riverbell through Cassandra's rift, she had immediately ordered Farmer Barth to gather the villagers in the square. Once everyone was in attendance, she told them how the capitol had turned on Riverbell for some far-fetched conspiracy theory. Around the capitol, Magistrate Fafnir was perpetrating the lie that the people of Riverbell had stirred up the skex horde in an attempt to help Lady Cassandra gain influence over the Council of Elders so they could overthrow the kingdom and join Malbec. The whole thing could not be more ludicrous to Elise and villagers. She knew they had no choice but to flee the village until things calmed down and they could convince the Elders that these were baseless accusations.

It was not an easy pill for them to swallow. The people of Riverbell had always and ever been dutiful to their kingdom. They were a simple folk, spending their days toiling over the crops they farmed and hunting for furs, which they traded with the nearby towns and capitol for other supplies. How could anyone ever believe Riverbell could do harm to the kingdom?

Elise had tried to explain that like it or not, that was their reality. However, it had only been a short time since the skex ravaged their own homes, leaving many too injured to take care of themselves. With no supplies coming from the capitol and no help from the nearby villages, they were in rough enough shape without having to also abandon their homes.

And so, some of the villagers vehemently opposed leaving.

Elise had tried to get them to see reason to no avail. "But Avery, if you stay here, you will not be safe."

Avery, the blacksmith, had scowled at her. "Not safe? What, from our own kingdom?" He shook his head in denial. "Nay, I think the only one not safe is yourself, on the run for some nefarious nonsense that Logan Walker got you into."

Several people rallied around the blacksmith, denying her pleas for them to leave. "I'll not be run off from my own home for some crime I did not commit!" one of the villagers yelled.

Another joined in emphatically. "If we run now, it'll just make us look all the more guilty! We need to stay here, where we belong, and wait for the arm of the law to come. They'll see we are innocent."

More chimed in with proclamations that "Baetylus would provide."

Elise could see she was rapidly losing control of the gathering. "Silence! The lot of you, be quiet and hear me out! I know this is hard. I know you are scared." The square fell silent and all eyes were on her. "You think the idea of fleeing our village doesn't terrify me as much as it does you? I'm just as scared of abandoning our home. But you didn't see what the magistrate is capable of. I did. They sent Corbin Walker over the wall into the wildlands!"

Many villagers gasped at this news. Corbin Walker was the epitome of a goodly young man.

"They are hanging people in the streets back in Fal. And I do not mean people like us. These are important men and women, completely innocent of their crimes but hanged nevertheless. Trust me when I tell you that our lives mean nothing to the people in power. They would just as soon throw us all in jail than let even the most remote possibility that we could be involved in some conspiracy linger." Elise could see she had them now. "And so we *must flee*. We need to escape now while we can. When this is all over and sorted through, we will return."

Most of the villagers were hooked at that point, but close to thirty had still refused to leave with them.

Elise did not like the idea of leaving anyone behind. She knew full well what Fafnir's men were capable of and could not stop thinking about those left behind. Now that everyone was settled in the caves, Elise had ordered Rimball and Rygor to accompany her back to Riverbell so they might try to sway the remaining villagers to join them.

Rimball was the most experienced hunter in the entire village. When he was not leading hunts, the hardened man spent his time acting as a sensei to the boys of their village, teaching the arts of using a spear and archery as well as martial combat that had been handed down for generations. He was easily able to scout out their path and keep them out of harm's way. Using his five-foot bo staff to balance his body, he deftly scaled the steep hill ahead of her and Rygor.

Rygor moved to the side so Madame Elise could go first, offering a hand for her as balance as she began climbing up the rocky slope.

Elise carefully followed the path that Rimball took up the hill. Try as she might, she kept tripping over her skirts, which were so long they reached her ankles. Every time she stumbled, Rygor was there to brace her, and Rimball looked back with annoyance plainly written on his face.

Elise brushed her long golden curls away from her eyes and blew out some air. She paused and thought for a moment. "Rygor, give me your knife."

The wiry man looked puzzled. "You want my dagger, madame?"

Elise nodded, holding her hand out expectantly for the weapon. Rimball stopped above to wait for them. Once Elise had the knife, which Rygor used to skin game, she hacked away the bottom of her skirt from the knees down.

Rygor caught one look at her exposed calves, smooth and covered in sweat from being trapped beneath the heavy skirts, and blushed like a fully bloomed rose, quickly averting his gaze to a set of trees growing crookedly from the hillside.

After Elise had worked the knife all the way around, freeing her legs from the restrictive cloth, she sighed and bunched up the material to throw it away.

Rimball's hand caught her by the forearm. Elise was shocked that he had moved so quickly down the hillside without making any noise, and she let out a tiny yelp. When she met his serious eyes, so dark brown they might as well be black pits, the hunter slowly shook his head without saying a word.

Elise gulped and dipped her head in a jerking nod, bunching the fabric and pushing it into the folds of her belt. Of course it would not be a good idea to leave evidence that they had been there, should Fafnir's men come looking in this area. She felt silly to not have thought of this on her own.

Rimball let go of her and motioned for them to follow him up the hill. The hunter's face was impassive, devoid of emotion. Elise had heard he could get like this on hunts but had never experienced it. Without another word, she followed him up the slope, this time without losing her footing even once.

Once they were at the top, Rimball lay flat on his belly like a lizard, working himself into an opening between an oblong boulder and some thorny shrubs. Elise wiggled in beside him, and Rygor resigned himself to trying to peek between their heads, crouching on his belly behind them.

Elise scanned the area. From this vantage point, they could see the valley of sloping hills that stretched from west to east around Mount Monkton, one of the tallest stalactites in Fal. The peak of it rose so high it almost reached the ceiling of the Fal cavern. Elise wondered what it was like for Corbin to be with the surface dwellers right now. She tried to imagine what it was like not to live in one giant cave with a myriad of stalagmites hanging from the jagged roof.

Far in the distance, she could see the Great Crystal floating close to the cavern ceiling, glowing a bright blue. Even from here, its light was warm on her skin, reminding her that most life in this cavern owed itself to Baetylus. She did not dare tell any of the villagers about Corbin's experience with the crystal and the false god's true nature.

Rimball scanned the landscape with his scope, a long leather tube held together by a cord around the middle. At either end was a lens made from the shell of a dead tortoise. Elise was not sure how it worked, but when the turtles were ready to die, they secreted an oily substance that calcified their shells. Over time, the river and sand worked down the material, turning pieces of their shell into a glassy substance. Hunters would scour the banks for the rare material once every tenth year, hoping to find some that they might sand down and polish into these lenses, which they would then trade to the nearby towns.

"Do you see anything?" Elise asked as quietly as she could manage. She thought for sure the hunter would reprimand her for speaking, but all Rimball did was shake his head and continue scanning.

Elise looked down into the valley and tried to make out her homeland. She could see the log cabins of Riverbell lining the west banks of the Naga River, but it was so far away, down past the hill and a couple miles over the fields they used for farming, that she could not make out any of the villagers.

Rimball tapped a finger in the dirt, gathering Elise's attention, and pointed at the village. Handing her the scope, Rimball waited until she had it up to her eye and then guided the lens until the village square came into her view.

The scope magnified objects so that she could see them much clearer than with the naked eye, except her view was curved, bent slightly by the lens, and the edges of it were smoky. At first she did not understand what Rimball wanted her to see. There was the village square, empty, and...wait, no it was not empty. Elise flicked the scope back a fraction to the left, and goosebumps crawled across her skin.

A large group of soldiers was corralling villagers into the square, while their leader yelled something at Avery the blacksmith. The soldiers had the rest of the villagers gathered in a circle, forced to huddle together, surrounded by Fafnir's men. The blacksmith fell on his knees, blocking his own wife and small boy, and clasped his hands together. Without being able to hear them, Elise knew the conversation. The soldiers wanted to know where the villagers were hiding, and Avery was begging for mercy, swearing his innocence. The soldier shouted again, pointing at Avery as he spoke. Avery said something, and the soldier snapped his head to look directly at Elise.

Gasping, she ducked her head low to the ground and dropped the scope.

Rimball patted her back. "They cannot see us. We are too far away." Whenever Rimball spoke, Elise always felt the hunter must need a drink of water. His voice sounded cracked and dry.

"They looked directly at me," she said doubtfully.

"Then our friends have given us away," Rimball lamented. "You will not want to see what happens next." He reached for his scope.

Elise pulled it toward her, rolling the leather tube away from Rimball. She shook her head, determined to see what would happen to her people.

When the lens came back up to her eye, Elise had to stifle another gasp. The lead soldier had stuck his sword through one of Avery's hands, which he must have thrown up to block the blade, and into one of his eyes. The angry soldier snarled and pushed the dead man off his sword with his boot. The rest of the villagers were screaming and crying. Avery's wife threw herself on her husband, hysterically shaking his body and clutching his face close to her own. Avery's little boy looked catatonic when the soldier hacked his blade across the woman's spine and shouted for his men to get to work.

Rimball saw all the color drain from Elise's face and gently pulled the scope out of her shaking fingers. She continued to stare at the far-off village with horrified eyes and a gaping mouth. When a great bonfire erupted in the center of the village, Elise finally turned away, tears uncontrollably clouding her eyes, though she fought hard to choke them down.

"What is it?" Rygor asked excitably, rising to try to see the village. "What's happening down there? Are Fafnir's men taking them prisoner already?"

Elise wanted to answer, but his words seemed far away, and she could not stop the grisly scene playing across her mind's eye.

"Yes, Rygor," Rimball answered for her, "the magistrate's men have come."

Rygor fell to his knees. He tried to ask more questions with trembling lips, but Rimball's tone had said it all. He did not need the scope to know their people were being executed. "Damn them," Rygor cursed. "Why didn't they listen to reason and come with us when they had the chance?"

Rygor had been very reluctant to accompany Elise on this journey. He had never needed any convincing when she arrived and told the villagers they were all in danger. Rygor had gathered up his wife and two children straight away and prepared to follow Elise, the new village Elder. When she asked him to accompany her back to Riverbell to convince the remaining villagers to join them, he had a hard time parting with his wife, who was absolutely terrified he would not return.

"The damned fools..." Rygor muttered again, angry at the villagers for not listening.

Elise slapped him hard across the face, and tears streaked out of her eyes. Rygor held his burning cheek and gaped at her. Elise was gaping right back, just as surprised as he that she had struck him.

"Don't you call them fools," she said. "Don't you ever call them that."

Rygor slowly nodded, feeling that he might begin weeping himself. Rimball insisted it was time to head back to camp, and Elise numbly agreed.

They were a good mile and a half away, heading southeast, when the winds shifted and the smells caught their nose.

"Mmm, I think someone's roasting chicken nearby," Rygor said, looking around the forest they were about to enter. Elise snapped her head up, looking as well, the aromas of cooking meat making her stomach growl. In the land of Fal, winds could travel far and fast with no sky above to escape into.

Rimball looked over his shoulder at them and shook his head solemnly. Rygor cocked his head to the side, furrowing his brow. Then the hunter's meaning took hold in his mind.

Elise too caught his meaning. Her stomach lurched, and she bent over to vomit in the grass. Rygor followed suit, unable to keep the contents of his stomach. Though he did not join in, the weathered old hunter could hardly blame the pair for their reaction. After all, who could be expected to smell the burning bodies of their fellow villagers without becoming ill?

The air was still filled with the smell of burning animal hide from the tent fires they had worked labouriously to put out. Without a river nearby, it had been hard, leaving them to rely on smothering techniques over a large scale of the burning Agma camp. If the jungle had not been so musky and humid, the fire would have likely spread out of their control, so Logan begrudged that there was at least one perk to the dank place.

The next day they slept in rounds while members of their party took turn keeping watch, staying alert both for the Agma, who only a night ago planned to sell them off as slaves, and for the raiding tribe of cannibal lizardmen, the Agmawor.

The chieftain had called them to his hut, a good-sized structure made of straw and mud with animal skins for a roof, for a private audience, attended only by Shaman Nan, his son Tokl, and a handful of the older Agma whose council he valued. No weapons were allowed in the chieftain's hut, not that the humans' equipment had been returned yet anyhow. They sat cross-legged, trying to blend in with the Agma customs as best they could.

"Tell us, Kyra Tarvano, what was your soft-skin tribe doing in our lands?" the chieftain inquired, holding a stone over the fire with wet ceramic tongs.

"My people are from Agarta," she replied, hesitating to gauge their reactions to her kingdom's name, which seemed to mean nothing to them. "It was...*is* a country far to the south of your jungle, where we are in danger from the jotnar. My people sent us north to see what the jotnar threat is like up here, in hopes of finding a safe haven."

The chieftain looked at Nan and smiled softly. "You lie to us," he stated flatly, turning the rock, which was beginning to glow red. Before Kyra could object, he held up a hand to silence her. "Have no fear in your heart of hearts, Kyra Tarvano of Agarta. Your reasons for holding truth locked away are your own. Branx does not judge you."

Kyra squirmed under the lizardman's gaze, uncomfortable at being so easily called out on her ruse. Wanting to change the subject, she asked, "What of the Agma people? Last I came through these jungles, I knew nothing of your tribe. Where did you come from?"

Stur winced, hoping she was not pushing her luck with the question.

This time Shaman Nan spoke for the chieftain, "The Agma have long dwelled in these jungles, Kyra. Since the time of creation, the Agma have wandered the jungle in our constant journey to avoid the grasp of the evil ice giants and avoid the Agma's cursed cousins, the Agmawor. Perhaps during Kyra's last visit you did not meet the Agma because we were not in this place. The Agma stay only for a short time before moving on."

Corbin found the idea fascinating; these lizard people were a nomadic tribe, always on the move to avoid detection.

"So you are also on the run from the jotnar?" Kyra asked.

"The Agma run not. By moving in constant cycles, we lessen the risk of enslavement, and the jungle provides sanctuary from the ice giants' prying sorcery," the chieftain explained, dropping the hot rock into a ceramic pot of water that Nan took from him after the steam dissipated.

"And what of Corbin Walker? You and your brother are not from the same tribe as Kyra's people," Nan coyly asked, as if she could see into the very depths of his soul with her single bloodshot eye.

Kyra shot him a look, and he could see she wished for him to make up some answer—something, anything, but the truth.

Corbin leveled his gaze at the chieftain, who waited patiently for his answer. "We are from there." He pointed to the soil in front of Branx's crossed legs. "Under the world of Acadia in a faraway land called Vanidriell."

Kyra took a sharp breath, furious that the fool had given away his hand so easily. And maybe he had, but Corbin was not ready to spread lies among these new allies. Nor did he believe the world should be staged to expect such things.

"I see. And you have come to the surface for what?" Branx replied, much calmer at the revelation than expected, while he nonchalantly added roughly peeled vegetable roots to Nan's pot.

Tokl snorted derisively. "Father, you cannot really believe this soft-skin fairy tale? This is ludicrous!"

The chieftain did not answer the impertinent question, merely shooting his son a dark glance for interrupting his conversation. Tokl withered under his gaze, and the chief motioned for Corbin to continue.

"Kyra is helping us search for Isaac, the man who will be the key to our land's salvation, freeing us from a powerful adversary who controls the minds of my people and feeds upon their souls." Corbin summed up their purpose with simplified clarity, though his quest was anything but.

The elder lizards in the tent bristled at his words, sending a low murmur rippling through the group. Even the chieftain and shaman fell to huddled whispering, as if the humans were not in the tent with them.

Corbin thought about peeking inside their minds to understand what they were discussing but did not let the idea take root. He would not live his life spying on all those he met. Just because he possessed ability over others did not mean he was justified to use it at his own whim. If he lost faith in the goodness of other people, along with everything else that had been shattered, what would there be left of the world to believe in?

Chief Branx finished speaking privately and gave a curt nod to Nan, who looked at the group of humans. As she spoke, she began grinding plants in a ceramic mortar. "We see your innocence in knowing, Corbin Walker. It is no mere *man* you search for. Isaacha be the very jungle around you."

Corbin screwed up his face, trying to grasp her meaning. Before he could question the shaman, Nan continued.

"There is a legend among the Agma as old as our firstborn. Long ago, the soft-skins dared to wage war against the mighty blue devils, the ice giants, the jotnar. Your race paid dearly for this transgression, burned away from the world like a rotting disease. A soft-belly unlike any other travelled the land in sorrow, filled with a deep despair, searching for his kin. One day he came to this land and laid down his life, too tired to continue his futile search and giving up on this mortal coil. It was then that this soft-skin blessed the land, sacrificing himself to create a sanctuary free of the jotnar's prying magic. Thus Isaacha came into being, spreading its miracle across the plains and giving the Agma tribes a safe haven to grow in number and become strong. So you see, ever do we walk in the loving embrace of Isaacha." Finishing her story, Nan stirred the herbs into her mixture. They smelled like jasmine and lemons melting into the hot liquid.

"So what does that mean for us?" Logan asked his brother doubtfully.

"Agma Crescent seekers will show you the way," the chieftain answered.

Corbin could see he was missing something. Even with Nero's language translator, there was a clear divide between the cultural meanings of words that was lost on him.

Nan caught his confusion and plopped the lid back on the pot. "Corbin does not understand? Kalilah and Tiko will show you the way." She spoke slowly and a little louder, as if it would help him understand better.

"Show us the way where?" Logan asked, sharing his brother's confusion.

"To the heart of Isaacha. Deep in the center of the jungle, where its spirit dwells," Nan replied, throwing the chieftain a wry look.

"But you said that Isaac-ha *is* the jungle," Corbin tried to reason.

"Tokl thinks it is more than their skin that is soft, Nan. How can we expect any less?" Tokl mocked. "Our esteemed shaman is trying to tell you that Isaacha, spirit of the jungle, holds his heart at its center. Kalilah is of age to take the pilgrimage and do the offering with Tiko as her heart's companion and moon guardian. Corbin will accompany the pilgrims to the White Tree, where Isaacha still communes with this plane. Does this make sense to your limited monkey brain?" he finished, knocking on his own scaled skull and laughing.

Corbin ignored Tokl's arrogance, thankful to have a straightforward answer. "So Isaacha is just a tree in the center of your jungle?"

The shaman glowered at them. "This is not accurate. The tree is where Isaacha's spirit slumbers, where the people commune with him when great things happen for the Agma," Nan corrected.

Logan looked at Corbin eagerly. This was something for them to go on. He could not be more delighted that they actually had a lead to follow, and it did not involve subservience to Kyra!

Corbin shared his enthusiasm, his heart daring to dream they were finally on the right path to find the answers they sought. "We humbly accept your offering, Chieftain Branx." He bowed his head toward the tribal leader.

Tokl snorted arrogantly. "These ones are not doing you a favor, soft-brain. Kalilah was already ready for the pilgrimage. All they are doing is moving it closer to the new moon to get rid of your cursed souls."

"Tokl will hold his insolent tongue," Brax snapped at his son, cowing the hunter's ego. "Tokl is not leader of this tribe yet, and until the dawning of that day, Tokl will not speak with authority for the Agma."

Kyra cleared her throat, drawing their attention away from the awkward exchange. "Chieftain Branx, we are grateful for your offer of assistance, but I must decline. I fear there are more pressing matters for us to attend to with the jotnar, and I cannot risk getting waylaid by a journey to your White Tree."

Corbin blinked as if openly struck by the hand of disbelief. Surely the marshal did not intend for them to pass up this opportunity.

Nan read the tension clearly and interrupted, ladling some of the broth she had made into a ceramic bowl with painted stripes. "Nan sees the soft-skins have much to talk about. You do this later, yes? For now we eat!" She offered Corbin the bowl, hitting him with the aromas of the ginger and lemongrass mingling in the hearty broth.

The silence was broken by a loud rumbling. Everyone looked at Bipp, who just shrugged with a sheepish grin. "What? My belly is as excited as my brain. I'm starved!"

The gnome laughed heartily and everyone joined in, forgetting their worries for a short time, sharing in the meal and joy of one another's company.

Corbin let it go for now, welcoming the group's fleeting bliss, but later he would need to handle this issue. Nothing was going to stand in the way of his quest. Nothing.

Daylight was beginning to filter through the jungle canopy. Even under the protective shielding of Acadian eyewear, dawn's radiance was like staring into a hundred fires to the Falians, and Corbin's eyes stung fiercely. Bipp complained about it and said he was going to bed with the rest of the weary Agma while the brothers worked out the details of their opportunity with Kyra. Corbin held his hand up to block the waves of daylight, peering through them in fascination that anything could exist so alive with energy.

"Here she comes." Logan nudged him, squaring his own shoulders for the upcoming debate.

Kyra walked around the hut with Stur, who carried a bundle. "The Agma have given us our weapons back," she informed them while Stur handed out the items.

"We are going to accompany the pair of Agma on their pilgrimage," Corbin blurted out, uninterested in skirting the topic at hand.

Kyra was slightly taken aback by his brazen nature. She was unused to people speaking to her in such a direct manner, and though she had come to expect it from the crude, cocky Logan, Corbin's open show of solidarity was unexpected.

Picking up on her surprise, Logan said, "You didn't really think we were going to turn our backs on this opportunity just because you said no, did you?"

As a matter of fact, she had, despite Stur's words of council. Kyra had thought these men understood her orders were final. "I cannot allow you to split from our group."

"The way I see it," Logan said, "we only agreed to help you scout out the area so you would help us search your ranks for Isaac. So now that we have a real lead, you have zero say in what we do."

"Kyra, nothing you can say will sway us from this path. If this Isaacha exists, we have to go after it in hopes of finding the answers Lady Cassandra said were out there," Corbin said as firmly as he could manage, wishing Kyra could see his point of view.

"There are fifty thousand people in the Citadel relying on us to find them a new home, safely free from the jotnar's grasp. My first priority *has* to be scouting out the area and determining if the ice giants are still a threat to our exodus. This has to take precedence over going to visit some fairy tale about a tree in the middle of the jungle that may or may not magically have the answer to your problems." Kyra was frustrated that the man could even comprehend turning his back on all the innocent souls back at the Citadel she was charged with protecting.

"Forget it, Corbin, the chick doesn't get it," Logan said, raising her blood pressure with his typical bravado.

Corbin held his hands out to soothe both of them. "The people you speak of in the Citadel, those are *your* people, not ours. *My* people are in Vanidriell, fleeing for their lives from soldiers who are unwittingly enthralled by a monstrous being." Logan shuffled anxiously, envisioning his people on the run. "We promised to come to the surface and check out the area with you. We have done that. Now we are going to follow this path to see where it leads."

Kyra shook her head, unwilling to hear his reasoning.

"Lady Tarvano, we cannot force them to continue on with us," Stur said, earning himself a cold look for speaking out of turn. However, the weapon master was not one to be cowed in the face of honor. "Nero *has* pointed out that the path Tiko will take to the tree leads close to Agarta's capitol," he reasoned.

"What good would that do?" Kyra asked. "Look at this place. Our civilization is gone, completely wiped from the land like nothing more than a forgotten dream. Look around you! Where once there stood a city that stretched for miles, now there is naught but this miserable jungle. Not even a hint of proud Agarta remains."

For the first time Corbin could hear the pain Kyra was masking behind that wall of bravery and under the heavy mantle of leadership. He saw, without needing to read her mind, that Kyra lived according to a set of rules he could never understand. He could also see that Stur struggled with himself, wanting to comfort Kyra in her sorrow but not daring to reveal his feelings and break decorum.

"Ah, now Nan hears the truth in Kyra." The shaman surprised them, walking into the middle of the debate. Not even Stur, the seasoned warrior of a hundred battles, had noticed her approach.

"I-I...uh...that is..." Kyra amused Logan, clambering for the right words to explain their conversation.

"Calm your spirit, Kyra. Nan will not spread your secret. So you are the ancient race of soft-skins that once ruled this land long ago. Much has changed since your people ravaged the world of Acadia." She calmly pointed her cane at Kyra's heart.

"We only wish to leave this world in peace," Kyra said.

"Nan thinks nothing less. The bones speak to me. They tell Nan that Kyra should follow the pilgrimage to Isaacha with her burrowing kin," the old lizardwoman said.

"Our path must lead to discovering the jotnar's present capabilities," Kyra said, unwilling to accept the call.

"Ah, but you underestimate the power of Isaacha. For who else but the spirit of the Agma land is better equipped to answer such a question?" Nan said, planting the seed of doubt in Kyra's mind. "No, Nan sees clearly—the answers Kyra seeks are Isaacha's alone to give." Her words rang with wisdom.

Stur faced his marshal. "Kyra, if what the shaman says is true, we can save much time by joining them in this. And perhaps we will glean more information about what happened to stop our exodus in the first place. There is as much value in knowledge of the past as there is in the present."

Kyra nodded, staring into his blue eyes, valuing the council of the man who had been her trusted ally for years. She had been so caught up in her course of action, she had forgotten the valuable teachings of her youth. If they could commune with this mystical being that was supposedly powerful enough to create an entire jungle as well as shield it from the jotnar, and which dwelled at the site of their ruined capitol, surely there would be value in it.

"Alright, we will join you on this pilgrimage," Kyra said.

Corbin sighed, deeply relieved by the news.

"But we will only travel as far as the capitol. From then on, you will be left on your own should you not accompany us back," Kyra said, turning her back on the men and heading to get some sleep before their journey. Though she had heard the wisdom of Nan and Stur and agreed with it, the marshal still felt an irrational frustration at being swayed from her determined course of action.

Stur shrugged and advised Corbin to get some much needed rest as well.

As they headed off to the hut the Agma had provided, Logan turned to address Shaman Nan with a smirk. "The spirits came to you, huh? Didn't I hear you telling Tokl something about them just being bones?"

Nan cackled at the young man's shrewd mirth. She found the pale soft-skin warrior intriguing. She reached up to lightly tap his forehead with her cane. "Nan thinks that soft brain is hearing things."

Logan laughed as the shaman winked at him and headed off to bed himself, ready for a new day filled with new adventures.

Chapter 5: Expedition

Four days had passed with them traversing the sweltering heat of the jungle. Four uneventful days. Corbin thought he could get used to this life, not constantly running from one life-threatening battle to the next. His heart panged for his homeland and the daily routines of honest, hard work that he had grown up enjoying.

The Agma guide Tiko knew much about the area, carefully leading them through safe paths and teaching the Acadians the inner workings of the alien environment. Corbin found more and more that he agreed with Logan. Though he had relished the jungle when they first arrived, the constant heat and musky odors were getting to be too much for him. To Corbin, it smelled like rotting garbage far too often. It was almost as if the jungle waited until he forgot about the rank odor, and then, when he least expected it, he would get a mouthful of the foul aroma.

Bipp managed to stay joyful during their trip, the jungle having no shortage of things for him to eat, from berries and fruits to an abundance of wildlife to hunt or trap. Between this and the naturally pure creeks and rivers, it was almost a paradise to the gnome.

Stur laughed heartily, circling Logan with his weapon drawn, mocking the young man with a feint of his sword. The two of them had found a common ground, bonding over Stur's mentorship in the art of warfare. When the weapon master originally brought up the topic to Logan, Corbin thought for sure his brother was about to lose his cool.

"What do you mean?" Logan had asked much more calmly than expected.

"Well," Stur said, "you have a natural swagger about you during a fight which makes you effective enough, more capable than most men I've seen at your skill level. But I also saw how sloppy you fought in the last two battles. Sheer instinct alone is not always going to get you there, my friend, and I would hate for that luck of yours to run out." The battle hardened weapon master hadn't wanted to offend Logan but was also being brutally honest.

Logan screwed up his face, mulling over Stur's observations for what Corbin was sure would be an explosive response. Logan thought over losing his sword under the monstrous crab, which by dumb luck worked in their favor, and of the spear which shattered in his hands against the Agmawor assassin's armor. Then his mind drifted to other battles Stur had no way of knowing about, to the multitude of times he found himself outmatched by the monstrous denizens of Vanidriell, and back to the most recent battle, when he had hit the assassin so hard he feared his mechanical hand was torn off.

"I'd eat my fist if you weren't right, Stur. I'm unconditioned and sloppy," Logan admitted. "I *would* appreciate some pointers."

And from that time forward, the two had spent hours sparring each time they made camp, with Stur walking his brother through different sword techniques. Logan was picking it up at an impressive rate, not that it surprised Corbin much. He had always known his older brother's potential, but daydreams and loafing about had always held Logan back.

Corbin smiled, turning back to the rest of their makeshift camp. Themis would be up soon, and dinner was just being finished by Nero and Kalilah. They had to sleep by day, the daystar's light being too bright for the three Falians' unaccustomed eyes, no matter what kind of protective gear they wore. He could not imagine trying to function in the intense daylight and was happy to be asleep in his bedroll by then, though he did feel guilty at not being able to participate in watch rotation due to this. Not that the Acadians seemed to mind guarding in short shifts as they were ordered by Kyra.

The group settled around the fire. The mouthwatering aroma of roasting onions mingled with rosemary and some sort of root vegetable like a potato made Corbin drool. Bipp looked over at him, reading Corbin's mind and wiggling his eyebrows in keen anticipation of supper.

"Pay no heed, Kyra. Tiko is not bothered by this one's questions," Tiko said in response to the android's ceaseless analysis of everything around him.

"As long as he is not disturbing you. Please let me know if that becomes the case. And don't feel that you are obligated to answer every little question," Kyra added, nodding for Nero to continue his line of questioning as she resumed stoking the campfire.

"Tiko, please explain the pilgrimage in more detail," Nero asked, unfettered by her disruption.

"As Tiko was telling this one, Kalilah will begin apprenticing the healing arts on her eighteenth month of the Blue Harper." The lizard hunter pointed up to the fading night sky at a small constellation of twinkling stars.

Corbin immediately regretted following his gaze, still uncomfortable with the vastness of space overhead. Most of the time he was at ease under the thick canopy of trees covering the jungle. However, today they had made camp in a small clearing with an opening to the skies above, and he was doing his best to keep his eyes downcast.

"Before Kalilah can be admitted to the healer den, she must seek a blessing from the jungle spirit Isaacha."

Nero nodded as was customary to fit in and be socially acceptable among humans, giving little thought to whether the same civilized constructs held for the Agma. "This is a rite of passage for the females of your species at eighteen years of age?"

"Tiko does not understand all of your words, soft ski—uh, Nero." The hunter caught his tongue, not wanting to use racial slurs with his new companions, who had proven to be honorable despite a lack of cultural knowledge.

"He means to ask if it's normal for your women to take this journey," Kyra elaborated, running a wet stone down the edge of her blade as she sharpened it beside the fire.

"No, Nero, most female Agma wish to lead honorable lives as hunters for the tribe. Kalilah was chosen by the healers' den on her naming day," Tiko answered.

"How many other healers have you escorted on this pilgrimage?" Corbin asked, accepting a small wooden bowl of broth from Kalilah, which Bipp was already wolfing down.

"None." The lizardman's response raised more than a couple eyebrows.

"You mean you have never made this trip before?" Kyra blurted out incredulously.

"Tiko did not say this. This one has made the journey twice in past risings. Never with a healer initiate, though," he explained, settling Kyra's frazzled nerves.

"So are you something like a guide for your tribe, then?" Corbin asked, understanding that the lizardman took things quite literally.

"Tiko feels your question. Not a guide. The first pilgrimage to Isaacha was for this one's name day, the second travel was for the Blood-father. This time Tiko travels for his bride, Kalilah." He was getting used to communicating with the humans, who spoke differently and used the same words for opposite meanings.

Corbin had not noticed the two Agma showing any signs that they were a couple. The idea that Tiko would make the pilgrimage with Kalilah to protect her was something he could relate to. He only wished he could be standing beside Elise right now, sheltering her from the storm of Fafnir's rage.

"So you and Kalilah are married then?" Kyra asked. She could see the lizardman did not understand and added, "Err, joined?" She brought her hands together, locking the fingertips as an example.

Tiko perked up, nodding that he understood her meaning. "Ah, Tiko sees. You mean to ask if we have sex regularly? Not until the pilgrimage is over. Then Tiko will enjoy his blood ceremony, *joining* with Kalilah forever. When an Agma warrior mates, it is for life."

Corbin chuckled at Kyra's flushed face and wide eyes. Apparently the stoic leader of the Acadians was not comfortable discussing the topic of sex, as the glowing red color of her neck attested.

"And what about Kyra and Corbin?" Tiko asked, wearing an innocent smile. "Have you been enjoying the sex with each other regularly?"

Now it was Corbin's turn to blush, practically choking on his food and spitting it out as Kyra snapped her head to look at him, mortified. He realized he had been staring at her with a stupid grin when the lizard had asked the unexpected question and quickly turned away, red-faced. "N-no, I mean, no way. I am engaged to be married to Elise Ivarone. I mean, even if I wasn't, me and Kyra, we're not a couple!" he stammered.

Kyra grumbled and stomped off to her tent, leaving Tiko to sit there feeling guilty. "Tiko offers apologies to new friends. It was not the intention to insult."

"Oh, no worries, I'm not insulted. It was a simple misunderstanding, that's all," Corbin said.

"Perhaps not for Kyra?" Tiko lamented. "She does appear as if my words offended."

"Oh, it wasn't *your* words, Tiko," Bipp corrected, "but it would appear my friend here needs a lesson on how to speak around women."

Nero made notes of the social exchange in his database.

"Huh?" Corbin said.

"It may be otherwise in your kingdom," Nero said in his disjointed, robotic way of speaking, "but in Agarta, it is perceived as cruel to publically announce you find a woman so unattractive."

Tiko agreed to the sentiment, nibbling on his dinner.

"That's not what I meant..." Corbin tried to explain.

"What are you gentlemen discussing over here?" Stur asked as he and Logan arrived at the campfire. Stur towered over Corbin, who sat in the grass, and wore the jubilant smile that was typical after his sessions with his new star pupil. Logan stood beside him, wiping the beads of sweat from his brow with a rag.

"Uh... I..." Corbin tried.

"Tiko was speaking of Corbin and Kyra's sexual prospects," Nero dutifully explained.

Stur's expression instantly shifted.

Corbin looked up at the pair. His older brother was ready to fall on the ground, barely containing his almost delirious amusement at watching Corbin squirm under the weapon master's deadly glare. Stur looked as though he were considering cleaving Corbin in two with the mighty sword he held with white knuckles. Corbin eyed the blade, gulped, and then hurriedly excused himself, retreating back to his bedroll.

Once he was out of earshot, all the men exchanged looks and burst into laughter around the fire.

Most of the camp went to sleep, leaving Logan and Bipp to sit around the fire.

"You've been smiling a lot lately," Bipp said. "With all that has gone on since we met Kyra and the Acadians, I'd think you would be in less than high spirits."

Logan raised a brow at the gnome.

"Oh, don't take me the wrong way," Bipp backpedaled. "I'm more than happy to see you enjoying life. It's just, well, it's a bit out of place."

Logan digested his friend's observation. He had been feeling quite optimistic lately, hadn't he? Should that be an odd reaction to their situation? Sometimes Logan felt like there was something wrong with him that he did not have the same reactions as normal people, like he was some strange creature whose emotional instincts spun in all the wrong directions.

"I guess, if I had to put my finger on it..." Logan rationalized out loud, trying to understand his feelings just as much as Bipp. "Geez, I don't know. I mean, well..."

Bipp grew concerned as his friend fell silent, staring into the glowing embers of the dwindling fire, which lit his face with flickering shadows. Logan wore a grim expression. It looked odd on the ever-smirking cynic, somehow misplaced or alien to his being.

"Bipp...did I ever tell you about my mother?"

Bipp suddenly felt very guilty for pushing his friend. He never imagined his curiosity would cause Logan to dwell in such a dark place. Logan *had* told him the story, one night after they had first met. It was late, just like this evening, and Bipp had just shared the tale of his own mother's death.

Logan's mother had died when he was just a lad. She had gone out to the river to do some laundry, and Logan had insisted on tagging along. His father wanted him to stay behind and help tend to his baby brother, but Logan was adamant on going, making the excuse that his mother needed help carrying the baskets. Of course both Melinda and Joseph knew their son better than to think that was his sole reason for going, but she caved in under his infectious smile.

While Melinda was trying to get the wash done on the riverbank, Logan kept whining that he was bored and wanted to play. When she refused, the boy slipped behind some trees to hide, forcing his giggling mother to play hide-and-seek with her mischievous son.

Logan was hiding across the trail from a badger that had slipped into the brush when she came around the trees. Melinda believed the badger rustling the leaves was Logan and he went along with it, barely holding back his giggles as she comically rounded the bush on tiptoes, anticipating the look on her face when the badger popped out.

Except when Melinda pulled back the brush, laughing and yelling, "Gotcha," she was not greeted by a harmless badger but the bite of a deadly black asp. The river serpent lashed out, scoring a hit on her shoulder that dropped her. She was dead before Logan could even reach the village to get his father for help.

The gnome nodded, sheepishly staring into the fire and chewing on the corner of his mouth. He shifted the glowing embers with a stick.

"Well, I sorta think the whole thing screwed me up," Logan said.

Bipp snorted. "I think it's to be expected that such an experience would cause anyone to become depressed."

"Nah, not in that way," Logan said. "I mean, sure I was just as upset as any kid could be, losing a parent like that. And then to have my dad take off as well, it was rough. But I think it really messed up my head. When I was growing up, sometimes I would wake in the middle of the night lost in a state of terror. Like, covered with sweat and just gripped with fear. I would try to find my folks to tell them how scared I was, and then it would hit me. They weren't there anymore."

"I'm so sorry, Logan," Bipp said, seeing the look of despair in Logan's emerald eyes.

"Hey, that's okay. When those nights came, it would make me remember." The firelight flickered off his eyes as Logan stared deep into the fire. He could almost see himself as a child in the embers, walking through Morgana's cabin alone in the middle of the night and calling for his mother.

"Remember what?" Bipp asked.

"How alone we all really are...and how insignificant our lives can be," Logan replied.

"Logan, you can't say such things." Bipp reached up and patted his friend's shoulder. Logan looked away from the fire, giving the gnome a wry grin.

"No, that's just it. For the first time in my life, I actually feel different. Since we began this journey back in Dudje, I feel alive. It's like for the first time I can actually do something that matters, you know? Like maybe we don't have to be so insignificant after all." Logan shrugged. "I think we're going to come through this on top, and I guess that's what is making me so happy lately."

Bipp nodded his agreement, pulling out his last flask of scrum and taking a long pull on it. They both sat in silence, staring at the crackling flames, the sounds of the jungle pressing in around them.

"What are you two troublemakers so depressed about?" Kyra asked, walking up to see the two staring into the fire with frowns.

"Oh, Bipp was just telling me about his constipation," Logan replied without missing a beat. Bipp spit his drink into the fire, the alcohol causing it to flare up for a moment so that they both had to jump back. They lay on their backs, laughing uncontrollably.

Kyra put her hands on her hips and shook her head. "You're like two children, you know that?"

The party got an early start as dusk rolled in, hoping to make some serious headway through the dense jungle that night. Logan was impressed by the two-hundred-foot trees that surrounded him and the layer upon layer of plant life in every shade of green he could possibly imagine, flecked with the vibrant blues and crimson reds of exotic flowers. Overhead, a small creature, resembling something between a monkey and a raccoon, had been following them for the last mile or so. Tiko had scolded him for feeding it a bit of his daily ration, but he just could not resist.

Logan was in a particularly good mood despite the thick cloud of low-hanging fog they had wandered into. He felt like he was on top of the world ever since he had begun bonding with the weapon master. Stur's combat training had Logan's muscles feeling tight in all the right ways, and his skills with the sword were getting better with each day that passed. He almost hoped they would encounter an enemy to test his mettle against, then instantly tried to retract the idea, thinking Corbin could hear his thoughts. He knew it was irrational; the mental shield Corbin had placed on Logan and Bipp prevented him from reading their minds without their knowledge.

"Bipp, where did your legs go?" Logan jested.

The gnome looked down to see the fog was all the way up to his waist now and let out a tiny yelp. Logan laughed while Bipp walked with his elbows lifted above the mist as if he were treading water.

"Bipp, the fog will not harm your well-being," Nero pointed out, attempting to use logic to temper the gnome's emotional reaction. "This is natural given the level of moisture lingering in the air of this area."

"Nothing natural about it. The stuff's spooky as a bat's smile, if you ask me," Bipp replied.

Stur chuckled, almost wanting to muss the big-nosed gnome's hair like a child but stopping himself with the mental reminder that Bipp was an adult and probably older than any of them. Unless, of course, you counted the time they had spent in cryo-sleep.

Their Agma guides came back from a scouting trip, crouched low to the ground, sliding through the dense jungle fog so fluidly it gave the illusion they were floating. If Logan did not know them, the lizard people would look quite menacing. Even so, he still had to fight his natural urge to ready his weapon as the reptilian humanoids approached.

"What did you find, Tiko?" Kyra asked.

"Tiko watches for tracks. The way ahead is still clear. These ones are very close to Isaacha's holy place on this plane." He pulled out a water skin to hydrate.

Kyra gathered the group to discuss their next move. "Let's break for lunch. I'll bet our gnome friend is itching to finish off that mushroom cake. Keep it short, though. I want us back on the trail in no less than an hour." She dismissed them to spread out into their own routines.

Logan almost walked right over Bipp, who had plopped himself down where he stood with only his silver hair sticking up over the fog. Logan shook his head, smirking. His friend just could not wait another moment before wolfing down his lunch.

Logan moved away from the group. The last time he had relieved himself close by, Kyra got all bent out of shape and called him a caveman—which he was, but something about the way she said it made him feel stupid. He steadied himself against a thick, ancient tree and let loose. He was just finishing when his new forest friend came skittering down the trunk to eye level.

"Hey little guy, you hungry?" He spoke in that uncontrollable tone people used when confronted with a cute baby. Logan pulled out his ration of unleavened flatbread and broke off small chunks, feeding them to the animal, which came right up to his palm.

"Would you stop giving away all our supplies?" Kyra snapped, making him flinch and startling the furry creature, which scurried back up the tree.

Logan spun to face the nagging crone, tired of her ceaseless nonsense. "Listen, *lady*, don't worry your pretty little face over what *I* do with *my* rations. Why don't you go mind your own business for once?"

Kyra huffed at his insolence, noticing that one of her men snickered at the comment. "How dare you? I am the-"

"Shut up." Logan cut her off.

Kyra's blood boiled even hotter. "Do you really bel—"

"Shhh!" He hissed, cutting her off again. "I mean it, stop talking! Listen...do you guys hear that?" Logan tensed up, slowly surveying the outskirts of their camp.

Stur rose, sensing Logan's seriousness, and pulled his blade.

"I don't hear nothing," Lars said from his seat beside Kyra.

"Exactly," Stur said, picking up on Logan's meaning.

All sound around them had died out, as if someone had flicked a switch for the jungle's soundtrack. This was odd, for the forest was generally filled with a myriad of sounds from the many creatures living in it.

"Something has the forest spooked," Logan said, moving closer to his team, who were already gathering in a defensive circle with their backs to one another. The Agma also perked up, gazing around for the source of the disturbance.

"Where is Erol?" Kyra asked, noticing the Acadian soldier was not in their midst.

"He headed over yonder to take a personal break, if you know what I mean." Lars pointed toward a copse of trees not far from where Logan had been standing only a moment before.

Logan and Tiko broke away from the group, sprinting to the area to see if their friend was okay. Logan almost bowled over the lizardman backtracking when the Acadian emerged from the brush alive and well.

Erol wore a bemused expression. "What's the big idea?" he asked innocently.

"We thought something happened to you!" his brother Lars complained, mad even through his relief.

"I'm fine...but I can't say the same for those bushes," Erol crudely jested, waving his hand in front of his nose. When no one laughed, he shrugged. "Everyone's a critic."

Logan took a deep breath to shake off the adrenaline rush, but he detected Tiko was still tensely scouring the area for some sign.

"What happened?" Erol asked, sensing he was being left out.

"Don't worry about it! Just get over here while we figure this out." Lars scowled in a way only brothers could get away with.

Erol nodded and started to move forward out of the thick undergrowth. Something growled, and a white flash streaked through the trees. Erol let out a scream as a mass of white fur dragged him back behind the tree.

Lars screamed for his brother, and Logan moved to chase after the creature. Tiko caught his wrist and shook his head. Erol let out a final cry that ended in a ripping noise followed by a gurgle. Lars fell to his knees in shock and Stur had to pull him to his feet.

"What is it?" Kyra asked.

"Dire wolves," Tiko said, his eyes darting back and forth over the fog that was seeping up from the jungle floor.

"Come back out here and fight, you bastard!" Logan screamed into the undergrowth.

The only response he received was a flash of glowing yellow eyes that penetrated the darkness for a moment. The eyes turned away, followed by the sound of growling and tearing flesh as the unseen wolf ate Erol. Logan shouted and flung his sword blade over hilt into the dense foliage. The dire wolf let out a yelp, and Logan motioned for his allies to come help finish the job.

An ear-splitting howl erupted from behind the tree, sending goosebumps over Logan's forearms. Even Kyra looked shaken by the primal sound. A myriad of howls broke through the night from the jungle to the east. The pack was answering the wounded wolf's call.

"What now?" Logan asked both Tiko and Kyra.

Tiko stood at attention, listening intently and sniffing the night air. "Now we run!" He turned and dashed into the jungle fog.

Stur lifted a babbling Lars from the ground and tossed him over his shoulder, shouting for everyone to flee.

"What is happening?" Corbin asked Kalilah under his heavy breathing.

"The dire wolves do come!" she exclaimed, her voice dripping with fear. "We are being hunted."

Logan's foot caught on something, sending him face-first into the dirt. His aching muscles felt too tired to keep moving. The fog was like a misty soup that covered the entire jungle in a blanket of grey-white mist, so thick they could barely see a couple yards in any direction. Stur helped him to his feet, offering to help balance his weight, but Logan shook him off, sure that the warrior must be growing tired after having carried Lars for so long. More howls rang through the trees, far closer this time than they had been.

"Blasted demon hounds, they've been chasing us relentlessly for hours!" Lars complained hoarsely, panting like an animal as he held his knees.

Kyra spun around to see what the problem was. "We have to keep moving!" she urged the men, prompting a solemn look of determination from Stur, who had unlatched his massive broadsword.

"We can't keep running, Marshal," Corbin said, reading the weapon master's thoughts and putting his back to the group to cover their flank.

"Everyone is tired," Stur said with a grimace, "and the damned beasts are still hot on our heels. I fear if we go any farther, we will be too weary to defend ourselves."

Kyra could see there was no talking her men out of this and had realized, over an hour ago, that this scenario was inevitable. "Logan, get in the middle of the group. You're already injured and completely defenseless," she called as he began walking into the thick fog.

"The hell I am," Logan barked, picking up the solid tree branch he had tripped over. "It'll take more than a little cut on the head to frighten me." His words were big, but the shaky feeling in his chest belied his true feelings. Logan did not care. He realized that if he did not muster up some strength of will here and now, it would mean his end. Pushing down the throbbing pain in the back of his head and the aching of his muscles deep down inside, he faced the east and snarled, ready to meet his foe.

As if in answer, the patter of feet and growls surrounded them on all sides, echoing off the trees. The dire wolves had already caught up with them!

Logan could not see the tenacious beasts through the thick mist and pushed his back up against the group, holding the forward arc formation they had created with Bipp lost in the foggy middle, slapping his hammer into an open palm.

Stur tensed, sensing movement close at hand. A ghost-white shape lunged out of the fog, catching the warrior on his side. He shouldered the pouncing wolf and would have taken a nasty gash if not for his flexible armor.

Another snarling wolf lurched in at Corbin, who ducked beneath its attack, slicing the beast's flank open with his raised voulge. Logan's heart surged with excitement over the devastating wound until he saw the matching line of blood across his brother's forearm.

"They're too fast!" Lars spat, angry at the entire damnable jungle.

Stur cut the air with his broadsword repeatedly, barely fending off one of the wolves, which clacked its teeth together, pacing slowly from side to side, waiting for its opening.

"Corbin, use your second sight!" Logan yelled. To Hel with keeping their secret from the Acadians. Now was as good a time as any to reveal his talents.

Kyra barely registered the implication, pulling her shield up just in time to block a wolf's snapping jaws. It was a flurry of white, knocking her over and thrashing her arm back and forth while massive jaws chewed on her shield. Logan gave the beast's face a thrashing of his own, flecks of his branch flying every which way until it finally released her shield. Tiko stabbed his spear at the growling wolf's face, but it loped back into the fog. Logan helped Kyra to her feet.

Corbin moved back into the fold and fell inside himself. It did not take long for him to find the stream of psychic energy coursing through the area. No fog could hide the sentient minds of the wolves from the psionic probing of Corbin Walker. His power had grown tenfold since his recent run-in with death in the ruins of Ul'kor. He could sense six of the beasts surrounding them, their minds glowing like candles in the psychic aether. Each of the wolves was easily two or three times the size of a regular canine, with only one thing on their animal minds—feasting on their prey. He twirled a finger in each monster's direction with his free hand, coating them with a glimmering blue outline that only he could see.

All around Corbin, his companions grew more and more frustrated at the futility of this fight, and the wolves sensed it. The idea of their prey weakening, showing fear, excited the beasts.

When he opened his eyes, Corbin was surprised to see Kyra down on one knee, holding his brother's scavenged weapon and lighting the wood on fire with flint. Logan had taken her sword and was fending off a wolf that had scored a vicious hit on Lars' ankle, tearing chunks of muscle and boot away.

"Stur, watch your right side!" Corbin shouted, shoving past the warrior and lunging forward with his voulge.

Stur thought him a madman until he heard the sound of the Falian's spear tearing through flesh and heard a yelp from the unseen beast. Corbin pressed on, confidently cutting a swath through the fog to intimidate another of the pack to stay back. Then, with a sideways thrust, he skewered the limping beast through the throat.

The wolves suddenly pulled back, quickly regrouping. Their glowing blue forms danced around Corbin through the fog, but he was not afraid. His blood pumped hard with adrenaline. He turned his back to them, psyching out one of the beasts, which came in hard. Before it reached him, Corbin did a backward sommersault, landing firmly behind the wall that was Stur.

Kyra's torch was in full bloom now, and she waved it around in an attempt to break up the fog. "Where are they, Corbin?" she shouted.

He pointed at two of the beasts on either side of them. No sooner had his finger touched on the direction than Stur's blade came down, clipping a swift-dodging wolf, which howled as the fine edge of the sword lopped off an ear. Kalilah lunged forward, throwing her spear in the same direction and skewering the beast.

Kyra ran out with her torch swinging, frightening the wits out of her wolf, while Bipp and Logan raced in, attacking the beast from both sides. Desperate to escape, it charged right over Bipp, but Logan cut deeply into the dire wolf's white fur with the tip of Kyra's blade. He dug the weapon in deep, and the wolf tried to shake him off. Logan clung to the handle, desperate to keep from being knocked weaponless to the ground, and was carried off into the fog.

"Tiko, go after him," Kyra shouted.

The lizardman charged toward the sound of Logan grunting and the beast's jaws clacking together. Logan sat astride the dire wolf, repeatedly punching the top of its skull while he clung to the buried sword with the unyielding grip of his mechanical hand. He saw Tiko coming and felt a wave of relief, unsure how much longer he could hold up. The lizardman hurled his spear straight for the beast's ribs and pinned it in place in the dirt. Logan screamed in triumph and finally released his grip, swinging around the wolf's side and falling to the ground. More yelping erupted through the white mist behind them as Stur stubbornly pursued another of the wolves.

Corbin could smell the pack's fear floating in the psychic aether at having two of their kin killed. This hunting tactic had worked for them for ages, since the time they were pups, and to have the tide turned was something they were not equipped to handle. The leader howled to his pack, retreating into the jungle away from the dangerous two-legs, leaving their slain kin behind.

"T-They are all gone...t-they fled!" Corbin announced in disbelief.

Stur walked back into view, tendrils of white mist curling around his grim, bloodied form, and lifted Lars from the dirt.

"Stur, are you...?" Corbin asked.

"It's not mine," he replied gruffly. "Help me with Lars. He is badly wounded."

Logan came limping out of the mist as well with Tiko at his side. He shook off the help offered by his brother and instead helped Stur brace Lars upright while Nero checked on the damage done, pulling off the soldier's tattered boot. Bipp choked on a dry heave at the chunk of calf muscle that was missing. He had to back away so he did not have to see it anymore.

"Ahh...I'm fine. It's just a flesh wound, eh?" Lars stubbornly joked, wincing as the wet air hit the gaping hole left from the dire wolf's claws.

"Aye, it's nothing you won't heal from, friend." Stur said, though his tone could not disguise the dire implications the weapon master truly felt. He placed a heavy hand on Lars' shoulder.

Bipp kept backing up, holding his stubby hands over his mouth to keep his stomach's contents inside. As he took another step, his heel came down to find the ground had disappeared. Letting out a yelp, he fell backwards, spinning head over heels in a little ball down the tangled hillside. The group could only watch in horror as their friend vanished.

"Logan, wait, don't!" Corbin called, reaching out to stop his brother.

It was too late. Logan had already abandoned Lars to the weapon master, recklessly running headlong into the fog after his friend. In an instant he too disappeared down the hillside.

Kyra motioned for them to move forward with caution. "Careful here, the ground slopes steeply downward," she said, lightly prodding the jungle floor with her toe through the thick fog.

Stur carried Lars and stood to the side for their more experienced Agma companions to lead the way. Tiko used his spear to balance himself and offered a hand to help Kyra down the hillside, which she nonchalantly declined, determined to make the way herself. The slope was steep enough to easily twist an ankle. Corbin was not surprised his brother and the gnome had tumbled down it.

"Well, the good news is we don't have to worry about that fog anymore!" Logan called up to them from the base of the hill.

And he was right. Tendrils of mist curled around the edge of the trees lining the area in an almost perfect circle. Thick roots from the jungle trees lining the sloping hillside ran down into a clearing, the knotty wood of them blanketed in moss.

It seemed unnatural how the wall of fog lingered in between the trunks above as if locked behind some invisible wall that divided the clearing from the greater jungle. From the moment they came through the barrier, it was as if a veil had been lifted, revealing the most amazing landscape.

The clearing itself was covered with rich green grass broken only by thick twisting roots from the surrounding jungle. The clearing was large enough to fit a small castle inside, and in some ways that was exactly what it held at the center, surrounded by slabs of moss-covered stones from the ruins of some ancient structure.

In the center of the clearing towered the largest tree any of them had ever seen, the likes of which they would most likely never witness again even if they wandered the world for ten lifetimes. The trunk was so wide it would take close to twenty men locking arms to circle it. The bark was white as the most pristine ivory with nary a blemish to be seen. The boughs were large enough to build a house on and were covered with leaves the size of Corbin's hand, each the color of tempered silver glittering in the light of the coming dawn. He had to crane his neck back to see the mythical tree's canopy. Its dizzying height was so unimaginable he almost lost his balance. He had to steady himself against Kalilah, who looked at the tree with awe and humble reverence.

"Bipp is knocked out cold," Logan called, reminding everyone that the gnome had fallen.

Corbin licked his dry lips. In those few moments he had forgotten all about his companions. Their journey, the wolves, all of it just washed away in that infinitesimal moment of wonder at the tree's majesty. He made his way carefully down the slope to Logan, crouching to check on the gnome, who was stretched out in the grass, snoring loudly. "Must have hit his head on the way down," Corbin said.

Nero ran a quick scan on their friend, confirming Bipp had indeed hit his head but adding that the sleeping had nothing to do with that and everything to do with fatigue.

"What about you?" Corbin asked his brother. "You look like you're in rough shape."

"I'll be fine." Logan smiled despite the painful bruises and scrapes covering his body. It was hard not to feel delight being in the presence of the mystical tree. "Pretty impressive, isn't it?" He elbowed Corbin, cocking his head toward the tree.

"She is something else, that's for sure. I mean, just look at this place." Corbin waved his arm around the sunken clearing, taking in the landscape with childlike wonderment. "It's like something out of one of Elder Morgana's fairy tales."

"Tiko has brought you to Isaacha," the lizardman proudly declared, crossing his scale-covered arms over his chest and bowing his long neck in reverence to the tree.

Corbin took a step back from the lizardman, thoughtfully filling his vision with the ancient tree once more. "Do you mean to say that we are here?" he asked in disbelief. Had his journey really come to its end? Was he really about to find the answers to save New Fal?

Tiko nodded, helping Kalilah strip off her clothing. Corbin averted his gaze from her strangely alluring breasts, ashamed to be aroused by anyone other than Elise, and a non-human at that.

Logan laughed hoarsely at him, wincing through the pain of his bruised ribs. Now that the adrenaline of battle was wearing off, he was aware of all sorts of aches and pains covering his bruised torso. Slapping a hand on Corbin's shoulder, he squeezed it to support himself, unabashedly admiring Kalilah's body while smirking. "Mm-hmm, what a sight." He whistled, heartily clapping Corbin's back.

"Logan, please..." Corbin did not understand how his brother could egg him on so, knowing the deep commitment he felt to his fiancée.

"*What?* We travelled all that distance, and a man can't even take a moment to admire the most magnificent spectacle of a tree there ever has been?" Logan coyly replied, waving toward the towering canopy then winking at his younger brother. Logan slowly hobbled after the Agma, leaving Corbin to stand there fumbling for words.

Kyra walked by, shooting him a mischievous glance. "Come on, lover boy. Enough gawking, let's get this show on the road," she teased. Corbin had to be the only man she had ever met who was such an utter gentleman toward women—other than Stur, of course, but he didn't really count. That man was practically a monk.

Stur could not help joining in her mirth at Corbin's expense as he walked down the hillside carrying Lars, who slept in his arms, long since passed out from the pain.

Tiko stopped at the bottom of the hill, letting Kalilah make the last leg of the spiritual pilgrimage alone. She stood naked, facing the mighty tree, before the stone idol of a gaping face that leaned crookedly in the soil and leaked a powdery lime moss from tiny carvings.

Their Agma guide held the shaft of his spear out to block the path, whispering, "Now is Kalilah's time of offering. This the healing maiden must do alone, friends."

The group silently accepted his request. There was something deeply energetic about this place, as if the very air itself was alive with possibility.

They were transfixed on Kalilah, who stood erect, her thin tail swaying back and forth with the gentle rocking of her softly curved hips. She was chanting something they could not make out, clasping her fingers together in praying hands that moved from her breast to the sky in thrusts of deepening intensity. Somehow the rhythm of her chanting, combined with her mesmerizing movement, had them all unconsciously swaying in time with her.

When Kalilah suddenly stopped, violently thrusting a rounded bone icon toward the sky, it was so startling that several of them gasped. In one fluid motion, Kalilah crouched low to the ground and slammed the bone effigy into her groin with a yelp of pain. Kyra lunged forward, screaming the woman's name in fear, but Tiko stopped her, wrapping his arms around the marshal. He held her tight and hushed her while rocking gently, as if she were a child who had woken from a nightmare. Corbin wondered if Stur would attack the Agma for touching his marshal but saw the warrior's acceptance of the situation written across his somber face. The weapon master understood they were witnessing a profoundly personal moment in Kalilah's life, one of immense spiritual significance that would impact her all her days to come in this world.

"Is she...okay?" Corbin mouthed, barely uttering the words to Tiko.

"It is the blood offering. Kalilah gives her first blood to Isaacha in exchange for the jungle's blessing as healer," Tiko replied, as if it were all the explanation necessary.

Rather than pry more information, Corbin went along, acting as if it made sense. The last thing he wanted to do was insult the Agma, who had risked life and limb to bring them to this sacred place.

Kalilah knelt on the slab of stone before her effigy, finishing her prayer. After long moments of silence, she finally rose, born anew in the eyes of the jungle. Tiko moved to meet her on the path, brimming with loving pride for her and taking her in his arms for the first time, sharing her tears of rejoicing.

The group turned away to give them some semblance of privacy during the intimate exchange. Corbin could see the ritual had disturbed Kyra. After a few minutes of whispers and laughter, the Agma came back up the grassy path.

"Isaacha has smiled upon Kalilah's path as a healer!" Tiko proclaimed to the world as the lizardwoman bowed, still holding one of his hands for support.

"Congratulations, Kalilah!" Kyra unexpectedly rejoiced, dropping her normal mask of seriousness, and startling both of the Agma with a tight hug. Catching herself, Kyra abruptly froze and moved the naked lizardwoman to arms-length. "Oh...uh...sorry," she said, trying to apologize for her impropriety.

To this Kalilah just tittered, throwing her head straight up to the pink dawning sky in glee. Holding Kyra's hand, she twirled the marshal in a circle and hugged her back. Tiko and Stur just looked to each other for a sign of what to do now that the women had clearly taken leave of their sanity.

As the women huddled away from the men to dress Kalilah once more, Tiko looked relieved. "Corbin, the time has now come for *your* blessing." He slowly nodded, pointing toward the stone statue down the path with the tip of his green snout.

Corbin looked anxiously to his brother, hoping he would be coming along. He did not need to ask; Logan was already leaning his weight on Corbin's shoulder, needing support to make it down the path with his weakened legs.

Corbin started to guide them but stopped short, a nagging thought rising to the surface. "Tiko, um, what do we do? I mean, are there certain words needed to commune with the spirit?"

"Corbin will know what Isaacha wants when the time comes," Tiko counseled, sounding like a wise sage confident in his pupil's readiness.

Corbin nervously blinked at the Agma before turning and making his way to the effigy, practically dragging Logan's weight along. Standing before the stone idol, he could see its size was deceiving, as it was almost as tall as Stur. Up close, it looked less like it was smiling and more like it was silently mocking his cause in leering laughter.

Logan slipped from his shoulder and slumped down to his knees on a stone slab that lay in the grass. It must have fallen over ages ago, the weight of it slowly sinking into the soft dirt of the clearing over the years. "What are you going to do now, offer some of your first blood?" Logan joked, leaning forward on the balls of his hands and wincing.

Corbin fell to the ground in prayer, falling into the only habit he knew, lying prostrate in front of the effigy and chanting an old Falian prayer of blessing. Instead of Baetylus' name, he invoked the spirit of the jungle, asking Isaacha to bless him with guidance, that he might see the path to saving his people. He begged the jungle deity to speak to him, falling deeper into a meditation of peace and echoing his words toward the stone idol in mental waves of psionic energy.

He did this repeatedly for close to an hour, pushing further and further into the dawn. The sky glowed a hot pink with misty purple clouds, and the air began to warm under the daystar's brilliance bursting over far-off mountains they could not see. The brighter it became, the more Corbin's frustration grew, his muscles tensing up as his subconscious mocked his futile attempts.

What was he thinking, after everything they had gone through in Vanidriell with the false god Baetylus? Had he really believed risking their lives on a wild goose chase through a deadly jungle was going to work? He had taken them far beyond their homeland, stripping them of their ability to save Elise and the villagers of Riverbell. Corbin tasted the bile in his throat, sickened by his idiocy. How could he believe that a stone statue worshipped by a primitive lizard race was going to somehow magically speak to him and give the answers to an unsolvable riddle, freeing the Falians from the mental prison of the crystal leech?

His frustration boiled over, shifting into fury. Screaming in defiance, Corbin lashed out, smashing the head of his voulge into the dirt with both hands over and over like he was swatting an evil fly that refused to die. He was so caught up in his rage that he did not even feel Logan relieve him of his weapon and then step back to let his younger brother's fury play out.

Corbin was so angry at the world, so filled with hatred for every unfair thing it had to offer. He felt the emotion fill him like a balloon with no release. In the background, he dimly heard Tiko begging Kyra to make him stop before he angered the jungle, and Stur was running to try to restrain him.

As tears streamed down Corbin's face, his voice boomed across the psychic aether, filling their minds and ears. He unleashed all his naked fury in one deadly beam of psionic energy filled with such raw power that all stood by stunned while a mind-boggling ray of light erupted from his forehead and eyes. The stone effigy was incinerated, carved in two by the psionic blast, which then harmlessly bounced off the ivory bark of the mighty tree behind it.

As his body closed off the channel of energy, Corbin hit the ground, lying on his back while chunks of remaining stone toppled to the ground from the ruined effigy. Tiko lay prostrate in the grass, pitifully begging the jungle spirit not to blame his people for bringing the soft-belly demon to the holy site, while Kalilah crouched close by, hysterically sobbing and shaking her head in denial.

Only a moment before, Corbin had been filled with overwhelming hatred, like an unquenchable fire suffocating his heart. But now, looking up at the serene sky, lit with dawn's radiance to the point that he was beginning to lose his vision amidst the myriad of pinks, oranges, and purples peeking through the fluttering silver leaves, Corbin realized that nothing had changed. Nothing he could do would change the world. He was simply not strong enough to change things. After all the power he had unleashed in anger, the world of Acadia still just kept on moving in peace, just as it had before he knew the surface existed and just like it would continue to long after his death. Corbin wondered what the point of it all was. Why try at all when you were too weak to alter the inevitable path of destiny?

The muscles in his back began to spasm against the stone slab, which twitched beneath his legs. Corbin looked around, puzzled, and saw Logan cautiously staring at the rumbling ground. Tiny pebbles danced across the slab of bedrock. A thin cloud of dust began to rise as the dirt shifted under the quaking, and Logan twisted his bruised body around, urging his feet to move. Corbin stared at him, at a loss for words, earning him a sharp slap from his older brother.

"Snap out of it, man. I think you pissed off that jungle god or something!" Logan scowled, spurring them to a run. The area was quaking so hard that the ground actually began to stand up under a cloud of falling dirt and dust. "I told him he should have given the jungle some of that first blood action!" Logan exclaimed to Stur as they caught up with the dumbstruck warrior.

The entire party fled to the edge of the hillside, scrambling up the grass on hands and knees to get away from whatever was coming. Logan turned to see the silhouette of a massive figure standing in the middle of the cloud of settling dust. He could not tear his eyes away as a gargantuan stone golem stepped forward from the wreck, shaking the ground under its considerable weight. The elemental being was made from the stone ruins that had littered the area, carved in much the same way as the ancient pagan effigy, with intricate patterns covering its blocky arms and hulking flat chest. Moss and vines still clung to it. Glowing green eyes probed the area, searching for the intruders until settling on the form of Kalilah, who still crouched in the grass, weeping in her hysteria.

Logan barely realized he was running on legs hardly strong enough to stay upright. It was as if he were watching the scene from above himself, dimly wondering why the stupid lizardwoman did not join them in flight. By the time he made it to Kalilah, the stone golem was already towering over her, standing eight feet tall, and readying lumbering hands high in the air to crush them both. Logan threw himself over the Agma woman, not knowing how else to save her, gritting his teeth and squeezing his eyes shut tight, bracing for death.

When none came, he wondered if death had been so fast that he had not even felt it. Another moment passed in silence. Corbin called his name from the hillside, and Logan opened one eye, scared to see what was left of himself. He found himself looking down at the face of Kalilah, frozen in terror and awe, staring back at him. Blinking to see if it were a dream, he fearfully craned his neck to look over his shoulder. The mighty stone guardian stood locked in place like a statue, clenched fists high in the air, wearing a serene face of obedience. Kalilah skittered away from Logan, shuffling backward through the grass as if realizing for the first time the danger they had faced.

"Wha—?" he mouthed, looking back and forth between the still goliath and his friends scattered on the hillside, who were all just as confused.

The ground began to tremble again as thick roots the size of small trees wriggled loose from the dirt, sending a spray of grass into the air. Five of the mighty roots worked their way backward toward the base of the mighty tree, curling upward into the air and braiding around each other. It was as if a mighty curtain had rolled to the side, revealing a perfectly arched doorway.

Bipp rolled over in the dirt, rubbing his eyes and scratching his bulbous nose, yawning. Stretching, he stood beside Logan, who had completely forgotten he was lying there, and pulled on his sleeve.

"Huh?" Logan blinked again, still lost in a state of shock, taking his eyes off the doorway and looking down at his friend.

"What did I miss?" Bipp asked, cocking his big head sideways at the strange stone golem, wondering who would make such a scary statue.

"YOU MAY ENTER!" a voice boomed from the doorway at the base of the tree, blasting through the air and pushing all the blades of grass backward.

Logan stood frozen in place, staring at the entrance, then looked at his companions, who wore similar expressions of disbelief. Looking back, he saw the gnome merrily heading down the path toward the tree. "Bipp, where are you going?" he asked incredulously in a high-pitched voice.

Bipp looked over his shoulder, innocently replying, "Fella just invited us in, didn't he? Don't know about you, but I'm not one for wanting to be rude. You coming, or you gonna play with that statue some more?" Winking, he continued inside under the arched roots.

Put like that, Logan saw no reason not to follow him inside the white tree.

Chapter 6: The White Tree

Once the nine companions passed through the towering portal of intertwined ivory roots, Corbin was greeted by the most unexpected sight. Rather than the hollowed out interior of a tree, they stood in the lobby of a massive tower. There was no ceiling. The tower seemed to rise all the way to the top of the tree and open to the sky above, funneling light down into the atrium crafted for a god's abode. The walls were made of the smooth, unblemished white wood of the tree. The round greeting area seemed to be twice as large as it should have been. Corbin even did a double-take at the tower entrance, wondering if they had walked inside a different building standing beside the magical heart of the jungle.

The sound of boots clacking across stone took his mind from the wonderment. Someone was racing down the steps above them, where polished stone staircases on either side of a balcony curved up to a central landing with a doorway that should, by all logic, lead back outside the tree. Yet mysteriously the steps continued beyond the door.

The clicking heels made an erratic shift in rhythm as their owner tripped over his own webbed feet, cartwheeling down the remaining few steps and crashing clumsily into the railing, almost toppling over the edge of the landing onto the startled group.

Quick as lightning, a frog the size of Bipp hopped to his feet, two red blossoms lighting up his shiny green cheeks. The figure straightened his heavy wool cloak, which was slightly too long for his body, and pulled the hood, which had flipped over his face, off his bald, amphibian head. The little fellow looked quite excitable and seemed more concerned with being seen falling down a flight of stairs than the idea of being hurt by such a tumble.

The diminutive frogman moved to the edge of the railing with a broad smile and opened his arms wide in an overly dramatic gesture. "Welcome most honored and esteemed guests of the great and powerful and magnificent mage Isaac!" His overly rehearsed greeting was in the squeaky, eager voice of a child.

Ah, so he's not just small. The frogman is actually a frogboy, Corbin noted.

"My name is Elijah, and I will be your humble guide today! Please follow me right this way to the Master's sanctum, where he awaits your arrival!" Elijah hopped up and down a couple times on large webbed feet, raring to go as they climbed the steps to meet him.

"Excellent, right this way!" He could barely contain himself, almost jogging up the stairs ahead of them.

The narrow passageway was a tight squeeze. Corbin imagined if Stur were any bigger, he would probably be stuck in the passage like the cork of a wine bottle. Elijah was moving so quickly he had to run back down the stairs several times to see if the group was still following.

As they went farther, Corbin held little doubt that the angle of these stairs should be impossible. They were set at an incline that would have brought them well past the tree trunk after only the first few steps.

Finally, the ascent came to an end, the passage splitting off in either direction to form curved halls of an even larger tower than the lobby first suggested. Statues of various knightly armors lined both sides of the walls, and Bipp almost leapt into Logan's arms when one tilted an empty visor to speak to its neighbor.

"Oy, what's all this rabble then?"

The other set of armor shrugged with creaky joints. "Looks like the frog has dragged in some more pets. Lizards and little people, no doubt."

Elijah stopped in front of an arched wooden doorway to their left, which by all accounts should open to the outside world but instead revealed yet another short hallway ending in a set of twin doors with an elaborate carving of a tree with small orbs floating around it on its face. Stur had to bow his head to pass through the portal into the cramped hallway. Beyond the twin doors, the room widened out.

A creature both mystifying and fear-inducing lay in wait. The beast had the head and body of a muscular lion, golden pelt and a fiery mane to boot, while the rear half of its body had hind paws like an eagle's talons, white feathered wings large enough to carry it, and a long lion's tail. As soon as it sensed them coming, the guardian was on its feet, letting out a roar so loud even Stur froze in his tracks.

For a split second, Corbin thought they had been led into a trap; the walls here were too tight to brandish his weapon and provide any semblance of defense. His fears were quickly put to rest, though, leaving only the lingering reminder in his head to watch their environment better in the future. Elijah was already upon the dangerous beast, berating it and shooing it into obedience.

"Oh, hush up, Shedu! Don't frighten the master's guests!" he scolded, cowing it into resting on the floor with paws folded over each other. Despite seeing the frogboy's seeming sway over the creature,

Corbin could not help gulping at a knot lodged in his throat as he walked by with Shedu's eyes hungrily tracing his every step.

Isaacha's inner sanctum looked much how Corbin would expect a mage's solar to be. The ceiling was domed with a fresco of animated stars and planets that slowly drifted around in orbit. The room was lined with bookcases, their shelves filled with dusty tomes. There was an armchair with torn purple fabric beside an antique globe of Acadia and a couple tables covered with scrolls and other odds and ends. In the center of the room stood a man he took to be Isaacha wearing a brown wool cloak that matched Elijah's and leaning on a white cane intricately carved with intertwining branches and topped with a man's face staring stoically into space, its handle shaped like a something between a crescent moon and a crab claw.

Isaacha himself looked nothing like Corbin expected. Since hearing the man was the powerful spirit of the forest, he had assumed the mental image of a white-bearded elder in white flowing cloaks floating in the air, much as Baetylus had looked when he pretended to be Corbin's God. Instead, Isaacha was tall and slender, with smooth ebony skin. He had no hair except the patch of white that made up his small goatee, and he gazed at them as if they could be a mirage through tangerine eyes that sparkled vibrantly in the daylight flooding through the room from a round, stained-glass window set in the wall to their right.

"Greetings, weary travelers!" Isaacha yelled. He winced and lowered his voice. "Please do sit." He waved to the chair then looked back at the group, silently counting their ranks and coming to a decision. "Or stand. Yes, standing would be better. There are not enough seats for all, I think. Yes, I am correct. Yes, stand." He nodded, emphatically agreeing with himself, then twirled his cane toward them. "How did you escape?" he eagerly asked while Elijah hopped to his side, eyes lit up, awaiting their explanation.

"Escape?" Corbin asked, not taking his meaning.

"Correct. Or is that not the right term?" He looked to Elijah, who shrugged. "Or were you freed? No, that can't be, certainly you would not be freed. What are your names?" Isaacha jumped from one question to the next.

Tiko pushed through the group bowing down low to the floor. "Great spirit of the jungle, Tiko is your humble servant."

Isaacha pulled the lizardman, who looked as if he might keel over in shock at being touched by the great jungle spirit, to his feet. He gently caressed Tiko's cheek with the back of his hand, his eyes filled with genuine love and warmth.

Bipp cleared his throat of a tickle, distracting the mage, who just as suddenly changed the course of his thoughts.

"Eli, look at this! It's a gnome!" he declared, delightfully pulling the excited frog toward them. "Hello there, good sir. What brings you all the way here from Vanidriell?" Isaacha asked, squatting down to Bipp's height.

Corbin was shocked to hear the mage speak the name of his homeland. His heart dared to fill with newfound hope that he had only a short while ago given up on as folly.

"Brillfilbipp Bobblefuzz, of the Dudje Bobblefuzzes and the Fustlehammers before them," Bipp said. "It is my extreme honor to meet your acquaintance, oh noble jungle spirit, Isaacha." Bipp bowed as if he had years of experience in high society.

Corbin shot his brother a dark look when Logan snorted at the gnome's civilized response.

"Ah yes, but please don't butcher my name with your underworld accent. I am Isaac the...well, the nothing. Just Isaac, and this is my apprentice, Eli!" Isaac shook Bipp's offered hand, awkwardly speaking louder than necessary in the small room.

Kyra stepped forward. "Master Isaac, my name is Kyra Tarvano, Marshal of Agarta. We have many questions for you and would love to get to know one another better, but for the moment can you be of assistance to my man here? Lars is very injured and sorely in need of serious of medical attention, I'm afraid."

The group parted, revealing Lars' limp, feverish body cradled in Stur's arms.

Isaac smiled uncomfortably, switched to a frown and then to a serious expression. "My dear girl, bring that man over here this instant." He recklessly swept the scrolls off a nearby table. Eli scrambled to catch a glass alembic before it hit the floor, bouncing it off his webbed hands several times before getting a firm hold of it.

Stur gently placed Lars atop the table, moving back so Isaac could inspect his wound.

"Hmm yes, I see. This man has lost a considerable amount of blood. What would do this? Crocodile...no. Ocreet? Hmm, could be, but the teeth are too widely set. Ah, I see. Dire wolf, yes?" the mage mumbled to himself. "Eli, escort our guests to their rooms. I have work to attend to." Isaac waved them away, focusing his attention on gathering vials of herbs and scrolls.

Kyra started to complain but was forcibly ushered toward the door by the small frogboy, who was much stronger than he appeared.

"Ah, uh, yes. Young man," Isaac addressed them, staring at Nero.

"Can I provide assistance, Master Isaac?" Nero inquired.

"No. Not you, robot, the lad behind you." Isaac had no time for the mechanical man and cared nothing for his feelings at being addressed as moving steel. He motioned for Logan to sit down. "Come over here and rest. I will see to you next." Isaac moved a pillow off his armchair as Logan slipped off Corbin's shoulder, welcoming the opportunity to get off his feet.

"Alright then, let's get you weary travelers to your rooms!" Eli beamed, ignoring Kyra's protests, and herded them toward the doorway like lost sheep.

"But, Master Isaac, there are so many questions," Corbin called, trying to keep his balance while the frogboy shoved him out the door.

"Yes, questions," Isaac said under his breath. "You are correct, I have many questions. Too true, my questions need answering." He ground some hilno cloves with his pestle. "We can discuss it all over a light snack. No, make that tea. No, not tea, we can have an early breakfast." He stirred some milky oil into the concoction. "Actually a late, late supper sounds right. No, a feast. Yes, that's what we need, a feast. A grand banquet in honor of your newly celebrated liberation!"

Corbin could see Isaac was not in his right mind. However, there was something about the man that comforted him. He sensed the mage was to be trusted.

Kyra moved to protest again, and Isaac flicked his fingers over his shoulder, magically slamming the doors in their faces and rousing his pet, Shedu. The mystical creature lifted its lazy head to give them a halfhearted rumbling growl that earned it a scolding from Eli.

Corbin sat in the dining hall with his companions, every bit as anxious as they, if not more so, as they waited on their host. Kyra shifted in her seat, uncomfortably adjusting the waist of the tight black evening dress Isaac had sent down to her room. The mage had had formal evening wear delivered to all of their rooms, and although the vest and slacks made Corbin feel silly, it was actually quite refreshing to get out of his unwashed traveling gear.

Bipp cleared his throat, downed another wooden mug of ale, and burped loudly in the overly quiet chamber. Giggling, the gnome excused himself and adjusted his green bowtie. The ceiling of the square room was high, and Bipp's belch carried across the white wood walls and over the crackling of the man-sized fireplace. Above the hearth, the massive bust of a boar looked down at the long wooden table where they were seated and excused Bipp, throwing the gnome into another fit of giggling.

A door opened at the far end of the room, and the boar's head announced the arrival of the Magnanimous Mage Isaac, who was trailed by a smiling, bright-eyed Logan, who had a little extra hop to his strut.

"Hey, guys!" Logan exclaimed. "Looking sharp, Stur." He fired an imaginary pistol at the weapon master, who looked quite pleased with himself. Isaac's chair slid back from the table of its own accord.

"I see we are all here," Isaac said. "How did everyone rest? Were your rooms to your liking?" His chair tucked itself back into the table without any physical effort on his part.

"The rooms were fine, thank you, Master Isaac," Kyra said, trying to be cordial, but she was impatient to get to the matter at hand. "Now if we could—"

Isaac held a hand up to silence her, looking around the room in a troubled manner. "Wait a moment...someone is missing!" he exclaimed in a high-pitched tone.

Logan leaned forward and spoke to the worried man in a low voice. "Isaac, Lars is resting in your solar, remember?"

"No. Not someone...something. Yes here we have it, little flames, we need candles!" Isaac snapped his fingers and a lit candelabra formed out of thin air on either side of the long table. "And flowers!" Again he snapped, materializing a grand arrangement of pungent gardenias as a center piece, a flick of his finger adding a white rose to Kyra's hair, which was suddenly styled in a royal fashion.

"Now, you listen here—" Kyra demanded haughtily.

"Listen? Ah yes, we have nothing to listen to! Do banquets normally have music?" Isaac asked the group.

"I believe they do, Master Isaac," Stur politely replied, feigning innocence and ignoring a dark look from Kyra.

A grand piano appeared by the fireplace, ivory keys playing themselves in a soft serenade that seemed fit for a King's court. Eli kicked open the side door with a webbed foot and carried in a tray twice his size while wearing a double-breasted cooking jacket and white chef's hat.

"Most excellent, dinner has arrived!" Isaac exclaimed, rubbing his hands together in delight as Eli placed a plate of steaming trout and sautéed vegetables in front of each of them in turn. "Yes, do dig in. No need for formality," Isaac allowed, referring to Bipp, who had already gobbled down two heaping forks full of the hot meal. The gnome sheepishly looked at his companions, giggled nervously, and then continued.

"Master Isaac, if I may?" Kyra asked, not touching her plate.

"Yes, you may eat," Isaac replied. "I just said as much, didn't I, Eli?" He leaned toward the frogboy, who agreed while climbing into one of the heavy oak chairs to sit at the table.

"No, what I meant was—"

"Isaac." The mage cut her off loudly while chewing a mouthful of trout.

"I beg your pardon?" Kyra replied, confused by his outburst.

"Not *Master* Isaac, just Isaac. Please, just Isaac."

She took a deep breath and slowly began again. "As you wish, *Isaac*. What I need to know—"

"I see. You wish to know about your man Lars, correct?" Isaac asked.

Kyra was trying to be patient, but when the mage interrupted her again, she jabbed her fork into the wooden table, bending the tines back against the grain.

"Oh my, you had a little accident there. Let me fix that for you." With a snap of Isaac's fingers, the fork was back in her hand, whole again. "Anyhow, Lars is in good shape. He will certainly walk again in the future. He just needs a couple weeks of rest to get him there. Corbin Walker, your brother has told me you have a request to make." Isaac turned his attention to the Falian and abruptly changed the subject, popping a marinated mushroom into his mouth.

"Thank you, milord. My people are in grave danger—" Corbin stopped when Isaac waved his hands in the air.

"Yes, yes, yes, I know. Logan has told me all about it. And Brilfillbipp, I am so sorry to hear of Ul'kor's plight. It truly saddens me to think about the fall of the center of gnome civilization. So off you go, then, Corbin, what's the request?" Isaac pointed his fork at the bewildered young man.

"That you help us save our people from the vile crystal Baetylus, milord," Corbin replied, speaking plainly. If the mage knew their predicament, how could there be a question as to what they might need?

"And how about you, Kalilah?" Isaac asked, turning his attention to the lizardwoman at the far end of the table, who practically choked on her fish at being addressed by the powerful spirit of the jungle. Tiko patted her back while she choked out the food and tried to rinse it down with water.

"Great spirit of our land, Tiko and Kalilah need nothing more than you wish to provide," Tiko answered for her, humbly bowing his head.

"I am *not* the spirit of the jungle or the land or milord or master or any other such nonsense. Honestly, you people. It's as if I'm speaking another language. I mean, I am speaking another language with the Agma, but you know what I mean, right, Eli?" The mage nudged his apprentice, who laughed, nodding. "My name is Isaac. Just Isaac."

"Are you not also the spirit of the jungle?" Nero inquired politely.

"Why is the robot man here? Does he even eat? He doesn't need food," Isaac asked Eli, then realized he had hurt the frogboy's feelings. "Not that it makes it any less important for you to be here," he quietly added to his apprentice. Corbin noticed Eli did not have any food in front of him.

"Isaac, no offense is intended, so please forgive me if this comes out the wrong way," Stur said, "but Nero is one of us. He has feelings just as much as any human...or gnome." He quickly added the last part in reaction to Bipp's raised brow.

"Yes, of course. I meant no offense," Isaac said. "Despicable things, these androids. I've had my fill of them for a lifetime, I have. But let me answer the tin man's question, as I do believe our Agma guests have a right to hear the response."

Tiko stared down the long table at the mage like a child about to learn the secrets of the universe.

"I *am* Isaac, not the spirit of the jungle, Isaacha, which is named after me. I am more like what you would call a guardian of the jungle— well, *the* guardian, actually. It is true that I have kept your people safe since creation, and it is true that the White Tree Isaacha cares deeply about your future. However, do not confuse me and it for the same thing," Isaac explained, holding a hand out toward the wall, which faded away, revealing the rich ivory branches beneath.

"Do you mean to say that the tree is some sort of jungle spirit?" Kyra asked.

"No. I don't *mean* to say it. I just did. Can't they hear me speaking, Eli?" Isaac was perplexed why they kept asking him questions he had already answered.

"What the Great and Powerful Isaac means to convey is that the White Tree does protect the jungle from outside evils. Yet without Isaac acting as the tree's guardian, life as we know it would not exist in this jungle today. The two have become one, where the one was broken," Eli tried to clarify, hoping his translation of the master's meaning was accurate.

"This is ridiculous," Kyra announced, pushing her untouched plate away and groaning.

"Why? What in the world could possibly be wrong with your food, lass?" Isaac asked in bewilderment. "Everyone else seems to be enjoying it. You're not a vegetarian, are you? Eli, I asked you to find out if they had any special dietary requirements! Is it the salt? It's hard to come by, you know. Maybe we put too much salt on it, Eli."

"What's a dietary requirement?" Bipp asked Logan from across the table, who just shrugged in return.

"That's not what I meant, and you know it!" Kyra shouted at the mage in frustration.

"Well, then, say exactly what you mean, woman," Isaac snapped right back at her.

"Isaac...once again, please do not take this the wrong way," Stur broke in. "I mean no disrespect, truly I do not. But when was the last time you actually interacted with other humans?"

Stur's question hung in the air. It was so plain to see, clear as day, that Corbin felt rather foolish for not picking up on it sooner.

The music gradually stopped, and Isaac stared at the ceiling, contemplating the nature of the question, dissecting the history of it, losing himself deep in thought, trying to grasp hold of the last time he had spoken to another living human. Blinking, he straightened and regarded his guests with a different manner altogether. Corbin felt the mage's presence fill the room as a twinkle entered his orange-flecked eyes, dancing in the candlelight from the center of the table. As he slowly took in the group, the mage settled his gaze back on Stur with focused determination, and the music resumed. However, instead of a ballad for the king's feast, it was slow and delicate, filling the air with melancholy.

"It has been far too long, good man. Far too long indeed. In fact, it seems ages since I last spoke to a real living being." Isaac's voice trailed off sorrowful, almost as if he were in mourning.

Kyra sat back stiffly in her seat, surprised by something. Corbin followed her line of sight and felt the same, realizing with astonishment that Eli had turned into a red clay statue. No, not turned—he always had been. The frog boy *was* a clay golem sitting on the chair, frozen in place, smiling at the group. He was eager to be part of the conversation but frozen, having turned inanimate.

"In fact, the last time I spoke with someone was back in New Fal," Isaac added, as if the surprising revelation of Eli's nature was not shocking enough for Corbin.

Color crept back across the frog's features as he became animate once more, and the little apprentice looked around, wondering why everyone was staring at him.

"So then you already know about the underworld land these men came from?" Kyra asked, receiving a curt nod in answer. "Isaac...do you know what happened to Port Wynd?"

"My dear girl...how does one ever forget the day the world crumbled?" Isaac replied sorrowfully, staring at the flickering light of the fireplace.

Corbin could not read him and pondered using his psychic talents to peer into the mage's mind.

"Best you not try that, lad, lest you be prepared for the horrors that await within." Isaac's turned to warn him, his tangerine eyes alive with swirling lights, gazing deep into Corbin's being. The mage had heard his thoughts! "Interesting that you have the sight. This is what we have been waiting for all these years." Isaac released Corbin from his penetrating gaze and changed the subject, as if it were of no importance. "Well, Kyra, I believe you had something you wanted to discuss?"

"I would have you tell me what happened to the kingdom of Agarta," she insisted.

"Your kingdom was burned to the ground, Lady Kyra," Isaac replied bluntly, casually sipping on his mug of mulled wine.

Kyra blanched, and the weapon master bristled in his seat at the callous delivery of such news. "B-but...s-surely someone..." Kyra began.

"When the mighty Citadels of Acadia tried to flee the planet, desperately hoping to escape the impending xenocide at the hands of the invading jotnar, they were all destroyed. The ice giants somehow knew about the plans mankind put in place and launched the most devastating attack Acadia has ever witnessed upon each base, laying waste to the twelve kingdoms in one fell swoop. The people of Agarta never had a chance after you abandoned them, Lady Tarvano. But don't let it keep you up at night. Had you stayed, surely none of you would be here today."

Kyra looked ready to murder the mage for his insensitivity, and Stur placed a hand over hers, daring to comfort the marshal. "Isaac, we can see that Port Wynd was destroyed. The very landscape has been altered from the explosion, according to our man Nero here." Isaac scowled at Nero but continued listening anyway. "What we need to know is if you have any insight into what happened that kept *our* Citadel from being harmed," Stur said.

"I was no more than a wee lad back then, but from what I have been able to garner over the years, I can tell you my theory on why your ship remained undetected. You see, the tree that I planted here ages ago protects the jungle from outside evils with very powerful magic from one of the nine ancient worlds. Powers so old, in fact, that they hail from a time and world we could not possibly remember. To the jotnar, flying overhead, this massive expanse of jungle is nothing more than miles of the wasteland leftover from when they ravished the land of Agarta with their foul sorcery. Whereas we see the land as it truly is, they see an elaborate illusion, so real to them they could even smell the acrid air of the desert." Isaac dispelled the illusion around the room, revealing the dizzying height at which they rested in the boughs of the White Tree and the canopy of the jungle beyond.

"What does this have to do with the citadel? I don't see what some magical tree has to do with anything," Kyra snapped at him. Corbin thought she was being unfair. She was acting as if Isaac were somehow to blame for her current plight.

"Well, that's the thing...as I have come to understand it, your vessel has a similar field around it. I can see the shield, which is at its core made from white magic, but have never found a way inside. Truly potent stuff, your wizards have there. I would love to know how it is done so I can try it out myself sometime."

Corbin noticed that the longer Isaac spoke, the more coherent and logical he was becoming.

"They sacrificed their eternal souls," Nero explained, meaning to help the mage with the knowledge he sought.

Isaac brooded on the idea of it. "Ah, blood magic. I see...that would do it. I think I'll pass on the trial and error learning method in this instance though, eh, Eli?" The mage and his apprentice shared a chuckle.

Kyra's fist slammed down on the table, rattling mugs and silverware against plates. "Those men gave their lives in sacrifice to their country! How dare you laugh at their expense?"

Isaac looked at her, dropping his mirth and replacing it with a look of disdain. As he stared at the group in silence, his shadow stretched across the wall behind him, growing in magnitude, and the fires of his eyes swirled with magical energy. "Do not speak to me of sacrifice, *princess*. Do not sit there and deign to judge that which you have no hope of comprehending. Instead of pouting like a mewling kitten, come out and say what you came here for." Without raising his voice, it somehow grew in power and intensity, cowing the Agma under the table in fear.

Kyra did not back down an inch, though her lip trembled in the face of the mage's power. "Tell us what you know of the existing jotnar threat."

"I will not." Isaac shrank back into himself. "Not when we have a lovely meal in front of us. For now we enjoy this moment. Tomorrow I will answer your questions, and you will hear my answers. Not a moment before."

Kyra's face was red with rage. She shook off Stur's hand, shoved her oak chair away from the table, and stalked haughtily out of the room, looking as if she could murder his pet griffin barehanded.

Logan could not help snickering to himself. For some reason he got a kick out of seeing Kyra throw her tantrum.

"You will please excuse me, gentlemen." Stur bowed to the group and gave chase.

"Was it something I said?" Isaac asked innocently enough.

"Master Isaac, will you tell us how to defeat the crystal and free our people?" Corbin blurted. He was beginning to doubt this man cared about any of their plights and could not contain himself any longer.

Isaac leaned down to speak with his apprentice privately. Though they were sitting at the same table, Corbin could not make out their words, which were muffled in an unnatural manner, indicating a spell was at work. When they were done, Isaac let out a long, drawn-out sigh and pointed a finger at Kyra's untouched plate of food, floating it over to Bipp. "We can discuss your options in the morning. For now, it is time to retire for the evening. It would seem my years of solitude have left me a bit rusty in the art of conversation. Also I fear I have troubled my dear Agma guests." Isaac rose to take his leave.

Tiko scurried from under the table to explain. "Oh no, mighty one, Tiko and Kalilah's reaction is not the fault of Master Isaac, but one of our own unworthiness."

Isaac did not respond but continued to walk away, upset with himself for not handling the situation better. As he left the room, Bipp called out his gratitude for the meal and lodging through a mouth stuffed with vegetables. Eli hopped down and began clearing the table.

Corbin looked at his brother. "What do you think?"

Logan shrugged. "I *think* we are at the mage's mercy. We have little choice but to wait until tomorrow and hope for an answer."

"I know you're right." Corbin hesitated for a moment. "It's just that we're so close, I can't imagine having to wait another night to find out what we need to do. Elise is down there all alone, fighting for our people..." Corbin muttered more to himself than Logan. "I'm going to head to my room to meditate. Are you coming?" He stood up, pushing his chair back in place against the table.

"Nah, you go on ahead. I'm gonna hang out here with Bipp a bit longer." Logan smiled, winking at his friend across the table, who was thoroughly enjoying shoveling the extra helping into his mouth.

Heading back to his room, Corbin found himself lost in thought, his mind playing out every scenario imaginable with Elise. He prayed that she was alive and safe, wishing he could speak to her at that moment. Not knowing was the worst part of it all.

The sound of whispering voices ahead caught his attention, distracting him from his thoughts. Without thinking, Corbin moved closer to the wall and slowed down, careful to not make a sound. It sounded like someone was having an argument. Leaning slightly around the corner, he could make out the conversation better.

"—doesn't make sense for us to trust him," Kyra said. She sounded a bit frantic.

"Lady Tarvano, we must believe that he is honorable," Stur said. "If the mage meant us harm, surely he would have unleashed his magical prowess upon us by now." Stur sounded as if he were trying to calm a frazzled cat that might bite his hand at any moment.

Kyra snorted. "You call those parlor tricks magic? Nothing but illusions, and minor ones at that, too. Filkinn, now there was a real wizard."

"Please, milady, do not say such things. I am sure the mage can hear your every word," Stur urged.

Even though Corbin knew he was referring to Isaac, his face flushed at the realization he too was eavesdropping on his friends. A feeling of shame washed over him and he moved to reveal himself but stopped at Kyra's next words.

"They can never find out."

"You worry too much, Your Grace. The Walker brothers and Bipp have proven themselves to be honorable men. We have to trust *someone*," Stur countered.

"I said no. I wish you would stop bringing it up," Kyra hissed, raising her voice above a whisper. Corbin could hear Stur shuffling under the berating. "I am sorry, Stur. I did not mean to snap at you so...after all you have done for me and the kingdom. It is just that I am scared. I mean, you say these things so matter-of-factly, but how do we really know this isn't an elaborate ruse to trap us?" Kyra whispered.

"Milady, if this were a trap, I do believe we would have been ensnared already." Stur hoped she would see reason and let go of these irrational fears that were eating away at her from the inside.

"And if it isn't?" Kyra slowly asked.

"Then I will kill them all. One by one, I will cut them down in the name of Kyra Tarvano, Queen of Agarta, last hope for humanity," Stur vowed with steely conviction.

Corbin gulped, letting his voulge slip from his hands and catching it only inches from the stone floor. He sighed at how close he had come to being found out and suddenly felt even guiltier for spying.

"What was that?" Kyra hissed, grabbing Stur's forearm and pushing him toward the corner of the hallway. The weapon master growled, pulling a thick glass dagger from the folds of his vest, and moved to catch their spy.

Corbin leaned back against the wall, his heart beating so hard he could hear it in his ears. How would he explain this to them? How could he possibly justify listening in on their private conversation? What if Stur attacked him anyhow? What could he possibly hope to do against the seasoned warrior?

"Better to just show yourself and spare us the trouble of chasing you down, dog," Stur ordered, rounding the corner ready to pounce. Kyra tried to move past him, pulling the ridiculous dress she was forced to wear for dinner up around her knees.

Stur straightened, relaxing his shoulders and sheathing the small blade.

"What's going on? Who is it?" she asked, seeing the calm look on his face, and ducked under Stur's elbow to see an empty hallway.

"Could have been anything in this tree. The place is magical, after all." Stur shrugged and guided her back to her room.

They said goodnight, and Kyra mentioned that in the future they should hold these discussions in her chamber, to which Stur blanched and stuttered that it would be inappropriate.

Doors shut one after the other and Corbin finally let out the air in his lungs, dropping to the floor from his spread-eagle perch against the ceiling. He had been using every ounce of strength to hold his body in place, pressed against the high ceiling of the hallway to keep out of sight. Quickly making his way past the Acadians' closed doors, he slammed his own shut, leaning heavily onto it and panting. Corbin knew he could not make sense of all he had heard, but one thing kept ringing in his head.

Kyra Tarvano is a queen?

Logan opened the door of his bedchamber to find a small creature standing in the hall, looking up at him. *Must be another one of them golems,* he thought, studying the strange creature. It had a round, bald head, beady black eyes, and wore overalls loosely strapped above long wavy arms and legs that ended in round nubs, like an octopus without the suction cups, all with waxy white skin.

Without saying a word, the strange golem turned away and headed down the hall. Shaking his head, Logan started to close the door again so he could lay back down for a bit longer, but was stopped firmly by one the creature's *feet.* The little bugger was fast! He had not even seen it come back.

"What do you want?" he asked, annoyed.

Instead of answering, it waved him on, its arms moving like some out of control snake.

Logan rolled his eyes. "You want me to follow you? Geez, why didn't you just say so?"

It was no use speaking to it, as it did not have a mouth from which to respond. Closing the door behind him, Logan followed it down the hallway toward Isaac's inner sanctum. *The wizard can make a flying pet lion, but his messenger doesn't speak. Yeah, cause that makes sense.* The white blobby thing shifted past the slumbering griffin and curled an arm to turn the iron door handle, letting him in.

All of his companions were waiting inside the room, staring at Logan as he entered. Kyra was seated on Stur's lap, Bipp was talking with the Agma, and Isaac was busy at work mixing a potion, his back to the group.

"It's about time you woke up," Kyra said.

Logan shared a look of mischief with Stur, who did his best not to let his smirk show in front of the marshal.

"First time I got some shut eye in a real bed for months. We don't all have the luxury of sleeping in glass tubes for centuries," Logan teased, plopping himself down in a chair and kicking his feet up onto a nearby table.

Kyra looked alarmed at his admission, darting around to see if Isaac had heard. The mage turned slowly to face them, wearing a smile that stretched from ear to ear.

Logan fell backwards in his chair, terrified to see the mage was not Isaac but the spitting image of an assassin he had seen only one other time in his life. Instead of the wizard they had been fooled into believing was Isaac, standing before him was the cold-blooded killer who had murdered one of his only friends, the goodly gnome Mr. Beauford.

"You bastard! What are you doing here?" he challenged the assassin, reaching for his sword. Panic flashed across his ribs like a tickle of lightning as he remembered he had lost his weapon battling the dire wolf.

"Have you lost your wits?" Stur demanded, standing up and pushing Kyra behind him.

The assassin grinned and walked backwards into the shadows, slowly raising his hand to point at Logan and laugh incessantly. His skin became as black as the shadows until all Logan could see were those taunting eyes.

Logan picked up his chair and hurled it across the room at the murderer, the wood shattering against the stone wall, catching nothing but open air.

"What is this madness? Why can't you ever stay out of trouble?" Corbin scolded from the doorway, his voice filled with contempt.

"C-Corbin...I—" Logan tried to explain, but he could not find the words. All eyes were on him, swimming with disappointment. Even Bipp, his only real friend in the world, stood with arms folded, tapping a boot and frowning.

"I knew we should have left you out there to rot," Corbin said. "You're nothing but a waste of air!" He spat on the floor by his feet, crushing Logan's heart with a mightier wound than any sword could produce.

"B-Brother, please...d-don't say such things. I'm sorry! It wasn't my fault." Logan crumpled to his knees, choking on the thickening air around him.

"The hell it wasn't. She would still be here with us if it wasn't for you!" Corbin shouted only inches from his face.

"Kyra is still here. Tell him, Stur. She's right there!" He tried to point behind the massive weapon master, who frowned down at him with open disdain.

Kyra moved Stur out the way, except it was not her anymore. Instead, his mother stood in her place, staring at him with eyes that were the very embodiment of hatred and disgust. She moved forward one crooked step at a time, pointing at her son and cackling. Logan clutched his face in terror, trying to pull the skin off as he screamed. No matter how hard or how loud he denied her, no words would come out of his choking throat, and his mother's legs broke off, revealing the body of a snake.

Corbin grabbed him roughly by the shoulders, holding his body in place for their mother and whispering softly in his ear. "Momma's going to teach you how to behave this time, but I still wish you were never even born at all."

His voice was icy cold, and the words stabbed at Logan's heart. Melinda's face split apart like a popped grape, tearing back like curled paper, and her jaws stretched open, revealing fangs and a slithering tongue that extended to wrap itself around Logan's throat.

"Say hello to mother, Logan!" Corbin diabolically laughed, joined by everyone else in the room, and stood above him while his mother cocked her head back and then snapped her wide jaws forward to eat his face.

Corbin thrashed violently, kicking the blade-tipped polearm leaning against the end of his bed to the floor. The sound of it clattering across the floor pulled him sharply from the nightmare. His sweat had soaked right into the bed, and damp hair clung to his face.

What the hell kind of messed up dream was that? he wildly wondered, sitting up. His heart still beat as fast as if he had just run a marathon. The stone floor was cold on his bare feet, and the skin on his arms was riddled with goosebumps. Grabbing a handful of water from the basin on his nightstand, he splashed his eyes and cooled his feverish forehead, working to rinse the salty sweat from his face.

As Corbin dressed for the day, he could not shake the feeling of the dream. It had felt so genuine and powerful. It was so vivid, in fact, that he actually felt guilt replaying the cruel words his dream-self had said to his older brother. He did not hate Logan. Far from it; if anything he always felt the opposite, that Logan had no time or patience for him. All through his youth, he longed for the sort of relationship other siblings in their village shared, but most of the time Logan never seemed to want him around.

He could not help trying to figure out some deeper meaning in the dream, but a rapping at his door shook him out of the reverie. "Come in," Corbin called.

The door creaked open, and the frog boy Elijah hopped inside, wearing blue overalls and a purple bandana. There were small flecks of yellow paint on his clothing. "Good morning, sir. I hope you had a good rest!" he announced in especially cheerful spirits.

"Oh yes, very much so," Corbin lied. "Please thank your Master Isaac for his hospitality for me." Corbin pulled a shirt over his head.

"Great to hear it, sir. There's nothing finer than a happy guest! Anyhow, the Master awaits your fine company on this most excellent morning, so you will have an opportunity to thank him yourself." Elijah gave him an exaggerated thumbs-up with his frog thumb, winked, and then hopped back to the doorway. "If you will just follow me…"

"Sure, no problem. Let me just grab my brother before we head over," Corbin said, following him out into the hallway.

"No need for that, sir. One of the jellyfish has already escorted him there!" Elijah exclaimed, leading the way down the curving hall.

When they rounded the corner to Isaac's inner-sanctum, a waxy creature just like the one Corbin had dreamt about walked by, looking up at the passersby. Goosebumps crawled across his skin again at the sight of its beady eyes.

"Oh, don't mind him, Master Corbin. The jellyfish are odd but also quite harmless, to be sure. Watch out now, Shedu, let us by." Eli gently waved the griffin out of their path, throwing Corbin a sly look. "Though I often wonder if they think, you know, the way I do? Don't say nothing, but I always thought it funny that Master Isaac could make a flying lion but he can't be bothered to give my helpers the ability to speak." Elijah chuckled, opening the door for him.

Corbin skirted past the frogboy, his head tingling from the sense of déjà vu. All the companions sat waiting inside the solar. Kyra had her arms folded as she leaned against the wall by Isaac's stained-glass window, and Stur sat beside her with Nero, leaning his heavy muscular frame forward and resting his arms on knees. Bipp was conversing with the Agma, and Logan sat back with his hands behind his head, feet kicked up on a nearby table, wearing a devilish grin. Based on the look splayed across Kyra's face, Corbin assumed his brother had just made some wisecrack she did not approve of.

"Good morning, I hope everyone got some decent rest," Corbin said, clearing his dry throat.

"Oh, it was as good as if the seven muses had come down and showered me in kisses," Bipp merrily proclaimed.

Logan laughed half-heartedly, though he did not say anything, staring expectedly at Isaac's back across the room, where the mage was working studiously with some glass beakers to concoct a potion. When the mage suddenly turned, Corbin noticed his brother flinch slightly and then let his shoulders slump in relief.

Corbin followed his gaze to the mage, half expecting Isaac to have changed into the assassin from his dream. He felt more than a little relieved himself to see the warm, slightly awkward, smile that Isaac wore as he took in the group.

Elijah hopped to his master's side and clapped his wet amphibian hands together gathering their attention. "Most esteemed guests of the White Tree, if I may have your attention? The Great and Powerful Isaac is ready to receive you."

The small room fell quiet as all eyes rested on the mage. Isaac carefully set down the potion he was working on and leaned forward on his tall staff. "I have given great deliberation to our conversation over dinner last night, and it is time we discussed your questions. Kyra, the world of Acadia is not the same land you once knew. The Jotnar Empire rules here with no equal. You will, of course, accompany me to the nearest city, where I have much work to do, and there you can complete your scouting expedition."

Kyra shuffled uncomfortably. She was expecting the mage to continue being obtuse and was thrown off by his forthright speech. Stur nodded, glad to have the mage's assistance in completing their mission.

"And what of New Fal, milord?" Corbin interrupted. "Will you tell me how to save my people?" He leaned forward over the back of his brother's armchair.

"No. I will not," Isaac replied, throwing them off. "You too will accompany me to Belikar, where you will aid in my mission to infiltrate the city using your psionic talents."

Corbin shook his head, denying the mage with a mounting frustration. "Absolutely not. You cannot expect me to just turn my back on the people of Riverbell, who are surely this very minute fighting for their lives against forces they cannot possibly hope to overcome, so that I might go gallivanting across the expanses of Acadia at the whim of some mad mage!"

Logan stood and patted his brother's shoulder, trying to calm him down.

"Oh, but I *do* expect it," Isaac said, "and it *will* be as I say. Your Falian family has been on the run for a couple weeks now at best. While I, on the other hand, have been awaiting your arrival for over a century and a half. Can you even comprehend what it means to watch as one unspeakable atrocity after another unfolds, helpless to act, for that length of time?" Isaac calmly asked him.

"Get off it, wizard. No one lives for that long." Logan waved away the mage's nonsensical claims and whispered for his brother to relax.

"Oh? So then Kyra and her men were not alive over two centuries ago?" Isaac asked, arching one eyebrow and directing his gaze at the Acadians.

"You know that's not what I meant." Logan replied, tilting his head and frowning thoughtfully despite himself.

"And your council of Twelve...are you going to tell me the Elders are not centuries old as well?" Isaac prompted.

Logan could not answer and looked to his younger brother for guidance.

Corbin stared at the strange mage, filled with curiosity at his claim. "Are you saying Elder Zacharia and the Council of Twelve, the rulers of New Fal, are actually over a century old?" he asked doubtfully.

"No. I am not saying anything of the sort. They are actually over *two* centuries old." Isaac coyly ticked his staff in the air, counting invisible numbers.

"But how can that be?" Logan asked. "The average age for a Falian is early fifties at best." He found himself unable to believe the preposterous claim. Logan thought it more likely the old windbag had lost his marbles living alone in the White Tree all these years.

"Well, that is interesting now, isn't it? We can discuss this further *after* our travels. For now, it is best if we prepare ourselves for the journey ahead."

"Isaac, milord—" Corbin began.

"Just Isaac." The mage turned to straighten the bottles of elixir he had just mixed, topping each with wax seals.

"Fine, *just Isaac*...we cannot travel with you to Belikar. My brother and I have wasted enough time nipping at Kyra's heels, hoping to meet you. Now that we have met you and it is clear you mean to offer us no means of support, it is time we take our leave and head back to Vanidriell to aid our people," Corbin said with a heavy heart.

Isaac looked over his shoulder, still busy gathering herbs and powders for the trip. "Oh no no no, my dear lad, you have it all wrong. I mean to offer you more than support, for I will be traveling to Fal with you so that I may personally assist in overthrowing the evil in that cursed kingdom."

Bipp snapped his fingers and whistled. With the mage on their side, the scales of power would shift considerably, giving them the advantage they sorely needed to go toe to toe with the corrupt Magistrate Fafnir and false god Baetylus.

"But you just said..." Corbin fumbled, while Logan slowly folded his arms and leaned back against the wall, regarding the mage in a different light.

Isaac motioned for Elijah, and the frog boy started packing his alchemical supplies in a small leather satchel that looked far too small to hold all the items. Turning to face the room once more, Isaac raised both hands level with his chest, swirling his ivory wooden staff around in the air to create a shimmering liquid dweomer. At the center of the magical pool, a scene painted itself, etching across the liquid with vivid clarity. The painting began to move, animated by his magic.

"Almost four centuries ago, mankind ruled the lands of our world in peace, living side by side with the other races of Acadia. Our world was filled with a blessed light from the grace of the gods who bestowed life upon us. Great kingdoms were erected during that time."

An image of a shimmering silver city floating high in the sky played across the dweomer, where humans, gnomes, gnolls, and bullywogs were going about their everyday business in merriment. Swiftly the scene faded to a dull grey, and the clouds gathered overhead, crackling with lightning and casting a pall over the grand city.

"But alas, this peace was not to be everlasting, for out of the shining light inevitably came the darkness, creeping like a shadow across the land. Some of the races of Acadia became ever more possessive. Their lives were not filled with enough to sate a slavering hunger growing in their ranks. They demanded more. Once the fruit begins to rot from the inside, it is not long before the maggots come a-calling. It begins to fall apart and lose its luster."

The city was abandoned, and the races of Acadia went their separate ways, erecting new kingdoms on the ground and abandoning the grace of the floating cities.

"The gnomes had their fill of this vile hatred early on and turned their backs on the other races, finding a home in the core of our planet, in the lands of Vanidriell, where they continued a life of peace and harmony with the world around them. While humanity, in all its cancerous conflicted treachery, raped the lands of their beauty so that they could erect empire after empire, claiming their sole right to rule the planet."

The skies of the floating dweomer filled with murky smog above each great kingdom, which began as a main castle at first then sprawled across the lands, burning down trees and scorching the landscape in its almost living growth.

"The wars began between two of the most powerful empires. No one remembers why. It could just as easily have been an argument over some moral stance as a fundamental disagreement over the color blue. Who knows? Either way, this set off a chain reaction which put our world into a war that raged for generations."

Across the dweomer, men and women were meeting on the battlefield to lock swords in a bloody conflict. Soon the swords were replaced with rifles. This turned into massive machines that rained unimaginable destruction. Children ran drills in camps, being raised as cookie-cutter soldiers.

"Mankind lost its way, falling from the grace of the gods. And then one day...the jotnar appeared."

The scene of carnage shifted to sands whipping around a desert plain. An army of humanoids marched through the dusty dunes, taller than an average Acadian man by a good two feet, with blue-grey skin and lustrous black hair which only hinted at being navy blue when the light hit it. Their silver eyes were offset by the glint of their sharp incisors. The muscular warriors carried all manner of weaponry, none of which were technological. They wore black steel armor, ready for the battle ahead.

"The jotnar found Acadia, though none know how or why. And once they were here, they began systematically destroying mankind. One by one, the greatest empires were taken over by this new race of blue-skinned ice giants. With a declaration, they claimed Acadia as their new home and gave all who lived here one, and only one, chance to lay down arms and swear fealty. The gnolls were the first to bend to their will. But mankind in its foolish pride would kneel before no one. And so the jotnar went about wiping humans from the planet in what many believed would be a massive xenocide."

The flowing dweomer shifted, and Citadels not unlike Kyra's ship were blasted from the sky by floating fortresses with ancient mystical weapons. Cities burned, and people were slaughtered. Their legacy was snuffed out like candlelight under the jotnar's falling fist of black steel. The dweomer melted in the air, disappearing back inside Isaac's staff, as he leveled his gaze at his engrossed audience.

"It has now been almost one and a half centuries since I first witnessed that Jotnar Invasion. That is how long I have waited for some glimmer of hope to infiltrate Belikar and fulfill my lifelong quest. So when I say I will assist you, know that I mean it in every sense of the word. However, that assistance will *not* be given until after we have seen my task through to the end. Besides, is there not some part of you that wishes to see what has become of the human race?" Isaac finished.

"Wait...I thought you said the humans were wiped out by the jotnar?" Bipp asked the mage, breaking the palpable tension that had settled in the room.

"So most thought when the Jotnar Invasion came, but the ice giants are ever the pragmatic devils. You will come with me and see for yourself what has befallen our people, no?" Isaac leaned on his tall staff, waiting for their answer.

Corbin felt as if his insides were twisted into knots, and he could feel an aching lump in his upper back, where the weight of this decision rested. How could he turn his back on New Fal to set out on this man's quest? Then again, how could he turn his back on such an immensely powerful ally to their cause? Judging by the grim look on Logan's face, he could see there was no choice left to them.

He leveled his gaze at Isaac, looking the mage square in the eyes before begrudgingly giving his answer. "We will accompany you on your quest. But only at your word that you will provide us the assistance we need when this is over and help save our people."

"You have my word on the honor of the White Tree." Isaac bowed.

Kyra smiled, happy to have the brothers joining them. Everyone began speaking again, and Nero prattled on in his android way about this being the wisest course. But Isaac did not join in their merriment, continuing to meet Corbin's gaze. He could see the weight of his decision was not lost on the mage, and could only hope that it was the right path.

Logan moved forward and patted Corbin's back, speaking low enough so none but Bipp and Corbin could hear. "And so we are set on the road ahead. I only pray we are making the right decision and that the people of Riverbell can stay safe long enough for us to get back and save them."

Corbin nodded, his mind drifting to thoughts of Elise and hoping much the same.

Chapter 7: Training Grounds

"I still don't feel that this is appropriate," Bertha said for perhaps the hundredth time, reluctantly handing over the bundle of garments to Elise.

Elise ignored the woman's protests and took the clothing behind a thick tree to get changed. As soon as Elise, Rimball, and Rygor returned from their expedition to the hills overlooking Riverbell, she had ordered Bertha to find her some clothes better suited for traveling. Bertha thought she meant a new skirt, since Elise's was torn. When Elise corrected her, insisting Bertha procure some form of trousers, the woman's bosom swelled so high, Elise worried Bertha might suffocate herself.

Bertha had given Elise a serious piece of her mind, saying it was not fit for the leader of their village to be prancing about dressed as a man. But Elise refused to put another able-bodied hunter, of which there were few left, in harm's way and was not about to go traipsing around the hills again wearing a dress. It had been hard enough traveling back to the caves, and she had no intention of slowing down their progress to Dure.

Bertha stared at her, mouth agape, as Elise stepped out from behind the tree in brown wool breeches and a plain grey tunic tied around the waist with a leather belt. The clothes had come from a young lad named Todd, who was barely twelve years old but tall for his age. Even though Todd was a young boy, the garments were still a size too big on Elise's small frame, but she made due, rolling up the bottom of the pant legs and sleeves.

Elise tied her blonde hair back in a bun. Since leaving Riverbell, it looked like a wild bird's nest. She fastened her father's dagger onto the belt and looked up at Bertha.

"By the All-Father..." Bertha gasped.

"You like it?" Elise teased, twirling for the heavy-set woman, who looked fit to pass out. Elise laughed at Bertha's response as Rimball made his way over to them.

"Everything is prepared, milady," he said. Rimball had his bo staff in hand and a short bow slung over his shoulder. The hunter had gathered a small pack of belongings and tied it across his back. He was ready to go, as should have been most of the villagers by that point.

The moment they had returned, Elise had spread the word that they needed to head for the forests outside the nearby town of Dure, putting good distance between themselves and Fafnir's men. She,

Rimball, and Rygor had kept word of what they had seen back in Riverbell relatively quiet, not wanting to panic the villagers.

It took half the day to prepare everyone for travel. There were still a great deal of injured folk from the skex attack traveling with them, and it would be slow going once they set out. Luckily, they had a good lead on Fafnir's men, thanks largely to Cassandra's magic.

"Rimball, let the people know we are ready to head out," Elise said.

Leaving the Monkton hills, the people of Riverbell travelled east with little opportunity to rest. It took a couple days to reach the forests that skirted the Gratuntite mountain range. Once in the forests, the remaining hunters of Riverbell made short work of finding their people a safe path to take. No one knew these woods better than the folk who lived nearby. Good luck to Fafnir's men trying to find them in these woods. They'd have better odds at finding a nugget of gold in Lake Ul'Toh.

Once everyone was safely camped, Elise began gathering up a small group of villagers to make the supply run to Dure.

"Are you sure it's safe to travel there, lass?" Gunter asked. Elise's father was a large man, towering over most of the other villagers, with broad shoulders and an even broader smile. Widely respected among the villagers, Gunter was all the family Elise had left. He had been sorely wounded during the skex attack and had been practically bedridden since. It took two men to pull his makeshift gurney, and Gunter was finally regaining enough strength to move about on his own, feebly supporting his weight on a y-angled oak branch he tucked under his armpit.

"You can't worry about me now, Da," Elise said, tightening the straps of her boots. "I'm not just your little girl anymore. I'm the village Elder, and it's my responsibility to keep everyone safe."

Gunter knew all of that and did not need reminding. "Ah, you could be the Queen of the Valkyries, and you'd still be my baby girl."

Elise stopped in front of him, taking hold of her father's forearm and reaching up to give him a peck on the cheek. His stubbly beard tickled her skin, reminding her of being a small girl and resting in his strong arms. "I know that, Da, I do."

Gunter smiled down at his daughter.

"You've just got to trust me on this."

He nodded, and Bertha helped him sit on a small cot beside his tent.

"She's got some sass, that daughter of yours." Bertha said with her hands on her hips, watching Elise make her way out of the camp with some of the hunters.

"Aye," Gunter replied. "I just feel so helpless stuck here while my little girl is out there where the magistrate's men might be about."

Bertha rubbed his aching shoulder. "Don't you be doubting. Elder Morgana knew exactly what she was doing, picking that one to be her successor. The girl's got fire in her heart and a head as hard as her father's."

Gunter could only hope Bertha was right.

Elise translated Rimball's grunt, holding up her clenched fist to signal the rest of their party to halt. Rygor slipped past the three villagers they had brought along on this journey. Several of the older folk had insisted she take more hunters with her, but Elise did not dare leave the camp defenseless. Not after what she saw back in the Monkton Hills. Perhaps Rimball was correct and there truly was nothing she could have done for those murdered villagers, but Elise would be damned if she put the rest of their people in the same position.

They had come down from the mountains around Mount Gruntuntite, making their way to Dure by cutting through the forest and bypassing the trade road. Elise did not need Rimball or anyone else to advise her that the roads were not safe. No doubt Fafnir's men were patrolling them for some sign of the missing villagers.

At the edge of the woods they came to the some farmland. Rimball was surveying the area for any signs of trouble before they headed out.

"Does he see anything?" Rygor asked, nervously shifting his eyes over the rows of maize. Nothing stirred in the field.

Rimball shot Elise a knowing look. She was beginning to be able to read the hunter's vague expressions. To most people, the man had one look: cold, dry, and wrinkled. But Elise knew better. It was very subtle, the way Rimball chose to communicate, pinching his eyes or pointing one finger at his ribs and circling it. He seemed to have a silent gesture for almost any situation.

Elise nodded and waved for the hunters to follow, though two of them were already on the move, having been tutored directly under Rimball as children.

Once in the fields, it was impossible to see over the tall stalks of maize that grew well past their heads, angling toward the hazy tangerine daylight of the great crystal floating close to the cavern ceiling in the north.

One of the hunters, Erik, reached out to tear off an ear of maize, but Elise caught him by the wrist. Erik was the same age as her and had grown up right alongside Corbin. "This is not ours to take," she said.

Erik tugged his hand away, scowling at her. "I'm hungry."

Elise shook her head. The rest of the party stopped, waiting for them to catch up. "We are all hungry, but that doesn't give you, or any of us, the right to steal the property of our neighbors."

"I ain't taking my orders from no damned girl." Erik turned his back on Elise and moved to take the ear of maize.

Elise wanted to scream at the big-headed dope that she was not some silly child. She was the new elder for Riverbell, and he should be listening to her without question. But Morgana had taught her better than that. To make such a proclamation would only make her appear weak.

"Rimball," Elise called.

The older hunter was at her side fast as wind.

"Erik here thinks that since we are all in grave danger, he can do as he pleases," Elise said. Erik had stopped moving and was nervously eyeing Rimball, who glowered at him. "Hold him down so I can show the fool of a boy what happens to villagers who break our laws."

Rimball moved forward, and Erik hopped back, holding his hands up in defeat.

"No need for that," Erik insisted. "I didn't even take nothing, honest."

Rimball stopped mid-step, satisfied with the young man's acquiescence.

"I do *not* make idle threats," she said.

"I understand, Elise," Erik replied, nodding emphatically.

"It's clear you are hungry, as we all are," Elise said, "but I will not tolerate my people resorting to petty crime. We cannot justify our crimes on the backs of those Fafnir brings to our table."

Erik nodded again, moving to walk away, but Elise stopped him with an upraised palm in his face.

"Where are you going?"

"I just...we said..." Erik stuttered.

Elise was happy to see the wind taken out of his arrogance. This was a good beginning. "What would Elder Morgana have done, had you spoken to her and behaved in such a way?"

Erik looked like a wilted flower, his head stooping low as he cringed. When he did not answer, Elise raised an eyebrow, prompting him to speak.

"Please, Elise, I—"

"You'll not have it any different from me, Erik," Elise said. "If you want act like a hotshot, steal maize from our neighbor, then tell me to mind my own business, you know what the price is."

Erik bit his lip and got down on his knees, ready for the caning he would have surely received from Elder Morgana for thievery.

Elise pulled up her gaze, making eye contact with each of the men in turn as she walked around the kneeling hunter. She pulled a thin reed from her belt and tested it out, swishing the plant in the air twice. It whistled with a humming sound.

"Put out your hand," Elise said.

Confused, Erik put out his right hand. The reed whistled once through the air, snapping over his knuckles. The damned thing stung hot and painful.

"Now get up and let's go," Elise said, moving past the prone hunter toward the town. "We have too much to do to waste time with your tantrums."

"T-that's it?" Erik asked.

Elise stopped on the spot and twirled to face him. Her face remained impassive, and she slapped the reed in her open palm. "Unless you feel it was not enough?" She raised an eyebrow.

Erik shook his head gratefully and hopped to his feet, thanking Elder Elise for her mercy and promising he would not try to steal anything ever again.

She moved to the front of the group with Rimball at her side. As they made their way through the rows of maize, Rimball spoke to her quietly out of the corner of his mouth. "You're a fast learner."

The compliment startled her, especially coming from the sensei who was infamously strict with his students. "I would not call twenty years of daily tutelage under Morgana *fast*," Elise said, "but thank you all the same."

If Elise did not know any better she might think her response made Rimball smirk.

As they neared the middle of the maize field, Rimball motioned for Elise to get ready. Someone was approaching.

The tall stalks gave way as a farmer made his way through the field on the back of a farming mole that looked rather bored. The man held a pitchfork at the ready. When he saw the group, he pulled his head back, blinking at them as if they were ghosts.

"Ho there, Jonathon," Rimball said, leaning on his bo staff and giving the man one firm wave.

"Well, bless my heart," Farmer Jon said, "if it isn't Rimball the Swift himself?" Farmer Jon was beaming. He pulled the reins to stop his mole and hopped off the saddle, spitting to the side as he did so.

Rimball moved forward and locked forearms with the man to greet him properly. "It is good to see you, old friend."

"Yes, and a damn sight unexpected at that, too." Jon shook his head, backing up to slam the pitchfork into the dirt. "Thought you was some more of them centipedes got into my crop again. Was going to stick ye through!"

Both Jon and Rimball laughed while the rest of the group stood by, silently watching the strange farmer.

"Are the magistrate's men around town?" Elise asked, breaking into their conversation.

Farmer Jon's laughter sputtered out, and he grew still, taking in the group with a grave expression. His lower lip bulged where he had tucked a rolled up buckleaf into it. Jon spit to the side again and rubbed his thick moustache, trying to find the right words. "Aye, they come and then they gone, and then they just come on over again."

That was not good news for Elise. "So the town knows we have been exiled?"

Jon scrunched up his face and twitched his moustache like a mouse. He shrugged and looked at Rimball. "Since when are you dragging girls through the woods?"

The hunter was quick to reply before Elise got her fires burning again. "Jon, this is Elder Elise Ivarone."

The farmer's eyes grew wide under his bushy red eyebrows, and he swiped the hat off the top of his head so fast that Elise thought he might be fit to eat it. "Beggin' your pardon, Elder Elise." Jon gulped, wringing the floppy straw hat in his hands. "I had no idea that was you. I mean, last time I saw ye girl, ye was just a wee lass, no bigger than a pot-bellied piglet bouncing on yer daddy's lap."

Elise saw Rygor roll his eyes and groan, thinking the farmer was in for it now. But she laughed. There was something oddly charming about Jon, though she was sure it was not the ring of frayed red hair that circled his bald head.

"No need for any of that, dear man." Elise gave Jon a slight bow in thanks for his greeting all the same. "But we would be interested to hear more about the magistrate's men before we head into town to speak with Elder Daniel."

Jon plopped the hat back on his head and looked between her and Rimball. "Don't think that'd be such a good idea just now, milady. Magistrate Fafnir has his men scouring the whole countryside looking for you folk. And to hear it told what happened down there in your village, we got a whole lot round here scared out of their wits. No, people are keeping an eye out for you. Might be best if you just head on back to wherever y'all are hiding out and lay low for a while longer."

Rimball grunted, squinting toward the town as if he could see lurking enemies in every shadow.

"Be that as it may," Elise said, "I'm afraid we've little choice but to speak with Elder Daniel about getting some supplies."

"Well, it's your perogative, Elder," Farmer Jon said. "Just you be careful in there. Ain't no place to hide if the lawmen come back into town looking for ye."

Elise nodded and motioned for Rimball to lead the way. The hunter bid his friend farewell, and they cut across the field in the direction Farmer Jon said would bring them right to the Elder's home in the center of the town.

Dure was a farming town, known throughout the kingdom for its quality livestock and produce. It was about twice the size of Riverbell with maybe three times more residents. Everyone worked the land together. They had a motto in Dure, "The farmer lives together by dawn or dies alone in the dusk." Elise had not understood it when she was younger, so Elder Morgana had to flesh it out.

"In Dure, they believe nothing matters more than a good day's hard work. No one owns a single crop, and the fields belong to everyone. As long as they are working together, the people of Dure are content."

Elise hoped that philosophy on life extended to helping out their neighbors in their hour of need.

She and the other Riverbell villagers were huddled on the edge of the maize fields, overlooking the dirt paths and stone buildings that made up the town. When Elise was a teen she visited the town with Elder Morgana to discuss trade agreements with Elder Daniel. At the time, Elise was in awe of Dure, thinking it quite grand with its fancy stone houses and carved out streets. The fountain sitting in the middle of town, where a natural reservoir flowed from the Naga River, was the most intricately detailed thing of beauty she had ever witnessed. But now, having been to the capitol city and seen what true grandeur meant, Dure did not seem as impressive to her somehow.

"I don't see any soldiers," Elise said.

Rimball carefully scanned the town streets, looking for any sign of ambush. The only people on the streets were residents of Dure going about their daily business. Rimball shook his head and moved out into the town without a word.

Elise motioned for Rygor and Erik to join them, but told the other two hunters to stay behind just in case. "Jimmy, if we don't return after two hours, get yourself back to the camp and move everyone eastward."

Jameson nodded, crouching down between the stalks.

Walking through town, Elise felt many eyes burning into her. Rimball held his head high, refusing to acknowledge the farmers openly gawking at them and muttering. Elise heard snippets of gossip as they passed the townsfolk. The words *exile*, *traitors*, and *doomed* came up more than once. She raised her head high in the air, ignoring the whispers.

As they came to Elder Daniel's home, a boy was just leaving the building. He took one look at their party and ran up the street away from them.

"Looks like Elder Daniel has already been informed of our arrival," Elise guessed.

Rygor was too busy looking down every street they walked past to respond, and Erik was probably too scared to speak. Rimball just grunted. Elise thought this was a fine lot fate had paired her with. They were just coming up the walkway when Elder Daniel's front door creaked open, spilling candlelight onto the front steps. Three of the townsfolk came out, but Elise noted Daniel was not among them.

"We have come to speak with Elder Daniel," she said.

One of the men gave her a polite bow. "I am sorry Madame Elise, but the Elder is not currently available."

Elise frowned. "You mean to say he does not want to be available, or that he is currently tied up in matters more important than the murder of my entire village?"

The man looked outraged at her proclamation, backing up until he hit the closed door.

A short woman, perhaps ten years older than Elise, put her hands together as if she were about to pray, then clasped her fingers instead. "Please, Elder Elise," she said, "you must understand the position your arrival puts us in."

It took Elise a few moments to recognize the grey-haired woman as Elder Daniel's wife, Elizabeth. "Madame, we do not come here to bring ill omens and carry our burdens to your husband's doorstep," Elise said. "We are only in search of supplies."

"Nevertheless, your very presence here puts our entire town in danger," Elizabeth countered without raising her voice in the slightest.

"Should we be foolhardy enough to offer you people assistance, just think what the Council of Elders would do to us. No, you must leave our town now, before rumors begin to spread that we are in collusion with your plots and deception."

"How can you believe that we would have any part in a plot to overthrow Fal?" Elise asked.

"This is what the Elders have spoken, and so it is true." Elizabeth firmly shook her head.

"Just as the magistrate would have it," Elise tried to explain. "This was never about a plot to overthrow Fal. It has always and ever been about that corrupt man's lust for power!" Elise's face was turning red, and her chest was heaving uncontrollably. She was worked up into a fervor and felt as if she might explode. Somewhere in the back of her mind, she wondered how Elder Morgana would have handled this situation. How would she have stopped her hands from trembling as Elise's now did?

Gathering her composure in the face of the impassive woman who stood between her and the Elder of Dure, Elise tried to start over. "I apologize. You understand I have a great deal to worry about at the moment."

Elizabeth bowed her head, acknowledging the weight of Elise's current plight.

"Elizabeth, please think on what you are doing to us. My people have only ever served the kingdom with integrity and devotion. I have scores of folk too injured to move on their own since the skex devastated Riverbell. You have always known us as goodly neighbors. Surely you do not believe we are capable of such vile deeds?"

Elizabeth frowned and looked at her shoes, contemplating the past. "I am sorry," she said, "but you will find no help here. It is time you left before we send out messengers to the lawmen patrolling the roads."

Elise started to beseech the woman's sensibilities again, but Elizabeth turned her back to them, slipping back inside the house and slamming the door behind her. The two men remaining on the stoop shuffled awkwardly to block their entrance.

"You cowards!" Elise shouted at the door.

She tried to rush up the steps, but Rimball grabbed hold of her waist, pulling her thrashing body away from the building. They were a good two blocks away before Elise came to her senses and ordered the old huntsman to put her down.

"I lost my temper," Elise admitted to the stone-faced hunter.

"You will need to control your anger if you are to become Morgana's successor," Rimball stated flatly.

"Well, so much for old friends," Rygor groaned to Erik, who just frowned and looked around like a lost puppy. "What are we going to do now?"

Elise surveyed the area. Townsfolk were staring at them and muttering to one another. But now she saw it differently. These common, decent people truly believed they had done something nefarious, that the people of Riverbell were working to overthrow the Council of Elders. Elise knew the whole thing was preposterous, but there it was in their eyes, staring at her with disgust and contempt.

"I think it's high time we get ourselves out of here," she said in a dry voice.

Rimball nodded, and they headed back to the maize fields.

"A rider!" Erik called out, spinning about and throwing himself in front of Elise with his spear at the ready.

A short, round-bellied man was racing up the street on the back of a donkey. When he reached them, the man hauled back on the reins, and the stubby jenny reared up, kicking its front legs in the air and clopping to a halt. The man was certainly a farmer by the looks of him. He tried to catch his breath, as if the horse had ridden him up the street and not the other way around. "Elder Elise," he wheezed, "I'm so glad I caught up to you in time."

"And who would you be?" Elise asked.

"Atric!" Rygor squealed, delighted. "Atric Afalmire, you old goat!" Rygor rushed around Elise and Erik to pull the plump man down from his steed and wrap him in a hearty hug. The two of them laughed, happy to see each other. Atric pulled back and patted Rygor's shoulder, staring into his eyes as if he were his son.

"You know this man?" Elise asked.

Rygor nodded emphatically. "Oh yes, this here is my Uncle Atric!"

"I certainly am." Atric gave him another hug and then moved back to his horse. "Oh lad, we thought we lost the lot of ye, after the news o' Riverbell being burned to the ground reached town." Atric caught himself, looking this way and that to see who was listening. "It's best you lot follow me back to the farm where we can speak in private. It's just up the hill here."

"Your Elder Daniel has made it abundantly clear we are not welcome in town anymore, Atric," Elise said. "I thank you for your kindness, but we are not here to put anyone in harm's way."

Rygor looked like a deflated balloon.

"To the nine hells with those fools." Atric spat on the ground from atop his steed. "Besides, the lawmen are patrolling the trade roads and scouring the countryside. They'll never think to look for ye at my place. Now come, follow me, and I'll get ye some supplies which ye'll no doubt be needing for the open road."

Atric kicked off his donkey, which trotted up the curving road. Rygor smiled hopefully at Elise with puppy dog eyes.

She gave in. "Very well. We can stay for a bit longer."

Atric's farm was on the western outskirts of town, which made Elise more comfortable as at least there were not eyes following their every move. When they arrived at his home, Atric was already dismounted. Two young lads came running from the field to greet them, joyfully throwing themselves at Rygor in celebration that he was still alive.

"Now you lads break it up. Dudly, I need you to run and fetch those supplies we talked about." Atric's son nodded, setting out around the side of the barn beside his house. "Elder Elise, I think it's best you lot wait inside the barn while my boys fetch that stuff. Don't know if you noticed, but there was more than one eager eye watching you come with me, and I don't feel too comfortable out here in the open."

"How long do think it will take for them to gather up everything?" Elise asked, stepping inside the barn. It was small, just big enough for Atric's six sheep when he needed to get them inside to keep them safe from scavenging roc bats. It was hot and stuffy, with an overwhelming smell of hay.

"Shouldn't be too long," Atric said. "Why don't ye go on and have yerself a seat. They'll be here real soon to take care of ye."

Elise squinted at the farmer, who was leering at her and walking backward out of the barn. Before she could yell, he pulled the barn doors shut in her face. Rimball darted past Elise, frantically trying to wrench the doors apart.

It was no use. Atric and his son had dropped the locking bars in place the moment the sliding doors were shut. It would take an ogre to break through that mechanism, though it was no more than a long wooden plank with deep notches in it gripping the prongs of the lock.

"Ain't no use trying to get out of there," Atric wheezed and chortled through the door.

"Uncle Atric," Rygor exclaimed, "what is this?"

"The magistrate has a fair bounty out on the little missus' head," Antric said.

Rygor looked dumbfounded. He opened his mouth but could not find any words. His shoulders slumped, he propped his forehead against the barn door, his voice barely a whisper. "B-but...I'm your family."

"Oh, don't you worry none, Rygor. Soon as them lawmen come on round, I'm gonna make sure they know you helped me bring the traitors here. Now why don't y'all get some rest. Them lawmen gonna be here soon enough."

Rimball growled and stalked away from the doors to pace back and forth around the room. Erik kicked the barn doors. "Atric, you bastard, I'm going to kill you when we get out of here!" he clenched and unclenched his fists, looking angry enough to tear down the wooden portal with his bare hands.

"I'm sorry, you guys," Rygor mumbled pathetically, his face hidden in the shadows of shame.

"This isn't your fault," Erik said somewhat begrudgingly. "That rat is supposed to be your family. If you can't rely on your own blood, then who the hell are you supposed to trust?" Erik gave Rygor one solid pat on the back and turned to plop his back against the barn doors. He cocked his head sideways. "And what is it you are doing?"

Rygor thought the man meant him, but when he looked up, Erik was staring at the center of the room, where Elise sat cross-legged. She held a fat onyx stone against her forehead and was whispering something. Rimball had stopped his pacing and stared at her with equal interest.

"Quiet. I need to concentrate to commune with her," Elise said without opening her eyes. "Lady Cassandra, I need you," she whispered to the stone. "Please answer me. I need you now."

Elise felt foolish sitting in the hay, whispering to a rock while the hunters stared at her as if she were mad. She had not spoken to the sorceress since shortly after Cassandra had created the magical rift to transport her safely back to Riverbell. She had tried to commune with her several times since then, when no one was around, but all attempts thus far had failed. Perhaps the cost of creating the rift was higher than Cassandra had initially let on. Maybe she had drifted away from the stone into the afterlife.

The Onyx began to warm in Elise's palms. *"Elise...is that you, dear girl?"*

Elise's heart soared to hear the sorceress's voice inside her mind. Erik's eye twitched when the core of the stone began to faintly glow green, pulsing like a beating heart. The hunters could not hear Cassandra's voice, so they did not see that the mystical stone pulsated with her every word.

"Yes! Yes, it is me, Lady Cassandra," Elise exclaimed out loud, "I...*we* are in danger. I need your help."

Erik looked to Rygor, who shrugged.

"Allow me to see your need, Elise."

Elise leaned her head back as the spirit of Cassandra entered her mind. She let the recent events play through her memories so that the sorceress could observe them.

"Do you see it, milady?" Elise asked hopefully. "Can you help us escape this trap?"

"Not in the way you mean, my dear." Cassandra's voice was like a distant song playing in her mind. *"To create another rift would take up far too much of my power, dwindling my being away to near nothingness."*

Elise opened her eyes, shocked to hear the woman could not help. The stone was so close she could see deep within the facets of its surface. Far away there was a tiny river with Cassandra sitting beside it under a green sky, speaking to her.

"Then we are doomed," Elise said. The heavy proclamation sent a shiver up Erik's spine.

"Do not lose hope so easily, Elise," Cassandra said, *"I never said that I could not be of assistance. Only that creating a rift is out of the question."*

A flicker of hope opened inside her heart once more. "Tell me, what can we do, milady?"

"Rise, let me see the room you are in."

Elise carried the stone before her, cupped in her palms. She made sure to show the sorceress all angles of the barn.

"Elder Elise," Rygor whispered urgently, his ear pressed against the barn door, "whatever it is you are doing, you best speed it up. I think I can hear riders coming up the hill!" Sweat beaded on the man's forehead, and he had a wild look in his eyes.

"Milady..." Elise said.

"Yes, I heard him," Cassandra replied before she needed to speak. *"Over there, at the back. No, not that way, go left."* Elise adjusted the direction of the stone. *"Yes, there. Do you see that?"*

Elise did not follow her meaning. "It's just a regular bale of hay sitting against the back wall of the barn."

Cassandra sighed. *"You are looking but you are not seeing. Try harder."*

"I'm not sure we have time for word games," Elise complained.

"Try harder."

Elise stared at the area, trying to make out what the sorceress wanted her to see. There was the bale of hay. The floor was strewn with the stuff. A shovel leaned against the hay. Surely Cassandra could not think they had time enough to dig their way out of the barn? Elise shook her head and ran her fingers over the wall.

And there it was. There was a gap between two of the wooden planks on the wall where a tiny sliver of crystal light came through.

"Rimball!" she said, pointing at the spot. The hunter was quick to comply, huddling behind the bale and digging his fingers into the gap.

"Best hurry. Uncle Atric's definitely talking to someone," Rygor urged. "And I think they are headed for the barn!"

The wooden plank was loose. Rimball gave it three good pushes, throwing his shoulder into it, until it snapped out of place.

"Erik, get over here and help him," Elise said.

The pair of them fell into it, desperately yanking planks out of the way.

"Why couldn't you just tell me this?" Elise asked Cassandra.

She could see Cassandra beside the creek inside the stone. She was pacing with her hands clasped behind her back. *Do you need my mastery over the magical plane to remove those boards?*

"No. Rimball and Erik are..." Elise began. She caught herself as the idea took root. "Oh, I see."

"You see what?" Cassandra prompted.

"I never actually needed your magic to get out of this barn. I just needed to look around the cursed room and use my eyes."

"That's it! They're outside!" Rygor whispered urgently. He backed away, staring fearfully at the barn doors.

Elise grabbed him by the shoulder and spun him around. They both ran to the back of the barn, and Elise began kicking at the planks. On the other side of the door, she could hear Atric boasting to the soldiers of his catch over the donkey's braying.

They cleared enough of the wood away to crawl out. Out of habit, Elise silently praised the crystal that she had not been foolish enough to wear a stupid skirt. The blasted thing would have gotten caught on the jagged planks for sure. Once they were all out of the barn Rimball reached in and pulled the bale of hay over the hole.

When the barn doors opened, they were already running through the rows of maize in farmer Atric's field. Rygor thought he heard his uncle shouting that they had escaped, but it was hard to make out over the braying donkey. They did not stop running for a second, even when they came upon their comrades, gathering them up for the wild flight. Not until they were clear of the fields and back inside the line of trees did Elise call for them to halt.

She looked back over the rows of crops. From this vantage point they could see over the heads of the stalks to the town beyond. Several riders were entering the town square and a couple foot soldiers harassed the townsfolk, no doubt searching for them. From this angle, she could not see Atric's farm. A pit of dread opened up in her stomach when she heard the bullhorn being blown from that direction.

"We need to leave this place. We are no longer safe here," Rimball insisted, turning and heading into the woods.

Elise frowned as in the town square a soldier punched a farmer in the stomach. She shook her head as the veil of the world was lifted, revealing to her the reality of Fal with such transparency and clarity that she almost laughed at the absurdity of it all. She frowned at the great crystal floating in the distance. The face of it seemed to be mocking her.

"I don't think we were ever safe to begin with."

Chapter 8: Practice Makes Perfect

"Logan," Isaac called from down the hallway. "May I speak with you privately for a moment?"

Logan looked down at Bipp and motioned for him to continue on without him. "I'll meet you in the lobby," he promised, both thumbs tucked into the straps of his backpack. Bipp nodded and headed down the rounded stairwell.

As Logan made his way toward the mage, he could see Isaac had changed into slightly different gear. His robes were the same thick brown wool, but he wore more rings, almost one for each finger, and had donned some sort of golden circlet around his forehead. It was ornately carved to look like branches of a tree intertwined in a delicate braided pattern with a miniscule emerald set in the center. He also wore a belt, which tied his robes around the waist and held several small satchels and pouches.

"Is this all you are taking with you?" Logan asked, pointing at the pouches.

Isaac looked alarmed for a moment, clapping his hands around his person to see if he had forgotten something important. After checking over his belongings and mumbling to himself incoherently, he replied, "Why, yes...yes, I believe it is all here. Why do you ask?"

Logan raised a brow. "Oh, uh, no reason. What did you want to talk about?"

Isaac motioned for him to step inside the doorway he stood beside. It caught Logan off guard for a moment, since he could swear only a moment before there had been no doorway there.

Stepping inside, he was immediately impressed. The room was larger than he expected, but that seemed to be expectedwhen inside the White Tree. Logan followed the mage down a spiral stone staircase carved into the wall of the round room, which was littered with all manner of relics.

Despite being packed with odd items, the room was not the least bit unorganized. In fact, there was a certain beauty about the way the place was arranged, with several dais holding artifacts. Mythic statues of various sizes and materials lined the walls alongside paintings and large murals of fantastic historic scenes. Even the tall columns, which were made of a series of rounded stones had small nooks carved into them holding items of some importance. The entire place was lit by four large crystal chandeliers overhead, each holding dozens of burning candles. The air was much cleaner than Logan would have expected, and he briefly wondered how the mage lit so many candles.

"Wow, this place is something else!" Logan said, excited by all the seemingly valuable items displayed in the wizard's gallery. "Where did you get all of this stuff?"

"Oh, here and there, you know how it is. I've spent many a year scouring the ruins of the forgotten Acadian empires since the jotnar laid them to waste, gathering up whatever magical relics or technological marvels I could find." Isaac was obviously proud of his collection, holding his waist with one hand and waving around the room with his staff while beaming It was the first time he had ever shown an outsider the room. "Stur told me of the recent series of mishaps with your weapons, and I thought perhaps I could help find you a suitable replacement."

Isaac guided Logan over to a raised dais which held a pedestal carved from the most luxurious marbled cherry wood weaving in and out of itself in an intricate braid. A long, hinged box sat on top of the pedestal, its wood so finely crafted it almost looked wet and soft, gleaming from the overhead glow of candlelight.

Isaac leaned onto his staff with both hands near his chin. "Inside is a very powerful artifact, the likes of which have never been reproduced in this world. Only a select few have ever even had the honor to wield it."

Logan licked his lips. If there was one thing that got him going, it was the thought of treasure, and this seemed to be the finest piece of loot he was likely to ever come across. He knew Corbin would have done the typical *"Are you sure?"* dramatic back and forth before accepting Isaac's offer, but Logan was not his brother.

"Well, I wouldn't want to turn down such a generous gift, Isaac. Thank you very much!" He eagerly rubbed his hands together and then snatched the object off the dais.

Except the box did not move. Logan looked at it, perplexed, and tried again. He tugged at it with all his strength, but the box would not budge.

"Eh...is it stuck?"

Isaac chuckled quietly to himself, amused at the young man's red-faced attempts to move the object. "Logan, you cannot hope to wield this weapon through sheer physical strength alone. It will only allow those worthy of its majesty to wield it."

"So I am not worthy?" Logan asked, wondering why the weapon had a problem with him. He felt silly thinking about weapons having any sort of sentience and quickly wondered if this were some sort of wizardly prank.

"Try asking Gandiva for its blessing to wield it," Isaac offered.

Logan suddenly felt quite foolish. He looked around the room to see if perhaps his companions were there, waiting to jump out and make fun of him. Shaking his head at the nonsensical notion, he studied the soft wood again, wondering what the appropriate way to ask a box for permission to lift it would be. Falling to one knee, he felt a wave of heat cross his face, embarrassed to be doing this.

"Oh, great and powerful Gandiva, may I be honored to use your weapon?" he asked halfheartedly, then stared at the box, waiting for some sign of acceptance.

Isaac slapped Logan's right thigh with the bottom of his staff. "Well? Stand up and see if it worked."

"Are you sure there's nothing more to it than that?" Logan asked, rising to his feet.

"What else did you expect it to be? Think the darn lockbox is going to clear its throat and give you permission?" Isaac asked.

Logan tentatively reached out for the parcel, sure that it would still not budge. After all, how could he be worthy of such an honor if this thing was so rare?

Isaac's eyes gleamed in delightful awe when the young man lifted Gandiva from the dais. Apparently the mage was as shocked as he that it had actually worked. Logan turned to smile at him, feeling like a schoolboy who just got the answer right after years of failing exams. The mage nodded, enthusiastically motioning for him to open the case.

Inside was the strangest weapon Logan had ever laid eyes upon. It was roughly the length of his forearm with a round nub on one end flaring up to a wide, curved edge at the other. It was made of a wood that was as white and flawless as the bark of Isaaca's mystical tree.

Confused, Logan looked up from the box. "It's...a club?"

"Club? No, no, this is much more spectacular than some blunt log, lad. She is called a boomerang. Pick Gandiva up and I will show you how to wield it," Isaac instructed.

"Oh...so the club is Gandiva? I thought that was the name of a spirit or something." Logan did not know what to make of the odd weapon.

Isaac was about to reply but bit his tongue. He had to remind himself that the young Falian's experience of the greater world was limited and that he was better served being spoken to as if he knew nothing, which he did. "As I said, Gandiva is *not* a club. What you see before you is a weapon that kings vied for. Many a knight battled to the death on long epic journeys for the dream of wielding this. You hold in your hands Gandiva, the god slayer, and she has chosen you, Logan Walker, as her hero. This is a far greater honor than you currently seem to be grasping, but never you mind that right now. Just take her out of the case."

Logan was not sure about this thing being all that the mage claimed, but did as he was instructed. When he lifted the boomerang it transformed in his hand. Lines grew across its face, carving the image of an eagle's wing, and the flared tip dyed itself in three strips of color, one orange, one red, and the last purple, giving it the appearance of some exotic bird's wing. Isaac's eyes gleamed with hidden fires, clearly impressed by the transformation.

"So...it's a wooden wing?" Logan asked slowly, sensing that he was wearing on the mage's nerves but still not grasping how this wooden club was going to help him fight.

"For the love of Asgard, boy, it's not a bloody flipping club." Isaac groaned. "Just...just flick your wrist."

Logan looked at the thing and tentatively flicked his wrist. To his astonishment, the weapon popped outward like a pocket knife, revealing a twin wing and shaping itself in an almost V-like angle. The boomerang made a clicking noise, locking itself in position. "Whoa..."

"Indeed. Gandiva manifests itself in many different ways. For you, she has become a boomerang." Isaac felt a little more comfortable at hearing Logan give the ancient relic the esteem it deserved.

"But how do I use it?" Logan asked, swishing the weapon back and forth like a sword.

"I have a feeling Stur can show you the art of wielding such a weapon, but generally one throws it at a target and then readies themselves to catch it when Gandiva returns." Isaac placed a gentle hand on Logan's forearm to stop the eager young man from throwing it and accidentally damaging one of his treasures. "Come now, we must get ourselves to the others and make ready for the open road."

Isaac was already halfway up the steps, moving spritely for a centurion, before Logan stopped him. "Isaac, wait. I...uh...thank you for this. I *do* appreciate what you have done here." Logan was not used to such conversations and was unsure what words to speak in a situation like this.

"Don't mention it, young man. Let us be on our way." Isaac smiled down at him.

They were almost to the lobby, coming down the last flight of stairs, when Logan asked him another question. "Did you say this thing would fly back to me?"

"Oh, yes. This way you can stop losing your weapons when you get frustrated and throw them at your enemies," Isaac teased, not missing a beat. Now Logan understood why the mage thought the weapon was a perfect match for him.

When they entered the lobby, everyone was already there, waiting to be on their way. Kalilah and Lars were saying their farewells. The lizardwoman was staying behind to help tend the Acadian's wounds. She was brimming with pride. This would be her first official act as a healer.

Stur marveled over Gandiva, telling Logan how legendary the weapon was. He showed him how to flick his wrist to close the boomerang back up and helped Logan secure it at his belt within easy reach. Isaac motioned for them all to follow him as he exited the White Tree.

"Good journey, Master Isaac!" Elijah called from his perch high up in the boughs of the White Tree, where he and the other golems stood waving. Even the seemingly lazy griffin Shedu roared, flying around the mage's home to bid its master farewell. Isaac stopped to wave back and told his constructs he would return before they knew it.

As they left the mage's tower behind, Logan could feel the excitement of the road ahead growing in his chest. He hid it from his brother, who looked somber at the prospect of putting even more distance between them and the woman he loved. That reminder was what Logan needed to keep himself in check. As eager as he was to embark on a new journey with a powerful weapon and cunning allies, he had to remind himself that Acadia was ever a dangerous land. And if he did not keep his wits about him at all times, the next moment might be his last.

They travelled for a good week and a half, with Isaac guiding their way and Tiko acting as their forward scout to ensure the path ahead was safe from danger. Corbin offered to search using his psionic abilities, which could detect other sentient minds hiding in wait, but Isaac insisted there was no need. Many of the jungle's dangers were not actually from sentient creatures, and he did not want them lulled into a false sense of security.

Isaac expressed some disappointment that they could not travel by day due to the Falians' sensitive eyes. After the third night of traveling in the dark, he had them gather around the fire to cast a spell over them. When it was complete, the world grew darker under the protective glasses Kyra had given them. When they removed the goggles, the world looked as it did to the Acadians, give or take varying depths of shade. Isaac told them he had cast a protective spell over their eyes to bend the light differently and make it so they could see.

And so they began traveling by daylight. In the mornings they moved swiftly through the dense, humid jungle, while at night, they gathered around a campfire, where both brothers trained. Stur spent hours teaching Logan how to properly wield Gandiva. It was a marvel to the group that when he threw the curved weapon, a blade edge lined its face, sharp enough to cut the leaves it passed through in half. Fearing the blade would cut his palm, it took Logan a while to get used to the weapon returning to his waiting hand, but eventually he mastered it. Stur told him that Gandiva was actually carved from a branch of Yggrdassil, the mythological world tree that connected the worlds of the gods with those of man.

While Logan trained with Stur every chance he got, Corbin learned more about his psionic capabilities with Isaac. The mage had chosen the path of elemental control, with a particular interest in Illusory magic derived from mastery over air. Corbin was one of a kind to him, most likely one of the last psionic mages left in the world of Acadia.

"But how can that be? Unless I'm mistaken, you did read our minds back in your tower." Corbin pointed out, scoffing at the idea of being called a mage himself.

Isaac waggled his pinky finger at Corbin, wearing a toothy grin in the light of the fire. "Ah, but I cheated. Ikol's Eye grants me the power to do so. I am fortunate to have been gifted this ring by my master." The ring on his finger glinted in the firelight.

As the days passed, Isaac worked closely with Corbin, fine-tuning his control over psionic energy, teaching him how to swiftly reach into his companions' minds and get the answers he sought without even needing to come in physical contact with them. He worked through Corbin's power to move inanimate objects using sheer force of will, something he called telekinesis.

One morning the brothers awoke to find both Stur and Isaac towering over them. Stur explained that it was time to test their new skills against real enemies. It would not be long before they were in jotnar territory, and they could ill afford to wait until a real fight stumbled on them to see if the men could hold their own.

The four of them set out alone, with Isaac leading the way to a site he had chosen for the test.

"Are you sure this is wise?" Corbin whispered as they crept up the perimeter of trees beside a tiny babbling brook. The vegetation here was overgrown just like everywhere else in the untamed jungle. Some of the plants had leaves so large his entire head could fit behind them unseen, and the air had a refreshing smell to it from the clean spring water that flowed over the rocks. They huddled together behind a stack of those plants set between several thick-trunked trees that curved to hang over the edge of the creek.

"Certainly there is nothing to fear from the imps," Isaac said. "They are dangerous to the layman unaware of his surroundings but not to the likes of you. Besides, we will be right here to assist should you need it," Isaac assured them, crouching with his staff supporting his weight.

"Here they come." Stur pointed to six creatures arriving in the clearing.

Each one of them was small, only about two feet tall, with round, lava-red bodies. They had no necks and very large teeth. Along their spines were rows of spikes, and they flitted through the air on undersized sets of bat wings. The imps made strange guttural sounds, seemingly communicating with each other. Four of them carried a slain deer to the ground and went to work feasting on it.

When the breeze rose up, Logan wrinkled his nose in disgust. "Ugh, they smell like vomit."

Isaac's eyes danced. "Yes, filthy little creatures, they are."

Logan looked at Stur. "We're going in."

Stur nodded. "Remember your leg movements and don't forget to carry through with your release, just like we talked about." Stur flicked his wrist as an example while Logan impatiently rocked his head, ready to get into the fight.

"And don't forget we are right here if you need us. Just call out the safe word," Isaac added, more to Corbin than his overeager brother.

"Right...*nuts*, got it. If we need you, we will call *nuts*," Corbin verified before signaling Logan to take the lead.

One of the plumper imps had torn a leg off the deer and was gorging itself against a large rock near their position. Logan pointed at it, then to Corbin, while he went the opposite direction. Corbin looked at the easy target, thinking it would be far simpler to just cut the wretched thing down with the blade of his voulge than to use psionic abilities, but that would defeat the entire purpose of today's outing.

Falling inside himself, he felt for the channels of energy floating through the air, seeing them as clearly as a beam of light that rippled across the ground, connecting all the impish minds as well as he and Logan in one great daisy chain. Tapping into the light, he followed it in a zip line to the imp's unsuspecting psyche, where he quickly went about adding the suggestion of memories to the gluttonous monster.

While Corbin was busy manipulating his target's memories, Logan slipped around to the opposite end of the clearing, flicking open his weapon and readying for the distraction to begin.

The other five imps were busy feasting upon the deer carcass when their sister suddenly stood and threw her deer leg down from the rock, hitting three of them from behind. In their foul, guttural language that sounded like croaks and burps, the angry little creatures demanded to know why she had done that. Instead of answering them, she stood on top of the rock and shouted down at the group, stomping her foot with each curse.

Logan did not know what kind of mental manipulation Corbin had worked in the female imp. Whatever it was, the others were visibly upset by her words, wasting no time swarming the lone imp to rip her to pieces. Watching it all transpire, Corbin felt a twinge of remorse. After all, the imp had done nothing to him, and he had just caused her death.

As the angered imps descended upon her in a frenzy of tooth and claw, a whistling sound streaked across the air. One of the imps turned around just in time to let out a gurgling yelp before Logan's bladed boomerang tore through his skull and returned to its owner.

The other four imps scattered in different directions, some taking flight while one tripped, rolling down the side of the rock head over heels. Hitting the dirt, it hopped to its stubby feet and ran to hide behind the deer carcass. Corbin let out a shout as he directed a wave of psionic energy at one of the monsters taking flight, aiming to switch its understanding of the world. The little beast suddenly believed that it was flying in the wrong direction and quickly altered course, smacking head first into the rocks beside the creek.

From Logan's vantage point, the confusion spell Corbin cast on the creature could not have been funnier. Even as it tried to fly away, dizzy from the collision, the monster's solid yellow eyes looked worried that it was suddenly walking upside-down, which of course it was not. Logan pulled Gandiva far back behind his head and let it rip, again whistling through the air to score a direct hit on the confused beast, killing it with one blow. His laugh was cut short when the weapon returned to his hand with one of the imp's severed arms still stuck to it.

"Logan, watch your head!" Corbin shouted in his mind, giving him enough warning to duck, narrowly dodging a swooping imp's clawed feet. Logan sprinted into the center of the clearing. He quickly dropped into a roll and scrambled over the carcass of the deer to find cover. When he landed with his back pressed against the deer, he found himself staring right into the face of a hiding imp. Logan recoiled out of sheer reflex, using the boomerang as club to knock the creature away in surprise.

Isaac muttered to himself. "How many times do I have to tell the lad it's not a club?"

The imp cried out as it flew through the air toward the steep hillside and right into a wall of vines. Except where it should have stopped against the vines, it passed straight through, revealing a cave hidden in the hillside, blending in perfectly with the surrounding landscape.

Logan did not even have time to register how odd this development was before a furious roar came from behind the wall of vines. His head perked up, and the flying imps all froze in midair, staring fearfully in the cave's direction. The imp he had batted inside came anxiously flitting out, looking both ways to find its companions.

Before it could join them, a drake the size of a large panther leapt from the cave opening, snatching the imp from the air with massive lizard jaws. The drake was a formidable jungle predator, large and muscular, covered with hard green scales all the way from its long tail, which ended in a spiky ball of bone, to its sharp, angular jaws. A set of long, yellow horns sat on either side of its ears amidst a crown of spiky cartilage and a hook of plating tipped over the front of the creature's snout. The drake's jaw changed to a copper color, which ran down its belly and matched the three long, hooked talons on each of its feet.

Logan scrambled to his feet and slowly walked backward, away from the fearsome monster. The drake finished gobbling up its catch and turned to face the other creatures that dared to disturb its slumber. Without hesitation, the red imps flew off in different directions while Logan turned around, running full steam back toward the trees, yelling, "Nuts! Nuts! Bloody goddamn nuts!"

Stur emerged from the edge of the clearing, pulling the mighty broadsword off his back, and Isaac pointed a staff in the dangerous dragonkin's direction. "Corbin, use your confusion spell!" the mage shouted, casting a pall over Logan to give him a temporary protective shield against physical attacks.

The drake pawed at the ground, raking large sections of dirt away with its front paw as it prepared to attack. It charged them with its head lowered, horns ready to skewer its prey. Corbin was already falling inside himself and sent his spell into the drake's mind, but it bounced off the magical creature.

"I-I can't get inside!" He shouted inside Isaac's mind. *"The lizard has some sort of protection against my magic!"*

As the drake closed in on Logan, Stur knocked him to the side, swinging his blade across the lizard's path. The charging behemoth saw the danger and leapt over the large mammal, smacking him in the head with the end of its tail as it flew by. If Stur had not been wearing his helmet, his skull would surely have been torn to pieces by the vicious blow. Instead the attack left him shaking as the impervious metal rang like a bell.

Seeing his newfound mentor take the hit knocked some sense back into Logan, who felt embarrassed at his panicked retreat. He shifted into a tight turn and let Gandiva fly, putting his weight heavily into the throw and scoring a direct hit as the beast was turning for another attack.

Scales went flying in a spray of blood as his weapon lacerated the predator's hind leg. The forest drake roared in pain and leapt for him so fast Logan could not hope to get out of the way. As the beast pinned him to the ground, Logan could only think about how disgusting its breath smelled, like something between rotting cabbage and sweaty feet.

Corbin cried out as he watched the massive lizard clamp rows of teeth bred for tearing meat apart over his brother's head, wriggling back and forth while it raked the talons of its hindquarters down his body to tear him apart.

A steady stream of ice spit forth from Isaac's staff, covering the monster's eyes. In a panic, the beast mewled, rolling off of Logan and clawing at the frozen icicles stinging its irises. Corbin helped his brother up in utter disbelief that he had barely suffered a scratch.

Logan only shrugged, saying, "Must have been Isaac's spell," before letting his weapon fly once more, bent on paying the lizard back in equal measure. Gandiva sliced open the drake's belly. When the boomerang returned to his grasp, Stur was already raining down a series of vicious blows onto the lizard's prone body, slaughtering the predator before it could regain its sight.

His bloodlust sated, the weapon master turned to face them and removed his helmet, laughing boisterously. "Well, so much for a safe training session, eh boys?" he roared.

Logan joined in his mirth, but Corbin could only halfheartedly chuckle, scratching the back of his head as he thought about how close his older brother had been to death.

"You are correct to think this way," Isaac informed him, sensing his thoughts and pulling him in close.

"If you weren't here, we would have been killed," Corbin lamented, unhappy to hear the truth of his own words.

"Mayhap that were a true statement, but I think not. You Walkers are a resourceful lot. I believe you would have come out of it in the end. Well...at least one of you would have, for sure," Isaac conceded.

Stur and Logan traded jibes over the mishap while they made their way back to the camp. Looking back at the drake's body, Corbin saw that the hungry imps had already returned and were feasting upon its remains. Not for the first time, he noted how weird and dangerous the surface world was and worried that they would never make it back to Vanidriell at all.

Chapter 9: Manta Bay

"This is a death sentence," Gustav said, shaking his head and crossing hairy arms over his barrel chest. A couple of the villagers agreed with him. Elise wondered if perhaps she should not have insisted they have this meeting publicly where all of their people could be heard. Things were getting away from her again, and last time that happened, she lost over thirty stubborn villagers.

"The gaps of Gratuntite—" Erik tried to reason.

"Are too dangerous for us to drag the women and children through!" Gustav insisted.

"Hey, now," Bertha warned, glowering at Gustav.

The bearded man recoiled a little under her withering gaze, but he was not ready to back down. "You know what I mean. It's not just a trip through the woods. Those passes are dangerous. Who knows what could be lurking inside some of those caves?"

"That's a risk we are going to have to take," Elise said.

"Why, because it doesn't matter if we lose a few folk, as long as Elder Elise gets us to the promised land?" Micum derided her.

Gunter hobbled over to the fire, leaning right over the flames to growl in Micum's face. He stuck a big, stubby finger in the other man's chest. "Don't you be talking to my daughter like that, you pig-headed oaf."

Micum looked like he might die then and there with the heavyset Gunter hovering over him, but Gustav came to his rescue, shoving Gunter away.

"You pick on someone your own size!" Gustav yelled, clapping his chest like an ape.

"That is enough!" Elise shouted, silencing everyone in the gathering. "You are behaving like infants. Now sit down and pretend you're adults so we can figure this out properly!"

Her father hobbled back to his place, leaning against his makeshift crutch with his back pressed against the tree. Gustav plopped himself down on a large rock, pouting, and everyone settled down.

"Micum, you asked why this is a risk we have to take," Elise said. "You think perhaps we might lose some of our friends and family on this journey, Aye, we might."

The gathering of villagers looked around at each other, surprised to hear the admission.

"Is that a risk we need to take?" Elisa continued. "Aye, it is. But not because of some ego you believe I have concocted for myself where I am stubbornly pressing Riverbell into danger. It is because we have no other options. This is it. We either make this move, or we sit here and wait for Fafnir's soldiers to find us. We might lose some of our friends and family on this journey, and don't you believe for a second that each and every one of their deaths will not haunt me until the day I die. But to stay, that is just sheer folly tantamount to suicide."

Gustav stared at his hands in shame.

"I know you are afraid, I'm scared too," Elise said. "Who among us isn't, given all we've been put through recently?" Villagers were nodding. "Now the question remains, do we want to lie down and wait for a death most certain?" Even Micum shook his head no. Elise felt more and more bolstered, raising her voice with each word. "Or do we want to grasp the glimmer of hope Bertha's plan represents and fight to the last fiber of our beings for our freedom?"

The people of Riverbell forgot themselves for a moment and broke into cheerful agreement. Even Gustav nodded, though it looked painful for him to swallow his pride.

Elise made her way back to her father and Bertha while the villagers celebrated their new course of action. "What will you do now?" Gunter asked his daughter.

"Well, we need to get the camp cleaned up and on its way," Elise began.

Bertha was quick to volunteer. "I'll be seeing to that straight away, milady. You should get some rest for the long journey ahead."

Elise shook her head. "I'll not be accompanying you. I've left instructions with Grey that he is to act in my stead as Riverbell's leader, just as before."

Bertha looked absolutely mortified. "But Elder Elise—"

"There are no buts about it," Elise said. "Your plan is a wise one. The villagers will be more than capable of making the trek through the Grantuntite pass without me. While you are doing that, I will be traveling with Rimball to beseech your cousins for help."

"I'm not sure..." Bertha said.

"Not sure of what?" Elise asked. "Are your cousins not going to be able to help us after all?"

"No, milady. That's not what I meant at all, but I suspect you know as much. Of course Samuel and Wallace will assist us." Bertha gathered up the apron of her dress, wringing the fabric with nervous hands. "Heaven knows I never understood why they moved all the way out to the outskirts of Fal, but now that we are in this mess.... Well, you know what they say, Baetylus always provides that which is needed, and it's not our place to question the all-Father's ways."

"And?" Elise asked.

"Well, it just isn't right for you to be putting yourself in harm's way when there are all these other able-bodied men that can accompany Rimball, milady," Bertha blurted.

"Agreed," Gunter said, circles of concern lining his eyes. "What is this all really about, dear?"

"When we were back in Dure, cornered like rats," Elise said, "Rimball and the hunters...well, they would have died if it was not for me. There are more than enough men and women with spears aplenty to defend our people through the pass, but who is going to look out for Rimball?"

"I'm sure that old man can take care of himself," Gunter insisted.

"No, this is my place. I can feel it in my bones." Elise was resolute. "Bertha, after the hunters and I meet with your cousins, you be ready by the archipelago in Toad Bay."

"Oh, milady..." Bertha moaned, seeing there was nothing more she could do to sway Elise.

Elise leaned forward and gave her father a tight hug. She felt like a child all over again in the man's strong arms. She stroked his bushy brown beard affectionately. "Get better, Father. I want to see you nice and strong the next time we meet."

As fearful as Gunter was about having his daughter head off into the fray, he could not help looking at the lass with swelling pride. He only wished her mother were here to see what a brave young woman Elise had grown to be. "You make sure there is a next time, you hear?"

Elise gave him a tearful nod and headed off to pack her things for the journey.

When the groups separated the next morning, Elise tried not to become emotional. She almost broke down seeing her father's forlorn expression.

She had tried to take a spear with her, but all the ones in camp were too long and heavy for her frame. She could try to wield one of the polearms, but it would probably do more harm than good. Gunter gave her an old short sword his father had given him when he was a boy. It had a solid weight and looked more like a long sword held aloft in her small hands. Rimball advised that she grip it two handed for better control. Elise proudly sheathed the blade at her waist.

They were far to the east now, and the woods hugging the base of the mountain range gave way. There was a decent expanse of open plains between them and the fords at the mouth of the Naga River, where it met Manta Bay and the waters of Malbec. Their destination was the small fishing port of Milua Isle. It was a place commonly known to harbor smugglers as much as fishermen. Smugglers like Bertha's cousins.

Thankfully there were no roads on this side of the river, since the area was scarcely traveled. This meant they were less likely to run into Fafnir's men, although that did not stop Rimball from insisting they take every precaution to travel unseen.

When they reached the open plains, Rimball showed Elise, Rygor, and Erik how to cut some of the tall, reedy grass and tie it around their clothing, creating a makeshift disguise.

"If anyone spots something suspicious, give the signal and be prepared to drop on your bellies," Rimball said.

"Understood." Elise helped Erik tie the reeds across his back while Rygor took care of himself.

The four of them traversed the plains crouched low to the ground, constantly surveying the area for enemies. It was not the fastest way to travel, but it was a damn sight safer than any alternative Elise could have thought up, and she would rather be safe than swift for the time being.

"What was all that nonsense with that stone of yours back in Dure?" Rimball asked her, speaking low enough so their companions could not hear.

Elise did not know if she was more surprised by the question or that Rimball was willingly speaking to her. "It was nothing. Just Elder business."

"Looked like a bit more than nothing," Rimball said without taking his eyes off their surroundings. "And in forty-eight years, I never witnessed Elder Morgana playing with black rocks that glow when you talk to them."

Elise knew the old hunter would not be easily shaken off. Should she just explain all about Lady Cassandra locked away in her pocket dimension deep inside the facets of the Onyx? "Look, it's not important right now. Just leave it be, okay?"

She studied Rimball's leathery face as he paced beside her, crouching low and brushing tall grass out of his path. The man was like stone, immaculate. She could see only the slightest hint of what was going on inside his mind. It was no wonder the old hunter had become the village sensei. You must need to have firm control over your nerves to deal with several generations of children.

"Was it magic?" he asked.

Elise caught her breath. Magic was forbidden in the Kingdom of Fal. It was the reason Cassandra had been put on trial in the first place, after sharing her secrets with Corbin Walker. "Uh..."

Rimball stopped, slowly craning his neck until his grey eyes locked on her own. Elise felt her blood freeze under the man's silent inquisition. "I see."

Elise felt the weight of those two words, so innocent yet callous. It was as if the seasoned hunter had just seen straight through her and passed judgment.

"It's not as if I'm a witch or anything," she said, for some reason desperate to defend her name.

Rimball nodded and continued his march. "It violates the All-Father's laws," he said, as if it were all that was needed.

"Those laws were set forth by the Arch Councilor, Elder Zacharia. Not by the Great Crystal." Elise replied.

Rimball nodded. "Sure enough, After he had a visitation from Baetylus during prayer, instructing him to do so."

Elise knew she had to watch herself carefully here. Her eyes flicked nervously to the cavern ceiling, where the light from the sentient crystal radiated from leagues away. She knew the reality of the crystal but dared not speak it among her people. If what Corbin said was true, then Baetylus could hear their words, if it was inclined to be listening, and could use its evil to sway the minds of the people of Fal, including Rimball.

Suddenly her mind was alive with paranoia. Was Rimball bewitched? What was this sudden infatuation with her stone? Elise knew he was not normally this chatty.

"Elder Morgana gave it to me," she lied. Rimball raised his brow. "The stone is a powerful artifact that only Elders may wield. There is a bylaw among the Council of Elders that we may use magical artifacts to protect our people from harm."

Rimball studied her out of the corner of his eye. Did he know she was completely full of it?

"I'm not sure I can stay with you," he said. Elise was stunned to silence. He suddenly looked guilty, torn internally. "I-I had a vision from Baetylus. I know it sounds crazy, but the All-Father visited me. The Great Crystal warned me to stay away from you...that you will lead me down the path to destruction."

Elise looked over her shoulder. Neither of their companions could hear a word he was saying, and they looked completely uninterested in their conversation. She had to think quickly, or she might lose a powerful ally. "We need you, Rimball. You cannot just abandon your responsibilities because of a dream." She could hear the rushing waters ahead. They must be close to the bridges.

"I-I don't know..." Rimball said.

"This is all a test," Elise blurted, louder than she meant. Her voice carried across the plains, echoing back after a short distance.

Erik cocked his head and called ahead to them. "Is everything okay, Elder?" Elise turned and pressed her finger to her lips, shushing the young man. "Geez," Erik said to Rygor, "she's the one yelling, and I get told to shut up."

Rimball's interest was piqued. "A test?"

Elise put on her best poker face. "The All-Father is clearly testing your nobility as a warrior." She spun the lie, not daring to speak the insidious truth of the Crystal to the fervent man. He was too torn and would surely see her words as open blasphemy. "Why else would Baetylus ask you to turn your back on those you love in their greatest hour of need?"

Rimball digested her explanation, silently brooding. As he moved through the tall reeds, one almost whipped back in Elise's face as it sprang back into place. The hunter nodded to himself. "That may be. I will think on your words, Elder."

"So you will not leave us, then?" she asked.

"I will accompany you at least to Milua Isle," he decided. "By that time I will hopefully have a better idea of the All-Father's true wishes for my path."

"Fair enough." When the hunter was not looking, she sighed with relief. She had averted disaster, if even for a short reprieve. If Rimball abandoned them, she saw no hope in reaching Bertha's kinfolk. She had no doubt that the evil crystal would continue trying to sway him, hoping to strip of her of the precious few allies she had. All the more reason for her to get her people to Malbec, where the false god held no sway.

The rest of the day passed by uneventfully, and that was just fine with the four weary travelers. The tall grasses continued all the way to the rocky banks of Manta Bay, the mouth of the Naga River. The bay marked the last leg of their journey, being the last stretch of Falian land before them.

"Looks like we made good time," Rygor said, as the four of them huddled on the edge of the plains.

"Hush now," Elise scolded.

"Let the man speak," Erik said. "It's not like there is anyone about—"

They all fell silent when Rimball raised his hand, holding it inches from Erik's face. Looking over his shoulder, the older hunter placed his finger to his lips then pointed northwest. They followed his direction.

Land bridges connected a myriad of fords leading out to Milua Isle, a small plot of land that the fishermen called home. They were so close to salvation. All they needed to do was make it across the network of low lying wooden bridges and contact Bertha's cousins, who would be able to pick up the villagers with their fleet of smuggling ships and transport them to Malbec.

However, as Rimball was pointing out, Fafnir's soldiers were hiding in wait all over the bridges.

"Damn the magistrate," Elise cursed. "He must have known we would try this."

"More likely he thinks we would take all the villagers across these roads to reach Malbec," Erik whispered, trying to count the soldiers' ranks.

"Aye, this *is* the central path to Malbec," Rygor agreed. "The old goat thinks to block our path."

"Then that is to our benefit," Elise said, drawing more than one odd look. She cocked her head and explained, "They are expecting a stream of villagers to come pouring out of the plains, unsuspecting of their trap. Which means four sneaky river rats have got a shot."

Rimball agreed.

"We should stick to the riverbank," Elise said, laying out a plan. "The waters around the bay are supposed to become treacherously deep out of nowhere, and the currents are said to be fickle at best. If we make it close enough, then it will be a short swim to bypass their position and use the bridges as shelter from their prying eyes."

"Which might not be that much of a problem anyhow, since they are watching Fal and not Malbec," Erik finished for her, impressed by the Elder's logic.

They all agreed it was as sound a plan as any. Rimball kept watch, counting beats until one of the guards looked their way. One by one they took turns slipping from the tall grass and sneaking across the rocky banks of the bay. Rygor barely made a splash when he slipped into the water, hobbling low so that it came right up to his neck. Rimball flicked his fingers and Erik did likewise, moving like a shadow across the large rocks.

Elise felt her heart pumping hard. When Rimball gave the signal, she froze in place, missing her opportunity. The guard shifted back to his post, watching in their direction for any signs of the Falian traitors. She felt foolish, caught under Rimball's frown.

"*You ready?*" he signaled. Elise shook the tension out of her hands and blew all the air out of her lungs, rocking her neck back and forth to loosen up. She looked at Rimball and gave a thumbs-up. The guard turned away to check the other side of the bridge, and Rimball gave the signal.

Staying low to the ground, Elise scrambled out of the tall grass across the rocky banks of the lake. She was surprised how cold the rocks felt. Their surface was slick, like a layer of invisible water clung to them. The tip of her boot lodged sideways in the crevice between two of the wet boulders and she lost her footing. Elise panicked, hearing the sound of her torso hitting the rock. It sounded like the cracking of a whip followed by a wet slap.

Erik moved to get out of the water and help, but she held her hand out for him to stay put. Shaking her head to straighten out the bank, Elise watched the bridge carefully. The guard still had his back to her. Too scared to rise, she stayed on her belly and groped down for the boot. The tip of it was too lodged to break free. Not daring to take her eyes off the soldier she blindly groped for the buckles of her boot and flicked them off with the swiftness of a master thief. The twisting tension was relieved when she slipped her foot out.

The guard began to turn in her direction. Elise moved across the rock on her belly with such an urgency she hardly paid any mind to the scrapes the rocks were leaving across her neck and forearm. The guard was just facing their direction when she plopped into the water with a tiny splash, falling in face first. He craned his neck forward, squinting to try to make out where the sound had come from.

The water was still. Wide-eyed, Elise leaned her back against the large boulder that jutted out from the bank, terrified to even breathe, Rygor and Erik on either side. They were safely protected from the soldier's view by the large rock and remained perfectly still until he finally looked away, heading to the other side of the bridge.

Elise did not even hear Rimball enter the bay and almost yelped when his head bobbed out of the water right in front of her. Her face felt hot when the hunter lifted his hand out of the water, holding her abandoned boot. Embarrassed, she took it and followed his lead as they skirted the banks.

Every time a soldier turned in their direction, they had to find shelter. Sometimes that meant splitting up into pairs. They came to the ford of rocks and used them as cover to make their way east, deeper into the lake and further away from the soldiers' watch.

Elise counted eight more of Fafnir's men as they moved through the water. Her legs were getting tired, and the water was growing colder by the minute. Rygor's lips were turning a pale blue and trembling. She realized her fingers were numb when she saw her hand touching a large rock but felt nothing.

Rimball gave them a signal. *"Just a little farther."* She nodded, her neck uncontrollably stuttering three more times before she gained control and followed.

They had to pass a couple more of the low land bridges, remaining under cover of the river boulders before getting to a point where the walkways were tall enough to swim underneath. All they had to do was get under them, and the rest of the passage should be easy sailing. The only problem was that a soldier kept lookout on either side of their entry point.

Rimball worked as a lookout, carefully watching as the men patrolled the bridge, looking past where the companions tread water, far in the distance to the plains and woods beyond. He gave the signal and they made a beeline for the bridge.

As soon as they were underneath, Elise hugged one of the wooden posts, relishing the reprieve it brought to her aching limbs. She did not even care that the green slimy residue clung to her clothing, though it stank like rotten fish. They all rested for a moment, using the beams as support to gather their strength.

"What's next?" Erik asked.

"We will pass right beneath their feet, completely undetected," Elise said.

When they set out again, keeping under cover of the bridge, they had to work in a straight line to remain hidden beneath the narrow walkway. Coming to the next soldier, Elise was surprised to see another guard had joined him. They were discussing the assignment. One of them was complaining about having to be all the way out here, insisting the villagers could not have gotten this far.

Elise cursed their luck. The path was blocked by horizontal support beams that connected the posts in an x formation. There was no way they were getting through without making a lot of noise in the water. Rimball pointed at them then made a circle with his fingers, directing their attention to the edge of the posts. They were going to have to skirt the beams to get by! It seemed like sheer madness with two guards patrolling right above them. All one of the men had to do was glance over the rail, and they would be caught. But there was no other choice.

"Hey, if the magistrate says get it done," one of the soldiers said, spitting over the edge of the walkway, "then we get it done."

"Still, seems like a waste of our time to be all the way out here when what we should be doing is combing the woods for them traitors," the other replied. The deep-voiced man looked like a weasel, but he flared his nostrils and twisted up his face at his partner's disgusting habit.

Rygor was the first to go, silently swimming around the post. Elise almost groaned when she saw how wide a circuit he made. Fortunately, neither guard seemed to pay any mind. Once on the other side of the support, Rygor looked back to see Erik holding his fist up over the water and biting his lip. He shrugged and motioned for Erik to follow.

"It would take us weeks to search those woods," the soldier countered. "Besides, I bet this beats having dungeon duty, like your buddy Ralph."

Erik slithered around the post, keeping his body tightly pressed against it. He did not see the jagged piece of wood beneath the water until it caught his leg. The edge of it tore his pants and cut a gash in the side of his calf. Erik flinched back out of reflex, splashing the water behind him. Elise almost hissed.

"What was that?" the other man said. When the soldier leaned over the rail to check the water, Elise held her breath. There was nothing there but bubbles and rings of water where Erik had been. The gentle waves of the lake quickly wiped away the rings left in his wake.

"Wow, look at you, getting all spooked," the soldier laughed, clapping the grim-faced man's back and pointing to the spot over the side of the rail. "It's probably just a fish, man, get a grip."

On the other side of the cross beams a frazzled Erik slowly rose above the water.

The man grumbled and shook off his friend's hand before pacing back to the center of the bridge. "You haven't seen what I seen. Them rats from Riverbell are some sneaky bastards."

"Ha, yeah yeah. You're just bitter 'cause you let that Logan Walker fella escape."

"Shut up! What do you know?" the man snapped. "He was like a damned devil when he got the drop on us! Even took out big Remy."

That seemed to impress the other soldier. "Wow...big Remy? Damn, that guy is one brute I wouldn't want to get into a tangle with."

Elise was next. She moved to the post on the opposite side, clinging to it and sneaking by without making any noise. Once they were all past the pair of soldiers, the group fell back into single line formation and worked east toward Milua Isle, safely under the cover of the bridges. The soldiers were all left behind now, but they still wanted to wait until they were far enough away before climbing up to the walkway, where their sudden presence would not raise suspicion.

"What was that guy talking about back there?" Erik asked. "How did he meet Logan?"

Elise shook her head. "I have no idea."

Rimball suddenly stopped, raising his hand for them to wait. Elise scanned the cracks between the boards above them, trying to see where the soldier was. In a sudden bubbling froth, the water parted, and a ridged back drifted past, cutting between her and Rygor.

"C-croc..." Rygor said with trembling lips. She could see the whites of Rimball's eyes under the bridge, and he slowly pressed a finger against his lips. The crocs were blind lake monsters, relying on their hearing and sense of smell to hunt the primordial waters of Malbec. Rygor shook his twitching head.

The croc moved like a silent blade cutting through the water. It was the king of predators in this terrain. To the casual observer it might appear as though some wooden flotsam with mushrooms growing on it was floating by. But when you are neck-deep, treading water as one of the large reptiles swam past, there was no doubting that you were in the presence of a croc.

The ridged back disappeared under the surface.

Erik looked as though he might lose his mind. "M-my...m-my c-cut," he managed to whisper.

The words hit Elise like a pail of ice cold water. Of course. Erik was bleeding in the water from his cut. The croc must have smelled it.

Rimball held a dagger in his palm and jabbed a finger straight up. They needed to get out of the water right away. Elise felt rough scales brush against her thigh. As the creature swam around her, she involuntarily shuddered, stifling a scream. Rimball snapped his fingers at the terrified group, gathering their attention. He pointed two fingers at his eyes then jabbed the dagger up toward the bridge again, more forcefully this time. Elise nodded. She could not help pinching her eyes shut as she forced herself to swim over to the post, fearing that the reptile would clamp down on her body at any moment.

Rimball jammed his dagger into the post. Once it was secure, he pulled another from his belt and used them to scale the slick beam.

The old wiry hunter was up and over the rail in a heartbeat, holding his arm out to help Rygor.

Elise did not open her eyes again until her knuckles ran into the post. Her gaze darted back and forth over the surface of the water, looking for the croc. Erik had not moved an inch.

"Erik," Elise hissed, "you need to get out of there."

The proud hunter was barely able to manage shaking his head. He was terrified. If he moved, the wound would bleed more, and the croc, which responded to sound and smell, would sense it.

"Look at me," Elise said. Erik tried but could not manage to move his stiff neck. "Look at me, Erik," she repeated, emphasizing each word.

He began to turn his neck, flinched back in place, then moved again so that his bloodshot eyes finally found her own.

From her pack, Elise pulled the bundle of fabric she had cut off her skirts a couple days before. She made silent motions to show him what to do, unsure whether the face Erik made meant he did not understand or that he had just peed himself. She chose to believe it was the former. "Wrap this around your wound so it doesn't bleed into the water," she said, dangling the fabric. Erik nodded.

Elise tossed the bunched cloth to him, but it fell short by a foot. When the fabric plopped onto the surface, the croc lunged. She could not help screaming upon seeing the long, snapping jaws break the surface. The croc's entire head was above water, thrashing about violently on the fabric, thinking it had caught its prey.

"Milady, you must stop screaming!" Rimball insisted.

Elise looked up. The hunter was reaching over the rail with an outstretched hand, urging her to grab ahold. She had not even realized she was still screaming and promptly clamped her mouth shut.

"Erik, now!" Elise urged the pale-faced man who was frozen in terror. "You must get out of there now." The croc had disappeared back underneath the surface.

"Elise, you must not speak," Rimball said. "You have to get out of the water."

She looked up at him. "But Erik...?"

"We cannot help him now," Rimball insisted, stretching farther over the rail. "Please take my hand."

Elise shook her head. She was not about to leave one of them behind. "Erik Ellison, if you don't get your sorry arse over here this very instant, I will be sure to tell Rosie Parkens about that time I caught you peeping at her through the bushes."

The glaze washed away from Erik's terrified eyes. "You wouldn't," he growled.

"Oh, yes, I would," Elise said, "and I'll tell her what a coward you were today as well."

Erik shook his head, blinking. She sighed when he began swimming over to her.

Elise pulled herself up the beam. Her foot slid across the slick surface and she lost her grip, splashing underneath the murky water. She rocked sideways, looking wildly around under the water. In the back of her mind, she wondered why the water looked green and grainy underneath, but the rest of her was focused on the shadow of the croc making its way toward them from the other side of the bridge.

Splashing out of the water, she scrambled up the post and snatched Rimball's hand. The hunter clamped onto her with all his strength and pulled her from the water. Elise wrapped her arm around the rail and flopped over the side, landing on the wooden bridge and staring up at the cavern ceiling far above.

Erik began to climb the post, hugging its slick surface like a bear climbing a tree. When Rimball came back over the rail to offer his hand, the other hunter was already halfway up. "I thought I was a goner there." Erik laughed nervously, accepting Rimball's hand.

Water flew everywhere as the croc erupted from the lake with snapping jaws right beneath Erik. He recoiled, pulling his knees up to his chest and screaming. The croc caught hold of his pant leg, tearing off a strip and almost pulling him right back down into the water.

Except Rygor was already at the rail and thrust his spear into the blind lake monster's face, scoring a good-sized gash across the top of its scaled muzzle. He went to jab again, but the croc disappeared under the surface, leaving a trail of blood behind.

Erik scrambled up the side of the rail. All he could do was rock on his hands and knees, staring at the wooden beams and heaving to catch his breath and steady his nerves.

"Thank the Crystal that's over," Rygor gasped, staring down at the water.

The sounds of men shouting came to them from the west.

"No doubt the soldiers have heard the ruckus," Rimball warned. "We need to be away from here before they arrive."

Elise nodded and rolled over, patting Erik on the back and telling him it was time to go. The man stank of fear.

Staying low so the railing was over their heads, they scrambled across the bridges away from the soldiers. Sounds of boots hitting the wooden walkways told Elise the soldiers were running now. She was about to say something to Rimball when the wooden rail in front of them burst apart.

The croc's head shattered the weak wooden rails, and it squirmed onto the bridge. "The devil himself has possessed this beast!" Rimball exclaimed, having never seen anything like it in all his years.

Elise snapped her head back to look in the direction of the great crystal, blocked by the curving heights of the Fal cavern. She stared at the wall of the cavern for a moment, knowing that behind it the Crystal lurked and suspecting Rimball's statement rang with more truth than he could imagine.

The croc shook free of the rail, scurrying onto the platform and shaking its long, ridged tail. Rimball had his bo staff ready, and Erik pulled free his spear, flipping it over his back so the tip was pointed down at the croc in front of them.

"I guess I pissed it off," Rygor said, backing away from the five-foot lizard with his spear ready.

The croc cocked its head toward him, opening and closing its jaws, which were lined with row upon row of razor-sharp needle teeth.

"You must be quiet and remain very still," Rimball whispered. Rygor nodded and continued backing away ever so slowly. Elise and the others had a slight advantage, being covered in the lake water, which would mask their scent.

"There they are!" a soldier shouted, spying their location from the walkways a good distance behind them.

The croc lunged forward, following the sound. Its legs were stubby and low to the ground, but for all that, the reptile moved fast as a serpent, barreling for them. Erik screamed, bolting to the side and hurling his spear into the croc's flank. The head stuck firmly in place, and the beast curved its body, swinging its long tail and knocking the man off his feet so that his face was only inches from its snapping jaws.

Rimball's staff slammed down on the monsters head, slamming its mouth closed so hard that several teeth shattered. The croc flailed up and down, slapping its tail on the walkway and shattering some planks underneath. It reared back away from them and let out a roar, deep and guttural, before scrambling straight for Rimball's position.

The hunter was already prepared, smacking the side of the croc's face and hopping up to balance himself on top of the bridge's wooden rail. Elise heard the soldiers shouting to their comrades, spying Rimball's move, and one of them was nocking an arrow only twenty yards away.

"Cassandra!" Elise yelled, gripping the Onyx in her palm. Lady Cassandra's spirit burst forth, sensing the dire urgency in Elise's voice.

The arrow narrowly missed Rimball, who moved with the litheness of a tiger, pouncing off the rail to land straddling the reptile's back. Rimball wrapped his arm around the flailing monster's throat and jammed his dagger into the side of its neck. Cassandra scanned Elise's thoughts, taking in the dangerous situation as three soldiers ran down the planks toward them with two more in tow.

"Rygor, now!" Rimball shouted, taking a hit on his back from the beast's snapping tail. The hunter gritted his teeth in pain but held the dagger firm and lunged back, pulling the heavy reptile upward so that its neck was exposed, stubby front legs clawing the air. Rygor thrust his own dagger deep into the reptile's exposed throat. It bucked hard away from him, landing on its side with Rimball's legs wrapped around its torso.

"Aim the Onyx at the soldiers!" Cassandra insisted. Elise did as she was instructed, thrusting the glowing Onyx toward a soldier running with his sword raised high.

A stream of blue fire spit out from the surface of the Onyx, wrapping the screaming man in flame. Elise backed away, stunned as the burning soldier ran back and forth, trying to find a way to put out the magical fire enveloping him.

Elise turned to look at her friends, in a state of disbelief at the violent magic. Rimball loosened his grip on the dying reptile and stared up at her with open horror. "So you *are* a witch," he accused.

Elise tried to deny it, but the shaft of an arrow buried itself in his shoulder, shocking her into silence. Rimball tried to react, but another embedded in his belly. The croc bucked hard, slapping the side of Rimball's head with its tail. The disoriented man managed to cling to the reptile as it rolled sideways, crashing through the wooden rails and taking him over the edge with it.

Elise ran to the shattered rail, screaming for the old hunter. But when she got there, all that was left were floating pieces of railing and bubbles where the croc and Rimball had fallen in. She fell to her knees, numbly waiting for him to resurface, and barely heard Rygor hit the planks as a soldier bowled him over.

All thoughts of escape were lost. The soldiers surrounded them now. Elise looked east, toward Milua Isle. Salvation was so close, yet they would never get there.

A soldier yanked her to her feet, slamming the pommel of his sword into her kidney, and the world went black.

Chapter 10: Land of the Giants

Corbin gazed down the rocky slope, past the desolate cracked plains below to the city of giants. Belikar was mightier than anything he could have ever imagined. The city stretched far and wide, sitting in an oval shape. It was completely surrounded by walls that loomed some thirty-six feet from the ground. That was practically double the size of New Fal's defensive border. Even more astounding, the city itself actually towered over the formidable barrier. He could not see what it looked like below the mighty walls, but the expanse that rose over the wall was awe-inspiring.

The city rose in concentric tiers, with one massive road that wrapped around the hillside over and over until it reached another set of soaring walls inlaid with towering buttresses. At the apex of the sloping city stood a series of castles surrounding a mighty palace fit for the ice giants. The dome-capped structure was connected by a long bridge leading to a fluted tower that reached up to tickle the very clouds above. Few, if any, trees dotted the winding road leading to the palace, and most of the city appeared to be completely devoid of plant life. Belikar was a series of hulking, cold stone and bleak, blue-grey rooftops.

"There have to be thousands of them inside," Logan announced, awestruck by the foreboding city.

"Somewhere in the realm of fifteen thousand, actually," Isaac said as he ducked between two large boulders, laying his staff in the grass.

"Shhh, keep it down, you fools," Kyra warned. "There is a watchtower just over the ridge." Kyra pointed over the edge of the dune. Corbin was so entranced by the jotnar city-state that he had been completely oblivious of the tower.

Weathered and built from ashy white bricks, the watchtower stood at the foot of the ridge's rocky slope. The whole thing leaned slightly to the left on rusting beams, and the long slits for windows around the top were empty, devoid of even the faintest hint of light from within.

"No need for worry," Isaac said. "This guard post has long since been abandoned. That is why I brought us to our current position. We are here to scale that very watchtower." The mage had spent generations keeping tabs on this city, watching, waiting, and planning for his moment to act.

"Have you lost your wits, old man?" Kyra asked. "There is no way of telling *who* or what could be in that watchtower. Even if we did know for certain that it's unoccupied, how would you propose we get down there without being seen from someone on the city walls?"

Rain drops began pattering across the dry, cracked soil around them. The cold drizzle sent shivers across Corbin's exposed arms. After all these weeks traveling in the overbearing heat of the jungle, his body was not prepared for the harsh winds whipping across the desolate plain of the Pal'nun expanse.

Isaac told them that the land here was cursed, doomed to stay cracked and barren for a millennia. Initially, the area had been destroyed by a mighty weapon the humans used to try to defeat the jotnar, scorching and battering the surface in a mountain of fire. The attempt did lay waste to an entire army of the brutal ice giants, but at too high of a cost. Soon after the jotnar won the war, they reclaimed these scorched lands and established the city-state of Belikar, fueling their magic by siphoning off the very life force of the surrounding lands, stripping nature of its ability to heal the wounded plains. *"I've oft wondered what it would be like to see these plains restored, but I was never able to truly hold on to that dream with no hope for the future on my own. But now that you lot are here, finally, we have a chance to reclaim our people's freedom,"* he had said.

Isaac regarded the marshal with fleeting interest. "Hmmm...old man, is it? Yes, I suppose that is the case. Listen here, Kyra, I have been scouting these lands for longer than your waking years. So if I say there is no one inside, then that's just the way of it." Isaac seemed offended that the marshal doubted the validity of his claim. "Besides, we will not be going down this hill exposed. That would be sheer suicide. No, no, she didn't think that, did she? Yes, she did, silly monarch. No, I will camouflage our descent."

Logan nudged Stur, who had to lay flat on his belly to hide behind the stones of the ridge. "What does he mean by that?"

Stur scrunched his face, trying to guess at which part the young man meant, and snapped his fingers, pointing to his clothing. "Ah, I see. You mean camouflage, right? The mage means he is going to hide us, blend us into the landscape somehow." Stur ignored the mage's verbal slip.

Logan wondered why Isaac hadn't just said that in the first place and looked down the ridge. The watchtower was a good half mile down the rocky descent. How could the mage hope to cover their tracks that far?

Isaac slipped from his perch and worked carefully back the way they had come, motioning for them to gather close. Ticking his staff in the air, he counted down through the group to himself, figuring calculations in his head. "Right then. I can't do everyone, there's too many of us for that. So we will just have to split up."

"I do not like that idea. My men should stay together," Kyra objected.

"Good gracious, lady," Logan said. "Do you have a problem with everything anyone says if it doesn't come out of your pretty lips first?" Logan rolled his eyes, amusing Stur, though the weapon master did his best to keep the smirk from his face.

"Before anyone gets too worked up, let me explain," Isaac said. "Tiko and Nero will stay here and set up camp. I can cast a glamour over one tent that will hide it from prying eyes both overhead and on the ground. As long as you both have enough sense to remain hidden, you will be in absolutely no danger whatsoever." Isaac pointed at the ground with his staff, muttering an incantation that slid the rocks outwards in a perfect ring, leaving a smooth bare hillside for them to erect a tent.

Kyra conceded, eyeing the swelling grey clouds overhead. Corbin shared her concern about the coming storm. "Can we even make it to that tower before the rains begin?" he questioned Stur.

The large man pulled off a gauntlet to lick his thumb and poke it in the air. "Not sure. Storm's brewing up faster than any I've seen before. No telling how much the weather has changed since we left."

"We just might beat the storm if we head out now," Isaac interjected, urging the men to finish setting up the tent. Corbin lent Tiko and Nero a hand getting their small makeshift camp in order, and they rolled most of the party's supplies into the cramped tent built for two.

Once Tiko and Nero were crouched inside, Isaac waved his staff over the top of the tent, muttering. The canvas shimmered, pulling into different shapes. Once his spell was cast, the tent was virtually invisible. The only way Corbin could even tell it still existed was that Nero still had the flap pulled open. Otherwise it blended in seamlessly with the rocky terrain.

"Well, that's something else, isn't it?" Stur reflected.

Isaac turned his attention to the group, asking them to huddle in closer and form a circle with him at its center. Swaying side to side, he chanted while working the head of his staff over each of them in turn, repeating himself over and over again. Corbin began to feel the world around him grow tighter, almost pulling against his body. The sensation was like being wrapped in a blanket made of air. Finally the mage finished, rubbing his tired eyes and mumbling that they were ready.

"But where's the disguise?" Logan asked. "I don't see anything different." He looked around to see if any of the others could explain, receiving similar frowns.

"Take ten paces back, my little non-believer." Isaac leaned on his staff, smiling, his robes fluttering in the growing winds. Logan thought the mage looked quite pleased with himself.

After hesitating a moment, Logan did as he was asked, feeling quite foolish for walking backward. However, when he reached the tenth step, everyone vanished into thin air.

Without thinking, he brandished his weapon and crouched low, his survival instincts getting the better of him. From the empty air in front of him, several of his friends began chuckling, and a hand reached out of the space to yank him back inside the magic bubble. Stur was still chuckling when he came into view holding Logan's forearm, and Logan looked around, surprised to see everyone again.

"That's one hell of a trick you got there, wizard!" he exclaimed.

Isaac gave a playful bow at the compliment. "So long as we stay tightly together, the glamour will conceal our whereabouts. But take heed, it will not mask your voices, so stay quiet as mice. Sounds can carry in dangerous ways across these cursed plains." He pointed his staff forward, signaling them to get moving.

The way down the steep decline was tricky, even more so since they had to stay tightly packed together to remain inside the glamour. Bipp had the idea of tying a connected length of rope around each of their waists to prevent any mistakes from occurring. It turned out to be two lengths to connect them all in one long daisy chain due to Stur's oversized frame. Once they had secured the rope, the way down was still tricky, but the stress of straying from the invisible shield was less overwhelming.

True to Isaac's word, they were just reaching the base of the watchtower, which looked much taller up close, when the rain suddenly shifted from a light drizzle to a full downpour, as if some god had decided to drain an entire waterfall over the desolate plains. The winds whipped up into a gusting squall, pulling Corbin's hood off each time he tried to cover his head, until he just gave up and let the rain run down his face.

"Can't you do anything about this weather?" Kyra asked the mage, hoping he would have some spell up his sleeve to keep them dry.

"Yes, indeed," Isaac answered, nodding with pursed lips. "I can climb this tower and get to shelter."

He directed them to begin climbing the rusty hooped rungs that rose up the side of the aging tower. Corbin followed the ladder up the structure with his eyes and felt the world spin as he craned his neck back to see the top. The tower mushroomed outward, widening at its apex, where a guard room sat above the leaning building. Above it, dark clouds obscured the moons and rushed past, spurred on by the roaring winds that drove the storm. The whole thing gave Corbin the illusion that the tower was swaying. Quickly looking down, he clenched his eyes shut, waiting for the world to stop spinning, reorienting himself.

"Okay, I'll go first since I'm the lightest," Kyra said. "Bipp, you follow, and so forth. Just make sure we keep moving and stay close...wait." Kyra second-guessed her plan. "Isaac, will the disguise hold if we are above you?"

"Yes, the glamour is a sphere, equal in height its width. Only Corbin and I can see it, but it is there, to be sure." Isaac waved them toward the ladder and threw Corbin a knowing wink.

Looking around, Corbin was not sure what the mage meant. He could not see anything different than his companions. Why did Isaac believe otherwise?

"You can see it. You just don't know how yet. Soon enough, though, soon enough," Isaac spoke in his mind.

After Bipp tested the rope around his waist to make sure it was secure, he nodded to Corbin. The gnome scaled a couple handholds and Corbin took a deep breath before grasping the bottom rung, determined not to look up at the sky again. Isaac tied his staff across his back and followed him, with Stur and Logan taking up the rear.

"I don't like you prying inside my mind, wizard." Corbin shot out the telepathic message, forcing himself to grasp the next rusty rung and pull his body up. The metal was so cold he could feel it right through his glove, which was quickly saturated with rainwater. *"I did not open the link between us so that you could eavesdrop on me."*

Isaac chuckled out loud and coolly replied, *"Ha, as if I needed to read your mind to know what you're thinking, boy."*

They were already a quarter of the way up the tower, which was swaying in the strong wind. Corbin did not dare look anywhere except in front of him at the weathered bricks while he felt for the handholds above. Below him, Logan and Stur were making jokes, though he could not make out their words through the howling wind and sound of rain splattering across the dry plains.

"I sense you are nervous," Isaac said. "Release your tension, lad. We must retain all our wits about us to avoid being caught by the ever devious jotnar."

Though he knew it was only an attempt to comfort him, Corbin could not control the swelling anger he felt, a typical human reaction when ego confronted fear. Denying the mage, he began to increase his pace, closing the distance with Bipp overhead.

"Don't worry about me. I'm fully capable of taking care of myself," he replied. "Why don't you just leave me alone and be quiet?" Over the course of their journey, he had been feeling more and more uncomfortable constantly being ordered around. First it was Kyra and now Isaac, who must clearly believe him as incapable as a child if he thought his constant supervision was so necessary.

"I see some guards," Logan alerted them, noting a pair of jotnar walking along the top of the city wall.

Corbin's muscles felt tighter than they should from such an easy climb. He knew it was because he was tensing up too much, given his extreme fear of looking toward the yawning sky above with its swirling clouds.

"Hmmm...you misunderstand me, Corbin. I think very highly of you in actuality. If you have feelings of inadequacy, surely they must spring from Elise and-"

"I said shut the bloody hell up!" Corbin shouted, his words swallowed by the wind.

Bipp stopped short to see what the ruckus below was all about, pushing his chin flat against his chest to get a glimpse between his stubby legs. Corbin was so lost in his frustration that he did not realize the gnome had stopped and reached up to pull himself onto the next rung, the same one Bipp's boot rested upon.

Bipp let out a yelp as the rung snapped from one side. He desperately hugged the wall as Corbin lost his grip and fell backward into the open air. He screamed for help as he slipped from the ladder, flipping over Isaac's back, and the rope yanked Bipp down with him. Kyra had no time to react, the skin from her bare palms scraping roughly against a rusty rung as she too was pulled off the ladder, screaming.

Corbin could see the ground swiftly rising up to meet him. A vision of Elise shot by, telling him to come back to her. Stur reached out and tried to grab hold of Corbin but only came away with a strip of torn fabric. Bipp thudded hard into Isaac, who was running through an incantation to become stiff as stone.

Corbin let out another cry of anger as he plummeted to his death, which would have sounded impressive had it not been cut off by the jerking motion of suddenly ceasing to fall and if his face had not smacked into the ashy bricks of the tower. A river of water ran down his upside-down body, blurring his vision, but he could still make out Logan holding him firmly by the ankle with his metal fist. Stur was bracing his older brother, and Kyra's legs were wrapped around the mighty weapon master's shoulders. Bipp had landed right on Isaac's head, his body bent over the mage and his groin in the sputtering man's face.

Corbin pulled himself upright and regained his footing below Logan, cutting the rope around his waist so the others could make their way back up safely. Logan and Stur were howling with uncontrollable laughter, teasing Isaac about his close encounter with Bipp, when Kyra hissed into the howling storm.

"Quiet, you fools." She motioned across the expanse, where the two jotnar patrolling the wall had stopped and were staring directly at the watchtower.

Corbin tensed up, and Logan reached for his weapon, but his hand was stayed by Isaac.

"Stop. They cannot see us."

Looking back across the plain, Corbin could see the mage was right. It was difficult to make out the ice giants' blue-skinned features through the storm, but he could see they were not actually looking at the tower as much as scanning the area around it. The companions had no way of knowing exactly what their enemy heard in that death-defying moment, and they all stood stock still on the ladder, replaying the incident to try to remember if they had shouted out, which indeed several of them had.

When one of the jotnar pointed directly at the tower, Corbin felt his stomach roll. What *had* they heard? He suddenly realized that he might be exposed, being so far below Isaac. As swift as he could manage, Corbin scrambled up the ladder, shuffling right over his brother like a squirrel, hiding back inside the shelter of Isaac's spell.

"Did they see me? Should I reach out and try to see inside their minds?" he frantically asked Isaac telepathically.

"No! We have no way of knowing whether they are magic users. The last thing we want is to have them feel the clumsy prying of a novice," Isaac quickly warned.

A blinding flash of lightning hit the top of a nearby watchtower, lighting up the entire area with brilliant electricity, and sparks showered down from its rooftop. It was so close that the entire watchtower they were climbing rocked from the storm's mighty blow. Bipp just about wet his pants in fright.

From the jotnar's perspective, the area they had heard sounds coming from was completely lit up, revealing nothing. Only a moment ago, they had thought there might be a boy climbing the old tower. The city youth thought they were clever, sneaking out and hanging around inside the abandoned watchtowers, though they had been warned many a time that the old, weathered structures were unsafe. But now that the lightning lit the area brilliantly, they could see nothing was there after all.

The taller of the blue-skinned guards slapped his friend's back. "Told you it wasn't nothing to worry about. It's nothing but the shadows playing tricks with your eyes again."

"You can't tell me you didn't hear it too," his partner said, feeling embarrassed at adamantly insisting he had seen a child on the tower.

"Come on, it's nothing. Just the wind carrying sounds from the lower pens," the guard replied, shaking his head and smirking. He placed both hands on his waist and cocked his head sideways. "Have you been drinking before your shift again?"

His partner looked away from the clearly abandoned tower and shrugged sheepishly, caught again. "Aw, come on. It's not like there's much to look forward to during our rounds on the wall, eh?"

Across the expanse, the companions let out a collective sigh of relief when the pair of guards turned away and calmly returned to their long circuit of the city walls. Corbin chanced a glance overhead to catch Kyra giving him a cold look. He would have apologized, except he also spied the yawning sky, storm clouds swirling in that neverending void above. Another flash of light broke the night and a lightning bolt cracked into a nearby watchtower. This one was so close the bolt nearly blinded them, leaving its ghostly impression on their vision. The entire area shook again from the force of natures' fury and their tower swayed hard enough to make Bipp yelp. Directly overhead a peel of thunder belched across the night sky, the sound of it was so loud Corbin could barely hear himself think.

"Best get ourselves out of this storm!" Stur called up to them.

Corbin knew he needed to forget his fear. He focused on moving up the ladder at a steady pace, and soon they were pulling one another through the tower door, which the wind repeatedly banged against the wall inside. Once they heaved Logan inside, Bipp and Kyra pushed the crooked wooden portal closed against the swelling winds. The gnome rested his back against the rattling door once they had secured the hook to lock it, breathing heavily.

"Wow. We never had no weather like that down in Vanidriell. Read about it some...but never imagined it'd be so strong," Bipp managed between gasps.

They were all catching their breath, and Stur had pulled a dry tunic from his pack, wrapping it around Kyra's slender frame to dry her off. On her, his shirt looked more like a blanket. Logan could not help chuckling at the sight, though for once Kyra did not become cross, taking the offering with a simple thanks and drying off her soaked olive skin. Corbin did likewise with a dry cloth from his pack, looking around the room to get his bearings.

They were in the watchtower, which had two floors. The one they were currently on was nothing but a stone room decorated with cobwebs and bits of tattered cloth around the arrow slits that made for spyhole windows. Each opening was three feet tall and about one foot across. Rain ran through them and down the walls on the right side of the room, the same direction the wind was blowing from. The only piece of furniture was a rotting wooden table set in the center that looked like it had not seen any use in decades.

"Looks like you were right, Isaac. Doesn't seem to have been a soldier in here for quite some time." Stur thoughtfully took in the room and made his way around Logan, who was laying some of his own belongings on the floor to dry. One of the latches on his pack had torn when he reached down to save his brother, letting water inside.

Stur followed Bipp up the curving wooden steps to the second floor loft while Isaac dried himself off using some sort of enchantment. Above them, Corbin heard Bipp let out a long whistle, clearly impressed by something.

"What have you found up there, guys?" he asked, moving toward the stairwell.

Bipp popped his head over the railing above with a big grin. "You have got to come up and see this!"

Stur was making his way back down as Corbin tried to go up the narrow steps. "Best do this one at a time. The platform feels a bit old and I don't want—" The warrior's weight snapped one of the wooden steps below him and he almost came tumbling down. Looking at the broken step, he grew a little red-faced. "As I said, it's not safe up there for all of us at once."

Corbin nodded and waited for the warrior to clear the steps before trying them himself. Testing each plank before shifting his weight onto it, he made his way to the second level. At the top, he could see the room was just as barren, except for the large, weathered, green apparatus that sat beside a shuttered window, which rattled against the gusts of wind outside.

"What is it?" Corbin asked the gnome, running his finger along the brass cylinder.

"It's a telly scope, if I'm not mistaken!" Bipp exclaimed, turning a hand crank on the apparatus's side that rotated the cogs, shifting the barrel upward.

"That's *tell-a-scope*, not telly. *Tell-a*," Kyra corrected from below. "Come down here so I can get up there and use the deivce."

Bipp scowled at the floor and rolled his eyes. "That's what I said, isn't it? Geesh, hang on to your girdle while I check this thing out."

Kyra paused to think for a moment then called out again. "No. Come back down. I already know how to use it. We don't have time for your games."

Bipp stomped his foot on the creaking planks, annoyed to be pulled away from such an amazing discovery, and stuck his tongue out toward the floor.

"And stop making faces at me," Kyra added, spooking the gnome half to death.

Bipp jumped and quickly made his way to the stairs while Corbin pulled the heavy machinery from the corner. The floorboards groaned as the brass scraped across them, leaving long scratches in the dust.

Once Kyra was on the platform, she wasted no time in checking the telescopic gears, spinning each carefully into place. Pointing the lens at one of the lower windows facing Belikar, she tried to look through the eyepiece. It was cloudy, smeared with a layer of black grime. She polished the glass lens with the bottom of her wet shirt, revealing a smooth belly that Logan spied from below through the railing. Stur gave him a cuff on the back of the head and growled to let him know he would not tolerate that kind of behavior.

Moving behind the scope, Kyra tried to get a glimpse of the city and slowly began moving the long tube using the hand cranks. "They used these to scour the land for hidden enemies. With this device, you can see miles away, giving your kingdom's defense the gift of time. There is no more precious resource than time," she mumbled to Corbin while searching the city.

"Ah, yes, of course, you are correct," Isaac agreed, floating across the scope's view and coming over the railing. Kyra jumped back, startled to see the mage flying through the air. "Have no fear, girl, I'm just shifting the density of the air to carry me. How is the view of Belikar?" he asked, tapping the mechanism with a ringed finger.

Already recovered from the momentary shock, Kyra straightened. "It's good, but the chamber is filled with dust, so the picture is a little fuzzy in spots."

"Hmm, shall we see if making it bigger helps?" he asked, though it was not really a question. Isaac pointed his staff at the window and cast his spell. A pool of silver water swirled into being, similar to the one he created for them back in the White Tree. Except instead of moving images of the past, this dweomer seemed to magnify the image of the scope, making it large enough that everyone could see from either level of the watchtower. Kyra smiled and turned the crank an inch at a time, slowly moving the scope along the city streets.

"Why is it dry down there?" Logan asked, immediately noticing that the city was not experiencing the same storm that raged around the guard tower.

"Looks like more magic," Stur brooded.

Blue-skinned men and women dressed in fine clothing were going about their business. Horse-drawn carriages traveled up and down the cobblestone road that curved around the city.

As Kyra moved the scope along the streets, she stopped and jerked it back. Something disturbing had caught her eye. A jotun was talking to some merchant and he held a leash, at the end of which a naked woman was bound by the throat. When the man's conversation was over, he waved goodbye and pulled his pet along, the human running on all fours to catch up. Kyra gasped at the sight, disgusted, as they all were, to see a person treated so cruelly.

"If that has you upset, Kyra, perhaps you had best leave the scope to me and turn away," Isaac said, waggling his fingers to keep the scope moving. He showed them that along the entire massive stretch of the city walls, only two guards were deployed, making their long arduous circuit.

"How can they have no other guards posted at the walls?" Stur said in utter disbelief.

"Interesting question," Isaac said. "Logan, what are walls for?" He floated down to the first level and touched down to the dusty floorboards.

"To keep invaders out?" Logan answered, sensing it to be a trick question.

"Correct. And since the jotnar have one hundred percent completely conquered the surface of Acadia..." Isaac prompted the weapon master.

"They don't have anything to fear," Stur said. "They don't *need* to guard their walls."

It was a sobering conclusion, yet another reminder of how drastically their world had been altered.

"B-but what about...what about rival kingdoms?" Kyra asked, also having a difficult time wrapping her head around the concept.

"My dear girl, the jotnar are not human. They do not war with each other, at least not openly, and never in the same way our own people once did in their folly," Isaac coldly explained.

Stur bristled at his underhanded insult. "Watch your mouth, cur. How dare you compare us to the ice giants?" He moved forward wearing a mask of disgust.

Logan pressed between them and held up a hand up. "Hey, whoa there. We're all friends here, remember? No need to get your blood pumping, big fella. Let's just calm down for a moment, all right? I mean, what's there to get upset over anyhow?"

Stur backed down, rubbing his left forearm in agitation.

"Certainly no disrespect was intended, noble warrior," Isaac said. "I do not mean to call in question *your* honor, nor compare anyone in this room to the evil ice giants residing in the city below." Isaac hadn't intended to set off the warrior with his rather accurate recount of history. The mage shifted his body to look up at Corbin, who was leaning over the railing above. "It is a difficult pill to swallow when you are confronted with our race's flaws. The sad *reality* is that when mankind ruled the surface of Acadia, they wasted all those years warring with one another and destroying the planet. Had our people not been blinded by generations of greed, they might have actually stood a chance against the Jotnar Invasion.

"Now Kyra, you have seen that our enemy is not watching the lands to the west and would most likely never notice you leaving until the Citadel was already in the heavens above," Isaac stated as the scope finished working back and forth along the city walls.

Kyra did not look as pleased as Corbin would have expected. "But you already knew this. Yet you dragged us here anyway?"

"Correct," Isaac replied.

"Wait, I don't understand. In fact, lately I feel like I never comprehend anything, while everyone else is in the know. Why would you make them come here if you already knew the city was not a threat?" Corbin asked the mage, working his way down the steps with Kyra in tow.

"To show them this," Isaac said in a sad voice, pointing toward his magnifying pool and working the scope with his magic again.

Instead of focusing on the walls, the image switched to the far side of the city and zoomed in. Hundreds of blurry pigs were squirming across the lens. Pinching his fingers, the mage focused the image, startling all of them with the sheer monstrosity of what they were witnessing. Corbin felt the acid sting of bile rising in his throat, realizing with sick fascination that the pigs were actually humans, naked and huddled tightly together in the mud, while a broad-shouldered jotun whipped some of them toward a pen.

"What in Toradin's stars...?" Bipp gasped.

"In Belikar, and the greater Jotnar Empire, humans are used in a variety of ways," Isaac explained, "this being one of the worst. What you see here are the poor wretches who have had the misfortune of becoming akin to cattle. These men and women are stripped, castrated, and raised for only one purpose. To become food." Isaac walked through the ghastly image, focusing the scope on a human who had died in her own filth, flies covering her open mouth.

"This can't be real. They conquered Acadia to make humans their dinner?" Logan said, wanting nothing more than to turn away from the image.

"Hardly their only purpose for coming to our realm." Isaac shifted the scope away from the ghastly scene, moving it through the streets until it found some more humans. "And not all of mankind's descendants are given this role. A good many are kept as slaves instead." The scope focused showed a young human maiden wearing a simple dress, carrying a basket full of bread. "These lucky souls are given the privilege of taking care of Acadia's conquerors."

Kyra moved between the mage and his magical pool. "You mean they turned us into errand boys and livestock?"

"Not quite the same thing. The slaves do everything. They pretty much run the city but have no rights or freedom. The lucky ones do the cooking, the cleaning, bathe the jotnar, etc. The unfortunate work the fields and tend the livestock, including the humans. Sometimes, if a jotun fancies it, they even have their way with them, although most end up being sent to the food pens after that. In a way, other than being cannibals, you could say they do all the menial tasks our own aristocracy used to demand of their peasants," Isaac calmly explained without batting an eye at Kyra's mounting rage.

Stur smashed his fist down on the rotting table, breaking it in half, and lunged for the mage. Isaac disappeared in a tiny poof of smoke and began laughing nervously at the weapon master as he floated over the ledge above.

"You *really* must calm your nerves, my brutish friend. This is not about you or your shortcomings. It's not your fault this happened. You were only one man. And taking it out on me is *not* going to fix the situation."

Logan pressed both hands on the growling weapon master's chest, warning him to stop before they made enough noise to alert the two guards coming back around the wall.

"Stop it this instant," Kyra snapped at Stur, who immediately turned away to stalk toward a corner of the room with his back to them. Logan looked on the normally reserved warrior with pity. He did not like seeing his friend in such anguish.

"I can't understand why he is reacting this way. I'm angered by the sight of Acadians being used liked dogs too, but why take it out on the old man?" Logan asked Bipp quietly.

"I imagine he feels guilty, leaving all these people to this fate," Bipp said. "Which is ridiculous."

Hearing the gnome's words, Stur turned, his inner turmoil painted across his face.

"If we are quite finished with our outbursts, there is one more thing for you all to see." Isaac moved the scope to a triangular building that connected to the palace walls on the top of the city's sloping hill. The scope zoomed in to center on a window near its base, enlarging the image further. This time Corbin sensed Isaac's magic was actually at play, magnifying an image the mechanism could not possibly see from this angle.

Deep in the bowels of the place was a dank dungeon, the walls of which were lined with cages housing humans. Jotnar and similarly attired dog-like humanoids were busying themselves at work using alchemical tools.

Two of the dog men were dragging a man from one cell by a metal collar around his neck. They led him to the center of the room, where a bubbling cauldron waited on a raised platform that had mystical symbols painted around it in a circle. A hooded jotun moved forward to press something against the terrified man's forehead, and one of the gnolls forced his mouth open so that he could shove a stone inside, forcing him to swallow it. They could see the jotun chanting something while the human screamed in pain, but thankfully words did not carry through Isaac's scrying pool.

When the robed jotun finished, he moved aside so the grim-faced gnolls could push the slave into the boiling cauldron.

"Blast it," Logan snapped at the mage, "I don't want to see this poor bastard turned into soup! What's the matter with you?"

"Shut your mouth and keep watching, boy," Isaac coldly replied without taking his own eyes off the spectacle.

Inside the cauldron, the man's flesh melted off his shoulders, and his eyes rolled back in his head, the shock of so much pain knocking him out. Soon his whole body was immersed in the boiling liquid as the hooded jotun chanted and sprayed flecks of green oily liquid into the cauldron from the mouth of a metal idol in his hand.

Kyra shuddered when a red, three-fingered hand rose from the bubbling surface and clamped onto the rim of the pot. At the end of each finger protruded thick yellow claws which grew like thorns before their eyes. A ghastly one-eyed, demonic face rose above the liquid, spitting the liquid out of its fang-riddled mouth. The gnolls helped the naked, red-skinned demon out of the cauldron, and it immediately kneeled before its new master.

Slack jawed, Corbin turned to face Isaac.

"This is the third way they use humans now," Isaac said somberly, "as fodder to summon creatures from the black abyss into our world."

With the ghastly ritual complete, Isaac pulled the scope's view out of the dungeon, resting it on the human cattle. Corbin could not believe what he had witnessed. His heart felt heavy in his chest. How could this be happening on the surface without the Elders knowing?

Even as he had the thought, he could hear his own naivety. Of course the Elders knew. Why else would they be so hell-bent on keeping their people in the sheltered confines of New Fal? How could they ever risk the safety of Vanidriell by allowing Falians to know the reality of the surface world? If the general population saw what Corbin had just witnessed, they would surely be compelled to return to the surface in force. Then again...maybe they would not. Perhaps the Elders were right in their way of thinking.

Isaac could see Corbin's inner turmoil and decided to ease the burden, focusing his attention on his brother instead. "Now you know why I have brought you here. I needed you to see with your own eyes what is happening to our race, so you can understand the weight of my need for your assistance."

"To do what?" Logan asked, already knowing the response he was likely to get.

"To liberate the humans," Corbin answered for him in a croaking voice. Looking at the magical image, his conscience confirmed the path he had no choice but to take. If he turned away from these people, if he turned away from this moment, how could he ever look the woman he loved in the eyes again? No, Corbin Walker was a man made of thicker moral fiber than that. To turn his back now would be to shatter the very fabric of who he was. He accepted his fate. "I will help you."

"Of course we will help you," Logan agreed, clapping his younger brother's shoulder. "I'm going to make these blue devils pay for this evil." Bipp nodded in agreement.

Isaac beamed, pleased and silently relieved to receive their support, but Kyra's face made him drop the grin.

"Do as you like, but know that we will not accompany you on this foolhardy quest," she said, shaking her head.

"But Lady Kyra, surely you cannot just turn your back on your people?" Isaac pointed at the naked humans huddled in the tight, muddy pen, waiting to be slaughtered for food.

"Those are *not* my people," Kyra replied. "We have over thirteen thousand souls back in the Citadel depending on me to get them off this miserable planet alive, and we are not about to turn our backs on *them* for some slaves."

"No, milady," the weapon master mumbled from the corner where he faced the wall.

"What was that, Stur?" Kyra gently asked, turning the man to face her. Stur had a stain on his face where tears had leaked out of his right eye. The weight of this was not lost on Corbin or his brother, who shifted uncomfortably, looking at the floor.

"I said *no*. I cannot turn my back on these people," Stur replied evenly to her.

"But...what are you saying? You're just going to abandon me and turn your back on *our* people?" Kyra did not know what else to say. Stur had always been the most loyal knight she had ever known.

"Milady, *you* cannot turn your back on these people either," he replied.

Kyra's eyes drifted to the magnified image. A small child was holding her knees tight against her chest, looking fearfully around her and shivering in the cold night air. Kyra turned away, staring down into her open palms, then regarded the weapon master. Their eyes locked together for long moments, unblinking.

"Milady—?" Isaac began to ask.

Kyra waved at him to stop speaking. "We will help you." She knew this was the right path even though every fiber of her being shouted to run back to the Citadel and get off this forsaken rock.

Isaac clapped his hands and rubbed them together. He snapped his fingers, and the magnifying portal dissipated.

"So what is your plan, anyhow?" Logan asked.

Isaac floated down to the first floor of the tight guard tower. "Why, Logan Walker, I am glad you asked. Do you know I have thought of nothing more than this moment for the last two centuries, playing out plan after plan in my mind, mapping each possibility and waiting for the right opportunity to strike?" With a wave of his hands, Isaac painted a picture in the air of ruins deep inside a jungle. Sitting in those ruins was a half-buried suit of white armor, helmet and all. "This is the Aegis, a relic from the kingdom of Ithiki, long since forgotten in the fading chapters of human history that it was born from," Isaac said.

Stur perked up and pointed at it. "How can it be that the jotnar did not recover this?" he asked, amazed to hear that the Aegis still existed.

"It's deep in the jungle, protected by the White Tree from the eyes of evil," Isaac enthusiastically answered, excited to share his vision with real people after all these years of solitude. Tapping Logan's chest with his staff, Isaac continued. "Logan Walker, you will lead a small group to recover the Aegis and bring it back to the White Tree. This will give us a major advantage in the battle to come." Isaac laid the task out before him, his eyes swirling with gold and tangerine flames of excitement.

"Sounds like my kind of adventure," Logan said, accepting the quest and trying to sound more confident than he felt.

"When should we set out?" Corbin asked.

Isaac looked over his shoulder at the young man. "Oh, no no no, you are not going with Logan. I need you here with me."

Logan shrugged at his younger brother, telling him it would be okay. Not that he was thrilled with the idea of leaving his little brother behind while he had all the fun, but it was probably best that he stay safe.

"But then, what are *we* going to do?" Corbin asked the mage, referring to the rest of the group.

A devilish grin spread across Isaac's face, and he all but drooled at the thought of finally putting his plans into motion. Clasping his hands together, Isaac replied perhaps a bit too gleefully, "Why, that's simple, my boy. We're going to break into the city of Belikar, of course."

Chapter 11: The Jotnar Cometh

Tryn Olvaldi, Marquess of Belikar, gritted his fanged teeth as he pulled the whip far over his shoulder and let it snap again. The barbed tips snapped wetly across the border guard's blue-skinned back, leaving ribbons of blood in their wake.

"Twenty-six," the prison gaoler counted for him, sneering at the kneeling jotun who had been tied up with his arms stretched wide to take the punishment. Blood pooled around the punished jotun in the small, dank torture chamber. The air was stale, with no windows, and there was a rack of torture implements secured to one of the grey walls, right beside where the marquess's hand-blade stood. The jotun was sworn to act as Tryn's personal bodyguard and would never leave his side.

Tryn looked at his instructor for guidance and confirmation that he had performed the lashing properly. Torture Master Pruett regarded the mish-mash network of wounds across the guard's back and stroked his thick, navy blue beard, which was finely kept. One would think a man who spent his waking hours administering pain would be a little more disheveled, but not Pruett. The torture master was ever one to take Duke Thiazi's direction extremely seriously, especially after having witnessed the jotun leader's might over the years. And so, following the duke's lead, Pruett did his level best to stay as neatly groomed as possible at all times.

He let go of his beard and turned to Tryn. "Your technique is getting better," he complimented, running a forefinger inside one of the cuts and popping the appendage into his mouth, "but you still need to work on your delivery. I mean really, Tryn, after all these months, why are you still sweating after a simple lashing?"

Tryn groaned. How did the torture master possibly expect him to whip a prisoner twenty-six times without breaking into some sort of sweat?

"It's those wiry arms of yours that are the problem," Pruett complained for the hundredth time.

Tryn rolled his eyes at the observation, a back-handed comment he had heard all too many times growing up. He was not built like the other jotnar who led the city, all of whom were naturally broad-shouldered and muscle-bound while Tryn, on the other hand, was quite, well, unexceptional. The marquess was of below average height for the jotnar, standing only seven feet tall, and his arms were a bit longer than they should be, though not thick like the warriors of his bloodline. They were muscular, but in a *wiry* sort of way. He wore his hair long, reaching down to the middle of his upper back, like the great jotnar sorcerers of myth he admired, keeping it plaited behind his head. His skin was a shade lighter than his father's, the duke. Where Thiazi had a broad, flat nose and a thick forehead—the strong, chiseled features of an Olvaldi—Tryn's nose was slender and his forehead softly sloped, with full lips and eyes the color of copper flecked with pink. All in all, for a son from a great warrior lineage, he looked soft and a bit average. If not for the teardrop topaz that had been embedded into the middle of his brow when he reached the age to be a "man," you might never even know he was the son of the most powerful jotun in all of Belikar.

"Spare me your endless prattling, torture master," Tryn sneered, baring his fangs at his mentor. "Either get on with some manner of education or take the guard's place."

Pruett eyed Tryn as if he were trying to decide whether to skewer the marquess's intestines or hug his pupil. "Ah, there might be some hope for you after all," he decided, pulling a whip from his own belt. "Now watch how it is done." Pruett pulled back on the whip with ease and cracked it with the merest flick of his wrist, scoring a hit across the border guard's back that bloomed crimson wider than any Tryn had struck.

"Twenty-seven," the gaoler cackled in the prisoner's face.

"It is all in the wrist. Forget about using the muscles in your shoulder and arm, you see?" Again Pruett snapped his wrist forward, never swinging his arm down, and scored another brutal lash, this one across the jotun's neck.

"Twenty-eight," the gaoler taunted, spitting in the tortured jotun's face to emphasize his point.

A rap came on the chamber door. Tryn's blade-hand, Fajik, moved to answer, his hand resting as it always did against the double-headed battle-axe strapped to his belt. As he murmured with someone at the door, Tryn tried his hand at the new technique. Pulling the whip back, he locked his bicep in place and flicked only his wrist. When he heard the whip crack through the air, his heart filled with exhilaration to think he had gotten it right, until he saw the gaoler howl and grab his bleeding cheek.

Torture Master Pruett regarded the strike with open disdain. "Better form, but perhaps we should keep the lashings to the prisoners and not my men?" he offered dryly, clearly unimpressed with the hopeless boy's lack of ability.

"Twenty-nine..." the prisoner groaned to the gaoler.

Pruett snorted, receiving a look of disbelief from his goaler. "Well, he *is* a funny one, isn't he?" The gaoler nodded begrudgingly. "Too bad this is not the local talent show, eh? Teach him a lesson for mocking your man," Pruett said to Tryn

Tryn nodded, pulling back the whip.

"Marquess, your lesson will have to wait until tomorrow," Fajik said, opening the door wider and standing aside for him to exit. "The duke has requested your immediate presence."

"Yes...well then." The torture master cleared his throat, eager to be on with his day and happy to be done with the untalented marquess. "I will see you tomorrow, milord." Retrieving the whip from Tryn, he gave a half bow and dismissed him, moving to offer the implement to the gaoler, that he might seek vengeance on the mocking prisoner.

Throwing a blue satin cloak over his shoulders, Tryn tied the high neck in place and moved to the hallway, happy to let the cooler dungeon air hit him. It was always so stuffy in the torture chambers, and the smell was grisly. He relished when the day's lessons were at an end.

As he walked through the corridors connecting the dungeons and the palace, his boot heels echoed across the walls like the clip-clop of a horse. "What does my father want?" Tryn asked his blade-hand.

"That is not for me to know, nor to say, your lordship," Fajik grunted, easily keeping pace just behind his master.

Tryn rolled his eyes. Fajik was ever the dutiful bastard to his father. What was the point in having a blade-hand, someone who followed you around day in and day out, everywhere you went, if you could not at least know with a certainty that he was your man? Fajik did not answer to Tryn. He worked directly for Duke Thiazi, a point of contention he made abundantly clear whenever he wished.

"Well, it can't be about my tutelage in the art of torture," Tryn reasoned. "I have only been at this new role for a couple weeks now, and for once, I think I'm actually getting the feel of it."

"I am sure you are correct, Marquess," Fajik gruffly replied, uninterested.

Tryn raised his eyebrow, looking at his bodyguard suspiciously. "Really? Is that it? Is my father moving me into another role already?" His blade-hand did not reply, only shrugged noncommittally. "This is ridiculous. All he does is bounce me around from one teacher to the next. How does he expect me to ever master any area of leadership if he doesn't leave me in one long enough?"

Tryn asked in exasperation. The last two years he had been thrown into "overseeing" eight different roles already.

"You mean like the battle master?" Fajik asked, feigning innocence.

Tryn scowled at the sarcastic reference, knowing the blade-hand was toying with him. The jotun seemed to take some sick pleasure in his failures. Tryn assumed it was out of jealousy that Fajik would never be as worthy as he, better than most all of the jotnar in Belikar due to his family lineage.

"That's unfair, and you know it. I didn't mean to cut the fool's head off. Besides, *he* was the one who insisted on not wearing full armor for our sparring match!" Tryn defended himself while his bodyguard smirked.

When they reached the upper level, Tryn could hear the soft sound of Siribel's singing, like a sad dove. The duke's section of the palace was richly appointed with a wide, blood-red central carpet running the length of his halls, to either side of which stood various suits of polished black steel battle armor. Gold plated sconces lit the area, though none were needed, as plenty of natural light flooded through the stained glass skylights high overhead the arched walkways.

As they came closer to his father's offices, they crossed the open doorway where the singing elf lived. Tryn caught a brief glimpse of Siribel behind layers of shifting white silk curtains gently swaying in the breeze from her ever open window. Siribel's sad purple eyes locked with his own from behind the oversized, gold-gilded birdcage the duke kept his oracle locked within.

"Marquess Olvaldi is here to see the duke," Fajik announced to the four armored jotnar standing guard outside his father's offices. One of the jotun nodded, popping inside the doorway to confirm the invitation was sent while the other three blocked the entrance with their sheer size.

"Been a while, Fajik," one of the older warriors commented, smirking at Tryn's bodyguard.

"Ho there, Balistor," Fajik grunted, in no mood for the veteran's chiding.

"How goes the babysitting? Is the tiny light-skin behaving himself?" Balistor taunted, his men howling with laughter.

Tryn puffed up his chest, sick of the ceaseless insults the cur laid on him whenever he was invited to visit his father. "Now see here!"

Balistor dropped his mirth immediately, bumping toe to toe with Tryn in three easy strides. The seasoned Palace Knight towered over him, his barbed black steel armor reflecting the light overhead directly into Tryn's eyes. "Now see what?" he spat, the hot stink of his breath beating down on Tryn's face.

Suddenly Tryn felt less courageous, stepping back from the warrior and clearing his throat while he looked at the floor. Balistor's men sniggered at the cowardly marquess, cowed before the smugly smirking palace guard.

The door opened, saving him from the embarrassing moment. "The marquess may enter," the returning guard announced, wondering what he had missed.

When Balistor turned to taunt the marquess again, he was gone, having already slipped around the jotun and headed inside the offices with a grimacing Fajik in tow. After they entered, Tryn let out a deep sigh, relieved to be away from the intimidating brutes.

The duke's office was a long rectangular room, neatly organized by his staff and kept clean as a whistle from the polished Pakassar ebony wood floors to the grey marble ceiling. The duke would have it no other way. Order and cleanliness were two of the most important principles he lived by. *"You can't run a fiefdom in chaos and dirt,"* he always said.

Tryn strode up to his father's long, rosewood desk, determined not to say anything foolish for once. Kneeling in front of it, with Fajik dutifully keeping guard at the doorway behind him, he waited. Many members of the duke's household staff hustled about, working with a bit more vigor than he was used to.

Something important must be going on, else why would father have summoned me? And what is everyone so worked up over? Tryn wondered, peeking up without un-bowing his head and watching his father sign some documents a jotun merchant was presenting. As soon as the man walked away, he was replaced by the head of the culinary staff, who presented the duke with several dishes to taste. Thiazi tried none of them, but pointed to the two he was most interested in.

As the last member of his staff withdrew, Duke Thiazi stroked his cheek absently while reading over some papers on his desk. Minutes stretched on with Tryn dutifully waiting for his father to address him before being allowed to speak. When his legs began feeling a bit unsteady, he dared to get the duke's attention by pretending to clear his throat. When his father made no reaction, Tryn tried again, this time louder.

Without looking up from his scrolls, Thiazi spoke and motioned for Tryn to rise. "Does the little rabbit finally feel like announcing itself?"

"My apologies, Duke. I assumed my presence was announced by your personal guard," Tryn replied, shuffling his feet as his father looked up with cold copper eyes in stark contrast to the indigo color of his skin and the near pitch black of his neatly cropped hair.

"So you believe a mere soldier should speak for you?" Thiazi asked, eyeing his son like he was looking at a stranger.

"N-no, father. I...just, I thought..." Tryn fumbled for the right words.

"Oh, stop your senseless blabbering. I have called you here with some important news."

Another jotun entered the office, making a beeline to stand just beside the duke. He ignored Tryn's presence entirely and addressed the ruler. "Duke Thiazi, Homm of House Harinndon has sent me to deliver these samples, my Lordship," the thin jotun servant announced. He knelt, offering a small open chest of miniature wine bottles resting on a red velvet cushioned lining.

"Ahhh, I have been expecting you!" the duke exclaimed, clapping his hands and eagerly rubbing them together. "And what are the varieties offered for our celebratory event?"

The servant looked thrown off a bit but quickly recovered, smoothly explaining what each bottle contained with a charming smile that Tryn found infectious and instinctively mirrored.

"Oh, but I simply must try the oaked-cherry. It is my favorite wine, after all," Duke Thiazi cooed, looking at his son with a broad smile.

"Yes, my Lordship, Lord Homm thought that to be the case." The servant pulled out the small bottle, uncorking it and presenting it to the duke with a flourish.

Thiazi laughed, a sound that did not suit him and always gave the impression he had some nefarious plan. Then again, he generally did. "Now, I can't be seen drinking at this time of day, my good man." The duke tapped a finger to his lips, mockingly pondering a solution. "Why, what would my son think of me, after all? I know, perhaps you should taste it for me."

The servant flinched, stepping back and looking as if he might be sick. "Me?" he managed to squeak through trembling lips. Everyone knew it was against Belikar law to drink in the presence of the duke without him taking the first sip. "Why, I simply couldn't, milord...not before you take the first taste. I *am* honorbound after all, milord." The servant squirmed under Duke Thiazi's leering smile, which rapidly faded into a grimace at the denial.

"I insist," the duke commanded. The servant looked around the room as if he hoped for some way of escape. "Now," Thiazi added, pushing the bottle across his desk toward the gulping jotun.

Tryn felt bad for him. The duke was known for making people break his laws just to punish them for his own entertainment, and the servant had really done nothing wrong. "Would it please the duke if *I* were to sample the wine?" he offered, hoping to spare the man and knowing any punishment received would be substantially lessened if it were for himself.

Thiazi grunted in annoyance at his irritating son's interference. "It would please me a great deal more than you could possibly imagine. But no, this sip is for Homm's servant."

Knowing he had no other option, the terrified servant of House Harinndon lifted the bottle with trembling fingers, beads of sweat rolling down his forehead, and took a quick swig. A single tear rolled from the jotun's right eye as he nervously swallowed under the withering grimace of the duke, who stared at him for a long moment.

"Well?" the duke prodded.

"It's..." The jotun looked sideways, trying to find the rights words. "It's fine!" he exclaimed, strangely relieved.

The duke smiled, his unexpected mirth contagious, and Tryn joined in, happy to see his father in good humor for once. The servant added to their merriment by smiling like a fool and waggling his eyebrows comically, knocking back another gulp from the bottle.

But before he could swallow it down, the man choked, spitting a spray of red wine all over Tryn's doublet. He looked bewildered, clutching his throat and sinking to his knees. The servant was suddenly racked with a series of spasms, tightening his knees to his chest as he clawed ragged strips of blue flesh away from his neck in a futile attempt to get something out. Tryn looked on in horror as his father roared with laughter, slamming his fist against the desk repeatedly. When the servant's body finally stopped convulsing, Thiazi opened a drawer and took out a long curved dagger, twirling it absently across his thick fingers.

"But...how did you know?" Tryn asked in utter disbelief.

"What? That the wine was poisoned?" Thiazi asked, staring at the jotun while his bloated throat expanded like a fleshy balloon. "Come now, son, you know better than to ask such silly questions."

Tryn nodded, feeling like an idiot. Of course the duke would know about an attempt on his life, a far too regular occurrence among jotnar nobility. The elven oracle Siribel, whom his father had caught long years past during a campaign in the realm of Alfenheim, had oft prophesied his various assassination attempts early enough for him to react. It was one of the things that had given Thiazi the ability to hold onto his title for so long in the dangerous world of jotnar aristocracy.

The dead servant's throat engorged and his mouth yawned open as a thick, slime-covered black leech slid out with alarming speed. Duke Thiazi wasted no time. Quick as a snake striking its prey, he flung the dagger through the vile parasite's body, pinning it squirming in place.

Tryn felt foolish for jumping backward when the leech appeared. He could see the duke was annoyed by the reaction as he called his personal guards. Entering the chamber, Balistor brandished his sword upon spotting the dead body, making a show of looking about the office for more attackers.

"Oh, drop it," the duke said with only mild irritation. "Have this dog sent back to House Harinndon, along with my little pet. Let Lord Homm know that I prefer the redleaf wine for the banquet, except with fewer notes of leech this time."

"But father, aren't you going to have Homm arrested for the assassination attempt?" Tryn asked, forgetting his place.

The palace guards fell silent, eyeing the pair. Duke Thiazi stood. He was an impressive jotun, wide and muscular. Even in his later years, he still looked as if he could easily toss one of his personal bodyguards aside. Stalking around the desk, he stood before his son, frowning, then sharply backhanded him across the face. Tryn did his best to stand up against the blow, knowing if he fell over, his father would just beat him all the worse.

"Don't you ever interrupt me when I am speaking, and don't you *ever* dare to question my orders again," the duke commanded, turning to address his men and silently cocking his head toward the door. The guards hurried to remove the dead servant, one of them holding the skewered leech at arm's length.

Returning to his seat in a manner only a member of royalty could possess, the duke motioned for his son to listen. "Now then, you may have noticed I am knee deep in preparations."

Tryn nodded, motioning for him to continue and not daring to rub the hot skin of his cheek.

"Belikar has a very important visitor on the way, and with only a two-day notice of arrival, at that."

Tryn shrugged noncommittally. "We have had visitors before. What is the big deal?"

The duke sighed, gritting back his frustration. "The *big deal* is that our visitor is none other than Archduke Marius himself."

Tryn openly gaped at the news, unable to believe his own ears.

"Ah, now I see I have your proper attention, and I can guess that you understand the implications of such a visit?"

"I do," Tryn lied, his mind racing to grasp the importance. *Why would a key member of the ruling dynasty be leaving the capitol to come to a backwater city-state like Belikar?*

The duke leaned back in his chair, stroking his tightly groomed black beard and thoughtfully eyeing the paintings of his forefathers that hung over his desk. "Finally, I can reclaim the birthright of our bloodline," he said, lost in thought.

"You mean the archduke is coming to invite us back to Vrykal?" Tryn blurted.

Thiazi shifted his gaze to his son. "Of course, he is. Why else would someone of his stature travel this far out from the capitol?"

"Does that mean the Emperor has finally forgiven the Olvaldi family?" Tryn asked hopefully.

"No, I doubt that very much. We Olvaldis will be living in the shadow of my grandfather's folly for years to come, I'm sure. Emperor Cronus is not one to forget things so readily," Thiazi said. His thoughts once again turned inward.

Tryn was surprised to realize that his father, the Duke of Belikar, who was always five steps ahead of his enemies, for once in his life did not have an answer. Thiazi was still trying to figure out what had prompted the archduke's imminent arrival.

"Then why is he coming? Have you asked Siribel?" Tryn asked, too excited by the news to guard his words carefully.

Thiazi scowled at him. "Of course, I've consulted with the oracle, what do I look like?"

Tryn quickly bowed his head, showing obedience and just the right amount of practiced fear.

"I've thought this through carefully since receiving the news. The short timeframe and presence of Archduke Marius can only mean one thing. The empire has finally taken note of my accomplishments. This must be an inspection. The archduke will no doubt want a tour of the fields and, more importantly, the dungeons."

Tryn perked up to hear this, puffing out his chest with pride. "I swear he will be pleased with the progress we have made in the dungeons, father. When the archduke sees the improvements I have made—in a very short time too, I might add—to the summoning potency, I assure you he will be more than impressed."

"You misunderstand me, as usual. *You* will no longer be in the dungeons when he arrives," the duke informed him, shaking his head and tapping a ringed finger on the arm of his chair. "I cannot risk you making a fool out of us. The experiments we perform in the dungeons will be a critical aspect of Belikar's worthiness to the archduke. If I was fool enough to leave you in control of the dungeons during his visit, you'd probably blow up the archduke or, even worse, make yourself look like the idiot you are."

Tryn did not understand. "What do you expect the Marquess of Belikar to do while the archduke visits?" he whined.

"If I could, I would hide you away. Better that than give you the opportunity to make a fool of me. However, since that is not an option, I am going to have you oversee the field slaves and food pens, starting immediately."

"But Father..." Tryn began, biting his tongue when he saw the dark flicker in Thiazi's eyes. "What I mean to say is, surely this is the wisest course. It certainly seems so to me. But I can't help wondering if the archduke will frown upon the idea of a marquess filling such a lowborn station in the city." He hoped his father would see reason.

"Again you reveal why these decisions are necessary." The duke leaned forward across the table. "Since you have come of age, I have put you in charge of all the roles befitting your bloodline and title. Yet in each task, you have brought embarrassment and shame to our house. See this for the favor it is, boy. If I leave you in charge of the dungeons and you make a mistake or say something foolish, the archduke will expect nothing less than your head."

Tryn gulped, eyeing his father uncertainly. "Father, surely you wouldn't—"

"What? Kill you to reclaim the Olvaldi birthright? Make no mistake, boy, I would do so in a heartbeat. That is why, rather than have to do such a terrible thing, I am moving you to oversee the slaves. A task even a trained weasel could handle." Duke Thiazi sauntered around the desk and pulled the young man to his feet so he could walk him out with a heavy arm draped around his shoulders. "Now be a good little marquess and make your way over to the slave pens. You will meet with the actual slave master, Overseer Ol'bron, who is expecting your arrival. Take the next two days to get the area into tip-top shape before Archduke Marius's arrival, and before you know it, we will be on our way, me back to Vrykal and you as the new Duke of Belikar," Thiazi cooed in his ear, leading his son out the entrance and waving goodbye.

With the door shut behind his son, Thiazi gazed across the room at the paintings of his ancestors. Finally he could reclaim everything his fool of a grandfather had lost for their bloodline. From the day Thiazi had murdered the old goat, he knew today would come. His life's journey had been to get their family back under the graces of Emperor Cronus. It had taken one murder after the next until he rose through the ranks of power in Belikar to claim the title of Duke.

Grunting, he pondered why such a great man as himself had been stuck with a weakling like his son, Tryn. Perhaps it was the god's way of punishing him for sacrificing the boy's mother that night? Shaking his head, he brushed away the notion. With Tryn overseeing the slaves, he would be out of the way during the archduke's imminent visit. Thiazi almost felt bad for the lad, knowing that his days would be numbered once the duke was invited back to the capitol. The nobles here would make short work of him, no doubt. As he possessed neither physical prowess nor sharp wits, it would not take much effort before Tryn was the one lying on the floor with a Bloat leech in his throat.

Though, the child *had* brought up a good point. In all the hullabaloo of preparing for Archduke Marius's visit, Thiazi had never once thought to consult his oracle, Siribel. He brushed aside the idea that the boy would think of something before himself and slipped into the adjoining room, motioning for the guard inside to leave and close the door behind him.

Thiazi stood in front of the towering golden birdcage and eyed his little treasure. Siribel was a spoil of war. He had claimed her as his own personal pet decades past, during a raid on Alfenheim to regain the Orathi Stones for the empire. Thiazi commanded only one of many battalions, but his had the good fortune to stumble upon Siribel's home in the Sylvani Highlands. He had enjoyed slitting her brother's throat while the elf witch was forced to watch. The thought of it brought a warm feeling across his groin even now. How she had begged for her life when they burned the rest of the warlocks and witches of her homeland alive!

The little elf woman stopped singing when he entered the room, hopelessly staring out an open window nearby carved into the stonework in the shape of a diamond. Themis' afternoon light framed her delicate features, her long golden hair covering her entire back and draped across the floor around her bare feet. Siribel's eyes were the color of polished amethysts, sparkling in the light that reflected off her fair skin.

"You were right again, my nightingale," Thiazi cooed softly, grinning at the elf like a Cheshire cat ready to play.

"When has it ever been otherwise?" Siribel asked, her voice sounding like musical notes playing sadly against the breeze.

"Aw, why the frown today, little witch?" the duke asked, feigning interest as he ran his thick fingers across the bars. Siribel shifted among the lush pillows that lined the floor of her prison, her ivory robes rustling, so she could face him.

"It is the day of my birth," she explained, unable to wipe the pout from her full lips and rubbing her small nose to hold back a sniffle.

"And why should your birthday bother you? Surely you are not worried about losing your looks in your old age?" Thiazi taunted.

Siribel was unable to lie to her master. He had a powerful curse cast on her long ago by his wife, only days before the elf prophesied that Tryn's mother would lead to her husband's death. Ah, Alendria, that was one murder he took little pleasure in performing. So, though Siribel knew what would come of it, she replied honestly and with little choice otherwise. "My age is not the problem. I was just thinking over all the decades you have kept me here in captivity, and it sickened me."

Thiazi growled, his face a mask of hatred. "So my accommodations are not good enough for the elven she-devil?"

Siribel shimmied to the far edge of the cage, bracing her back against the gold bars and shivering.

The duke's face melted into one of calm reserve, and he forced a smile. "Ah, don't get worked up sweet Siribel. I've only come for another telling,

my dear. Tell me what I need to know about our unexpected visitor."

The elf bowed her head in acceptance, crawling to the center of the cage and sitting cross-legged. She leaned her head back to stare up at the ceiling. Sharply her head jerked backward even farther as her eyes became pools of black with the very stars reflected deep beyond their cores. The future opened before her as she rocked back and forth. The oracle recited the many paths of destiny through her vessel, her dual voice ghostly and ethereal.

"The dark stranger will give you everything you deserve.
Forever will the Empire be altered.
Belikar will soon become of great interest to Emperor Cronus,
And the Olvaldi name will be whispered in fear."

The vision passed. Siribel slumped forward, rubbing her cloudy eyes to clear her vision, and found the duke standing over her, inside the cage, with a bullwhip in hand.

Leering, he praised her. "That's a good little pet. You see, witch? Soon enough House Olvaldi will rise to power once more."

Siribel shook her head and whimpered, scurrying backward away from the duke.

"Ah, but first to celebrate your birthday," he cruelly promised, pulling the whip taut with both hands and stalking toward the oracle.

Corbin watched his brother's small group as they worked their way across the desolate expanse, back toward the jungle, with a sense of melancholy. Their separation was abrupt and unexpected. He had been shocked to hear how readily Logan accepted Isaac's plan. It was not an easy decision to split up, and he had been surprised when Logan spoke with the voice of reason.

"What's there to think about?" Logan had asked. "It's not like we have much choice. We need the mage to help us in New Fal. Besides, how could we ever turn our back on those people down there?"

Corbin shook his head. "I don't dispute any of that, but splitting up feels wrong. After all we have been through...I'd rather we stuck together." He had only just begun having a real relationship with his older brother, who until recently had alienated him his whole life. It took an enraged battle with each other for Corbin to finally understand the source of his brother's angst, his feeling of responsibility for their mother's death when he was a child.

"You just want to go on an adventure," Corbin said lightly.

"Perhaps there is more truth to that than either of us realize," Logan admitted. "But there's something else tugging at me. It's as if all these years I have been asleep, daydreaming as life drifts past me. Now, at this time, in this place, *I can make a difference*...and for the first time, I want that. I want to feel like my life matters, like people actually care whether I live or die."

Corbin had stared at him in awe. Who was this person standing before him, speaking with his brother's voice?

Logan shrugged and cuffed him on the shoulder. "Aw, don't go getting all teary eyed on me, now."

They shared a nervous laugh, and then Logan rummaged in his pack. He pulled out a pendant on a brass chain. Corbin's eyes locked on it, and then they did get teary. It was Elder Morgana's pendant, the one she always wore during Sunday ritual. Logan placed it in his brother's hands.

"Take this. I carry it to always have a piece of her with me. Hold onto it, and you will know that I am close behind and will always return—after my dazzling victories, of course."

Corbin had chuckled and locked hands with his brother to bid him farewell.

Now that they were parted, a dark cloud hung over his heart. Though he trusted Logan to hold his own, Corbin could not help the nagging feeling that splitting up on the dangerous surface world was somehow a mistake.

The rains were finally dying down, leaving only occasional gusts of wind, and the three moons above began to shine through the fleeing clusters of storm clouds. As much as he would not miss the swelter of rain, there was a certain nostalgia in being beneath a closed roof again, even if it was just a blanket of clouds. Now that the moons were poking through, their light cast long shadows across the ridge and the desolate plains that lay between them and the city walls. With his brother and Bipp gone, Corbin suddenly felt very naked and alone in a vast world with no end to the heavens.

"We must be off now, lad," Isaac said, placing a comforting hand on the young hunter's shoulder. "You will see your brother again by this time next week."

Corbin gave a nod, pursing his lips, and followed the wizard back to the top of the ridge. Isaac squinted down the shaft of his staff, which was pointed at Belikar.

"Okay, Isaac, how do you propose we make it across this stretch of desert wasteland unseen?" Kyra asked the mage, surveying the cracked landscape for an idea herself. "There's not exactly a lot of cover down there."

Corbin could see that though she had agreed to help on this task, Kyra was none too happy about it. The marshal was clearly someone who was used to getting her way, regardless of the implications, and even though she knew in her heart that helping the human captives was the right thing to do, she was still having a hard time coping with not having her choice in the matter.

Isaac looked back at Kyra, Stur, and Corbin, blinking and licking his lips like some mad hermit. Corbin fleetingly worried that the mage had forgotten who they were, based on the blank look in his eyes. "Yes, of course. We can't use my cloaking spell—too much risk of having one of you trip outside the circle. And besides, we will want to move faster than that."

"If we can't use your shield, then what are we going to do?" Corbin asked, confused as to what alternatives they had.

"Ah, hold still and stop asking so many questions, the lot of you," Isaac ordered, slowly circling his staff over each of their heads in turn. As his staff moved back from Corbin's forehead, he could see a thin, wispy strand of glowing blue energy flowing from his face to the tip of the ivory wood.

"What is that stuff?" he gasped.

"So, you *can* see it, can you?" Isaac asked with mounting interest, without turning away from waving the staff over Stur. "What you see is a reflection of your person. I imagine you can see the energy flows since you are tuned to the psychic aether." As he finished with himself, Isaac aimed the staff straight up to the clouds, where a globe of the blue light emerged and descended over each of them, tightening toward the crowns of their heads. Corbin was beside himself, looking to see if his comrades shared in the spectacle, but neither seemed to notice. They were more intent on watching Isaac and oblivious to the glowing bubbles of energy forming around their heads like halos.

"And...there," Isaac said, standing back to admire his handiwork, "we are all set. Ready when you are!"

The companions looked at each other for some clue as to what the mage was talking about. As far as Corbin could tell, nothing had changed, with the exception of the luminescence clinging to their crowns.

"Is this some sort of silly prank, mage? Where are our disguises?" Kyra asked, folding her arms across her chest and cocking one eyebrow skeptically.

"At this level we look the same, but from above, the world sees a vastly different visage, I assure you." Isaac pointed across the plains toward the walls of Belikar. "Any guards looking down on us will see nothing more than four mangy, wild coyotes running across the desert wasteland."

"Running?" Stur groaned. The warrior could move fast as the wind when in battle, but never did he desire to run.

Isaac nodded. "Yes, we must aid in the illusion the guards will see. Not many coyote found walking at a steady human pace around here." He tapped his staff on Corbin's chest. "Now I'll need for you to add to this enchantment. Alone I can create all manner of illusions great and small, but they are limited to sight only and will not change our voices, which may carry on these cursed winds."

"But, what about that musical instrument—a piano, I believe they are called—the one you summoned for our dinner party at your home?" Corbin asked, his curiosity piqued. "That illusion played music and everything."

"A very observant one, you are. I can see why you were chosen to receive the gift of psionics. The piano I like to summon during meals is made from nothing. It's easy to alter nothing into any illusion imaginable, but that's not what we are doing here. I'll explain more on the way, but be prepared to do exactly as I say to keep our true identities hidden."

Corbin agreed, and the mage beckoned for them to follow, using a spell to propel his body along at a good jogging gait, hovering just a few inches above the cracked desert soil, with the group in tow.

Corbin joined them, staying quick on his toes as they raced down the stone ridge toward the watchtower they had used only hours earlier. His arms tingled with goose bumps, thinking about how terrified he felt climbing back down the iron ladder, and he vowed no more tall buildings for him anytime soon. He felt the wave of nausea wash away as they left the creaking tower in their wake, heading for the looming walled city beyond.

"You see, when nothing exists, it is much easier to let your viewer believe...well, anything they can imagine. However, when something as complex as a human already occupies space and time, there is that much more to hide, lest your illusion be frail indeed," Isaac explained, gliding a couple inches above the ground beside Corbin.

Corbin could think of another time when a robed man floated beside him as he traveled across an expanse, giving him a sense of deja vu. He shook off the feeling, hopping over a large jagged stone in his path. Isaac was nothing like the devious entity known as Baetylus, that evil crystal which had fooled his people into believing it was a god while it fed off their life source, like a parasite leeching off its unsuspecting host.

"So if I understand you," Corbin huffed, trying to keep his breathing steady while he ran, "it would be easier to make a rock look and sound like a coyote than a human?"

Isaac's eyes widened. He had not expected the boy to comprehend his meaning so easily. "Why yes, that is correct. But can you tell me why?"

Corbin found it amusing when the mage acted like a school teacher with him, but he answered anyhow. "Well, a rock has no breathing, no movement, and no sound of its own. It is dull and inanimate, therefore it has less to mask. Whereas a living being would have a certain way of moving and would make all sorts of different noises that you would have to mask."

Isaac was even more impressed at the young man's ease in grasping the fundamental principles of illusory magic. "Well, well, lad, most impressive. We may even be able to begin training you in some of the Illusory arts soon enough. Oh, watch your step!"

Corbin was beaming proudly at the mage and only narrowly missed stumbling over a dried husk of a snail shell the size of a small dog, its owner long since decayed back into the dust of Acadia.

Kyra giggled at his clumsy mistake. "Watch your toes, *Merlin,*" she teased, playfully winking at him before increasing her pace to leave them in her dust. Even after the heavy downpour, there were no puddles left on the craggy terrain, all of the water having seeped into the neverending network of jagged cracks that covered the stripped soil. Isaac seemed to think the marshal's joke funny indeed, speeding up to join her.

"What's a merlin?" Corbin asked Stur. Instead of replying, the weapon master shook his head, boisterously laughing at his ignorance. When they hit their first mile of running, Corbin could see the large warrior was sweating profusely around his forehead and neck. He had even taken off his battle helmet and set it inside his pack, hoping to get some cool air on his face.

Isaac fell back to Corbin's side, warning Kyra to stay close by. "Here they come again, lad," he said, pointing along the far end of the wall where the two guards appeared once more, working their monotonous circuit around the city. "As we get closer, there *is* the off chance those thugs will hear our talking or maybe even Stur's grunting." Isaac pointed a thumb over his shoulder at the red-faced, panting weapon master. Corbin noted that despite his struggle, the warrior's pace did not slow in the slightest. "I want you to use your telepathic powers to tap into their minds—"

"You want me to read their thoughts from two miles away?" Corbin asked, exasperated at the crazy request.

Isaac scrunched his face, wrinkling the tight skin on his forehead. "No, nothing of the sort...unless you can manage it while doing this...but nothing so mundane. No. First and foremost, I want you to enter their minds and plant the tiniest, faintest hint of a suggestion that we are coyotes. So if they should happen to glance our way, they will not hear humans or see coyotes running at an odd pace, but instead let their subconscious mind fill in the blanks." Isaac set the task before him. Corbin could not help feeling nervous at the mage's request, which was asked as if it were some simple rudimentary task for a psionicist.

"Umm...okay," he conceded, halting to press fingertips to his temples and fall inside his own mind.

"Oh no, you mustn't stop moving, boy!" Isaac snapped, making Corbin jump out of his skin in fright.

"Okay, you don't need to yell. Good grief." Corbin scowled back at him, resuming his steady gait. The mage made no move to apologize, waiting expectantly for him to work his magic.

Corbin let his arms shake, wiggling them behind his back as he ran, trying to loosen up the tension growing in his shoulders. Pressing fingers against his temples, he let the psychic aether enter his body. It was not an easy task while moving, the cord of psychic energy fluttering about like a butterfly before he was able to catch hold of it in a steady stream. Once he had a firm hold of the chain, he aimed it across the desert plain, toward the top of the wall, forming a psychic bridge that he could cross to the minds of the wall patrol.

Isaac could see the curved, silvery bridge form and smiled at the Falian's potential. He had been waiting for centuries to meet one such as this.

Corbin directed his mind over the bridge. It burst forth faster than he intended, zipping across the projection and startling the mage, who clapped him on the back of the head, knocking him out of the trance.

"Owww! What in the crystal are you doing?" Corbin complained, gingerly rubbing the tender spot on his head while making sure to keep up his pace.

"Not like that. You have to go slower," Isaac reprimanded.

Kyra frowned at the magic user. "You don't need to hit Corbin to make your point, mage."

"And if I hadn't knocked him out of that trance, he would have just alerted the guards to our presence," Isaac huffed haughtily, unhappy having to explain his actions to the unenlightened.

Kyra looked alarmed at the prospect and gave Corbin a shrug, jogging back over to Stur. He was on his own with the mage. They were rapidly closing in on the city, with only another mile and a half left to go.

"Hurry now, lad. We are running out of time. Try it again...but don't rush it this time," Isaac commanded, waving his hand for Corbin to continue.

Again he channeled the psychic aether and funneled it to the top of the wall as a conduit between his mind and the guards. This time, however, he only gave himself the slightest nudge to move across that bridge, which was difficult since he also had to remain focused on running half-blind without tripping over rocks. Once his psychic form made it to the wall, he swirled around one of the patrolman's minds, gently pushing against it to enter without being detected. Immediately upon entering, he was overwhelmed with the jotun's thoughts and conversation.

"I don't see how she expects me to do that and still be calm in the morning," the guard said to his colleague. His thoughts were filled with visions of a dark blue-skinned woman scolding him around a dinner table while simultaneously rolling naked across a red satin bed, rocking her head back and moaning.

Corbin blocked out the ice giant's filthy thoughts and focused on the matter at hand. He whispered in the back of the jotun's mind that all he saw were coyotes running below. With the task complete, he quietly drifted out and wrapped himself around the other patrolman's mind.

"Look, I'm telling you, if you don't put these courtesans in their place, they will take you for everything," the second jotun urged his partner. His mind was filled with whipping a naked, blue-skinned courtesan while she sat on all fours, begging for more.

Corbin's physical body gagged at the sight of the strips of flesh hanging off her whipped skin. Stur had to grab his arm to keep him from falling over. The guard was counseling his friend on what he would do with one of the city's prostitutes, but his thoughts were so ghastly and perverted, Corbin was having a hard time staying focused. Instead of whispering his psychic command, it came out as a shout, ricocheting around in the giant's mind and setting off alarm bells.

"Eh...what, dogs, is it?" the patrolman asked his friend, who looked downright puzzled.

"What are you talking about? I didn't call her a dog!" he replied indignantly, anxiously looking around as if he feared the courtesan would somehow hear their conversation.

"Shhh...shut up for a second." He stopped, carefully looking out at the desert plain below.

Corbin rocketed back to his body, snapping his head up toward the clouds with such force he was lucky not to bite off his own tongue. Stur felt the jerking and grew deeply concerned, steadying him and urging him to keep moving.

"What did you do?" Isaac asked, suspiciously gazing up at the wall, where one of the guards was pointing at them.

"I think I may have pushed a bit too hard..." Corbin answered meekly. He threw himself into a sidelong dodge as a bullet whizzed by, ricocheting off the dry ground at his feet.

"Ha ha, did you see that?" the patrolman cackled sadistically from the wall. "I almost had the mangy little mutt!"

"Would you leave the coyotes alone? What are they doing to us?" his partner asked, pushing the barrel of his partner's rifle down and taking the wild pack of coyotes out of the eager jotun's view.

"Damned amateur!" Isaac howled. "Get a move on before we get clipped!" Without another word the mage propelled forward. No one needed to be convinced. It was another mile to the wall, and they were completely exposed.

"Well, at least they think we're wild dogs, huh, mage?" Stur huffed sarcastically, extremely annoyed at being forced to run even faster. Another bullet clipped the cracked soil.

"Come on, seriously, you better stop before you rouse up Commander Erruza," the patrolman pleaded.

Without lowering his rifle, his partner cackled. "All we do all day long is walk around this wall, talking to each other. You can't seriously tell me you don't want to blow off a little steam and play target practice with these hounds?" he asked, letting off another round that narrowly missed the darkest mutt's head.

With a shrug, the patrolman conceded to his partner, chuckling at his own hesitation and deciding to join in. Pulling his musket off the shoulder strap, the jotun steadied the barrel against the wall as he took aim. "Five pence says I get one before you do."

His devious friend smiled at him. "Oh, you're on."

"Now they're both shooting. I think they saw through your little ruse!" Kyra shouted in alarm as a volley of bullets rained down at them.

"Nah, the sick fiends are just playing target practice!" Isaac replied, impressively twirling his staff just in time to deflect a bullet that would have lodged in his crown. "If we can make it to the wall, I'll throw them off our scent!"

"Darn, I thought I had that one for sure!" the brash guard brooded, wondering how the dark mutt had avoided the bullet.

"*If* we make it?" Corbin repeated, lunging over a large crack in the ground. They were still at least a quarter of a mile out from their destination. Close enough to hear the jotnar's laughs carried on the strange wind but still far from safety. "Isaac get ready!" he called out, recklessly stopping to snatch a rock and throw it as hard as he could away from their group.

"Watch out!" Kyra shouted, tugging him forward before a shot could take him out, lodging into the soil at his feet. Isaac did not follow his lead until Corbin reached out his arm, channeling energy into a telekinetic wave that he used to carry the stone away from them. Not wasting any time, the mage cast an illusion of a coyote over the rock.

The patrolman who had just missed the wild dog stopped to rub his eyes, swearing he had just seen the hound split in two, each half heading in opposite directions.

"Double to the jotun who gets that one that headed out by itself!" his normally laidback partner exclaimed. It was good to see his friend blowing off some steam for once, biting his thumb to the system a bit.

Below on the plains, the companions took full advantage of their reprieve as the two guards aimed round after round at their diversion. Corbin had to let go of his telekinetic hold as the rock came to the end of his limitations, looking almost as if it were hanging in the air on a leash that began moving backwards.

"What in the fires of Asgard is that mutt doing?" the brasher jotun guard exclaimed, steadying his aim at the mangy, backwards-running coyote. He fired, and the mutt stopped and fell dead on the ground. He howled with excitement, proclaiming himself the victor.

His partner grunted. He quickly aimed his crosshairs at the original pack, his scope settling on the smallest coyote's muzzle. It would be a nice and neat kill. He steadied his breathing, focusing on the target, and squeezed the trigger.

"What in Ymir's name do you bilge rats think you're doing up here?!" the wall commander Erruza shouted behind them, startling the guard so hard that the butt of his rifle jerked hard into his jaw and fired, the bullet whizzing just past Kyra's exposed head below.

"Oh, um...uh..." his partner tried to explain.

"Did I ask you to speak, maggot?" The commander was fired up, still wearing his sleeping attire and bare-chested, followed by two other armed men. "Is there an attack on the city?" he asked the patrolman's partner.

"No, Commander, there is not," the brash patrolman dutifully replied, standing at attention and setting his rifle tightly against his side.

"Sir, we were just shooting at some coyotes, sir," the unwise jotun added, finally finding his voice.

The commander gave him a look that could rot milk then motioned for one of his men. The newly arrived patrolman smashed the butt of a rifle into the jotun's face, dropping the man to the ground with a bloody nose. Moving over to the parapet, the commander looked out at the desert. There were no coyotes to be seen. The commander motioned for his man to lift the bloodied patrolman back to his feet. Moving right up to the jotun's face, he said, "Do you see any dogs? I don't see any dogs."

Trembling, the guard looked out at the desert, where the lone pup lay dead and the pack huddled next to the base of the wall. "Y-yes sir, j-just a co-couple," he replied, pinching his leaking nose.

The commander furrowed his brow, looking over the edge of the wall and straight down at its base, where the jotun had pointed. What the commander could not know was that before he had a chance to spy them, Isaac had already switched his illusion to match that of the ground. So the commander saw nothing.

"Come here, you half-wit," the commander ordered, pulling the guard to look down to the base of the wall. "Where are these dogs you idiots were shooting at?" he asked, pointing out at the empty desert.

"Uh, ummm, I..." the patrolman fumbled.

The commander grabbed him by the throat and heaved him straight over the edge. The patrolman screamed through the air until his body met the ground and broke at weird angles only twenty paces from the hidden party.

The commander sneered at the other patrolman standing at attention. "Next time I'm trying to sleep, keep it quiet up here, maggot!" he howled, adding, "Constantine, take this hapless twit to the marquess for a good whipping."

Below, Corbin sighed, loosening his muscles and strapping the voulge back in place across his back. No one needed to give voice to how close death had just been. Instead they focused on the task at hand, following Isaac to a nearby culvert covered with a rusty grate. The wide tunnel was used to drain excess water from the city's lower level and reeked of foul waste left to rot for years in the unclean pipes.

"This is our way in," Isaac instructed, motioning for Stur to lift the loose grate aside so they could enter. Ducking under the heavy, rusted thing, the mage made his way inside and motioned for them to follow.

Kyra stopped to take one last look at the eastern horizon. "I hope your fool of a brother knows what he is doing out there," she said before ducking under Stur's arm.

Corbin followed her lead, moving to brace the opening from the inside so that Stur could squeeze in after them. "Don't you worry about Logan. He may seem reckless, but he's really become much more responsible over the last few months. Those guys will be fine out there with him in the lead," he replied, though by the pitch of his voice, Kyra thought perhaps even Corbin did not truly believe the statement.

The daystar was beginning to set in the east, painting a wave of hazy violet dancing with rivers of pale pink across the rapidly darkening sky. They had been traveling hard without any rest and had made it to a break in the jungle. The companions were greatful for the reprieve from the tangled undergrowth. The rocky area overlooked a wide range of mountains, and they were surprised to see how high up they had come. The jungle surely felt as if they had been climbing upward but not to the dizzying height they now found themselves. Tiko advised that they skirt the treeline for a while, sticking to the rocky cliffs, which made for easier travel.

The Agma had gone ahead to scout out the land some time ago, and Nero found himself waiting dutifully for his other two companions, standing among the wide fig leaves that covered the ground at the edge of the tree line.

He could hear Logan returning from his foolhardy errand but could not quite determine the exact distance until, suddenly, the young swashbuckler burst from the brush, looking like a madman.

"Run, you idiot, run!" Logan cried, barreling through the thick brush and almost tripping over a vine in his path while clutching a purple, speckled egg the size of his upper body. Nero almost twirled in a perfect three-hundred-and-sixty-degree turn as Logan barreled into him, running right past to put distance between himself and the jungle.

"Outta the way, robot!" Bipp warned, hot on his friend's heels.

"Logan, I assume that you experienced complications in your plan?" Nero asked, raising the volume of his voice to project farther as he ran to catch up with the pair.

As if in answer, a bone-rattling squawk came from the dense jungle behind them. The sound of it encouraged Logan and Bipp to run faster.

"You might say that!" Logan called back over his shoulder, shifting his attention to something behind Nero as a noisy rustling came from the tree line.

Nero chanced a glance back at the jungle and saw a great black-feathered bird burst from the trees in a spray of leaves. The bird was easily Logan's height, running swiftly on two long legs that ended in elongated talons which looked like they could do some serious damage. The cassowary snapped its long neck forward, trying to stab at the back of Nero's head with a sharp gray beak. The feathers around the bird's anger–filled, black eyes were a shock of white that ran all the way back over its head.

"Told you both this was a bad idea!" Bipp reprimanded them, insisting he had been against Logan's plan to steal the oversized egg for supper.

Logan picked up speed when he heard another of the feathered beasts exit the jungle in pursuit. "What are you talking about? This was all your plan!" he yelled at the complaining gnome, hopping over a break in the narrowing path and motioning for his companions to follow him into the brush.

"That's what I meant, isn't it!" Bipp howled back as the second cassowary closed in on them, easily picking its way over the rocky ground on long legs made for this type of travel.

"Watch your step!" Logan warned, stopping for only an instant before shifting left. The ground fell away to their right, straight down the sheer edge of a cliff. Bipp and Nero had no time to see just how far down it descended as they blindly followed Logan in their mad scramble to keep away from the snapping beaks of the enraged birds. Nero deftly pivoted at such a tight angle and with such half-crazed speed that the bird hot on his heels almost went tumbling right over the edge of the cliff. Flapping its small wings to catch its balance again and swinging long legs back toward the ground, the bird barely avoided the plummet.

The larger cassowary darted diagonally, not wishing to knock its partner off the ledge, and hopped over a large rock jutting up through a patch of tall grass. Instead of sliding through the bird's legs like he normally would in such a predicament, Bipp hopped onto its back, straddling the monstrous bird's thick neck and clinging for his life.

The cassowary tried snatching him off its back with one of its legs, but it could not reach him and began hopping around in a circle, violently shaking its head, trying to dislodge the hitchhiker.

"Stop messing about!" Logan yelled, seeing his friend in trouble and doubling back to save him. Nero beat him to the punch, diving to the ground in a roll that took the monstrous bird's legs out from under it.

The gnome flew through the air, landing on his feet already running to escape the other cassowary, who was squawking incessantly as if spitting a stream of curses at the egg bandits.

Thankfully the bird stopped to help its companion up, licking its feathers back in place and making sure it was okay.

Spying his opportunity, Logan directed them to dash through a copse of wide trees. They moved through them quickly, and he skidded to a halt, suddenly realizing it was a dead end. He tossed the egg without warning to Nero, who caught it with ease. "Get over to the other side. I'll slow them down!" he ordered, pointing across the narrow ravine in front of them.

Bipp's eye followed the cliff down—it was so steep the bottom became nothing more than shadows—and then to the fat, moss-covered tree that Logan meant to use as a bridge across the gap. The gnome felt a rolling sensation in his tummy. "You sure that's the right way?" he asked, trying to buy some time. Nero was already halfway across the makeshift bridge.

Logan crouched with his boomerang ready to fly toward the copse of trees, which he expected the cassowaries to emerge from at any moment. "C'mon, you're not going to let a machine make you look bad, are you?" He smirked over his shoulder at the gnome.

Bipp whistled. "Damn thing's probably programmed not to fall or something like that," he grumbled, testing his weight on the old trunk. When he heard the dual squawking again, it gave the gnome a little more incentive to cross, and he scurried to the other side without so much as a thought of slipping.

When the giant birds rushed out of the tall grass, Logan was ready for them. He cocked his arm far back behind his head then snapped it forward, twirling the bladed boomerang over the birds' heads.

"Oh bloody Hel, he missed," Bipp groaned.

"Bipp, I believe our somewhat reckless leader has a different plan," Nero pointed out just as the weapon reversed course, spinning to return to its owner. But not before knocking the bough of a tree off with a loud crack. The limb crashed down on top of the cassowaries, burying them under a rainfall of bark, branches, and leaves. Logan was already almost all the way across the narrow gap when he caught Gandiva and gave it a kiss in delight. The pile of debris was already shifting when he hopped off the tree on the other side.

"Logan, I do not believe they are going to stay trapped for very long," Nero said as the tip of a sharp beak smashed through one of the thick branches.

"Yeah, yeah. Help me get this thing out of the way, Bipp!" Logan hurriedly harnessed his weapon and motioned for the gnome to grab a section of the large tree, while across the gap, one of the birds shot out of the temporary trap, shaking leaves out of its feathers. Logan's face turned as red as the sky where the daystar had dipped behind a wall of trees, straining under the exertion of trying to move the dead tree. Bipp told him to stop and advised they count it down to three, which seemed to help shift the log's weight only a fraction of an inch.

"Master Logan, the cassowaries are free, sir," Nero calmly informed them, holding the large speckled egg like a baby.

"Tell me something I don't know," Logan grunted, slipping in the dirt and slamming his shoulder into the tree, which refused to budge.

"Wait wait wait," Bipp howled in frustration, "the damned thing is connected!" Logan did not follow his meaning until he saw Bipp begin slamming his hammer down on a thick green vine that stretched from the grass to wrap around the trunk.

"Master Logan, the cassowaries are preparing to cross, sir," Nero updated.

Logan looked up to see one of the large birds tentatively feeling for a foothold on the tree on the other side of the ravine. Cursing to himself, he fumbled for his boomerang. Keeping it closed, he battered the vine Bipp was working on. The black-feathered bird called to its companion, who followed it onto the tree. Both friends worked that much harder to cut the vine loose.

When the vine finally snapped in half, the entire tree groaned and rolled two feet sideways before shuddering to a stop. Looking up, Logan was sorely disappointed to see the larger bird still on the log, shifting its long orange legs and digging six-inch talons into the mossy bark. Once the cassowary steadied itself, it lifted its head with definite determination, flexing its long neck and giving a long squawk.

"Master Logan, the—"

"Would you shut the hell up for five filthy seconds so I can think?" Logan snapped, cutting off the android's warning.

Bipp motioned for him to come over to where he had found another vine and leaned over the edge of the cliff to awkwardly strike at it. Logan scurried across the dirt, shoving his friend out of the way as he went to work furiously hacking at the vine.

The large bird stopped to answer the cries of its squawking companion, which had jumped off on the other side when the tree shifted. If he did not know any better, Logan would think it was telling the smaller bird to hurry up and join it. It turned to face them again, and Logan locked eyes with the cassowary. It squawked loudly and ran full speed across the log.

"There!" Logan announced triumphantly as the vine snapped free with a loud pop. "Throw your back into it!" he ordered the gnome, throwing his weight into rolling the fallen tree off the edge. Both friends fell on their bellies, with dirt in their faces, as the entire log rolled away from them with a loud splintering racket. The last of its dead roots pulled free from the other side of the gap, where the other cassowary quickly hopped back off, flapping its tiny wings to balance itself. Logan clenched his fist in victory as the larger black-feathered beast fell away, down the long, deep ravine along with the mossy log.

"Ha!" He jumped in the air, celebrating while Bipp hopped up to do a little dance of his own. "Thought you were going to get us, didn't you?" Logan called across the ravine, taunting the lone remaining bird.

"What is happening here?" Tiko asked in astonishment, returning from his scouting to find them dancing at the edge of the cliff.

Looking a little embarrassed at being taken out of context, Logan gave one more awkward giggle and put Gandiva away. "Oh, hey, Tiko...didn't see you come back. When did you get here?"

"Only a moment ago did I return," Tiko answered, still taking in the strange scene. When his eyes settled on their pursuer, he stiffened, pupils suddenly dilating. "What the...is that a cassowary?"

"A casso-what-are-we now?" Bipp repeated, rubbing the dirt off his bulbous nose.

"Relax, Tiko, ain't nothing to worry about. The buzzard can't even fly," Logan said, trying to quell the lizardman's sudden anxiety.

"We must flee the area straight away, Logan Walker!" Tiko warned in a sudden, inexplicable state of panic.

Unfortunately for the party, it was already too late. Themis' rays completely disappeared far to the east, and the silky blue, ringed moon Clotho already peeked over the tree line to the west, where the jungle wrapped around the cliffs of the mountainous landscape. At that moment, the source of Tiko's cryptic fear became apparent.

As the moonglow of Clotho rested on the cassowary, its high-pitched squawk turned into a gurgling noise. Unable to move, Logan watched in horrified disgust as the giant bird's bones cracked and contorted in unhealthy angles, popping sounds turning his stomach as the cassowary shifted shape into a different bird altogether. Within seconds, the flightless cassowary was changed into a demonic version of itself, one with red, webbed wings ending in talons at their tips. The cassowary stretched its wings and looked across the gap at the mammals that had just killed his female mate and let out a deep-throated caw from a razor sharp beak that protruded a good foot and was now lined with rows of teeth.

"Oh boy...I think you better give him back his egg," Bipp mumbled, slowly walking backward away from the cliff's edge. Logan gulped and absently reached for Gandiva.

With another gurgling caw, the demonic, man-sized bird leapt high into the air, opening its wings wide and swooping across the ravine. Logan readied his weapon to attack and was aiming for the swift-moving creature when Tiko's spear whistled over the chasm, plunging straight through the monstrous cassowary's long neck. The force of the blow flipped the bird head over heels in midair. Twirling in a downward spiral, the dead monster descended into the shadowy chasm.

Logan turned to regard the lizardman with both awe and esteem, clapping his shoulder in congratulations. "Well done, Tiko. Talk about perfect aim!"

Tiko regarded the careless human with a frown. "Tiko takes no pride in killing the cassowary. This one should be giving tribute to the proud bird's sacrifice, given so that we may live."

Logan shook his head, not comprehending the lizardman's meaning. Tiko moved past them and knelt beside the edge of the cliff, giving prayer to his vanquished foe.

"Nero believes the Agma find all life sacred, giving the highest regard to death," the android explained, handing over the purple, speckled egg to his temporary leader.

Logan looked back at his Agma companion, grimly nodding. He could see the robot was correct and felt more than a little guilt for forcing the lizardman to kill a bird that was only trying to defend its nest. Not one to dwell on matters such as these, he gave a helpless shrug and beckoned for the group to set up camp for the night. If they were going to rest for the evening, this was as good a spot as any.

The ringed moon Clotho was far overhead, while its sister Artopos slid behind it in a swirl of greens and creamy yellow, lighting up the night sky brighter than anything Logan had ever experienced in Vanidriell. For him, the nighttime was almost as bright as the Acadians experienced daylight. He relished these nights on the surface that were everything he had dreamt about as a child. They had made camp right on the cliffs, at the edge of the jungle, which was alive with a chorus of insects and animals waking for the evening. To him the racket sounded much like the jumbled voices of a village celebration. With so many different denizens trying to communicate, it was hard to pinpoint just one. Looking across the crackling fire they had started, he guessed that Tiko was still upset with him. With his bone dagger, the lizardman was sharpening a long branch he had scoured the nearby copse of jungle to find.

"What are you going to use for the spear's tip?" Logan asked the Agma, attempting to alleviate the palpable tension and make conversation.

"Tiko will use this," he replied curtly, pulling a sharpened stone from a heavy pouch hanging at his waist and presenting it to Logan.

Logan walked around the fire to inspect the object, pricking the skin of his thumb against its razor edge. Flinching, he shifted the finely carved stone to his other palm and sucked the blood off his thumb, leaving a copper taste in his mouth.

"This one must be careful when handling Tiko's handiwork," Tiko said, retrieving the pointed stone to store safely in his pouch until he was done carving the new spear shaft.

"That's a pretty impressive trick to do with a stone," Logan complimented, squatting down on the bare soil next to him.

"Tiko's people are long practiced in the ways of survival, Logan Walker," the Agma explained, pulling the blade of his bone dagger across the length of branch.

Logan nodded, biting his cheek. "Yes. I understand the Agma only take what they need from the world...right?"

"It is good Logan embraces an understanding of Tiko's way of life," the Agma replied, continuing to whittle away at the knotty branch. "Tiko's people know that we are one with the jungle and every breath taken has a meaning."

"Sure, I get that...but there is no shame in killing that cassowary monster before it attacked us," Logan said. Bipp overheard and slapped his own forehead at his friend's mistake.

"The cassowary is no more evil than a flower," Tiko replied calmly.

"Hmm...you mean no less evil than that monstrous crab that killed our friends? Or maybe you meant the dire wolves that ate Erol and chased us to the White Tree?" Logan countered.

"Tiko cannot fault the dire wolves for hunting prey. It is their nature, much as it was the cassowary's nature to defend their nest," Tiko coolly explained, determined to help the mammal understand the ways of the jungle.

Logan thought on it, almost seeing the perspective in its entirety as he stared up at the mighty ringed Clotho floating in the sea of stars above. He spoke in a low voice. "And what of the Agmawor? Are they too just living out their nature?"

Tiko's knife jerked, snapping the branch he had been carving in half. The lizardman set the two pieces aside. "No. Agmawor are pure evil," he said with gritted razor-sharp teeth, leveling his vertical eye slits with Logan's. Tiko regarded him with all the seriousness he could muster. "It is Tiko's nature to be one with the jungle. The Agmawor have made a choice , a way of being, to kill their kin and eat their flesh. This is not only most unholy, but pure evil...much like the jotnar and human struggle."

"Tiko...I am sorry," Logan apologized. "It was never my intention to offend you."

Tiko reached over, and for a moment Logan thought the lizardman meant to attack him, but instead he pointed a scaly finger in the center of Logan's forehead. "Tiko will never fault this one for opening what is here."

Bipp smiled warmly across the fire, happy to see the lizardman forgiving their ignorance of his culture. Logan reached over and placed a hand on Tiko's forearm, shaking it and smiling to show he understood and agreed.

"Dinner is ready, Master Logan," the android announced, breaking up their bonding moment. Two of the folding frying pans he kept in his pack were filled with cooked egg.

"Nero, you really have to stop speaking so formally. It's just...creepy," Logan said. He looked at the Agma he had just made amends with. "You too, Tiko. You don't need to say your name every time you talk to us."

Bipp agreed with a silent nod, getting his small plate ready for dinner.

"Tiko needs to understand how Logan Walker will know we are referring to ourselves if not by stating our given titles," the Agma asked, while Nero spooned a large helping of the omelet onto the drooling gnome's dish.

"I don't know, what do normal people say? I, me, we..." Logan stood, brushing an ant off his pants while Bipp snatched the spoon from the distracted android to get a larger portion. Tiko rose as well, heading to the fire. "You're going to eat dinner with us?" Logan asked, puzzled to think the Agma would eat the egg after everything that had happened.

Tiko gave him an odd look, showing a bit too many of his sharp teeth for Logan's comfort. "This one...*I* would not want to dishonor the kill by wasting the bounty," he said, throwing Logan a wink before skirting past him to a place beside the fire.

Logan stood silently for a moment, realizing the lizardman had just smiled for the first time since they met, ghastly as it was to behold, and let out a hearty laugh then joined his friends for dinner. After filling their bellies with the bountiful amount of cassowary egg, they told tales for a while until deciding it was time to get some rest.

Logan agreed to take the first watch, settling against a large, cool boulder within the crackling firelight of the camp. Bipp was already snoring as soon as his head hit the bedroll, and Nero placed himself into a hibernating mode that he said recharged his core reactor, whatever that meant.

Looking once more to the starry heavens above, Logan saw the third moon had risen, resting in the sky far away from its sisters. Decima was in the shape of a crescent tonight, and he noticed that if he pinched his eyes almost shut, she looked like the great crystal that floated above his homeland.

Logan sighed, thinking of his village deep inside the core of Acadia, leagues beneath their feet. He thought back on the days when he would hide behind hay bales, daydreaming of adventures in the kingdom of Malbec, where brave explorers went to find their fortunes. How he had longed for a life of excitement outside the dull confines of his small farming village. He thought about how naïve he was then, when the idea of living in the capitol city of Fal was something he was sure he was bred for. How quickly those dreams had shattered, like a splintered chalice under the foot of a stomping troll, when he finally went to the capitol only to find it was filled with corruption and lies. Thinking of everyone down there right now, living under the deception of those Elders, filled him with rage.

The fuzzy crescent moon above blurred as the warmth of the campfire danced across his closed lids, and he settled into the rock.

A shrill cry broke through the night as a swarm of skex rushed past him in a flutter of insect wings. Logan popped his eyes wide open, looking half-crazed as he was startled awake. Confused, he shivered, feeling the prick of the frigid night air on his skin. The campfire had burned down to nothing but glowing embers, bogging down his jumbled thoughts.

"Help me, you bastards!" Bipp howled again from somewhere in the camp.

Logan hopped to his feet as his companions stirred from their slumber, and Tiko soon appeared at his side. The gnome was not in his bedroll, and the strange shuffling sounds of wings shifted his attention to the air. The only moon left in the sky was Atropos, its tiny twinkling celestial body too far away to give any real light to the landscape. Logan's heart pounded like a drum in his ears as he searched around the dark area in vain.

"Get off me, you damned rodents!" Bipp howled again, a little farther away. Logan snapped his head in the direction of his friend's voice and made out multiple shadowy forms with flapping wings flying into the jungle.

"Bipp!" he shouted, hopelessly reaching out for the gnome. Nero was also on his feet, readying an arrow.

The gnome managed to twist around enough to face them, scowling at Logan. "You fell asleep during watch again!" he managed to accuse before being hauled into the canopy of trees and out of sight. One after the other, Nero's arrows whistled into the leaves only moments too late.

"No!" Logan howled in despair, moving to give pursuit.

Tiko grabbed his arm, spinning him about. "There is naught we can do for the little man, Logan. He belongs to the jungle now," he said with remorse.

Logan roughly shook the Agma off him. "Shut your damned mouth! We are going in there after our friend. Bipp does *not* belong to those things!" He knew the lizardman was referring more to the fact that finding Bipp was almost certainly impossible in the dense jungle, but his adrenaline was pumping hard and he felt entirely irrational.

"Nero agrees with Logan. We must give pursuit. Let this one gather our things," the android agreed, snatching Bipp's bedroll off the ground and moving for his boots.

Logan snatched up his own pack. "Forget the rest of it, we leave now," he brusquely ordered, leaving no room for debate and heading into the jungle. His companions looked at each other helplessly and quickly followed suit.

As soon as they entered the thick tangle of trees and vines, the air grew thick and musty again. Tiko ran right past the limp, winged body lying on the ground, but even through Isaac's dweomer, Logan's Falian eyesight could see it clear as day. "Hold!" he called, moving to flip over the slick red body in the tall grass. An arrow shaft had lodged straight through the dead imp's throat, scoring a sure kill by Nero.

"Little bloody monsters. How did they find us?" Logan growled, seeing it was one of the devious creatures he and Corbin had hunted with Isaac.

Tiko leaned forward on his newly carved spear to regard the plump monster. "Tiko doubts this is from the same pack Logan hunted. These creatures are known for staying close to their nests, and we were leagues from here when you went out to practice."

Logan raised his head. "Wait...that means they're still close-by?"

Tiko nodded, looking around the trees for some sign. "Yes, the imps must be within five or six miles of this place to be hunting for food."

"Five or six miles? That's not close at all!" Logan said, feeling his sudden surge of hope crushed by the thought of aimlessly wandering through the dangerous jungle for days, searching for Bipp. Not that it mattered, because he would search for months if it came to that.

"Master Logan, I have found a trail," Nero announced, motioning for him to come see. Across the ground, the grass was wet with spatters of blood.

"You must have hit two of them!" Logan remarked, excited to have a lead. "If we follow this, we should be able to track them!"

"I judge your logic to be sound, sir," the android agreed. He calculated the angle of spatter and pointed in the direction they should head.

For hours the group raced through the jungle, stopping each time they found blood so that Nero could direct their course. The night grew long until even Atropos had descended over the horizon to the east. Logan quietly panicked many times, fearful that they had lost the trail of his best friend. He was plagued by nightmarish visions of the imps feasting on the screaming gnome, but just when he began to lose hope again, they would find a puddle of blood that had leaked from the wounded imp.

After a time, Tiko stopped in his tracks to inspect the grass ahead of them and then groaned. A stone lodged itself in Logan's throat at the sound, and his body was racked with fear, able to guess what the Agma was studying on the ground. "What is it?" he frantically asked, shoving past the lizardman.

Lying in the grass was a dead winged body, pierced with an arrow through the shoulder. Logan sighed in relief to see the corpse was not Bipp but the imp, which had finally bled out.

Then the weight of the discovery settled upon him. "I-If the imp is dead...th-then...then..."

"We have lost our friend's trail," Tiko solemnly finished, crushing Logan's soul under the weight of those words. "I am sorry, Logan Walker."

"Silence...you must be quiet." Nero hushed them with an upraised hand, listening toward the treetops.

"What is it?" Logan asked, cut off again by the android's waving hand.

Without speaking, Nero pointed up to the high boughs of a thick tree on their left. It was no different than many of its other hulking, reddish-brown cousins pressing in around them, its thick branches sprawling in every direction overhead, reaching all the way to the roof of the jungle. Logan started to ask the android what he was thinking, but Nero placed a finger to his lips and tapped his ear, signaling for them to be quiet and listen. Logan did as he was instructed, but all he could hear were the typical sounds of the jungle. Insects chirping, birds cawing, strange felines calling to each other, and...snoring. Somebody was snoring in the branches overhead! In fact not just some*one*, but a bunch of creatures.

Tiko put away his spear, plucking a dagger from his belt and digging it into the bark so he could scale the tree. Nero did the same with the tips of two metal-shafted arrows. The trees in this jungle were so wide that all three of them could scale it and still there was room between them. Though it twisted and made his wrist ache, Logan used the sturdy grip of his mechanical hand to dig into the soft bark and make his way up, straddling the sappy tree with his legs.

They were a good thirty feet off the ground when the snoring grew much louder. Close by on a branch fat enough for two full grown men to stand side by side, the pack of imps were huddled in a pile, lying against each other with fat red bellies rising up and down in time with their snores. Slipping onto the fat branch as quiet as a cat, Logan hunched over, creeping up to the monsters.

His hopes surged as he spied Bipp passed out on the opposite side of the monsters, tied to the branch with a vine. Logan pried a small piece of bark from beneath his foot and tossed it against Bipp's forehead to wake him. The gnome stopped snoring to shift and mutter something about Clara in his sleep. Taking a deep breath, Logan pulled a couple more pieces, throwing them in rapid succession. He was just readying to toss another when the last tapped the gnome's nose, which wiggled back and forth, twitching, before Bipp scrunched his face and sneezed. Tiko fell flat, his belly against the branch, and Logan flinched, catching his breath and shuffling back away from the imps, several of which had stopped snoring.

When one of the winged devils rolled to its side, shimmying closer to the warmth of its pack, and they all resumed snoring, Logan finally let the air out of his lungs. Looking back over the group, he was startled to see Bipp staring back at him, his eyes filled with anger.

"You fell asleep again," the gnome whispered between gritted teeth.

Logan held up his hands to lower the gnome's voice. "I know, I know, let's just—"

"I can't believe you did this to me again," the gnome growled. "It was your turn at watch..."

"Logan, what does the gnome mean? Has he been taken by imps before?" Tiko asked in a low voice, unable to contain his curiosity.

"No, I...would everyone stop talking? We have to get him out of here!" Logan urged in a hissing whisper. Tiko nodded, acquiescing, and Nero secured himself with his back pressed against the trunk of the tree and his bow drawn. Behind Logan, Bipp began to growl loudly.

"I said keep your mouth sh—" Logan turned to see one of the imps awake and baring its teeth at the intruders. Before he could stop it, the winged monster emitted a throaty chirping sound, waking its pack.

Logan let Gandiva fly, catching the beast on the side of its head and zipping past the pack to slice through Bipp's binds. The stricken monster grabbed its bruised head and growled at the human who strangely held out his hand. It never even realized what happened when the returning boomerang cracked clean through the back of its soft skull, dropping the vicious beast to the jungle floor below.

A volley of arrows filled the tight pack of monsters, urging them to scatter in all directions. Some were not fast enough to escape the deadly barrage, as Nero relentlessly let his projectiles fly, while others sharply angled back in to claw at their attackers' faces and torsos with the talons on their three-fingered hands and feet.

Tiko caught one with the tip of his swinging spear, cutting a deep line across its chest. When the creature howled and clutched the wound, he skewered it, flipping the trapped imp to his feet to kill it by shoving the spear down through its chest.

Logan had taken down another of the creatures in midair with a heavy hit from Gandiva and was weaponless when its kin swooped toward him. Logan blocked the attack but lost his balance and fell off the branch. One of his nails bent backward against a think chunk of bark as he held on for dear life. The imp made a strange cackling sound and swooped toward the defenseless human. Or so the imp thought, until Logan knocked the air out of it with a sharp blow to the side of its winged body from his metal fist.

Only two of the devilish monsters remained, and they decided it was time to retreat, swooping low to the jungle floor and zipping out of sight. Logan caught his returning weapon and slammed it into the branch, using it for leverage to climb back up. He ran over to help Bipp, who was untangling himself from the torn vines.

Once he was free, the gnome gave Logan a couple kicks to the shins. "Bloody hell, I could have been imp breakfast!"

Logan backed up, futilely trying to block the angry gnome's feet. "Okay, okay," he pleaded, palms raised in defeat, "I'm sorry! I'm so sorry, Bipp! You don't know how scared I was thinking we had lost you."

The gnome stopped, folding his arms over his chest and turning away from his friend, grunting to himself.

Logan tentatively reached out, turning the gnome to face him. "You can't possibly imagine how sorry I am. No more falling asleep during my watch," he swore, crossing his fingers over his chest as a sign of his vow.

"Well all right...not like it was *all* your fault anyhow," Bipp said, reluctantly forgiving him. "Did anyone grab my boots? My damned toes are freezing."

Nero unpacked the gnome's boots, happy that he had stopped to grab them.

Tiko walked up beside Logan so they could stare out at the sprawling jungle beneath them together. It was a canopy of shadows and trees. "Tiko is happy we could save Bipp from his fate. Logan was correct in making us give pursuit," he admitted.

"We never leave our own without throwing everything we've got into it," Logan replied, explaining the code of honor he had just that moment decided he would forever live by. "There's just one thing left we need to figure out."

Bipp turned to look back at his friend. "Oh, what's that, then?"

Logan pointed out at the thick jungle that stretched in all directions. "Well, only problem we have now is... where in the nine hells are we?"

The reckless pursuit had taken them far from their destination, and the group was most certainly lost in the middle of nowhere.

Chapter 12: Infiltration

"The exit is just ahead," Isaac promised for the third time. After having led the party down wrong tunnels several times, he was losing credibility in Corbin's book.

Kyra groaned. The stench of the sewer tunnels was getting to her. They had been making their way through the network of tunnels for some time now. It felt like an entire day may have passed since they had narrowly escaped the wall guards' attacks. The air was unbearably thick, wafting with stomach-wrenching odors of rotting refuse. The tunnel system was used to funnel waste and rainwater out of the city and built to accommodate the jotnar, so the tunnels stretched wide and tall. The majority of the tunnel was taken up by a wide channel of flowing rot, with only a narrow walkway on either side for them to shift across. As if the putrid stench were not enough, the walls were also caked with rotting buildup and black mold that they tried to avoid.

"Wait, what was that?" Stur motioned for them to stop, cocking his head to listen.

"It's probably just another rat," Kyra remarked, dismissing the warrior's caution. They'd already had to take down two of the dog-sized rodents since entering the network of sewers.

"No, that's not it," Corbin countered. "Stur is right, this is different." He wished she would be quiet so they could get a grip on what was coming. It sounded like a mob of people!

"Relax, that is just the sound of the city above," Isaac said. "This means we have arrived at our destination." His revelation alleviated their concern, and he pointed his staff at the ceiling at the end of the tunnel where it sharply curved. Gathering them toward the spot, Corbin could see there was indeed a covered porthole above his head with small holes punched through it. A faint greyish glow haloed around Isaac's staff. He lightly set it against his chin and began softly mumbling.

"What is he doing?" Corbin whispered to Kyra. She replied with a shrug and began inspecting the porthole.

The glow faded and Isaac opened his eyes. "Above us is a storehouse for grains. This is a safe place for you to make your entry into the city."

Kyra flinched as if she had been struck. "Wait. What do you mean? Aren't you coming with us?"

"Absolutely not," Isaac scoffed, as if she had just asked the most ridiculous of questions.

"So it's okay for you to send us into a city swarming with jotnar, but the *mighty mage Isaac* is too precious to be put in harm's way himself?" Kyra snarled, shaking her head in disgust. "You see, Stur? This is exactly what I told you would happen. How can we ever trust a wizard?"

"My dear girl, I am *not* a wizard," Isaac said, sounding as if his feelings were hurt by the title. "I'm a mage." Slumping his shoulders, Isaac gazed down at his feet and muttered, "Seems like such a simple thing to keep straight. Don't know why she is having such a tough time of it."

"Kyra, please, let's hear the man out," Corbin interjected, seeing no point in idle bickering at a time like this. They had already committed to infiltrating Belikar. There was no turning back now, though he sensed that would be her line of reasoning soon enough.

Isaac's eyes became focused and clear once more as he pondered Kyra's question. "Yes, stay still while I work, no speaking. I need absolute concentration to cast the dweomer." He guided each of them into position so that they formed a triangle with him at its center. "Now before I begin, Corbin, you will need to reach out and cast an orb of silence above the grate, so that none hear us from above."

Though they had discussed the spell in the past, Isaac had given little instruction on how to carry it out, insisting they would get to it before it was time. "Isaac, I still have not been trained—" Corbin began.

"Yes, yes, I am sure you will be fine. Just think of it as wrapping the psychic energy into a shield that silences nearby subconscious suggestions that there are noises coming from beneath their feet." The mage hurried through his education, not giving Corbin much to go on.

"But how do I actually cast the spell itself?" Corbin asked, at a loss for how to proceed.

"How should I know? I'm not a Psionicist, am I?" Isaac snorted, as if the question were ridiculous.

Corbin just stood slack-jawed, staring at the mage, who had already moved on to rummaging through his pouches for the ingredients needed to cast his dweomer.

Stur placed a heavy, calloused hand on Corbin's shoulder. "Never mind him. You can do this," he reassured. Corbin looked at Kyra, who held his gaze and nodded in solemn agreement. These people believed in him. Not that they had much choice. And yet...

Resolved to do his part, Corbin easily fell into his innermost being, meditating to channel the psychic aether flowing in thick curving streams all about him. Above, he could sense the minds of many human slaves hard at work loading their day's labors into wooden crates. Creeping into the nearest psyche, he tried to get a sense of their awareness to background noises. He found it was nothing so transparent as their immediate thoughts or even their emotional state. Wandering across the amygdala, he could sense it was a powerhouse for protection, constantly checking on all the sights, sounds, smells, and other sensory input around its owner to keep them safe. Like the flick of a switch, he turned off the idea that strange sounds from below their feet were anything but normal.

Stur gave Kyra a thumbs up, seeing that Corbin was smiling with satisfaction, lost in his meditative state. Once he had found the path, it was easy for Corbin to send out a psychic message to all the brains in the area, including the jotnar guards, who were not above the mental need of an amygdala to tell them when to fight or flee. In fact, if anything, theirs seemed hyper-sensitive. Once he had the mental suggestion in place, Corbin pulled the energy in on itself, shaping it into a semi-circle that he laid over the sewer grate like a psychic dome.

Letting out a deep sigh, he opened his eyes to find Isaac regarding him with deep interest. "Is it done?" the mage asked. Corbin nodded. "You found the amygdala awfully fast. Your control over the psychic aether is getting stronger by the day," Isaac remarked, impressed with the young man's quickening mastery.

Kyra's brow furrowed at his remark. "You mean you knew what he needed to do?" She received an innocent shrug from Isaac in response. "Then why didn't you just tell him how to do it? What is the point of all the deception?" she pressed, angry that he would play games with such important situations.

Isaac ignored her and centered his response squarely on Corbin. "If I tell you how to do every little thing, what will you do when I am not around? How will you think for yourself when you are constantly relying on my guidance?"

Kyra scowled at the mage. His reasoning was sound, but this was no place to be giving philosophical lessons, in her opinion.

"Your true power comes from within," Isaac continued. "It is not mine to give or to instruct. Do you understand?"

Corbin thought on it for a moment, his head bowed and his lips pursed in a slight frown. Like it or not, the mage was right. He *was* beginning to lean on him for every little use of his newfound abilities. For Corbin, it had been nice to finally have someone he could get advice from. His last mentor, who had given him the confidence to stand on his own, had turned out to be a false god. Baetylus was not an experience he wanted relive.

"Okay, what now?" Kyra asked, eager to take action on their quest.

"I will begin." Isaac carefully opened a brown canvas parcel he had plucked from his pouch, revealing a miniature blue spruce tree with delicate boughs and tiny needles. The entire tree emitted a hazy blue glow, lighting up the walls of the dank sewer. Even Kyra gazed on the glowing tree with awe, lost in the beauty of the mystical plant. The three of them flinched as one when Isaac began snapping off its branches.

"Each of you will need to hold onto one of these," he instructed, tossing the delicate branches to each in turn. Corbin was surprised how soft the bluish needles were against his palm, like the fabric of a blanket yet spiny and rigid.

Once Isaac had given them each a branch, he began muttering his incantation. The remains of the tree floated in front of his chest while he swirled his staff around in a wide circle, fingers deftly moving along the shaft faster than Corbin's eyes could follow. From the center of the miniature tree trunk, a triangular turquoise glyph grew, swirling with asymmetrical living patterns and expanding so that it extended across the tunnel, with Isaac and the tree at its center, while the pointed tips rested on each party member.

Isaac's muttering grew louder and the air around them swirled, whipping away the muck clinging to their clothing. Corbin watched in fascination as not only the debris but his companions' very appearance began to be blown away by the wind. Kyra's face morphed to that of a man with greasy black hair hanging in front of mud-colored eyes and skin bronzed from a lifetime of toil under the desert daystar. Stur was quickly shrinking in stature, hunching over as his bulky muscles were stripped away, leaving behind an emaciated man with similar features to Kyra. Judging by their expressions, Corbin deemed his own appearance was undergoing a similar transformation. Their armor was disguised in the illusion of worn rags, strips of filthy cloth barely covering their chests and loose brown pants that were torn and worn down around the knees and ankles.

The swirling air began to slow as Isaac finished casting the dweomer. The miniature tree still floated in front of him, though with a fainter glow to it, and the mage leaned heavily against his staff, weary from the effort of casting the elaborate illusion. Corbin moved to help steady him but was waved off.

"I'll be alright lad, no need to worry." Isaac weakly shook his head. "The dweomer is intact. I believe I can hold it for two, maybe three days at best, so you must make every minute in Belikar count," he explained, feebly pressing a hand against the nearest wall for support.

"So you need to stay behind to keep the spell going?" Corbin asked.

"That is correct. I must continue focusing on the illusion to keep it intact," Isaac said, making Kyra feel guilty for her accusations. "You must keep your piece of the Xanth tree safely hidden from the jotnar. If they are lost, so too will be your personal dweomer, revealing your true nature as outsiders to all."

Corbin loosened his grip on the delicate branch and it in his palm with reverence.

"You must do your best not to become separated. It is difficult enough keeping a spell of this magnitude going without also having to search for each of you. I will try to stay in contact through Corbin's mind, so do your best to get in and out quickly."

Kyra squared her shoulders, which now looked like a young man's, and motioned for them to boost her up to the porthole. Peering through the small slits, she gauged there was no one about and pushed the grate out of the way so she could crawl through the opening. Once they were all out of the sewer, Corbin peered down at Isaac.

"Remember," the mage cautioned, "you only have two or three days at best to find some chink in the city's defenses before you must get back here so we can escape undetected."

The party signaled they understood and Corbin slid the plate back in place, covering the entrance to the tunnel.

The granary was an oddly shaped building, a bit more like the inside of a gargantuan rounded anthill than a proper warehouse. Some slaves were hustling about, shoveling wagons of ground grain into crates for storage, while others ground the grain between fat slabs of rounded stone that they turned using jutting handles so large two slaves needed to push it at the same time.

Corbin could see the only guards were positioned at the entrance to the mill. Were the humans so beaten into submission that the jotnar did not even worry over the possibility that they may try to escape? Kyra looked disgusted, watching the slaves toil tirelessly for the benefit of their masters.

"Should we make our way out through the back?" Corbin asked her.

"I don't think that would be wise. This is probably our best bet for infiltration. It is unlikely that the jotnar know every human who works the granary. If we were to be out on the street, we would be exposed without knowing the lay of the city. We would be best served to act as if we are one of these slaves," Kyra reasoned, making up her mind and motioning for them to follow her.

When they moved toward a group of workers, none of the other slaves paid them any notice, naturally assuming they were just other slaves sent in to work the granary. Corbin and Kyra quickly busied themselves with shoveling grain into the crates, while Stur helped push the grinding stone, motioning for one of the men to move over.

Under the warrior's considerable strength, the stones lunged forward, sliding easily across the grain with such speed that they pulverized it into flour. The feeble, middle-aged man beside him crashed face first into the dirt floor, losing his grip under the unexpected increase in speed. Stur stopped to help the man up, making sure he was okay.

"You are a strong one then, eh, lad? Look scrawny enough for a scab, but you must be strong as an ox to move the grinding stone so," the slave remarked, brushing the dirt off his chin and regarding Stur curiously.

"Must have just had a good night of sleep is all," Stur said, trying to brush off the astute observation.

"Yeah, right, that'll be the day," the man admonished, moving back into position on the wheel. Stur was about to scramble for some other explanation, realizing the slaves probably rarely got their share of rest, when a whip cracked across the air, tearing the middle-aged man's tattered shirt open and knocking his face into the handle.

"Get back to work, you lazy scabs! Who said you could stop?"

Corbin turned about, surprised, expecting to see an unnoticed jotun guard. Instead, to his astonishment, another human held the whip. Except where the rest of the rabble was filthy, wearing tattered, unwashed rags, this man looked well fed and wore a clean white toga with a purple sash that wrapped around his waist and ran up and over his left shoulder. Stur was equally bewildered to see a human keeping guard over the slaves.

The slaver seemed to notice their peculiar behavior, gritting his teeth and flicking the whip at Stur's face. Instead of a leaving a thin red line across his cheek, the whip tore a gash across the illusion of his shirt, showing only bare chest. Despite the visage that Stur was a slave of average size, he was in reality much larger in stature. Corbin looked at Kyra, worried that their cover had already been blown. Ever so slightly, she shook her head, motioning for him to continue working like the surrounding slaves.

Though momentarily confused that his whip had struck the slave's chest rather than his face, the slaver recovered quickly. "What do you think you are looking at, scab?" the foul man hissed, whipping the fallen slave once more to emphasize his position. Stur knew better than to respond to the slaver and bowed his head, feigning fear instead. "That's more like it, whelp. Help the lazy scab up and get back to work!"

Stur moved to assist the older man, who was bleeding from a gash where his forehead had connected with the wooden handle. The slave shook him off, scowling at Stur in resentment.

"Why would that man be helping the jotnar?" Corbin whispered to Kyra as Stur resumed pushing the wheel, slowly this time so as not to draw any more attention.

"Shhh," one of the women working the piles of grain beside them demanded as quietly as she could. "Keep quiet before the two of you get us all in trouble," she warned.

"Well?" Corbin projected his thoughts into Kyra's mind, startling her so that she missed the crate, clipping the side of it loudly with her shovel and spilling grain on the ground. The guard snapped his head in their direction like a good little guard dog. Kyra gave the man absolutely no signal that she had messed up, continuing to shovel as if nothing had happened until he lost interest.

"A little warning would be nice," she said mentally. "I have heard of this sort of thing happening when one country occupies another. To save on resources they would allow certain citizens the right of policing their own people. In exchange they receive slightly better accommodations or short-term privileges," Kyra replied.

"That is absurd. How could a man sell out his own race just for some better scraps at the dinner table?" Corbin admonished the very thought of the man's genetic betrayal.

Kyra was not surprised by his naivety. The Falian had admitted to living his life sheltered in the underbelly of the planet, raised in blissful societal ignorance, after all.

"I'm sorry, but I do not believe it is ignorance to find his actions unacceptable," Corbin snapped at her, clearly offended by her thoughts.

Kyra grunted, helping the other woman move a new crate in place to cover her slip. "Speaking telepathically is one thing. But that does not give you the right to read my thoughts, Corbin Walker," she chastised him, making his cheeks turn rosy, even under the bronze skin of his disguise.

He knew Kyra was right. Though he had not done it intentionally, he had no right to listen in on a companion's thoughts. Corbin made a mental note to be more vigilant in not abusing his power, or letting it linger longer than it should. There was still so much about the art of psionics he did not grasp.

"Besides, for all we know, this man's position has afforded him safety for his entire family. After all these people have been through, who are we to judge his motives?" Kyra added, moving on to the next crate.

Corbin eyed the slaver while he had his back turned to them. Kyra had a point. There was no way for him to know what despicable things these people had been put through over the years. *"Does that mean you think what he is doing is justifiable?"* he asked Kyra.

She stopped mid-shovel to eye him with cold, steely resolve. *"Absolutely not. After we take this city back, I am going to hang every last one of these jotnar sympathizers,"* she vowed.

They stood motionless for a few moments until Corbin gulped down the knot stuck in his throat. Even under the disguise of a greasy, filth-covered slave, Kyra was one scary woman.

A bell tolled, marking the hour and breaking the uncomfortable mounting tension. The guard began whipping the ground around the group's feet, and more slavers were showing up to help him. The slaves mindlessly put away their tools and huddled into a mass, four across, then headed out of the granary, being herded like livestock by the jotnar sympathizers, who continued barking out orders and whipping the ground by their feet to keep them moving.

Stur fell in line next to them as the companions made their way into the city. *"Now what?"* Corbin asked Kyra, gathering Stur into their telepathic conversation.

"Now we follow the slaves and try to get the lay of the land. Keep your eyes and ears open and be ready for anything," Kyra counseled them.

Stur nodded, and Corbin resolved to follow suit, more than a little nervous to see what lay ahead in the dangerous city of Belikar.

The cool night air was comforting on Tryn's face. For him it was like the feeling of freedom. Safely away from the palace grounds, he found a little more swagger in his step, his high boots clicking against the sloping cobblestone streets. There was nothing better than these secret excursions away from the suffocating confines of nobility.

Pulling the hood of his brown wool cloak tighter around his face, the marquess bowed his head politely as he passed some workers unloading a carriage of goods. Every time he made it past someone undetected, his blood pumped harder. It was thrilling to walk among the common rabble, none the wiser that their future duke was close at hand.

The moonlight and street lamps lit the streets well enough on the higher section of the city, but here, almost halfway down through the city, artificial light gave way to the looming shadows thrown across the cracked cobblestones by the buildings around him. Tryn liked to pretend he was a spy during these secret midnight rendezvous in the city, slipping from one shadow to the next as carefully as he could manage. He liked to make a game of remaining undetected from those still walking the streets at this late hour.

The Ogre's Fist was not too far now. It was one of his favorite taverns, a place his father would never dream of allowing him to go alone. *"Too many seedy braggarts,"* the duke would say. What would people think to see the marquess in such a place?

Tryn snorted derisively to himself as the tavern came into view down the hill on the curving road, its lights splayed across the cobblestone through unwashed windows. When the door opened, Tryn was hit with the raucous sounds of a scab band playing for the jotnar's entertainment. The place was crowded this evening. No doubt everyone had a little extra coin in their pockets thanks to the last-minute preparations taking place all over Belikar for Archduke Marius's visit.

Tryn slipped in unnoticed, blending into the crowd and making his way to a small, uneven table in the corner. He liked this place, though the floors were constantly sticky from spilled tankards of ale, and the foul cantankerous odor that wafted off a group of unwashed jotnar workers nearby was enough to turn your stomach. Despite that, he liked to sit here, unnoticed, with no one coming up to give him false smiles, and no warriors here to taunt him. No one to regard him with that look he was all too familiar with, the one that said, *"How is this little runt the marquess?"* No, on nights like this, when he was able to slip out of the palace undetected, he found himself at his absolute happiest.

Tryn absently watched a group of jotnar playing a game of cards, as he flagged down a passing barmaid. "What'll ye have?" she asked, shifting her long black braids over her shoulder and leaning forward so he could get an eyeful of her ample cleavage, which was accentuated by the shimmer she had powdered onto her indigo skin.

"Pint of moon ale," Tryn ordered, disguising his voice with a rough edge that was unnecessary, "and keep 'em coming." He tossed a copper carelessly on the table, and it spun in place like a top until the barmaid snatched it up, rolling her eyes and heading to the bar.

Tryn watched in amusement as a gnoll pickpocket worked her way through the crowd of patrons watching the stage. Her partner across the room was sending hand signals to keep the dog girl aware of the heavyset jotun guard sitting at the end of the bar, and keeping a mindful watch for the owner. Tryn rubbed his lips thoughtfully, realizing that the two canine humanoids were not concerned about the bouncer. When the furry brown pickpocket sidled over to the tavern guard and slickly dropped some of the coin in his waiting palm, Tryn all but snickered to himself.

His thoughts were interrupted when the barmaid slid a tankard across his small table in a rush, the moon ale swilling over the sides in a foaming pool. Tryn had to resist his urge to quickly sop up the spill. Such reactions would not be normal of an Ogre's Hand patron. Regardless of how many times he had been in these seedy taverns, he could not quell the urge to at least wipe down the outside of his wooden mug, which had specks of crud dried onto it like glue. As he sipped the bitter ale, the band's time came to an end and they cleared off the cramped stage.

"Next up we have a rare treat for ye scallywags!" a squat, big-bellied jotun announced. Tryn hoped it would be a scab battle-match. He enjoyed watching the little humans kill each other for glory. "At the bequest of his *lordship*, Baxter the Bastard—" The patrons all laughed, along with tavern owner Baxter. "—I give you my wingless dove, Annabel," the jotun finished with weak flair, hobbling off the stage on a bad leg.

Tryn cared little for human singing. It always sounded like a whining cat in heat. Instead he watched a group of jotnar fistfight over a spilled drink, musing how simple-minded the commoners were.

He groaned, realizing that after the archduke's visit, *he* would likely be the fool in charge of this rabble, leader of the entire city-state, to be exact. Tryn wondered if he could step aside and give the position to another, perhaps some jotun noble more worthy than he of the responsibility. Yes, he could relinquish the title and leave Belikar for the Gray Tower, a place he properly belonged. Long had he dreamed of joining the ranks of those great jotnar magic users, taking on the mantle of apprentice under one of the master sorcerers.

Glumly, he silently shook his head and stared down into his own sad, half-cloaked face reflected in the black ale he held between his cupped hands. No. His father would never allow such a thing. Even leagues away in the capitol, Thiazi would no doubt still have a firm grip over his life.

His reverie was broken by the sound of an angel singing in the back of his mind. For a moment he wondered if he had suffered a split from reality to hear such a magnificent voice in a seedy place such as this. However, once his eyes landed on the stage, he saw the melody's source.

A gnoll sat on a stool, wearing a forest green jerkin with a white tunic underneath and matching green breeches. His pawed feet tapped in time to the music he played on a fairly tuned lute, and one of the dogman's wrists was strapped to a leash attached to the metal collar around the human female singer's throat.

Instantly upon seeing her, Tryn was taken aback. For the most part she looked just like any other bronze-skinned scab. Long, unkempt brown hair ran down to her bottom, and grimy scraps of clothing loosely hung around her. But there was something about the curve of the human's shoulders, the fullness of her supple lips, or maybe the strange, sorrowful gleam in her uncommonly blue eyes that caught his attention. As she sang, Tryn found himself riveted by the rich melodic timbre of her voice, like a robin singing as dawn appeared over the mountains.

Are you ready, you few,
To resist with all your might,
Stand your ground in the fight?

Are you brave enough,
Will you join our path to freedom?
And stick to it with your burning hearts.
For your strength may easily be wasted,
If you stand up to the Aesir all alone.
When to some sad tales, your name is marked,
One more proud jotnar hero who failed all on his own.

A life mighty and free,
Just the same as boughs of the world tree.
And yet strong, like dwergaz steel,
That's so longing of the old fires,
It provides us with strength for our fray.

Facing the dullness, the hatred and sway,
Dear companions in rage, dear jotnar in fight,
Know that time and timber will reclaim our right.

When the exotic little slave finished the chorus and moved on to her second round, Tryn noticed her voice had entranced many of the tavern patrons, like silk and honey washing over their ears. The gnoll pickpockets were using it as a prime opportunity to relinquish the distracted drunks of their valuables, and the tavern owner leaned forward, resting his elbows on the sticky bar with his chin cupped between rough blue hands. The longer she sang, the more Tryn's heart seemed to ache. He felt a strange sensation in his belly, watching the delicate creature perform.

A rough-looking group of jotnar, close to the stage, began heckling the performers. "Look here, we gots us a dog playing for a scab!" a short, round-bellied jotun announced, flinging some walnut shells on stage.

The human's expression did not waver as the hard shells hit her skin, and a ripple of laughter erupted across the tavern. It was as if someone had given the patrons a firm backhand to bring them back to their senses, having forgotten for a moment that they were actually bottom feeders. Most of the tavern's denizens went back to their business, but a few joined in on the fun, tossing insults and whatever scraps they could find onto the stage.

Baxter motioned for his bouncer to intervene. He did not want a mess to clean up and quite enjoyed when Kallix brought the lass to his tavern. Tryn thought he was sure to see a physical display of prowess when the large man sidled over to the offending tables. However, rather than knock a couple of their skulls together, the bouncer started exchanging clever jibes with the unruly drunks, cleverly distracting them from the human performer. Tryn was impressed by the display.

He was knocking back his second ale when one of the card players nearby threw his chair backward as he lunged over the table to wrap his large hands around a gnoll's throat. "Cheatin' furry bastard, I'll kill ye!" he howled. Before the bouncer could make it to the card table, the gnoll had plucked a small dagger from his fur and jabbed it into the accusing jotun's side several times. Chaos erupted around the table, thrilling Tryn with its vulgarity. This was one of the things he so enjoyed about the lower city taverns—you never knew when blood would be spilled.

He watched in amusement, thinking to signal for another drink, when, out of the corner of his eye, he caught something else of interest. The group of heckling jotnar rabble had moved away from their table and surrounded the stage, and the short, round-bellied one climbed the platform, leering at the human. Tryn felt his eye twitch and blood start pumping hard in his veins. He did not know why it should matter to him. It was not as if this was an uncommon occurrence, and what should it matter to him what happened to a scab?

Tryn was shocked to find he was already moving through the crowd, pressing for the stage. As he neared it, he could hear the fat jotun taunting the slave girl, who was doing her best to continue singing despite her obvious terror. The jotun jerked her head back by the hair and whispered something lewd into her ear. Her eyes widened like saucers, filled with dread. And yet she continued to sing.

Tryn climbed the stage from the side as the offender grabbed a handful of the human's breast, licking her cheek while his men snickered.

"Take your hands off of the scab," Tryn ordered, looking down at the stout jotun with a courage he never knew he possessed.

The group laughed even harder, thinking he was joking.

"Now," Tryn added, channeling his father's tone and air of leadership. All the while the human kept singing and the gnoll continued to play out his tune.

Two of the larger jotnar moved to teach this lout a lesson, but they were halted by their plump friend. He looked up at Tryn, wondering why in the seven kingdoms this lanky hooded jotun cared whether he toyed with the scab slut. "What's the matter, pal, you got a crush on the little scab?" he teased, running his hand down her belly and into the folds of her clothing, finally stifling her song under fearful tears.

"I am warning you," Tryn growled. The gnoll dropped his lute, throwing the human's leash to the ground and scurrying off the stage.

"Warning me what?" the jotun snarled, spitting on the human and turning to his friends, who began climbing the platform and surrounded the cloaked stranger. "Looks like we got us a human sympathizer, fellas."

Tryn's face felt hot, suddenly aware that many eyes were on them, watching the spectacle of a jotun defending a scab on stage. He was more shocked than the spectators when his whip cracked across the air, licking the fat-bellied jotun's face with its barbed tips. The fat man squealed, shuffling backward and gripping the stinging line of blood across his lips. He mumbled something incoherent, and one of his companions roared to his friends to tear Tryn apart.

Before they could move forward, Tryn tore his hood back, revealing himself in front of the common filth, his face a mask of indignation. The four jotnar stumbled, gaping that the marquess himself stood before them. It seemed to Tryn that everyone in the tavern gasped.

Upon seeing the teardrop of topaz on the unmasked jotun's brow, Baxter called, "It's the bloody duke's son, you twits." And one after the other, the patrons and workers alike fell to their knees. Tryn looked across the tavern, a swell of pride blooming in his chest as adrenaline pumped coarsely through his veins.

"My humble apologies, yer lordship. I meant no disrespect, sire, honest to me mother's grave," the toad-like jotun whined, his bleeding face pressed to the filthy stage floor. As much as Tryn relished the swift change in attitude, he knew he needed some excuse as to why he had stopped the jotnar from their lewd act.

"I was enjoying the little scab's song. It displeases me to have my enjoyment taken away," he growled, pacing slowly around the prone man. "Now, what was it you called me? Oh yes, scab sympathizer." Tryn felt as if he were someone else, observing the events from the outside.

The fat jotun squeaked again, knowing he was in for a world of hurt before Tryn's whip even touched his back. The marquess thrashed the insolent pig over and over, letting out all his rage on the stage, his lashes cutting deep wounds that even Torture Master Pruett would be proud of. Ragged strips of flesh hung where his whip tore across the fat little bastard's exposed arms, his neck, and even his skull. When the squealing little pig rolled unconscious to his back, Tryn continued to beat him, ripping apart the jotun's flabby, blue-skinned belly.

When his rage finally played out, Tryn turned to face the horrified patrons. Collecting himself, the marquess smoothed back his hair with trembling hands and addressed the beaten jotun's friends. "Get this dog out of my sight," he ordered in a shaky voice. "And *never* interrupt me again," he added, hearing how dumb it sounded and wincing inside. "Well? Get back to it!" he barked at the tavern.

Everyone quickly made an effort to go back to their festivities. Coiling the bloody whip, Tryn returned it to the folds of his cloak and crouched down to tap the prone human's shoulder. When his finger touched her, the woman jerked and let out a squeak, terrified she was about to be beaten.

Tryn grasped her jaw between slender, gloved fingers, pulling her face up to look at him. Inspecting the scab for a moment, he wondered why the woman made his belly feel so warm. "Get up. You are coming with me," he softly ordered, realizing it was a bit too kindly spoken and worrying that those nearby would get the wrong impression. But what was the right impression?

The human did as she was told, trying her best to stand up on shaking legs in the presence of the vicious marquess and quickly wiping the tears from her eyes.

As Tryn made his way to the door, he made an extra show of pulling the woman by her leash, roughly yanking on it when she did not keep pace.

Just as he neared the exit, the bow-legged entertainment master cut in front of his path. Raising his hands diplomatically, the jotun merchant smiled broadly at him. "Why, Marquess, where *are* you going with my merchandise?" he asked innocently, though his greedy eyes belied the jotun's true intention.

"Wherever I want. Step out of my way," Tryn replied evenly, trying to move around him.

The opportunistic man continued to smile, blocking his way once more. "My Lordship surely would not take away his humble, lowly, servant's goods without some form of recompense, eh?" Kallix shrugged, speaking loudly enough for all nearby to hear and adding, "After all, the law is the law, and one cannot take a slave unless a fair bargain is struck, correct?"

Tryn snickered at the merchant's tenacity. He knew the jotun was correct. The law was set up to stop over-eager jotnar from killing slavers or stealing their wares to increase their own rank. It was a law the duke had set up after doing exactly that to rise in power, and it was one he brutally enforced.

"Get out of my way," Tryn repeated, forcing a smirk onto his face as he flicked a gold piece to the jotun, who practically drooled as he snatched the coin from the air and stared down at it as if it were the most beautiful thing he had ever seen.

Yanking the human's leash, Tryn exited the building, the cool night air washing deliciously over his face again. Looking back over his shoulder at the woman and the tavern beyond, he let out a heavy sigh, relieved to be out of the dangerous pit of vipers.

"Well, that was most unexpected," Fajik announced, revealing himself where he leaned with his arms crossed in the shadows by the tavern window. The blade-hand regarded Tryn with marked interest. "Not your usual night out, I would say."

Disarmed, Tryn bobbed his head back and cocked an eyebrow. "What are you doing here? How long have you been watching?"

"My dear marquess, I am *always* here. You didn't actually think I would let you sneak out of the palace without keeping tabs did you?" Fajik smugly replied, snorting at his charge's naivety.

"But the ale...?" Tryn exclaimed.

"Yes, yes...I fake it. It takes a lot more than a couple pints of honeywine to get me drunk," Fajik answered.

Tryn felt foolish. All the times he had slipped out of the palace, thinking he was alone and exploring the city, his bodyguard must have been silently following him. Of course the blade-hand could not let him wander around alone. If anything ever happened, the duke would have the jotun's head.

"But on to the real question," Fajik continued, pushing away from the wall and walking toward them. "Where are you going with the scab?" He moved her hair back to inspect the woman's face with curiosity.

Tryn slapped the leering bodyguard's hand away. "Back to the palace."

Fajik gave him a dark look, both surprised and annoyed to have the marquess get physical with him. "We have plenty of slaves. What do you need another human for?" he asked, carefully gauging the marquess's response.

Tryn looked at the overly suspicious man, then at the human singer, who was dutifully staring at her feet. What *did* he need her for? Why in the world had he whipped that jotun over this scab?

He gave the most plausible answer his mind could muster. "The scab is going to be my personal concubine."

Fajik smiled shrewdly. He liked the sound of that, and he liked the marquess's change in personality. Both reeked of power, something which many had been waiting for the duke's son to exhibit for years now. "Well, then it looks like we better sneak you *and* your new pet back into the palace then, eh?" Fajik smirked, regarding the marquess in a new light.

They were lost. Nero had no way of determining their position. His tracking skills were completely dependent on a point of reference, some familiar landmark he could calculate by. And since the entire surface of the land had been altered and overgrown, he had no way of guiding their course. Tiko had never been in these parts of the jungle, warning that they were avoided at all costs by the Agma. Fortunately, he did not need to know where they were to lead them in the proper direction. All Tiko needed were the stars as his guide, so at least they were headed north again.

The party stopped to rest several times. Hiking through the sweltering heat of the jungle was too much for the Falians to take, although Nero was perfectly fine, merely adjusting his core exhaust to adapt to the changes in climate. Even with the weariness that came from traveling under the hot surface light, which heated the jungle like an oven, Logan could not bring himself to fall asleep. He did not know if it was a guilty conscience playing tricks with his mind, or if it was more a matter of how uncomfortable he felt with sweat dripping out of every pore in his body. Either way, while the others rested, he stayed awake, alert and vigilant to face the next unseen enemy.

Tiko was correct about the area being dangerous, though Logan was not sure it was worse than any other place they had been since coming to the surface. At one point they almost walked into an entire nest of baby malbrix, man-eating plants whose long vines waved about at the prospect of trapping animals to feed on. If Tiko had not blocked Bipp's path with the length of his spear, the little gnome would surely have become plant food.

Another time, Logan had stopped to admire some flowers around the base of some thin, oddly angled light-green trees that broke into segments as they reached for the jungle canopy. The flowers had three rounded petals that were a silky purple blending with a freckled white center, the stamens sticking out at him like teasing tongues. He found them intriguing and was lulled in by their heady perfume. Tiko did not know what they were called but seemed equally enthralled.

If not for Logan's near-death experience in the winding tunnels that led to Bipp's homeland, Dudje, he may have ended his journey right then and there. But thankfully, a nagging tickle in the back of his head made him look around the tall grass, where he saw several rotting carcasses of other animals that had wandered too close to the dangerous orchids. He felt lucky to have realized the flowers emitted an intoxicating endorphin which lulled its prey into sleep. Bipp grumbled that the flower's poison would not have worked either way, since Nero would have been immune and woken them up. Logan laughed it off, as the gnome was still a little miffed over being taken by the imps.

After marching all night and halfway through the next day, they came to an area that felt cooler. At first Logan did not recognize the implications of the change, relishing the gentle breeze that offered some slight reprieve from the torturous heat of the musty jungle. He was smiling and had an extra pep in his stride when it dawned on him.

"Wait a minute." He stopped, raising his arms to halt the group. "Where there's a breeze, there is an opening!"

Only Bipp understood his friend's meaning, having also lived his life in the claustrophobic confines of the Vanidriell caverns. Tiko was shaking his head, so the gnome explained, "The jungle itself is kind of like one giant cave. The air here is mostly trapped inside due to the thick canopy of trees and pressing cluster of vegetation. So if there is a nice breeze like this, then..."

"There must be an opening!" Logan happily finished for him. "Come on, guys, follow me!" He excitedly waved them on and ran in the direction of the cooler air. Logan was so excited by the prospect of escaping the muggy heat of the jungle that when a long viper crossed his path, he did not so much as hesitate, jumping right over it as if it were nothing more than another vine.

The sounds of rushing grew louder as they moved through to the edge of the jungle. Soon the way ahead grew brighter, which neither he nor Bipp cared for, since the daylight stung their eyes. But still he ran toward it gleefully, like a child going to a party. Bursting from the cramped confines into open air, cool and crisp against his damp skin, Logan spread his arms wide, spinning to embrace his freedom.

"Hee hee hee, you look like an idiot," Bipp teased. The gnome mocked his movement, spreading his stubby arms wide and spinning while laughing.

Logan grew a little red-faced, but everyone was equally happy to have found a way out of the never-ending labyrinth of trees. The ground only stretched forward from where they stood about twenty feet, jutting out in a long, toothy peninsula that rested high above a gently winding stream. Logan could see far into the distance from here. A long mountain range curved around them, as if nature had created it as a barrier to protect the jungle.

"Is this what you call a canyon?" he asked Nero, marveling at the sheer magnitude of the ravine below.

"In Nero's estimation this would be considered a gorge by geologists," Nero replied pragmatically.

"Either way, it's impressive." Logan stared out at the sprawling network of ravines, which were lush as any forest he had seen in Vanidriell with trees and all manner of plants dotting the steep cliffs and a blanket of green following the shallow river below them.

"Can you get a better angle on where we are now?" Logan asked, hoping the android recognized some nearby landmark from this vantage point.

Nero flicked a seamless compartment on his wrist, punching some keys to engage the override on his global positioning system. Within moments, numbers in strange patterns flickered across the front of his face, hovering in the air as a hologram. The planet of Acadia came into view, zooming in to their location, and the screen flickered out of view again.

"Nero does see our current position, Logan Walker," the android finally answered. "Take a look at that large mountain to the northeast. If Nero is correct, that formation matches with the peak of Mount Soltus. With that landmark, the directions are clearer."

"Seriously, you have to stop that third person crap. It's getting annoying," Logan said, cocking an eyebrow and nudging Bipp for a little backup.

"Understandable, Logan. This one will do his best to fill your request," Nero promised, giving a stiff bow.

Logan rolled his eyes. It was like talking to a machine. *Then again, I am talking to a machine, aren't I?* "Okay, Nero, shoot. Which way do we go from here?"

"Based on Master Isaac's estimation and Lady Kyra's notes, the Aegis is in the ruins of Ithiki. Now that this one has re-triangulated our position, it is abundantly clear that we head in this direction, which will take us north." Nero pointed out over the edge of the cliff.

"Hmm, that's going to be tough," Logan mumbled, thinking out loud while he looked down the steep cliffs. "We can manage it if we head down into the ravine, but that's going to be tricky."

"Yeah, and it looks like a good two-hundred foot drop," Bipp said, peering over the edge. "We trip on this slope made for mountain goats, and that'll be all the gods wrote for us. Maybe we should try a different route."

The way down was a path of crumbling rocks and loose weeds barely clinging to the face of the cliff, and to make matters worse, the lower half was sprayed with a light mist from the wind blowing across the frothing waters of the stream below.

Despite the gnome's protest, all members of the group were able to descend the dangerous slope in less than an hour. By the time they reached the bottom, Logan could feel the sweat soaking through his clothes, just as badly as it had when they were in the jungle. Except now the stiff breeze blowing through the tight valley pressed his wet tunic uncomfortably against the skin of his back.

Reaching the base of the gorge, they all stopped to break for a bit. Logan used the time to switch shirts, splashing the clean water of the stream against his chest and face to cool off. He thought it was the most refreshing water he had ever tasted. Bipp dunked his head below the surface then shook his silver hair and mutton chops like a pup drying off.

Logan decided the simplest route would be to follow the stream northward. If at any point it veered too far off track, they would decide a different path, but until then, sticking to the small river nestled at the base of the canyon would provide them with food and water for their long trek. Everyone agreed with this reasoning, and they marched on through the late afternoon.

At times they hit spots where vegetation had taken hold in the bedrock lining the stream, but most of the trail meant hopping from one outcropping of smooth river stones to another. Nero reasoned that the water level must actually come up quite a bit higher, and Logan was grateful that was not currently the case. Not only was the breeze which shot up the canyon a godsend for him, but the daystar was finally beginning its descent, already disappearing over the lip of the other side of the gorge.

The farther they travelled, the more the stream widened, and the gorge began to curve sharply in places, always coming back to head north. Gradually the stream widened into a proper river.

"Wow...would you look at that!" Bipp exclaimed, stopping to regard a waterfall around one of those bends.

The left side of the steep slope was covered with tuberous, leafy vines and thick green moss in this area, with a rounded overhang of rock jutting out from the gorge wall. It looked like someone had cut the rock away at its base, leaving an overhang that protruded almost to the center of the river below it. The entire bulging rock face was covered with a thick carpet of green and brown moss which hung over it like an umbrella, and a stream from the cliff face high above poured down over it, spreading across the moss in frothy rivulets.

"It looks like a giant umbrella!" Nero exclaimed uncharacteristically.

"More like a mushroom cap," Bipp added enthusiastically, stepping back and craning his neck to see the top of the falls.

Logan did not bother asking what an *umbrella* was, knowing there was much the Acadians found commonplace that had been forever lost to the strains of time. Anyway, he did not need to know what one was to appreciate the beauty of the waterfall gently cascading off the strange outcrop of rocks into the river below.

Wherever the water hit the river's surface, it glowed, shimmering in a vibrant, blue-white, iridescent halo across the surface of the river and drifting out from the outline of the waterfall in vibrant tendrils.

"Why does it glow like that?" Logan asked Tiko, moving closer to the majestic waterfall. The air here smelled clean, and the cold spray flecking his face invigorated Logan.

"Never have I seen anything like this, but Tiko suspects this is the work of witchcraft," Tiko replied, mystified by the incandescent display.

"There is nothing mystical about it. The water only seems to glow, when it is in fact the bioluminescence of—" Nero tried to explain.

"Wow, way to make something beautiful boring. Sorry I asked," Logan cut him off, not wanting to ruin the moment.

Bipp folded his arms, regarding the display with childlike wonder. "Sure is beautiful, though, eh fellas?"

"This is a great place for us to rest awhile," Logan decided.

Opposite the waterfall, the other gorge wall also curved out from the cliffs, forming an outcropping. This one was much smaller and half hidden behind a curtain of overgrown, leafy vines hanging down to the river stones and waving gently in the breeze.

The face of the cliff behind him shifted in Logan's peripheral vision. Without thinking, he spun with Gandiva in hand, ready to strike at whatever lurked among the wall of vines.

Something massive chuckled, sounding like bits of gravel rolling together across sand. "Look what has come into my home, uninvited," the gravelly voice said, as if it were speaking to an unseen companion.

Logan gave his friends a glance to see if they had any idea what was lurking behind the vines. "Who goes there?" he called. "Show your face, coward!"

The polished river rocks rattled at their feet as a hill giant stepped out from behind the rocky alcove. The ghastly humanoid stood a good fifteen feet tall and half as wide, with broad, bulky shoulders. Its arms were as big as tree trunks and were slightly too long, giving the creature a knuckle-dragging posture.

"Who are ye calling coward, little one?" the hill giant roared, spraying spittle on Logan's face and blowing his hair back as if a brisk wind had come through. The giant glared down at him with flared nostrils, grinding the crooked teeth of its overbite. Logan could picture this monstrous humanoid chewing stones with that ridiculously large mouth, and a pit opened in his stomach as he spied the necklace of humanoid skulls hanging around its fat, hairy neck.

The giant was almost bare from the neck down, with what looked like the remnants of a ship's sail draped over one shoulder and tied around the waist by a thick, knotted vine. The makeshift clothing hung down to the giant's knees and was filthy from years of use without any concern for washing.

"Great, we are going to get eaten by a guy wearing a skirt," Bipp groaned, slowly stepping back, readying to flee.

"What did ye just say?" the giant demanded in a booming voice.

Bipp yelped, ducking behind Tiko, who shifted his spear into a defensive posture. "Think we best get outta here while the getting is good," the gnome moaned.

The giant bent over, listening to him, and stomped his foot so hard that they almost lost their footing. Roaring with laughter, the hill giant picked up a massive boulder and lifted over his head. "Just ye try and run, little puny morsels. Grog will shake the ground and flatten you with his ball," Grog warned, lifting the boulder higher in the air to prove his point.

"No no no." Logan hopped forward and held up his hands. "There's no need for that! You have us. We are your prisoners."

"My *dinner*," Grog corrected, working his lower jaw and gritting his teeth while lifting the boulder again threateningly.

"Right! Right. Your dinner then," Logan quickly agreed, nodding and motioning for his friends to do the same.

"Good little morsels. Get inside now," Grog ordered, dropping his boulder to the ground, which shook the area and knocked Tiko off balance.

Lifting the vines aside, the hill giant motioned for them to enter his lair. The area was littered with bones picked clean of their meat and tatters of animal furs. To the far end of the alcove was a large, shoddily built cage made of tree stumps crudely tied together with vines.

"Get my fire going and make it good and high. Grog likes to cook over a crackling flame," Grog ordered.

He kicked Logan as if he were a rat, knocking him across the lair. Logan worried the giant's blow might have broken something in his back, as it was harder than anything he had ever experienced. His companions quickly helped him to his feet and went to work moving the massive pieces of stacked wood in place to build the fire.

"What are we going to do?" Bipp urgently whispered while they carried a log.

"Don't know yet, but I'll think of something," Logan said. "We just have to buy some time."

"Quit yer whisperin' fore I just eat ye raw!" Grog grunted.

Logan motioned for Tiko to slow down. They were building the great bonfire too quickly, and he needed more time to sort out a plan.

Grog seemed to forget himself and went to work picking bugs out of his grimy beard with sausage fingers that ended in moldy, cracked yellow nails. When he found one, he would flick it to the ground, and the bug would scurry away. "Get a move on, ye river rats!" he barked, seeing through their ruse.

The second time they began to slow down, the giant grew angry, punching the wall and slapping them out of the way to light the fire himself. Once the flames were high enough, he turned to the group, licking his blistered lips and rubbing his hands together.

"Wait wait wait!" Logan pleaded, raising his palms to halt the giant's grasping hand.

Grog looked down at him with a frown. "What does the morsel want? Please don't let them be wantin' last wishes again," he said, adding in the last part as if he were addressing someone beside him, though there was no one there.

"No, no...uh...." Logan desperately searched for an idea to get them out of this mess, looking all around.

"Time's up, little morsel. Grog wants his snack!" The giant ground his teeth and reaching down for him again.

"Wait!" Logan yelped. "You can't eat on an empty mind, can you?" he hollered, saying the first thing that came to him.

The giant stopped, looking confused. "What does it mean?"

Logan was fumbling for an answer that would not cause him to get smashed to a pulp when Nero spoke up for him. "Perhaps Grog would enjoy a good story before his meal? I hear such things aid in a giant's digestion."

Grog tilted his head, looking puzzled. "Hmm, Grog does like stories. What is this tale? Does it contain giants? Grog does not want to hear stupid morsel's story if there are no brave giants."

"Oh yes, of course! This is a tale with a most brave giant who is as cunning as he is wise!" Bipp said, scurrying around Logan to face the giant.

Grog rubbed his belly, which growled for food, and crunched his teeth together. "Grog does not know...maybe one morsel first then story?" he debated with himself.

"Oh, but after this tale, Grog shall have as many morsels as he chooses!" Logan offered, swaying the hill giant, who begrudgingly sat back down with a thud.

"Okay, little morsel...but no tricks, or Grog will smash you to jam," he warned, waving his hairy hand for the gnome to begin.

Bipp walked over to the giant's monstrous feet and began his tale.

At one time and in one place, imagine a king who had seven sons whom he loved more dearly than anything else in the world. One day when they came of age, he sent them out to find princesses they could wed. The king only sent six of the brothers out, giving them all manner of lavish jewels and clothing along with the finest spices to present as tokens to their future brides. The king kept his youngest son behind, as he could not bear to be apart from all seven at the same time.

When they had traveled to many different kingdoms, searching far and wide and meeting many princesses, the brothers at last came to a place where a queen had six daughters, more lovely than any they had ever seen. At once the brothers determined to court the girls, winning their hearts and setting back off for their homeland. But as they were on their way, one of the princes realized they had been so lost in the youthful joy of love that they had forgotten to find a wife for their youngest brother. The princes lamented their mistake, for they sorely wanted to return home to their father and spend the rest of their days with the beautiful princesses, but none could ever be happy knowing they had forsaken their brother.

A wandering peddler came upon them then, overhearing their plight, and offered to give the princes information about a beautiful maiden sure to win their brother's heart in exchange for some of their gold. The brothers agreed, and he told them of a valley between two hillsides where they would find her.

Arriving at the hidden valley, they passed a steep hillside in which a giant had built his house. The giant was sometimes an old man, and sometimes a gnome, for he had the power to change his appearance at will. Hearing the six brothers and their six princesses, he came outside and called them in closer.

"Have you a maiden living here, good man?" one of the princes asked.

"Oh, surely I do, good lad. Tie your horses up and come around back so that I may present her."

The brothers were excited, and they did as the old man asked. Except when the twelve of them walked around the back of the cottage, there was only the old man waiting for them. Before anyone could speak, swift as the devil himself, the giant used his gift of the evil eye to turn *them all to stone. He moved them in front of his cottage for decoration and licked his lips at the bounty of horse meat that had dropped into his lap.*

"Ha, stupid feeble-brained princes lost all that good meat," Grog snorted.

"Surely." Bipp bowed. "What else can you expect when matching wits with a hill giant?"

Grog smiled in contentment. "That was a good story. Now I eat."

"Oh, but the best part is yet to come," Bipp countered.

"Truly?"

"Oh, yes. Why not make yourself comfortable? There's no sense in hearing such a fine tale of a giant's cunning without a nice soft pillow." Bipp waved his hand for his companions to get moving.

Logan, Nero, and Tiko carried a heavy sack of spoiled grain from the corner, pushing it behind the giant's back. Grog grumbled his agreement and pulled it up behind his neck, resting back to hear more of the gnome's tale.

The king waited and waited for his six sons to return. However, the more he waited, the deeper he fell into despair. "I will forever live without happiness in my heart," he lamented. "Not until my sons return home will I smile again." And he determined to never show happiness.

"Father," his youngest son Anders said to him early one day, "I must go out and search the land for my brothers."

The king was stifled by the fear of losing another son and demanded he stay. "I shall never allow you to leave, for then I would be left here all alone! If you leave, I will not be able to live in this world any longer. My sadness will consume me!"

Anders could see there would be no way to convince his father, so he gathered some lazy honeysuckle leaves from the garden, then ground them into the king's stew and served it for dinner. Once the leaves did their trick, the king fell into a deep sleep, one that could only be broken by the root of the very same plant. Anders lovingly laid his father in bed and ordered for a horse to be brought to him, instructing that the king was to be cared for but not woken before Anders returned, lest he die from sadness upon discovering his seventh son had also left the land.

When the young Prince had ridden for quite some time, he came upon a griffin lying in the road. The beast was not able to move its wings and fly away, so several carts had ridden right over it. "Are you alright, good griffin?" Anders asked.

The griffin limply lifted its neck and cried, "Oh, dear human, give me a morsel of food. I am starving and have no strength to move."

"I do not have much to offer, but what I do have is yours." Anders hand-fed the winged lion, whose strength returned. Soon enough the griffin was flapping its wings in the air above him, merry to be alive.

"I owe you a debt, little human. Whenever you need, just call me and I will come!"

Anders did not see how a griffin could be of much use to him, but he nodded politely and set back on his way.

Now when he had traveled a bit longer, he came across a winding brook, and in it lay a great catfish stuck upon a dry rock. It flapped about, but no matter how hard it tried, it could not get back into the water. "Oh, sweet human, please shove me back into the water again, and in return I'll help you whenever you're in need!"

Anders shook his head, chuckling at the idea that a fish could help him. His stomach began grumbling. "Well, the help you can give me can never be that great, and I am sorely hungry," he said, and the catfish knew its time was up. "However, I will not stand by while you lie there helpless and choke to death. There is no honor in that." And he threw the fish back into the stream to swim merrily away.

After this, he went on his way for some time until he met a great wolf which was so famished that it crawled pitifully along the road on its belly. "Dear human, do let me eat your horse. I'm so hungry you can see my bones. I have not had anything to eat for weeks now."

"No," said Anders, firmly shaking his head. "You cannot ask this of me. First I came upon a griffin, and I was asked to give it my food, which I did. Then I came across a great catfish and was asked to spare it, which I did. And now you ask for my horse! It cannot be given. Without this steed, I will not be able to ride through the land and find my missing brothers."

"Nay, dear human, but you can help me," the wolf named Graylegs whined pitifully, slinking in closer to the prince, "and in return, I will let you ride on my back, taking you as far and wide as you wish. For I can show you where your brothers have gone!"

Grog's rumbled with laughter. "Only a human would trust a wolf."

Bipp feigned astonishment. "Do tell, dear Grog. Share with our base minds what should be done in such a circumstance."

Logan and Nero pushed a stone mug of filthy water beside Grog, who lay on his side, deeply interested in Bipp's story.

"Can't trust a wolf," Grog said. "They're no good for anything but shishkabob."

"Ah, that would explain why the giant so easily fools Greylegs," Bipp said, motioning for his companions to put more wood on the fire.

Grog pouted. "Don't give away the ending, morsel."

Bipp bowed low and promised not to reveal any further details. As Logan and Tiko dropped another log on the fire, he continued.

Without hesitation, Anders gave his horse to the wolf, which gobbled it up and regained his strength. Anders took the bit and saddle and put them on Graylegs, who was so strong after his hearty meal that he set out right away for the giant's valley with Anders on his back. "When we get to the valley," said Graylegs, "I will show you the giant's house where your six brothers and their princesses can be found."

After a long while of riding, they came to it.

"See, here is the giant's house," said the wolf quietly as it slinked along between the trees, "and there are your brothers turned to stone along the riverbed, and away yonder is the door to the house, where you must surely go."

"I dare not go inside that house," said Anders. "The giant will kill me for sure!"

"No, never!" said the wolf. "When you get inside, you will find a princess he keeps prisoner, and she will tell you how to put an end to the miserable wretch. Only mind you listen to her instructions carefully!"

Full of doubt, Anders went inside the large house carved into the hillside, determined to be brave though he was filled with fear. When he entered, the giant was thankfully away, but true to the wolf's word, he found a princess sitting in one of the rooms, sobbing, and she was more beautiful than any he had ever seen in his life. "Fair maiden, why do you cry so?" he asked, startling the princess from her sorrow.

"Oh, heaven help you! However did you get in here?" said the princess upon seeing him. "It will surely spell your death, for none can defeat the giant who lives here!" Anders rashly drew his short sword, vowing to free the fair princess by battling the giant. "You silly prince, the giant has no heart in his body and can never be defeated that way."

"Well...I am here, so we must find a way, and I will see if I cannot free my brothers that have been turned to stone just the same. We must try, or what is the point of our miserable existence?"

The princess found hope in the young prince's brave words. "If you must try, I have an idea. Creep under the bed and listen to what he and I discuss carefully." Anders nodded eagerly and the princess held the blanket for him to shimmy under the bed. "But you must be quiet as a mouse or the giant will hear you and kill us both." Just as she let the blanket drape over the bedside, the giant returned home.

"Ha! I smell a man in this house!" the giant roared, dropping his sack to the floor.

"Yes, I know. It does stink awful," the maiden said. "This morning a magpie did fly by and dropped the finger bone of a man into your chimney. I tried to get it out of the house as fast as I could, but for all that, I could not get the smell gone."

The giant contented himself with her explanation and said no more about it. When night came they went to bed, and the princess dramatically sighed several times until the giant asked her what was wrong.

"There is one thing I would like to ask you, but I dare not."

"What is that one thing, little princess?" the giant asked.

"Only that I wonder where you keep your heart, since I know you never keep it with you," she asked innocently.

The giant laughed at her audacity. "Now there is something you have no business wondering on, but since you must know, I hide it under the door sill."

The next morning the giant got up and gathered his things, setting out for the day. No sooner had he left the house than Anders came scrambling from under the bed, making a beeline for the door sill. He and the princess dug a deep hole, searching for the heart, until they finally realized the giant had tricked her. Covering the hole back up, they gathered some of the prettiest flowers from the riverbank and covered the spot with them before Anders crawled back into his hiding nook under the bed.

The giant returned home, dropping his sack in the corner and sniffed the air. "Hmm, by my eyes and limbs, I smell a man in my house again!"

"Yes, I know," the princess answered, feigning frustration, seemingly absorbed in fixing his meal, "for a magpie came along and dropped another bone in the chimney this morning. I scrubbed as hard as I might, but alas the foul odor seems to not escape your keen senses."

Satisfied with her answer, the giant ate his dinner and then went to bed. On his way into the bedroom, he stopped to look at the flowers strewn across the doorway.

"What have we here? Who has laid these flowers on my doorstep?" he asked.

"Why, it was me, of course," the princess replied.

"Why would you do that, then?" the giant asked.

"I've grown so very fond of you that I could not help scattering them there, now that I know your heart is hidden underneath," she answered, batting her lashes.

"Silly girl, surely you did not believe I would keep my heart under the doorway?"

When they lay to sleep that night, the princess asked him where his heart could truly be hidden, and the giant grumbled. "As sure as I am that it is none of your business, I am touched by your gesture today, so I will tell you true. My heart is actually behind the cupboards in the kitchen. Now get you to sleep."

Anders listened, anxious to have morning come. All through the night he stayed awake, unable to sleep, until finally the morning arrived and the giant left his house once more.

Once again, as soon as he was out, Anders scrambled from beneath the bed and helped the princess take down all the cupboards. They searched the walls with his pickaxe to find the giant's heart. "I fear the vile trickster has fooled us again, dear princess," he despaired as they set everything back up again before the giant returned. The princess laid flowers all about the cupboards, hoping to hide the mess they had created.

When the giant returned, Anders was already safely hidden under the bed once more, and the princess was cooking his supper.

Bipp paused the tale, studying the hill giant's face for some sign that he was still awake. Grog's breathing was heavy, and his head leaned all the way back against the sack of grain.

Logan motioned for Nero to gather up some rope and pointed at the giant's feet. One of his fingers grazed Grog's toe, and the hill giant let out a long burp, lifting his head and looking around in confusion.

He squinted red-rimmed eyes shrewdly at Logan, who stood beside his feet. "Eh, what is the morsel up to?"

"Who, him?" Bipp said. "Logan was just getting ready to give Grog a footrub so you can enjoy the rest of the story."

Logan shot the gnome a dirty look, and Bipp shrugged helplessly.

"Hmm." Grog smacked his dry lips. "Grog would enjoy a footrub. Good idea, morsel."

Logan had to step back as Grog shifted his foot, pushing it close to Logan's face and waggling his toes. Logan sucked in his breath and turned his face away from the stench before pressing his hands firmly into the filthy soles of Grog's feet.

The hill giant rumbled in pleasure and motioned with a waving finger for Bipp to continue.

"Where were we? Oh yes, so the giant returned home and came into his house with a snuffle, snuffle..."

"What is this? I smell a man in my house again!" the giant roared, throwing his sack into the corner and shuffling the chairs around in search of the intruder.

"I know. I only wish I could get the stink out of your house, for not a moment after you left this morning, that damnable magpie flew by and dropped another finger bone down the chimney! I did scrub the floors and the hearth for hours, but I fear the stink is lingering on my hands," the princess complained, feigning her distress.

The giant looked at her with one eye closed. 'Where are these bones you keep finding then, sweet little child?"

Anders's heart froze, fearing the princess had been caught in her lie, but she was made of quicker stuff than that. "Oh, my strong giant, I threw them right in the river to float far away from here. They can go stink up some other wretch's house and leave yours to peace."

Satisfied with her answer, the giant sat down to eat his supper, noticing the pretty flowers strewn all along the cupboards. "Hmm, what's this, then? Who put flowers all over my cupboards?"

"Why, it was me, of course," she replied.

"And why would you do such nonsense?" the giant asked.

"I am so very fond of you I could not help myself, for once I knew where you truly keep your heart hidden, I had to lay some flowers around it," the princess answered.

Though the giant did not care for such tomfoolery, he could not help feeling his heart melt at the princess's gesture. "You silly girl, did you really believe I would keep my heart in such a place?"

After they went to bed for the night, the princess asked where he truly kept his heart so that she may not make a fool out of herself again.

"Though it is none of your business, I can see you truly care for me, young princess, so I will tell you the truth this time. I do not keep my heart on me, I never buried it under the doorframe, and I would never hide it behind the cupboards," the giant teased her.

"Then where could it be?" the princess asked.

"Over the hills and far away, in a black lake lies an island, on that isle stands a temple, in that temple is a well, in that well lives a silver duck, inside that duck there is an egg, and inside that egg doth my heart truly hide. Now get you to sleep for morning will be upon us soon enough." And with that the giant rolled over to sleep.

In the early dawn, before Themis rose over the river valley, the giant headed out for the day. No sooner was he gone than Anders scrambled from beneath the bed. "I must set off at once, dear princess, but fear not, I swear I shall return to free you!"

In the valley beside the riverbank, he found Graylegs waiting for him. Anders told the wolf all that had happened inside the giant's house and told him they must set out at once to find this temple on a black lake. At once upon hearing this, Graylegs perked his ears and bade Anders to get on his back swiftly, for he had come across this very temple in his travels. Away they went, across rivers and over hill, until after a long afternoon of running, they came upon the lake. The prince despaired, for there were no boats about to bear them across the lake to the isle, but Graylegs told him, "Do not cry, young prince. Remove my bindings and jump on my back. I will get us across."

Anders had heard the tales of wolves crossing water with their hapless victims tricked into riding on their backs, but he trusted this wolf, believing in the bond they had shared, and so he removed the saddle and jumped on Graylegs's back. True to his word, the wolf swam all the way across the lake, bringing him safely to the isle.

They came to the temple but could not get inside. The doors were locked and the keys hung high up in the tower, where only a giant could reach. Anders did not know how he could get them.

"Do not fear, young prince. Did you not say the griffin owed you a favor? Only call for him now and see if it can be fulfilled."

Anders did as the wolf suggested, calling out to the sky for the griffin, which soon appeared swooping down from the clouds. The griffin was more than happy to help him and flew up, fetching the keys and dropping them into the prince's hands. Anders quickly unlocked the front doors and made his way inside the temple, seeing the well at its altar and knowing the giant had told the truth.

When he came to the well, there was indeed a silver duck swimming around in circles. The prince cooed softly for the bird, calming the mallard so he could snatch it from the water. But alas, as he pulled the silver duck from the well, the egg slipped from its body into the deep water below. Anders was beside himself, trying to retrieve the lost egg. How could he ever get it out again?

"Do not fear, young prince, for did you not say that the great catfish also owed you a favor? Who better to retrieve the egg? Just call for him and let's see if he will fulfill his promise," Graylegs advised.

So the king's youngest son called into the water for the catfish, which appeared fast as a fish might and listened to his story. Happily the catfish retrieved the egg, spitting it over the lip of the well for the young prince to catch.

"Squeeze the egg!" said the wolf at once. Anders gripped the golden egg tightly in his palm, adding pressure enough to squeeze it without breaking. Many miles away, the giant fell down hard in the dirt of his valley, clutching his chest in pain.

"Squeeze it again!" said the wolf. Anders gripped it tight in his palm, putting more pressure on the egg.

Across rivers and over hills, the giant tried to make it to his doorstep, to strike down the princess who surely must have retrieved his heart through some witchery, but as he moved to open his door, the pain wracked him again, and the giant screamed, sprawled on the ground in pain.

Anders called out to the griffin and bid it to fly back and tell the giant that he had his heart. If the giant wanted to live, he must change the young prince's six brothers and their six brides back from stone and promise to leave them in peace. Hearing the griffin's message, the giant readily agreed, using his evil eye to change them back. Once the curse was lifted, he begged the griffin to tell Anders to leave him in peace now. When the griffin returned, Anders's heart soared to hear his family was safe once more, and he smashed the egg to the stone floor of the temple, killing the wicked giant forever.

With the giant destroyed, Anders rode back to the valley on the back of the wolf, and there stood his brothers, all six alive and well, celebrating with their six princesses around the stone body of the giant. Running inside the house, he was elated to find the young princess free and waiting for him. They returned to their kingdom to wake their father.

When the King was given the root of the lazy honeysuckle in some tea, he woke almost immediately, rubbing his eyes to see all seven of his sons with all seven of their beautiful brides standing around his bed chamber. The King was so overfilled with joy that he threw a feast to end all feasts. Everyone in the kingdom came to celebrate, and many say the festivities were so much fun that they are still celebrating them today in the stars above us.

When Bipp finished the tale, Logan blinked several times, slowly realizing they were all so entranced by the story that none of them had even noticed that the hill giant had finally fallen deeply asleep, snoring loudly and lying on his side with his large hairy belly hanging out.

Logan put a finger to his lips and pulled the length of rope Nero had retrieved from his pack, motioning for the android to grab the other end. Tying the ropes together with a tight knot, he bid Tiko run over to the wooden cage and secure one end while he and Nero wrapped the other end around both of the giant's repulsive-smelling ankles. Once it was secure, the four of them slowly rolled the large boulder away from the hungry hill giant, stopping in ice cold dread when the boulder groaned loudly across a piece of bone.

Grog stopped his snoring, mumbling in his sleep about the evil eye and rolled over heavily, facing away from them. With a collective sigh, they continued moving the boulder until it was clear of the alcove and they were outside in the cool night air.

Wasting no time, Logan bid them to run for their freedom. The party was just leaving the area when Tiko's foot kicked the skull of some animal, which loudly clanked across the river stones and splashed into the water. As one they froze in place, turning to see if there was any sign of Grog waking.

"Damned lucky the big stupid oaf sleeps like a baby," Bipp whispered.

From behind the wall of vines, the hill giant roared, waking up to find he had been deceived by the tricky little morsels. Slamming hairy knuckles into the ground, Grog tried to rise, falling on his face when the rope caught him.

"Run!" Logan screamed, shoving Tiko to move.

Grog grabbed the rope tied to his ankles with one hand and tore it free. Roaring again, he burst from the curtain of vines, dragging the man-sized wooden cage, which was still attached to one ankle. "Grog will smash puny morsels!" he promised, snatching the boulder in his rage and lifting it overhead.

"Only thing you're going to be eating tonight is Gandiva, monster!" Logan yelled back, dropping to a crouch and flinging his weapon as hard as he could.

The spinning boomerang's blade sliced across one of Grog's eyes, blinding him with a flash of searing pain. The hill giant howled so loudly the entire valley shook with his anguish, and he let go of the boulder to clutch his face. The heavy rock came down hard on his crown, knocking the giant face first into the river.

Catching the returning weapon, Logan did not wait to see if the hulking monster was dead and urged his friends to run as fast as they could. He wanted to put as much distance between them and the blood thirsty giant as possible.

Chapter 13: A Place to Lay My Head

After leaving the granary, the group of scabs was herded back to their living quarters, which were behind high concrete walls patrolled by both human and jotnar slavers armed with whips and swords.

Immediately upon passing through the gates, Corbin had two distinct impressions. First, the place had a sour odor that burned his sinuses, as if the entire area had not been washed in months. Judging by the desperate condition of the human slaves, he guessed that was probably a good assumption. Secondly, the feeling of being trapped in a cage suddenly washed over him. And for a man who grew up in the claustrophobic caverns of Vanidriell, that was saying something.

Pulling his companions aside, while the slaves dragged themselves to their shanty houses, Corbin asked in a low voice, "What do we do now?" He looked in either direction to be sure they were not being watched.

"Just act normal," Kyra insisted.

"Yeah, but what is normal? I mean, look at this place." He pointed out their obvious predicament. Kyra took his meaning, looking around at the fetid wooden shacks that were really no more than hovels. Slaves piled into the cramped shacks like zombies, setting about preparing their meals for the afternoon before being sent back out to the fields to help harvest more grain. The scabs worked from dawn till dusk.

"Corbin's right, our options seem pretty limited. Either we join them and hope no one notices we're in their home, or we stay out here, which is going to raise suspicion if the guards catch wind of it."

As if on cue, a whip cracked across Corbin's back, stinging through his invisible leather vest and forcing his body a few steps forward. "Get to your shack, maggots. You know better than to stand about!" a human slaver barked behind them. They had not even noticed him coming around the corner.

Corbin gritted his teeth, catching a look of caution from Kyra, and swallowed back his urge to bash the despicable slaver's head in. Nodding instead, Kyra pushed them on down the path with the slaver keeping a steady pace at their heels. They had to pick up their speed when he whipped Corbin again, barking, "Get a move on!"

"Where are we going to go?" Corbin asked, his mind racing for ideas and settling on the grim reality that he might have to kill the slaver and blow their cover. Before he could brandish his disguised polearm, Kyra pushed them all up two crooked steps and inside a nearby shanty. As they entered, Corbin quickly made a headcount. Ten slaves lived inside this creaking shack! Six sat around a makeshift table, eating maggoty bread, and another four were doing chores around the one room. All of them stopped what they were doing to turn and stare at the trio who had unexpectedly barged into their home unannounced.

Before anyone could speak, Corbin flinched, knocked forward by another crack of the whip, which this time tore a strip of skin off the back of his neck.

Kyra quickly moved to see if he was injured, receiving a whiplash of her own across the chest. The slaver was getting frustrated that his whipping was not making the despicable scabs bleed more and decided to have the leather maker take a look at it for repairs later in the evening.

Corbin nodded, pushing his companions behind him to face the slaver, who was making his way across the rickety porch. "What the hell do you think you are doing?" he asked in more of a snarl than a question, slowly shifting cold eyes around the room to take in everyone. To Corbin's astonishment, the shanty's residents went back about their business as if nothing were happening.

"I beg your pardon, sir, we don't—" Corbin said but was cut off by the man's whip snapping across his belly.

"Not you," the slaver sneered, pointing at Stur, "him. The scab what don' know how to speak none." The warrior looked beyond odd in his disguise, shrugging noncommittally at the sadistic guard. The slaver mocked his gesture, making it look a bit more oafish. "Nothing? What, you too dumb to understand me, scab? Lemme spell it out so a dumb scab like you can understand it." Pacing, he squared up level to Stur, though Corbin knew it only appeared that way, given the dweomer Isaac had cast. In reality, the slaver was standing with the top of his head roughly around Stur's neck. "What are you filthy scabs doing coming into Maggs's shack?" he asked slowly, pronouncing each syllable as if he were talking to an idiot and pointing at the older woman by the counter who was breaking apart half a head of cabbage for their meal. "I know you scabs is dumb and all, but you did just hear me tell you to get to yer home, didn't ye? Or does a worthless scab like you need his filthy ears cleaned out?"

The room fell silent as the slaves stopped what they were doing, realizing there was no way they could get out of being involved in the slaver's punishment. The men and women sitting stared fearfully at the splintered table top, hoping the slaver would not call on them. Their rheumy eyes were filled with the burden they carried, sore and red with a distant glaze. Corbin could almost hear their thoughts, as if they were wondering out loud, *When will this nightmare end? Why was I ever born into this world?* It was a look of sheer hopelessness and an almost crazed despair.

"We're staying here with Maggs," Stur explained with zero humility in his voice.

"Oh really?" The human slaver clearly doubted this, staring hard at Stur and cocking his head to the side. "Is this true Maggs?" he asked, never taking his eyes off Stur.

Corbin almost bit his tongue, realizing he needed to act quickly. Lashing out with his mind, he entered the older woman's head and dropped the seed of a memory. Maggs stopped what she was doing, blinking several times and rubbing the back of her head as she stared at the countertop before turning to respond. "Sure enough, they been sent down here, Master Benjamin. Got word just yesterday evening from the Overseer hisself."

The man scrunched his face up at the odd, unexpected reply. He looked the older woman up and down with newfound interest. "Are you sure?" he asked.

Corbin probed the man's mind. The slaver was unsure what to make of Maggs's response. She had never been one to lie, yet how could the Overseer send down three new slaves without giving him any notice? And why were they full grown, when new shipments of scabs sent down were generally still young'uns? Maybe they were from the servant class? That would explain their odd behavior. *I don't know, something seems off here. They speak awful strange like, even for house slaves, and I can't see old man Milton parting with no scabs.* The slaver pulled a filthy handkerchief out of his back pocket, wiping a layer of sweat off his brow and blowing his nose, while he ruminated on the odd circumstances, deciding he best call the Overseer to the cabin and get to the bottom of it all.

"Yes sir, we be from the servant class," Corbin blurted, adjusting his twang accordingly. "Been sent down what to help out with the harvest. Master Milton said the granary been shorthanded and we need to fill in for a few weeks. Said he just paying a gambling debt to the Overseer, and after this they even as far as he concerned." As he spoke, Corbin planted a seed of understanding in the man's mind, making his words that much more palatable.

The slaver nodded thoughtfully, turning back to Stur. "Well, why didn't ye just say that in the first place, ye stupid scab?" The warrior just stared back at the slaver with dead eyes. The man snorted. "Listen at me. What am I talkin' about? This is one stupid scab, to be sure. Just look at him, clearly dumb as a box of rocks." When no one laughed at his joke, the man sneered and spit a gob of phlegm in Stur's face. "Now ye scabs stay out of trouble, ye hear? I don't want to have to come back here and sort ye out none." And, clearly disappointed at the missed opportunity to dole out a beating, he stalked out of the cramped shack.

As the slaver stepped off the porch, everyone in the room sighed, shoulders dropping as the threat of a whipping passed. Corbin roughly sat down, pushing his back against the creaking wooden slats of a wall and resting his elbows on his knees.

"Are you alright? Did he hurt you?" Kyra asked, kneeling beside him, filled with concern.

"Eh? Oh yes, I'm fine," Corbin said. "Most of the lashes hit my leather armor. Though I am a bit sore around the neck." He reached back to rub the spot and winced when the dirt on his gloved fingertips stung the wound like acid. He pulled his hand back to eye the tiny smear of already drying blood. Seeing the wound, Kyra shook her head, thinking he was being stubborn, and pulled out a cloth to clean it. Corbin blocked her advance. "No, really, I'm fine. The effort of sending out psionic commands so rapidly just drained some of my strength is all. Stur might be the one who needs looking after."

The warrior chimed in, "No, the idiot hit my armor too, not that he could know that to look at us. Best we save some of this chatter for a more private venue, though?" he advised, tilting his head toward the slaves, who were all sitting around the table, doing their best to pretend not to be listening.

Seeing the strangers' attention, Maggs hobbled over to plop down a filthy, cracked wooden tray with a couple pieces of stale, maggoty bread and a chunk of cabbage. "I see the servant class ain't got no sense enough not to be traipsing around in front of slavers and running yer mouth in whispers," the older woman complained, shaking her head with her hands at her hips. "No sir, we gots some uppity scabs up in here, with no sense at all."

"Thank you, Miss Maggs, we certainly appreciate the hospitality," Kyra said, picking up the tray from the dirty floor and handing pieces of the bread to her companions.

"Don't you be sweet talking me none," Maggs warned. "Ain't nothing worse than a scab trying to put on airs. I ain't no Miss."

Kyra tried to placate the woman with a nod while bringing the bread to her mouth. When her eyes caught the wriggling movement of a fat maggot, she let out a yelp and tossed the bread back onto the tray, uncontrollably wiping off her forearms, suddenly feeling that the little creatures must be crawling all over her.

"Tut tut." Maggs shook her head in disgust. "You see that, Roger? What I tell ye? Can't be trustin' no scab living the high life in the servant class. What is it, darling, you scared of a little protein?"

Roger stood up from the table to retrieve the tray. Like most of the slaves, his clothes were filthy, and he smelled like a mixture of rotten onions and sweat. "You sure is right, Maggs. Now don't you worry none, though, I ain't going to waste nothin'," he promised, gobbling up the bread and a tossing hunk to the nearest slave. The group of them had a laugh at the horrified expression on Kyra's face.

Everyone abruptly stopped when a bullhorn was blown from up on the wall surrounding the slaves' living quarters. Without so much as a word, they dropped their things and headed out of the hovel, ready for another half day of labor. Corbin shuffled to his feet, following the quickly growing line of slaves back out of the area as the horn continued to blow. On either side of the steady stream of slaves paced more human slavers, barking orders for the scabs to move faster at the ends of flicking whips. Corbin looked around the swelling crowd of workers for a way out.

"There's no sense in staying behind. We can't risk any more attention from the slavers," Kyra counseled, looking down at her feet so the slavers could not see her lips moving.

"Besides, it would seem we have a new member to our party," Stur added, ever so slightly motioning to their rear. Corbin casually glanced over his shoulder, locking eyes with a young teenage boy who was staring at the trio. The boy quickly snapped his head away, his face flushed.

"He was one of the slaves back in the shack. It's just a coincidence," Corbin reasoned.

"More likely he is curious about the new *scabs*," Stur replied, not concerned about the boy trailing them but noting it so they knew parting from the crowd would not go unnoticed. Not that he saw a way for them to do so anyhow.

Rather than returning to the granary, the companions realized the slaves were being led to the fields. Apparently late afternoon was a good time to harvest the grain. Right when the blazing daystar overhead was in just the right position to weigh down on them like an exploding juggernaut.

Corbin followed the lead of several slaves, plucking a hand sickle from a pile of tools and heading down a narrow row of stalks to get to work. For hours they worked side by side with the slaves, bowing their heads low whenever a slaver stalked past.

"Why don't they just fight back? It's not like they do not have weapons available," Corbin asked, referring to the sharp, curved sickles, which would do some serious damage if employed properly.

"With what training would they manage this? And where would they go? Look around you. These poor souls move from one walled prison to another, living like caged animals," Kyra pointed out, beads of sweat running down her brow in an unending river.

"At least they could try. I would rather die than live like this," Corbin replied, unhappy with the idea that anyone would be forced to live this way.

"I think if you put it in perspective, this is the only life they have ever known. It's easy for us to say they should fight to the death for freedom when we have tasted its cool waters," Stur said. "You have but walked a few hours in their shoes. Think how the spirit can be broken when your entire existence has been nothing but as an animal bred for work."

Corbin frowned, looking away from the mighty warrior in shame. He suddenly felt foolish for his complaints.

"And even if they somehow made it past all these guards and over all these walls, what awaits them outside the city but a desolate wasteland?" Kyra added, looking around at the broken slaves with despair filling her heart.

"It is we who must be their sword and shield," Isaac intoned in their minds. The mage had been listening in on all of their conversations through Corbin's psychic bond since entering the granary. *"When there are those in need, it is the lions that must rise and devour evil."*

Kyra nodded, agreeing with the mage's perspective.

Their conversation was cut short when an elderly man suddenly flopped limply to the dirt, passed out under the sweltering heat of Themis, Acadia's blazing star. No sooner had the man fallen than a slaver was there with his whip, shouting for the lazy scab to get up and get back to work. When the old man did not move, the slaver became angry, kicking him in the legs. Without warning, Stur dropped his sickle and ran over to the pair. Kyra stopped Corbin from following, trusting in her weapon master to handle himself and trusting he would not give away their disguise.

The slaver stepped back to let the newly arrived scab approach the old man, watching with irritation as Stur crouched down and tried to wake him. Feeling the slave's forehead and checking his tongue, Stur looked up with a frown. "This man is dehydrated. He needs water and rest."

The slaver's laugh sounded like the braying of a horse. "What, ye turn int a doctor all a sudden? He ain't dehydrated, just lazy. Now get the scab up!" he ordered, kicking the old man's bony legs again.

"Please, sir, just a little water, and I can help him up." Stur hoped the slaver would see reason.

"Oh, just a little water, is that all? Sure, I'll give him some water." With a sick glint in his eye, the slaver let his breeches loose and pissed on the old man's face. Stur backed up with a snarl, rising to face the slaver.

"Still think he won't do anything rash?" Corbin asked, sharing a doubtful look with Kyra.

"We better get over there," she said. The two of them moved to join their companion.

"What're you looking at, scab?" the slaver hissed. When Stur did not reply, the man shoved the warrior to the ground and raised his whip to strike.

At least, that was what he meant to do. Except when he shoved Stur, the man did not budge, not even an inch, and the slaver rebounded, falling on his backside in the dirt. This set the slaver off in a fury, and he hopped to his feet, cursing. The infuriated man rained down a flurry of blows. Except none of them were aimed for Stur and instead hit the unconscious old man. Stur threw himself on top of the defenseless elder, taking the unyielding volley of lashes in his stead.

Corbin had just arrived on the spot and was ready to intervene when a brooding jotun strode over on the back of a fine black mare.

"What in the seven hells are you doing, Oswould?" the Overseer spat, freezing the slaver's fury in place.

The jotnar sympathizer turned about like a spring, bowing low to his master, and explained. "Overseer Ol'bron, I was trying to get this loafing scab back to work, and this other fool—"

"What part of *keep everything orderly* did you not understand?" Overseer Ol'bron growled. "The marquess is coming through for his midday inspection any minute now, before the archduke arrives, and I don't want any problems."

"Yes Master, but—" the slaver began, cut off as the overseer grabbed him by the neck, lifting the slaver up to his height atop the horse and choking him.

"Are you questioning me, dog?" he growled, baring his purple gums and fanged teeth.

"Overseer Ol'bron, Master, if it pleases?" The slaver from earlier cautiously approached, distracting his jotnar master. "If I may, Master? These troublemakers *were* causing a fuss earlier."

The jotun dropped his captive to the ground, taking interest in his slaver Fergus, whom he trusted. It was hard to find a good lapdog these days, so many of them being worthless scabs, but Fergus was different. He was not just obedient but clever as well, a particularly magnificent dog to have around. "Go ahead," the Overseer allowed.

"Seems they be sent down here by Master Milton on loan. Guess they don't teach them servant class scabs how to do no proper work, eh?" the slaver said, smiling to see the lines of blood and peeled skin across Stur's exposed back.

Overseer Ol'bron straightened in his saddle, taking his clever lapdog's double meaning. If these scabs were Milton's, then he would expect them back in one piece, else the Overseer would be on the hook to repay their purchase price. "Well, get this damned area cleaned up before the marquess arrives," he growled to Fergus. "And you three scabs, bring these men to the healers," he added.

Corbin was surprised to hear a voice mumble, "Yes, Overseer." Just beside him stood the curious teenager from earlier. The boy scurried to help the gasping slaver to his feet. Corbin and Kyra helped Stur rise, balancing his heavy weight with an arm around each of them.

When the overseer stalked away, Fergus called over two slaves to take the old man to the food pens. "Well, at least he'll be getting something to eat," Corbin whispered to Kyra before it dawned on him that the slaver was referring to the human kennels that they had seen from outside the city.

"Hey, kid," Kyra called to the boy helping the slaver walk in front of them, "you know the way to the healers?"

Without slowing, the boy shot them a quizzical look. "Of course, I do. Geez, who doesn't know where the healers be?" He looked the trio up and down. "You servant scabs sure is something strange."

"Yeah, kid?" Corbin muttered. "You don't know the half of it."

To get to the healers, they needed to make their way out of the walled farming area, passing several other walled sections of the city, where slaves toiled in various tasks, before arriving at their destination. Corbin knew he should not be surprised to find that the healers' quarters was nothing more than a network of connected tents. Why would the jotnar construct an actual building dedicated to keeping the slaves healthy when they forced them to live in such squalor in the first place?

When they arrived, the group was sent to the backroom of one of the larger tents and told to wait for Healer Eir. The area was broken up into smaller rooms using goat skins as makeshift walls. It was odd, the way the quarters were arranged, as if you walked down a hall with tents acting as rooms. Each tent was completely blocked off with the exception of windows cut into the wall facing the "hallway," which were lined with a thin layer of netting. This way the jotnar standing guard inside the healer's area could keep an eye on the slaves and ensure no one tried to slip out undetected.

Corbin helped Kyra lay their injured friend, who was still fairly dazed from his beating, on a low wooden cot.

"Hey, what are you doing?" the teenager asked, sounding terrified but wearing a scowl. "You know slavers have first right. Scabs is for the dirt, where we belong."

Corbin looked at the dirty floor of the tent then at his injured friend before replying through gritted teeth. "He's staying put. Put the slaver on the ground...where *he* belongs."

Kyra looked unsure whether that was the wisest course, but Corbin's grim expression told her there would be no debate. When the teenager did not move to comply, Corbin huffed and wrenched the slaver from his arms, dropping the despicable jotnar sympathizer to the dirt and glaring at the shocked boy until he backed away. The three of them took a seat on the floor, brooding over the situation with their backs to the tent wall.

"The only reason we even seeing Healer Eir is 'cause of the slaver." The boy pointed at the man who was raggedly gasping on the ground. "Don't see how giving a scab priority over a slaver is gonna turn out right for us."

The comment interested Corbin, but not for the same reason that the boy meant. "Is this Eir important?"

The boy looked at him as if he had just asked if the sky was blue. "Are you daft? You must be one of them dumb scabs who don't know any better, huh?"

"We're from the servant class," Kyra chimed in. "Things are much different with us *scabs*."

The boy seemed to swallow the explanation, nodding. "*Healer Eir* is the head of all the healers down here. She been looking after us scabs for a long time now, the way Big Earl tells it," he answered.

The flap to their small enclosure opened, and a pair of jotnar, a male and female, made their way inside. Both wore the same short-sleeve cotton shirts and matching breeches that were standard for the healer class. The cream-colored fabric seemed to glow in rich contrast against their blue skin.

The woman, who Corbin assumed was Healer Eir, stopped in her tracks, looking back and forth between the two injured humans then down at the trio sitting on the floor, puzzlement plain in her expression. "Did you bring these men here?" she asked.

"Yes milady," Corbin replied with a slight bow of his head. Eir wrinkled her nose at the odd title, but the jotun next to her snickered, earning himself a look of annoyance.

"Why is the slaver on the floor?" she asked coldly.

"There was only one cot, milady," Corbin replied, feigning ignorance.

Healer Eir let out a sigh, peering out the netted window. "Walizer, help me switch them before a guard happens by," she ordered without taking her eyes from the opening. She grasped Stur's shoulders while the other healer grabbed his feet. After they placed Stur in the dirt and switched the slaver into the cot, Corbin watched as they examined the jotnar sympathizer. He sneered at the slaver, whose face was turning a pale shade of blue, thinking that the man would probably be happy to find his skin almost the same color as the jotnar. When they were finished with the slaver, he lay still, deeply asleep.

When Healer Eir felt Stur's ribs, Corbin noticed she seemed curious. Asking her colleague to feel something, she looked over her shoulder at the pair. He realized with fright that she had probably felt that Stur's ribs were not where she was pressing. Fooling the eyes with a dweomer was one thing, but to trick the trained hand of a healer would require a bit more magic than Isaac's illusion alone.

Corbin shot his mind into the woman's mind, perhaps a bit too forcefully. He caught his breath when she snapped her head to regard him for a moment, looking as if she had heard some odd noise, before returning to her work and whispering something to the other healer. The male jotun's eyes shifted in their direction while she spoke, though Corbin could not hear what she was saying.

"I think she knows something is up," Corbin warned Kyra telepathically, who already shared his concern. He decided it would be best if he entered the healer's mind to see what she was thinking.

"That would be ill-advised, lad," Isaac chimed into their telepathic conversation. Forgetting himself, Corbin quickly looked around.

"Keep still, Corbin!" Kyra insisted. The healer was looking at him again with a furrowed brow, wondering why the human was behaving so oddly. He tried to shoot her an innocent smile, though it

came out clumsy and even more suspicious. Eir nodded toward them, saying something to her counterpart.

"Isaac, why do you speak caution," Corbin asked. *"I believe we are in danger and swift action must be taken."* He was unable to hide his frustration in the clear channels of thought.

"Oh, there is no doubt you are both very much in danger, as you have been from the moment you entered the city. However, it is not uncommon for healers to be practiced in the art of psionics, lad. I would tread lightly around this one if I were you. Even from this distance I can feel that the jotuness reeks of magic," Isaac advised.

Finishing their work, the healers wrapped a clean strip of cloth all the way around Stur's torso. "He's going to need a few days of rest," Eir said to her companion.

"Little chance of that happening." The other healer shook his head. "More likely Ol'bron will have him back in the fields tomorrow."

Healer Eir walked up to Corbin, Kyra, and the boy. She towered over them at seven feet, reminding Corbin that they were indeed in a city of giants. Eir carefully studied the slaves with a furrowed brow. Corbin did his best to remain calm under the healer's scrutiny. Frowning, she stepped out of the room with her partner.

"I think we better act quickly," Corbin said as he and Kyra watched the jotuness emphatically speaking with her partner in the hallway. Whatever she said prompted the jotun to stop and look at them suspiciously. Corbin averted his gaze.

"We need to get out of here," Corbin thought, starting to rise. Kyra grabbed his thigh, pushing him back down before he could stand. Outside the room, Healer Eir nodded, and the jotun walked away with an urgency that left a yawning pit in Corbin's stomach.

"How can we leave without Stur?" Kyra asked. Corbin was afraid to take his eyes off the healer, who was peering back into the room. He felt dread. The look in her eyes left little doubt that they had been found out. When she turned her back and walked away, Corbin was quick to his feet, running over to Stur's unconscious body.

"Grab his legs. We have to get out of here," he urged Kyra, propping Stur up and slinging one of the warrior's arms around his neck. The heavy warrior mumbled something incoherent, and a thin line of drool ran down from the corner of his mouth. "Quickly now, before they return," Corbin urged.

The boy looked at them, his eyes puddles of fear. When he jumped up to run for the door, Kyra snatched the boy by his soiled collar and clamped her fingers over his mouth, muffling his screams.

"Quiet now," she hissed. When the boy did not comply, she produced her short sword, ramming the pommel into his gut and knocking the wind from his lungs.

Choking on vomit, the boy bent over and retched across the dirt floor. Trying to catch his breath, wild eyed with terror, he scrambled back, holding one palm up and begging her to spare his life.

Kyra leaned forward with one hand on her hip and the sword pointed at the boy, bobbing the pointed tip with each syllable. "Keep your mouth shut, or I'll have to run you through, you hear?" When he pitifully nodded, Kyra put her weapon away and grabbed Stur's feet.

"Going somewhere?" Healer Eir asked from the doorway, holding the flap open, two armed human guards and her companion standing behind her. Corbin froze in place, eyeing Kyra, who was reaching for her weapon. The guards entered, moving to either side of the pair and pointing six-foot iron spears at them.

"Put the patient down," Eir said, short and steady, while the jotun tied the tent flap closed behind him, leaving a human guarding the entrance outside.

Kyra steadied her gaze on Corbin and nodded. They carefully set Stur back on the dirt floor and stepped away from him, ushered into the far corner by the sharp heads of the spears.

After they sat back down beside the boy, the doctor stood over them with crossed arms. "Who are you?"

"We ain't nothing but scabs fit to serve, ma'am. Ain't doing nothing but moving him to the other side of the tent. Not like a slaver gonna be none too happy wakin' up next to no scab what got him here." Corbin was impressed by Kyra's swift reaction. Her clever words would have been enough to avoid a beating by most slavers, maybe even some overseers as well, but Healer Eir was not so easily duped.

"You think we are idiots?" Eir asked, drumming her fingers against a toned bicep. "Between me and Bugge, we have seen all the human slaves that work in the farming class and a good deal of the servant class as well. And neither of us has ever laid eyes upon either of you." Eir emphasized each word, letting the weight of them sink into her captives' heads.

"Be ready on my signal," Kyra thought, her eyes darting from one guard to the next, gauging how fast she and Corbin could take them down.

"I'll take my guy and then go for the jotun healer by the flap," Corbin replied, firming his resolve.

"You see, Eir, what did I tell you? Check out the way the human is glaring at you, like he's not even afraid," Bugge said, pointing at Corbin, who did admittedly look fit to kill the healer.

"There is something off here," Isaac broke in. *"Talk with her for a moment. There is no need to take action yet."*

Corbin would have ignored the mage's telepathic intrusion if not for the spear tip that suddenly pressed against the side of his throat.

Eir crouched, putting her softly curved face in line with Corbin's. "Let me ask you again, and this time I'll say it nice and slow so you know I'm not buying your little act. Who are you, really?"

"We are from the house of Milton, sent down to the granary to fulfill a debt owed by our master," Corbin replied.

"Lies! They are telling lies, Eir!" Bugge blurted a bit too excitably. The jotun healer began anxiously pacing back and forth, wringing his hands. "They've found out. I told you this would happen eventually."

The healer quickly made her way to Bugge's side, rubbing his back to comfort him. "Let's take it easy now. We don't know any of that is true."

"How can you say that?" Bugge stopped with an accusatory finger aimed at Kyra. "Where else could they be from? They're the duke's spies!"

Eir was trying to quell the jotun's mounting hysteria calmly, but when Bugge raised his voice, she snapped. "Would you be quiet? Or do you want to bring the entire camp down on our heads?" she hissed. Bugge tightened his lips, nodding in shame at his outburst. "Now just let me get to the bottom of this."

"Corbin, use your power to read her!" Isaac shouted in his mind.

"But you said—"

"Yes, yes, but if she had the gift, she would have already used it on you instead of this hack job of an interrogation," Isaac said.

Corbin argued no further, seeing the wisdom in the mage's reasoning. Like a bullet, his mind raced inside the healer's mind, probing tendrils blanketing the woman's thoughts. He did not have to go far to hear her conscious mind. There were two competing worries raging inside her. The first was a hope that the human female in another tent was going to get better. The poor slave had been raped the night before by a group of guards who liked to beat and molest the slaves whenever they could, a vile trio she despised but could do nothing about.

As if this were not odd enough to Corbin, her second emerging thought was one word which shocked him so much he uttered it out loud.

"Resistance?"

As the word fell from his lips, Healer Eir's face turned pale and the humans at either side of him gasped.

Bugge flew into a nervous rage. "You see, they know! Duke Thiazi knows! What are we going to do?"

Eir looked terrified yet still in control enough to order her men. "Kill them." When nothing happened, she repeated the command. "What are you two doing? Kill them."

"We...c-can't h-h...Eir...," One of the soldiers struggled to speak, his jaw clenched tight under Corbin's overpowering telepathic command for the men to remain still.

Standing up, Kyra casually brushed the shaft of the guard's spear aside. To the jotnar's disbelieving eyes, the small slave plucked a finely crafted short sword from the air.

"This jotuness is confusing to me. How can this be?" Corbin's mind raced as he focused on holding the guards' will in place like a vice.

"Let's be done with this. Our cover is blown," Kyra said aloud. "Let's kill these four and be away from this place."

"No no no no. Find out more, this is a rare opportunity," Isaac said.

"What is the resistance?" Corbin asked the healer, who stood stock still in fear.

"H-how did you d-do that?" she asked with trembling lips, pointing at her men with a finger that would not stay in one place.

"The same way I am doing this," Corbin replied.

Eir felt the cold edge of a black steel dagger against her throat.

"Ei-Eir...I c-can't stop...," Bugge said with his eye twitching, trying to control the jerking movements of his arm, which seemed to have a mind of its own as it held a knife to Eir's throat.

"Don't fight it. We wouldn't want you to accidentally slit her throat now, eh?" Corbin said in a voice so cold even Kyra was surprised. "Tell me about the resistance. Now."

On the outside, Corbin was cool and calculating, while inside he was grasping to maintain control over the guards and both jotnar, battling their will with the sheer force of his telepathic need. When Eir's trembling lips closed tightly together in an act of defiance, he felt as if he would burst.

Isaac sent him a quick suggestion, which he gladly put to use, snapping his fingers and commanding the guards to sleep. When the men fell limply to the floor, the human at the door barreled in, having heard the commotion. He had no time to call for help, as Kyra's leg snapped his legs out from under him. She knocked the man out cold with one blow to the jaw.

Astonished, Eir openly gaped at Corbin. *"What are you?"* she thought, her mind bubbling with concern that the guards were dead.

"I'm a human, or as you would say, a *dumb scab*, and they are not dead, just in a deep sleep. A *really* deep sleep," he answered. "Now tell me about the resistance."

Corbin was curious to feel relief wash over her that the guards had not been killed. "I'll tell you nothing. You are better off killing me," she said defiantly, raising her chin higher and pressing the tip of the dagger against her throat.

Corbin could see her mind clearly, now that he was not spread so thinly. Visions of humans she had cared for raced across it, scattered and jumbled in her fear, but one kept rising to the surface.

"Greyson?" he said, and a flicker of fear arced across Eir's eyes. "Who is he? What is the resistance?" Corbin asked.

Bugge stopped fighting against the pull on his arm, his eyes growing wide.

"How are you doing this?" Eir groaned pitifully, a tear trickling down her cheek. In her mind, an image flashed of her and the bearded servant class slave named Greyson shaking hands. Corbin opened up the psychic aether to Kyra, showing her his probing, and she stepped back, astonished.

Isaac shared their shock. *"A human sympathizer."*

"A human what?" Kyra asked. *"How can this be? Are you saying some of these ice giants actually feel bad for the humans?"* Kyra thought the idea was ludicrous. The very concept of a human-jotnar bond flew in the face of everything she had experienced from the blue-skinned devils.

"From what my scrying has revealed, yes. Over the years, as new generations of the ice giants have matured, there seems to be an emerging school of thought growing among a small portion of them. I have witnessed some of these sympathizers exhibit extreme acts kindness," Isaac replied.

Kyra thought the mage must surely be toying with her.

"Do you...," Corbin began, unsure. "Are you *sympathizers*?" he managed to ask. Kyra scowled at the idea, ready to run the giants through before she and Corbin could be infected by their lies.

"You'll never take the resistance! Tell your master that humans and jotnar *will* live free of the empire's oppression!" Bugge vowed, baring his fanged teeth at them while tears streaked down the cheeks of a tight-lipped Eir.

Kyra blanched. The jotnar were ready to sacrifice themselves in the name of protecting humans. It was unbelievable to her.

"Keep your voice down. We are not here to kill you," Corbin warned, fearing the guards would hear the jotun's shouting and come running. He released his hold on Bugge, whose dagger went flying across the room with his hand finally back under his control, his straining muscles releasing. Both jotnar quickly stumbled backward, moving away from the dangerous humans. "However, you would do well to remain quiet or I might have to change my mind," Corbin added, wondering if the pair of them were going to try to flee the room. "It appears we are on the same side, so tell me more about this resistance."

Eir was confused, exchanging a questioning look with her partner. "First tell us who you are, really," she said. "The only humans we do not know are those in the upper houses. How can we know for certain that you are not one of Duke Thiazi's spies?"

"Show them," Isaac said.

Kyra clenched her jaw. "Don't do it, Corbin. We can't trust them," she said, never taking her eyes off the pair.

Corbin kept his eyes on them as well, reaching into his tunic. Eir flinched at this, thinking he was going to pull a weapon. When his hand came back out holding a glowing, miniature tree branch, both of the jotnar were immediately puzzled. Walking over to Stur, Corbin gently placed the branch on the warrior's sleeping chest and took a couple paces away, revealing his true form.

Eir staggered sideways and grasped her partner's arm, seeing the pale-skinned human dressed for battle.

"Now then, Healer Eir, my name is Corbin Walker, and I can easily strip all the information I need from your mind," he lied. "But since we are clearly both on the same side here, why don't you just tell me all about this resistance of yours?"

"Do you need help with that, Your Lordship?" the valet asked, moving in to button the high neck of Tryn's purple embroidered doublet. Pulling away from him, the marquess slapped his servant's hand away in annoyance.

"I can take care of it myself," he insisted. After buttoning the tight neckline, he pointed for his shoes. "Leave them on the bed and get out."

"But Marquess, I..." the valet began then withered under his master's glare. "Yes, milord." The light-skinned jotun bowed before making a haughty exit from Tryn's bedchamber.

Hearing the door to his apartments click closed outside the room, Tryn sighed, leaning on a bedpost for balance and slipping on one of the tight dress shoes. *Finally, a chance to breath,* he thought, relishing the privacy. All day long he could only think of coming back to his quarters to gaze upon the human he had taken from the Ogre's Fist.

Annabel sat with her back to the marquess on a cushioned bench at the end of his bed, as he had instructed, producing the most delicate melody from a small, ornately carved wooden lute he had brought up for her. While he brushed his doublet to ensure there was not a speck of debris on it, something which the duke would surely frown upon, he stared at the strangely fascinating human. She certainly looked different after he had his household staff clean her up. Whatever they had washed her hair with gave it a rich luster. Tryn had never known the color brown could look so lush and inviting.

"Palace servant attire suits you," he complimented, turning to grab his belt from the wardrobe. "This is much better than those droll rags your previous master had you in."

Annabel shifted uncomfortably on the cushioned bench, continuing to pluck out her song without daring to look in his direction.

"You can speak to me, you know. I told you as much last night. There is nothing to worry about. I'm not tricking you into conversation so I can punish you, not like the duke, he would certainly delight in that kind of mental torture." Tryn suddenly pursed his lips and stopped talking. *What am I doing, speaking to a human like this? Have I lost my wits?* he wondered, tightening his belt. *Does she even understand what I am saying?* He bit his cheek. The human certainly gave no outward sign that she understood him, and he knew so little about the creatures that he really had no idea what their comprehension level was.

Annabel could feel the inquisitive gaze of her new master like fiery pinpricks on her soft neck. She could feel him standing beside his wardrobe for long minutes while she continued to strum her melody, until she half wondered if the marquess was still there or if he had left the room. Daring to peek over her shoulder, Annabel was so shocked to see that the jotun had moved close beside her that she jerked, yelping and plucking the wrong note with a high-pitched twang.

Tryn decided she did understand him. Reaching down to run his long blue fingers through her soft hair, he tried to speak to her again. "Do not fret, little one. A single foul note does not ruin such an enchanting song."

He did not know what had come over him. Tryn had heard stories of other jotnar nobles becoming bewitched by humans and keeping them as sexual pets. However, he could never truly understand what they saw in the weak little creatures. They were certainly better suited to washing floors and raising crops, and when their duties were over, being recycled into meat to fill the larder.

As he let her hair fall back in place, cascading down to her waist, the aroma of rosehips tantalized him. "Ah, the maids certainly did well in cleaning you up." He gently pushed the instrument out of her hands and set it on the bench so he could stand the human up. With her back to him, Tryn pressed himself against Annabel, leaning down to get a whiff of the hair curling around her neck. "Yes, you smell lovely. Quite like the little flower that you remind me of."

As the words fell from his lips, Tryn felt silly. Why was he standing in his room speaking to a human this way? Yet he found he could not help himself, and he slowly turned Annabel to face him.

"Look up," he commanded as if telling a dog to sit. The human promptly looked directly up at the ceiling. Snickering at the creature's simplistic mind, Tryn corrected her, more gently this time. "Not like that, not at the ceiling. Look at *me*."

"My lord?" Annabel squeaked, flinching and looking down at her feet again as if she were bashful at the thought of looking him in the face.

No, not shy, Tryn realized. *The poor thing is terrified.* Suddenly he felt ashamed that such a lovely being was scared of him.

"There is nothing to fear. You will not be punished. Look at me," he softly prodded.

Annabel tentatively raised her head. When her eyes caught his smiling mouth, she jerked her head back down nervously. It took her several tries before she was finally able to look up at him. In the human's chocolate eyes, he saw an innocence he never dreamed one could possess. Tryn bit his lip, feeling the longing that worked its way up his stomach as he took in her beauty. To him, Annabel was like a fragile flower ready to bloom. *What is this feeling?* he wondered, tracing the contours of her full lips with his eyes.

"Such interesting little dots you have on your face," he remarked, referring to the orange freckles around her button nose. Tryn reached out, wanting to see the contrast of his light blue skin against her soft bronzed cheek. When his fingertips brushed against her skin, Annabel flinched as if she was about to be struck. Tryn was surprised to find himself quickly pulling back.

"You don't have to be afraid. I'm not going to hurt you," he said, trying to calm her fears, nudging the woman's chin back up to look at him. Tryn could see she was truly afraid of him, the tears welling uncontrollably in the corners of her almond-shaped eyes. Another wave of guilt washed over him. Though he had done nothing to warrant her reaction, Tryn felt embarrassed. "Why are you upset? Tell me. I swear I will not punish you."

Annabel looked down to her feet, unable to meet the marquess's eyes.

"Come on, now, I'm being more than fair with you. Out with it," he urged.

Still staring at her feet, Annabel began to mumble, somehow finding the words though her throat felt tight. Tryn could barely understand her. He half wondered if maybe he was wrong and she could not understand him after all, when a word broke through her mumbling.

"Concubine?" he repeated in a clear voice. "Oh yes, concubine. I forgot I told Fajik as much back at the tavern, didn't I?" He snapped his fingers. "Ah, it all makes sense now. Of course you are scared, you poor thing. How could I expect anything otherwise? All this time you must have been sitting here, wondering when I meant to take you for my pleasure," Tryn gave voice to her fear. "You must be beside yourself, speculating whether you are worthy of such a coupling, eh? Fret not, my sweet little angel, though you are a human, I still deem you up to the task." Tryn didn't pull away this time when she flinched while he soothingly stroked her warm cheek. Feeling her skin shuddering uncontrollably, he noticed her legs were wobbly and made a decision then and there. "Besides," he began, unsure he should be saying such things, "I will not take pleasure with you until you are ready for it."

Annabel jerked her head up at his promise, staring the strange jotun in the eyes with intrigue. Something about his smile disarmed her. He did not seem to be toying with her. The marquess seemed to be genuinely attempting to quell her nerves. For a moment her heart froze. Did he know? How could he? Was this a test? Had they found out after all?

They stood like that for long minutes, and Tryn's expression softened even further. He seemed in awe of the look in Annabel's eyes. It was one of intelligence and understanding. He was dumbfounded to behold such a look of clarity in a human's gaze and tried to remember if he had ever even bothered to look one of the creatures in the eye before. Humans were supposed to be ignorant savages that served no better purpose than as tools. Yet here before him was this delicate creature looking into his eyes as if she could read his soul. He suddenly ached to hear her story, to hear all of her hopes and fears.

Her own inner thoughts tumbled like cards as he lovingly stroked her cheek, and Annabel somehow found herself rubbing against his comforting hand, her eyes closed and a warm smile spread across her lips. Tryn could not remember a time when he felt such happiness.

When someone knocked on his chamber door, they both shook violently, backing away from each other, startled.

Tryn quickly gathered himself, straightening his doublet and moving for the door. When he opened it, Fajik was there, waiting for him.

"We better get moving, Marquess. Your father will not like it if you are late for the archduke's arrival ceremony."

"Yes, of course. I was just tying up some last minute preparations," Tryn replied.

The blade-hand looked over his shoulder into the room, where Annabel sat at the end of the bed, absently staring at the lute in her hands. "Yeah, I bet you were," he leered with a lusty smile.

Normally Fajik's misplaced remarks would irritate Tryn, but at this moment he was relieved for the misunderstanding, finding his actions both confusing and a little unnerving. Without another word, he closed his bedroom door behind him and followed the blade-hand out to the highest reaches of the palace.

As Tryn stepped out onto the roof, the hot afternoon settled heavily around him. "I see father has had the air docks cleared off," he observed.

At the pinnacle of Belikar sat the duke's palace, which was several stories high, the top of which opened out onto a landing strip built to house the warships and cargo vessels the empire had used to claim the land centuries ago. With Acadia conquered generations past, there had been little need for the strip other than for small cargo vessels, which funneled goods back to the floating capitol city Vrykal, far in the north among the Valarin mountains. The Empire itself had moved away from the larger flying war machines, as they took a great deal of magical energy to operate and became obsolete once the invasion of Acadia was complete. The landing strip atop Belikar normally housed stacks upon stacks of crates and was largely unused. Duke Thiazi had ordered everything cleared away, wanting to make a solid first impression with their royal visitor.

Not one for idle chatter, Fajik grunted in agreement, following dutifully across the narrow walkway, which doubled as a wall surrounding the palace grounds. They made their way over to the rest of the awaiting retinue on the air dock. Several of Belikar's highest ranking earls stood in attendance among the large greeting party, their lower class jotnar servants in tow. At the group's center stood Duke Thiazi dressed in a suit of black steel plate mail armor emblazoned with a scorpion, his family crest, on either pauldron. A finely woven purple cloak billowed in the wind behind the duke. It was the type of outfit one would only wear during a royal ceremony or festive procession. In the real battlefield, a soldier might as well paint a big red X on their back rather than wear such finely polished armor.

"Your Lordship," Tryn greeted his father, bowing down to one knee respectfully.

"Yes, yes, rise, boy. The archduke will be here any moment," Thiazi impatiently fussed, looking out over the ramparts into the clouds while blocking the light of Themis with one hand.

Tryn blanched, noticing each House representative had gifts in tow. He had not thought to present the archduke with anything! Why did no one mention this piece of decorum to him? He worried himself sick, his belly beginning to squirm at the thought of bringing shame to his father's house. *There has to be time, I can get down to my quarters and find something,* he frantically thought, all but biting his nails in distress as he stepped to the side, thinking to make his way back to his room.

"Where are you going?" Duke Thiazi snapped, roughly pulling his son back in place at his side. "Stand still. I see the archduke's vessel now." He pointed across the sky to an oblong shape quickly making its way to the city.

Suddenly Tryn forgot his anxiety, beholding the massive airship with awe. The *Goliath* was almost as big as one of the castles surrounding the palace, pill-shaped with tall, jutting spires both below and on the rear deck, which held spinning, hollow rings as large as the platform they stood on. Tryn had never seen a magneska conduit before. The airship's spires were a perfect blend of air magic and procured Acadian technology, keeping the vessel afloat in the sky using powerful magic that used the magnetic field around it. Each cargo vessel that visited Belikar had similar units but on a vastly smaller scale as those supplementing the massive warship's spires, which crackled with energy. While the cargo vessels relied on sails to grab the wind, the archduke's vessel had turbines on either side, propelling it forward through the clouds faster than the simpler cargo ships could ever hope to travel.

As the gargantuan airship came closer, casting a long shadow over the city, Tryn had to block the daystar to see the solid steel mast, which was carved into the roaring face of a dragon. The air around them whipped around in sharp gusts as the hulking armored craft slowed to dock against the tower. This close, Tryn could only stare in wonder that anything so large could move through the sky, his eyes filled with its bulk. The *Goliath* was as large as a small city in its own right. Archduke Marius must need a small army to fly it and man the cannons peeking out from its sides and deck.

"Put your tongue away, boy," Duke Thiazi said with a wry grin over the whipping wind as the airship settled into the housing, "and witness the glory of the capitol."

Tryn noticed his father stood a little taller, with a glint in his eye. It was a rare occasion to see the duke looking so optimistic, yet the moment of his lifelong pursuit for redemption was finally at hand. Tryn smiled back at him, puffing up his own chest, ready to face the archduke with pride.

The *Goliath's* engines died down, leaving a ringing in Tryn's ears. Workers firmly docked it in place floating in the sky above the city, and the long, curved bottom of the hull whirred open like a drawbridge, connecting to the palace dock. The smell of the engines dying down burned Tryn's sinuses and brought a cloud of stinging black smoke into his eyes, something his father must have foreseen, having covered his mouth with a gauntleted hand.

Duke Thiazi motioned for his men to begin playing the empire anthem on horns and drums while a retinue of soldiers in full military garb marched out of the ship and down the plank, tapping the base of their long halberds on the ground in perfect synchronicity with each other. After a good twenty of the jotnar soldiers arrived, each stopping before the retinue, slamming their long polearm to the ground, and standing at attention, the archduke emerged, making his way down the airship bridge.

Archduke Marius was far from what Tryn expected. The jotnar leader looked nothing like the powerful warriors he had grown up around. He was of average height, standing only nine feet tall, with a light blue skin similar to Tryn's own. Wrinkles lined the old jotun's face, and his hair was wild and unkempt, a shock of black and white that ran down to his shoulders and matched his shortly cropped moustache and beard. Marius walked with a short staff, more like an oversized cane, carved from the impenetrable icy heart of a frost dragon, the tip of it even chiseled into a likeness of its former owner, a leering dragon head. Tryn could see the archduke's eyes radiating like two glowing golden orbs. He was shocked to realize that the jotun was not a warrior at all, but a wizard!

He only caught a brief glimpse of the leather armor the archduke wore beneath his long crimson cloak as it blew open on the higher ramparts before the royal visitor stood in front of the greeting party with his entourage close at hand and the armored soldiers at attention behind him. Tryn was impressed by the whole spectacle, which was clearly fashioned to intimidate the onlookers.

Duke Thiazi put a clenched fist to his chest, elbow pointed out to face the archduke, and bowed low. The Belikar earls followed their duke's lead. Standing erect once more, Thiazi greeted his guest. "Royal Archduke Marius of the First Blood and House Valkar, Third in line to the Emperor's throne, it is with great honor and deep humility that I welcome you to—"

"Archduke Marius wants your men to stop this infernal racket!" the royal man-at-arms ordered.

The people of Belikar were visibly shocked to witness their duke so rudely interrupted, an act that would surely earn an order of execution from their short-tempered leader. To Tryn's surprise, the duke himself looked at a loss for words, staring back at the grim-faced archduke. However, Thiazi quickly recovered from the intentional slight, waving for his men to stop the music with a withering gaze.

He began again. "As you wish, Your Excellency. As I was saying we are—"

"Archduke Marius is wondering why you have not greeted him properly as of yet," the man-at-arms interrupted again, though Tryn was certain the archduke had not spoken a word or given any signal to his heavy-set jotun lackey. When the duke made no move to do anything different, the warrior rolled his eyes and sighed as if he were bored. "It is customary to present yourself by kneeling before the archduke," he educated them, speaking as if their slight was droll.

Darin, one of the duke's most trusted earls, looked to him for guidance, receiving a curt nod. They all fell to their knees.

"That is better," the man-at-arms confirmed.

Archduke Marius walked over to the duke and stretched out his arm for Thiazi to kiss his ringed hand, before stepping back. "You may rise," he allowed in a sharp voice.

The humbled Thiazi rose, towering over the archduke yet looking greatly his lesser at that moment. Thiazi cleared his throat, starting over again with his rehearsed greeting. "Royal Archduke Marius of the First Blood and House Valkar, Third in line to the Emperor's throne, it is with great honor and deep humility that I welcome you to my city, Belikar. I have prepared a magnificent feast in your honor and—"

The archduke raised a hand, silencing Tryn's father, who was growing visibly flustered. "Duke Thiazi *welcomes* me to *his* city?" Marius asked his men, who remained stone-faced. "Last I checked, Belikar was a city-state of the empire, no?" Marius directed the steely edged question to his father.

Thiazi furrowed his brow. "Yes, of course, my liege. I certainly meant no disrespect." Tryn frowned, seeing Earl Homm smirking at the duke's situation, which seemed to be rapidly deteriorating from his plans. If Tryn did not know any better, he would guess the archduke was testing his father, a dangerous game to play.

Looking around at the nobility surrounding the duke, Marius sneered. "Yes...though it *does* give one an ill feeling to think that this backwater excuse for a city is actually part of the empire."

This made Earl Homm's smile grow even wider, and he turned his fat neck to gloat with his men while the duke stewed. When the gloating earl turned back, he flinched to find Marius standing directly in front of him.

"And who are you?" Marius sneered.

"Me? Uh, I am Earl Homm of House Harinndon, Your Excellence. It is my utmost privilege to be in your presence." The earl quickly recovered.

"It is? And why is that?" the archduke snarled.

Homm faltered, his mouth opening and closing, at a loss for words. Licking his lips, the earl snapped his fingers, signaling his human servants to present the gifts he had brought. "Offerings from the House of Harinndon, Your Lordship," Earl Homm explained with an overly melodramatic flourish of his arms that made the earl's double chins flap. When the archduke did not move, Homm meekly pointed toward the ornately carved boxes again and bowed so low Tryn thought the fat jotun might tip over if he bent any farther.

"Hmm, gifts, eh?" Marius muttered, moving over to the presents and flicking them open. "You certainly seem to be enjoying the conversation your duke and I are having," he pointed out while perusing the goods. "Perhaps you agree that he is a buffoon for offending me with his paltry welcome?"

Homm slowly nodded, closing his eyes with an unflattering smirk and smugly grinning at the duke when Marius turned his back.

"Zain, dispose of the Earl of House Harinndon," the archduke callously ordered as if he were asking the man-at-arms to bring him his lunch.

Without any hesitation, the armored warrior took three great strides forward and ran his broad sword cleanly through Homm's gaping mouth, quicker than the earl could even blink. Everyone in the retinue stepped back with a gasp as the earl bled out on the stone platform. All except Duke Thiazi, who stood motionless, completely devoid of emotion.

The archduke began pacing in front of the group, thoughtfully drumming his long, ringed, fingers along the edge of his cane.

"Shut your mouths!" Zain brusquely ordered, quieting the emotional group.

Marius strode up to Tryn's father again, squaring his unblinking gaze with the unfazed duke's. They studied each other for long minutes that stretched out in the uncomfortable heat of midday. Finally the faintest smile cracked across the old archduke's face. "You knew I would kill the earl, didn't you?" he accused.

It was the duke's turn to smile coyly down at the older jotun. "And why would I want such a thing?"

The archduke made a sound like leather being torn. It took Tryn a moment to realize he was laughing. "Perhaps because it is common knowledge that I will not abide open disrespect toward one's betters, or because you are apparently not as stupid as you look?"

Thinking his father would surely kill the archduke where he stood for such an insult, Tryn let out a pitiful groan. He felt his insides turn to jelly when both men snapped their heads to glare at him. The archduke seemed to almost float over to his spot, mesmerizing Tryn in the swirling fires of his golden eyes. Tryn knew the archduke was sizing him up, measuring the worth of the fool who dared to make a sound in front of him. Somewhere far away from the licking flames of magic that were grazing across his soul, he could see his father, in his peripheral vision, looking at Tryn with open disgust.

"I'll not attend any banquet." Marius said. "I've no time to waste on such frivolous affairs. Also, I hear you actually employ human cooks in the palace. I'll not have scabs breathing on my meal." The archduke abruptly broke off his gaze, flicking his frozen cane toward his man-at-arms.

Zain began shouting orders to his men. They dutifully fell into formation and began marching for the palace.

Duke Thiazi, though clearly upset to hear the banquet he had spent the last several days carefully planning would not be necessary, bowed respectfully. "Would you like to begin the tour on the morrow, Archduke?"

Marius turned, true curiosity etched across his ancient face. "Tour?" he asked, as if he had never heard the word before, leaning in toward Zain to speak privately. Tryn heard him mumbling something, but it was inaudible. He could make out nothing more than, *"Inspection, eh?"* Finishing his conversation with Zain and arching an eyebrow, the archduke smirked, taking in Thiazi with a wolfish grin. A great many of the movements the royal jotun made reminded Tryn of a wolf. "Yes, of course, the inspection. The morrow sounds adequate. We will begin after first light," Marius agreed, turning his back to a pleased Duke Thiazi, who bowed with a gleam in his eye.

Tryn realized things had actually played out much to his father's liking. Not for the first time in his life, he found himself impressed with the ever strange and calculating ways of his father.

"And send this one to accompany me," the archduke added as an afterthought, disarming the duke when he pointed the end of his cane directly at Tryn.

Thiazi forgot himself for a moment, exclaiming with stupid disbelief, "My son?"

The archduke regarded them both in turn. "Wait, *he* is your son? Hmm, I would expect the firstborn of the *legendary* General Thiazi Olvaldi to be a bit more impressive. Are you sure this gangly youth came from your loins?" The archduke snickered, pleased with himself. "Interesting... yes, send the lad along to accompany me on my entire tour of the city. He will act as my personal escort on your behalf." The matter settled, Archduke Marius turned his back on them and made his way to the palace.

Tryn felt his insides turn to mush, and he spun to apologize to the duke. "Father, I..." he began, faltering under Thiazi's menacing scowl.

"Save it for later. I have to ensure the archduke and his men get to their quarters properly," Thiazi growled, brusquely shoving past his wretched offspring. As he sauntered after the entourage, he added over his shoulder, "I'll come by your apartments tonight to groom you on escorting a member of the royal family. You will not let me down."

Tryn bowed respectfully. Though he knew the evening's education was sure to come with a lashing for his groaning mishap, his heart soared to think the duke would actually be coming to his very own apartments and personally grooming him for the upcoming task. He could not believe his luck, glancing back up at the *Goliath* and wondering what else the next couple days had in store for him.

Beads of sweat rolled off Logan's brow, trickling down from his thick mop of walnut hair. They had travelled for two days straight, virtually racing to their destination. There was no doubting that they had left the angry hill giant far behind, eating the dust of their hard flight.

Nero was having an easy time of it. In fact, Logan would even say the android seemed to be enjoying itself, using his stores of data to calculate which buildings once stood among the ruins and guiding them along based on the invisible information playing across his robotic vision. Nero was recording a mountain of data on the changed landscape.

Signs of the long extinct civilization slowly began to emerge from the impenetrable jungle soon after they climbed out of the gorge. First it was the fractured remains of what must have been a wall surrounding the kingdom, which was now no more than a series of fallen, jagged yellow stones set in a semi-uniform array, with weeds and trees growing between their shattered remains. But then, as they travelled farther into the area, the ruins became more frequent. Out of nowhere, they would come across an arched stone doorway, resting alone in a clearing, or steps leading up to nothing.

Soon enough, signs of drakes became evident.

"The place looks to be swarming with them," Bipp pointed out. They had found droppings and tracks all around the ruins, indicating there were a good many of the monstrous lizards calling the place home.

"The Ithikins are said to have raised drakes as pets and used the larger ones as mounts," Nero explained. "It is possible that left unchecked, their population has greatly increased."

Logan deemed it would be wise if they traveled the rest of the way with weapons drawn and in defensive formation, putting Nero in the back with his short bow and having Tiko lead alongside Bipp.

By the time they reached the center of the lost kingdom of Ithiki, Logan's skin had turned the red of a shiny lobster left under the sweltering heat of Themis. His pale Falian skin was completely unused to this kind of exposure, and he was regretting their decision to travel by daylight in hopes of gaining back some of the time they had lost during their brief capture at the hill giant's camp.

"Tiko, do you have any remedies for this?" Logan asked the lizardman in hopes he held some other secret jungle knowledge to relieve his stinging skin. The day before, the lizard had given him some roots to chew on, which he promised would help keep Logan awake and reinvigorated. They worked like a miracle, clearing up his hazy, sleep-deprived perception and giving renewed strength to his aching muscles.

But alas, Tiko knew of nothing to help with the sunburn covering Logan's exposed arms, neck, and face, explaining, "The Agma do not have such soft-skin problems. Our body is made for Themis's radiance."

"Okay, no need to gloat about it, pal. I'm in enough pain without the bragging," Logan snapped at him.

"Master Logan, I know of a plant you can rub on the problem areas to alleviate the pain and help in your body's regeneration," Nero offered, promising them he would keep a lookout for it in their continued travels.

After some time, the android perked up, announcing he had found the plant. Logan's face screwed up when he looked at the gangly pointed plant riddled with spiky protrusions. "You're kidding, right? I'm not rubbing that thing across my arm. It hurts enough already without adding a row of cuts to my skin!"

Logan was flabbergasted that the android even suggested he try this method. Up until now, he had only been keeping himself moving by thinking there would be some sort of relief on the road ahead. To find that, after all that anticipation, it was doomed to end in bust, he could feel his blood beginning to boil. Visions of popping the robot man's head off and putting it back on in reverse ran through his heat exhaustion-tainted thoughts.

"Why are you smiling at him like that?" Bipp asked his friend cautiously. "It's creepy."

Nero reached barehanded for a clump of the leaves, which surprisingly broke off rather easily, and turned to show the bounty to Logan. "Master Logan, you misunderstand. It is not the outside of the elo that you rub on the affected area, but the juices inside," he said, squeezing a blob of the clear gelatinous stuff onto his palm to show Logan it was safe.

"Looks like a donkey's spit, you darn hunk of bolts," Logan grumbled, refusing to accept the strange fluid.

"Geez, you need some rest, man." Bipp rolled his eyes, nudging Logan to get his attention. "Do you even realize what a jerk you've been for the last couple of hours?"

Logan looked down at his friend, who usually dwelled in a perpetual state of joy. Beneath the pounding headache, he could see there was something wrong and knew the gnome did too. Yet each time the party stopped to rest, try as he might, he still could not fall asleep.

"Yeah...I guess those arabica leaves are starting to lose their affect," he admitted, his way of apologizing to the group. Logan accepted the android's offering. The spiky plant was unnaturally soft and smooth to the touch, dripping a thick clear juice directly onto his forearm that was sticky yet satisfying, as if someone had just taken a cool damp cloth and placed it over his burns. "Wow, Nero, this is amazing!" he exclaimed.

"Yes, it is in my databanks that the plant would be seen as such," Nero replied in his choppy robotic manner.

"Why don't we take a short rest and get you some shut-eye before you pass out from exhaustion?" Bipp asked, waving at a good resting spot in the grass.

Logan was just about to agree with his friend, squeezing another gob of elo onto his neck, when Tiko interrupted them. "It appears that time has come and gone my friends," he said, pointing past a hillock nestled between two nearby trees, "for this one believes we have reached our destination."

Ducking under a low hanging vine covered in grey moss, Logan crept between the trees to look down the small hill. The area was bumpy and rugged with the broken remains of an ancient structure. Sandy yellow monoliths that could have been the remnants of a building's support beams and columns jutted among the thick blanket of green grass waving in the breeze. The jungle was just as overgrown here as anywhere they had been during this perilous journey, yet somehow it held an almost mystical feel, as if magical energy from aeons ago still lingered nearby.

"This is a holy site," Tiko said reverently, kneeling in the grass to offer thanks to the spirits.

Logan looked at his gnome friend, who squirmed uneasily while gaping around at the strange glen. Bipp felt his stare. "For once I gotta say I agree with the lizard," the gnome said, nervously tapping his lips. "Something is off about this place."

"Yeah, I know what you mean. I feel it too," Logan agreed. Looking at the creepy monoliths, he tried to pinpoint where the energy he felt was coming from. "It's almost as if something is...I don't know, beckoning to me or something."

"Ohh, now you're giving me the willies. Knock it off. The only reason you feel that way is 'cause you're out of it from them weird leaves the lizard gave you. And all this exposure to Themis' daylight isn't helping any. And, oh yeah, did I mention you need some rest?" Bipp cut into him, not willing to sit around and listen to ghost stories.

"Wait!" Logan unexpectedly shouted, making the gnome jump straight up in the air with fright. "Look over there, past those walls!" He pointed beyond a row of fallen blocks of stone, where the daystar's light reflected off something shiny.

Scurrying down the hillock, they wove through the glen, making their way past the ruins toward the mysterious object.

"Now that's odd. I haven't seen no trees like these anywhere else we've been," Bipp commented, referring to a grove of willow trees with fat, gnarled trunks and thick, drooping branches blocking their view.

"I believe Master Bipp is correct, sir. The willow trees are a phenomenon not typical to these climates," Nero observed, ducking under the long, sweeping tendrils of branches that were tickling Logan's neck as he made his way beneath the boughs. All his nervous energy was eerily replaced by a sense of overwhelming calm in the presence of the gently swaying trees.

"Come on, Tiko, this is no time to be lazing about," Logan called to the lizardman, who was still kneeling in the grass, praying. He felt the irony of those words coming from his mouth after years of being known as the village slacker.

Past the thick curtain of weeping branches, they found a wide meadow, the perimeter of which was lined with weeping willows set in an almost perfect circle. It was much like the clearing around the White Tree, a fact he was certain was not mere coincidence.

The Aegis lay directly in the center of the mystical grove. Half buried in the soil and overgrown with moss and vines, it was much like the rest of the ruins they had seen since entering Ithiki, but there was no mistaking what this magnificent suit of armor truly was. The ancient relic was gargantuan by human standards. Even with it lying on its side, Logan could see it must stand twelve feet, nearly as tall as the hill giant they had encountered and just as wide. The white armor was dirty and unpolished, yet it still sparkled where Themis' rays danced around the heavy shoulder plate that was in view.

"Have you ever imagined seeing anything like this?" Logan asked Bipp, trying to take in the sheer size and scale of the armor.

The helmet was fully enclosed and came to a sharp crease at the center from the nose down, with an eye slit large enough for Logan to stick his forearm into, though given what might be lurking in that dark crevice, he thought better of the impulse. Large, tarnished golden wings rose from either side of the helmet, and a crest of white hair rested on top, like the mohawk he had cut into his brother's hair one night when he was asleep. The chest plates were half-buried in the soil, but what he could see indicated the armor was thick and came to a jutting crease in the center, with massive pauldrons on each shoulder shaped in the visage of a snarling griffin's face, each decorated with gold plating. Even on its side, the whole suit of armor hulked over their heads as the party slowly moved closer to inspect it.

"Isaac didn't say it would be so...huge," Logan said in awe, running his natural hand across its cold metal surface, tracing the intricate patterns that worked along the edge of each overlapping layer of the chest plate. "How are we going to get this thing out of here?"

"Typically the dragon slayers were manned, like a tank," Nero explained.

"What in the hell is a tank?" Logan asked, cocking his eyebrow and walking down the length of the suit.

"Nero apologizes, Master Logan. To put this in simpler terms, you have to get inside and control the Aegis," the android explained, pointing at the helmet.

"He ain't big enough to walk around inside this thing!" Bipp countered, snorting. "Maybe I can get in one leg, and you can get in the other, though," he sarcastically added.

"No, I think he's right, Bipp," Logan cut in, cocking his head as whispering voices carried on the breeze. He felt as though they were trying to communicate to him, trying to tell him something about the Aegis. Logan tried to understand it, but the feeling was already gone. He frowned and rubbed his eyes. "We need to figure out how to get inside this thing." He rapped on the breastplate, which rang hollow, echoing off the wall of willows surrounding them.

The gnome trusted his friend's intuition and immediately set about trying to figure out how to open the hulking armor. "There's an inscription here on its leg, but it's written in no language I've ever seen," Bipp pointed out.

"Wow, I'm floored," Logan jested, smirking down at him. "Finally a language the world-famous scholar Bipp does not know!"

Bipp rolled his eyes and shoved the human away from him.

"Master Logan, this is written in an ancient Draconian dialect. Nero can decipher it," Nero announced.

Tiko gasped behind them, having finally finished praying and made his way into the grove.

"Pretty neat, huh, lizard skin?" Logan said, motioning for his Agma comrade to come closer. The humble lizardman looked mortified at the idea of being inside this holy circle but crept forward anyway, tip-toeing as if he feared waking the sleeping armored giant.

"Master Logan, Nero is done. The inscription reads:

Óðinn-son armor is wrought,
Mithril and lightning kissed by Dain.
Blessed by Nain, to face Bahamut, the Morningstar,
Fallen from grace and cursed to roam the abyss.
Possess true honor and keep the heart of a serpent locked inside,
The Aegis, Dragonslayer, bringer of justice, will rise.

"Hmm, what do you suppose that means?" Bipp asked.

"I'm not sure." Logan contemplated the odd inscription. "Nero, what can you tell us about the Ithikins? Perhaps if we know more about them, it will help us understand this better."

"From the limited data I have, it seems the Ithikins were a strange people. They were one of the older empires on Acadia, tracing their lineage to the distant past. The Ithikins claimed that their ancestors were brought to Acadia by the ancient Vanir."

"Yeah...that just brings up a whole multitude of other questions for me," Logan said. "Is there anything else? Anything we might use to understand how to open this thing?"

"Let me see. They were not one of the largest empires but all Kings on Acadia seemed to revere the Ithikins and valued them as allies. Many tried to steal the Aegis from them, but none succeeded. Their House standard is a white dragon flying across the moon. Their main crop was—"

"A drake," Tiko replied.

Logan snapped his fingers, emphatically nodding in agreement. "Yes, that's it! 'The Heart of a serpent locked inside.' We need the heart of a drake to open this thing!"

"Good luck with that. Been seeing their damned tracks for days now, but the damned things are more like phantoms. Haven't seen one yet," Bipp complained, not looking forward to tracking one of the fearsome creatures.

"No, Logan Walker," Tiko said, pointing at the armor, "*a drake!*"

Tiko hopped back, flipping his spear over his shoulder and crouching low, pointing it defensively above them. Logan spun about as the shadow crept over him. The green-scaled drake flicked its long pink tongue overhead, looking down at the food from its perch on the shoulder plate of the buried armor.

"Fall back!" Logan called, shoving Nero by the chest without taking his eyes off the dangerous predator.

With a hiss, the drake opened its wide jaws and spit a stream of fire at him. Logan barely kept enough sense to roll out of the way, letting Gandiva fly toward the hissing lizard's scaled flank. The drake pounced from the armor, charging in to take him down, and the boomerang flew harmlessly past.

Tiko let out a war cry, stinging the drake with his spear as it ran past and distracting the predator just long enough for Logan to scramble madly out of harm's way. But not before being bowled over by a hit from one of the beast's solid shoulders, which tossed him sideways into the tall grass. The drake was a swift predator, spinning about to spit another stream of fire at the exposed Tiko, bathing him in flames.

Nero let loose a series of well-aimed arrows at the monster's face, but only one of them lodged deeply between its breastplate and neck. As the forest drake growled, flicking its tongue to try to remove the stinging shaft, Logan ran to help his Agma companion. He was shocked to see the lizardman still on his feet in an offensive stance, unfazed by the scorching fire, and readying a burning spear to hurtle at the beast.

Sensing the danger, the drake leapt into the air like a tiger, flicking its long, armored tail at the incoming spear and snapping it cleanly in half before landing with another low growl.

Bipp rushed in, ready with his hammer, but Logan pulled him back. Logan flung Gandiva at the beast's face and then, without warning, grabbed the gnome by the collar and belt to spin him around and hurl him toward the monster.

The drake watched Logan's deadly weapon spinning through the air right for its head. It was preoccupied with side-stepping the blade when Bipp landed in the grass by its feet and smashed its talons to pieces with his hammer. At the same time, another arrow dug deeply into the creature's exposed mouth.

The beast howled, throwing its head into the air and roaring like a lion. Bipp stepped back, keeping his eyes trained on the enraged monster and trying to figure out a way out of this mess. He flinched when Gandiva tore straight through the back of the lizard's long neck, practically beheading it. Bipp barely got out of the way as the drake fell heavily to the ground, pinning his ankle under its weight.

Logan was laughing victoriously as they rushed in to free the gnome from under the slain dragon kin. "Could have warned me," Bipp muttered in embarrassment.

"Are you kidding me? We just took down a forest drake!" Logan replied, lost in jubilation over their victory. His smile was infectious, and Bipp could not help but join in. It took all three of them to roll the heavy beast over onto its side and free the gnome.

"Are you wounded, Master Bipp?" Nero inquired, crouching down to inspect the gnome.

"Nothing I can't dance off," Bipp replied, though Logan noticed he limped slightly when he tried to walk.

"Tiko, how come you weren't hurt when the drake's fire hit you?" Logan asked the Agma hunter.

"Tiko explained this to Logan. The Agma do not burn," the lizardman replied, shrugging as if it were nothing.

"Yeah, that's when we were talking about sunburns," Logan said, looking at the Agma's scale-covered skin. It was completely unblemished from the fire. "Oh, never mind. Good to know, though. I'm just happy you're still alive!"

"Logan must take the heart of his kill now, while it is still fresh and pure from the rot of death," Tiko urged, slapping a spot at the base of the beast's throat and handing Logan his bone dagger.

"Sure, whatever you say." Logan took the tribal weapon hesitantly. He had gutted plenty of game while hunting with his dad as a kid, but never anything as large as this. "Hey, Bipp, at least we can eat *this* lizard, eh?" Bipp snorted, though the inside joke was lost on their companions. "Tiko, do us a favor and climb up that tree. Keep a lookout so no more of these beasts can catch us unaware."

The Agma nodded at his wisdom, heading for a thick-trunked willow to scale.

Logan ran the bone knife over the tough leather hide of the drake's underbelly, straining to saw a jagged gash through the skin where Tiko had indicated. Once the cut was large enough, he reached inside, wrinkling his nose in disgust at the fetid odor and feeling around for the heart. He was up to his forearm before he pulled out an oblong crystal the size of Bipp's skull.

It pulsed with a bright purple light from deep in its core, surrounded by a black glassy surface. Logan felt like he was six again, kneeling in the grass beside the slain beast and thanking it for its sacrifice that he may reap the bounty. He felt foolish doing so but went along out of respect for his father's memory, who would surely have insisted they pay proper homage to the great creature, giving its death meaning. When he lifted the crystal heart toward the sky, it was as if a serpent whispered behind his ear while slithering around his neck, and then slipped into the light, taking the pulse of the bloody crystal with it.

"What is it?" Bipp asked, concerned to see his friend's face drain of all color.

Logan shook his head. "Nothing...probably just need that rest, like you said," he replied, too embarrassed to tell his friend what he had just experienced. He quickly changed the subject. "Now we just need to wait for nightfall, when the moons are out, so we can awaken the Aegis." He wrapped the purple and black crystal with a cloth and slipped it inside his pack, which lay beside the armor.

Bipp leaned against the drake and beamed, folding his stubby arms proudly across his chest. "We actually did it. Now we can get back to Corbin and Kyra!"

The hoot of an owl came from the trees. Logan turned toward the sound, wondering why Tiko was making such funny noises.

A spear dug itself into the drake's belly, shuddering in place only inches from the gnome's bulbous nose. Nero crouched low, narrowing his eyes to try to see where the weapon had come from, but the tip of a pointed spear against the back of the android's neck stopped him cold.

All around them, agmawor closed in, sliding out of the tree line and rising from the tall grass like snakes, surrounding each companion with over a dozen spears held ready to impale.

Nero looked at his feet, where he had set the bow and arrow to attend to Bipp, then up at Logan questioningly. Logan slowly shook his head, certain that they were far too outnumbered and stood no chance of escaping through sheer force.

The blue-green lizardmen moved aside to let their leader through. He was a lean Agmawor who wore the skulls of Agma on his shoulders and their teeth around his long neck as a necklace. He gave Logan an evil, sharp-toothed grin, flexing the dorsal fin on his crown and looking at his second-in-command.

"Bind the filthy soft-skinned invaders. Queen Nadja will be pleased to see the bounty we bring her," he ordered.

"Yes, Rahl," one of the lizardmen answered, moving forward with a length of vine in his hand.

Logan scanned the trees coolly, careful to not giveaway his thoughts. Tiko mind as well be a shadow, he was nowhere to be seen. Logan could only hope the agma was able to slip away unseen. He looked to the armor, gauging how long it would take him to make it past the cannibal lizards. It looked like he could make it in time to start the unit...*if* he knew what to do and *if* he knew where to put the heart. It was a lot of *ifs*.

The leader, Rahl, suddenly grabbed Logan's jaw with his claws, roughly pulling his face to look up at him. "Stupid soft-skin has filthy ideas, this one sees. You try nothing. You are Agmawor property now."

Logan spit directly in Rahl's face, shaking his head free from the humanoid's clawed hand. A flash of stars washed across his vision as a sharp blow cracked across the back of his skull.

"Pick up the soft-skin. He has a date with the witch queen."

Unlike the Agma, these lizardmen laughed, and it sent shivers up Logan's spine. He could only imagine who or what the witch queen was.

Chapter 14: Deliverance

Fafnir's men had bound Elise's and her companions' wrists behind their backs and marched the three villagers back toward Fal, west across the network of interconnected land bridges, stopping once they reached the mouth of the river. Baetylus's light was fading to a dull, hazy blue. It was getting late, and they made camp for the evening at the top of a small hill overlooking the lake.

A pair of the ruffians headed off to send word of their capture to a man named Rodger. He was apparently one of Fafnir's righthand men who had been placed in charge of the various bands of soldiers scouring the countryside for her people. Elise did not try denying who she was, not that it would have helped her any after her gruesome display of elemental magic. They had her, and it was only a matter of time until they had the rest of the villagers.

The soldiers were cooking some fish over the crackling fire, celebrating their victory with a bit of drink. Elise and her two remaining companions were left tied around some nearby trees, Rygor and Erik around one and her around the other.

"Elder Elise," Erik called in a low voice for the third time. He had been trying to get her to speak to him since the soldiers left them tied there, but Elise just stared blankly at the grass by her feet. "C'mon, woman, you've got to snap out of it. We have to figure out a way to get out of this."

Elise shook her head. "No."

"What the hell does she mean, no?" Erik asked his friend. Rygor had a hard time speaking with his lip cracked and swollen under a double set of black eyes. The soldiers had given him a severe thrashing and he had not been fast enough to block his face as Erik had. Rygor shrugged. Any bravery he once possessed had fled in the face of hopelessness.

"I mean no," Elise mumbled. "I'll not be trying to escape. That's all I've been doing for weeks now, and every time I do, someone else gets hurt. Someone dies."

Cassandra was listening in. She had not left their side since Elise was captured, drifting in and out of Elise's mind like a swirling fog. She had implored Elise to take action the moment the soldiers tried to take her, but the girl was a stubborn one to be sure. *"Elise, my dear girl, hear my words, I beg of you,"* Cassandra said, though the others could not hear her words. *"I know you are afraid, but you must be brave right now."*

"I'm not afraid," Elise hissed.

One of the soldiers perked up. "You be quiet over there if you know what's good for you."

Another of the men laughed, spilling some of his drink into the fire, which made the flames crackle that much higher. "Yeah, keep yer mouth shut, or we can come over and help you plug it up." He hopped away from the flames, patting a bit of fire that took hold on his pant leg, throwing his comrades into howling laughter. Elise ignored the soldier.

Erik scowled. "Milady, keep your damned voice down."

Elise ignored him too.

"What happened to Rimball was not your fault," Cassandra insisted.

"Of course it was my fault," Elise replied. "Did you see the look in his eyes after I let you burn that poor soldier alive?"

"I think our Elder has lost her mind a bit," Erik whispered, watching the young woman talking to herself. She did look quite mad too, with her blonde hair all frayed and her eyes red and swollen, staring at the grass while her head bobbed up and down. Rygor glumly shook his head at the insanity of it all, rubbing his aching forearm where one of the men had kicked him repeatedly. "Lisie," Erik said, calling her by her childhood nickname, "gather your wits. This is serious."

"The lad is right, you need to stay focused," Cassandra said.

Elise looked up, staring Erik hard in the eye. "I am focused," she snapped. Erik frowned, trying to make sense of her words. Elise rolled her eyes. "Don't you see? This is it. The magistrate is bent on capturing me. It was stupid and selfish of me to run in the first place. Well, it ends now. I'm staying here, where I can't cause anyone else to be hurt. First it was Lady Cassandra, then it was blacksmith Avery and his pig-headed family...and now Rimball. I can't do it anymore, Erik. I'm no leader. I'm just a cursed girl from Riverbell."

"Lisie, you can't say that." Erik looked wounded, as if the idea of her breaking somehow physically hurt him. "You're not just some girl from Riverbell. You're our Elder, and we need you. Magistrate Fafnir's corruption is not your fault." He searched her for some sign of acceptance but she did not say a word. "And what about me and Rygor? Will your conscience be at peace leaving us to the mercy of these soldiers?" Elise shook her head and went back to staring at the grass. She knew wherever she went, people would die, and there was nothing Erik could say to change her mind.

"Damnation," Erik said. "Looks like we're going to have to do this on our own." Rygor nodded feebly.

"Hmm, do tell," a soldier said as he walked between the two trees, pulling up the front of his breeches and tying the cord. "What exactly is it that you'll be doing on your own?"

"Uh, I..." Erik was at a loss for words. He had not heard the soldier relieving himself in the trees. If he was not fastened so tightly against the tree, he might have managed dodging the soldier's boot, which planted itself squarely in his gut. Erik vomited all over his chin.

"Little rats!" the soldier grabbed Erik's collar and spat in his face. "You think you're going to escape what's coming to ye?" Letting go, he kicked Erik again, this time across the thigh. "When the magistrate sends word, we're going to hang you by your neck from this very tree, ye damned traitors."

"No, please stop! Leave him alone!" Elise pleaded, fighting against her bonds.

Weasel-face scrunched up, the soldier turned his crooked nose in her direction. His upper lip twitched in a curl and he sauntered over to her. "Aw, the little witch wants me to stop," he taunted, kneeling beside Elise and smirking at Erik. He ran his hand through her tangled blonde hair, stroking it as if Elise were a pet. "Don't ye worry nothing, darling. We ain't gonna hurt ye." He snarled, tugging back her head by the clump of hair in his hand. "Just gonna use ye like a five pence wench while yer men watch from their nooses!"

Elise cried out, trying to pull her head away from his hand. Erik yelled, "You go straight to Hel, you damned rat-faced bastard!"

The insult only seemed to egg the soldier on, because he began laughing. "Aw, c'mon lad," he goaded, looking over his shoulder and filling his free hand with Elise's breast, "don't tell me ye never wanted to see the little wench get done proper."

Erik's face was red and lines of blood streaked through the sleeve of his shirt as he fought his restraints like a madman. "You get your filthy hands off of her! If you do anything to Elise, I'll kill you with my bare hands!" Rygor fought his restraints as well.

The weasel laughed at them even harder. He gave Elise's breast a slap then backhanded her across the face. Erik began screaming like he had lost his mind when the man pushed her squirming legs apart and wriggled between them. He leered, inches away from her face. "Oh, you is going to taste right sweet, aren't ye, witch?"

Elise spit in his eye and bit the man's hooked nose. She growled like a feral animal when he tried to pull away, clamping down her teeth even harder.

He punched her in the stomach hard enough to make her gag, hobbled backward, almost falling, and grasped his nose. When he looked down at his hand, it was covered with blood. "You miserable little wench," the soldier growled, pulling his dagger from his belt. "Now I'm going to cut ye open while I screw yer brains out!"

Elise was going to respond, but something about the soldier's face confused her suddenly. It twisted from a snarl to a look of utter disbelief as an arrowhead popped out through his right eye socket. The rat-faced soldier was dead in an instant, falling face first into the grass and rolling down the small hillside toward the fire.

Behind Erik's and Rygor's tree crouched Rimball, with his bow still in hand in a perfect fighting stance.

Elise was too astonished to say anything. Down by the fire, she heard the sounds of battle as Malbecians rushed the camp, brutally cutting down the drunken soldiers. Rimball made short work of cutting the rope around Erik's and Rygor's chests. Erik dropped to his side and flipped his bound wrists through his legs so that Rimball could cut them free. He handed a dagger to the young man so he could free his ankles and Rygor as well.

When Rimball came over to Elise's tree, she felt lost. "Am I dreaming?" she asked. Rimball shook his head, grim-faced as he cut the rope around her waist, freeing her body from the tree. "B-but...but...you died," Elise stammered. "I watched you die."

"Did you?" Rimball asked.

"Yes?" she said feebly.

Rimball worked the dagger over her wrist bonds. "Not that those arrows didn't sting," he said, pulling aside his collar so she could see the bandaging around his shoulder, "but it takes more than that to kill me. Once I hit the water, I knew our best chance for survival would be to swim off and find Bertha's cousins. We had to search a good portion of the bay before we found you." The rope snapped free and Elise rubbed her sore wrists. The hunter flipped his dagger around, offering her the handle.

"You want to help me...even after seeing me unleash Cassandra's stone?" Elise asked, tentatively accepting the blade.

Rimball stared at her, just as stone-faced as ever. "I would *never* abandon my people."

Elise felt a wave of emotion wash over her. Tears blurred her vision as she hacked away at the cord binding her ankles. Perhaps some of Baetylus's grip was loosened when the hunter left Fal? She felt so grateful to have the old man alive, it was hard not cry.

But Elise was determined to meet the Milua Isle fishermen with pride and wiped away the tears, steadying herself and using the tree to help her rise. Her legs tingled from poor circulation, and she had to wiggle them as she walked to get the blood flowing properly again.

Erik was coming back up the hill with her pack. "Thank you," Elise said, still feeling lost in a dream. Her eyes said so much more to the man who only minutes before was ready to die for her honor. Erik nodded once then turned away, searching for anything else to look at other than the Elder.

One of Bertha's cousins, a staunch man with a thick red beard, ran his blade through a dying soldier's throat, putting the corrupt lawman out of his misery. Elise flinched but forced herself to watch the men who were killing in the name of her people.

"It did not take much to convince the smugglers to help us," Rimball said, standing beside her. "They hate Falian lawmen almost as much as they love their cousin Bertha."

Elise nodded grimly. "How much did they ask for?" she asked, cutting to the heart of it.

"Just about all we have to offer," Rimball replied. One of the smugglers shouted a warning. There were riders coming from the west.

"We must fly!" Bertha's cousin Samuel called to them. Elise needed no convincing, running with all speed down the hill.

"Wallace has a boat waiting for us on the banks!" Rimball said from behind her, looking over his shoulder at the incoming lawmen. The soldiers were barking for them to halt, and a crossbow bolt took one of the smugglers in the back of his calf. The man howled and stumbled forward, but his brothers were there, pulling him up.

Elise slowed for a moment, wondering if they were better off standing their ground and fighting. "Don't stop!" Erik yelled, almost knocking her over when he ran by and tugged on the sleeve of her tunic. Elise regained her balance and began running again, with Rimball at her heels.

Another bolt flew by, sticking into a tree. She could see the water just ahead. There was a good-sized boat waiting for them, and several of the smugglers were already scrambling aboard, pulling the anchor and readying oars.

"We'll never get offshore in time!" Rygor yelled. Elise tripped and tumbled down the hill head over heels. Something hard hit the side of her head. She was stunned for a moment, disoriented, staring up at the cavern ceiling high above. In the distance, she could hear her fiancée Corbin yelling, "Keep running," followed by the sounds of wild dogs and gunshots.

The vision faded and Rimball was above her, lifting the Elder to her feet and saying something to Erik as he handed her off.

"What?" Elise asked, feeling the wet spot on the side of her head. Her fingers were sticky and red.

All the sounds around her bloomed into being like a thunderous wave. "Get her on the boat now!" Rimball said to Erik.

Elise realized what was going on. "No! Rimball, this is suicide!" She tried to pull the hunter back toward her, but he twisted away. She screamed and flailed to get away from Erik, but the hunter was much stronger than her and he heaved Elise over his shoulder.

Rimball looked Elise in the eye with his steady gaze.

"Don't do this, Rimball. Not when we just got you back. We can make it out of here *together*."

"There are too many of them, milady. Get out of here while I hold the line," he said.

"No, Rimball..."

"Elise, our people need you. You are our only future and I believe in you." Rimball turned his back to her and stalked back up the hill toward his enemies.

Elise tried to fight against Erik, but the men and women onboard the ship helped pull her over. Try as Elise might, she could not help sobbing and screaming for the hunter as the ship moved away from shore.

Up the hill, the soldiers had to get off their horses. The hill was too steep and rocky. Rimball took two of them down with his bow before they even got close. Six more soldiers closed in on him in a semi-circle, swords drawn. They moved in cautiously, like trappers cornering a tiger.

Rimball flicked his bo staff off his back and did a sideways spinning kick, sending the closest man stumbling back to avoid getting a boot in the face. Rimball caved in the side of another man's face with his bo staff and immediately back-flipped to get out of the path of another's blade. One of the soldiers ran in at him, thinking to catch the hunter off guard, but Rimball landed low to the ground and swiped his staff across the man's feet, dropping him to the ground, where he slammed the tip of the bo staff into his gut then forehead.

"The old man might just make it...," one of the sailors said in awe.

Rimball took down two more soldiers before they fell on him.

Elise had to look away. She refused to watch Riverbell's proudest hunter being murdered, but the look of horror on Rygor's face told her all she needed.

Elise Ivarone did not look back at the shore again. She would not let Rimball's sacrifice be in vain. The Elder of Riverbell stared toward the kingdom of Malbec, toward the future, toward salvation.

Healer Eir leaned back against the lone cot, running the tip of her finger across her blue lips, digesting all that Corbin Walker had told her.

Kyra was relieved that the Falian was not so foolish as to reveal all of his cards, telling the jotnar nothing of the nearby Citadel where thousands of Acadians were fast asleep in stasis chambers. She was impressed by his skill at twisting the truth, telling these supposed members of the "resistance" that he was from a faraway planet that the human race had fled to during the Jotnar Invasion, and that he had been sent to scout out the city and determine how to free the human slaves from the oppression of the jotnar and bring them to their new home.

In return, the healer had told them all about the underground resistance growing in Belikar, which was supposedly made up of a couple hundred jotnar and gnolls.

"You mean the gnoll race still lives?" Kyra interrupted, surprised to hear the dog-like humanoids had survived. She had been certain that after the jotnar were done with the humans, they would turn on the lesser races of Acadia.

"Oh yes, the gnolls were never the target of Emperor Cronus. In fact, soon after the wars began, the gnoll nations swore fealty to our people and helped in the war effort," Healer Eir explained, going on to flesh out how she had helped form a network the humans could use to safely communicate with the resistance. At first it was quite difficult to get the humans to understand that they could trust the movement, and many resistance members died because humans informed on them out of fear. But over time the resistance was able to grow and flourish to the point that there were now members in every slave class, working behind the scenes to convince their people that rebellion was necessary. "We just need a catalyst to spark the revolution, and I think that could be you!" Eir finished eagerly.

Kyra shook her head, unsure. She did not have the luxury of telepathic empathy, nor did she share Corbin's idealism. Unlike him, she had actually been alive during the jotnar culling, witnessing firsthand the horror and devastation as hundreds upon thousands of humans were senselessly slaughtered. Her mind drifted back to the moment she left the Kingdom of Alonn after they had declared fealty to the jotnar. With her ship only miles away, she watched in horror as the peaceful nation was obliterated under the mighty war machine that was the Jotnar Invasion. They never even had a chance. The screams from that day still echoed in her head.

"How do we know we can trust her?" she asked Corbin. "It seems highly suspicious that a jotnar doctor would risk everything for the sake of a human." Kyra turned back to Eir. "How are we supposed to believe this is not part of some elaborate ruse to quell a human uprising that has been festering in your midst?"

"We are not doctors," Bugge answered for Eir. "Not like you mean, anyhow. We do not use straight *science*, as your race did, though we have adopted a good deal of your people's advancements."

Eir snorted derisively at this. "Yeah, all the parts that would help fuel Cronus's military might, a skill your people seemed particularly adept at."

Ignoring her sarcasm, Bugge continued, "By human definition, we would be considered veterinarians." Noting Kyra's dark look and the way her knuckles whitened around the pommel of her short sword, he quickly added, "Strictly speaking in the oppressive perspective of our leaders, of course. We *are* healers. It is in our nature to heal and nurture those around us, thus the obvious course to understanding that your race is equal to us, not beneath."

Corbin directed his thoughts to Kyra. *"They speak the truth. These people truly care about the slaves. I can see it in their minds and feel it in their hearts."*

"But how can we ever trust them?" Kyra asked, unable to shake the shackles of skepticism that gripped her.

"I don't believe we can. But do we really have any other choice?" Corbin responded.

"It would appear the gods have left this to chance," Isaac said from the sewers deep beneath their feet. *"Though I believe this to be a fortuitous turn of events for us. We hoped to find only a chink in the armor of Belikar, but instead may have found an entire network of weakness to exploit."*

Heeding her companions' council with the understanding and acceptance that there really was no better alternative at this juncture, Kyra finally put away her weapon, which looked as if it disappeared into thin air to the jotnar and human guards. Stepping back, she gave

Corbin a short, firm nod and placed her own branch on Stur's sleeping chest, revealing her true form to the awe of the room.

"Then it is decided," Corbin confirmed. "We will join you in this cause." He bowed slightly and offered his hand to Eir. The healer looked beside herself with happiness, quickly shaking his small hand.

"If you expect our help, I'll need to know exactly what your plan is," Kyra said, suspending her own disbelief at the surreal situation. The marshal would never have imagined a time could come where she would offer help to the jotnar, no matter what the circumstances.

"With you on our side, we can finally convince Fivan to join our cause," Eir said, her voice full of hope.

"Who is this Fivan, and why is he so important?" Kyra asked, shifting fully into the role of strategist now that her course was set.

"He is the leader of the field slaves, a great man respected by all," Eir explained.

"Your companion does not share your high esteem of him?" Corbin asked, noting Bugge flare his nostrils at the suggestion that Fivan was a *great man*.

"We share different perspectives," Eir admitted.

"Fivan is stubborn," Bugge said. "We have approached him dozens of times, trying to sway the old man to our cause, but he always turns his back on us." One of the human guards nodded in agreement.

"He is afraid for his people," Eir justified.

"I think what he is *afraid of* is losing his favor with the Overseer," Bugge countered. "The old goat is just another slaver in the making."

"How can you say that after all he has done to keep his people safe? Fivan is a good man. He is just trying to do what is best for his people," Eir admonished her companion, who looked slightly ashamed at the proclamation.

"You still have not said why this man is so important to your cause," Kyra interrupted, rapidly growing annoyed with the jotnars' petty squabbling. "Surely one slave leader cannot sway the minds of the thousands of jotnar in this city not in your resistance?"

Eir straightened and explained, "There is only one thing my race recognizes, and that is power. Whether through strength of will or physical prowess, should we defeat Duke Thiazi, the fealty of the city will automatically fall to the victor. Fivan is largely seen as the unspoken leader of the field slaves, the largest community of humans living in Belikar. With the support of Fivan, we will add such numbers to our cause that we may have a chance of taking the palace by force."

On the ground, Stur groaned, sitting up and clutching his wounded side. "What in blasted damnation are you pair prattling on about?" he growled, holding out his arm for Corbin to help him rise. At first the room spun, but the ever stubborn Stur planted his feet and shook off the feeling.

"You should really get more rest," Eir advised.

"It'll be a cold day in Hel before I take orders from a blue-skinned devil," Stur growled. He had been listening to a great deal of their conversation while *resting* in the dirt. "Besides, there is no way I'm going to stay here on my back while the two of you head into that pit of vipers," he added, handing Corbin his magical branch, which slipped Isaac's dweomer back around his form.

Eir bowed her head in acceptance of the human's unshakable bond of honor, though she genuinely would prefer for him to rest until he was well enough to move around.

"What makes you believe that this Fivan can be swayed by us where your attempts have failed?" Corbin asked.

"All you need is to reveal your true nature to him. Once Fivan sees that a human *can* live a free life as well as the amazing magic which you possess, he will surely join our ranks," Eir said. "Once you have his allegiance, send word, and we will arrange a meeting of the resistance to flesh out our battle plans."

"That settles it, then. We will go find this Fivan and convince him to join the resistance," Corbin agreed. "But how will we get word to you?"

"We have many eyes and ears in the city. Once you have Fivan's confidence, find a jotun named Gaurmin in camp. He will deliver your message," one of the human guards instructed.

The group discussed some more details so that Corbin and his companions knew where to find Fivan and how to approach him without raising suspicion. Healer Eir preferred for them to wait until the morning to set out, but both Kyra and Corbin disagreed, wanting to head back straight away.

"And the child?" Eir asked. Kyra had completely forgotten about the teenage boy who had accompanied them to the healers.

"I've modified both his and the slaver's memories, so even if they subconsciously heard some of our conversation while they were in my induced sleep, they will have no recollection of it upon waking," Corbin explained. He saw the boy as a liability and would not risk the lives of thousands on the overactive and unpredictable hormones of a teenager. "He stays here."

After saying their goodbyes, the group headed out of the healers' tents, back toward the field slave quarters with a small scroll in hand, proving where they had been. Corbin was not only surprised but also slightly perturbed by the slaves' indifference when no one questioned their return to Maggs's hovel without the boy.

Night had fallen over the city and the moons were high in the sky when they settled down for the evening.

"We need to get some rest," Corbin explained in response to Kyra's questioning glare.

"But you told Eir there was no time," she reminded him.

"The lad only said it because he doesn't trust the bastards any more than we do, Kyra," Stur explained.

Corbin nodded. *Though Stur's only half right,* he thought, looking down at the tiny magical branch in his palm. Several of the leaves were curled in on themselves, dried and dead. He knew they'd best make the most out of the time they had left, because it was soon running out.

In the morning, they were awoken by a bullhorn being blown on the perimeter of the wall. Corbin's back was stiff. Sleeping on the rickety floorboards was far worse than lying in a grassy forest. He thought Stur would need help rising, but the proud warrior was already up and about with the slaves, readying for the workday. The slaves were barely awake before their keepers came barking for them to get to the granary.

As they shuffled along with the crowd of bedraggled humans, Corbin noticed more than one odd look their way. Apparently news of Stur's activities the previous day had spread throughout the camp. Most slaves had already marked him as a dead scab walking.

Without a word, each of them headed to their familiar tasks, Corbin and Kyra shoveling grain into the empty crates, and Stur moving the heavy stone wheel to grind the grain into flour. Kyra advised they remain as low-key as possible today and reprimanded Stur for losing his temper the previous day. The warrior knew better than to question her orders, and so the morning passed with no surprises.

As the afternoon rolled around, they became almost lost in the repetitive labor they were dutifully pretending to perform while keeping a keen eye out for slavers and the Overseer.

"It is almost time," Kyra said, judging they were ready to make their move based on Themis' position overhead.

As if on cue, a slaver gave three short blows on his horn, signaling it was time for the quick break Eir had told them about. Without missing a beat, Corbin laid down his shovel and followed Kyra between the crates and out past the rows of waiting slaves. As they made their way around an oversized trough being filled with food, Stur said, "Where are those jotnar going?"

Corbin followed his gaze, seeing a pair of armed jotnar making their way to the back of the granary. They seemed full of purpose, heading in the exact direction of the sewer entrance. *"Isaac, I think your cover may be blown!"* Corbin thought in alarm.

"Nonsense, lad, they are nothing more than a standard patrol. Worry yourself naught and get to Fivan," Isaac replied, unconcerned with the patrolling guards, secure that Corbin's masking psionic shield would keep his low chanting muffled.

"We are almost there now," Kyra replied, motioning Stur to one side while she worked her way around the other, circling a pair of human slaves that kept watch while their esteemed leader ate his lunch, removed from the swelling crowd around the trough. The unarmed slaves were caught off guard, roughly pulled behind the stack of crates by the Acadians and strong-armed until they calmed down.

Fivan moved to rise, ready to shout at the sudden attack, when Corbin held his hands out and smiled. "No need for alarm. We are not here to hurt you. We just came to talk."

Fivan grimaced. He was old by slave standards, with thin, grey hair around the crown of his head and a loose, wrinkled face. Corbin could see he must have been impressive by slave standards as a youth, with a broad-shouldered build, square jaw, and flat nose that had deteriorated in his old age and left him crooked and bent. However, he did still possess the same foreboding stance. Pulling his dirty robes around his legs, Fivan sat on the ground once more. "Got a strange way of showing it," he said.

Kyra and Stur led Fivan's men back and had them sit beside their leader while Corbin plopped down in the dirt opposite the old man, waiting for Kyra to join him.

Fivan gave a curt nod to his men and resumed his meal. "Who are you three?" he asked. Corbin could see the old man was making an effort to show that their abrupt intrusion meant little to him.

"We are your friends," Corbin replied.

"To be sure? Normally my friends have a name and a good reason to disturb my lunch," Fivan coolly replied, biting a strip of meat off a greasy drumstick. Corbin noticed his lunch was not the same slop being served to the rest of the rabble, and his clothes seemed just a little less filthy.

"We have no time for your banter, old man," Kyra said.

The men on either side of the slave leader bristled at her impertinence, but Fivan held up his drumstick, signaling for them to relax. "Ah, a man who gets to the point. I like this fella," Fivan said. Corbin snickered. It was easy to forget that everyone saw Kyra as a male slave. "So tell me, what is it you came here to discuss?"

Kyra looked around. The slavers were fully intent on goading the scabs, and none seemed concerned with the old man or with whom he was conversing. Deciding it was safe to speak, she said in a low voice, "You need to join the resistance."

The old man coughed and sputtered at her bold proclamation, chicken catching in his scraggly beard. One of his men moved to help, patting Fivan's back and offering a drink.

"These scabs bothering you, Fivan?" a slaver asked gruffly from behind them with whip in hand.

Fivan held up his hand. "No, no, everything is fine. Just went down the wrong pipe, Frederick," he assured the slaver, who searched their expressions for a sign of trouble.

"Okay, but let me know if you need anything," the slaver said and stalked away.

"Are you mad?" Fivan hissed, clenching his fists as soon as the slaver was safely out of earshot. "You can't just walk up to me and make such a statement. I don't even know you lot."

Kyra ignored his outrage and continued. "We have come here to help free your people. I am Kyra Tarvano and this is my companion Corbin Walker. Our trustworthy friend there is Stur Skorsgard."

"Oh, look lads. We got us Her Highness and her man-at-arms come back from the dead," Fivan said, his voice dripping with sarcasm. "And I'm the Archduke of Canterbury." Fivan rolled his eyes and laughed with his men.

Kyra bit her lip, cursing herself for using her real name. She had assumed the slaves were uneducated, but it seemed Fivan knew a bit of Acadian history.

A metal dagger appeared in her hand, plucked from thin air, as far as the slaves were concerned. It was tempered from fine Agartan steel, the like of which had not been seen in Acadia for centuries. The sight of it made Fivan's laugh catch in his throat, and his face grew serious.

"If you waste any more of our time, I will gut these two buffoons and be long gone before that fool of a slaver can even think to come over here." Kyra's voice was cold and determined. They had very little time to have this discussion, and she could not afford to waste it convincing the old man just to talk in the first place.

"Where did you get that?" Fivan asked slowly.

"As my companion here has already informed you, we are here to help rescue your people from captivity. We are from a faraway kingdom, where jotnar do not exist. The resistance has sent us to ask you to reconsider joining their ranks," Corbin said, worried that Kyra might actually stay true to her word and cut down the other slaves.

"You are Thiazi's men, then," Fivan stated as a matter of fact.

"I just said—" Corbin started.

"Yes, yes, I heard your outlandish claims," Fivan said, cutting him off with a scowl, "and I'm not so daft as to mistake the threat of your dagger neither, young man. Go tell your master, the Duke of Belikar, that I've never been nor will I ever be a part of this mysterious *resistance* he believes is festering."

Kyra shot the man a look that could have melted steel, but he had called her bluff. She had no intention of cutting Fivan or his men down and remained still as the old man rose. Before Corbin had a chance to react, the horns were blown again, signaling the break had passed, and whips cracked to get the slaves back to work.

"This conversation is not over," Kyra promised the old man.

"It is for me," Fivan replied, casually motioning for his men to follow and heading back into the granary.

As they made their way to their previous posts, Corbin sought Isaac's guidance. *"What should we do? He does not seem to be easily convinced."*

Kyra cut in while retrieving her shovel. *"What do we expect, coming to him with such a story? How can we blame the old man for being a skeptic?"*

"It would appear," Isaac added, *"that you will need to get the nonbeliever alone and show him your true nature."*

"But how can we hope to do that?" Corbin asked. *"Our next break is not for hours yet, and we don't dare try to find him in this warehouse for risk of raising unwanted suspicion."*

"I have an idea on that," Stur chimed in to the telepathic conversation, while grunting under the strain of moving the grinder. His bandaged back was not enjoying the physical effort. *"First we—"*

"Hold, someone is coming!" Isaac shouted in their minds, the alarm in his voice clear as a bell.

The slavers unexpectedly blew their horns again. The men and women all around Corbin raised their heads, puzzled by the signal. There was not a moment lost for questions, as they were quickly rounded up at the end of whips and told to line up against the outside wall of the granary for the archduke's inspection.

Kyra quickly spotted Fivan among the gathered slaves and worked her way through the pressing group of uneasy people to get to him. Fivan had his men at either side, but Kyra and her companions sidled in right between them and the old man.

"They are saying it is the archduke," Corbin informed Isaac, unsure whether he had caught the slavers' comments. Up and down the line, slavers paced, whipping the slaves and barking for them to remove their clothing.

"Not there, here!" Isaac corrected in a panic. *"Someone is coming down into the tunnels!"*

Using his connection to the mage, Corbin could see through Isaac's eyes, which darted back and forth, peering down the tunnel to his left. The splashing of footsteps announced there were indeed several people approaching. Corbin could feel the fear clinging to the mage as the old man gently floated above the floor and fled out of sight around the corner.

Kyra nudged Corbin, motioning at the other slaves, who were beginning to take off their clothing. He did not understand her urgent look of concern, but then it hit him: They could not remove clothing that was not really there in the first place! Their choices were to remain clothed, practically begging for a lashing and drawing unwanted attention, or remove their armor, which would stick out like a sore thumb among the tatters of filthy clothing at the humans' bare feet.

"Isaac, you must alter our dweomers!" Corbin said, pressing his back tighter against the warehouse wall to avoid being spotted still clothed by the slavers down the line.

"Easier said than done!" Isaac complained, stopping with his back against a grimy sewer wall, crouched just around the corner from where he had been. In the background he could hear the search party still wading around in the muck not too far away.

Corbin felt his heart racing. Fivan stared at him with a serious expression, wondering what the wide-eyed, panic-stricken scabs were doing.

"Hold, I'll have it in only a few moments," Isaac whispered in Corbin's mind. The mage had to work hard to change their appearance, only able to guess at what it would look like. His magical hold over

them was not as strong, being farther away and distracted to boot. *"There,"* he said, finishing the incantation and blowing on the small, glowing tree floating above his palms.

Before Fivan's eyes, the strangers' clothing vanished, leaving them naked against the wall, just as a slaver was making his way down the line. The old man gasped, as did his companions and some nearby slaves, who grabbed each other and stumbled away from the three.

"What's this, then?" the slaver asked, spotting the sudden commotion. Fivan was fast to gather himself, and his men wisely fell in step.

"But he...they...," A slave to their left fumbled for words, unable to comprehend what he had just witnessed. His mumbling earned him a sharp rap across the chest, sending him tumbling to the dirt.

"Out with it, man? What's the big hubbub?" the slaver demanded.

Down the line, Corbin could see another slaver taking interest in the weasel and knew he had to act quickly. "I think the scab was just in awe at seeing the size of my manhood," he jested, momentarily channeling Logan.

The slaver stared blankly at Corbin then began laughing hoarsely. "His manhood...oh, that's rich." He waved down the line that everything was all set to his partners, who fell back into a formation of their own as the sound of hoofbeats came from around the warehouse. Corbin's shoulders sagged and he puffed up his cheeks, exhaling in relief. Fivan could not stop eyeing them.

"Isaac, are you still there?" Kyra asked.

Isaac sent them the telepathic equivalent of a nod. From where he hid, pressed against the tight corner of the sewer tunnel, he could see the two jotnar guards Corbin had warned him of earlier.

"How did they find out you're down there? Has my field of silence failed?" Corbin asked anxiously, while he watched a sleek, golden carriage pulled by black mares arrive in front of the granary, far down the line of slaves.

"No, I can still sense the field is there. At least I believe so...wait a moment." Isaac carefully wrapped the tree and placed it inside the folds of his belt, channeling a new spell that wove a small circular glyph in the air, allowing him to hear his trackers' conversation. *"Hmm...they seem to be discussing something about detecting a strong magical presence in the tunnels. I think they were sent down here by...a city wizard,"* Isaac slowly replied. It was expending a good deal of his energy to stay afloat over the sewage, keep up their disguise, cast the listening spell, and hold his telepathic link at the same time.

"Just stay out of sight until they leave," Kyra said coarsely. Corbin knew she did not mean to let her annoyance at the turn of events show, but nevertheless a flash of thought permeated into the group's shared conversation. "If I had more real soldiers here, none of this would be happening." Hearing her own impulsive thoughts bubble to the surface, the military leader blanched.

Archduke Marius emerged from the carriage with a small entourage of jotnar. They were speaking about the granary operations, pointing out how the production line worked to the brooding archduke. The group was too far down the line for Corbin to understand them properly, but it was obvious the archduke held an extreme distaste for humans, snarling at the scabs with an upturned nose.

In his mind, Corbin could feel Isaac's fear grow tighter, slinking farther down the tunnel to keep out of view of the tenacious guards continuing to make their way in his direction. Without speaking to the mage, he knew that if Isaac were pulled too far away, the dweomer would weaken, perhaps revealing them to all.

"And these humans work solid fourteen-hour days with no complaints," Marquess Tryn bragged to the archduke, stopping to feel the bicep of a naked male. "Just look at them, hearty and firm. Good stock we raise here in Belikar, strong enough to last into their late thirties before needing to be put out to pasture." Tryn clapped the slave's arm. The man stood impassive, staring blankly past the jotnar rulers.

"Interesting. So you still refer to them as humans, eh?" the archduke asked, inspecting the slave as if he were a horse. Marius gave the human an unexpectedly firm backhand across the face and stepped back. "Hmm, you are correct, though. The scab does not so much as whimper."

Tryn was surprised but said nothing about it. "Ah, yes...as I said, this is the strongest human in the flock."

Marius leaned toward the younger jotun. "The best you have to offer, then?"

Tryn nodded, eagerly hoping to earn the archduke's approval. "As you requested, and I would be more than happy to give him to you as a gift, Your Lordship, so that he may serve your House as well as he has served Belikar."

"Are you a born liar or does it take effort on your part?" Marius calmly asked the marquess, who stepped back, shaken at the abrupt accusation. "Or perhaps you have been around your dimwitted father too long and it has dulled your wits?" Archduke Marius tightened his eyes, studying Tryn's reaction. He could see the young jotun had much potential, all of it being wasted under the leadership of his father. "Yes, that does seem to be it. You're not a liar, are you? Just a moron."

Corbin tensed as the archduke made a beeline for Kyra, stopping just in front of her. "This is your strongest scab," he proclaimed, slithering around her like a snake and sniffing her shoulder. Kyra did her best not to flinch at the unexpected attention.

When the marquess approached, Corbin thought surely they would be recognized as infiltrators. It took all of his willpower to remain still. However, the jotun noble did not seem to share the same knowledge about humans as the healers. A sideways glance at the overseer told Tryn that the man Marius was inspecting was nothing special.

"Archduke Marius, surely I can procure you a finer human than this?" Tryn offered, waving his hand back at the slave they had walked away from. Marius eyed Kyra once last time. Corbin's heart was beating so hard in his chest he feared the jotnar would hear it.

Marius growled, glaring at his tour guide over Kyra's shoulder, which he ran a razor sharp talon across. "This is exactly what is wrong with our empire today. Too many young fools raised by buffoons. These are *not* humans. They ceased to be so when we conquered their filthy species. What you see now is a scab, good for nothing more than wallowing in their own shit. It's beyond me why we even keep them around. They are not even fit to lick my boots." The archduke roughly shoved Kyra aside and grabbed Corbin by the back of his head, forcing him to his knees. "This is the only position a scab should ever be in when in the presence of nobility," he sneered.

Fivan quickly dropped to his knees at the dangerous jotun's statement, which was immediately followed by everyone down the line. Marius let go of Corbin's head, looking down at the slaves with only the faintest hint of being impressed before returning to his lecture.

"When I ask you for your strongest scab, your answer should be that there are no strong scabs." Marius sneered, rapping his staff on the ground. "If I ask for the *best* scab you own, your answer should always and ever be that there are no *good* scabs, let alone *best*," he added, placing the base of his short staff against Fivan's temple and knocking the man sideways to the ground, where he remained, knowing better than to move.

Tryn regarded the great and powerful leader, one of the mightiest jotun of his empire, with deep interest. He did not understand the cryptic archduke's perspective. Surely the humans were strong enough to do many of the tasks that jotnar no longer did on their own? But, though he may be naïve, Tryn was no fool, and he gave Marius a formal bow. "I am humbled in the face of your teachings, Archduke."

Marius grunted, thinking the boy had much potential indeed. He was a fast learner.

"Corbin, we're in trouble. I've nowhere left to run," Isaac groaned, looking back and forth between a pile of rubble which blocked his path and the approaching jotnar, who saw him and pulled out their swords.

"Not yet, we need a little more time," Corbin urged.

Marius snapped his head over his shoulder at an angle Corbin did not think possible. "Eh, what did you say, scab? Time? Time for what?" Marius glared at him with fire-soaked eyes. Corbin's palms grew damp and he twitched, breaking eye contact and staring at the ground, trying to look as pitiful as possible.

"Archduke?" Tryn asked, puzzled by the man's outburst. "Are you okay? No one spoke, sir."

Marius looked between Corbin and Kyra, inspecting them with swelling interest.

"Sir?" Tryn prodded again, concerned that the archduke had been out in the afternoon heat too long.

"Eh?" Marius said. "Oh, yes, have it your way then, young Tryn." He sneered at Kyra and flicked his attention back to the marquess. "This one smells of a scab bitch anyhow, and I like my meat virginal."

"Meat, sir?" Tryn asked, confused by the archduke's strange behavior.

Marius scowled at him. "Come now, boy, don't act so daft, just when I was getting optimistic for your future." Marius waved away the notion with a circle of his short staff and paced away from Kyra, back down the line.

"It's now or never, Corbin," Isaac groaned both out loud and in their heads. The jotnar guards were grinning sickly at him, circling to either side and clenching their swords.

"No, Isaac, we need more time!" Corbin begged, watching the archduke's back carefully.

Their disguises began to flicker. As startled as the slaves were to see the illusion fade off and onto their bodies, none of them made a peep, fearing the wrath of Marius more than whatever witchcraft was at play.

"Looks like we found us a little runaway scab. Commander Erruza will find this quite interesting," one of the jotnar leered, wading through the filth toward Isaac. "'Course, we don't need the scab alive. She can always pull one of those necromantic tricks to make the little piggy squeal, eh?"

"*I am sorry, my friends,*" Isaac lamented, both psychically and aloud, fully exposing them by releasing his hold on the dweomer.

The line of slaves was shaken when before their very eyes Corbin's, Kyra's, and Stur's disguises melted away. Where once there stood three average scabs, now were a warrior built like an ox, a short pale man with long raven hair, and the most beautiful woman any of them had ever beheld. Fivan covered a woman's mouth before she could scream in fear at the witchcraft before them.

Thankfully the jotnar retinue had their backs to the group. Down the line, Marius stopped once more in front of the muscular human Tryn had offered, oblivious to the commotion the trio was causing. "I'll take him."

Tryn nodded and gestured for the overseer to have the slave cleaned and brought to the palace for servant training. While the pair was speaking, Marius waved his hand, signaling his man to slice the scab's throat.

Tryn stumbled forward. "But...what? I thought you wanted to take him."

Marius feigned ignorance, looking back at the marquess with mild amusement. "I *am* taking him. This is a fine piece of tenderloin you have raised. I look forward to eating it in about a week or so." Tryn raised an eyebrow, broadcasting his unspoken question. "Oh, I like to let the meat rot a little before cooking it. Makes for a more succulent treat." Marius cackled at the marquess's wrinkled nose.

"But I thought you wanted him for a servant. If it was meat you needed, we have stores of that in the chop house." Tryn felt stupid for not understanding the archduke's needs sooner, wondering if his father would have made the same mistake.

"That garbage? You mean the leftover scraps of your dying or invalid scabs? No, I only eat the younger ones, and I like a lot of muscle on my steak," Marius explained, enjoying how Tryn's human slavers involuntarily squirmed as he spoke.

In the sewers, Isaac backed toward the rubble, as his pursuers closed in.

"Nowhere for you to run now, little scab. Might as well just let us get this over with nice and quick," the overly talkative jotun guard goaded him, moving close enough to swing his sword across Isaac's face. Except when he swung, the ebony man flickered, the sword cutting through thin air and cracking so hard across a block of tumbled stone that the force vibrated up the sword painfully into the soldier's hand and he almost bit his tongue when his teeth clacked together.

"What—?" the other guard began, cut off by the sudden reappearance of Isaac, who let a bolt of lightning fly from his staff into the jotun's chest. Grinding his teeth uncontrollably, the soldier tried to let go of his weapon but clutched it all the harder with muscles coursing with electricity. When he hit the sludge, grinding his teeth hard enough to shatter a fang, the jotun could see his partner writhing in the electrified sewage beside him, choking on the filth with a gaping scream that would never come.

"Quickly now, Isaac!" Corbin shouted in the mage's mind, forcing the telepathic connection though the mage had severed it.

Marius stopped short, swinging his head to peer down the line at the strange slaves once more. "Why are those scabs standing like that?" he hissed with a wild look in his eyes that scared even the overseer. Down the line, the slaves stood at odd angles, blocking his view of the scabs he had been interested in earlier.

"Frederick, move those scabs back into formation!" Tryn called, trying to add the proper weight of command into his voice.

The human slaver moved forward, barking at the slaves to get back against the wall. But his whipping only seemed to make the chaos worse, as men and women fell over each other on the ground, howling in pain.

"Isaac!" Kyra prodded urgently, panicking as the slaves created the unexpected barrier around them.

Tryn growled at his man's incompetence, snatching his own whip from his belt and stomping over to the ridiculous outbreak. With four sharp flicks, he had the slaves all back in line, their backs firmly pressed against the warehouse wall.

Marius was beside him, eyeing Kyra and Corbin suspiciously. "What were the two of you just discussing, scab?" he asked, moving his face up to Corbin and sniffing the air. "I heard you. Don't try to deny it."

"It was me," Stur mumbled, stepping forward to Kyra's alarm.

Corbin thought about using his magic against the archduke, swaying the jotun that he had heard nothing after all. *"Don't you do it, lad,"* Isaac whispered. *"This is a powerful wizard, no doubt about it, to have heard your telepathy. You'll never get so far as to enter his mind before he lays waste to all of you."* Though his heart wrenched at the idea of Stur facing this cruel jotun's punishment, Corbin did not dare to reply to the mage deep in the sewers.

Marius brooded over Stur, moving fluidly to his side so that as he spoke, his fangs were against Stur's earlobe. "What did you say?"

"It was me, Your Lordship. I cannot help it, I mumble when I'm nervous," Stur said weakly. Kyra knew the proud warrior was putting on an act, but it did not bother her any less to see the weapon master cowering before one of the blue-skinned devils.

Marius growled in Stur's ear and motioned for his man-at-arms. In his heart, Corbin knew there was no way he would stand by while his friend was butchered, and he slowly reached behind his back, grasping the center of his voulge.

"Mark him," the archduke commanded, "and also his friends here, who think I am a fool who doesn't see them all for liars." The man-at-arms slashed a cut into Stur's shoulder while his men took care of Corbin and Kyra. "And add the old goat there," Marius said, pointing at Fivan. "He has too much sway over the rest of these scabs." The archduke had not missed Fivan's lead when he had fallen to his knees earlier. Satisfied, Marius turned to his royal tour guide. "This *has* been an interesting tour of your scab facilities, but the granary will be our last stop for the day."

Tryn bowed humbly before the archduke, exhilarated to hear the mighty leader's praise. "Shall we convene on the morrow?"

"You may come get me in one day. I have other matters to tend to with your father tomorrow. You will show me around these dungeons Belikar is supposedly famous for," Marius ordered, turning his back on Tryn and heading to his carriage. "Oh, and don't forget the marked scabs. They will make excellent fodder for an experiment I would like to show you."

Tryn could not believe his luck. The ancient gods must surely be smiling down upon him for the day to have turned out so well. He quickly ordered a pair of slavers to tie the bundle of meat up in the rotting house and mark it for delivery to the archduke in exactly a week, adding that none were to touch the slaves Marius had personally selected for experimentation. As he walked away from the line, allowing it to be broken up, he could not help feeling excited that the archduke himself was going to be teaching him.

The slavers were in rare form, whipping the heels of the crowd and barking for them to get back to work.

Fivan roughly made his way through the crowd, grasping Kyra's shoulder and spinning her in place to speak. "You better explain who in the hell you are and just what in blazes is going on."

"Oh, so we have your attention now?" Kyra replied with a wry grin.

Chapter 15: The Witch Queen

Marching through the swamps with Bipp and Nero at his side and agmawor at his back, Logan replayed the past couple weeks. When they came across the first totem, which was nothing more than the severed head of an Agma mounted atop a crude wooden spear stuck in the ground, he snapped out of his ruminating over how they had gotten in their current predicament. One look at that rotting head told him it was time to stop dwelling in the past and focus on staying alive.

The marshlands soon shifted back into the dense jungle he had come to hate. Signs of the approaching Agmawor camp became more frequent as they came across more and more of the ghastly totems marking their territory. A group of Agmawor guarding the outskirts of their camp came out of the thick foliage to greet Logan's captors. There was quick talk of a high priestess named Luana, and then the hunting party was on their way again.

When they came to the wall, Logan was surprised. "How did these primitives build this barrier out here in the jungle?" he whispered to his companions. The yellowed stone wall loomed ominously and looked grossly out of place in the wild forest. It was at least seven feet tall and overgrown with a blanket of vines crawling across its cracked surface. Agmawor rested on top, keeping a lookout.

"This is not of their creation," Nero countered. "We are likely at the site of Ithiki's zoo. These walls must be remnants from that time."

Logan shared a puzzled look with Bipp and asked, "What is a zoo?"

"The people of Ithiki collected a wide variety of species, which they put on display here for all to see," Nero replied.

Why would people want to put animals on display? Logan wondered. The whole concept seemed barbaric to him.

Bipp whistled. "Must have been built well, to have held up all this time."

They passed through the wall into the Agmawor camp. All vegetation seemed to have been stripped from the campgrounds, most likely lost under the trampling feet of its denizens. The place was a network of tents, wide at the base and narrow at the top, made of animal skins. The ruins of Ithiki stood here and there between the rows of tents, and the smell of burning wood filled the area.

Agmawor were everywhere. Logan was astounded by the sheer volume of lizard people living in this place. They easily doubled the Agma tribe in number. It was no wonder the blue-green cannibals easily overpowered their nomadic green cousins.

As they were led through the dusty camp, groups of curious Agmawor approached, prodding the strange soft-skins before being driven away by a hissing Rahl. The prisoners were shoved across a crudely built platform over a ten-foot drop. As they crossed, Logan thought the bottom of the pit was moving until he realized it was packed with snakes of all colors and sizes.

"Halt!" Rhal commanded, lining Logan, Bipp, and Nero up shoulder to shoulder in front of a cave opening. Several stakes with severed heads decorated either side of the cave. Rhal tapped his spear on the solid rock at their feet and chanted, his voice echoing into the cave entrance. Someone inside replied with another chant that ended with all of the hunting party kneeling, foreheads pressed to the ground. When Rhal saw the soft-skins were not also kneeling, he quickly gave each of them sharp blows to the spine, forcing the prisoners to their knees.

Logan heard the approaching entourage before it emerged from the cave, led by a set of muscular Agmawor who each carried large cudgels made from some sort of carved bone and wore the skulls of wolves as helms. Three robed Agmawor acolytes followed, leading the high priestess.

The high priestess was tall and slender by Agmawor standards, and naked beneath the loose brown robe she wore. Her scales were much paler, more green than blue, and she wore the talons of a drake around her neck, with wide plumes of black feathers standing upright from the back of her collar. She carried her thurible, a long interlinking chain that ended in a hollowed-out censer, with great care. Logan had seen Morgana use a similar item to burn incense during prayer to Baetylus, though he suspected in Luana's hands it held a more devious purpose. The exotic-looking lizardwoman studied the kneeling soft-skins intently, with cold eyes and a frown, before moving aside to make room for the witch queen.

Nadja was carried out of the cave on a large litter by four broad-shouldered Agmawor who wore nothing but bone necklaces. The litter was wide, covered with layers of animal fur as padding, and the servants carried it with long poles painted in the blood of their enemies. Nadja leaned back amid the soft furs, her creamy white skin draped in a nearly translucent, green silky fabric that fell from her shoulders in delicate layers around an ample bosom. The witch queen wore a look of boredom as she was carried out of the cave, but when her eyes rested on the strange humanoids, the Agmawor leader perked up.

The servants stopped and knelt, remaining perfectly still with the poles of the litter resting horizontally across their backs.

"What are these delightful little creatures we've been brought, Luana?" the witch queen asked the high priestess with a mischievous glint in her eye.

"Never have I set eyes on soft-skins such as these," Luana replied, staring at the odd creatures. "They are too light to be escaped jotnar slaves, and this one—" She pointed at Bipp with the end of her long wooden staff. "—is *most* peculiar."

"Which is their leader? Bring it closer," Nadja commanded of Rhal.

The Agmawor hunter was quick to comply, prodding Logan with the tip of his spear. Logan could not stand up fast enough for the lizardman, who kept poking at him incessantly.

Logan stood before the witch queen, her litter set at the height of his waist. She studied him with a lustful grin. She was not like the other Agmawor, he saw. She almost looked human, with long, shiny black hair cascading down her shoulders and curling around her waist, and a heart-shaped face. When she shifted slightly on her resting elbow, he could see her skin was actually covered in tiny white scales that glittered in the daylight, and her ears had no lobes. Nadja's eyes met his own. They were almond-shaped and the same emerald green as Logan's. Her nose was small and delicate above deep red lips shaped like a cupid's bow. If not for the feral look in her eyes and scintillating scales, which no human could possibly possess, he would swear the witch queen was one of his own kind.

"Does it speak?" Nadja playfully asked her high priestess.

"Why have you brought us here?" Logan asked. "You have no cause to hold ill will toward me and my men. We have done nothing to you."

Nadja feigned shock, covering her giggle with slender fingers that ended in needle-sharp talons. She gave him a throaty laugh and flicked her free hand at Rhal. The hunter punched Logan hard in the kidney, grunting for him to keep his mouth shut in front of the Queen. Logan almost fell down from the staggering blow.

Nadja giggled some more as he gritted his teeth through the pain. She was impressed by the soft-skin's strength of will. "They have done nothing to the Agmawor?" she asked. "Is that correct, high priestess?" Logan could see the witch queen was toying with him.

"There were reports of strange soft-skins murdering members of our hunting party a couple weeks ago," Luana replied grimly.

"And what have you to say to that, soft-skin?" Nadja prompted, smirking at him.

"My name is Logan Walker, not soft ski—" Logan replied, cut off by another jab from Rahl's spear as he hissed for the soft-skin to answer the queen. Grunting, Logan turned to give the smug lizard a hateful glare. Looking back at the witch queen, he regarded her for a moment then nodded, smirking back. "I see the stories of you are true," he said.

The queen arched a thin eyebrow. "Oh? And what stories might those be?"

"That Nadja, Queen of the Agmawor, is as wise as she is beautiful. Being here in your presence, I can see why these lizards follow you so," Logan said, giving the witch his most charming smile.

Bipp rolled his eyes and moaned under his breath, "We're dead now."

However, the Queen's smile grew wider at the compliment. When her hunter moved to strike the soft-skin for his insolence, she held up a hand, signaling it was okay to let the man speak.

"And where, pray tell, have you heard these stories of me?" Nadja said.

Logan feigned a dumbfounded look of disbelief and snorted. "Why, all across Acadia. From the land of the giants to the empires of man, the name of Queen Nadja is spoken with great reverence to your beauty. Except now that I am here, to bear witness and behold you with my very own eyes, I can see those tales pale in comparison to your angelic beauty."

The witch queen giggled, leaning back farther and letting the folds of her silky robes fall to the side, revealing a perfectly shaped breast. Logan's eyes instinctively rested on her milky white bosom, its cherry rosebud hard in the exposed air, and he gulped. His mouth grew dry and his face burned hot under her mischievous eyes. Nadja enjoyed the way the soft-skin grew embarrassed and tilted her head farther back than should be possible, laughing raucously. Logan joined her, grinning stupidly, and the Agmawor hunters grew uncomfortable.

Suddenly the Queen shifted her shoulder forward, twirling as she slithered across the litter and pressed her face close to Logan's. The laughter caught in his throat as the witch queen regarded him with cold amusement. This close, he could see each tiny scale that covered her skin and smell her musky odor, like that of rotting flowers.

"Such pretty lies." Nadja grinned, running a razor-sharp talon across his chiseled jawline and pressing it just above his throat. "For a dirty little *hu*-man."

When Logan's eyes betrayed his surprise, she let out a malicious grin and swirled away from him. Bipp groaned again when the witch queen's robes split apart, revealing the white and orange striated lower body of a snake.

"Tell me, little man, do I still look appealing to you?" Nadja laughed, coiling her body back and rocking in place.

Without missing a beat, Logan replied with a smirk. "No. You are even more so, Your Majesty." He bowed low to the writhing snake woman.

While the high priestess looked annoyed with the soft-skin, the queen seemed to be enjoying his flattery. Slithering forward, with her lower body still coiled under the robes, she circled Logan, running her talons across his shoulders and giving his bicep a firm squeeze. "And what of my question? Did you murder my hunters at the Agma camp?" she crooned in his ear, long forked tongue flicking to tickle his lobe.

"Well, most alluring queen of the jungle, if it is true, what the high priestess says, that we were involved in the murder of some of your men, then surely they were not fit to be in your tribe in the first place. What, to be felled by such weak hands as ours?" Logan reasoned, turning his head to speak directly to the snake woman, who licked her lips lustfully while looking him up and down. Logan was not sure if she wanted to make love or eat him for lunch, though his gut said it was a little of both.

"There, the strange creature has as much as admitted it," High Priestess Luana snapped, drawing the queen's attention away from him. "Let us be done with this foolishness and send them to be gutted for the feast."

Nadja curled back onto the litter, away from Logan, feigning a pout. The witch queen thoughtfully tapped her crimson lips with a talon, looking to the sky. Her eyes lit up like two gemstones caught in a ray of starlight, an idea forming. "No," she said.

The high priestess looked stunned, blinking stupidly at the queen. "No? But Your Grace, the laws are unbreakable in this regard."

"Oh yes, my high priestess, they are unbreakable. But these soft-skins will not be wasted as meager food for our feast," Nadja said, coolly grinning as she goaded the high priestess. "Surely you agree that Seti has brought us these curious creatures for a purpose?"

Luana kissed her right hand and weaved it around like a snake over her heart at the mention of their god, Seti. When she was finished, the rest of the Agmawor in the area did the same. "Does our great Lord speak through you, my queen?" she asked fervently.

"He does." Nadja's eyes were crazed. "Seti does not want these *hu*-mans used as fodder for our feast."

Logan let out a sigh of relief, surprised his flirting had actually worked.

"No, the Great Serpent demands they be sacrificed!" Nadja exclaimed. Her smile stretched unnaturally from ear to ear and her eyes glowed with a fiendish hunger as she laughed sadistically at the look on Logan's face.

Logan could still hear the maniacal sound as they were led away by the high priestess and her two acolytes through the tribe of Agmawor to a set of cages. He thought of making a run for it, as Rahl and the other hunters had followed Nadja into the cave to receive their reward for bringing the bounty back to camp. Logan shuddered to think what it could be, remembering the look of lust on Rhal's face as he followed the witch queen inside.

The cages were made of bone tied together with cut vines. They were built low to the ground, forcing prisoners to crouch or sit in the dirt. One of them was wider around and held maybe a dozen Agma, all male, waiting to be butchered for the Agmawor feast. The smaller cage stood empty.

Stopping in front of the smaller of the two, the high priestess waited in silence while the Agmawor guards scrambled to bow before her, practically licking the holy woman's scaled feet.

"Enough groveling," Luana said, brushing them off with a kick. "These three are not to be harmed in any way. They are for Seti and he *will* receive them unblemished."

One of the guards, a squat Agmawor who looked and smelled like he sorely needed a bath, groveled. "As it should be, High Priestess, but can't this one just have a little taste? It is so hungry."

Luana sneered at the pathetic prison guard, pushing him down to the dirt and producing a curved dagger from her robe. "If this one is too weak to abide Seti's fasting, then perhaps we shall place him in with the Agma."

Still groveling, the lizardman skittered backward and begged for forgiveness, the fin on his head softened to a flop. Luana granted him mercy and ordered him to cut the prisoners' bindings. When the high priestess and her acolytes left, the guards stood upright again, opening the cage and shoving the soft-skins inside.

"This is a fine pickle we're in," Bipp grumbled, rubbing his sores wrists.

"Well, at least I think I know where they are planning to do the sacrifice," Logan said.

"And how would you know that?" Bipp asked, more than a little annoyed with their situation.

"Because it's right behind you," Logan said, nodding his head over the gnome's shoulder.

Beyond a few nearby tents, a long flight of wide, worn stone steps worked their way up the side of the hill. They were clearly left over from some grand Ithikan building. At the apex, the steps flattened out into a landing that looked like it had been altered to be a platform. At the back of it stood the frame of an arched stone doorway, with no door and no walls. At the bottom of the steps, on either side, stood crumbling statues of a mighty serpent.

Bipp whistled at the ominous ruins.

"That is what you humans would call *ironic*," Nero flatly stated.

"Why is that, then?" Bipp asked.

"The sacrificial altar seems to be none other than the entrance to the zoo's famed lizard house," Nero explained. "It is recorded that the country boasts the highest variety of cold-blooded creatures that exist in any zoo. They even have, or *had*, a basilisk on display."

Logan had read about basilisks in one of Elder Morgana's books, *Mythic Monsters of Acadia*. "Hmm. How did they manage that without turning everyone to bloody stone?" he asked, testing the strength of the cage's bars while the guards were busy squabbling with each other. Their prison was made of solid bone tied firmly together. There was no way they were going to get out of the cage by breaking it.

Logan kicked one of the bones in frustration and turned around, plopping down in the dirt. They were trapped, alright. He felt his blood boiling at the thought that this was one mess they were not getting out of. How could he have been so stupid not to have had Tiko scout the area for enemies sooner? He hated himself for being so inept and for being so foolish as to think there was actually something worthwhile he could do in this world. At that moment, all he wanted to do was curl up in a ball and forget he ever existed in the first place.

"What are you doing?" Bipp asked, exasperated.

Logan scowled at his friend and rolled over. "What does it look like?" he said, clamping his eyes shut. "I'm getting that damned rest you've been prattling on about the last couple days."

Bipp shrugged at Nero and sat on the ground beside Logan.

The first day they were in the cage passed by with nothing particularly interesting happening. They came up with several ways to escape, all of which were useless. The Agma in the nearby cage refused to talk to them. It seemed the captured lizardmen had resigned themselves to their fate and just sat about staring blankly at nothing. At night the Agmawor liked to chant war songs and dance naked around bonfires.

The second morning, one of the guards unexpectedly opened their cage when his partner went away to fetch some water. The humanoid had a crazed look in his eyes, and Logan immediately guessed his intentions. "The high priestess warned you not to touch us," he quickly reminded the lizard.

"This one cares not. His belly is empty. Hilk just has a tiny taste, no one notices," the guard hissed, the dorsal fin on his head flexing and becoming ridged as it grasped for Bipp, licking its lips.

"But your god...," Logan warned.

"Seti be damned. The fasting is killing this one," Hilk whined. "Get over here, little beastie." He crawled just inside the door of the cage, trying to grab the squirming Bipp. Logan pulled the gnome behind himself, shuffling backward toward the rear of the cage.

"If you really cannot abide by your god's laws, then go ahead and have a taste of me," Logan said, offering his exposed wrist.

Hilk stopped trying to get at the gnome. The lizardman quickly looked over his shoulder to see if his partner was returning yet, then nodded for the soft-skin to hurry up. Logan crawled toward the entrance and offered his hand to the drooling Agmawor, who promptly clamped down on a finger.

The sound of the lizardman's teeth breaking against the unbending metal of Logan's mechanical hand was loud enough to make even the semi-catatonic Agma take notice. Before the cannibal could make any noise, Logan gave it two sharp jabs in the jaw with his metal fist and wrapped his arm around its neck. Applying force, he choked the air out of the flailing humanoid's body. It was hard to get a good grip in the cramped cage. He took a couple ragged gashes across his forearm from the guard's clawed hands until, finally, the lizardman stopped struggling. Logan kept squeezing anyhow to be sure the bastard was dead.

Unfortunately, the other guard returned and was already calling for help before they could escape the open cage. Nearby Agmawor went for the high priestess, and Luana sent an acolyte to see what the problem was. The devoted disciple of Seti deemed the dead guard had been punished by the Serpent God for touching their sacrificial offering. He *was* warned, after all. The remaining guard accepted their verdict but gazed at the prisoners with a blood-curdling look.

When night fell again, celebrations broke out everywhere. Bonfires were lit all around the camp, and naked Agmawor danced around them. Several Agma were pulled from their cage and sent off for slaughter, fodder for the feast. After the twin moons rose in the sky, the lizard people began putting on costumes, wearing animal skins and acting like different jungle creatures. A group of naked female Agmawor chased a laughing male around their cage and then back toward the bonfires. Every so often, random Agmawor would come up to their cage and taunt Seti's offerings, poking and prodding the soft-skins.

One such Agmawor was just heading toward them, crouching and covered head to toe in the skin of a wolf. As it sidled up to the back of the cage, Logan scowled. "Why don't you go throw yourself in a bonfire or something else equally useful?"

"Tiko does not believe that would be the wisest course," his friend whispered from behind the disguise. Bipp got excited and made to hop up, but Logan held him back, throwing a look at the unsuspecting guard's back. Bipp nodded, taking his meaning, and settled down.

"How did you get in here undetected, friend?" Logan asked, keeping his voice down and watching for the guard.

"Tiko has his ways," the Agma replied, flashing a toothy grin behind the furs and reaching into the folds of his wolf skin. Tiko produced Bipp's trusty hammer and Nero's short bow, with three arrows, which he carefully slid between the bars.

"I see you have been busy," Logan snickered. "Where did you come across these?"

"Let this one just say that the hunter Rhal will not be attending tonight's festivities," Tiko explained. Logan's heart soared when his Agma companion produced Gandiva from beneath the wolf skin, sliding it between the bars

"Oy, what is it doing over there?" the guard growled, hopping to his feet and running around the cage with spear in hand. Tiko remained calm, still crouched close to the bone bars. "Answer this one! What did it just hand the soft-skins?"

"Come closer, so that this one may show you," Tiko encouraged.

The guard lowered his weapon, leaning in to peer curiously at the masked lizardman's open hands. When his fingers twisted and the bone dagger suddenly appeared, the guard's eye slits grew tight. He jumped back, but his calls for alarm were abruptly cut off when one of the caged Agma seized the opportunity to lock the guard in a chokehold through the bars of their prison. Unfortunately, the Agma was weak from being imprisoned without food or water for days, and the guard was writhing for his life, making it difficult to keep a firm hold. Tiko was there in a flash, stabbing the guard repeatedly in the chest and stomach. As the Agmawor fell limp, the imprisoned Agma pulled his weapon in between the bars.

Tiko quickly moved to the cage, pulling back the wolf's head to reveal himself. The Agma gasped when he saw his comrade's face. "Tiko! It's really you here to rescue us! How many came with you? Where are they? How did you get in here?"

The questions came out like floodwater and Logan called over, "You better get your friends to settle down before the whole camp knows what we are up to."

Tiko nodded, looking back to his tribe mates, and whispered, "The soft-skin is wise. These ones must keep voices low, Kol." But he grasped his friend's forearm in a firm, warm greeting between the bars all the same.

"Where are the others? How many are here?" Kol repeated in a lower voice. Tiko cast his eyes down to his feet, unable to meet his friend's gaze. "Kol sees. Tiko is alone. Does the chief know Tiko is here?"

Tiko shook his head. "Shaman Nan sent Tiko to guide the soft-skins in search of Isaacha. It is a long story that we have come to be here, but I will not leave you, my blood brother."

"Come on, come on," Bipp urged.

Remembering himself, Tiko tossed a bone dagger to the gnome and moved around to the other side of the cage. The lizardman dragged the dead Agmawor around to the front and positioned his body to make it appear as though he had fallen asleep. Bipp worked his little hands as fast as possible, sawing through the wrapped vines that secured the cage door, while Tiko worked on freeing the Agma.

"These ones must be quick. The Feast of Serpents is almost underway," Tiko warned, tearing away the vines of the cage with fervor.

"What is this festival they are celebrating?" Nero asked, unable to quell his ceaseless hunger for knowledge, no doubt a byproduct of his programmed secondary directives.

"Agmawor worship the evil snake god, Seti," Tiko explained. "Every time of the twin full moons, they have a great celebration in Seti's name, giving offerings to keep him appeased for another couple months, lest their evil Serpent God grow unhappy and wreak havoc upon Agmawor tribe."

"Get out of the way." Logan pulled Bipp away from the gate, which still had two vines tied around the base. He gave the bone door a series of blows from his shoulder, finally bending the opening wide enough so that they could crawl out through the top. Bipp snatched the knife back and scurried over to their rescuer, helping the Agma cut the bindings on the other cage.

"The Queen ordered us to be sacrificed to Seti," Logan informed him, which gave Tiko pause for only a moment before he resumed unwrapping the bindings.

"It is good this one is here, then," Tiko said.

"Why, what is the sacrifice?" Bipp asked, though he was certain he did not want to know the answer.

Tiko licked his lips and said, "The chosen for sacrifice are given a decision. One option is to take the Rite of Seti, where you are given a choice of drink. If the offering chooses correctly, the drink is not poison, and it is decided that one has been gifted with mercy by the Great Serpent."

"That sounds horrendous," Bipp said. "What is the other option?"

"To be disemboweled alive before your head is taken off. It is said the witch queen even makes love to the writhing bodies of Seti's offerings while their entrails are being pulled," Tiko said, pulling the last vines away and throwing the door wide so that his Agma friends could escape. The lizardmen were so weak from lack of sustenance that some needed to be dragged.

"Sounds like the Rite of Seti is the way to go to me," Bipp said, blanching when he heard the words come from his own mouth. "Not that I would want to do either!" he quickly added.

"Tiko's friend would think so, but it is said the rite is fixed. All drinks are poison, and it is a slow painful death, much worse than the disembowelment," Tiko gravely replied, directing his companions to the shadows behind the cage.

Logan sneered at the barbaric practice. "At least with the poison, you don't have to bump uglies with that snake witch," he spat.

Tiko worked to secure the door, so that passing Agmawor would need to walk all the way up to the area before they spotted there was a problem. "This is true. The witch queen does not make love with the victims of the rite. Instead, she has them castrated and eats their organ while they watch."

Bipp gulped. "Thank the gods we're getting out this place."

Logan's face turned white as he looked over the gnome's shoulder.

Hearing the snarling Agmawor behind him, Bipp frowned. "We aren't getting out of here, are we?"

Logan slowly shook his head and held up his arms in surrender. A group of ten armed Agmawor stood behind the high priestess, spears ready to skewer the soft-skins, while another group surrounded the weakened Agma.

"Where is it you think you are going?" High Priestess Luana asked without a trace of amusement. Nobody had a response fit for giving voice.

Within moments they were corralled back into their separate cages. The high priestess stopped her men from placing Tiko with the Agma, saying if he wanted to free the soft-skins, then the infidel was *fit for sacrifice.* The wolf skin, bone dagger, and spear were taken from Tiko, but no one thought to search the rest of the party for weapons.

"Now we're really screwed," Bipp groaned, gripping the bars and frowning at the feast.

Packs of the lizard people were left to stand watch around the cages. An entire horde of Agmawor began gathering at the base of the stairs across from their prison. Great bonfires were set to either side of the steps and behind the arched stone doorway on the platform.

"That is the gateway to Seti's realm, only reached during the twin full moons," Tiko explained, following Logan's eye to the blazing doorway.

As the moons rose overhead, the Agmawor grew calmer. Loud animal-skin drums began beating, announcing the witch queen's approach. Nadja towered over her subjects on her litter, carried by her oiled servants up the steps with the high priestess and a procession of robed acolytes in tow. The firelight gleamed in Queen Nadja's devious eyes, which ran over her followers with zeal. When they reached the platform, the litter was set before the blazing doorway, outlining her snake body through the wispy garments she wore.

The high priestess began the ceremony with a prayer to Seti. All of the Agmawor fell to their knees, worshipping the serpent god. Logan regretted to hear that the sacrifice would take place before dinner. Not that he wanted to watch the Agma prisoners be eaten, but given the alternative, he did not want to have his head cut off, either.

The four of them were ushered out of the cage and marched past the rows of chanting Agmawor. Logan could feel hundreds of evil eyes on him as they walked through the swaying horde. He tried lying to himself that he was not intimidated, but the overwhelming hatred directed at them was almost more than he could bear. The world seemed to shift, stretching in obscene angles. Logan wondered if this was what Lady Cassandra felt as she was being led to her execution. He could see his body walking up the steep stone steps, with the witch queen waiting at the top, speaking with her subjects, as if he was removed from the situation.

"The time is here, my blood," Nadja said. "Hark as the twin sisters bloom full, opening the gateway to Seti's realm!"

She slithered back and forth with her silk robes opened wide to display her naked upper torso. The witch queen was wrapped in a black boa, which encircled her arms and ran its diamond head between her oiled breasts. Logan gagged on the smell of her putrid rot, only accentuated by the burning pyre heating her snakeskin.

"Seti calls to me!" Nadja informed the tribe with arms stretched to the moons. The Agmawor began groveling in the dirt. Throwing her head back toward the moon, Nadja clasped her hands together as if begging. "Oh, Dark Father of my tribe, I hear your words. Speak through me, your blessed servant, that the tribe may bathe in your might! Give us understanding Seti, my father, my holy master, my lover."

Logan and his friends were lined up before the writhing witch queen. He watched the vile creature as she sensually danced back and forth, summoning the spirit of their snake god. Beside her, High Priestess Luana was deeply lost in prayer with her eyes closed. The plumes of her high-collared dress whipped back from the heat of the blazing inferno in the doorway. Despite Nadja's four naked servants and the five guards that had brought them up the steps, Logan could probably gut the witch queen before they were able to take him down. If Logan Walker was going to die, he would be damn certain this witch was coming with him.

"Logan Walker, *hu*-man, great Seti has spoken. The Golden Serpent will allow you to give your life in his name," Nadja said, holding her hands to the sky while rocking on her snake body.

"Oh, what an honor," Logan dryly replied.

The black boa slithered up her arm until its head was at the tip of her fingers. Nadja shifted so that she reached out to the companions as she spoke. "It *will* be your life's honor to give your soul to Seti. You are truly blessed."

"More like cursed, you mean?" Logan snarled at her. The witch queen feigned shock at his words, though he could see she was secretly amused by him.

"Come now, child," Nadja crooned, leaning forward and running her talon across his chest while her long, forked tongue caressed his cheekbone, "give yourself to Seti so that he may show you true pleasure in your last hour."

Her breath was hot and smelled like an unwashed casket. Logan shuddered, brushing the Agmawor queen's hand away. One of the guards stepped forward to punish him, but Logan bent down, twisting his body to grapple the fighter around the waist, and heaved the lizardman into the flaming portal. The other guards moved with great speed, gripping him from all sides and holding the weak soft-skin still, arms pinned to his sides.

Nadja laughed, truly delighted by his fighting spirit. Working her way closer to his body, the witch lifted his leather jerkin above his naked belly. "What fire inside this one," she leered, licking her pale lips as she ran the cold tip of a sacrificial dagger around his belly button, drawing a thin line of blood. "How Seti will enjoy tasting of your...fruits." She cackled and suddenly plunged the knife into his pants, pressing the sharp blade against the bottom of his groin. Logan tried to pull away, but the four guards held him firmly in place. "Now tell me, little *hu*-man," Nadja said, running her tongue across his tightly pursed lips while tickling him with her fingernails, pressing harder with the knife, "which of your friends would you prefer to watch give themselves to Seti first?"

Logan was too terrified to even speak, fearing that the wrong word would set the mad witch off and wishing to hell the blade was anywhere else. In his peripheral vision, he could see Bipp squirming and biting his fist. Not for the first time, he wondered how he had gotten them into this mess. Why did he have to drag poor Bipp on his journey? Why had he not just left the goodly gnome back in Dudje where he was safe?

From some inner source of strength, Logan mustered up the nerve to spit directly in the witch queen's face and growl, "Go to Hel, you evil hag."

Logan closed his eyes tight, ready for the knife to dismember him. But instead Nadja laughed. When he opened his eyes, she was using her long tongue to lick the spittle from her cheeks and nose. The massive swarm of Agmawor below seemed equally delighted. Logan had no way of knowing the Agmawor tribe took great pride in strength, and a sacrifice that showed such conviction of will was sure to please the Serpent God.

Nadja pulled the knife from his pants, licking the tip with a gleaming lust in her emerald eyes. "Oh, you are a stubborn one. Seti will like that."

Before Logan could form a response about where Seti could stick it, the witch's talons elongated, and she gripped his jaw with the strength of a lion. Logan's mouth was forcibly popped open as Luana plucked a small red snake from her robes and dropped it inside. Logan tried his hardest to grind his teeth together and chew the squirming thing, but the witch's grip was unshakable, and the snake slithered down his throat. Nadja suddenly locked her cold wet lips around his mouth, ramming her long tongue down his throat to push the snake further inside his body. Satisfied, she pulled her tongue out and ran it across his face, tickling his ear before pulling back.

Tiko groaned for his friend and began to beg the Agmawor leader for mercy on Logan's soul. High Priestess Luana made her way over to the prostrate Agma and placed a hand on his crown, giving him the blessing his warrior heart deserved.

Nadja looked on with amusement then redirected her attention to Logan. "It would appear your friends will watch *you* go first instead," she said with a devilish grin before turning to her executioners. "Remove the *hu*-man's clothing!"

Nero shook off his guard and stepped forward. "Take Nero to be the first, Your Grace!"

Logan shook violently, trying to get away from the four Agmawor restraining him, and yelled, "No, Nero!"

At first Nadja tilted her head to the side and cocked a thin eyebrow at the soft-skin's demand. Never had a sacrifice shown such courage in the face of their imminent death. Usually by now, they would all turn to puddles of whimpering mush, mewling for freedom. Hearing the pain in Logan's plea, her crooked smile spread unnaturally across her face, and Nadja slithered over to Nero. Curling around his body, so that his legs were buried beneath the weight of her snakelike bottom half, Nadja brought her face close to his own. "*Hu*-man, if you are so ready for Seti's embrace, then let us accommodate that need."

"If Nero is correct, the choice in my death is my own to make, is it not?" he asked innocently.

Nadja curled her lips, baring her teeth at him, determined to enjoy his death as she chose. However, the high priestess quick to butt in. "The child of man is correct. Seti demands that he choose his own path to sacrifice."

Nero nodded thoughtfully. "Then this one chooses the Rite of Seti."

Nadja dropped her annoyance in laughter. She had assumed the soft-skin would take the easy way out and demand he be stabbed through the heart.

The high priestess paused. "Are you sure this is the manner you would choose?" Luana asked, giving him an opportunity to back out.

Nero nodded, firm in his resolve, while Logan begged his friend not to do it.

The high priestess led him over to a wooden table, where various cups of dark liquid were scattered. Some of the vessels were carved from wood, others the horns of hunted game, and others yet were made up of carved Agma bones. "The Rite of Seti is set before you," Nadja informed Nero loudly enough for all to hear, her voice booming across the gathering below. "You may choose one vessel only and must drink of it fully. If Seti sees your soul fit, he will spare it and bestow the Blessing of the Chosen. If he desires to taste of your essence, the vessel will be filled with poison from an adder, which will course through your body for hours in an excruciating pain you have ever only imagined possible."

The witch queen tapped Nero's soft, perfectly shaped nose with her talon and drifted back to face the worshippers. "The soft-skin has entered the Rite of Seti. Let him choose, and the Great Serpent himself will judge whether his soul be worthy!"

The Agmawor fell into a sweltering frenzy, shouting and cheering over the proclamation. It was a strong sacrifice indeed that would willingly choose death by poison.

Nero ran a finger over the many vessels, seemingly deep in thought. He stopped, turning to look at his companions with a frown. "Nero is sorry, my friends. Tiko was correct. They are all poison."

Logan screamed for him to stop, but the android snatched up a vessel and knocked back its contents in one swig. The crowd below cheered even louder for the soft-skin's unflinching bravery, and Nadja mocked him with laughter. Nero gripped his stomach, side-stepping and stumbling. He stared at the ground, off-balance as the poison coursed through his body.

"Seti has chosen! The sacrifice will be long and painful!" Nadja shouted with sick glee. "Bring me his member," she commanded the acolytes, who moved forward to steady the dizzy soft-skin.

Except when they approached, Nero unexpectedly straightened, holding the Agmawor warriors at bay with an upturned palm. The android smiled at the witch queen and stretched his arms wide. "Seti has blessed my soul as a Chosen. The poison is gone!"

The crowd below fell silent with mouths agape, rocked by the proclamation. They watched in anticipation as the high priestess made her way over to check that the soft-skin's claims were true. She felt his forehead. There was no fever. He should be burning up already! And his belly muscles were not tightening, nor were his eyes dilated. The soft-skin had actually passed the Rite of Seti!

"H-he...," High Priestess Luana stammered in disbelief, stepping back from the soft-skin and looking down the steps to her tribe. "He speaks the truth! The soft-skin has been given Seti's blessing!"

The horde erupted into celebration, knocking drums and dancing around in circles at the miracle. Seti had blessed their feast with a Chosen, something that was unheard of!

Queen Nadja interrupted their merriment. The bonfires danced in her eyes as she scowled. "This is trickery! The *hu*-man is deceiving us!"

Hearing her wild accusation the crowd grew calm again. Had the soft-skin deceived their god somehow?

Luana grimly shook her head. "There can be no trickery against Seti, master of deception. If the Great Serpent has seen this soft-skin fit, who are we to question his divine judgment?"

Nadja's mind raced to comprehend how the soft-skin had pulled off his deception. She had only ever ordered the poison of an adder to be set out. It was the deadliest of poisons, and no living creature, other than herself, could taste even a sip without falling dead within the day. "Have him try another. Surely if this is no trickery, then Seti will spare him once more!"

The high priestess shook her head defiantly. "The Rite of Seti has been passed, as is our law set forth by Seti himself. The soft-skin has been seen fit. No further trials are necessary."

Nadja's eyes sharpened at the high priestess's insolence. She wanted nothing more than to tear the lizardwoman apart but knew that all eyes were on her after that statement.

Nero broke the silence. "Nero will prove he is worthy! Seti blessed this one with his forgiveness once. I trust the Great Serpent will do so again."

The witch queen narrowed her eyes, unnoticed by the cheering Agmawor, who were chanting for the soft-skin. His willingness was even more suspect to her. Any rational being would be relieved to have gotten through the rite, but this one was going in for seconds? The whole thing reeked foul to her keen senses.

Without waiting, Nero snatched up an Agma skull with both hands and poured the dark, sour liquid into his mouth, letting it overflow down his jaw in greasy rivulets. When he was finished, the android held the skull up to the moons and gave praise to Seti. The roar of the Agmawor was deafening. They had never witnessed one blessed by Seti in all their years. The soft-skin was a miracle gifted to their tribe.

Nadja hissed, feeling in her bones that the soft-skin was deceiving them in some way. "The *hu*-man blasphemes our god with this trickery!"

"Our eyes cannot be fooled, Nadja. The soft-skin has taken two full vessels and is alive to give testament," High Priestess Luana countered.

The witch queen slithered across the platform to pluck an acolyte into her arms, setting the scared lizardman down in front of the wooden table. "The soft-skin has somehow changed Seti's blood to water. Watch, even a lowly novice will survive the Rite!"

Luana moved to stop her witch queen before she violated their holy practice by forcing the Rite of Seti upon an unchosen. However, the serpent woman was far too fast. Moving with alacrity and smiling knowingly at Logan Walker, she forced a wooden cup of the poison upon the helpless acolyte.

After he had emptied the vessel with shaking hands, the witch queen pulled it away and waited. The acolyte's lips quivered with fear. When nothing happened, she began to slap the base of her tail against the stone platform excitedly. "You see? The blood of Seti has been switch—"

Her triumphant declaration was cut off when the acolyte fell down the steps, wracked with spasms. His muscles contorted weirdly, and thick white phlegm bubbled around the corners of his mouth.

Logan seized the moment, shaking free from his dumbfounded captors and shouting to the crowd, "You see? Nero *has* been chosen by Seti. The queen is the one who is committing heresy!"

The crowd sweltered with anger. Some of it was directed at Nadja, who had displeased the Great Serpent, while some was directed at the soft-skin who dared to question their queen. The lizard people began calling for his body to be torn apart.

Nero's arms flew back behind him and his chest puffed forward. High Priestess Luana stepped back from his oddly angled body and bit her lip. Nero's eyes suddenly erupted with twin beams of light, which he would normally use to help illuminate the path for human travelers, and the priestess shrieked, cowering on the ground with arms raised to ward off the human.

"How dare you question my judgment?" Nero's voice boomed over the crowd, amplified by the booster in his voice modulator. He let his eyes run slowly over the stupefied Agmawor. "Seti has spoken, and you *will* obey. The soft-skins are to be freed along with their Agma brethren."

That was where he messed up. Logan could see it written on the faces of some of the Agmawor. The idea that their god, who was never known for his benevolence, would spare the weak and pathetic Agma reeked of deception.

"He speaks heresy! Seti would never release the Agma!" Nadja hissed, pointing an accusatory talon at Nero, who let the lights die in his eyes. "Kill the *hu*-mans!"

Logan knew they were doomed, Nero's ruse was up. Yet none of the guards moved to touch the Chosen. How could they risk Seti's wrath if they were wrong?

"You cowards! If none of you has the stones to do it, then I will kill the soft-skin myself!" Nadja lunged forward with twin fangs suddenly elongated and her sacrificial dagger pulled back, ready to thrust into Nero's chest.

She was stopped cold when the High Priestess cast a magical cloud of black gnats in the witch queen's face and pulled Nero behind her. "I cannot allow you to harm the Chosen! Seti has spoken!"

Nadja waved away the insects and stretched to her full height, the flames casting her long, writhing shadow down the steps. "How dare you interfere with your queen?" she hissed, tossing her black boa on top of an unsuspecting Bipp.

Logan lunged to free his friend, falling to his knees and trying to pry the snake away. But the harder he tried to remove it, the tighter the black snake's grip became, like a vise choking the life from his friend.

"Step aside and let me have the *hu*-man, and I will consider forgiving your insolence," Nadja continued.

Luana stood firm. "Never! What you speak is blasphemy. Seti has chosen him and even you cannot change that!"

The crowd was quickly dividing between those who believed blindly in their god, Seti, and those who believed in the wisdom of the witch queen.

"So be it!" Nadja snarled, her face becoming a mask of hatred as she unleashed a stream of poison from her mouth on the high priestess. Luana quickly spun her thurible, calling forth a wall of thick vines, which erupted through the stone platform to deflect the poison.

As the two powerful women locked in battle, the horde of Agmawor below fell into absolute chaos as civil war was thrust upon them.

Logan pulled Gandiva and used it to batter the black boa's body to no avail. He shouted for Bipp to hold on, though he was certain the gnome could not hear it. His face was turning a purple color under the constricting boa. Flicking the weapon open, Logan frantically searched for the snakes head.

Nadja called forth a wave of serpents, which seemed to pour out of the folds of her robes from some dark place. Slithering across the stone, the snakes tried to bite Luana's bare feet, but the high priestess was quick to react and sent forth a stream of acid from her spinning thurible, melting them.

Tiko helped Logan pull the snake's head back so that he could run Gandiva's blade across it, sheering the constrictor's head off. Beheaded, the body finally loosened, leaving Bipp gasping for air and weakly trying to uncoil the black serpent from his body. With Bipp free, Logan looked around at the carnage. In a matter of minutes, the Agmawor tribe had plunged itself into a bloody massacre. Luana was calling forth another round of thick vines to block the witch queen's spells. "I wonder which of them will win?" he asked.

"Tiko thinks it best we are not here to find out," the Agma wisely advised. Logan readily agreed. There was no telling who would be the victor or whether the rest of them would even be spared. If they were going to escape, now was the time to make their move.

Tiko tossed the semi-conscious gnome over his scaly shoulder as Nero ran to meet them. When they descended the stone staircase, the sounds of Nadja's triumphant laughing erupted from the platform.

Hopping off the last step, into the swelling wave of chaos, Logan turned to see the evil witch queen looming over High Priestess Luana, who was wrapped in the queen's coiled snake body. A look of sick delight burned in the queen's eyes and she opened her jaws wide, revealing long, dripping fangs. Without hesitation, Logan threw everything he had into Gandiva. The ancient weapon whistled through the air up the steps. Nadja blinked for a moment, wondering what the sound was, before the boomerang tore through her shoulder, ripping it apart.

Nero let one of his arrows fly into the face of an attacking Agmawor, and Tiko snatched a spear from the dead grasp of a lizardman lying in its own blood. When Gandiva returned to Logan's grasp, he took one last look at the platform. Freed of the snake woman's body, the high priestess regarded him with astonishment for saving her life and turned to face the screaming witch queen with steely resolve.

"We have to free the Agma!" Logan shouted, letting Gandiva tear a path through the fighting crowd of Agmawor. They made their way quickly through the battle, with most Agmawor either too enthralled in their bloodlust or too afraid to touch Seti's blessed one, Nero, who led their charge. The handful of lizardmen that *were* foolish enough to challenge them met sure deaths at the hands of Logan or Tiko.

Once they got back to the cages, Tiko threw a spear inside and put Bipp down for a moment. The imprisoned Agma worked on vines from the bottom while Logan hacked at the bindings on top.

"Hurry, my friends," Tiko said, throwing the door wide. "Away we must be!"

Together they raced for the walls. As they neared the gate, a large Agmawor stepped into path, slapping a heavy bone cudgel in his palm and growling, his blue-green dorsal fin flexing and rigid. Logan moved to take the brute down, but the Agma shoved past, falling on the warrior with their scavenged spears.

Logan had to scream for them to stop. The Agmawor was long dead, and they were still slashing away at his battered torso. "Sate your revenge some other time. We need to get out of here!" he shouted.

On the platform, Nadja whipped her snake tail at the high priestess, who jumped back and called forth the powers of the jungle. A fat vine burst from the stone platform, pummeling the maddened queen in the jaw and shoving her back into the flaming doorway. The flames licked her skin, spreading like a wave across her body, ignited by the oils she had rubbed on for the ceremony. The witch queen screamed as she burned, thrashing back and forth, crushing the wooden table and shattering a stone column. The high priestess shot forth vines to bind Nadja's wrists to the doorway, pulling her arms wide and clamping roots over her thrashing body so that she could burn alive under the twin full moons.

"None may defy Seti!" Luana swore triumphantly.

As Logan and his companions ran past the stone walls of the perimeter, away from the evil Agmawor camp and its bloodthirsty civil war, he could hear the witch queen's howls, and they made him smile.

Chapter 16: Summoner

Hrar curled his nose as he approached the slave quarters and the unwashed stink of the place hit him. The jotun servant was not accustomed to being subjected to such squalor, spending his days fetching things and delivering messages for the marquess. Hrar was a loyal servant to Marquess Tryn, whom he respected even when others turned their nose at the jotun noble's odd nature. In truth, Hrar quite liked the marquess, seeing his everyday acts for what they were. He knew somewhere deep down inside, the marquess possessed the strength that a Belikar ruler needed. Once he ascended to the inevitable position of duke, the rest of the city would see the same, and Hrar was sure his hard work and unflinching loyalty would pay off.

Two lazy jotnar guards leaned against the stone wall beside the gate, drinking as the marquess' page made his way down the hill. "I come to pick up the shipment of marked scabs for the marquess," Hrar informed them, though they hardly seemed to care, waving him on with a grumble for interrupting their conversation. Hrar huffed and crossed his arms. "Well?"

One of the guards seemed annoyed at the soft little jotun, rolling his eyes at his partner and standing up. The guard was tall, a good foot more so than Hrar, who gulped when the hard jotun leaned forward. "'Well' what? You want a parade for doing your job?"

Hrar surprised the rough guard by barking right back. "Who is it you believe you are addressing? I am not some commoner come calling for you to practice your insolence on! Before you stands a member of House Olvaldi, and you would do well to remember that fact, pig!"

The guard stared down at him, blinking his eyes and wondering whether the small jotun had really just shouted at him. When the servant was still there after a couple more blinks, he turned to his friend, and they both began laughing at the funny little deliveryman.

Inside the slave quarters, past row upon row of cramped shanties, Corbin and his companions were locked deep in conversation with Fivan. Kyra had wisely dismissed the slave leader's insistence that they explain themselves back at the granary.

Corbin found himself greatly worried that the leaves of their mystical branches were all but withered at this point. Time was running out, and he knew they needed to make the best of what precious few hours they had remaining.

To make matters worse, when the workday was over, armed slavers came to gather the four of them. The marked slaves were moved to a special holding cell at the back of the slave's living quarters. The place was no more than a sloppily built wooden shack, with one entrance that two slavers guarded. Blood stained the wooden floor and feces were dried in one corner, telling Corbin that the place had been used for far more grim circumstances.

Fivan was certainly a man of power, as much as a slave could be expected to possess. The slavers respected him enough to let him be, trusting that the human leader would make their jobs easier by keeping his people in line. Fivan saw his role as a protector of the scabs, who knew no better, and if left to their own devices, would surely have ended up food for the jotnar by now. It was little challenge for him to have the slavers bring them some rations from his home despite being ordered not to feed the prisoners. And the two jotnar sympathizers guarding them even respected his request to wait outside so that the four of them could converse in private, huddled in a circle on the filthy floor.

Kyra had gone over the lie Corbin weaved for Eir, giving just enough information to explain their purpose but not enough to leave either of their homelands exposed.

When she was finished weaving her tale, Fivan stroked his wild grey beard. "But how can this be? You say there are actually other humans living out there, far away over Belikar's walls, free? It's a heavy piece of bread for one to be swallowing." Kyra solemnly nodded in response. "And you say the resistance knows of this?"

"Not only do they know, they welcome our help," Corbin added, jumping on the cynical old man's moment of doubt.

"I swear I will have both your heads if you do not stop it this instant!" Hrar whined, stomping his shoe on the ground. This made the drunk guards roar that much louder with laughter. One of them had to cover his face to block the view of the funny little page, punching the wall to release some of his laughter.

Hrar's face was puffed with pink splotches on his blue cheeks, looking as if it would explode. He was so frustrated with the guard's disrespectful behavior that he kicked the dirt. He needed to figure out how to order these jotnar to do his bidding. "Well, the two of you are clearly drunk," he pouted, raising another peel of uncontrollable laughter from the jotnar.

"Sav and Niv, what is going on over here?" Overseer Ol'bron clopped up on a black mare out of the shadows. Hrar felt his intestines shrivel up under the ominous glare of the angry jotun. The overseer was making his rounds and would not broach any tomfoolery, not while the archduke himself was in town.

Both guards straightened up, clambering to retrieve their spears and hide the ale. "Nothing, Master Ol'bron. We were just having a chat with the marquess' little errand boy here, that's all," one of the guards, Sav, was quick to respond, bowing dutifully as he finished.

"I am not an errand boy!" Hrar snapped at the pair, though he quickly reconsidered his tone under the sharp hawkish eyes of the overseer.

Ol'bron sidled his horse closer. "You are wearing the insignia of House Olvaldi. Are you from the palace?" he asked.

Hrar puffed out his chest and shot the guards a smug look. "Indeed I am, Overseer Ol'bron. I have been sent by the marquess himself to retrieve the marked scabs for delivery to the dungeons before first light."

"Then you *are* an errand boy after all," the overseer stated with no trace of humor.

Hrar opened and closed his mouth, unable to think of a response, then lowered his face to the ground, stepping back from the mounted jotun with a frown and a nod.

One of the guards snickered and received a sharp kick to the chest from the overseer, knocking him to the dirt and shattering the bottle of lager they had been trying to hide. "Did I say you could laugh?" he shouted. "It's not bad enough I've got the archduke prowling around my fields? I need you two louts getting drunk and harassing a man of the palace as well?"

The guard whimpered, rising to his feet again on shaking legs. His chest felt like someone had dropped an anvil on it. Both of them began spitting out a stream of apologies to the overseer.

"Shut your drunken mouths!" Ol'bron barked, backing his horse away from the pair and pointing the reins at Hrar. "Niv, escort the marquess's errand boy to the marked scabs for retrieval." Niv quickly moved to comply. "And have some scab slavers accompany him back to the dungeons."

In the holding shack, Fivan considered the implications of joining the resistance. "Let me see you," he said. Corbin moved closer to the old man, catching his face in the moonlight, which was just filtering in through the wide cracks of the splintered ceiling. "Not like that. I want to see you as you stood in the granary," Fivan explained.

Corbin looked to Kyra for guidance. The slavers could walk in on them at any moment. She dipped her head slightly and reached inside her shoulder pocket to grab the magical branch.

The old man gasped when the three of them removed the branches from their proximity, setting them on the floor and exposing their true selves. Fivan reached out a trembling hand to touch Corbin's face. He needed to feel the man's pale skin to tell himself this was not some dream. Corbin leaned forward and grasped the old slave's hand, which looked almost black against his Falian skin. Fivan recoiled as if he were stung.

"So you see we have given you the truth of it," Kyra said. "Now give us your answer. Will you join the resistance and stand beside us as we free our people?"

Fivan stared at her, taking in her soft features and long black hair tied back from her face. "I...uh..."

A sharp rap on the door broke their conversation. Outside, one of the slavers whispered insistently, "Fivan, they are coming for them scabs. Best you be out of there straight away."

Stur hopped to his feet, pulling out his mighty broadsword. "What does he mean by that? Where are you off to?"

Fivan gulped at the warrior's ominous presence, staring from him to the deadly weapon and choosing his next words carefully. "There was never any intention for me to go to the dungeons. I've a replacement waiting outside as we speak. It won't matter much to the masters. One scab is just as good as another to them."

Kyra held up her hand, signaling Stur to back down. "It's not a problem," she said. "Now we don't have to figure out how to get you out of here with us. You staying behind is all the better, so you can rally the slaves. They need a leader right now, someone they trust. Someone they respect enough to follow into battle when the time comes."

Fivan nodded, agreeing with her.

"So you *will* join the resistance?" Corbin asked, eagerly pulling off his glove and holding out a hand for the man to shake.

"If you live through the night, then count me as a member." Fivan spit on his palm before grasping the pale-skinned man's cold hand with a firm shake.

Another series of sharp raps made the door rattle on its weak hinges. "Fivan, you must be out of there now," the slaver rasped.

Corbin helped the old man rise on feeble legs, holding his aching back for support, as the others quickly retrieved their branches. Fivan tapped on the door, signaling he was ready to leave. When it opened, he turned around, silhouetted in the doorway. "How will I know when we shall meet?"

"We will send for you," Kyra replied cryptically, unsure exactly how they would even find the jotun named Gaurmin that was supposed to deliver their news to Eir. It seemed to be answer enough for the slave, who was impressed by the strange ways of these foreigners.

As soon as Fivan was outside, slaver roughly shoved his replacement into the cramped shack. Corbin caught the frightened decoy before he could fall.

Hrar was only ten paces away when he heard the slavers slam the door shut again, not even noticing the old man who stole away through the shadows between the nearby hovels.

"Get that door back open!" Niv barked. The slavers jumped to comply, throwing the rickety door wide and calling for the scabs to come out and line up in front of the shack. The smaller page walked around them, smugly inspecting the marked slaves. Corbin suspected the jotun was putting on a show of it for the guard's benefit.

Deciding they were fit to travel, Hrar spun on his heel and addressed the slavers. "The two of you will accompany me on order of Overseer Ol'bron. We are going to escort these scabs to the dungeons."

The slavers blanched, bowing before the jotun. They made short work of huddling the slaves together, whips in hand. Corbin noticed the jotun guard's look of annoyance at the spectacle.

When they passed the thick stone walls, leaving the slave quarters behind, they saw another guard getting whipped beside a tree by the overseer himself, who only stopped for a moment to brush the hair out of his eyes and glare at the entourage. Hrar gave him a nervous nod and picked up his pace, glad to be away from the stench of the place, though he was certain it would take a couple weeks to wash the stink off his clothes. They travelled through the night, up and down the quiet city streets in silence. As far as he was concerned, there was nothing much to discuss with the guard, and he was not even sure if the doomed scabs could speak, not that he had any inclination to talk with the animals.

"Ho, there," a drunken jotun hollered as he stumbled from a nearby alleyway. "Is that my friend Niv?"

Hrar rolled his eyes; of course the guard's friends were drunkards too. "We have no time for this," he groaned to Niv, who was smiling back at the stumbling jotun. "I want to be done with this delivery and in bed before the moons set."

"Ah, hold your horses, *yer majesty.*" Niv slapped Hrar's chest with the back of his large hand to halt the page. "I don't see no overseer around to bail you out this time," he added, low enough so that the slaves could not hear, and sauntered over to the drunken jotun with arms wide open. "Ho, there. What are you on about at this hour? Bet you had too much of that piss Loral is serving over at the Purple Wench, eh?"

Hrar grunted and folded his arms across his chest, resigning himself to wait.

"Master, perhaps we should—" Hrar cut off the slaver who had dared address him with a snarl, delighting in how the scab curled into a bow and backed away.

"Wait...what are you—" Niv took a quick step back and tried to swing his iron spear out in defense.

Suddenly, Hrar felt as though he were in a dream, seeing two more jotnar step from the shadows of the alleyway. One of them grabbed Niv from behind while the other slit his throat in a spray of blood that hit a nearby building. Niv tried to scream, but nothing would come from his throat.

It was hours later when Hrar came out of his stupor, still standing with his arms spread wide and letting out a weak scream that died in his overly dry throat. The moons were high overhead now, marking that many hours had passed. *But how can that be?* he wondered, his mind racing to comprehend what was happening.

To his astonishment, Niv had completely vanished. Hrar ran to the alleyway, calling for the slavers to follow. Niv was nowhere to be seen. It made no sense. How could an eight-foot-tall warrior just disappear into thin air?

"Did you see where he went?" he asked the slavers. When no one answered him, Hrar spun about angrily, ready to give them a lashing.

The world kept spinning around him when he realized with soul crushing dread that not only had the slavers disappeared, but so too had the marked scabs.

"The archduke awaits your arrival below," Marius's man-at-arms informed Tryn as he entered the outer chamber to the dungeons. The marquess hurried down the dark stone steps, deep into the bowels of the dungeon, ignoring the rows of cells he passed in the narrow passageway, each housing dozens of moaning humans inside.

Down another flight of dark steps, he entered the forge proper. The room was larger than the torture chamber on the opposite side of the building, stretching wide with a vaulted ceiling that came to a point. At the ceiling's center was an open atrium. Tall cages sat on either side of the impressive room, filled with moaning humans waiting to be used as material for the forge. Leaving Fajik behind at the entrance, Tryn crossed the room and climbed the steps that rose to the higher summoning platform. It was carved from rock and positioned immediately below the open atrium.

Flickers of torchlight danced across the archduke's face, giving a fleeting illusion that the jotun was a slavering demon. Tryn blinked quickly, knowing it to be a trick of the light, and found the archduke's glowing eyes hungrily following him. "I apologize if I am late, Your Lordship," he said, bowing with humility.

Marius waved off his apprehension with a flick of his free hand, the other leaning on his short staff. "This is the expected time, I wanted to come down and get a good look at the demon forge before we began. And it is a good thing I did, else we would have wasted our valuable time together correcting your summoner's amateur arrangements."

Behind the archduke, Summoner Luz scowled at the insult, brushing gold ink across the stone floor to finish the corrections. Tryn snapped his eyes away from the necrophage, worried that the archduke would hang the jotun for such insolence. "There were corrections necessary, Your Lordship?" Tryn asked, genuinely interested to learn.

"Not that I should have expected much more. Belikar is, after all far behind the rest of the Empire in current events." Marius shrugged, and pointed his ice staff at the intricate glyph, half carved and half painted in the center of the stone floor.

Tryn ignored the slight, though he was surprised to hear the archduke voice his disdain so openly and casually. It was common knowledge that the city was considered a backwoods kingdom, which was just one of the many reasons Duke Thiazi desperately wanted to return to the capitol and restore honor to his family name.

"*Novice* Necrophage Luz had some sloppy excuses for runes, and several of them were even incorrect," Marius continued. "Also *your* alignment was all off. Things will work much better once the soft-headed jotun finishes the preparations."

Tryn examined the glyph to see what he meant. The circle itself remained the same, perfectly carved with a large outer and smaller inner ellipse. Intricately carved runes ran between them. He could see a big difference in the ancient Jotic symbols, each line cleaner and more rigid than before. At the center of the circle was painted a new star, the symbol for Themis, which Acadia orbited, whereas in the past it had been the star from Jotunheim, the world where the jotnar had been imprisoned for a millennia. At the edge of Themis was another perfect circle with a crescent moon inside. At each of the four corners of the inner circle, a new orb was carved and then painted with gold dust. Each of these had strange symbols which Tryn was unfamiliar with inside of them.

"What are these new orbs?" he asked thoughtfully, still staring at the work.

Marius's eyes glinted in the torchlight, and he grinned, which was an ugly thing to behold on the archduke, looking grossly out of place. It was more like the leer of a hungry jackal than an expression of happiness. "These are the ancient necromantic symbols for the stones of power, stolen from us and spread across the seven worlds."

"But there are only four depicted here," Tryn said with a frown, counting them over again as if he had missed something obvious.

"For today's *alterations* and with the pathetic quality of ingredients we have at our disposal, four will be more than sufficient," Marius explained, raising his nose in the air at the mention of their paltry ingredients. He tapped each orb in turn. "Here we have Vanaheim of the ancients. This one is Niflheim of the dead, and there is Muspelheim, our forsaken homeland. And then there is Svartlheim of the shadowkin."

"The preparations are complete, Master Marius," Luz said, bowing low to the stone floor. "I will have my disciples bring us the fodder while I retrieve the rest of the ingredients you requested."

Marius gave the necrophage a curt nod and waved for him to get back to work. "Where are those scabs I asked you to bring?" the archduke inquired, looking over Tryn's shoulder and down the steps. "When you arrived, you were alone."

Tryn shuffled uncomfortably under the archduke's withering glare. "I expected them already to be here, sir. No doubt my page will arrive with them shortly." At least he hoped so. Where was Hrar? He had given explicit instructions to bring the marked humans here no later than dawn. He decided to whip Hrar for his inexcusable tardiness.

"Very well, we can begin by practicing on some of the other filthy vermin at our disposal," Marius said, shifting his attention to the two thick-skinned red demons that were approaching. "So these are the byproducts of your handiwork?"

"Yes, yes, they are," Tryn proclaimed, proudly beholding his necromantic work. The pair of demons stood a bit squatter than a human, with heavy bellies and thick red skin that shone wetly in the firelight. They had three stubby fingers on each hand, jutting tusks from their mouths, and a lone eye in the center of their bald heads.

The archduke raised his navy blue eyebrows and frowned slightly. "Not bad, given the dismal conditions you have had to work with and the lack of a real education." If Tryn did not know any better, he would say the archduke was almost giving him a compliment. Flicking his hand, Marius sent the demons to retrieve a piece of flesh for him. Tryn stood a little taller, watching his creations stalk toward the cages.

"Why do you do this?" Marius asked him.

Tryn was thrown off by the question. It was fairly common for his betters to tell him what to do or why he was incompetent at it, but at that moment he could not think of a single incident when someone had actually asked him *why* he had done something.

"Why do I work the necromantic forge, my lord?" he asked. The archduke gave a curt nod, staring at him as he waited for an answer. Tryn shifted, looking around the wide room. "Well...I guess I enjoy it. When I am down here experimenting with new creations, it gives me a feeling of contribution to our people. Perhaps one day I can come up with a demon that will help us in our struggle."

The archduke looked very pleased with his young charge's answer. He could see Tryn in a way none had ever tried. Under that judgment, Tryn felt as if he had some measure of worth and potential, which indeed the archduke did see in him.

When Luz returned, he carefully placed various ingredients where Marius instructed, fresh herbs over the Vanaheim circle, dried pig intestines around the Svartlheim circle, and a copper bowl filled halfway with the fresh blood of a virgin at the very edge of the crescent moon.

"No cauldron?" Tryn asked, slightly perplexed by the missing pot. Where would they place the human in order to perform the transformation? Marius snickered at his ignorance and shook his head, making Tryn feel three feet tall again.

The cyclopes returned, pulling a naked man who struggled weakly and sobbed for them not to kill him. When they reached the platform, the slave went limp, dropping himself to the floor in an irrational attempt to slow the demon's progress. For a flash, Tryn's heartstrings were pulled, picturing Annabel being dragged to her doom by the cyclopes. However, the moment passed in a blink, and he shook off the notion, flicking his whip at the demons to hurry their delivery. One of the hellspawn dropped the man's arm and delivered three sharp blows to his face, disorienting the slave, who drooled blood.

"Come on now. Get the flesh to the altar. No more delays," Marius said, stepping aside so that the monsters could drop the barely conscious man into the circle. Marius said, "I prefer to have them wide awake for these rituals. It takes some of the delight out of it otherwise. Keep that in mind for the future."

Tryn perked up. The archduke pictured a future where he would still be educating the marquess? This was exciting news indeed. "I will make sure we can hear their screams next time, Your Lordship," he promised with a bow.

"Oh, we will hear him scream, there's no doubt about that," Marius cackled while Necrophagenecromancer Luz lit some incense inside the hollowed out skull of an elf child. Marius began skirting the circle, tracing patterns across the surface with a tendril of green smoke that was emanating from the tip of his staff of ice. Once he had encircled the entire summoning area, the archduke began to chant in the guttural tongue of the ancient shadowkin. Tryn was impressed by the old jotun's mastery over the ancient language, though he knew such an esteemed member of the Empire should easily know such lore.

The air around the platform began whipping in a whirlwind, rising from the summoning circle as Marius's voice also grew, echoing in a heavy bass across the area. Tryn had to take a quick step back, taken by surprise, when without warning the stone floor buckled from the center of the glyph. A spider web of deep cracks spread from the center and continued to splinter along the surface, stopping when they reached the edge of the protective circle. The human had a mad look in his eyes and white foam bubbled from the corners of his dirty mouth. Tryn watched in sick fascination as the stone peeled downward, like the ragged skin of a moldy orange, revealing a pit of flames. Raw magical energy crackled from the archduke's eyes as he continued the chant, raising his staff higher into the air and pointing a bony finger at the slave, willing the universe to bend to his will.

The flames began to rise from the pit, which must have been a gateway into some hell. The fires scorched the human's writhing torso. As his skin blackened, Tryn's stomach growled uncontrollably at the aroma of grilling steak. The fat under the slave's chin caught fire, lighting him up like a howling candle, and a crackling beam of black energy shot from the tip of Marius's ice staff. When the lightless black energy entered the slave's forehead, a concussive blast of air erupted from the pit. Every torch in the room was suddenly snuffed out, leaving them in utter darkness as wafts of smoke fogged the area. Tryn choked on the smoke, waving it out of his stinging eyes and covering his mouth. The smell of cooked meat still lingered deliciously in the room, and he could make out Luz fanning away the murky cloud on the other side of the summoning circle.

"What happened? Why didn't it work?" Tryn asked the shadowy outline of Marius, still choking on the sulfuric smoke which was finally beginning to dissipate up the shaft of the atrium.

"Who said that it did not work?" Marius asked. The archduke was never one to enjoy others' doubt over the effectiveness of his abilities. "Behold the minotaur for yourself."

Tryn looked at the center of the summoning circle. A demon rose from the floor with the head of a bull and the muscular body of a hardened warrior. The beastly demonspawn stretched out his arms, clenching his hairy fists and roaring toward the ceiling. Across the circle, Luz crouched low to the floor, looking as if he were afraid the demon would turn and kill him where he stood. The demonspawn finished its furious roar and sank to one knee, bowing its black-horned head to the archduke. Tryn was flabbergasted to see such an impressive summoning from just one human, but what it did next was truly dumbfounding. The monstrous humanoid actually spoke.

"I am yours to command, Master."

Marius looked quite pleased with himself, moving forward to stroke the minotaur's furry brown crown. "Yes, you will do quite nicely. Luz, get my new minion cleaned up and suited for battle."

The necrophage snapped his head up, looking terrified to be the creature's caretaker. "B-battle, milord? Are w-we going to b-be under a-attack?"

"Are we going to battle?" Marius repeated the necrophage's question as if it were the stupidest thing he had ever been asked. "What in the hell do you think we are doing on this wretched planet? It's no wonder you backwater Belikarians have not died of outright stupidity before now!" The archduke flew into a rage, kicking Luz down the steps and beating him about the legs with his small staff.

After he had let his rage play out, Marius stepped back and commanded the necrophage to rise and do as he was told. When Luz led the freshly born minotaur away toward the demon cells, Marius turned, facing Tryn with that same sickly jackal grin.

"That was most impressive, Archduke. I never fathomed such creations were possible to summon within this forge." Tryn bowed, which seemed to please Marius even further. "Only, where is it that the creature came from?"

"His is a lost soul, pulled from the foul Hydra Azelban's army of shades," Marius said. "The moon dragons' ranks have swelled so greatly and her grasp covers so much of Alfenheim that she does not even notice as we pull her minotaurs into our service, fodder for the battle ahead."

The marquess stood in uncomfortable silence, shifting slightly under the archduke's penetrating gaze.

"What is it? What do you wish to ask me, Tryn?" Marius beckoned. Tryn looked at the floor, shuffling his feet again and shaking his head. The archduke sidled up to him, wrapping his fingers around the young jotun's shoulders and patting them. "Tryn, I see much potential in you. The duke has been a fool to waste your talents all these years." Tryn's eyes flickered toward the dungeon entrance at the proclamation. "You fear him, I see. It is true that Thiazi is a powerful warrior and a cunning strategist. But that does not excuse his stubbornness to have insisted you follow the same path. Any duke or duchess in their right mind would have sent you to the Grey Tower years ago for a proper education in wizardry."

Tryn felt the fires of his soul stoked at the mention of his lifelong dream. Marius could see that desire clear as day and continued slithering around him, stroking the tender flesh of Tryn's chin to make the marquess look at him.

"You will be my apprentice. I have decided it will be so," Marius said. "Now there can be no secrets between us. Out with it. I want to hear this question that is lingering in your mind."

Tryn blinked and swallowed back the lump in his throat. "Well, it's only...you mentioned a battle, but Belikar has not seen war since the Great Cleansing." The marquess winced slightly when the words fell from his lips, as if the archduke might suddenly change his mind and beat him for his ignorance.

Marius did look displeased, frowning, but not angry. He pulled his hand away from Tryn's face and drummed bony fingers across the shaft of his staff. "Tell me, Tryn, why did we come to Acadia?" Marius asked, without any condescension.

Tryn thought it over, wondering if this was not some trick question, careful that he did not blurt out the wrong answer. "To escape the bonds of our imprisonment in Jotunheim?" Tryn asked, his face growing hot when Marius nodded. "I'm right?" he blurted, immediately feeling like a fool.

"You are half correct." Marius brooded, staring down at the freshly healed stone floor, where not even a hint of a blemish remained after the summoning. "It is disgusting to see that our younger generation has fallen so far from the path...though in truth it is equally interesting to me." With his cloaked back to Tryn, Marius asked, "Tell me, young Tryn, what do you actually know of our imprisonment?"

Tryn recited their history, feeling like he was back learning his lessons with Tutor Balgos. "The Aesir, usurpers of Yggdrasil, stole our lands and denied us entry. When the mighty jotnar armies met them on the battlefield, they were deceived by one of our own, Hlér, who was under the spell of Óðinn One-Eye's black magic. The cowardly Aesir refused to meet us in open battle, fearing our prowess, and instead cast a dark spell over the jotnar, banishing our people to the inescapable reaches of the barren, icy plains of Jotunheim."

"Spoken like an apt pupil," Marius complimented mockingly, "but do you know *how* the Aesir managed to steal our homeland in the first place?" Tryn frowned. "Ah, it is as I thought. You have learned nothing of our history. Tell me, have they at least educated you on how the first gods came to be?"

The corners of Tryn's mouth quirked upward, happy that he knew this one. "In the dawn of time, before the worlds were born, there was nothing. Out of that abyss, the land of Niflheim grew, cold and dark as a black dragon's undying heart. To the south of this land was Muspelheim, land of the giants, filled with roaring fires and lava. Between them was the great emptiness, the void, Ginnungagap. From Niflheim, ice waves floated out of the great spring Hvergelmir, the origin of all living creatures and that place to which we will return upon crossing over into death's embrace. When the ice waves found their way deep into the void, the heat from ever-burning Muspelheim melted the ice and it began to drip, and from it grew the giant troll Ymir, the mighty jotun god. As Ymir slept, the sweat from under his arms grew giants, and his legs coupled to create Adhumbla, the nurturing cow giant. Ymir's children suckled upon Adhumbla's milk, growing strong and sharp of wit. One day Adhumbla, in her own aching hunger, found a large salty rock of ice that had fallen from the ice waves, and licked its salty surface. The first day she licked the rock, human hair emerged. The second a full head, and by the third day, fair of features, great and mighty Buri was born. And thus the first gods were created."

The archduke paced around the circle, moving ingredients the bedraggled Luz had returned with into position. "And what of Ymir?" Marius asked.

"Father of the giants? When the giant troll died, his body was dragged back to Ginnungagap, and the remains were used to create the world. Blood became the oceans, flesh turned to the lands, bone was used for mountains, hair became forests and plains, and teeth were made into rocks. However, the giants saved his eyelashes, long and beautiful, to use in the first great forge, building Acadia as a gift to the humans." Tryn moved closer, trying to see what the strange chalky powder was that Marius spread over the circle in a downward triangle.

From the far side of the dungeon, one of Tryn's men came running toward the platform.

"And how was it that Ymir came to be dead?" Marius calmly asked, pouring a line of blood in the center of the circle.

"Marquess, sir," Tryn's man interrupted, trying to gather his attention.

Tryn motioned for him to wait, scowling at the fool for his impropriety. Returning his attention to the archduke, who was still crouched around the circle, directing Luz in a new arrangement, Tryn answered with shame. "Archduke, I am your unworthy servant that I do not know the answer to this. I always assumed Ymir died of old age."

Marius rose, almost floating over to the marquess in one fluid motion. "This is the problem," he muttered, more to himself than the marquess. "We are losing our way, and that fool Cronus is doing nothing about it." Tryn was astonished to hear the archduke speak the emperor's name with such open blasphemy. "Ymir was an immortal, something only those of the purest bloodline can hope to attain in this day and age. Time alone could not slay the mighty creator of all," Marius said, baring his rows of razor-sharp teeth and looking very much as if he might spit. "No, great and mighty Ymir did *not* die of old age. Our God of Gods was murdered."

"Murdered?" Tryn said, staring dumbly at the archduke.

"*Murdered,*" Marius confirmed, the mask of disgust still painted across his face. "When Borr, first son of Buri, mated with the jotuness Bestla, their unholy union brought forth the first Aesir, curse upon our existence. It was their three sons, Vé, Vili, and Óðinn, who murdered Ymir out of their jealousy for his unyielding love and favor for the jotnar. With Ymir out of the way, the cretins took the jotnar homeland while our people were lost in mourning." The fires in Marius's eyes flared. "So I ask you again, why did we come to Acadia in the first place?"

Tryn felt his own blood boiling at the thought of the benevolent god Ymir being murdered in his sleep by the treacherous Aesir. "We came here to escape our bondage in Jotunheim *and* to seek vengeance on the Aesir usurpers."

Marius grimaced. "Correct. Filled with resources, Acadia is our chance to reclaim the fatherland and lay waste to the treacherous Aesir. It is here that our ranks have grown again. It is here that we are training our armies to meet the usurpers on the battlefield. It is from Acadia that we will reclaim our mantle as overlords of the seven worlds once more!" The archduke fervently waved his staff about as he spoke.

Tryn found it inspiring to be in the presence of the great jotun. "How will we do this your Lordship?" he asked, excited at the prospect.

"Believe it or not, the human scum are the key to everything," Marius said, gathering himself, though the gluttonous gleam still lingered in his eyes. "Unfortunately, we did not realize it until we had nearly eradicated the scabs."

"How can the humans be the key to our victory over the Aesir?" Tryn asked.

"We waste these scabs on menial tasks that only serve to weaken our ranks. Our empire is festering with laziness," Marius said.

"So we shouldn't use humans as slaves?" Tryn asked, carefully choosing his words. What the archduke was saying bordered on heresy, but a part of Tryn flickered with an unexpected hope, suddenly picturing his gentle Annabel.

"Absolutely not," Marius replied. "Humans are far too useful a commodity to waste on picking grain and cleaning chamberpots. Fodder for the forge, this is what we need to use the scabs for. With these new methods for summoning I've discovered, we can create an army of demonspawn! For each worthless lump of human flesh, we can create a powerful soldier, ready to fill the frontlines of our assault against the Aesir usurpers."

Tryn frowned and looked back at the cages of humans. He pictured Annabel sitting among the emaciated slaves waiting to be dragged into the summoning circle. It pained him to think of her used that way. Surely Annabel was more than just an ingredient or fodder as Marius put it. Tryn's eyes moved over the packed cages, and he wondered if any of these humans knew Annabel.

What if she has brothers or sisters among these poor wretches? The sudden revelation consumed him. Could these humans be no different than her? What if they all had thoughts and feelings?

It was as if a veil were lifted from his face, revealing the suffering souls before him. All his life he had believed that humans were nothing more than savage animals that served no better purpose than biding the jotnar's will. Now he saw row upon row of terrified prisoners, and all he could picture was his sweet, delicate Annabel peeking out from their filthy ranks. A yawning pit grew in Tryn's heart as a vision of Annabel being thrown into the circle of summoning and ripped apart by the demon fires assaulted his senses and gripped him with terror. "H-How many of the h-humans will we need?" he asked, trying to hide the curious trembling of his voice.

Marius circled the marquess, leering, the torchlight flickering across his maniacal grin. "All of them. Every last one. I have already ordered the entire herd from Falzar to be sent here. In two weeks' time, we will begin gathering up all of the scabs in Belikar and bringing them to the dungeons."

"That soon?" Tryn asked. Inside he was shouting at himself to shut up, but his heart suddenly ached irrationally over the idea of losing Annabel. How could he have such strong feelings for one of the humans? And if his feelings were real, how could he allow Annabel or any other human to be turned into a demonspawn?

"Not soon enough. We would have started two decades ago if I had my way. It will take time to train the younger generations in warfare. They have grown lazy and wanton with scabs waiting on their every whim. Then there are the newly spawned demons we will also need to train in warfare and, of course, the gnolls, whom we will use as fodder to bolster our front lines alongside the demonspawn." The archduke was speaking pragmatically, but his excited, wolfish grin grew more and more with each word. "By the time we are ready to march on Asgard, the Aesir will have no hope of stopping our forces."

Tryn tried to pretend he was as excited as the archduke, but inside he could not shake the tormented feeling that Annabel would soon become a demonspawn. Thankfully, Marius did not seem to notice, ordering Luz to step back away from the circle. "Now then, where are those slaves your servant was bringing?"

Tryn looked to his man, who anxiously paced at the base of the stone steps. "Marquess, sir. T-That is w-what I need to tell you," the page whimpered, looking as if he might be sick at any moment.

"Out with it, man, what is it?" Tryn snapped, in no mood to be made a fool in front of the archduke.

With a sideways glance, hoping perhaps there was a way he could escape the situation, Hrar tried to deliver his news. "Well...the slaves you sent us to fetch, sir...well...they...they're..."

"Yes, yes, what of them? Where are they?" Tryn snapped, sneering at the jotun's sniveling incompetence.

Hrar gulped, looking over Tryn's shoulder at the fierce archduke, who also glared down at him. "They've disappeared, my lord. The slaves are gone."

Chapter 17: Parting Ways

Logan Walker waved farewell to his new Agma friends as they disappeared into the jungle on their way back home. They had traveled together all through the night, putting a great distance between themselves and the Agmawor camp. But now, with their goals heading in opposite directions, it was time to say goodbye to Kol and his companions.

The Agma had insisted Tiko join them, but the lizardman would have no part in it, refusing to separate from his new friends and their task. He asked only that the Agma tell his tale to the chieftain and report that he was safe and alive. Besides, Kalilah waited for him back at the White Tree. So the Agma headed back to their camp, and the companions set out for the second time to retrieve the Aegis.

The group stopped to rest, and this time Logan fell fast asleep. When he awoke, it was with a feeling of complete refreshment. Back at the Agmawor camp, he had kept beating himself over not sensing the cannibals closing in on them sooner. He vowed to never be in that position again and wanted to be sharp of wit.

By the time they returned to the circle of willow trees where the Aegis lay, dawn had come and gone, leaving the heavy afternoon daystar to rest overhead, baking the jungle like an oven. Sounds of animals could be heard all around them as they neared the sacred grove: birds chirping, woodpeckers searching for food, squirrels chattering, and somewhere, nearby, the growling of a drake hunting for prey.

"Well, Morgana always used to say that second time's the charm," Logan said, breaking the silence as they entered the clearing. "Or was that the third time?"

The drake's carcass had been nearly picked clean by wild animals. Logan shuddered, wondering how many dire wolves or imps it had taken to leave the pile of bones and sinew that remained where the drake had been slain.

The Aegis was no less stunning on second discovery, half buried in the soil and overgrown with weeds. The four of them had weapons drawn as they approached the ancient suit of armor, dwarfed in its shadow, and kept their eyes peeled for wandering drakes. Logan pointed at the helmet with two fingers then twirled them in the air, making a circle. Tiko followed his lead and made his way around the Aegis, skirting an unburied boot so he could scout the area. Once they were satisfied they were alone, weapons were put away.

"Tiko," Logan asked, "do you mind giving us some eyes in the air?" The lizardman nodded and scaled a nearby willow, surveying the jungle for approaching enemies. "Right then, where were we, Nero?" Logan asked.

The android ran his fingers over the inscription he had translated a couple days ago. "It would seem the armor is brought to life by the heart of a dragon. Seeing as the beasts have not been seen in close to four centuries, we determined the drake's heart should suffice."

Logan nodded. "However, we could be wrong, and then this whole journey has been for naught." He sorely hoped that was not the case and searched the tall grass for his pack, which had been left when they were captured.

"We just have to figure out where to put the blasted thing," Bipp grumbled, scaling the armor in search of a solution. He pulled his stubby legs up onto the armor's breastplate and, precariously balanced, walked across the arm and carefully inspected each fold in the armor. He had to brush off dirt and tug away vines which had long ago latched themselves to the Aegis.

Logan spotted his pack, snapping his fingers and pointing at it. When he opened it, a foot-long centipede darted out of the interior, slithering like a snake on hundreds of tiny legs. "Yuck," he said, brushing away the intruder and grasping the purple and black swirled crystal. It was heavy as marble, filling his whole palm.

"Any luck figuring out where we put this?" Logan called to his friend, blocking the daylight with his forearm to get a look at Bipp on top of the armor. Bipp shrugged, lost in thought as he searched. "What do you think, Nero? Any guesses on where we put the drake's heart?" Logan asked, walking over to Nero, who was studying the inscription for clues.

"Nero is not made for guessing, Master Logan," the android explained. "It is in my programming to apply logical reasoning on the best possible course of action. This is based on a series of—"

"Whoa, whoa, settle down, I get it." Logan patted the androgynous man's back. "So what is your best reasoning then?"

"Nero does not have an answer," the android replied, frowning that he could not be of more use to them.

Logan gave the forlorn android a warm smile. "Listen, Nero, what you did back there…that was really something." Before the android could interject, Logan shook his head and continued, "I know, I know, you're going to tell me it's only in your programming or some other such nonsense."

"I think I found it!" Bipp exclaimed, almost slipping off the curved breastplate in his excitement.

Logan chuckled at the gnome. "Okay, I'll be there in one sec. Now you listen to me, Nero. What I saw back at that Agmawor camp was not some hunk of bolts running through its *directives*. That was pure intuition and ingenuity. I don't think you can be *programmed* with that kind of behavior."

Nero felt something inside his wiring tickle, a familiar echo in his binary circuits that drifted into being with Logan's appreciative smile. Logan held out his hand and grasped Nero in a heartfelt handshake, and Nero knew, for the first time in his life cycle, that he had truly made a friend. He did not know how to feel about the revelation, or how the strange concept of '*feeling*' was coming over him in the first place. However, when Logan clambered over the armor to meet the gnome, who was pumping his legs and struggling to pull thick vines away from a corner of the breastplate, the android was surprised to feel a smile spread across his face.

"Let me see what you have there," Logan said, taking Bipp's spot. He tore away the vines with his mechanical fingers, plucking the thin tuberous growths like candy ribbons. Beneath the mass of intertwined growth was a solid breastplate, curved to a point at the upper center. "Hmm, nothing here," Logan muttered.

"That's where your untrained human eyes deceive you," Bipp teased, sliding under Logan's arm to wiggle his way over the breastplate. With the vines cleared away, the gnome easily ran a stubby finger across a hairline joint, knocking on it at intervals until he came to a spot that did not echo as hollowly. With a greedy little laugh, the gnome pressed an unseen button, popping the armor open to reveal a small chamber just big enough for a dragon's heart.

Logan gaped at the opaque, smoky crimson crystal inside. It was three times larger than the one he had taken from the drake but splintered into three pieces. Bipp carefully fished out the shards and motioned for Logan to hand him the drake's heart. The gnome's hair began to stand up as he lowered the crystal into the chamber. Energy crackled from within the tiny portal, trying to connect with the raw power source, and it made Bipp look like a mad scientist. Though, gauging by his satisfied grin, Logan could see he was not harmed in any way. Bipp carefully let the heart slide inside the tiny chamber. Light began building up in the core of the drake's heart, and he quickly pulled his fingers away before closing the lid.

As the cover fit in place, the faceplate of the helmet slid back, and the entire chest began to slide down toward its feet. Logan grabbed Bipp just in time to save him from tumbling over the side while trying to keep his own balance atop the moving sheet of mithril.

"Great leaping lizards of Baradin!" Bipp gasped, looking inside the exposed chamber. From Tiko's perch in the tree, he too could see the skeletal remains of the Aegis's last owner.

"Who was he?" Logan asked no one in particular. The man had been tall, but his flesh had long since rotted away, and the scraps of cloth remaining were nothing more than formless tatters.

"Looks like a king, no doubt," Bipp whispered, eyeing the skeleton's gold crown, which was still intact if a bit tarnished. The crown came to three points, each adorned with a different gemstone—a ruby, an emerald, and an amethyst. They matched the three gems set into the pendant hanging off a gold chain around his neck, set in an upward V shape.

"What do we do with him?" Logan asked, licking his blistered lips.

"You're always talking about wanting to search for treasure. Well, here you go!" Bipp said, jubilantly laughing at their good fortune. Logan shared his friend's mirth, but inside he felt hollow at the prospect of picking this honorable man's corpse clean.

The two of them worked together to pull the skeleton out of the chamber. It was surprising how well the bones had held up over time. Bipp figured it had something to do with how sealed off the body was from air all these years. The gnome wanted to just heave the skeleton over the side of the armor, but Logan insisted they carefully take it down and give the lost king a proper burial. Nero pitched in, and they dug a makeshift grave in the soil with their bare hands. When the shallow plot was ready, the pair stripped the king of his treasure. Logan placed the crown in his bag and put the chain around his neck. Bipp took the king's five rings and placed them one by one into his pouch, but not without biting them first to see if they were real gold. When they were done, the three of them lowered the king's skeleton into the grave.

"Should we say something?" Bipp asked.

Logan felt that it would be appropriate but had no idea what would be good. "Nero, do you know any burial speeches or something from Ithiki?"

"Perhaps it is proper to say:

Farewell ye brave wanderer,
Set about on your final journey.
May the light of Yggrdassil bathe your soul,

And may the Valkyries find you in the halls of Valhalla.

With that said, they patted down the dirt, covering the stranger and bidding him farewell. When they were done, Logan climbed back up the armor and stretched, cracking his knuckles in clasped hands. "Okay, here goes nothing," he said, climbing into the chamber and lying on his back, facing the sky.

There were holes inside where he felt his arms and legs should go. Once his limbs stretched all the way, his feet came to rest on something that clicked in place, closing around his leather boots. Logan's heart thundered in his chest, but he did not relent. Probing with his fingers, he found bars to either side that pulled into his palms. Another clicking sound came as gauntlets magically formed around his hands, and the entire breastplate began to close again.

"Are you okay in there?" Bipp hollered up the side of the armor.

Tiko could see Logan and shouted down from the tree, "His head is still above the chest, where the helmet is."

But as the Agma spoke, the faceplate too slid back in place, and a great whirring sound erupted from deep within the armor. For a flashing instant, Logan felt the inescapable terror of one locked in a coffin, buried alive. But just as suddenly as the feeling was upon him, it washed away. Inside the Aegis, he was rapidly covered in a metal suit of armor his own size. When he moved inside the magical suit, the massive outer armor of the Aegis copied him.

"Step back," he said, his voice carried by some mystical means, growing in volume from the helmet. Trusting that his companions had done as instructed, Logan moved the mighty armored hand down to the ground, pushing away from the soil to pull the other arm from the ground in a cloud of dirt. He was amazed to feel each fingertip graze the soil, though his hands were firmly tucked away deep inside the armor. Once both arms were free, he was able to get the armor to rise, dirt tumbling off the Aegis in rivulets and layers of vines tearing away from the ground. When he stood fully upright, he was at eye level with Tiko, twelve feet up in the tree. Bipp and Nero stood below him like two toys to be played with.

"This is the coolest thing we have ever done!" Bipp called up, jumping up and down. Logan gave him a thumbs up and began laughing.

"Well, my friends," Logan said in a booming voice, "I think it is time we got back to the White Tree and showed our companions what the ice giants have to look forward to!"

The short, round-bellied jotun slaver, Kallix, peeked around the corner, looking both directions down the palace hall. The soldiers were all busy gathering for a meeting with the duke and no one was about. Now was his chance. He had waited for almost a week, sneaking in and out of the palace grounds for some opportunity to be alone with his former companion Annabel. Ever since the marquess had swept away with the slave girl, he had kept her under tight lock and key.

Kallix shuffled into the hall, making a beeline for the door to the marquess's apartments. He paused in front of it, making a pretense that he was readying to knock while he checked once more to see if anyone was about. Without a second thought, he let a pin slide into the keyhole, expertly working the lock. He heard the click of the mechanism unlocking and cracked open the door, slipping inside and gently letting it close behind him.

He stood in silence, cocking an ear to listen. He needed to be absolutely certain Annabel was alone. *Hmm, quite a lavish abode for a nobleman who can only afford one gold piece for my slave,* he brooded to himself, taking in the rich design of the royal apartment. Once he was sure there was no one else in the rooms, he headed toward the back.

Before he made it halfway across the room, the bedroom door creaked open. Kallix froze midstride.

Annabel stuck her head out the door and locked eyes on him. She studied him ruefully, up and down, before stepping out of the room with a wooden club in hand.

Kallix appraised the club and chuckled. "Never could sneak up on ya, girlie."

Annabel grinned wolfishly and set the club down against the wall. She ran across the room and greeted him with a hug.

He smiled warmly and hugged her back. "Oh girlie, I've been so worried about ya." He pushed her back and held her shoulders, studying her eyes. "Has the bastard done ya any harm?"

Annabel shook her head. "No, he's actually been quite…caring?" It was hard for her to make sense of the way the marquess acted and even more difficult to give words to how that made her feel.

"Well, at least that's something then," he brooded.

"What took you so long?"

Kallix' cheeks grew red and puffy. "There's gratitude for ya. It's not so easy sneaking into the royal palace, you know."

Annabel giggled and clapped his shoulder. "I'm only teasing you, ya old toad." He chuckled at that. "But seriously, I was beginning to think you were never going to get me out of here."

Kallix's face grew serious.

"What is it?" Annabel asked.

"The resistance wants you to stay put."

"What? How could they abandon me after all I've—"

"It's not like that. Think about the opportunity we have here. To have a member of our ranks right in the very apartments of the marquess hisself?"

Annabel had thought about it. She had thought long and hard of the fact that she was living in the palace. It was the last place she'd ever expected to find herself. For years they had been plotting how to gain agency inside the place with nary an opportunity. It was next to impossible to get the servants living here to join their cause and even less likely that one of the royal family would take on an outside slave. The jotnar were notoriously paranoid toward outsiders.

She squared off with Kallix. He was clearly torn about the idea of leaving her here, but there was something greater on his mind at the moment and she needed to know what it was. She arched a brow and folded her arms across her chest, throwing him a shrug.

Kallix knew that gesture. Annabel was silently telling him to get to the damned point. He reached inside his vest and produced a finely carved dagger. "They want you to cut the marquess down."

For once Annabel was startled. She took a step back and gasped, quickly snapping her head to the apartment entrance. "Put that thing away," she snarled, gently pushing down on his forearm.

"Not to worry, girlie, there are no soldiers around. Trust me, I've been biding my time for this conversation. We are completely alone."

Annabel shook her head uncertainly. "If one of the duke's men finds you in the palace with a weapon..."

Kallix scowled. "Don't ya think I know that? Come on now, take this and tuck it away somewhere safe." He took her wrist and turned it, gently placing the dagger in her palm.

"But, I...I'm no assassin."

"Tell that to Merchant Kellermen."

"That was different," Annabel almost whined. "He discovered our secret. I had to..."

Kallix held up his hand. "I know that. No sense in dragging it all up out of the bog again. Listen, they want you to do this as soonas possible. There is something big stirring, and you may not have much time."

"But..." Annabel's voice trailed off, her eyes downcast to the floor with a frown.

Kallix studied her for a long moment. "What's the matter? This is what we've been working toward for years now. Don't tell me you're having doubts. I've told ya a hundred times, the only way to change our city is to take it by force."

"I know that," she insisted, "and I agree. We will only ever succeed through strength of force and indomitable will."

Kallix smiled proudly at her. "That's right. Then what's eating at ya?"

"It's just, the marquess, he's...he's not a bad person," she mumbled.

"Not a bad person? He tortures jotun in the dungeons and turns humans into demonspawn. How much worse can he get?"

Annabel nodded reluctantly. "I know...you're right. But the way his father treats him...sometimes it seems like he's as much of a slave as the rest of us, just in a different way."

Kallix placed a hand over hers, gently folding her fingers over the hilt of the dagger, and pushed her chin up to look at him. "Think about your mother. This will strike a massive blow to our enemies. Your actions here could be the difference between failure and securing our victory in the rebellion."

A fire grew in the back of her eyes. Annabel clenched her teeth and firmly nodded. She accepted the mantle of responsibility that the resistance was placing on her.

"It will be done."

Chapter 18: Resistance

"The room is right back here," a tall jotun resistance member name Gaurmin informed Corbin and his companions, wearing a devilish smirk as they made their way deeper into the granary warehouse.

Corbin found he quite liked the roguish jotun, who had rescued them from the marquess's errand boy. He felt no compassion for the human slavers when they were cut down in the street. The idea of it made Corbin frown in contemplation as he walked around tall stacks of crates. His sensibilities screamed that it was wrong for him to feel any sort of affinity toward one of the ice giants. After all, their kind had driven his race to the brink of extinction. Yet his gut said that this was right. Not for the first time in the last couple months, Corbin realized things were not always as black and white as he once believed, growing up in sheltered Riverbell. Sometime it was more like varying shades of grey. *But then was it right for me to feel such hatred toward the slavers, who themselves were merely victims of this cruel world?* he wondered, not broadcasting his thoughts to his companions.

They traveled all the way to the back of the warehouse, a lot farther than the slaves normally worked. The group came to a doorway, guarded on either side by more jotnar, each armed with tall iron spears. Stur fought his urge to reach for his broadsword, an instinct born from years of fighting these creatures. His heavy muscles flexed at the sight of the jotnar as he worked his hand open then closed.

"Rest easy, these are our allies," Gaurmin said, seeing the human struggling with himself. The jotnar stepped to either side of the giant wooden doors and bowed before opening them. Kyra awkwardly bowed in return, feeling unsure that she should ever do so for one of the blue-skinned devils.

"The resistance awaits your arrival inside," Gaurmin said, gesturing that they should enter while cautiously looking back the way they had come.

"I don't understand," Corbin said. "What is this place? How can the resistance meet back here without alerting the city watch?"

"This portion of the granary was an old processing plant which long ago fell into disuse. It was originally created to replicate human weapons." Gaurmin saw Corbin's puzzled expression and explained further. "When Emperor Cronus first conquered Acadia, he was deeply intrigued by Acadian technology, believing it would give our race the edge needed to destroy the Aesir. However, as time passed, our people realized they would not need to worry about battles with the Asgardians anytime soon, and so they experimented less and less with human weapons, which are inferior to the soaring magic and battle prowess of the jotnar anyhow."

"I see. Are you not joining us though?" Corbin asked, surprised to find he felt disappointment at the idea of parting ways with the cavalier jotun so soon.

Gaurmin shook his head, once more motioning for them to enter. "My men and I will wait out here and guard the chamber. Hurry now. They are all going to begin the meeting soon."

"All?" Corbin asked Stur, who never took his eyes off the armed jotnar surrounding him.

When they entered the wide room, Corbin was alarmed by the sheer volume of people inside. It was a perfect place for the resistance to meet, since a network of tunnels under the city connected at the base of the large warehouse. When Corbin and the others came through the door, they were greeted by a crowd standing on a landing that ran around the large, two-story factory room. Eir waited by the doors, ready to greet them with a warm smile, and Fivan stood at her side. The pair of them were surrounded by not only jotnar but also humans and gnolls, all deeply engaged in discussion and debate. Eir motioned for them to follow her down a nearby flight of wooden steps to the lower level, where even more resistance members waited.

"Feel like sardines in a can here," Stur complained out of the side of his mouth to Kyra. When they reached the center of the room, a slender jotun with white streaks in his navy blue shoulder-length locks held up his hands for silence. It took a few minutes for the noise to die down as eye upon eye rested on them.

"We're like the prize ham at a festival," Corbin muttered. It was hard not to be intimidated under the watchful scrutiny of all these resistance members.

"My dear friends, I thank you for meeting us here tonight, and on such short notice," the group's leader began, circling as he spoke. His voice carried well in the acoustics of the room.

Before he could continue, one of the gnolls growled down from the rampart. "What's the big idea calling us all together like this, Ezekiel?" Sparked by the dog-faced humanoid, dozens of others chimed in, voicing their outrage at taking such a risk and demanding to know why all the subterfuge.

Ezekiel waved his hands in the air until everyone quieted once more. "Please, my friends, hear me out. Long have we toiled behind the scenes, doing whatever we can to quell the hatred that has been bred into our society, that burning anger which the older generation cannot put behind them."

Corbin saw many nods behind pain-streaked eyes. He tried to imagine what horrors these humans had endured. For the first time he was also able to see it from the perspective of the jotnar, imagining what it would be like to stand by, helpless for years, as defenseless innocents were tormented both physically and mentally. How would he be able to live with himself? How would he ever be able to share a moment of happiness with Elise? Knowing that others were being tortured, beaten, abused, and even murdered, how could he live with himself in any other state than resigned despair?

That was what he saw in the eyes of the resistance as their leader spurred his people on with the announcement that Fivan had finally joined their ranks. When the old man stepped forward, he was greeted with a great ruckus of clapping and many huzzahs.

"Oh, but that is not all the news we have to share with you!" Ezekiel continued, feeding off the wave of hope moving through the crowd. "For today, I would like to introduce you to our newest allies. This is Kyra Tarvano, Marshal of Agarta. The marshal has a massive army of trained warriors who even now are waiting on the outskirts of Belikar for the time to strike. And that time is now!" Ezekiel announced with fervor, waving his clenched fist in the air. Ezekiel's elation grew as the crowd went mad at his proclamations, cheering and stomping their feet in glee.

"Hold," a rough-looking older jotun shouted above the din, raising his arms to silence everyone that he might speak.

Ezekiel scowled. "What is it, Mundas?" Corbin heard members of the resistance groaning at the ever-cynical older jotun.

Mundas gripped the wooden rail for balance and addressed the gathering. "How can we trust these newcomers? Who is to say these three, whom none of us have ever met before, are not in actuality spies who came here from the archduke's airship?"

The question hung openly in the air, planting the seed of suspicion in many of the resistance members' minds. "Mundas speaks pragmatically," a gnoll called out. "I mean, who among us beside Eir has vouched for these Agartans we have been hearing whispers of?"

And just like that, the room erupted into chaos, members arguing and debating over the best course of action.

Ezekiel had to call over the din several times before everyone quieted so that he could speak once more. "My friends, please calm yourselves. I can feel you, I hear your trepidation. Who among us can be expected not to harbor some fear at this moment, now that our time to overthrow the evil duke is at hand?" Every eye intently followed the leader of the resistance as he slowly turned to address the balcony above. "But you must not give in to these base fears, for they are senseless! The moment we have fought for all these years is being thrust upon us, and we must snatch it and rejoice. It is only together that we will knock down these walls of oppression!" The group was getting excited at their leader's almost fanatical speech. "Now I ask you, my friends, will you join me in this fight?"

Kyra was impressed by Ezekiel's ability to sway the crowd, which only a moment before was ready to debate for hours. Everyone was back to cheering, including the cynical Mundas. Ezekiel opened his arms and smiled at the balcony then proudly turned to Healer Eir.

Eir was just about to speak when the smile faded from Ezekiel's face, replaced by a puzzled frown. Everyone in the back of the ramparts was rapidly falling silent. At the rear of the room, on the balcony, one of the participants was laughing heavily.

Corbin narrowed his eyes as the crowd began to part, revealing Gaurmin. The jotun's eyes were bloodshot, wide and crazed, and he wore a crooked smile as he laughed at them. The crowd grew stiff and indignant over the rogue's hysteria, as if they were the butt of some inside joke only he knew.

"Gaurmin, what is the meaning of this intrusion?" Ezekiel asked, aggravated by the rogue's interruption. When the jotun continued laughing without a response, Ezekiel shouted, "If you have some apprehension in our course of action, don't just stand there laughing like a fool. Spit it out!"

The rogue abruptly stopped laughing and his face grew serious. He looked directly at Corbin with a twitching eye, taking two steps forward. "I...I'm sorry."

Gaurmin's face turned a pale blue and blood began running from the side of his mouth and nose. The crowd stumbled backward out of the rogue's way as he took two crooked steps forward and fell over the rail, landing with the crunch of his skull hitting the wooden floorboards. Gasps abounded upon seeing a sword firmly stuck in the rogue's spine.

Duke Thiazi stepped into the room in full black steel armor from neck to toe, slowly clapping his hands and sneering at the trapped men and women. The fear that hit the crowd was so substantial that Corbin thought he could actually smell it, acrid and bitter. The crowd started to flee, but armed soldiers quickly filed into the room, surrounding the outside of the upper landing with crossbows in hand.

"Having fun, little children?" Duke Thiazi asked, laughing at Ezekiel, who stood below, opening and closing his mouth. "My, my...what *are* we all doing out so late?"

"Duke, I...," Ezekiel began.

Thiazi held up his hand to silence the jotun, pressing the finger of his gauntlet against his lips. "Shh, hush now, Ezekiel. There is no worry to be had. After all, why should one of my earls need fear forgetting to invite me to his little soiree?"

"You bastard!" a human screamed, throwing herself at the duke with a dagger in hand. With little effort, Thiazi barely turned, catching the would-be assassin by her throat and lifting her in the air. "My, what feisty entertainment you have for us this evening," he said, before motioning for his man-at-arms, Balistor, to come forward with his long bronze spear. Thiazi laughed as he dropped the flailing woman onto the spear so she could writhe in agony.

Thiazi turned his attention back to the crowd. "That's the thing about these humans you so dearly love. They make far better pets than soldiers. For example...," The duke motioned for Fivan to come to him. The old man dutifully scurried over to his master, getting down on all fours and leaning in as the duke lovingly patted his head.

The dog! He ratted us out. Kyra's growl ran through Corbin and Stur's minds, along with a flashing image of her bashing in the old traitor's skull with a mallet.

"Well, at least now we understand how he survived this long," Corbin murmured to his companions.

"When given the choice between freedom and servitude, the scabs will always choose the latter," Thiazi said, as if he were addressing a meeting of his intellectual peers. All the while he stroked Fivan's head, and the old man closed his eyes and smiled warmly at his master's affection. "What you lot have failed to comprehend is that which a scab truly fears. The idea of having to make their own choices terrifies these pathetic creatures. They depend on us. They *need* someone to keep them tame, and the scabs know it. Deep down in their hearts, they know it."

Corbin wondered if the duke was trying to convince some of the jotnar resistance members in the room of the righteousness in the jotnar way of life.

"Lies!" Eir shouted, interrupting his self-righteous bravado. "Humans are people! They feel the same emotions as you or me! These creatures are fully capable of logic and *deserve* to live productive lives in the eyes of the gods."

The crowd of resistance was bolstered by the healer's brave words, murmuring in agreement.

"Oh, my dear, dear Healer Eir, you dare to call me a liar?" Thiazi asked, feigning that her accusation wounded his honor. "Do I skulk around in secret meetings, plotting the overthrow of my government? Do you see *me* breaking the laws of our emperor? No! That is a hapless existence that only you choose to live. How easily everyone forgets what Acadia was like before we came here. The scabs deserve freedom? Tell me, Eir, what did the scabs do when they had that privilege?" Thiazi waited for the healer to answer, but she could not, looking at the floor instead. "Ah, but the truth is a stinging blade, isn't it? Because even beneath the layers of fantasy you all are mired in, you know the truth. The humans fought wars. That's what they did. They fought wars over who deserved the most land, and all the while they stripped the world of every natural resource they could get their greedy little paws on."

Kyra was filled with an overflowing hatred for the duke. It was so strong Corbin and Stur could feel it in their minds. Except she did not hate him for all the reasons one would expect. Kyra despised the duke because she knew in her heart he was correct.

"The humans were no different than wild animals when we came here. Can you even imagine if they were allowed to travel to the other worlds? Why, surely the disease-infested scabs would spread like a cancer, stripping and destroying. We did them a favor, gave the weak little animals a better life in servitude to us. But just like every good pet—" Thiazi bit his lip and gripped the top of Fivan's skull firmly in his giant armored palm. "—there comes a time when you just *have* to put them down."

Baring his fangs, the duke snapped Fivan's neck, dropping the traitor to the floorboards and laughing at the horrified expressions surrounding him.

Thiazi's amusement was cut short when a dagger spiraled through the air directly for his head. He narrowly managed to avoid the sharp blade as it drew a line of blood across his high cheekbone. Feeling the cut, Thiazi's copper eyes opened wide as saucers at the blood on his fingers. "You dare defy me?" he roared at Stur, who had thrown the blade.

Kyra stepped forward, blocking the warrior as her companions took her cue and tossed their branches to the floor, dispelling Isaac's illusion.

Looking as if he had suddenly gone mad, the duke stared at the three of them in open shock, tightly gripping the wooden rail. "What madness is this?"

"Come down here and fight like a human, you coward!" Corbin shouted, flipping the voulge over his head and getting into a fighting stance while Kyra unstrung her shield, which twirled into place, and brandished her short sword threateningly.

"Kill them! Kill all of them!" Thiazi roared, tearing a chunk of the rail away and flipping his black steel broadsword over his head.

Crossbows twanged all around the room as men and women began shouting, pressing against the armored soldiers. Entire rows of resistance members fell under the brutal assault, but in the close quarters, the soldiers had no chance to reload their weapons and had to step back from the maddened mob. The duke had sorely underestimated the will these people would have to stay alive. Half of the soldiers were beaten to death before they managed to get their weapons drawn. But then swords and maces began tearing through the unarmed crowd.

Corbin ran like a panther through the throng of people, hopping on the wooden rail of the staircase and running up it to meet the duke in battle. Stur took a more direct approach, throwing himself like a ram into the first soldiers down the steps. Corbin could hear the first giant's bones cracking as Stur squeezed him with the strength of an ox. Kyra viciously laid waste to any of the duke's men that dared get in her way. Deftly, she rolled over Stur's back, stabbing then flicking back and guarding his flank.

When Corbin reached the top of the steps, he had to somersault off the railing, over an eight-foot-tall warrior's swinging blade. Landing on his toes, Corbin fell to a crouch and swept his leg across the dangerous jotun's shins. When the warrior hit the ground, Corbin rolled on his side and shoved the tip of his voulge into the jotun's throat.

Before he could rise, the duke was already there, thrusting a broadsword at the strange pale-skinned human. If Kyra had not made it to the top of the steps and thrown herself at them, Corbin would have lost his head. Instead the duke's broadsword clanged like a bell across the marshal's shield as she and Corbin tumbled backward. They had to be quick on their feet and were immediately lost in the swirl of bloody chaos.

When Stur reached the top of the steps, a giant cleaved the gnoll he had just saved nearly in half, the blood spattering Stur's chest and face. Wrenching his sword from the furry humanoid, the giant laughed at Stur's look of rage. "Are you next, little scab?" he asked.

Stur roared like the lion emblazoned on his shoulder plate and leapt in the air to smash the foul giant's helmet into the side of his face, shattering the jotun's broad nose underneath. The brutal soldier heaved his sword at Stur, who deflected it with his own and moved in with parry upon parry. The giant was bewildered to find himself being driven back by a puny human and furiously fought back. This was what Stur had hoped for—he had seen too many powerful fighters let rage cloud their judgment and fall on the battlefield. Watching every move the powerful jotun thrust at him, Stur found his opening, flinging his own body sideways to knock the fiend back and sweep his massive broadsword across the cretin's throat.

Stur did not even wait around while the disbelieving swordsman clutched his throat, which spouted a spray of blood through his fingers. Shifting his attention to a nearby soldier fighting several humans and a lone jotun, Stur flinched to see one of them cut down. The resistance was sorely outmatched and underequipped for this battle. Where the duke's men had black steel armor and finely crafted weapons, the resistance members wore leather or robes and brandished daggers or rust-riddled weapons.

Duke Thiazi was cutting down humans left and right, blood soaking the front of his armor. He was searching for the pale-skinned scab and his pretty little sidekick. Corbin caught sight of the jotun over the shoulder of the giant he was locked in combat with. Without hesitation, the duke growled, running in and cutting down his own man to get at Corbin. Madness filled the duke's eyes as he lusted for the intruder's death. Before he could reach Corbin, Kyra ran across his path, flinging herself upward so that her shield jarred the duke's jaw, shattering one of his teeth.

Spitting blood, Thiazi swung his sword with such fury that Kyra was knocked heavily to the floor, where she lay on her back, dazed. Corbin jabbed his voulge for the duke's chin, but the giant was quick to react, snapping his head to the side and catching the shaft with his hand, stopping it just before it pierced his skin. Corbin tried to wrench the weapon back, but Thiazi's grip was unyielding, and he looked at the pale human with a devious grin before pressing one boot onto Kyra's shield, which she had weakly brought up to block her chest.

"Is this what you meant by fighting like a human, scab?" he growled, pressing his heel harder onto the pinned woman. Corbin tried to shove forward, throwing his body into the maneuver, but the giant just laughed at him, wrenching the voulge from his grip as if plucking a toy from a child. "It's a pity I have to kill such a pretty little thing, but you really should learn to protect your possessions better, boy," Thiazi said, taunting him with a vicious, bloody smile as he pressed harder on Kyra's screaming body.

Corbin ducked as the duke swung his stolen voulge at him. "I see you jotnar are as dumb as you look," he goaded the giant, provoking another swing, this one much harder to dodge. "I guess if you had any brains in that fat head of yours, you would know." Corbin shifted his body into a feint for Thiazi's side, then leapt out of the way as the blade of his voulge crashed into the floor.

"Know what?!" the bloodthirsty duke howled, wishing the scab would stay still.

Kyra's blade tore straight through the duke's armor, goring Thiazi's thigh like a stuck pig. "That Kyra Tarvano is nobody's possession!" she snarled, twisting the blade and pulling it free. The duke roared in agony, dropping the voulge and stumbling backward.

Their victory was short-lived, as Corbin noted more of the duke's men flooding into the building. There was no way they could reach the exit, not through that sea of armored giants cutting down the resistance members as if they were weeds.

Thiazi roared again, gritting his shattered teeth and standing tall despite the river of blood flowing from the deep wound in his leg. Thiazi pointed the tip of his broadsword at Kyra. "You will die this day, every last one of you. And when I am finished drinking your blood, I *will* find your people hiding outside my city, and I *will* kill every last one of them!" Thiazi's eyes were bloodshot and spittle flew from his purple lips.

The entire building began violently quaking, stopping most of the battle in its tracks. Human and giant alike looked around for the cause, terrified the building was suddenly going to fall around them. Thiazi was shouting for his men to fall back, knowing this was not of his doing, when the floor exploded outward in a blinding flash of light.

Through the shower of stones thundered a dragon, its body one long serpentine coil of golden scales completely ablaze. The ice giants scrambled over one another to get out of the way of the fire, which terrified them more than any other thing in the world could. It was too late for five of the soldiers, as the dragon barreled through the bottom of the rampart with snapping jaws, tearing away a large section. The giants screamed in terror as they fell into the beast's gaping maw, and it began spitting streams of fire in every direction, setting the room ablaze.

Kyra ran to the ledge, looking down the crater into the sewers, where Isaac commanded his spell, white light spilling from his eye sockets. Corbin snatched his voulge from the floorboards and joined her, calling for Stur, who was busy using his body as a shield so that the resistance members did not get burned. When he saw what the young hunter was pointing at, Stur felt a surge of hope, directing the resistance members nearby to follow him down the steps.

When they reached the bottom, Isaac shifted the dragon to blast a fireball into the far wall, opening a large hole for the trapped people to escape through.

Eir ran to them to help, but Corbin held her back. "No, you must go! You have to hide and prepare. We will be back!" he vowed.

The healer reluctantly left them, fleeing the building with her people in droves. Knowing he could wait no longer, Stur said a blessing for those who could not reach her and let his sword shatter the beams holding the steps so that the duke's men might not follow. Without another word, he hopped down into the exposed sewer and ran after his friends while Isaac tied off the spell to play itself out for hours. By the time the duke realized the fires were not even hot, the remnants of the resistance members were flooding the streets and slipping into the night.

"This is not the way we came earlier!" Corbin said.

"It's close enough," Isaac called back.

"Are they following?" Kyra shouted over the deafening roar of the dragon illusion they had left behind.

"I see none, milady!" Stur replied.

Soon they came to a sewer entrance, different than the one they had entered the city through, and Isaac pointed his staff at the grate, letting loose an explosive bolt of lightning, which bent the bars outward. When Corbin went to slip through the bent iron, the mage halted him. "Step aside, lad," he instructed, casting a cloud of freezing mist over the red hot metal. "Stur, if you please."

Stur gave the gate a heavy kick, shattering it into shards and stepping through so that he could help his companions from the other side. Kyra hopped easily through the opening, but Isaac needed help, using his staff and Stur's shoulder to balance himself.

"Damn it. We're not alone, guys," Kyra warned.

Five yards down the length of the wall, a group of five armed jotnar waited outside their original sewer entrance to the city.

"I told you we were close," Isaac bragged, and Corbin suddenly thought it was probably a good thing after all that they had not found their old path.

One of the jotnar pointed at them with a raised sword, calling for his comrades.

"Better make this quick," Corbin warned, as they readied to fight the armored fiends. A flick of fire raced past his shoulder, crashing into the center of the ice giants, who flew in every direction to get away from the flames.

Isaac made time for a quick wink and then ran away from the city. It did not take the stunned companions long to follow, hoping to put enough distance between themselves and the city of giants before Duke Thiazi caught wind that they had escaped.

From the top of Belikar's eastern wall, a brooding Duke Thiazi watched the three strange humans fleeing across the desolate expanse below.

Archduke Marius rushed up the parapet, snarling his outrage. "What is this, Thiazi? Is this how you run your city, letting weak-minded fools conspire revolution against the Empire?" Thiazi did not even bother looking in his direction. The insolent response only furthered Marius's anger. He gazed out over the wall to see what was so important that the duke could not answer him, and his eyes went wide. "You are letting them get away? Shoot the scabs down!"

Thiazi's soldier lifted his longbow high into the air, but the duke raised a hand to stop him. Marius slithered into his view. "How dare you overrule my order?"

The duke finally met Marius's eye. "I know why you are really here," he said, coldly revealing his newfound knowledge. "You're not here for some empirical inspection."

The archduke blanched and his upper lip twitched nervously. The duke had paid good gold to Marius's man-at-arms for the knowledge. The archduke had fallen out of favor with the emperor and was banished from the capitol city indefinitely, sent to Belikar where he could not cause any more problems for Emperor Cronus.

The archduke quickly recovered his composure. "Inspection or not, the emperor will hear of this. And what do you believe he will do to you when he learns you let a resistance fester?"

Thiazi rubbed some of the dried blood out of his beard, returning his attention to the fleeing humans. This far away, they looked like tiny ants running up the rocky hillside beside his weathered watchtowers. "I suspect he will invite me back to the capitol, while you stay here to rule Belikar, *Archduke*."

Marius scoffed at the duke's outlandish claim, wondering if perhaps the jotun had lost too much blood during his battle. He *was* bleeding pretty steadily from a wound in his thigh.

"I see your confusion," Thiazi said calmly, "and here I thought *you* were supposed to be the smart one. Tell me, Marius, what does one do when they have a rodent problem?" When Marius did not reply, Thiazi directed his attention to the tiny dots that were just reaching the top of the rocky ridge. "Here I'll help you. They find...?"

Marius looked at the duke with a newfound respect. Thiazi was far more clever than he had initially realized. "You find their nest," Marius finished just as the humans disappeared over the ridge.

Duke Thiazi smiled darkly, nodding and never taking his eyes off the ridge.

"It's getting late. Decima has almost set," Bipp called up to Logan. "We better stop and rest soon."

Logan nodded inside the Aegis, and the giant helmet tilted in Bipp's direction. "Let's just go a little farther," he suggested.

Bipp's belly grumbled, but he agreed. They probably had a good hour and a half of daylight left, and it was wise to use every minute of it. The jungle had broken a couple miles back, and they were walking alongside a deep canyon, which seemed to plummet all the way into the depths of Vanidriell itself. Nero said in his time, the broken path was a road used to connect kingdoms, though barely a hint of it still existed. There was not much grass here, and the trail was covered with layers of trees that also dotted the cliffs, somehow staying alive on their rocky perches.

In the distance they could see clusters of the green mountains and rolling hills that bordered the jungle. As Themis set, it washed the sky in a rich pink light, giving the cottony clouds a purple silhouette that made Bipp feel like he was on top of the world. Bipp held a deep love for the caverns of Vanidriell, and he knew there was as much beauty down there as the surface of Acadia had to offer. But for the first time since coming aboveground, he truly felt at peace.

The ground rumbled as a massive oblong boulder rolled down the steep rocky hillside to their right. "Avalanche!" Logan howled.

The group scattered in opposite directions, rushing to get out of the way. The heavy boulder tore an entire tree free in its descent. Logan knew he could not hope to run without risking trampling one of his companions under the armor's wide feet, so he braced for the impact instead, dropping to one knee with a shoulder down. He counted his good fortune as the boulder skittered past him, shaking the ground and rolling over the edge of the cliff. The broken tree trunk came rolling for his legs, and Logan smashed a fist down in front of the kneeling suit of armor to create a barrier that the trunk rebounded off of, falling harmlessly over the edge.

"Geesh, *that* was a close one!" Bipp said, standing up and brushing the dirt off his legs while his companions gathered themselves.

Logan agreed. In fact, it was a bit too close. He scanned the hillside through the wide slit in his helmet, his head stopping with a jerk as he spotted the cause of the avalanche.

Rushing down the hill and roaring like a mad beast was the hill giant Grog, wielding the trunk of a tree as a club.

"Get back!" Logan warned his friends, spreading his armored feet and crouching to meet the giant's charge.

Grog came on, fiercely swinging the tree across Logan's armored chest. The giant was surprised but not deterred when the strange armor caught his club in midair. The force of the blow made Logan take two giant steps back, coming dangerously close to the cliff's edge. He tore the weapon from his attacker's hairy hands, and the enraged giant assaulted his face with a mighty blow, cutting the skin of his dirty knuckles open against the unyielding Aegis.

"Thought ye could escape from me, did ye?" Grog shouted in his voice like stones tumbling together. One of his eyes was covered with a fresh scar where Gandiva had torn it apart.

Logan reared back and gave Grog a heavy blow to the belly, knocking all the air from the gargantuan brute. Grog stumbled back and gasped, holding his midsection in disbelief. "Not so easy to pick on someone your own size, is it?" Logan asked, swinging an armored fist for the giant's face.

Grog deflected the fist with his forearm and grappled the Aegis's midsection. Grunting, the hill giant heaved with his legs and slammed Logan onto his back. Scrambling to stand over the armor, the monster smiled, thumping his chest with a hairy fist. "You've another couple feet to go yet to stand as tall as a hill giant, boy. And ye'll never have the strength of Grog!"

Logan kicked the hill giant's shin, forcing him to hop away in pain so that he could get off the ground. But by the time he got up, Grog was already rushing in to throw his arms around the Aegis's waist in a tackle. The pair of them rolled across the grass until Logan was on his back with his head hanging over the lip of the cliff and Grog sat on his waist, pummeling the suit with blows.

Logan caught the giant on the side of his temple with a blow. When he went to add another, the beast used both hands to pin his arm down under a heavy leg, stinking of mold and sweat. Logan panicked, realizing there was no way to deflect the blows and wondering how much the mythic armor could withstand before it would buckle, crushing him inside.

The giant stopped suddenly, feeling a prick in his belly. Wrinkling his brow, Grog plucked Nero's arrow from the side of his fat stomach and snarled at the little creature. "Just stay still, puny morsel. I will be with you soon."

Bipp held up his fist beside Nero and shouted right back at the giant. "You leave my friend alone!"

Grog laughed again but stopped short when Tiko's spear dug into his throat. The hill giant roared down at the small lizardman, wrenching the spear free and tossing it to the side. A steady line of blood flowed from the wound.

Logan used the distraction to free his arm, giving Grog another sharp blow to the jaw and ramming his knee into the behemoth's back, hurling him face first over the edge of the cliff. Bipp cheered.

Logan rolled the armor over and made his way slowly to his feet again. He was amazed to find the hill giant had not even made a dent in the Aegis, but his head was still ringing from the blows. "Ugh, I'm going to have a headache for a bloody week after that thrashing," Logan said to his friends, stooping in a crouch and catching his breath. "We just can't get rid of that big smelly bastard, can we?"

"I think he had a crush on Nero," Bipp said, giggling. "Probably been dreaming about him since the moment we left!" The gnome nudged his android companion to get him to laugh along.

Behind Logan, Grog roared, hurling a large rock over the edge of the cliff, where he was quickly pulling his body back over the edge. Logan threw his armor directly in the path of the massive rock before it could crush his companions. It bounced off the snarling griffin on his pauldron, spinning the Aegis around so that the charging giant was able to tackle him from behind. Again Grog rained furious blows down on Logan, this time each one ringing across his spine. If not for the armor, the blows would have turned his body to mush. When Grog saw his punches were accomplishing nothing but bloody knuckles, he tried to wrench the helmet free.

Logan grunted under the giant's crushing weight, forcing both of his hands in place on the ground so he could push himself up to his knees. Grog wrapped his legs around the Aegis's midsection, determined not to let go as he continued trying to wrench off the helmet from behind. The sound of metal warping told Logan he needed to do something fast or the hill giant was about to get his way. He tried to blindly punch over his shoulder several times, missing the squirming giant each time.

"Logan, you got to do something quick!" Bipp said, scared the giant would kill his friend.

Logan grunted. He was thrashing about, to shake the giant off, but the tenacious monster's grip could not be broken. "I need a bloody weapon!" he howled, hearing the sound of bending metal once more.

The pommel of a sword shot out of the Aegis's back, blasting Grog so hard in the face that it knocked the brute clear across the cliffside trail. He landed with a ground-shaking thump against the hillside.

Logan was confused. "What was that?" he yelled.

"A sword!" Bipp said, pointing at his back.

"There is a sword on the back of the armor!" Nero shouted at the same time.

Logan reached behind his head to grasp the hilt and pulled forth the massive sword, which extended once more after it was pulled out. The Silvlari Draconian Blade was brilliant, glinting in the light of the daystar. It was almost as long as the armor it sprang from. Logan used the weapon to pivot his weight and stand, just as Grog was making his way to his feet again, looking slightly dazed.

"Isaac was right, this armor really is amazing!" Logan said. Squaring out his feet, he asked the armor for a shield. The snarling griffin pauldron on his left shoulder popped free into the air, where he caught the shield in his grasping hand.

Grog growled, spitting out a fat, cracked yellow tooth, and picked up a boulder.

"Let's try that again, shall we, big boy?" Logan mocked the filthy giant.

Grog let the boulder fly, and Logan charged forward, cutting the stone in half with the mythic blade and smashing the shield across the hill giant's face. The two of them danced in a series of gruesome blows, and Bipp had no idea how the monster was still standing. Each time the sword cut a deep gash in his thick, pasty skin, the giant returned with a bone-jarring blow, throwing Logan on the defensive.

Grog clasped both hands together in a giant fist, throwing all of his considerable strength into pummeling the side of Logan's helmet. The blow jarred the head of the Aegis at an odd angle. As Logan stumbled backward, clearly dazed from the blow, his massive shield clattered over the edge of the cliff.

"Aw, the little pork chop lost his toy," Grog teased.

Bipp howled for his friend and was as surprised as Grog when Logan's sword ran clean through the giant's chest.

Grog took one step back, staring in dumb fascination at the blade, and grasped the pommel to try to pull it free. Dark brown blood oozed from his open chest.

"Not too funny now, is it, you filthy beast?" Logan asked, growling while he tried to straighten out the helmet so that he could see straight. The thing was set at such an odd angle that he worried that the giant had caused permanent damage to the ancient Draconian armor.

Bipp watched in horrified slow motion, unable to stop it, unable to shout out a warning, unable to save his friend.

Grog clamped his rotting teeth together, drooling a line of bloody spittle, and snarled at Logan, throwing himself forward. Before Logan knew what was happening, the hill giant tackled him, clasping his arms around the Aegis's waist and throwing both of them far off the edge of the cliff.

Tiko was so stunned that he staggered backward, recoiling from the horror as Bipp raced for the edge, howling for Logan, who they could see plummeting down into the yawning canyon, his silver-armored hand outstretched for them to catch him, though it would never be possible.

Bipp fell to his knees, the world ripped from his heart, as his dear friend Logan Walker fell into the yawning abyss.

"Nooooo!!!!" Corbin sat up, screaming into the night. All that remained of the campfire beside him were some glowing embers.

Stur had been keeping watch and raced over. Kyra quickly rolled out of her blanket with sword in hand.

"No, Logan! No!" Corbin screamed hysterically, covered in a cold sweat.

"Corbin, what is it, lad? What has happened?" Stur asked, shaking his friend by the shoulders. Kyra grabbed some water and splashed it in Corbin's face, hoping to wake him from his nightmare.

Corbin shoved the waterskin away. "I'm not dreaming! My brother...Logan." Corbin sobered up, staring blankly into the embers. "Logan is dead."

Kyra shared a concerned look with Stur, but the warrior looked grave. They knew Corbin delved into the mystical arts, and Stur was not sure whether this was just a dream or something else.

"It was only a dream, Corbin, just a dream." Kyra tried to comfort him, placing a hand on either side of his panic-stricken face and forcing him to look her in the eyes. The hardened marshal felt her own heart break at the look of anguish splayed across his face. She remembered that look only too well.

Corbin fell against her and began sobbing uncontrollably, calling out for his brother as Kyra continued trying to convince him it was just a dream, rocking the broken man gently in her arms. Stur looked across the embers at Isaac. The mage sat staring down at the soil, frowning forlornly. Stur knew that whatever Corbin had seen was more than just a mere dream.

It took the rest of the night to calm Corbin down and convince him that everything was alright. "You will see, when we get back to the White Tree, Logan will be waiting for us with his cocky smile and the Aegis to brag about. You will see," Kyra said.

But when they arrived, they found none of their companions had made it back to the White Tree yet, and neither Kalilah nor Elijah had any word from them.

Kyra consoled Corbin once more. "They are surely on their way back as we speak. You will see. By this time tomorrow, Logan will return with larger than life tales about their journey to get the Aegis."

Corbin could not sleep that night and waited outside the tree for his brother to return all through the rising dawn. Kyra and Stur waited with him after they woke.

Finally, when the afternoon rolled around, Corbin saw that Kyra was right, and his heart lifted to see Nero making his way into the clearing, followed by Tiko leaning on a freshly cut spear. He craned his neck to see his brother. Bipp stalked into the clearing with swollen red eyes and slumped shoulders. When the gnome looked up at Corbin sitting on the ivory roots of Isaacha, he tried to explain how sorry he was but only managed to begin sobbing once more. Kalilah rushed over to the anguished gnome, wrapping him in her arms as he wailed anew at the loss of his dear friend.

Kyra moved toward Corbin, whose heart felt cold and hollow, but Stur pulled her back. "He needs to be alone," he said. Kyra knew the weapon master was right but could not help chasing after Corbin anyhow as he made his way back inside the White Tree.

"Corbin, I'm so sorry for your loss. I..." Kyra said, standing in his path. She meant to say something grander, something that conveyed how saddened she was that he had lost his brother. Something to explain how she understood his pain and that he had friends who would always be there for him. But, as was most often the case, the agony of losing someone choked the wisdom and beauty from her words.

Corbin stared at Kyra as though she were the most despicable monster he had ever set eyes on. His face was a cold mask of hatred as tears streaked from his angry eyes. "Don't stand there and pretend as if you care. This is all your fault," Corbin said, snarling at the shocked marshal. "If we had never come out here with you in the first place, following that mad mage around, my brother would still be alive!"

"Corbin, I understand what you are feeling—" Kyra said breathlessly.

Corbin snorted in disgust. "As if you feel anything. How can you, when you don't have a heart yourself? You're no better than that bastard Thiazi, using us as tools for your war. To you, we are just a means to your end. Get out of my way. I'm done with the lot of you!"

Stur pulled the shocked Kyra back, holding the marshal tight as Corbin ran past them into the mage's tower.

"Don't you listen to the boy. He's just lashing out in pain," Stur comforted, feeling a bitter sorrow for his friend.

Kyra looked back at the sobbing gnome. Bipp's face looked so wrong lost in the throes of despair that she began to weep herself. For the first time in centuries, she began to sob, pushing her face against Stur's chest.

Ever since the jotnar arrived, her world had been plagued by death and despair. One after the other, every person she cared about had suffered under their shadow. Logan was one more in a long line of brave heroes to fall in his quest to overthrow the invaders, and to see Corbin in such anguish was more than she could take.

Kyra turned her gaze skyward and vowed to the gods that she would punish the duke for this. The entire jotnar race had better run and find some dark hole to hide in or go back to whatever hell they came from in the first place, because Kyra Tarvano would make them pay dearly for the death of Logan Walker.

Chapter 19: Stratagem

"Taking defensive measures is the wisest course of action for us to take!" Earl Alban insisted.

Tryn had just walked into the war council room. The duke, several of his most trusted earls, and Belikar's newly appointed military generals stood around an oak table, debating strategy with a map of the nearby lands sprawled across it. They all had their backs to the marquess, and even if they did notice him arrive, they most likely would not have acknowledged his presence anyway. Tryn only hoped that the duke was too caught up in the strategic debate to notice he was late to the council.

Balistor, general of the Belikar army, a newly appointed title, countered the earl, stroking his black braided beard. "In over two hundred years, Belikar has never once been attacked from the outside. What proof do you even have that this is going to happen?"

"My source?" Earl Alban sneered at the broad-shouldered general. "You speak to me of sources at a time such as this? My source is—"

"Yes, yes. So the earl has already informed us at least a dozen times. But how can we trust the word of a human informer?" Earl Istaf brusquely cut off the indignant Alban.

Thiazi grimaced at the squabbling jotnar lords. "When Ol'bron returns from his expedition, we will know more. Until then, it is prudent to look at this from all angles."

"And how do we know Ol'bron will even return?" Earl Astif asked. The war council rebuked his statement with daggers in their eyes. "What? You can't tell me none of you are thinking the same thing. Every band of warriors we have sent out has thus failed to return."

Duke Thiazi growled, "Overseer Ol'bron is a hardened veteran of the Ullevi war. He fought alongside me as we sacked the Alfenheim city and laid waste to Ullr's elven chattel. This is not some hapless lackey we have sent out, but a seasoned warrior. Ol'bron has seen more battle than an Erathi gladiator and is not likely to be defeated by a bunch of scabs. He *will* return soon, most likely with a sack full of the heads of those who would stand before him." Everyone fell silent under their leader's scrutiny. It was clear the duke was not in any mood for bickering. "What we need to focus on is how we are going to root out the rest of these insurgents before they are allowed to escape the city."

"No one has seen Healer Eir since the resistance raid?" Earl Alban asked, gesturing to Commander Erruza, head of the city guard, for confirmation. The jotun shook his head solemnly.

"Well, how many of the traitors *did* we find?" Earl Rike asked, pulling the sleeves of his robes back and leaning forward.

"We are making progress, my lords," the commander said. "Today in the markets, my men were able to capture twenty of the resistance members." Erruza tapped the city map, indicating where the group had been caught.

"And yet there are still hundreds more roaming the city, scabs and jotnar traitors free to plot and plan their next move against the empire," Marius interjected from the doorway, drawing everyone's eye. The war council quickly turned and offered the customary bows to the archduke. Marius stalked in without acknowledging any of them, pointing the tip of his short staff directly at the commander. "If we were in Vrykal, this jotun would have had his entrails pulled by now for his incompetence."

Erruza bit his lip in a most unflattering fashion, making him look much like a chastised bulldog.

Duke Thiazi sneered. "Well, we are not in Vrykal, most *esteemed* Archduke."

"Indeed," Marius replied, raising his nose in the air at the thought of Belikar being compared to the jotnar capitol.

Thiazi ignored the slight and continued, "And since we are not in Vrykal, *I* will determine the fate of my subjects, incompetent or otherwise."

Marius motioned for Tryn to join him as he parted the earls to lean over the weathered map of Belikar. "Oh, and what a splendid job you have been doing, my dear duke. Twenty days since the human attack on Belikar and still you have not captured them?"

Tryn winced. Thiazi gritted his sharp fangs together, glaring at the archduke as if he might reach across the table and choke the life out of the old jotun.

Tryn could not help but stick up for his father. "B-but we have sent Ol'bron out with his legion to search for signs of the human camp." He knew his uninvited interruption, though it was to defend the duke's honor, had misfired. The blood vessel in Thiazi's forehead throbbed, and he could see in his father's eyes that a defense given by Tryn made the duke look that much more incompetent in everyone's eyes.

"Oh, Overseer Ol'bron, you say?" Marius mocked them. "You mean the jotun who spent his days guarding scabs and allowed this uprising to swelter under his very nose? Well, that's different, then." Marius's sarcasm made Thiazi bristle, but the archduke was relentless in his condemnation, shifting his attention to Balistor. "Tell me, *General*, how many scouting parties does that make now? I think we have sent out a couple already, no? What was it two, three...?"

General Balistor looked as if he would rather be boiled in oil at that moment, shifting his eyes down to his thick calloused hands resting on the table and answered in a low voice, barely audible, "Twelve."

Marius's eyes lit up, ablaze with disgust. "Twelve! Twelve groups of Belikar's finest sent to track four pathetic scabs! And not one of them has returned to the city. Yet we keep sending out more fodder for the fire?"

Thiazi slammed his fist against the table, rattling the brass markers set around the map. "Enough! We did not come here to listen to your prattling, old man! When Ol'bron returns—"

"Oh, didn't I mention?" Marius said, cutting off the duke with a vindictive sneer. "The overseer returned only an hour ago. I've brought him here now."

"Well, why didn't you say so?" Earl Alban said, a bit louder than was wise.

The archduke signaled the guards, and the doors were opened so Ol'bron could be brought in. Last time Tryn had seen the slave master, he stood tall and proud, a seasoned warrior respected by all. However, the jotun Marius's men had to drag into the room, his steel boots dragging across the stone, could have been another person altogether. Ol'bron's face was caked with dried blood, which was also spattered across his armor. The jotun was mumbling incoherently under his breath. Duke Thiazi was at a loss for words, shocked to see his trusted champion in such disarray.

"Ol'bron, what has happened?" Earl Istaf asked. "Have you found the rebel camp?"

The ragged warrior looked up, flinching under Thiazi's gawking, and looking around the room, puzzled as to how he had gotten there. "Eh? What is the castle? Where are the wolves?"

Tryn had never seen the overly proud overseer show even the slightest hint of fear. Yet here he was with wild eyes darting about the room, shying away from the shadows. Ol'bron tried to force himself to speak again, but something caught his eye against the wall, and he cringed away from Marius's men, trying to flee the room. Tryn looked where the overseer was staring, but there was nothing there.

Thiazi sidled around the table to stand before his champion. He gave the jotun a heavy backhand square in the jaw, knocking some semblance of awareness into the madman. "Snap out of it, Ol'bron!"

The distant fuzziness faded from the overseer's eyes for a moment, and they focused on the duke standing before him. Ol'bron slowly nodded.

"Now tell us what you saw out there in the desert," Thiazi said.

"Desert?" Ol'bron asked. "Yes...yes, there was supposed to be a desert." Tryn could see Ol'bron was trying hard to sort through his jumbled thoughts. "No desert. It was a jungle, an ancient deep jungle!"

The war council groaned, and Thiazi rolled his eyes. The warrior had clearly lost his wits. All around Belikar, stretching for miles in every direction, was nothing but desolate wasteland. The nearest land that even remotely resembled a small forest, let alone a dense jungle, was leagues to the north by the Nasik Sea.

"And what of the humans?" General Balistor asked. "Did you at least find their camp? Can you show it to us on the map?" Balistor pushed the map toward the crazed overseer, hoping at least they could get that much from him.

Ol'bron looked down to the table, licking his lips and curiously inspecting the markers. He plucked one from the table and brought it close to his eye, squinting at it. It was a bronze carved square with a bored hole through the center, the symbol for wall guards. Staring through the hole with his bloodshot eye aimed at the duke, Ol'bron replied in a haunted voice, "They were deep down, deep inside the trees, whispering on the wind. There were hundreds of them hiding in the holes...no, thousands. Thousands of the scabs...and their creatures. They are coming for us, Duke! They are coming for us!"

Thiazi leaned away from the insane jotun with a sneer of disgust. "Get this hapless fool out of here," he ordered.

As Ol'bron was pulled from the room, heels scraping across the stone, he began shouting like a madman. "No, you must listen to me! There are thousands of them! They are preparing for war! War, I tell you!" As he passed Tryn, Ol'bron's eyes went wide, and he plopped the brass marker into his mouth, swallowing it and laughing hysterically.

The doors slammed behind him, but they could still hear the lunatic's ravings far down the hall. The room erupted in debate, the earls all bickering once more.

Thiazi scowled, standing in front of the open window with his back to them, brooding at something in the distance with his hands clasped behind his back.

"Father...Duke, what are we going to do now?" Tryn tentatively asked from across the room. Thiazi did not so much as give him a sideways glance, lost in thought. "Have you consulted the oracle?" Tryn continued.

The war council grew silent, eager to hear what the duke had to say. Siribel was no secret to the people of Belikar. The duke had paraded her through the streets when he returned from the war, and many spoke about the oracle as if she were some witch that the duke used to defy death. There was more truth to these rumors than any could ever guess, but the duke never spoke openly about her abilities.

Thiazi did not answer his son's question right away, offering him a glowering look over his shoulder instead. Finally turning to the marquess, he answered, his voice quivering with pent rage, "Of course I've used the elf bitch. Do I look like a fool that needs his useless son to bring up the obvious?"

"No, Duke, sir. I just...," Tryn tried to explain, but the anger was almost wafting off his father, and so he backed down, looking at the floor and bowing with a step backward.

"And what did she say? If you may be so bold as to share this insight with your war council?" Marius asked, genuinely interested to hear what the oracle had seen.

A blue-skinned messenger burst into the room, his body covered in sweat from running all the way across the city, straight from the raven's tower to the palace. Thiazi snapped his head toward the young jotun, motioning for him to come closer, and they turned their backs to the council. Tryn tried to hear what the boy was saying, but his voice was muffled, speaking in urgent whispers. He heard only one phrase, when the messenger's voice raised uncontrollably.

"Jotnar army!"

Thiazi cocked his head back and pivoted to face Marius with a furrowed brow. "What did you do?" It was an accusation more than a question.

"My duty to the empire," Marius replied coolly. "So Duke Caeruleus has sent the army I requested? This is good news. I was worried your sharp shooters had taken down all of my ravens before they made it over the wall."

Thiazi stared hard at the overly smug archduke. "We do not need any assistance from that wretch. The matter is well in hand."

"What are the two of you talking about?" General Balistor cut in, unsure what had just happened.

"The archduke sent word to Vimur in the West. Our wizards have caught sight of them marching for Belikar," Thiazi explained.

Tryn did not see why that was an issue, but the look that spread across the war council was mixed. Some were obviously relieved to know reinforcements were coming. Others blanched at the idea of needing help. It flew in the face of their honor to be seen as weak, and the general's face was riddled with rage, matching the duke's.

"How dare you interfere in the military concerns of our city!" the general said.

Marius glowered at the disrespectful jotun. "How dare I intervene? Who is it you believe you are speaking to? Do you think I am the Duke of Belikar, unable to tend to my own affairs?" As the archduke spoke, like a wolf circling its prey, he lifted his ice staff level with the general's chest. The earls wisely shifted away from the enraged military leader. "I'll not be spoken to like some common noble who you think to bully with your insecurities." The general looked frightened and stared at Marius with an almost pleading look in his eyes. "Belikar *is* a part of the empire, as deplorable as that thought may be. I would have to be a fool to stand by and do nothing while you simple-minded oafs lose the city to an infestation of scabs."

A crack of black light shot out from the ice staff, slamming into the general's chest and knocking him against the wall. The groaning military leader begged for mercy as Marius siphoned off his life force, feeding on the energy that radiated back into his bony hand. With a flick of his wrist the spell was over, the black light licking back inside the staff, leaving the war council to stand in fearsome awe in a wide circle around the fallen Balistor, who groaned on the floor.

Thiazi silently glowered at the archduke as he sauntered out of the room, the guards scrambling to open the doors for him. When Marius was gone, the duke growled at his men. "Get the stupid bastard up. We have work to do!"

"B-but the archduke just said...," Earl Istaf interjected, shutting his mouth under the duke's rage. "Yes, my liege." He bowed and moved to help the general to his feet.

"Father...what will you do?" Tryn asked, not seeing what alternatives the duke had left.

"Go down to the dungeons and get to work. I want a hundred demonspawn summoned in the next week," Thiazi said.

"In a week?" Tryn asked. "But to get that many summoned in such a short time...it's impossible. We would need to work nonstop, and even then, there is no way we can meet those numbers."

Thiazi considered cutting his son in half at that moment. "Then I suggest you get started right away. I don't care if it kills you. Get it done."

Tryn gulped, because he knew the threat was not an idle one. "And which humans shall we use as fodder for the forge?"

"It matters not. Use up what you will. Any human not turned to demonspawn will be executed before the week is over anyhow. It's time for a culling," Thiazi decided. "Instead of trying to weed out the rats, we will begin mass executions." He dismissed the marquess and turned to address his men. "In the meantime, we will begin preparing every soldier in Belikar for war. We are going to march on the humans before the Vimur army gets here. I'll not have that bloody bastard Caeruleus stealing our glory and stripping my honor."

Tryn was still in a daze when he left the council chamber. He did not even notice Fajik join him from behind, eager to hear the news. "What did the duke say? What was wrong with Ol'bron? He looked mad as a hatter."

At first Tryn ignored the blade-hand, his mind racing through the potential implications of Thiazi's orders. Finally, after Fajik repeated his line of questioning several times, Tryn snapped back, "I'm to summon a hundred demonspawn."

Fajik stopped midstride, staring at Tryn, dumbfounded. "A hundred demonspawn?" he repeated. When Tryn did not stop to engage him, the blade-hand ran to catch up. "But...I don't understand."

Tryn spun around, frustrated with the incessant interrogation. "What? What is it you don't get? We are sending out an army to crush the human outlaws, and Thiazi is going to execute every single one of the creatures living in Belikar."

"I understand that, all of it," Fajik said. "But if the duke wants you to summon that many demonspawn, then why are we going to your quarters? Shouldn't you be headed straight for the dungeon forges?" Fajik asked, pointing out the obvious.

Tryn stupidly looked around them. He had not even realized he was heading back to his quarters, yet here he stood before the door to his apartments. He stood in silent contemplation for a moment, staring at the door and wondering why he had come here. But Tryn knew why. It had been lurking in his thoughts for days now. He just had not found the courage to give it voice.

"Marquess, shouldn't we get—" Fajik began to ask, cut off by Tryn's scowl.

"Wait here," Tryn commanded, entering his apartments and closing the door in the blade-hand's face.

The marquess cut across his living quarters, making a beeline for the bedroom. When he opened the door, Annabel jumped and let out a weak yelp, startled by his abrupt entrance. The fair-skinned human quickly kneeled before her lord, bowing her face obediently to the floor.

Tryn snatched her hand and pulled her up gently. "Oh Annabel, I've been such a fool," he admitted, disarming the slave and cupping her delicate hands between both of his. There were so many things he wanted to say to her. Tryn wanted to confess his love to her, to tell Annabel how she had opened his eyes to the gross injustice her race had been put through. So many things to share with her, but the only one he could manage was, "We have to flee the city. The duke is going to have all humans in Belikar executed by the week's end."

Annabel trembled, alarmed by the dire news. She looked at the marquess's caressing hands with open confusion. "But...all those people?"

"I know, my dear sweet dove, but there is naught we can do for them. It is for your own survival I fear most," Tryn replied with tender eyes, pulling her closer to him.

Annabel studied his face. "B-but Marquess, the duke...he is your father." She shuddered, terrified of the warm feeling blooming in her chest at the jotun's touch.

Tryn shook his head. "Only in blood. I've never been his son in any other way, and I'll not stand by as he murders the woman I love!" The proclamation was given with every fiber of his being. Annabel gasped at the marquess's admission of love and pulled back from him. "What is it, my love? Tell me, I will hear you," Tryn implored.

Annabel moved to the closet, terrified in her heart that this was all a ruse, and thrust aside the doors. Standing in front of the open wardrobe, she turned with quivering lips and stared Tryn directly in the eye.

"What is it, Annabel? Please, you must tell me," Tryn beseeched her.

"We are not alone," Annabel said.

From inside the closet, a blue arm pulled back the hanging clothes, and Healer Eir stepped out, dressed head to toe in a hooded brown cowl. She bowed slightly to Tryn and stood beside Annabel. "Good evening, Marquess. It would appear that we have much to discuss."

Chapter 20: Malbec

It was a beautiful morning in Port Panipo, the epicenter of Malbecian trade. Blankets of evening fog had receded off the banks, and the mantle of Kahô, the Mighty Volcano, was glowing a vibrant orange, lighting the entire kingdom in a warm mixture of yellow and tangerine. The multicolored cave finches were out in flocks, their merry song celebrating the dawn. The diminutive birds swooped down to clean the docks with hungry little beaks, eating most anything and delighting in the slop littered across the docks, leftovers from the fishermen's previous day's toils.

Things kicked off early in the Port Panipo, with sailors preparing to leave at the first radiance of Kahô's dawn. Elise wondered if it was a prerequisite to working on a boat that you had to grow the scraggliest beard around and wear suspenders with croc-skin overalls.

Mornings were not as long on this side of the cavern, with no light from the floating crystal of Fal, and their day was actually opposite to the neighboring kingdom, with nighttime here during Fal's day and vice versa. There was not a moment to be wasted, with plenty of fish calling from the sea and eager adventurers to transport to the Tu'Pùqa Isles. Boatswains were already barking at their able seamen to prepare the decks and load their cargo. Heavy fishing equipment was being carefully carried on board and set in place. It would be necessary to bolt down the fifty pound cranks, and the boatswain were there to ensure every last one of them was secured. When hunting the powerful aquatic creatures of the Maka Sea, all precautions had to be made, for should even one of those bolts not be set properly, the entire unit could tear off the deck, placing many sailors in jeopardy. Despite rigorous morning protocols, it was a grisly scene all too many a sailor had witnessed in their time.

Everything was normal this morning, the regular hustle and bustle of the port ringing through the early morning air. All except for the approach of riders, as Falian lawmen came upon the docks in force.

A dozen of the overly proud soldiers from their neighboring kingdom prowled the wharfs in search of something. The sailors grumbled. It was too frequent a circumstance that these men came from the west to harass fishermen in search of smugglers. Many wondered why King Glanery tolerated the foreigners' behavior. Some said it was because he had no spine, while others claimed it was because he dared not risk the profitable trade they made with New Fal, reminding everyone that Falian coin lined all their purses. Either way, it *had been* a beautiful morning until the soldiers, in their fancy black leather, swaggered upon each ship to harass the seamen.

"Hey, you there," a soldier named Dal said again, "answer me when I'm speaking to you."

The boatswain was helping his seamen load heavy wooden crates. He passed one up the loading plank and then turned to face the foreigner with a scowl you could scarcely see beneath the frayed curls of his black beard. The sailor was built like an ox and in no mood for the Falian's shenanigans. "What do you want, leech?" he said, only half interested.

Dal pulled his head back, looking as if he had just smelled something rotten. "Leech? Is that how you address a man of the law?"

"Ain't no Malbec pikeman standing 'fore me," the boatswain, Oris, said, turning his head to spit on the dock. "Don't see nothing but a bottom-feeding leech where he don't belong."

Dal curled his upper lip at the fisherman's disrespect, threateningly placing his palm on the pommel of the sword hanging from his belt. "Now you listen, seadog—"

"No, *you* listen," Oris barked back at him so loud several nearby seamen stopped what they were doing to watch. It would sure start the morning out right to see crazy Oris knock the senses out of one of the pompous Falian lawmen. "We got real work to do around here, and your yapping is getting in the way. So get to the friggin' point and tell me what you want already." The soldier blinked several times at the brash sailor without speaking. Oris rolled his eyes and told his men to get back to work, and the cargo loading assembly line resumed.

"Dal!" a Falian soldier called from the opposite end of the docks, waving for him to join them. Relieved by the escape, Dal leaned his head to the side and pointed a finger at the rude sailor. "I'll be back for you later," he promised, though he hoped to never see the man again.

Oris grumbled as he helped pull another heavy crate up to the boat. "Yeah, yeah," he called down to the Falian. "Go on now, your girlie is calling you." Several of the nearby fishermen laughed at Dal as he quickly made his way down the dock, averting his gaze from the unruly seadogs. He finally looked up again once he caught up to his friend, who was urging for him to move faster.

"What is it, Pete?" Dal scolded, suddenly regaining his false bravado in the face of another Falian. "Can't you see I was in the middle of an interrogation?"

Pete flinched at the reprimand. "Listen, Dal, Captain Rodger thinks we found the ship, but the seadogs are refusing to let us aboard, so Rodger says we might have to use force."

A couple yards farther down the dock, Dal's captain had soldiers gathered around him as he argued with a red-bearded sailor. "Look, I already told you, there is nothing to fear from us. If you have nothing to hide, then let us aboard!" Rodger called up to the sailor on deck.

"And I already told ye that ye can stand out here bellyachin' all day long, and it still ain't gonna make me lower my plank to let ye filthy theivin' land slugs aboard," the sailor said, taking a deep swig from his foaming mug of ale. He seemed quite drunk, slurring his words and laughing at Captain Rodger's face, which was quickly turning red, a bulging vein in the center of his forehead. "Ye Falians be getting worked up something awful fierce, don't ye?"

"You say there is nothing to hide, yet you won't let us aboard," Rodger said. "My man here tells me he saw this exact vessel transporting known fugitives from New Fal's borders. By Falian law, you are ordered to open your vessel for inspection."

"It's a good thing I don't give a rat's wet arse what yer man there says, then," the sailor taunted, slapping his own belly and laughing some more.

"That's it," Rodger said. "You leave us little choice. If you do not comply with my orders in the next minute, we *will* seize your property, under Council Decree Twelve-Zero." The sailor ignored him, waving his hand for the men to go away and leave him to his drink. "Okay, men, prepare to scale the hull!"

The Falian soldiers swarmed to the edge of the dock, and one of them leapt across the distance between the wooden planks and the hull of the transport vessel. With daggers in each hand, he quickly scaled the side of the ship. Everyone froze when an arrow went clean through the soldier's shoulder, knocking him into the water, where another pierced his chest.

Dumbfounded, Rodger ran to the edge of the platform. His man floated face down in the dark water, pools of blood fogging up around him. "This is insanity!" he snarled. "You dare to defy the law of New Fal?" He was even more alarmed when he looked up and took a couple steps back.

Four men held bows with arrows nocked at the ready, locking the Falians in their sites. The drunken sailor stood firm and grim-faced now, with his arms folded across his chest and mug of ale held steady.

"This is an open violation of Two Kingdom trade law!" Rodger warned.

"Already told ye we don't care about yer stinkin' laws," the sailor said. "Now piss off before we turn yer stupid skulls into pincushions." He threw his mug at Captain Rodger's feet, splashing ale all over his polished leather boots.

The two of them stayed locked in a staring contest for several long minutes. Dal would have bet they would have stayed that way for hours, except sounds from the entrance to the wharf caught everyone's attention. Rows of pikemen poured into the harbor, clad in beige tunics and brandishing the trademark three-pronged tridents of the Malbecian King's men. At least two dozen of them made their way down the docks toward the altercation.

"We might have a problem, lass," Wallace, the red-bearded sailor, muttered to the leader of Riverbell.

Elise tried to peek over the edge of the ship's hull from where she hid behind a crate, but a sailor pushed her head back down.

A smug smile broadened across Captain Rodger's face as he saw the Malbec reinforcements arriving. "Oh look, your lawmen have arrived," he gloated.

Wallace pinched his lips and brooded down at the dead man in the water.

"Not much to say now that you're screwed, eh loudmouth?" Rodger said. "Nothing worse than a cowardly braggart."

"Ho there, Falian," the captain of the guard greeted Rodger, arriving on the scene. She was tall, clad in silvril armor with a rapier hanging from her belt and her chestnut hair cropped in a bob. "I am Reisha, Captain of the Phaestus Guard. What goes here? A spot of trouble perhaps?" She took in the scene with an extreme air of authority. Pikemen fell in place on either side of them, aiming their tridents at the ship. Before Rodger could offer a response, she snapped at the sailors, "You men up there, lower your weapons. I don't want a stray arrow pricking one of my men."

"Goodly met, Constable. I am Captain Rodger of Fal. I come here as an envoy for Magistrate Fafnir, who sent us to search for known terrorists that were seen fleeing the borders of New Fal in a ship not unlike this one," Rodger said, shaking Reisha's hand as he explained their purpose on the wharf. He was pleasantly surprised to feel the firmness of her grip. "These dogs are violating the law, refusing entry to the Council's lawmen."

"Hmm," Reisha said, turning to regard the sailors perched on their ship above. She had to hold a hand over her eyes to block out some of the growing light from the surface of the volcano in the distance. "What say you to these accusations, sailor?"

Wallace fidgeted his thumbs over the purple suspenders that held up his pants. "Well...if I had to say anything, it'd be that their claim is a crock of bat dung." A peel of laughter broke out among his men and the pikemen below joined in.

Reisha turned from the boat to face Captain Rodger. "Well, there you have it. Wallace says you're full of it." She shrugged and gestured for the Falians to head toward the exit of the docks. "It seems you should be on your way."

Rodger stared open-mouthed at her, as if he could not believe the words that had just come out her mouth. "B-but...by order of the Council you mu—"

"We must nothing," Reisha countered. "These sailors say they do not have your *fugitives,* and so your business here is at an end. Now take your leave."

"You insolent pig!" Pete stepped forward with sword in hand.

Reisha moved like a fox, sidestepping the soldier's swing and planting her knee firmly in his groin. When Pete hit the ground, clutching himself, she ran her sword clean through his throat.

Rodger stepped back from the formidable fighter, motioning for his men to put their swords away without taking his eyes off of her. The pikemen surrounded them in a circle, and the sailors above held bows at the ready. "Th-this is madness," Rodger growled. "You are violating the Falian-Malbecian alliance."

Reisha steeled her resolve like an iron goliath, burning holes through his big words. "Get off my docks," she warned for the last time.

Rodger snarled at her and motioned his men to submit. As they made their way off the docks, sailors laughed and began pelting them with rotten fish and other refuse. Reisha was close on their heels with six of her men, while another group of pikemen waited at the entrance to the docks. Sailors began to follow them as well, carrying harpoons and slapping clubs in their hands. Oris glowered at Dal as they passed, and the young foot soldier could not help gulping.

"Get our mounts. We ride straight for Fal," Rodger ordered.

Dal nodded and moved to untie them but stopped short when the tip of a trident came up under his neck. A pikeman gritted his teeth and pushed just hard enough to back Dal off. He complied with hands held in the air.

"These elk have been commandeered by the wharf master," Reisha said from behind them. Rodger looked as if he wanted to tear her apart limb from limb. "Now get out of my town and don't ever come back, or losing a few elk will be the least of your concerns."

Rodger balled his fists so tightly that his nails dug right through his leather gloves into his palms. "King Glanery will hear of your open treason against the council," he vowed.

Reisha cocked her head. "Oh, thank you, I almost completely forgot to deliver the king's message," she said, feigning innocence. "His Royal Highness wants you to make sure your Magistrate Fafnir understands that he knows *everything*."

Dal did not understand the woman's cryptic message, but it seemed to have a massive impact on Captain Rodger. He grew stock still as a sobering look spread over him, and he unclenched his fists.

"That's right...*everything*," Reisha said, as if reading his thoughts.

Rodger turned his back on the pikemen and ordered his men to get moving. As they made their way with due haste out of the port, Dal looked over his shoulder to see one of the pikemen kicking Pete's dead body over the dock with a splash.

He looked back at Rodger. The captain was a brute among brutes. To see him nervously scanning the area, as if his worst fears had just come to life, made Dal feel nauseous.

Back on the wharf, Reisha made her way to Wallace's ship once more. "Ho there, Captain!" Wallace greeted.

"Wipe that stupid smile off your face and tell the Riverbell woman to get out here," Reisha ordered.

Wallace was about to deny her claim when Elise slipped past him to look down at the captain.

"Elise Ivarone, Elder of Riverbell?" Reisha asked. Elise was too scared to speak. She nodded once. "Goodly met, milady. King Glanery requests your presence on the middle hour. My men will escort your companions to the Gnome's Ruby, where we have rooms waiting."

Elise could not believe her ears. The people of Malbec were openly offering them sanctuary! It was like a dream come true. "Captain Reisha," Elise said, standing a bit taller and raising her head as she gathered her courage, "there are quite a bit more of us than a single inn can hold, I fear."

"Oh?" Reisha tilted her head, looking to Wallace in curiosity. "How many are there, then?"

In answer, Wallace gestured to the two vessels beside his own. Row upon row of Riverbellians walked toward the rails, astounding

Reisha by the sheer volume of villagers the elder had managed to save from the Falian lawmen. She looked back at Elise with profound respect and smiled warmly. "I'm sure we can find good Malbecian homes for everyone, milady."

Elise felt as if she would pass out, staggering sideways into Eric to support herself. Their long journey was finally over! *We did it, Corbin! Our people are safe!* she shouted in her mind, hoping her fiancée could hear her somewhere out there. In the back of her mind, Elise felt Corbin hugging her, content to hear the news.

"Oh, and Elder..." Reisha said from below.

"Yes?"

Reisha beamed. "Welcome to Malbec, milady."

"Corbin, please let me in," Stur said. "I just want to talk to you, lad."

Corbin blinked several times, the foot of his bed coming into focus as he drifted out of his meditative trance. How long had he been out of it? The rapping on his door sounded again, patient, unwavering. *How long has Stur been knocking?* he wondered.

When Corbin opened the door, Stur looked relieved, an edge of concern traced in the corners of his eyes. Stur frowned as he looked over his unkempt friend. Corbin could see the Acadian was concerned, but he could not find any part of himself that cared. It had been two weeks since the news of Logan's death, and Corbin had confined himself to his room for almost the entire time. The golems had brought him food, but barely any had been consumed, and Corbin had refused to see most everyone with the exception of Bipp, who was also having a rough time mourning the loss of his friend.

"Corbin, lad," Stur said, as the young Falian absently crossed the room to sit on the end of his bed, "you have to come out of this room sometime, my friend."

Corbin nodded in agreement, tapping his knee and rubbing his face. "I know you're right."

Stur blinked. "I am?" He did not think it would be so easy to convince the grieving man to rejoin the living. Perhaps he should have forced his way into the room days ago.

"Yes, you are," Corbin nodded. "In two days' time, when your people march for Belikar, I will be leaving the White Tower." Corbin noticed the look of relief beneath the warrior's thick beard. "Oh, you mistake my meaning. I will not be leaving to join you in battle. I'll be starting my journey back to Vanidriell."

Stur slowly shook his head, digesting the young man's plan. "Corbin."

"There's no point in trying to talk me out of it. This is the wisest course. With Elise and the villagers from Riverbell now safely secure in Malbec, there really is no other reason for me to stay here on the surface."

"You can't believe that. You're a fighter through and through. I refuse to believe you'd turn a blind eye to those in Belikar who need you."

Corbin stood up and paced back and forth. "You're wrong, Stur. You don't even know me. If you did, you wouldn't say that. I'm *not* a fighter. I'm just a scared hunter from Riverbell who got caught up in something bigger than himself. My place isn't here," Corbin insisted, stopping to gesture around the room. "I belong in Malbec with Elise, where we can forget the lies and scheming of the power-hungry and raise a family together in peace." Finishing, he leaned against the wall and folded his arms over his chest.

Stur silently regarded the brooding young man for a moment. "You know I cared deeply for your brother. He was like kin to me."

The uncharacteristic display of affection threw Corbin off. His face twisted into a mask of despair, and he turned away from Stur, too ashamed to meet his gaze. The pressure in Corbin's chest made it hard to breathe, and he suddenly found himself fighting back tears.

"His death weighs heavy on my soul, lad, just as much as it does yours."

"Don't," Corbin managed through gritted teeth, fighting back the pain. "Just leave me be and go fight Kyra's stupid war."

Stur's brow furrowed. "This war is not Kyra's. Every human on Acadia has been set on this path from the moment the ice giants arrived. Placing the blame for Logan's death at her feet does his legacy no honor."

Corbin rubbed his throbbing temples and shut his eyes. Even closed, they burned. He was so sick of everyone trying to talk to him about honor and righteousness, as if any of those concepts would bring his brother back from the depths of oblivion. His dream of Logan falling into the yawning abyss, desperately reaching out his hand for someone to catch him, flashed across Corbin's mind again, and he gritted his teeth, begging it to go away.

"What do you want from me?" he asked, lashing out in anger. "Did Kyra send you up here to convince me to fight for her? One more champion to die on her front lines?"

"Kyra has nothing to do with me coming here. The marshal is still on her way back from the Citadel after overseeing the awakening," Stur replied calmly. He was not going to get into a shouting match with Corbin. The young man was clearly in pain and knew not what he said.

"Cold-hearted witch," Corbin mumbled under his breath.

Stur stalked over to pull a wooden chair in front of Corbin, sitting so they were nearly face to face. "You name Kyra Tarvano a cold-hearted witch? Aye, there might be some measure of truth to that these days. However, you cannot pretend to know what she has gone through to get to this point." Corbin looked up at him. "She wasn't always like this. There was a time I can remember...," Stur stared at the wall, his mind reflected inward, and a sad smile crept over him. "Well, it was a different time. I can't just sit back and watch the same thing happen to you, lad."

"You mean back when she was still queen?" Corbin asked.

Stur looked slightly astonished to hear their secret spoken aloud. "You know? But how?" His mind played back their journey. "Oh, I see, that was you in the hall listening in on us."

"Even if I hadn't heard it then, it would have been obvious by now. The two of you are not very good at hiding it." Corbin was filled with too much sorrow to care if Stur was angry with him for unraveling their little deception.

Stur pursed his lips tight and stroked his beard thoughtfully. "I suppose it was only a matter of time before it came out anyhow. With so many of my brethren now awake, it would not have done to keep her secret from you, our trusted companion, any longer. So you know that Kyra is queen, but you have no idea the pain she went through to claim that mantle."

Corbin found himself intrigued, forgetting the aching in his chest for a moment. "What happened?"

"Before the war got out of hand—no, that's not the right way to think about it. Before we realized the implications of the war, Kyra was so different, such a free spirit. She never took anything seriously, always telling everyone she met that they needed to enjoy life to its fullest. She believed we could unite the warring kingdoms through fancy balls and lavish feasts. She defied her father, the king, at every turn, insisting the wars were foolish, barbaric systems, completely unnecessary. It used to throw King Alfred into a right fit to have his daughter berate him so in front of anyone who would listen.

Sometimes I think she just did it to humiliate him, she was so rebellious. And the worst part of it was that her acts of defiance were actually working. Three kingdoms declared peace under bonds of friendship Kyra and a handful of other young aristocrats forged. Somehow those frivolous dinner parties were actually working! But how could anyone believe that drinking and dancing would erase the decades of bitter rivalries forged over time?

"Kyra's father was finally seeing the light. He was away at a peace summit to get the other four kingdoms to join the Eastern Alliance and declare a time of peace. That was when the first jotnar emissaries reached Agarta. Despite the queen's disproval, Kyra granted an ice giant *ambassador* an audience with them in the king's hall, where she and her mother waited for him." Stur paused, his eyes growing dark. "Ten of the king's guard died before I was able to finally overcome that jotun wizard and his infernal black magic. When it was over, I was so terrified he had killed both the queen and princess, but when the dust settled, there was Kyra, sobbing over her mother's charred, murdered body."

"And what about the king?" Corbin prodded, too engrossed in the tale to remember his anger.

"He never made it back alive. The peace summit was a trap. The jotnar had manipulated King Ilrec to set the whole thing up so that they could get all of the rulers in one place. It was a slaughter. After the queen's murder, Kyra locked herself away in her chambers, much the same way you are right now. When news of the king's assassination reached her...it was horrible. The woman I knew all those years—the carefree, adventurous lass who always made everyone around her smile—she vanished that day. That version of Kyra was shattered from the inside out against the mantle of responsibility thrust upon her. The young lass was suddenly Queen of Agarta in a time when mankind faced certain annihilation. But Kyra was always a tenacious one, and she pulled herself up, determined to meet the enemy in open battle. When it became clear that none of our efforts could hope to beat the unstoppable force that was the Jotnar Invasion, Kyra decided to flee the planet, vowing to return one day and make sure the ice giants could never hurt another race as they did the Acadians."

When Stur finished his story, he sat in silence, staring at the wall. Corbin felt shame that he had so callously compared Kyra to the jotnar.

Stur broke the uncomfortable silence. "These ice giants and their insatiable hunger for power have destroyed so many innocents, destroyed the lives of so many good people. Don't let them take away who you are, lad. I care too much about you to stand by idly as you let them murder your spirit."

"Like you do for Kyra?" Corbin asked quietly. Stur looked alarmed and snapped his face away, embarrassed. "You *do* love her, don't you?" Corbin asked. At that moment, the proud weapon master looked so sad and alone that Corbin forgot all about his own choking sorrow and felt pity for his friend. "Why don't you just tell her?"

Stur shifted his chair back slightly and shook his head sorrowfully. "It wouldn't be right."

"Because she is your queen? Surely such bindings do not still hold after all that has happened," Corbin said.

Stur ignored him, standing up and sighing. "Look, what I want you to understand is that dwelling on your own misery can give no justice to Logan's memory. Making his life and actions meaningful, that's what gives him honor. If you turn your back on this struggle and slink back down into the planet, you will forever regret running away, whether we win on that battlefield or not," Stur proclaimed, moving for the door. "You said I don't know you, and that may well be true for most things. But there is one thing I do know. The man I have come to know as Corbin Walker could never forgive himself for turning his back on those in need. And there has never been a people more in need than those poor wretches in Belikar. Now you have a decision to make, and whichever you choose, I'll respect it, but make sure when you make that choice that it's with both your heart and soul aligned." As Stur finished, he closed the door behind himself.

Corbin stood in the silent room, staring at the closed wooden door for some time. He opened his clutched hand to stare at the moon pendant resting in his palm, and in the back of his mind he could hear Logan speaking.

"All these years I have been asleep, daydreaming as life drifts past me. Now, at this time, in this place, I can make a difference...and for the first time, I want that. I want to feel like my life matters, like people actually care whether I live or die."

Corbin clutched the pendant, and clamped his eyes shut, feeling as if his chest would explode. All he wanted to do was scream loudly enough that the gods themselves would cower. As a tear streaked down his cheek, he gave up. Corbin threw the pendant across the room and fell on his bed, sobbing into the pillow for long minutes.

When the wave of sorrow passed, leaving a dull throbbing ache in his chest, he sat up and straightened out his shirt. His eye caught on the floorboards, where the moon jewel rested crookedly between two wooden planks. Corbin stalked over and picked it up, cradling the last piece of his family in his palm.

Without another thought, he opened his mind, racing across the psychic aether to find Elise, who was fast asleep in her bed. Corbin nudged her awake.

"What is it, my love? Are you in danger?" Elise asked in a panic, worried that something else had happened to him.

"I am...no, not in danger, fear not," Corbin replied, surrounding her with his essence and warmth.

Elise could sense the hesitation in his voice. "But?"

Corbin resolved himself. "Elise...we need to talk."

Chapter 21: Final Countdown

Kyra regarded the magical image of the area that Isaac had projected and which floated in the air outside the White Tree. She had called for one last meeting to review their plans before setting out for Belikar and was in the company of several Agartan military leaders, whose troops had been arriving for the past couple days. The entire time Kyra had been away, her scientists had been carrying out the orders to continue waking the military.

"We will come at them from this hill, here," Kyra said, singling out the ridge they would use to enter the battlefield.

"It would be wise if we armed our men with the MZ42's, my lady," Stur said.

"That it would, if enough of them actually survived the strains of time," Dorn said. "We have an extremely limited arsenal of Acadian rifles, Your Grace, and those that we do have are in fairly rough shape. I can have maybe a dozen or so ready for the battle."

Kyra shook her head. "I only want reliable weapons in the hands of our men. The last thing we need is for a firearm to take off one of our soldiers' hands in the middle of a war."

The group agreed. Dorn felt fairly certain he could have a handful of them safely ready in time, but that would be it. If they were going to win this battle, they would need to rely on strategy and swords.

As they were speaking about Isaac's place in the battle, a white stallion with a diamond of black on her head galloped up to the edge of the tree line. The rider dismounted and came carefully down the sloping hill into the glen.

Kyra stopped what she was doing and motioned for Stur to follow as she stepped forward to greet the woman. "Ho there, Engineer Stana," she greeted, moving to the slope and holding out a hand to help the clumsy scientist.

Stana looked as though she might trip at any moment and eagerly grasped Kyra's hand, running down the last part of the hill while holding onto her red hair, which was tied in a bun at the back of her head.

"What have you to report?" Kyra asked. "Give me some good news."

"Pfft, wish that I could, marshal," Stana said, straightening her belt so she could tuck her oversized shirt back in where it had come loose from riding the horse.

"How many?" Kyra asked with hands on her hips.

"Well, we were able to repair an atomizer for one of them and—"

Kyra cut her off before she could recite her engineering work, knowing that once Stana began, she could go on for hours. "How many?"

"Three," Stana said reluctantly.

"Three?" Stur asked. "How in heavens can only three be left? We were transporting at least a dozen!"

Stana shook her head and bit her lip while she tried to explain. "The best we can tell is there must have been some sort of explosion to cause all that damage."

"What would have triggered it?" Kyra asked. The entire group was interested now, curious what had happened in the Citadel while they slept. "Was it the spiders?"

"The spiders *could* have caused the explosion," Stana said. "Óðinn knows they chewed through their fair share of equipment to get at the cryo chambers. And we lost almost all of the livestock before the arachnids even went on to the human chambers." She motioned over her shoulder at the white stallion at the top of the slope. "But this...this was something else. There are no other signs of the arachnids in the vault."

"Three then?" Kyra asked again, turning to Stur and sharing an unspoken thought. Stana nodded. "Then we will just have to adjust our plans. Isaac, can you bring up the..."

Kyra fell silent and everyone followed her gaze to the White Tree. Corbin Walker and Brillfilbipp Bobblefuzz stood by the entrance, staring at the group. They were dressed for battle. Kyra had ordered brigandine armor custom made for the gnome. It matched Stur's in color, with indigo padding across the chest and arms, except the standard on each shoulder was the face of a roaring gnome with a waterfall coming from his mouth, the standard for Dudje. Corbin wore overlapping scale armor that stopped at his midsection over a bodysuit of hardened leather armor with his usual accessories. His shoulder padding was rounded hard scale as well, but with no emblems.

Kyra tentatively approached the Falians.

"Kyra," Corbin said, nodding and holding out his hand for her.

Kyra grasped his forearm and he grasped hers. "Are you...?" she asked.

"Going home?" Corbin finished. "Yes, we are." The marshal's heart felt deflated, and Stur's shoulders slumped at the news.

"However, we're not leaving for that journey until we help you free our brethren from enslavement in Belikar. That is, if you'll still have us."

Kyra's eyes widened, and she smiled as if she were suddenly a little girl again. "It would be our utmost honor to have you both at our side during this battle, Corbin Walker."

Stur stepped forward and happily clapped the side of Corbin's shoulder, almost knocking him over.

"Kyra, I hope you can forgive me. The things I said...," Corbin said.

Kyra held up her hand to silence him. "There is no apology necessary, Corbin. Your brother's death is a bitter pill to swallow. Would that I could take away that suffering that so many of us know only too well." Kyra frowned, averting her gaze to the high boughs of the White Tree. "But now...now we will make the jotnar pay for *all* the loved ones they have stolen from us in their wretched war. We will march forth for Logan. We will tear down our enemy's walls for King Alfred. We will throw the heathens into the abyss where their black souls will be lost forever for their crimes."

As Kyra spoke, the Agartans each bowed their head and mumbled names of the loved ones they intended to avenge. Corbin realized in that moment that his brother was another in a long list of casualties, men and women who had lost their lives fighting against the jotnar invaders. He was at once filled with a profound sorrow for all those lost souls and a deep honor to be among those brave enough to still stand up to the tyranny, something he intended to do unto his dying breath.

Bipp stepped into the center of the group and held his hands at his hips. He wore a grim expression that anyone who knew him had a hard time looking at. "Well, let's go kill us some ice giants."

Tryn cracked open the door of his bedroom to see if anyone was waiting outside the chamber. There was no one in his apartments that he could see. Closing it, he turned to address Eir and Annabel. "If all that you say is true, then we need to get you out of the palace immediately."

"It is too dangerous for me to attempt leaving, my lordship," Eir explained. "This is why Annabel has been kind enough to stow me away in your personal apartments...the last place Thiazi's men would dream of checking."

Tryn chewed on his lower lip, eyeballing Annabel. She was just full of surprises. "We are both on the same side of this," he said after a moment's contemplation. "I will not let my father exterminate all of the humans as if they were some sort of rodent infestation. Annabel is not a rat...she is...I *will* keep her safe."

Annabel smiled meekly at the marquess's declaration.

"But how can we get out of the palace unseen?" Eir asked.

"I will disguise you with some of my own clothing and escort you to the palace entrance myself," Tryn said. "From there you will be on your own." He moved past the healer and began rummaging through his closet, throwing garments over his shoulder onto the bed.

Eir wasted no time throwing his clothes on over her own. Even with her clothes underneath, the outfit was a couple sizes too large. "I'm not sure this will not raise suspicion," she said.

Tryn shook his head and plopped a hat on her head that sank down to her eyebrows. "No soldier in the palace will dare question you if I am at your side," he proudly declared, puffing up his chest. He frowned as a cloud crossed his face. "Except one."

"Marquess, what is the matter?" Eir asked.

"Follow me. Annabel, you stay here," Tryn said. Eir trailed behind him into the apartments, skirting plush couches and expensive tables. He lifted a heavy vase and handed it to the healer, silently motioning for her to hold it over her head. Confused, Eir did as he suggested. Tryn motioned for her to stand behind the door as he opened it. Fajik was leaning against the wall beside the door with his arms crossed.

"Fajik, come in here for a moment," Tryn said to his blade-hand. "I would have a word with you."

"Oh?" Fajik straightened and sauntered into the room. When he was just about to walk past Tryn, the marquess shoved him hard from the side and yelled to Eir, "Now!"

With a yelp she smashed the vase down on the blade-hand's head, knocking Fajik to the floor. Tryn quickly looked both ways down the hall to see if anyone had heard the commotion then slammed his door shut. Fajik was knocked out with a goose egg growing on his crown.

"W-what now?" Eir asked.

"We need to find something to bind him with. When Fajik wakes, he will not be a happy camper," Tryn said, looking around the room for an idea.

Annabel opened the bedroom door. "Would this work?" she asked, showing him a length of his bed sheets.

Tryn nodded and waved for her to bring it over. He lifted the blade-hand's feet while Eir and Annabel wrapped the sheets around them, binding his ankles.

The three of them almost jumped out of their skins when someone began banging on the door to his apartments. Tryn held a finger to his lips, motioning for them to get back behind the door to his bedroom and stay quiet. The knocking continued, and someone began frantically calling his name. Tryn cracked the door and poked his head into the hallway to find one of his errand boys.

"What is it?" he hissed.

"Marquess, sir, they're here!" the boy blurted.

Tryn screwed up his face. "*Who* is here? What in Ymir's name are you going on about, child?"

"The army of scabs, master. The scab army is right outside the city!" The errand boy trembled at the thought of war on their doorstep.

Tryn blanched and looked down the hall, expecting to see an army of humans and jotnar come around the corner to fight at any second. He tried to swallow, but his throat had suddenly grown dry.

"Sir?" the boy said.

Tryn turned and nodded. "You are relieved, page. Go find your family and get somewhere away from the battle."

"Yes sir." The boy bowed and ran down the hallway, disappearing around the bend before Tryn even had the door closed.

The bedroom door stood open, and Annabel stared at him fearfully. Tryn darted across to her. "Eir, if you are to make it out of here alive we must leave immediately." Eir nodded and moved past Annabel. Tryn put both hands on the fair human's shoulders and bent down so she could look him right in the eye. "As soon as we leave, lock the doors behind us." Annabel's eyes went to Fajik lying unconscious on the floor. Tryn followed her gaze then snapped his face back to her, giving Annabel a little shake. "Focus. He is not a threat to you in there. These doors were built to withstand a full scale assault. There is no way Fajik is getting inside. Do you understand?"

Annabel slowly nodded. "Good now get in there and lock the door, and no matter what happens, do not open it unless I am knocking." Annabel closed the door, turning the three locks and sealing herself in his bedroom chamber.

Soldiers ran down the hall outside his door, heading for the walls as loud horns began blowing all across the city.

"Come, Eir, we have to get you out of here before it's too late!"

Chapter 22: Strike

Corbin watched in morbid anticipation as Kyra's foot soldiers howled, racing down the rocky ridge toward the watchtowers. Thirty men came down on the right slope while another thirty swarmed around the left ridge. It was impressive to see the military precision with which they broke off into groups of fifteen men, approaching the towers with each raiding party holding their long oval shields in a locking formation over their heads to deflect the barrage of arrows.

The jotnar frontline archers, waiting in the watchtowers, must have been sorely frustrated to find the humans so well organized. However, the ice giants were also a stubborn lot, continuing to rain down arrows on their approaching enemies, who were slowly making their way down the rocky slopes toward the base of the defensive watchtowers.

An Acadian broke formation, slouching to the side and yelping when an arrow pierced straight through his ankle. As soon as the man stumbled, another arrow ran through his neck, dropping him to the ground. Corbin flinched, tensing up and readying to run down the hill and save him. Stur had to grab him by the shoulder, solemnly shaking his head as a volley of hungry projectiles littered the fallen soldier's exposed body. As much as the weapon master hated to see his men die, once you were out of formation in a scenario like this, there was no saving you.

With the opening in their left flank, another man in that group took an arrow in the thigh. He fell and another arrow tore through the side of his skull. But still the raiding party continued to march on.

Once the Acadians reached the bases of the archer towers, the wall of shields broke slightly to allow the riflemen access. Weathered Acadian muzzles broke through the gaps of shielding and fired into the wooden archer towers, blasting away splinters as bullets ripped into the baseboards. The guns were spectacular, putting anything Corbin had ever seen in Fal to shame with the exception of Morgana's rare laser rifle. He could hear the shouts of wounded jotnar from inside the towers. Though they were his enemies, Corbin did not relish the soldiers their agonizing trap. It seemed a filthy way to die, unable to meet your enemy face to face in battle.

"Can they overcome them all with this tactic?" Corbin loudly asked Kyra over the ringing in his ears from the shots below.

Kyra shook her head, flinching to see another of her men go down as an arrow flew right into the small gap a rifleman was aiming through, piercing his eye. "No, the guns are only a diversion to keep the jotnar from understanding our real motives."

Corbin understood her meaning as the shield men surrounded the base of a tower and began throwing grappling hooks up to the higher beams. The riflemen were relentless, firing round after round into the steep sides of the towers as the hooks secured holds. When their platoon leader shouted, the shield men lowered their defense and all ran in the same direction with taut rope wrapped around their forearms. The jotnar inside screamed, thrown to the floor or knocked against the wall as the entire tower violently shifted on its rusty support beams.

The smell of gunpowder came up the ridge on the wind, and Corbin could hear one of the shield men shouting to his men, "One...two...three...*heave!*" followed by the grunting of the remaining eleven pulling in unison. One of the archers inside managed to steady a shot, planting an arrow into an Acadian's exposed spine. This only seemed to spur his countrymen on that much harder as they gave another countdown and tugged.

The nearest tower was being worked in a similar fashion. Though only eight men remained in that raiding party, it came down first. The sound of rusty metal bending hurt Corbin's ears, even from way up on the top of the ridge, and he only dimly heard Kyra screaming down the slope for her men to move. The group scattered in different directions as the tower fell. Screams rang out before it crashed to the ground, shattering in an explosion of wood and dust.

Another tower came crashing down. Corbin felt the surge of excitement diffuse when the crashing tower took down two soldiers before they could clear away from the area. In the blink of an eye, the men were lost beneath a pile of debris. All that remained of the destroyed tower were broken planks and a cloud of dust.

One of the jotnar in a nearby tower managed to let loose an arrow, slicing through a soldier's shoulder. The man howled in pain as blood began spurting out of his torn muscle and let go of his rope. One of the other Acadians in his party shouted, concerned for his friend. He let go of his own rope and whipped his rifle in place, sending a series of ear-splitting shots into the tower through one of the thin windows. His commander howled for him to fall back in formation, but the soldier ignored him, screaming and firing his rifle until the archer was finally hit, falling face first through the window opening.

The rest of the raiding party moved in to help their comrades, and the bloodthirsty soldier was able to pull his friend behind a shield, protecting the fallen soldier while he used his one good arm to send a series of shots into the tower.

"One...two...three...heave!" the commander bellowed. The metal beam finally groaned, twisting under the force of their pull. As the tower leaned, the entire base of the wooden room above snapped off the rusty beams. "Run!" a soldier screamed in terror.

Corbin watched in sick horror as the tower smashed into the ground, rolling sideways like some giant wheel down the slope as the soldiers raced to get out of its path. A jotun archer flopped out as it spun, landing on the rocky ridge broken and bloody.

"Look away, Kyra," Stur advised his queen.

She shook her head, determined to see the fate of her men "I'll not diminish their sacrifice by not looking. These men will be remembered forever in our history as those who forged the way for the rebellion," Kyra said. She was determined to be the leader the people needed at this moment in time.

Corbin understood the honor in her words but also noted that, despite her conviction, Kyra winced as six of the men were crushed underneath the rolling watchtower, their blood-curdling screams enough to give the most stalwart warrior nightmares. Finally the tower exploded against an exposed boulder, stopping in place, broken and silent.

When the dust settled, they could see only one tower remained.

"What are those men doing?" Kyra asked incredulously.

The twelve soldiers that remained in that group were not engaging the watchtower with grappling hooks as they had been ordered. They were climbing the iron rungs of the watchtower with one hand, while blocking arrows with a shield that protected them and almost the entire exposed soldier behind. One of the unshielded soldiers looked up the ladder to find an arrow whistling down between his eyes.

Stur growled. "That's Ryker and his men. I should have known he would try something like this. Bastion overheard the thick-headed mule complaining about your tactics yesterday," he said, his blood boiling as the dead soldier fell and knocked two more off the ladder to their deaths. "Though I didn't think he would actually do anything about it."

The lead shield man, Ryker, reached the top of the rusty ladder, and an archer appeared in the doorway, slamming his short sword against Ryker's shield. The metal clang echoed around the tower. Ryker flipped his shield and caught the jotun's forearm before he could pull away. With a sharp tug, he wrenched the ice giant over the edge of the tower, and his screaming face hit the rocks like a cracked egg. Ryker disappeared inside the tower, and the sounds of clashing weapons resounded. With the jotun clear from the doorway the rest of his men easily made their way inside.

"Why would he risk so many men to take one of the watchtowers?" Corbin asked, not comprehending why the Acadian would be so rash.

"He clearly believes it is to our advantage to possess a higher position on the battlefield from which he hopes to engage the city walls," Kyra pointed out, a trace of admiration lingering in her voice.

Corbin saw it now. This tower was much closer to Belikar than the others, and with proper longbows, an archer just might reach the top of the wall.

The remaining raiders were bolstered by the rogue group's bold move and ran to help them. Stur gave two sharp blows on his horn, calling the soldiers back as was previously agreed. Most of the men dutifully returned, but three of them were too lost in their excitement to pull back and began scaling the tower to join the rogue soldiers.

Corbin could see that Stur was aggravated by their disobedience. In war, a soldier was expected to follow their general's tactics to the tee. It was not about one man or woman; the things they did were for the overall good. The weapon master could not complain too much, however, as arrows began to fly from the tower, taking out jotnar on the parapets of Belikar. The small band of raiders was scoring a tremendous victory for the Acadians.

A flash of light erupted from the city wall. Thiazi had commanded two of the city wizards to let loose a powerful spell, unleashing a massive fireball at the captured watchtower. A ball of flame half the size of the tower crushed the side of it in a fiery explosion.

Corbin cringed. He could hear the trapped Acadians screaming in agony as they were burned alive. The soldiers still climbing the tower were shaken off like flies, plummeting to the ground. Some of them still lay there broken and moaning when the tower fell in on itself, dropping burning cinders onto their heads. Kyra pinched her eyes shut at the loss and looked away from the grizzly scene.

From the high walls, Thiazi grinned triumphantly, watching as the building burned across the desolate gap of cracked desert.

"Seems a waste of good magic, expending so much energy for one tiny tower," Marius complained behind him.

Thiazi snarled. He was getting fed up with the old archduke's constant criticism. Thiazi would have responded, but it was obvious the two wizards *were* drained from casting their powerful elemental magic, so he found himself on the defensive instead. "Only a quarter of their men are still alive, a heavy victory for us."

"Of the scabs we can see, that is true. But how many wait over those dunes, I wonder?" Marius pointed out.

Thiazi thumbed over his shoulder, where Marius's airship was docked above the palace. "My men can see far from your airship. There are only a couple hundred more scabs, all of them simple infantrymen. It's a shame that the *Goliath* is not equipped with better weaponry that we might use to lay waste to the filthy scabs."

"The vessel's weaponry is sufficient for my needs," Marius said. "We have had to modify it to hunt down sky pirates in the last couple decades, but *Goliath* can still hold his own." Marius pointed out the massive cannon barrels.

Thiazi grunted, flaring his nostrils at the jotun who was supposed to be his superior. He half wished the humans actually could break past his fortifications just so he could use it as an excuse to snap the smug archduke's neck and blame it on the invasion. Moving past the thought, he motioned to his man on the wall, who waved a large orange banner in the air toward the inside of the city.

By the city gates, General Balistor saw the signal and howled at his men, "Release the demons!"

"Here come the monsters Eir warned us about!" Kyra announced.

Corbin looked where she was pointing around the curve of the city wall far to the left of the ridge. A swarm of demonspawn poured out of the city gates. Some were red-skinned cyclopes wielding large wooden cudgels and others bull-headed minotaurs, with cudgels or heavy two-handed battle axes.

Kyra took to her horse, pulling hard on the reins. The white stallion whinnied, kicking its front hooves in the air as she turned the mount about to face the army.

"This is the moment of our glory! Follow me and we will show Thiazi what we think of his abominations! To arms!" she howled, spinning about and thrusting her sword toward the rushing horde of monsters on the desert plain.

The Acadians roared as one and raced down the ridge, singing a war song. From Thiazi's perspective on the wall, it looked as if an ant hill had just erupted, spewing forth angry humans. He laughed at the pathetic display.

Corbin joined their ranks, gritting his teeth and racing to meet their enemy in a head-on assault. The ground shook from the weight of the two armies. He could feel his heart pumping hard in his chest, anticipating the battle.

When Kyra blew hard on her horn, the army was moving so fast they almost fell over one another trying to halt. As planned, the front two lines knelt in the dirt, raising shields with men in between thrusting spears through the gaps, bracing the long poles by shoving them into the dirt.

It happened so swiftly and the demon swarm was so close that they did not have time to slow their furious charge. Corbin had only a fraction of a second to brace himself against the long wooden spear he had dug into the dirt before a cyclops ran right into it, the shaft tearing into its belly and out through its back. The enraged demonspawn tried to swing its heavy wooden club at Corbin's head, but the deft hunter spun in the dirt to escape the dying monster.

He felt pity for the cyclops as it fell dead, knowing that at one time it had been human and wondering if that person were still in there somewhere, watching in horror but helplessly trapped.

Stur rammed into Corbin with his shoulder, blocking an incoming battle axe with his long broadsword. The weapon master's face was a mask of determination, shoving back the weapon and throwing the minotaur off balance before cleaving its head clean from its dark tan body.

"Pay attention, ye fool!" he howled at Corbin, punching the headless torso in the chest to knock it out of his way.

Corbin spun around, meeting another cyclops demon in battle. He blocked the monster's swinging club, though the weight of it rang across his voulge, making his hands numb. *Better not try that again,* he thought, dodging his attacker's wild swings.

The cyclops had him working hard on his feet to stay away from its swinging club when a soldier near him was cleaved across the midsection by a minotaur. Distracted by the gruesome site, Corbin almost took a blow to the knee by the cyclops. He jumped so the weapon swung beneath him, but it nicked his ankle and threw him off balance. As Corbin went down, he thrust his voulge hard into the demon's exposed neck. A fountain of blood spewed over its red skin as the one-eyed monster dropped to the ground, clutching the spraying wound. Two more men were killed by the minotaur before three of them worked together to take it down.

Corbin felt dizzy from the pressing swarm of demons and men locked in bloody combat all around him. His world was filled with the sounds of clashing metal and screaming death.

He was quickly thrust into battle again as a minotaur stomped over a dying cyclops's head to get at him. The bull-faced humanoid was much larger than him and swung its mighty battle axe one-handed with ease, wielding it as if it were a short sword. Even though he was stunned by the demon's agility and sheer strength, Corbin did not let that distract him from carefully watching the bovine behemoth's movements. He worked quickly, turning on the balls of his feet to swing his voulge in a circle and deflect a blow, running the axe blade down the length of his polearm and head-butting the monster in its hairy chest. It was like headbutting a pile of bricks. Corbin saw stars, and he thought the minotaur laughed, a braying sound.

Blinded, he nearly lost his hand blocking the demon's furious back-handed swipe, the axe chipping away a piece of his Falian steel voulge. Corbin had to roll with the force of the blow, spinning sideways and desperately pulling up his voulge in time to deflect another hit. He jumped backward as the minotaur followed through, reversing and swinging his axe in an upward arc.

Corbin crashed into a cyclops's back trying to keep away from the blow, knocking the one-eyed demon forward to one knee. The soldiers fighting that monster quickly took the advantage to sting its face with their short swords, but not before it hurled its club like a dagger, crushing in the side of an Acadian's skull.

Corbin leaned his upper body against the dead cyclops, pulled his knees up to his chest, and double-kicked the approaching minotaur in the stomach. When the bull-headed beast lurched forward, he was already spring-boarding off the cyclops and swung his voulge down through the bull's crown.

Thiazi grimaced from the parapet. The humans were faring much better against the demonspawn than he had anticipated. He caught Marius's expression out of the corner of his eye and saw the archduke was similarly concerned.

"Perhaps if we had more time to suit them up in appropriate armor?" Marius asked broodingly, watching as the tide began to shift.

Thiazi nodded in agreement. The archduke's idea for a demon army was sound. They just needed time to train and equip the monsters. "It would seem the scabs might get closer to the walls than we anticipated," Thiazi acknowledged. The fact that the ground was littered with far more dead humans than demonspawn did little to alleviate his annoyance.

Stur tore his way through the battlefield. Where Corbin's arms were burning and his strength was waning from the nonstop combat, the berserk weapon master seemed to have a neverending fount of energy.

Another cyclops hopped in Stur's path, and the powerful warrior hit the demon's bone cudgel with his broadsword so hard it splintered and cracked in half. Corbin was busy dodging another demon when he saw Stur punch his enemy square in the nose, almost knocking out the demon, before running his broadsword through its chest and throwing it aside to move on to the next enemy.

Corbin blocked another battle axe aimed for his neck and danced sideways around a minotaur. He punched the demon's ribs several times, releasing the blade in his gauntlet with the last blow. The weapon slid over the top of his fist, digging into the monster's body. The minotaur flew into a rage, howling, and snatched Corbin's wrist as it tossed its battle axe to the side. The demon wrenched Corbin's arm up with such force that it tore a gouge through its own side before popping out the blade. Corbin tried to pull away from powerful demon's grasp but found the strength of a bull to be a formidable force. The minotaur lifted his hand up and slammed the blade sideways, shattering it against one of its curved black horns. Corbin felt his voulge fall to the ground as the minotaur wrapped its free hand around his neck.

Instead of waiting for his neck to be snapped like the blade, Corbin punched the minotaur square in the jaw, releasing his other gauntlet blade. The weapon thrust right into the demon's face, tearing a bloody gash that sliced over bone and through muscle.

When Corbin hit the ground, released from the beastman's grip, he landed on his back and stared up at the sky in a daze. The air was so serene and majestic, a crystal blue afternoon sky and birds circling overhead, waiting for the battle to be over so they could feast. He had no time to ponder the wonder of the world, which seemed oblivious to their struggles for survival, as a cyclops suddenly kicked him hard in the side of the face.

Corbin flipped over onto his belly and tried to rise on shaky knees, but he had to bend almost backward to dodge a swinging cudgel. The bone club still nicked the tip of his chin enough to knock him sideways and tear away some flesh.

Out of the madness Kyra darted like a cunning thief, slipping between the cyclops's legs and running her sword up through the demon's groin. She bought Corbin enough time to find his dropped voulge and recover, making it back to his feet.

Then, just like that, they were caught up in battle again. He could hardly believe it was over when they dropped the last of the demonspawn around them.

Corbin gazed around the battlefield in a suspended state of disillusionment. The ground was wet and sticky from the pools of blood, and the desert was littered with the torn bodies of both human and demonspawn alike. Kyra's horse looked like a ghost where it lay dead among the demons. Corbin felt as though the world were spinning.

He faced Kyra, who was looking around as well, her eyes red and swollen like that of a crazy person. The mad-eyed marshal looked up at him and smiled, raising her sword in the air and screaming in victory. One by one, the entire army of Acadians joined in the battle cry, glad to be alive.

Corbin felt himself following suit, but it was as if someone else were there cheering, and not for victory but because they had somehow just cheated death.

Chapter 23: The Moxy

Thiazi slammed his fist into the stone wall of the parapet, his black steel gauntlet leaving a spray of sparks in its trail. The demonspawn front guard had been completely destroyed. It was not that Thiazi expected the demons to persevere, he just thought they would eliminate more of the humans. Yet the scab army had crushed his frontline far swifter than the duke could have imagined.

"How many of them are left?" he growled to his scout at the top of the archer tower built into the city wall to his left.

"Our demonspawn took out half their number, my lord!" the soldier announced proudly, as if this were good news.

Marius grumbled, brooding over the side of the wall at the fallen demonspawn. He knew that with better equipment and training, the summoned creatures would be a more formidable force. However, to be defeated by the scabs so easily...it did not bode well for his plans to impress the emperor with an army with which they could destroy the Aesi. Marius fearfully looked sideways, quickly trying to calculate some way to turn this to his advantage and keep the news of his epic failure from reaching Emperor Cronus's ears.

A messenger ran past him to the Duke of Belikar. "Master, the Vimur army approaches!" he announced, almost bowling right into Thiazi.

The duke looked to the southeast, rubbing the scabbed wound across his high cheekbone with two armored fingers. At that moment, Thiazi looked like a feral cat trapped in a corner with no way out but to eat its own leg. He eyed Marius in a way that gave even the cold-hearted, manipulating archduke pause. "I'll not have those smug Vimur bastards stealing the glory of my victory," Thiazi muttered.

"It is best we wait until Caeruleus's soldiers get here. That way we can cull the scab rebellion in one fell swoop," Marius reasoned, only slightly regretting that he had rubbed his involvement in recruiting Vimur in the duke's face.

Thiazi quickly surveyed the battlefield. The humans had ceased their cheering and were falling back into defensive formations all along the ridge. They were like little rats, moving to pick at the fallen debris of the towers. His face screwed up in puzzlement.

"What are they doing down there?" Marius asked, giving voice to Thiazi's unspoken question. He saw one of the humans waving her arms at a man at the top of the ridge.

"Do they still have anyone behind the ridge? I thought you said this was all of them!" Thiazi bellowed up to his man on the archer tower.

The soldier shook his head in confusion, focusing his scope at the land beyond the ridge. "Master Thiazi, there is no one else there, sir. I don't kno—"

Thiazi jerked his head and scowled at the jotun. The soldier's face grew pale blue and his purple eyes widened so that the pupils were tiny pinpricks.

"What is it?!" Thiazi howled at the gaping scout.

Kyra gave the signal, and Nero turned to face the opposite direction. Below him, the sand stretched empty to the casual observer. The android flashed his eyes in a series of illuminating bursts, sending the signal to Isaac, who waited on the other side of the ridge.

The mage slammed his staff down into the sand, releasing the immensely powerful illusion over the waiting army. Thousands of Acadians stood at the ready, swords and spears in hand. A select few even had some scavenged and scrapped pistols.

In front of the rows of soldiers, three hovercrafts powered up.

The jotun soldier's eyes looked ready to pop out of his head. He could only dimly hear the duke shouting for him to respond as he looked on in utter disbelief as the real Acadian army was revealed. The jotun was so shocked that he did not even hear the duke come up the stone steps and only knew he was there when the mighty jotun wrenched the scope from his eye to see what he was gawking at.

Thiazi gazed across the ridge and saw the army. It was at least five times larger than they had estimated the humans could muster. The duke grabbed his scout roughly by the collar.

"Master, please, please don't. I swear they were not there before!" the jotun pleaded for his life, seeing the crazed look in Thiazi's eyes.

"Then where did they come from?" Thiazi roared in the scout's face, baring his fangs.

"They just...they just appeared!" the soldier all but wept.

Thiazi tossed him to the side in disgust and waved down to Marius. The archduke waved a black banner down at the city guard who eagerly awaited orders. Commander Erruza nodded, and Earl Alban waved a black banner in acknowledgment.

Erruza turned to address his waiting battalion of city guards. "Duke Thiazi has just given the order. Execute all humans in the city and any jotnar that are stupid enough to get in our way! Give no quarter!"

His jotnar saluted and headed off in groups to spread the word.

When Thiazi raised his scope to see the hovercrafts lifting off the ground, he could already hear the cries of scabs being cut down in the streets below, and it made him smile. "Bring it on," Thiazi muttered under his breath and waved down to Marius again.

The archduke could not see what was over the ridge but knew it must be formidable indeed for Thiazi to pull the trigger on losing so much merchandise. However, he shook his head, resolutely denying the duke's new command. "We should wait for the Vimur army to arrive at their flank," he countered.

When the duke came down out of the tower, Marius could see the jotun was not in his right mind. Thiazi shoved the archduke back and swung the blue banner himself, signaling to his army waiting by the gates of the city.

"You dare touch me!" Marius snarled back.

"Shut your mouth and watch the glory of Belikar unleashed, old man!" Thiazi growled, gripping the wall and leering over it at the spectacle about to unfold below.

Corbin had to cover his ears as the hovercrafts zipped past his group. They had worked together to remove the rusty metal beams of the fallen towers from the ridge, clearing the way for Kyra's amazing war vehicles. Each hovercraft was a long oval with an open cockpit protected only by a curved piece of glass that Stur said would shield the driver from debris. On the back of each vehicle was a single Gatling gun that required two experienced engineers to operate. The entire bottom of the floating unit employed a pulse technology not unlike that which the jotnar now used in their mighty airships, and on either side of the curved vehicle rested a small propulsion engine which stank of burning rubber.

One of the vehicles hummed to the left while the other two cut around a pile of scattered debris and headed right, all three driving straight for the walls. Kyra and Stur had joined a group of soldiers to his right to watch the brave crews try to open a path into the city.

When they reached the proper range, the hovercrafts flew in opposite directions, letting loose a volley of bullets at the parapet. Stone crumbled and split off in sections as jotnar riflemen fell to their deaths, and Thiazi had to throw himself backward out of the guns' deadly path. The hovercrafts zipped back the way they had come, forming a long figure eight, and then headed back for the wall.

Behind them, the Acadian army poured down the hillside, and Stur moved to command them into different squadrons. Corbin ran over to meet Kyra as she bit her lip, watching the brave engineers tear through the wall's defenses again.

"Good, good, now we are ready," she murmured to herself.

"Queen Tarvano, the city gates are opening!" one of her men hollered, pointing at the large gates to Belikar far to the left of their position.

"He's releasing the army!" Corbin gasped, but Kyra looked enraged.

She turned to Stur and pointed her sword in the air, then toward the blue-skinned giants pouring from the city gates.

"Are you mad? How can we hope to defeat that army in open combat?" Corbin asked.

Kyra was too engrossed in the hovercraft's progress to turn away. "We have to defend the hovercrafts. If they don't make it through the wall, then all is lost," she explained.

Corbin knew she was correct, but still, it seemed insane to him to send out the troops.

The ruined plains lit up when one of the hovercrafts exploded, a ball of fire crashing into it from above. Isaac ran down the ridge to join them, holding his robes up around his knees to avoid tripping down the treacherous slope.

The hovercrafts pulled sharply back in opposite directions. One of the women was hurled from the vehicle when a lancing arc of lightning tore through her chest from the tip of Marius's staff. The hovercraft zipped sideways to retrieve the fallen soldier, but when they saw the smoking hole in her charred stomach, they continued right past the body.

The archduke howled down the wall for the Belikar wizards to ready another fireball, his eyes alive with blazing orange fires. Marius released another bolt of lightning, this one tearing into the hood of the only fully manned craft. The unit slowed, shuddering as its motor burst into flames. The pilot and engineers were trying to escape the vehicle when a ball of fire slammed down on them. One of the screaming men fled from the burning vehicle, lit up like a torch, until he fell down face first, burning alive in the dry dust of the desert. Bullets tore the pilot's body apart, putting the man out of his agony as the last remaining hovercraft flew by.

Kyra leaned forward, gripping the rusty beam in front of her. The lone hovercraft stopped just out of range then turned to face the wall. Corbin could hear its motor revving as the pilot readied to go in. Blue hot flames burst from the twin jets and the unit lurched forward. Marius let a stream of lightning fly, but the pilot deftly dodged to the side. A ball of flame came down toward the vehicle, but he turned the unit almost ninety degrees to avoid it and then veered straight for the wall.

"He's going to kill himself!" Corbin suddenly realized.

Kyra dug her nails so hard into the metal that one splintered, though she barely flinched. "We *must* get past the walls before Thiazi's army makes it to our position."

It was all the response she gave. Corbin knew it was the right thing to do. After all, did not the good of the many outweigh the needs of the few? Still, he felt nauseous thinking that the pilot was willing to sacrifice his life on a chance.

The spells began to shoot down ever faster and more reckless than before. But the pilot was in the zone, every fiber of his being in tune with the craft. Every time it looked as though a spell would obliterate him, the hovercraft performed some amazing maneuver to dodge it.

Finally, Marius scored a hit, his lightning arcing down from his staff and tearing into the right propulsion engine. It exploded, hurling the hovercraft bottom over top sideways, grinding the metal hull across the cracked ground.

When the unit landed, smoking and battered, the gunner lay a couple yards away in the dirt. She tried to stand on bloodied legs, but a ball of fire engulfed her as it hit the ground.

Corbin heard Bipp groan. He was surprised to see the gnome next to him. He had been so absorbed in the kamikaze maneuver that he had not seen Bipp join him.

Kyra looked down to the ground at her feet. Her gamble had not paid off. Corbin looked to the southeast and saw the Belikar army marching toward them. Stur was moving the Acadian soldiers into position, ready to face their enemy if need be.

Then Kyra bit her lip and leaned forward, excited by something on the plains.

Corbin looked back to see the final hovercraft still on the move. When it had stopped rolling, the pilot gunned it, narrowly evading another fireball and darting for the wall like a snake, swerving and weaving to retain control with only one engine and fires covering the back of the unit. Corbin imagined he could hear the pilot's scream tear through the psychic aether when the hovercraft crashed head first into the wall.

The explosion was massive. Balls of flame spewed in all directions, shrapnel propelled high into the sky, and a flume of black smoke erupted from the site.

Thiazi raged at the wizards' failure, rushing over to grab one of them by the throat. "You call yourselves masters of the arcane and yet you can't even stop a single human carriage!" he snarled, hurling the terrified, white-haired jotun over the parapet.

Thiazi turned to grab the other wizard, but the wiser jotun had fled back into the city.

Corbin was shocked to see a jotun fly off the side of the wall. His robes flapped wildly in the air, and the wizard disappeared inside the billowing black smoke that wafted up from where the hovercraft breached the city.

Despite the loss of their comrades, Acadians were cheering all around him. Kyra ordered the charge, and the entire army swarmed across the ruined plains for the opening.

Isaac swooped over Corbin's head, floating on a chariot of light that moved with the speed of a lightning bolt. He tried to keep his eyes on the mage but had to focus on not falling with the army racing all around him. The mage's chariot of light raced ahead of them and disappeared into the plume of smoke wafting off the city wall.

General Balistor shouted for his warriors to intercept. They were close now, and it would be a cold day in Hel before he let some scabs swarm into Belikar like rodents.

As the Acadians raced forward, the smoke began to clear, and the cheers died out. The hovercraft had indeed pierced the wall, but the hole was barely large enough for two men to fit through at a time. There was no way they would be able to use it as a strike point.

Bipp stumbled as he slid to a stop beside Corbin. "We're in for it now," he moaned, rubbing his bulbous nose nervously.

Corbin knew the gnome was right, as the ice giant army was rapidly closing the distance to their position. Bloodlust danced in the ice giants' eyes, and they easily outnumbered the Acadian army three to one. From his perch in the wall's opening, Isaac shot a bolt of fire from one of his rings. The magical flames scorched through a line of giants in Balistor's front ranks.

Without knowing where it came from, Corbin felt a surge of inspiration and shouted at the top of his lungs, "For Acadia!"

The Acadians braced themselves, chanting the battle cry as the two armies collided. It was like two tidal waves of steel crashing together in a flurry of blood and screaming.

Stur was in an absolute frenzy as he thrashed about, violently cutting down jotnar left and right. Corbin was in rare form, falling to his knees to avoid a swinging blade and piercing a jotun's midsection with his voulge, tearing right through the soldier's leather armor. Bipp spun around his friend's side and shattered a nearby jotun's knee cap with a well-placed blow from his hammer. When the blue-skinned devil fell forward, Kyra drove her shield into his face with such brutal force it snapped the ice giant's neck.

The battle raged on for nearly two hours of hand-to-hand combat, and Corbin was growing tired. His muscles ached, and he found it harder and harder to keep up his swift movements. It seemed for every jotun they put down, two more appeared to take their place. And the ice giants were a fearsome enemy, most of them towering over the Acadians by a good foot and a half, strong as bulls, and many were cunning warriors. The jotnar dressed in leather were much easier to dispatch than the armor-clad warriors among them. The black steel plate mail was considerably more difficult to puncture, and those warriors were cutting through the Acadian army with ease.

Corbin did a back flip, kicking one of the armored warriors in the helmet as he spun. When he landed, Bipp was already throwing his body into the giant's calf, knocking the dangerous warrior to his back so that Corbin could slam his voulge down on the jotun's groin. Even though the armor deflected his blade, there was no doubting the maneuver still hurt the giant, as he yelped and let go of his weapon to grab himself.

Corbin lunged forward to decapitate his foe but a dagger lodged deep in his shoulder. He staggered back in shock, spotting the jotun who had thrown it leering at him. The giant ignored her fallen comrade entirely, stepping over his groaning body to reach Corbin with a spinning flail in hand. Bipp crushed the front of the fallen giant's helmet in with repeated blows from his hammer.

Corbin quickly threw himself to the ground in a roll, avoiding the jotuness's spike-tipped flail as the iron ball crashed into the ground where he had been. Bipp moved to aid his friend but was quickly intercepted, locked in combat with another warrior who emerged from the swelling battlefield. Corbin could smell the stink of death as he stumbled across the ground, dragging himself on elbows past the bleeding bodies of Acadians piled over a dead jotun. In his peripheral vision, he could see the jotuness snarl as she pulled back on the chain and whipped the spiky steel ball at him again.

He rolled left, wrenching the dagger from his shoulder and hurling it into her throat all in the same movement. The warrior looked shocked, tossing her helmet off and clutching her throat for the weapon. Her face was a quivering mask of disbelief as her hand found the hilt of the dagger. With one last gurgle she fell face first onto the bloody soil, driving the blade deeper into her throat.

When the crowd parted, Corbin briefly caught a glimpse of Stur locked in battle with General Balistor. The weapon master looked tired and off balance. Both the human and jotnar soldiers were keeping a wide berth of the combatants. Corbin saw a litter of dead bodies around them, marking what had happened to those foolish enough to try to join in.

Balistor swept his weapon down to cleave the battered Stur's shoulder, but the weapon master suddenly leaned far to the left, ducking under the blade and slapping the flat of his greatsword into the jotun's legs. Corbin expected Stur to pounce on the fallen general, but instead he leapt back out of reach. This proved to be genius, as Balistor kicked out where Stur had been standing. When the general moved to rise, Stur hopped back in and headbutted him square in the face.

It all happened in a flash, and then Corbin's view was blocked once more by the swarming battle raging around him.

"There are too many of them!" Corbin shouted to Kyra over the sounds of clashing steel. He was not sure she could even hear him, but the queen nodded in agreement, never taking her eyes off the pair of jotun she was fighting nearby.

Corbin sucked in his breath when one of the jotun swept a blade across Kyra's neck. But the marshal was too swift for such a maneuver and even seemed to have been luring the jotun to perform it in the first place. In one fluid move, she rolled under the jotun's arms and brought her kopis up under his armpit from behind. The tip of her blade poked through the top of his armor, and she pivoted to the left, throwing the startled jotun directly into the path of her other foe's crashing mallet. The heavy two-handed hammer caved in the jotun's helm, and Kyra already had her blade free, swinging her body around the falling soldier.

Corbin lost sight of her as three more ice giants joined their fallen comrade. The last glimpse he had was of Kyra smashing one of them in the kneecap with her shield while swinging her short sword around in a twirling maneuver to block another incoming attack.

Beside him, Bipp took a sharp blow to the side, which cut a ragged line across his bicep. Losing Kyra among the swarming jotnar and seeing Bipp wounded, Corbin had a sudden certainty that they would all die on this battlefield. He knew the best he could hope for was to try to rescue the gnome and get them out of there.

Forcing himself up again, he screamed, falling on the ice giant that had wounded Bipp with such savagery that all those nearby moved out of the way, fearful that the crazed Falian would take them down on accident. Blow after blow cut through the leather clad jotun's defenses, until he was left a bloody mess on the ground.

Once he was out of the way, Corbin shuffled back and gashed the side of another jotnar's face. "Bipp, we have to retreat!" he shouted over the din.

Bipp shook his head in the wrong direction, disoriented from the blow he had taken. The gnome looked around and saw the pressing jotnar army laying waste to the Acadians. There were far too many of the ice giants, and it had never been the plan to face them on the open battlefield.

From the west, a loud bullhorn sounded, emitting three deep blows, like a death knell. The Vimur army had arrived, and it was too late to retreat.

"We're doomed," Bipp croaked dryly.

Chapter 24: Unknown Soldier

Over the ridge to the southeast, the horn blew, announcing the arrival of Duke Caeruleus's army. The unexpected signal stirred everyone from their battle. It was eerie how the battlefield suddenly fell silent as all eyes moved to the west, where a blue-skinned warrior on horseback was blowing the bullhorn. At that moment, the Acadians realized their deaths were at hand, and true dread filled their hearts.

From the city walls, Thiazi sneered contemptuously at the arriving *cavalry.*

"What in the black heart of Óðinn?" one of his men hollered, gawking through his spy glass at the army.

Marius smiled broadly to see the ridge filling with mounted jotnar. "You see, Thiazi, here is a *real* duke, come to save your incompetent arse."

Thiazi threw down the scope he had taken from his scout, punched away a hunk of stone from the parapet, and snarled at the archduke, "You fool, those are not Caeruleus's men!"

Confused, Marius recovered the scope and saw what everyone on the battlefield was looking at. Row upon row of Agmawor and Agma alike lined the ridge on the backs of red elks. They were bobbing spears up and down in the air as they chanted a name. High Priestess Luana twirled her thebis, green energy trailing from the skull as she prepared her spell, glyphs floating around her shoulders.

Corbin could not believe his eyes. What were the lizardmen doing here? Pebbles and fallen weapons began to rumble around his feet as something incredibly heavy made its way over the ridge.

Now it was the jotnar who felt dread in the pits of their stomachs as the glorious Aegis stepped over the ridge, surrounded by a virtual horde of green- and blue-skinned lizardmen. The white and silver armor glistened in the heavy afternoon rays of the daystar, its long, tattered blue cloak flapping in the wind, emblazoned with the insignia of a dragon, and Logan Walker pointed the Aegis's sword toward the jotnar army.

"Hear me, foul and wretched ice giants. I am Logan Walker, master of the world dragon slayer, the Aegis. With Seti's blessing, I have climbed out of the very bowels of Hel to meet you here on this battlefield, and this *will* be your day of judgment! Now prepare yourself for death!"

When Corbin heard his brother speaking through the powerful ancient artifact, his heart soared and tears of joy welled in the corners of his eyes. Logan lifted the sword high toward the heavens and screamed for his army to attack.

On the battlefield, Stur roared at the proclamation, and the entire war started anew as if it had never stopped. The Agma and their Agmawor cousins rushed down the slope, howling like wolves, meeting their enemy from behind while Kyra and the Acadian army pressed them from the front.

Like many of his compatriots, Corbin was filled with renewed vigor, adrenaline pumping hard through his veins. He became like a demon himself, brilliantly deflecting the blows of the terrified jotnar and cutting them down alongside his companions. He caught a glimpse of an unfazed Kyra joining Stur, the two of them falling on General Balistor with an unparalleled fervor. Bipp shouted gleefully and hustled in beside Corbin, ready to crush their foes.

Thiazi watched, dumbfounded, as the Aegis, which towered over his jotnar and was twice as wide to boot, cut a swath through their terrified ranks. Something inside him snapped when he saw jotnar begin to flee from the Aegis's path like cowardly dogs. It was as if the mystical armor was cutting down grass rather than proud Belikar warriors.

Marius grabbed the duke's arm and shouted, "You must close the gates!"

Thiazi shook the old devil off and signaled for his men to seal the city back up. The jotnar scrambled to the heavy crank and began lowering the stone to close the massive city gates.

Logan heard the groaning of the gates shutting and shifted his armor around to face the city. A brave jotun tried to attack him from the side, but Logan deftly blocked with his forearm, taking a blow that did not so much as scratch the mystical armor, and cut a deep gash across the ice giant's chest. The jotun looked down at his black steel breastplate torn open like tin, and Logan smashed his attacker's helmet inward with a mighty blow from the Aegis fist.

Shifting his attention back to the gate, Logan said, "Aw, why are you shutting the doors so soon? The party hasn't even started!" Leaning forward, he placed one hand on the ground and readied the Aegis to sprint.

Thiazi saw the move and howled down to his men, "Get those gates closed now, you incompetent morons!"

Logan sprang forward, and the entire area shook as the massive suit of mystical dragon armor bolted for the gates. Inside the

Aegis, he furiously pumped his legs, trying to make it to the wall before the massive wooden doors could be sealed.

Thiazi screamed again for his men to close the gates, threatening to behead any jotnar standing by idly watching. All in the area fell upon the crank, knowing there was no such thing as an empty threat when it came to their duke. Logan grunted, seeing the gates pinch closed, and Thiazi sneered a foul smile.

The grin was wiped away just as fast as it had appeared, however, when Logan pushed himself into an even faster sprint. He lowered the head of the Aegis and threw up a forearm, meaning to use the armor as a battering ram.

None of the jotnar celebrating their success in closing the gate had a chance to get out of the way. The Aegis burst straight through the city gates, splinters of wood flying in all directions. With its counterweight destroyed, the heavy stone pendulum plummeted down, crushing a gaping jotun. Logan slid on the Aegis's widely placed feet, trying to stop his momentum as he brought his sword down, cleaving the lone surviving guard nearly in half.

Corbin saw his brother crash through the city gates and side-stepped from his enemy, skewering the jotun in the neck between the folds of his armor. With the giant slain, Corbin worked backward through the crowd away from the line of jotnar. He waited until there were several lines of Acadians between him and the enemy horde before falling into himself, reaching his mind past the city walls to find Eir. Her mind glowed like a beacon just outside the slave quarters.

"Eir, we have breached the city walls!"

Though she was eagerly waiting for the news, the resistance leader jumped at the human's booming voice in her mind. She nodded her understanding and shouted for the rebellion to begin.

Her band of resistance fighters burst from the shadows and out of a nearby temple, screaming for freedom from the tyranny of Duke Thiazi. The slavers on the wall were dispatched with a flurry of arrows. Before the first jotnar even hit the ground, an arrow through his throat, Eir was blowing on her own small horn, signaling to the slaves that the movement had begun.

Slaves burst out of their hovels, screaming for freedom. They fell on the jotnar and human guards, who were going through the camp and executing the scabs one hovel at a time, with anything they could find—frying pans, broken chairs, planks of weathered wood pried from their crooked hovels.

A group of four jotnar sympathizers were taken unaware when a mob of slaves came upon them. The tallest of the human slavers puffed up his chest. "Get your sorry arses back into your homes, scabs. There's a curfew in effect!" he commanded, snapping his whip across the chest of an approaching scab holding a rotted wooden plank.

The teenager stopped for a moment to look down at the line of blood forming on his dirty skin. When he slowly brought his gaze level with the slaver, the man gulped at the bloodshot, rheumy-eyed look of absolute determination on the scab's face. "That'll be the last time you whip one of your own kind, traitor," the teenage boy growled like a feral dog.

When he stepped forward, the slaver suddenly backed up, holding his unsteady hands in the air and dropping the whip. "N-now come on...y-you know...I had no choice! I'm just trying to survive, s-same as you!"

"Everyone has a choice!" the boy screamed as the mob descended upon the cowering slavers. The boy was like a mindless beast, raging as he bludgeoned the slaver to death, flecks of rotted wood flying into the air along with pieces of the jotnar sympathizer's skull. When he finally stopped beating the slaver, the boy's face was covered with tears, and his fingers shook uncontrollably.

Corbin could see through Eir's eyes as she took in the scene of carnage they had just wrought upon the human slavers. She could see the teenage boy and the resistance dispatching the last of the jotnar guards rushing to stop them. The boy raised the shattered remains of his makeshift weapon in the air and screamed for his freedom. Eir was stopped in her tracks by the sound as the entire camp of human slaves took up the chant. Her heart filled with a burning happiness so bright and true that it was scary. After all these years, the hour had finally come, the rebellion could actually succeed, and Eir raised her own hand to the sky and joined in with the battle cry.

Thiazi watched the breach of his city wall with horror that quickly melted into a near hysterical rage. Looking back and forth from the battle below, which was rapidly turning in the Acadians' favor now that their despicable allies had shown up, and the waves of humans pouring out of the slave quarters, he felt the blood in his forehead sizzling.

Marius eyed Thiazi cautiously as the duke rounded on him, his face a snarling visage of pure irrational rage. "Now, Thiazi...we must stay calm. This is no time to be turning on one another," Marius advised, carefully stepping away from the advancing jotun. He was alarmed at how easily the duke's will seemed to have broken.

"You...you're cursed! This is all your fault! Everything was fine until you showed up!" Thiazi spit flecks of white foam as he stalked toward the archduke.

"I would watch myself, Duke Olvaldi." Marius held up a hand to ward off the duke, but he could see that sanity had left the Belikar leader. The archduke knew he was in very real danger in such close proximity to the hardened battlemaster.

"I am going to peel the skin from your bones!" Thiazi growled, lunging forward like a madman and wrapping his strong hands around the archduke's neck. He squeezed the older jotun's throat so hard his eyes bulged. Thiazi bared his fangs, the vein in his forehead throbbing as if it might burst.

Marius's tongue lolled out of the corner of his mouth as he felt the world tighten up around him. He cursed himself for sending his man-at-arms to the *Goliath* only moments before to ready it for takeoff should it be necessary to escape. Marius scrambled to push away the overpowering duke, but the jotun battlemaster could not be deterred. Even when Marius scraped three long, ragged lines across the duke's face with his nails, the warrior did not budge, flexing that much harder.

Marius's peripheral vision was clouding, murky spots forming as the duke shook him, pressing so hard Marius was dimly aware that his neck might actually snap before he was choked to death.

He weakly pressed the trigger on the side of his middle ring, unleashing a fount of drake's fire from the eye of his topaz. He fell to the floor of the parapet as Thiazi screamed, batting at the left side of his face where the flames took hold.

Thiazi shook the black steel gauntlet off his left hand and slapped at the flames that scorched the right side of his face with the palm of his leather glove, desperately trying to smother them. When the fire was finally put out, his sinuses were filled with the mingled smells of burning hair and cooked flesh. With his right hand he punched the stone wall, sending a spray of chipped stone over the edge.

One of his men ran to his aid. "Master Thiazi! Are you okay, my lord?" the soldier asked, trying to see if the duke was injured. When Thiazi turned to face him, the soldier's eyes widened and he vomited while clasping his knees. The left side of Thiazi's face was melted from ear to jaw, and his hair had been completely burned away, leaving the whole area smoldering.

Thiazi saw red as the soldier reacted to his damaged face. He snarled and backhanded the soldier across the face, eager to get back to Marius. The duke was even further enraged when he found Marius was no longer on the wall, having escaped while Thiazi was quenching the fire licking his face. Below the wall Thiazi saw humans swarming the food troughs, freeing their kin.

How could all this be happening? Everything had been assured. This was to be his finest moment, his crowning achievement. How did it all go south like this? His mind raced to pinpoint where he went wrong while blood-curdling rage filled every bone in his body.

Thiazi suddenly stopped and snapped his head toward the palace like a feral dog that had just caught a scent. "That little elf witch! She lied to me," he snarled.

Soldiers scrambled to get out of the insane duke's path as he bolted for the palace with his sword drawn.

Annabel rushed past the swell of servants trying to flee the palace. One of the older maids seized her hand, trying to tug the marquess's freckled handmaiden along with her. "Ye must escape while ye can, lass. The whole palace is under siege by the duke's own warriors!" the old woman begged. Annabel shook her head and pulled away. Her course was not set for flight. The round woman shrugged and turned to flee. If the fool of a girl did not want to escape, who was she to risk her own neck?

Annabel cried out in horror as the old woman turned the corner and ran blindly into a jotnar palace guard's sword, impaling herself. The woman looked up, confused, at the leering ice giant, and blood ran out of her open mouth.

Annabel screamed as another three guards came around the corner with blood-stained weapons drawn. She quickly fled in the opposite direction, the sounds of the guards cutting down fleeing human servants echoing in her wake. As she rounded the corner, Annabel caught a last glimpse as a group of newly arrived resistance fighters clashed swords with the palace guards.

She had to find the marquess. He had left his apartments a while before, insisting it was urgent he retrieve something from the library. Then chaos broke loose. Annabel could not stay in his apartments once she heard Fajik break free of his bonds and stomp out into the palace. The duke's men were going room to room, rounding up the remaining human servants and executing them on his orders. If she wanted to survive and make it out of the palace, she needed to find the marquess.

Bursting into the palace library, she frantically looked around for him. This part of the palace was eerily quiet with only the echoes of war coming from an open window somewhere behind the stacks. The long chamber was empty as far as she could see, though she thought she heard someone sobbing beyond the rows of shelving. The long oak tables had been abandoned in a hurry, with open books and parchment lying in disarray.

Annabel walked quickly past the study area. "Tryn!" she called, her voice bouncing off the high ceiling. She slowed her pace, scanning the rows of shelving, irrationally hoping for some clue to where Tryn had gone.

The sound of a table leg scraping loudly across the floor behind her made Annabel jump. She spun, startled to find a palace guard only a couple paces away leering at her with sword in hand. "Told you it wasn't none of them resistance fighters!" he called over her shoulder.

Annabel was too scared to turn around. Another jotun suddenly emerged from behind the shelving and spun her about by her shoulders.

"So you did!" the weathered older jotun warrior replied, running his hungry eyes down the length of her. Annabel tried to squirm free, but the guard gave her two quick raps to the side of the head. Annabel crashed sideways into the table, and the jotun gave her a hard slap on the backside while his partner laughed hoarsely. "Where you going, scab? Ain't no running to be had, not from a pretty little scab like you."

Annabel tried to scream out Tryn's name, but the guard grabbed a handful of her hair, wrapping her long chestnut braid in his fist and slamming her face into the table. Dazed, she fell limply to the floor with blood running from her nose.

"Bring her along, then!" he ordered the younger guard, who willingly complied, running over to them with a twisted smile. The younger guard grabbed another fistful of her hair so he could drag her along the floor.

The doorway to the library was blurred and spinning in her vision, and it disappeared around the corner of a bookshelf as the guards dragged her toward the back corner of the library, where a group of ten other human servants waited. Two other jotnar guards watched over the slaves, who knelt at the end of spears pointed at their chests.

Tryn's blade-hand stood over the humans, and he turned to see what his men had caught. "Ah, what have we here?"

Annabel eyed the three dead bodies at the end of the line of slaves. They were sprawled face first on the floor, like carelessly discarded dolls.

"Just another scab trying to escape, Fajik," the younger guard grunted, dragging her to kneel before the jotun.

Fajik leaned forward to brush the hair away from her face and laughed to himself. "Well, if it isn't the marquess's little whore! This is a fine catch you've brought us. We'll have lots of fun with this one before we're through!" The guards joined in the blade-hand's mirth. Fajik noticed Annabel's nostrils flare and the look of revulsion on her face. "Oh, what's the matter, dear? Are our warrior-class cocks not good enough for the likes of a nobleman's wench?"

When Annabel did not reply, the younger guard backhanded her. "Answer the blade-master, scab!"

Annabel wiped the blood from her lower lip and straightened as well as a person could manage while kneeling, so she could stare the blade-hand in the eye. "Shouldn't you be out fighting for the city?" she asked contemptuously.

"Oh, isn't that precious?" Fajik asked the older guard. "The little slut is concerned with the war." He dropped his smirk and replied with a solemn expression, "The city's lost, lass. Ain't nothing more we can do out there."

"So you're going to hide in here where it's safe, picking on defenseless people?" Annabel snapped. One of the women, a cook, began sobbing harder.

Fajik scowled at the cook in annoyance. "Oh no, you've got it all wrong, lass. We're not hiding. Me and my boys here, we're fulfilling the orders given to us by the duke himself." He walked over to the last man in the line of humans. Stopping to stand over the kneeling servant, a friendly porter Annabel had the good fortune to speak to several times, Fajik explained further, "See, if we were to go outside the palace, then who would be here to put down all these stray scabs?"

The porter gasped, trying to move out of the way, as the blade-hand ran his sword into the man's chest. The cook began to sob hysterically, and the rest of the slaves squirmed, terrified to be next.

"You're nothing but a coward." Annabel glared hatefully at the blade-hand.

Fajik only laughed coldly and shifted his attention to the cook. He stroked the side of her tear-streaked face with the tip of his bloody blade and snatched the woman's jaw, squeezing to open her mouth, where he placed the tip of his sword. The cook froze in fear as the sharp edge brushed against her tongue.

"Finally the hag shuts up," Fajik said to the other guards, who snickered. "Looks like all she needed was something to fill her mouth!" With a lustful gleam in his eyes, Fajik quickly pulled the sword out of her mouth and ran it down the woman's chest, tearing open her blouse and exposing her ample bosom. "Have some fun with her lads!"

He shoved the cook into the corner, where the dead body of another house maid lay, her skirts in tatters and her throat slit. Two of the guards moved to the corner to have their sick pleasure with the sobbing woman.

With their attention off Annabel for a moment, she slowly moved her hand between her thighs, reaching into the folds of her dress for the hilt of her dagger. Her fingers had just brushed the warmed pommel when Fajik turned to face her again. Her body froze in place while his eyes traced a path down to the exposed flesh of her thigh.

"Hmm, look at this, boys. The whore can't wait to get started!" he exclaimed proudly. Fajik sauntered behind her kneeling body and pressed himself hard against the back of her head. Reaching down, he grabbed her throat from behind with one hand, squeezing just enough to make her open her mouth wide, and stuck his dirty, blood-crusted thumb inside.

Annabel dutifully sucked on his filthy finger. It tasted foul, like copper shillings, but she fought past her revulsion, distracting him while she wrapped her fingers around the dagger inside her dress.

The blade-hand leaned forward, his breath hot and sour in her face. "That's a good wench," he leered, upside down from her angle.

Annabel slowly pulled the dagger along the length of her inner thigh, never breaking eye contact. "Mmm, it *is* nice," she mumbled.

"Old habits die hard, huh?" Fajik asked. "I hear the way you moan for the marquess when I'm listening by the door. Most scab sluts just do it 'cause they have to, but you...you actually get off on screwing His Lordship, don't you?"

Annabel nodded and sucked his thumb harder, readying to strike.

"Are you going to moan like that for me?" he teased, as if he were talking to a lover and not some captive.

Annabel nodded once more and then bit down on his thumb and lashed upward with the dagger.

The blade-hand wrenched his hand from her mouth before she could get a good grip with her teeth and caught her wrist before the dagger could strike. He began laughing. "Did you really think I could be caught unaware so easily?" He squeezed her wrist so hard it went numb, and the dagger clattered to the stone floor. With the weapon gone, he punched her hard in the side of the head, knocking Annabel over and pushing his knee into her back. "Now I'm *really* going to have me way with you-ough...ugh."

At first Annabel thought Fajik must have hit her hard enough to damage an eardrum, as his words were gurgling and incoherent, but then she saw the expressions of horror on the other slaves' faces. The blade-hand fell beside her, the light fading from his eyes, clutching the knife that jutted from his bleeding throat while blood pooled around him.

Tryn was already on to the next guard, whom he dispatched easily, and then he spun to hurl another dagger deep into the last guard's chest. The two jotnar that were having their way with the cook stopped suddenly.

"Get away from the human, you savages," Tryn ordered.

The guards held their hands in the air and backed away from the sobbing woman. "My liege, we only—" the older guard began.

"Shut your mouth, deserter!" Tryn snarled, putting on his best front. "The war is *outside* the palace, not in here with defenseless humans that cook and clean up after us!" The guards bowed low, shame blooming in their faces to be called out by the duke's son. "Now get out there before I report your cowardice to my father!"

The guards bowed a couple more times, scrambling for their weapons and pulling up their breeches. When they turned to leave, Tryn buried his sword into the back of one of their skulls. The younger guard screamed that he was a traitor and tried to run away, but the marquess wrapped a whip around his throat from behind, yanking back on it so hard the guard's neck broke.

Annabel was on her feet, standing protectively in front of the kneeling humans, when Tryn turned. "Come, all of you. We must get you out of the palace immediately. There are palace guards executing humans left and right," he said. Annabel could see his hands shaking from the rescue. The humans huddled past him, not needing another reminder. "Come, my dear," he said softly, holding his hand out to Annabel. "We have to get you to safety before more of the duke's warriors arrive."

Annabel looked down at the blade-hand, his eyes staring like a dead fish up at the rafters and blood pooled around his throat. "But...he was your friend," she said.

Tryn spit on the dead jotun and grasped her hand tightly. "The second he decided to threaten you, he was a dead man. Besides, he was a real bastard."

Hand in hand, they raced out of the library, speeding down long corridors. Everywhere they turned, the resistance was locked in battle with palace guards. Annabel saw the strange humans from another land had reached the palace to aid in the revolt. As she and Tryn ran toward the palace rooftop, Annabel caught a glimpse of the open doorway to the oracle's room.

"Wait, the elf!" she insisted, trying to pull away from the marquess.

Tryn would not release his grip, shaking his head as they ran past the room. "There is no time for her. Your life is too important to me. Only the gods may save the elf witch now."

When Thiazi rounded the corner, his armor wet with the blood of those foolish enough to challenge him, he narrowly missed seeing his son flee for the rooftop. When he saw the open doorway to Siribel's room, visions of bathing in the elf's blood filled his half-crazed mind. Stepping inside, he slammed the door shut behind him, bolting it in place so none could intrude on them.

"*Siribel*," he crooned into the room, "I'm back, my sweet little dove."

Thiazi worked his way toward the back of the room. Curtains of silk flapped gently in the soft breeze carried in through the open window by her cage. As Thiazi moved closer, the cage could be seen through the nearly translucent cream-colored curtains. "Come, my little sparrow, it's time for you to sing for me," he taunted, brushing aside the last curtain with the tip of his sword.

The cage was empty. Thiazi roared, kicking the golden bars so hard they bent inward. He spun to face the room, sniffing in the air. "I know you are in here, you little lying witch!" Thiazi snarled, gripping his broadsword and licking his lips. "Come out here so I can see you!"

When no one answered, Thiazi made his way toward where he believed the elf was hiding. A piece of fabric brushed across his raw, burnt cheek, sending a wave of tingling nausea over the proud duke. He bit back the pain and hacked down the curtain rod, dropping an entire row of silk cloth to the floor. "Hiding is only going to make the punishment harder on you!" he promised.

Something shuffled to his left, and Thiazi slashed the heavy broadsword, taking down another line of curtains. No one was there. "I just want to understand how you did it. If you come out and tell me, I promise to go easy on you."

Something moved to his right. Thiazi took down more of the curtains, but still no one was there. His frustration bubbled, frothing from his blood in a heavy wave of near hysterical rage. The duke began blindly hacking away at the curtains, tearing down row upon row of them and screaming, "Tell me how you broke the curse! Tell me how you lied to me! Tell me!"

He was more than mildly surprised when a falling row of curtains revealed a robed human with ebony skin staring at him in shock. Thiazi snarled at Isaac and cleaved him in half with his broadsword. The blow was so strong it slammed all the way through the intruder's body to the floor with a crunching noise like breaking glass.

Thiazi was puzzled by a puff of smoke as the human dissipated in a cloud of purple. When the smoke cleared on the breeze coming in through the window, he saw the tip of his broadsword was lodged in an oblong crystal as fat around as his hand. Isaac's laughter swirled around the room, taunting the duke.

"Damned magic-users," Thiazi grumbled. "How dare you laugh at me, you worthless scab?" he howled, understanding now how Siribel had escaped her cage. "I'm going to tear you limb from limb and make the elf witch watch!" he vowed, moving to find the taunting man. Except his muscles would not respond!

"I think not, Duke," Isaac teased, his voice seeming to come from all sides in a swirling circle. Isaac stepped out from behind a row of curtains, waggling his fingers at the duke and grinning.

"What is the meaning of this sorcery?" Thiazi snarled, struggling to regain control of his body. "Release me at once or I'll—"

"Or you will what?" Isaac asked in a deeper voice, his form suddenly growing larger before the paralyzed jotun. As his shape grew in size, so too did his voice, which boomed in the duke's ears. "Nothing. That is what you will do—nothing!"

A glimmer of fear bloomed inside Thiazi's stomach. He cowered in the face of the human's impressive display of magical prowess. Duke Thiazi was suddenly painfully aware that this diminutive ebony man possessed a power far greater than he had ever imagined one of their kind could.

"Wh-who are you?" he asked, still growling and fighting against his magical bonds.

"I'm just another *scab*. One who has waited centuries to put your kind down like the rabid dogs you are!" Isaac announced, words he had repeated in his head for ages while he waited, planning for this moment. The mage shifted his attention to the duke's right. "But it is not to me that you will be answering this day, *Duke*."

Out of the corner of his eye, Thiazi could see a form emerge from between the silk curtains. It was Siribel, her long, golden tresses swaying in the gentle breeze, covering her eyes in a dark shadow. "No...I...," Thiazi muttered.

Isaac pointed his staff toward the jotnar leader's head. As he pushed down in the air, so too did the duke fall to his knees. When Siribel came to his side, Thiazi's eyes flickered up to her, panicked and lined with hatred at the same time. "How did you do it, you witch?" he snarled, baring his fangs defiantly at the elf.

Siribel leaned close to the duke and brought her lips to his ear. Isaac could hear her whispering something to the vile ice giant. He saw the jotnar leader's eyes suddenly grow wide with terror. But before Thiazi could utter another word, Siribel ran his letter opener across his throat in a deep gash. The blood ran out like a river, down the front of his black steel armor and across the floor while the once mighty, brutal, and unyielding Duke of Belikar sputtered incoherently.

Siribel stood there coldly regarding him, watching patiently as the jotun who had tormented her for decades, the vile bastard who had murdered both her brother and husband before her very eyes as they begged for mercy, the bastard who had cursed her to live inside a gilded cage and stolen her visions, finally died. Siribel's face was expressionless through it all.

Finally Isaac came up beside her. "Are you ready to leave your prison now?" he asked in a dry voice.

Siribel nodded. "I have been ready since the day I dreamt of your arrival, Isaac of the White Tree." She turned her back on the dead leader of Belikar and followed the mage out of the palace for the rooftop.

Annabel screamed, jumping out of the way as a palace guard tumbled down the steps that led to the rooftop.

Tryn looked just as shocked but was determined to get them out of the dangerous eye of the battle. He sidestepped the groaning warrior, who wore a deep wound across his face, and grasped her shaking hands in his own. Steadying her, Tryn looked deep into her eyes. "We must remain calm. I do not know what we will see out there, but we *must* stay together at all costs."

Annabel meekly shook her throbbing head. All the heat and excitement was making her sweat, and she had to wipe her eyes to see clearly.

"Alright...ready?" Tryn asked.

Annabel nodded, and he pulled her past the dying guard and through the doorway into the heat of midday. As soon as they exited the building, the deafening roar of war loomed over her. Swords clashed. People were screaming and dying. She could smell the smoke from a nearby noble estate set ablaze by the rebellion wafting across the rooftop, stinging her eyes much worse than sweat could. She was forced to hold her forearm over her face and blink hard, her eyes tearing up in the smog.

Tryn took in the grisly scene for only a moment and then pulled her into a run once more. They dashed past the resistance members and duke's warriors fighting all around the area. Above them, the mighty airship of Archduke Marius loomed overhead, its engines creating such a loud racket she could not hear the marquess's endless line of encouragement. The *Goliath* was whipping up the wind, tossing her hair around wildly.

Tryn suddenly stopped and twisted her to the side, screaming as a spear flew past Annabel's shoulder. The jotun who had attacked was dressed in full body armor emblazoned with the banner of House Valkar, marking him as one the archduke's men, and he charged full speed for the pair. Annabel thought the ice giant looked like a wild dog guarding its master's den.

Tryn roughly tossed her to the side, preparing to meet the attacker head on. The guard hit him with such force that the marquess almost went over the edge of the low wall around the roof, barely catching hold of his attacker's iron collar in time.

Annabel looked in both directions, trying to find some way of escape. Everywhere she turned, there was only the promise of more madness. The bloody battle raged all across the area as the resistance tried to block the archduke's ship from escaping. When she looked back, Tryn was squirming around the guard and shoved the howling ice giant off the roof.

Running over to her, Tryn shouted something Annabel could not understand, holding out his hand. Tentatively she accepted, and he helped her rise. Once she was on her feet, the marquess tugged, and they were running through the carnage again.

The booming sound of the airship lessened enough for Annabel to hear her own huffing as they ran down the slope that led from the rooftop to the palace gardens below. Tryn screamed at a confused guard to get out of his way. The ice giant looked puzzled as to why the duke's son would be running away from the airship. He tried to tell the marquess he was going the wrong way, but a broad-shouldered human, far bigger than any slave Tryn had ever seen, fell upon the soldier. Tryn shook his head at Annabel and skirted the fight, lunging for the garden below. They raced past beds of black roses and mounds of crimson babybells before Tryn finally stopped to catch his breath.

Tryn let go of her and put his hands on his knees, gasping to catch his breath and coughing out the acrid smoke burning his lungs. Annabel pulled the hair away from her face where it clung to her sweaty brow.

The marquess looked over his shoulder, back at the palace, and began to laugh. "We did it!" he exclaimed between laughs, still catching his breath from their flight. "We actually escaped the palace!"

Annabel gave a nervous laugh in response, and Tryn straightened, moving closer to her. He wrapped his arms around her in a warm embrace. His strength was too overpowering for her to resist, and Annabel found her face pressed against his chest.

Tryn's heart was beating hard as happiness filled his soul. Gently stepping back with his hands on her shoulders, Tryn bent down to look Annabel in the eye. The marquess smiled affectionately. "You are safe now, little one. Now we can get out of the city and be together forever." His eyes were filled with the wonder of what their future had in store, and he moved to kiss her gently on the forehead. He could taste the saltiness of her skin against his purple lips.

That's odd, Tryn thought, feeling the sting on his chest. Looking down, he saw the dagger buried all the way to the hilt in the center of his tunic.

Confused, he staggered back, and Annabel let go of the weapon as blood began to run down the handle onto her creamy white skin. Tryn felt the world tighten up around him. "B-but... my love?" he tried to ask, dumbfounded by what was happening.

"Your love?" Annabel asked, her face contorting into a mask of disgust at his words. "What can your kind know of love? All the jotnar can ever understand is hatred and ownership."

Tryn fell to his knees, the strength of his legs giving out. He reached across an endless distance for Annabel to hold him.

Unrelenting, she backed away out of reach, hands shaking at her sides. "I'll never let you touch me again, you sick bastard!"

Tryn looked up at her with a profound sadness that melted through her veil of denial. "So much anger...so much hatred," he muttered to himself, understanding the cracks in their world. "My sweet, sweet Annabel, I am so sorry. Life has been quite unfair to you. If my death can take away this hatred that has festered in your heart, then so be it."

Annabel could not believe the marquess's words. Tryn fell backward, the world spinning around him. Overhead a dove glided on the wind, disappearing into a gray cloud.

Annabel lunged forward, catching the back of the marquess's head as a single tear ran from her twitching eye. Tryn smiled warmly up at her face, his heart at peace. "It's okay, my love...it's okay."

"H-how can you forgive me for this?" she sobbed, trying to comprehend how the jotun could smile at the woman who had just murdered him.

Tryn reached up, cold trembling fingers wiping away her tears. "Don't you see it, Annabel? I would cross an eternity of stars for your love."

Annabel's dam of denial over the love she felt for this jotun broke. Howling in despair, she begged him not to die. She clutched at the wound, swearing it was not that bad, that they could get help in time. When Tryn did not respond, she pulled him roughly up to his knees again, shaking the dying marquess and screaming at him to stay with her.

"Hold still! I'll take care of the blue devil for you!" an Acadian called over her shoulder. Out of the corner of her eye, Annabel saw the man hurling his spear toward Tryn's chest. She screamed for him to stop and lunged in front of the marquess's body, taking the spear clean through her own chest. Tryn hit the ground with a crack, and the woman he loved fell beside him.

"What in the hell did you just do!" Stur shouted at the soldier, roughly pulling the man away from the pair.

On the ground, lying on her side and facing Tryn, Annabel slowly stretched out her arm, fingers weakly trying to grasp his hand. "I love you too," she gasped, blood running down her nose and out of her mouth onto the stone.

Tryn's mind shattered in despair. He wanted to howl, to rage, to destroy the entire world. Yet all he could do was watch feebly as the light faded from her eyes and tears rolled out of his own.

Stur felt his heart break at the pair of lovers, a jotun and a human, sprawled across the ground and reaching for one another. He turned a cold eye on the soldier, who was shaking.

"What did she go and do that for?" the soldier asked. "I was trying to save her before that filthy jotun could hurt her."

"He wasn't hurting her. She was trying to save his life," Stur corrected sadly.

"Ho there, Stur!" Isaac called as he rushed down the sloped path into the garden.

Stur shook himself out of the forlorn moment, noting that the mage was accompanied by the fairest woman he had ever seen. "I see you were able to rescue the oracle," he remarked, spotting Siribel's pointed ears and motioning for the other soldier to get back to the fight, which he did readily enough.

"How goes it here?" Isaac asked, looking around at the raging battle.

"We are pressing the duke's remaining jotnar hard from the eastern side of the city. The lower boroughs have been taken, and most of the noble estates have surrendered. It shouldn't be long now before we find Thiazi."

"The duke is dead," Siribel said.

Stur knew he should feel some sense of victory, but after what he had just seen... Looking back at the dead woman, Stur grumbled when he saw her jotun lover was gone and she lay there with dead eyes, reaching out to no one.

"What is it, man?" Isaac asked, as a look of concern crossed the warrior's face.

Stur turned away from his brooding, shaking away the notion and focusing on the task at hand. "Nothing, it's nothing. We should part ways. I've still work to do here. We are going to make a push for the archduke's airship."

"I fear the time has passed for that opportunity, my friends," Siribel cryptically informed them.

"What do you—?" Stur began to ask, but the *Goliath* suddenly whirred into life, slowly lifting up into the sky.

"Archduke! I've plotted a course for the capitol, my lord!" the airship captain explained to his liege as the angry wizard entered the bridge.

Marius nodded then thought of something and held up a finger for the jotun to wait. He turned his attention to his banner guard. "Take this jotun to my personal quarters and then report back after you've secured a necrophage to tend his wounds."

The banner guard nodded and carried the lifeless Marquess of Belikar away.

"Sir?" the airship captain prodded, waiting for orders and wanting to be away from the massacre below.

Marius strode over to the viewport, looking through the thick glass pane down at the city. "We are not leaving yet. These scabs want a fight with the Jotnar Empire?" Marius snarled. "Then let's give them one." He pointed his bony finger at his air marshal. "Fire the cannons!"

Stur howled for his men to get back, waving for them to retreat from the rooftops as the airship began turning above the palace. A heavy fireball burst out of the cannon, the sound of it like thunder crackling across the sky. The cannonball exploded through the rooftop of a nearby noble estate at an angle and engulfed a group of resistance fighters in flames.

"Fall back! Find cover!" Stur howled again, though it sounded muffled through his ringing ears.

Marius cackled gleefully at the humans scrambling in all directions. The airship twisted around, heading for the mass of the Acadian army, raining devastation down on the city as it went. "Release the tungsten spears!" he ordered.

Corbin watched in horror as the airship shuddered, releasing its payload. A flat spear as tall as a house tore from the base of the vessel. When it crashed through the nearby buildings, the ground quaked under the impact, splintering and rising in a crater around the immense weapon of destruction.

"*Logan!*" he shouted telepathically, pointing a warning finger at the airship.

Logan was surrounded by eight jotnar warriors in black steel armor. He elbowed the closest jotun in the side of the head, knocking the ice giant away from him, and pulled back, swiping his mighty blade in a wide semi-circle to keep the encroaching band of jotnar at bay. Looking up to see what his brother was referring to, he was startled.

"Destroy that abomination!" Marius ordered. Clouds of steam spit from the weapons control panel as the pressure built up for another release.

Logan slid his right foot back, forming a T-shape, and spread his legs wide as he crouched in the Aegis and pulled the mystical armor's sword all the way back around him.

Marius's eye twitched, seeing the armor move into an offensive pose. "Release the damned spear! Release the tungsten now!" he screamed. The airship rocked as another deadly tungsten spear released, this one aimed for the Aegis.

The Aegis twisted sharply as Logan channeled every ounce of strength he had into his throw. The Aegis's sword whipped through the air like a dart, flying fast as an eagle. With a massive explosion, it ripped into the hull of the airship. At the same time, the ground shuddered as the tungsten spear pummeled the Aegis, driving the ancient armor down hard into the shattered cobblestone.

Isaac gasped as the *Goliath* spiraled in reverse, completely out of control as the lower section of the airship fell away in pieces, which fell on the city like meteorites. He waved his staff in the air then stopped and thrust it forward with both hands, aiming a bolt of lightning at the blade stuck through the ship's bridge. His magical blast channeled through the Aegis blade, sending a web of electricity crackling across the entire hull.

The magical towers atop the archduke's airship exploded one by one in blue-ringed fiery blasts, each one breaking the sound barrier and sending out huge concussive rings of air. The devastating attack hurled the remains of the Goliath down onto the city. The palace roof was crushed as the exploding ship crashed into it, and the ground quaked as if it would fall from under their feet. Stur fought hard to retain his footing while the world shook.

Corbin ran for his brother, who was lost under a cloud of smoke and dust where the tungsten spear had hit. He screamed into the smoke, choking on the acrid taste of burning metal. The ground where Logan had been was sloped in a crater with the crushed remains of the Aegis at its center, stuck to the ground like a ragdoll by the archduke's weapon. When Corbin reached the armor, armored jotnar were already climbing down after him, looking at the wreckage for signs that the armor would come alive again.

"Logan!" Corbin screamed again. Surely the fates could not be so cruel as to bring his brother back just to take him away again?

Through the ringing in his ears, he could dimly make out a whirring sound as the Aegis's breastplate opened halfway, getting caught on the tungsten spear buried through its waist. Corbin climbed over the hot mithril, caring not for his own safety and waving away the smoke. Logan's metal hand came over the lip of the opening, and Corbin grasped it. He gave a heave and pulled his brother, choking on the grey smoke, out of the armor. Logan's forehead was cut open, and black soot covered his cheeks, but for all that, he was alive and well!

Commander Erruza pointed at the armor and called his soldiers to arms. "Look, my friends, he is only a human! Now is our chance. Destroy the infidels!"

The jotnar shouted and raced down the shattered crater with their swords raised.

A whistling sound came just before Gandiva crushed the commander's breastplate, throwing the jotun onto his back, dead on impact. When the weapon returned to Logan's hand, every jotun in the area had stopped and was staring at him fearfully.

"Yeah...I'm *only* a human," Logan taunted. "Come and give it your best shot."

"Jotnar warriors of Belikar!" Kyra called from the top of the crater as wafts of smoke parted to reveal her form. The crushed, burning palace could be seen over her shoulder in the distance. "Duke Thiazi is dead. Your defenses have been laid to waste." As she spoke, more Acadians began to appear through the smoke, slowly coming down the slope for the jotnar. "The empire could not save you, for you have lost this war. Now you have a choice. Do you want to die, or do you want to live?" As she asked the question, the look of grim determination on Kyra's face told the soldiers that she would gladly kill every last one of them if she had to.

One of the larger warriors let his sword and shield clatter to the ground, and he fell to his knees with his hands behind his head in surrender. Logan smiled across the distance at the marshal as the rest of the horde followed suit and fell to their knees.

Corbin grasped his brother's forearm, helping him down from the armor, and gave him a hearty hug. "I thought we'd lost you!"

"Can't get rid of me that easily, little brother." Logan laughed, though it hurt his side, and slapped Corbin on the back, choking down tears of joy before breaking free.

Together they surveyed the city around them with immeasurable awe and profound humility. Somehow against all odds, Kyra's army had overthrown the jotnar. The city was sacked, the battle was over, and for the first time in over two hundred years, the humans of Belikar were free.

Chapter 25: Departure

It had only been several weeks since the revolution, but to Corbin Walker, it felt like an eternity. Every fiber of his being ached to get back to Vanidriell and save his people from the slavering hunger of the false god Baetylus. However, in the days following the great battle of Belikar, there was much to be done.

Everyone marked it as a miracle that Logan had walked away from the Aegis with only minor wounds. It was his second brush with death since coming to possess the mystical armor. When asked how he had survived the fall from the cliffs, Logan told most people made up fantasies. "I rode the dragon's tail to the daystar and was blessed by flying apes," or "I guess years of practice falling out of trees finally came in handy." Then there was Corbin's favorite, "The Valkyries themselves came down to bring me to Valhalla, but I told those angels of death, 'No thanks, ladies. I've got a war to win, and I'm running late.'" That was the one that made Kyra groan, though she was overjoyed to see the Falian alive and well. Particularly since his arrival turned the tide of war in their favor.

It was Tiko who explained what really happened. Apparently, when they hit the bottom of the canyon, Logan landed on top of the hulking hill giant in an iridescent pond, crushing the monster but narrowly saving Logan's life.

The Agmawor were praying around the pool for Seti's guidance. The pool was their scared shrine to the dead, and Logan had fallen from the sky in the dead center of it. When the Aegis arrived, the Agmawor marked it as a sign their god was not upset with them for the recent civil war and dragged the massive suit of armor to High Priestess Luana.

When Logan spoke to them, Luana knew who he was, remembering the soft-skin's voice from the day she took power over her people. The high priestess had wanted an end to the bloodshed between the Agmawor and Agma for quite some time and saw Nero's blessing from Seti as an opportunity to gain the power to do just that. In fact, when Logan arrived, she was already meeting with an envoy from the Agma tribe.

Logan explained what was happening and resumed his pilgrimage back to the mage's tower. Luana declared this to be a sign from Seti, and soon Logan found that both the Agma and Agmawor were following him to his destination, laying their spears at his feet and begging for the gods' blessing. The lizards knew the jotnar would eventually find their hidden jungle and did not want to wait around to see what the blue-skinned devils might do to them.

The rest, as they say, was history, or at least that was as much as Tiko was able to garner in such a short time.

The Agma and their cousins only stayed for a couple days after Belikar was taken. With the glory of battle over, there was not much more to keep them there, and the lizard people ached to part ways and get back to their sacred jungle.

Logan asked Tiko if he would join them in their journey back to Fal, but the proud hunter bowed graciously and declined. He was eager to be wed to Kalilah and start their family. His place was by her side, no matter how much he yearned to accompany his new friends on their adventure. Kalilah was a healer now, and she was never needed more than after the battle at Belikar.

They were sad to see the lizardman go but parted as friends, promising to see each other again one day.

There was much work to do tending to the wounded and rounding up the jotnar prisoners.

"What will you do with them all?" Corbin asked Kyra as they walked out of the dungeons where the ice giants were locked in cells.

"We do not know yet," Kyra said thoughtfully.

"And there is still no word of Archduke Marius?" he asked.

A cloud settled over Kyra's eyes and she shook her head. "It troubles me greatly that we have not found his body in the rubble as of yet. If even one of the jotnar got out..." she let the thought hang in the air. "Anyhow, I suspect it'll take a great many debates and consultations with Belikar's new leadership before we can make decisions on the fate of the remaining jotnar."

Many humans were calling for the immediate execution of all jotnar. Unfortunately, that included those of the ice giants who had helped overthrow the evil rulers of the city. Then there were those who wished to move on and offer forgiveness, allowing the jotnar to live side by side with them or else be exiled from the city, never to return.

The whole thing was a heavy moral dilemma for Kyra who, being leader of the massive army that occupied the city, was now Queen of Belikar as well as of the Agartan people. She was forced to keep the jotnar resistance members segregated from the rest of the population, to Eir's great sadness.

"It's only for the time being," Kyra explained with a heavy heart. "Just until we can sort through this mess." She did not enjoy having to treat these jotnar, who had risked everything to free the humans, like prisoners.

Eir nodded her understanding. "They need time to work through the pain. We all do really. Though I fear it will never truly be lifted from their souls after generations of enslavement. I only hope the people see that some of us stood by them and accept us in their hearts."

Her words stung Corbin, and Logan argued passionately against separating the two races. But in the end, Kyra had to do what was right to keep all her people, human and jotnar alike, safe from harm while the world they knew changed around them.

And so several weeks had gone by, and now the companions found themselves outside the city of Belikar, exchanging their farewells. The walls above were lined with Acadians watching the departure of the strange heroes from another land.

"Are you sure you can't stay longer?' Kyra asked. "There's still so much to do, and your council would be greatly valued." She smiled, hoping to tempt the heroes into staying one last time.

"Would that we could, Queen Tarvano," Corbin replied, tying his saddle packs closed and tenderly patting the red elk she had gifted them. "But our journey is far from over, and it is long past time we got back to our own land to help the people of Fal."

Kyra smiled with a wisdom beyond her years and stepped to the side so that Stur could come forward. The warrior wrapped Logan in a hearty bear hug, lifting the cavalier man from his feet and shaking him about. "Ah, I am going to miss you, lad!" He laughed heartily as he tossed the young man around like a babe before setting him back down.

Logan straightened himself out, laughing as well. "Geesh, show me how you really feel, old man!"

Stur bristled. "I'll give you old man!" he roared, pretending as if he would attack the Falian who had become his dear friend as well as apt pupil.

"Come, my friends, it is time we set out on our journey," Isaac called from where he sat on the back of his own red elk.

Corbin nodded and turned to bow to his friends before mounting. Bipp sauntered past Logan, who was trying to get on his own mount as gracefully as possible, though it looked comical as he kept failing in the attempt.

"Queen Tarvano, this is for you." Bipp bowed low, holding out a small shiny object in his lifted hands. "A gift to remember us by."

Kyra carefully took the tiny metal object. It was a carving of their group—Bipp, Stur, Tiko, Isaac, Logan, Corbin, and Kyra—all looking very noble and ready for battle with weapons drawn. At the center of the carving, tiny clock hands ticked. The timepiece was breathtaking, and she was humbled to receive it.

"Oh, Bipp," Kyra said, "as if we could ever forget you. This is too kind." Kyra placed a hand over her heart and gave the Agarta oath of allegiance. "May the bonds between our people be forever tempered by friendship and good will." She leaned down to give the gnome a kiss on his forehead that made him blush three shades of red and giggle nervously. Stur smirked at the gnome.

"You done, lover boy?" Logan said rolling his eyes. "Come on, you heard the mage. It's time to go already." Reaching down, he helped Bipp onto the back of his elk, and the four of them turned their mounts to leave.

"Goodbye, Falians," Kyra called. "Nero will be waiting for you at the White Tree. May the gods show favor on your journey, and may we cross paths again in this world before the next!"

Kyra dropped to one knee as her friends left. All along the wall, Acadians and freed slaves cheered for their heroes. The people of Belikar were still watching as the Walker brothers disappeared over the ridge, led by Isaac the mage back to their homeland.

"But how will we get back to Vanidriell?" Logan asked as the jungle came into view ahead. "The bridge to Ul'kor has been destroyed."

Isaac leaned back in his saddle to regard the Falian with a devious glimmer in his eyes. "There are many roads that lead to Vanidriell, lad, many roads indeed." With a mischievous wink, the mage spurred his elk to trot faster for the tree line.

Corbin laughed at his brother's surprised expression and urged his red elk to give chase. Bipp nudged Logan to go after them, and Logan smirked devilishly at his little friend.

"Looks like we're going home, buddy!" he exclaimed then whooped and spurred his own mount after them.

Epilogue

Elise Ivarone had had an amazing day. The King's men had come from the capitol of Malbec to meet with her that morning. They offered terms of sanctuary to her and all the people of Riverbell, promising that the King himself would hear her words of ill omen over the revelations of Baetylus's true nature.

"You did well today!" Cassandra intoned proudly from within her stone, which radiated warmly against Elise's chest. *"Your people are in good hands here. King Glanery is a kind and wise ruler."*

"Thank you, Lady Cassandra," Elise said as she walked up the creaky steps to her room at the back of the inn.

Cassandra noted an edge of melancholy to the young woman. *"Don't you worry, my dear girl. Corbin will be back among us before we know it,"* she wisely assured.

In her heart, Elise knew Cassandra was right, but it had been so long, and the couple had been put through so many struggles. It felt like a distant dream that her fiancée would return one day.

Elise was so distracted in her reverie that she did not notice her door was partially open when she entered her chamber. She was already halfway across the room, dropping her pouch on the round wooden table, when a man cleared his throat by the bedside.

Elise jumped back, scrambling to hold her dagger out with shaking hands toward the man sitting in her armchair with his legs crossed.

"Hello, *Madame* Elise. It has been too long since we last saw one another," he crooned in his scratchy voice, leaning forward into the light of her flickering oil lamp so that she could clearly make out Fafnir's face.

Elise spun to flee the room, but her path was blocked by an ebony man who stepped from the shadows with an evil smile just a few sizes too big across his face. The tip of his saber pressed against her throat, stopping her dead in her tracks. Elise was too scared to even breathe as she felt the cold tip of the blade against her skin.

"Now is that any way to behave? And after I've traveled all this distance to see you again," Fafnir teased, rising from his seat and making his way around the bed to stand behind her.

"Cassandra...," she whimpered.

"Tut tut," Fafnir wagged a finger over her shoulder. "We don't want our conversation cut short by black magic, do we?"

Fafnir's man traced a delicate line down her throat to the center of Elise's breasts then snapped back, slicing open the inside pocket. Catching the Onyx in his hand, he presented it to Fafnir, who greedily snatched it away. The magistrate peered deep into the eye of the stone, shocked upon seeing Lady Cassandra looking up at him with immense hatred from inside her pocket dimension.

The surprise quickly faded into a look of devious intention, and the magistrate's crooked smile grew longer. "Well, well...what have we here? If it isn't the Lady Cassandra herself, back from the dead," he cooed gleefully. "Oh, we have so much to discuss, my dear lady, so much indeed." With another wolfish grin, Fafnir dropped his new prize into an enchanted red velvet pouch that dampened all magic.

"Well then, Elise Ivarone," Fafnir snickered, "it's time you came with us. I believe we have some unfinished business to attend to, eh?"

Elise looked from the doorway to the grim-faced assassin in front of her. He was still tracing the tip of his blade around her heart and grinning like a Cheshire cat. "B-business?" she asked.

"Why yes, dear woman." Fafnir cackled, heading for the doorway. "There is still the matter of your execution to attend to, after all."

The assassin moved so fast that Elise did not even have time to yelp as his fist drove into her jaw, knocking her out cold.

Fafnir's man tossed her over his shoulder and headed past the magistrate, who held the door open for him. Fafnir grinned to himself, relishing the thought of seeing the look on Corbin Walker's face when he found out his love had been hanged to death, and closed the door behind him.

"I have her, All-Father," Fafnir told his Crystal God, who was miles away.

Baetlyus coiled within itself with hungry satisfaction. Its plan was coming together, and soon enough it would walk the lands of Vanidriell. Then Fal and all of Acadia would bow before their Crystal Lord.

FOLLOW THE ADVENTURES of the Walker Brothers and their companions, in book three of the series, NECROMANCER'S CURSE, coming Summer 2015.

Become an Acadian today to receive free exclusive short stories at http://www.davidmatthewalmond.com and to keep up to date on everything Acadia.

If you enjoyed the novel even half as much as David enjoyed writing it, there can be no finer gift than a review! More reviews equals higher visibility in e-rankings for new readers to even see the book exists. Please share your thoughts on Amazon's review section http://www.amazon.com/dp/B00RHBOCU4 it would mean a great deal to the author!

Bipp's tall tales based on the Scandinavian Folktale *The Giant Who Had No Heart*.

Acknowledgments

To all the fans of Acadia who have come after me with an enthusiasm I could never have predicted, this volume is for you. But especially for Rich and Jeni who continue to be my rocks.

D. M. Almond is a figment of your imagination. His works are only the byproduct of a deeply interesting dream you are now having due to consuming an overabundance of pizza before bedtime. Your parents warned you about days like this, but you just didn't listen. Alas, the pepperoni could not hold its grip upon you and you must now wake up.